MISSION OF THE KINGS

MISSION OF THE KINGS

¤

The Overlords

A Novel

J. Michael Squatrito, Jr.

Mission of the Kings
The Overlords

The Overlords books may be ordered through Internet booksellers or by contacting:

J. Michael Squatrito, Jr.
www.The-Overlords.com

Edited by Laura Vadney
Cover design by Patrick Thompson

ISBN: 978-1077604810 (pbk)
Printed in the United States of America

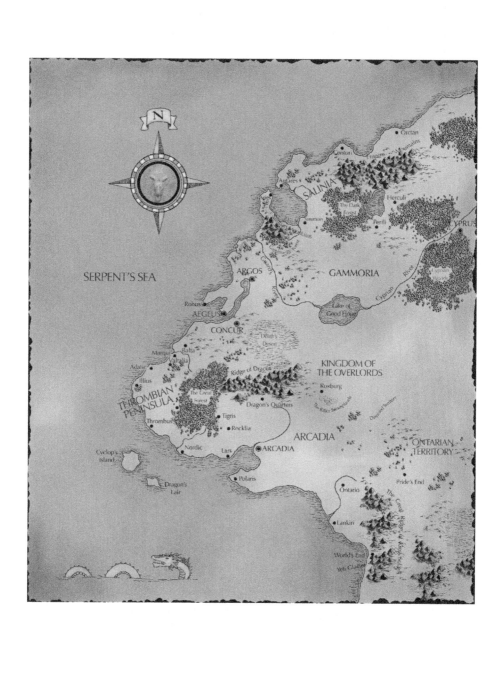

Prologue

A steady snow fell from the wintery sky, large snowflakes dancing from the heavens. The weather in the Empire mountains region could be brutal at times, but today the bone chilling temperatures felt like home to the creature that trudged through the knee deep snow.

Naa'il's Scynthian mind raced with worrisome thoughts. Less than a month ago, humans had destroyed the outpost that he and his comrades had constructed near the coast of the Thrombian peninsula. Worse yet, he allowed the detested race to capture him. The juvenile shuddered at the thought, but memories of the fires the humans had set to his compound kept him warm during the many cold nights since his release.

Steam spewing from his mouth, the Scynthian found a tree to lean against, resting his tired body. The beast would have died of hypothermia weeks ago if not for the coarse, thick hair that covered his body. The rough terrain made it hard for trekking and his lack of adequate supplies kept his survival tenuous at best. Naa'il took his gaze upward, away from the thick coniferous trees and to the rocky incline before him. With flakes brushing his face, the young beast concentrated, knowing that a few miles beyond the rise stood Mahalanobis – his home.

After a moment of rest, the Scynthian lowered his head, exhaled deeply, then continued his trek. Along the way, Naa'il reflected on the people who had held him captive and their inexplicable decision to set him free. Swinkle, he recalled, picturing

1

the small human in the green cloak, and Harrison the warrior. Fools, both of them, he thought. A Scynthian does not set prisoners free. Yet, he could not find a reason to hate them, which disturbed him more.

Naa'il reached the apex of a steady incline, then shimmied down the other side. His people's city lay ever closer. After plodding through the thick snow again, the Scynthian made an abrupt stop. Straining his green, cat-like eyes into the distance, Naa'il allowed his other instincts to take over.

"Smoke," he said, sniffing the late afternoon air. Burning. Naa'il's heart began to race. Quickening his pace, the juvenile hiked along the rocky trail, his brain churning. Maybe a bonfire, he rationalized. Or a sacrifice. His heart told him otherwise, though.

Hungry and near exhaustion, Naa'il pressed onward, the ensuing darkness better enhancing his race's pronounced visual advantage. The Scynthian knew that a vast city rested on a plateau between two massive mountains. Trekking closer, thick billowing smoke blew in his direction, tantalizing him to follow its trail.

Naa'il jerked to a halt, bringing a large, clawed hand to his head, the onset of a headache taking him by surprise. The juvenile then dropped to one knee, the pain getting worse with every passing second.

Something's not right, he told himself. Must help. Channeling an inner will, Naa'il rose to his feet and continued toward his home. The snow fell sideways now, intermingling with the smoldering ashes. Lifting his eyes, he saw the final bend in the trail that led to his city loomed mere steps away.

The Scynthian found large rocks jutting from the deep snow. Placing a strong hand on one of them, he gripped a nook, then sprung himself forward. Naa'il placed his chest against the formation, peeking his head over the rise. The young beast's eyes widened in shock at the sight.

His head pounding, the Scynthian did his best to block out the droning pain and evaluate the situation. His eyes darted in all directions, finding every section of his city set ablaze, the heat from the flames warming his face in stark contrast to the cold that continued to grip his backside. Just when he felt a sense of helplessness, he heard the moans.

Naa'il focused on the horrific sounds. Many times he had heard shrieks of horror from his defenseless enemies along with screams and shouts of excruciating pain. However, the anguish he heard now came from his kindred.

Squinting into the distance, the juvenile saw eight figures rushing from the city. Half of them pressed their hands to their heads as they scampered away from an invisible being. Then the unthinkable happened.

Naa'il watched in horror as a huge beast emerged from the smoky carnage. The monster took on the form of a two-headed dragon with dark metallic green scales covering its body and an underbelly a shade lighter. One of the heads spewed flames toward the hysterical Scynthians, while the other locked its gaze on two that had dropped to their knees. The Scynthians on the ground continued to press their hands against their heads, their moans turning to shrieks of agony.

From his perch, the juvenile's brain called for him to help his comrades, but his inner will kept his feet entrenched in place. His eyes glued to the scene, he watched as his friends suffered for the last time. The two Scynthians lowered their hands, blood flowing from their eyes and ears before their bodies slumped to the ground.

Naa'il's heart pounded double time and he held his breath. At that very moment, his own head started to feel warmer, his brain inexplicably heating. The Scynthian spun away, diverting his eyes from the scene and pinning his back against the jagged rock.

Near trembling, the juvenile did his best to recall the teachings that his masters had preached, but instead all his memories brought back were feelings of fighting, rage, and death. Then, a most unusual thought sprang to his mind, a purely human trait and not something any rational Scynthian would entertain.

Naa'il recalled his conversations with Swinkle, the small, unarmed human that treated him unlike anyone in his life. This insignificant being preached non-violence, shying away from confrontation if at all possible. The Scynthian shook his head, knowing this line of reasoning went against his core beliefs. However, Naa'il understood the direness of his predicament.

3

Though the beast's head continued to radiate heat, he knew he had to peek over the rocks again. Gathering all the courage he had, Naa'il gazed over the formation, finding all his comrades dead, blood flowing from their orifices. The dragon focused on the burning structures before releasing a blood-curdling screech. The sound rattled Naa'il's bones. To his surprise, three more two-headed beasts joined the first monster. They stared at each other and, without making a sound, the four began to flap their massive wings to head in Naa'il's direction.

The juvenile ducked and pinned himself against the cold rock once again. Naa'il could hear the sound of the flapping wings, each second bringing them closer to his position. With no god to pray to, the Scynthian made an unusual decision. Channeling a human voice, he asked Pious to protect him at this moment, to save him from the horror that had befallen his friends. Unsure of even how to pray, Naa'il did his best.

The monsters flew off, oblivious to the horrified Scynthian, leaving him alone, rattled and scared. Naa'il watched for a long time, until the four massive beasts became nothing more than diminishing pin pricks in the darkening sky. Over that same time, the young Scynthian realized that his head started cooling and no longer throbbed.

Feeling a bit better about his situation, Naa'il found the courage to glance over the rock again. The city continued to burn while his comrades remained motionless on the ground, but any imminent danger appeared gone. Though he was just a juvenile and still learning the ways of Scynthian adulthood, a most mature thought entered his mind. His elders had reinforced in him the importance of recovering their race's most sacred artifact in the case of total catastrophe. Gazing at the smoldering metropolis and understanding the gravity of his homeland's current predicament, he realized that the time had come to enact emergency protocols.

Naa'il knew he needed to help his friends and anyone else that remained in the city, but they would have to wait until he completed his new mission. Without hesitation, he started his trek down the mountainside, each step bringing him closer to his battered home. Yet, with all the uncertainties swirling inside his head, he refused to forget that Pious had allowed him to survive.

C H A P T E R 1

 Q

The pounding in Harrison's head grew stronger. The young warrior, his vision blurred from an apparent head injury, tried to rise from the ground. A vicious tug stopped his forward momentum. The unmistakable clang of metal scraping against a hard surface meant only one thing. Harrison did not need his warrior training to realize that someone had chained his arms to a stone wall. The young warrior, doing his best to regain his senses, shimmied backward until the bonds slackened. With a huff, he rested his backside against the cold wall.

His head still buzzing, Harrison brought his hands to his face, finding iron cuffs digging into his wrists. Gritting his teeth, he dropped his arms by his sides, alleviating his pain. Panning his surroundings gave him a better understanding of his predicament; someone had shackled him to a wall in a prison cell. But where?

Without warning, the metal door to his chamber flung open, slamming into the stone barrier, creating a thunderous crash. Harrison stared wide-eyed as a large figure loomed in the doorway. The young warrior took no time in recognizing the being. The Scynthian warrior stepped into the room, then shifted to his right to allow a second savage to enter.

Harrison focused on the beast's red arm bands, knowing that the markings signified his leadership status. The Scynthian unsheathed a long sword from its scabbard and pointed it at the defenseless human.

In a low, guttural tone, the beast bellowed, "Arcadia is ours! Your pathetic attempt to reclaim your city is over. You will bow to our new sovereignty!"

The young warrior heard the Scynthian's words, yet something did not register. His language sounded too clear, Harrison reasoned to himself, too understandable. Too intelligent?

The Scynthian leader had more to say. Taking a step closer to his captive, he thundered, "Your losses are colossal and your leadership is in disarray!"

Harrison opened his mouth to rebuff the beast's charges. Though his jaws moved, he could not speak. The young warrior, astonished at his sudden lack of communication skills, tried again with the same result.

Both Scynthians saw the human's pathetic attempt at speech and the perplexing expression on his face. "Isn't that sweet!" chided the lead fighter. "The prisoner's trying to talk!" They then began to laugh, buckling over in hysterics.

Harrison glared at his captors, his blood simmering. The young warrior tried to formulate words, but again speech eluded him.

What's happening to me? His eyes darted and his heart pounded. *Why can't I speak?* Harrison focused on the laughing Scynthians. *I can't speak, but they can!*

The Scynthian chief, curtailing his laughter a bit, lowered his blade and pumped his comrade's chest with his fist. Wiping a tear from his eye, he said, "Go fetch this creature's leaders." The beast then exhaled heartily, trying to regain his composure, the way someone does after witnessing a hilarious event. A moment later another Scynthian warrior returned.

Gesturing to Harrison, the head fighter said, "Show him what's left of his superiors!"

The young warrior's eyes widened in shock upon seeing the enormity of this beast. The Scynthian was huge, his body taking up the entire doorframe. The monster entered the room, taking two purposeful steps toward Harrison. The young warrior felt his body tense, doing his best to remain motionless. Shifting only his eyes, he brought his gaze to the bloody objects in the savage's hands.

In one smooth motion, the giant beast tossed the items in Harrison's direction. The severed heads of Bracken Drake, Brendan Brigade, and Octavius and Caidan Forge landed with a soft thud on the young warrior's chest before rolling onto the cold floor. Harrison's eyes gravitated to the jagged base of each neck, realizing that these savages had not severed the heads off their bodies with a well-sharpened blade, but had torn them off instead. Each head faced the shackled human, eyes wide and terror-filled, mouths agape, their final screams muted.

Harrison's head darted from one bludgeoned body part to the next, his brain churning, trying to make sense of the scene before him. He opened his mouth to scream, but nothing happened.

The three Scynthians witnessed Harrison's pathetic attempt to yell, then laughed in hysterics again. While the young warrior looked on in horror, the largest Scynthian moved closer to his position. Taking his boot-covered foot, the beast kicked Harrison hard in his side, driving through his ribs, shattering them to pieces. The Aegean hollered in pain. However, this time he heard his own loud, horrific scream.

"Be quiet!" said the voice next to him in a hushed but panicked tone. "You're going to alert every Scynthian to our position!"

The young warrior instinctively reached for his side, finding no sign of injury. Bonds no longer shackled his wrists and the chains that had secured him to the wall had disappeared.

Murdock removed a tankard from his belt, took a rag, and doused it with water. Taking the wet cloth to his friend's head, he said, "That's a nasty wound." Harrison recoiled, the wetness stinging his open gash.

"What happened?" The Aegean tried to gauge his situation, which had become challenging at best. "Where are the Scynthians?"

The ranger grimaced, realizing that his friend had suffered a more dangerous injury than he had first suspected. "They're around. You need to see Swinkle."

7

Harrison took his eyes all about the room, doing his best to recognize his surroundings. He no longer sat in a prison cell that was for sure. Instead he found himself lying on the floor of a windowless room. A floor covering made of coarse animal hairs twisted between his fingers, the warmth of a glowing fire in a hearth, the smell of food cooking in a pot, a mantle containing quaint knickknacks. A residence?

"Where am I?" muttered the young warrior before his vision began to swirl, resembling rambling hallucinations through a kaleidoscope.

"Don't worry about that now," said Murdock, still addressing the wound. "We need to find Swinkle."

Harrison saw something move across the room. A door slowly opened behind the ranger, allowing a bright light to enter the space. A large figure stepped into the glow as soon as the portal opened, forming a shadow that loomed in the doorway. Harrison recognized the Scynthian warrior and watched in horror as the beast raised his blade. The young warrior stared at his friend who continued to tend to his injury, oblivious of the oncoming creature. The Scynthian raised his weapon in a strike position.

Harrison tried to warn Murdock but, just as before, nothing audible exited his mouth. Instead, he heard his friend's continued conversation.

"Swinkle has bandages and that healing power of his," said the ranger, dabbing the blood from Harrison's forehead. "He'll be able to—"

The Scynthian's blade sliced clean and deep into the ranger's back. Murdock buckled forward, dropping his blood-soaked rag. Harrison stared in disbelief. His friend's eyes bulged as the monster struck him again.

Harrison screamed in vain and, to his horror, still heard nothing. He brought his focus back to his mortally-wounded friend, finding him gagging. Blood began to spew from his mouth as he gasped for air. As the Scynthian raised his sword one more time, the ranger coughed, raining copious amounts of blood across the young warrior's face.

Harrison's eyes flitted and he tried to regain his focus. "Harrison, stay still," said the robed figure. "You have sustained a serious head injury." Swinkle continued to mumble a prayer and again tossed holy water onto the confused fighter's face.

This time the young warrior shuffled away from the man in front of him. "Who are you?" he exclaimed, eyes wide, his heart thumping fast and hard.

The young cleric raised his hands, realizing his friend's state of confusion. "It is I, Swinkle. You need to relax so that I can help you."

Harrison's eyes darted in every direction. "No, you're not!" He then made a visual scan of the area, trying in vain to develop a mental picture of his surroundings for the third time.

"Where's Murdock?" he asked before clutching his aching head in his hands.

Swinkle took a cautious step toward his friend. "He's with the others, helping to beat back the Scynthians."

The young warrior still did not trust his situation. "How do I know you're really Swinkle?" Harrison's wild-eyed expression swept all about his new environment, finding the two in the living area of someone's home, though not the same one he witnessed moments ago.

The holy man raised his palms to his friend. "Harrison, listen to me carefully. We're still in a heated battle, fighting to save Arcadia from falling into Scynthian hands." Swinkle took a cautious step toward his friend.

"You were in a battle with two of the beasts, but one of them smacked you in the head with their weapon. I need to tend to your wound right now."

Harrison's head throbbed as he tried in vain to remember the melee. "If what you've said is true, what happened to the Scynthians?"

"Brendan and Murdock came to your rescue and defeated the beasts. They then dragged you in here and summoned me to help you." Swinkle maneuvered closer to Harrison. "I really need to treat you."

The young warrior needed to hear more. "How long have I been here?"

"Probably a couple of hours," said Swinkle, cocking his head from side to side. "Give or take."

"Two hours! Have I been unconscious all that time?"

"For most of it." Swinkle arched his eyebrows and raised his hands toward his injured friend. "May I?"

Harrison knew Swinkle would never harm him and, with no more questions to ask, nodded his approval. The young cleric positioned his hands close to Harrison's head wound and began to pray. A soft white glow enveloped his damaged scalp, stopping the loss of blood, and healing the injury a bit. A moment later the light ceased and Swinkle eased away from his friend.

"My prayer will help for now, but you are in no shape to continue fighting," said the young cleric.

Harrison took a hand to his head, running his fingers over the gash, finding that the throbbing had subsided. Confident that he was no longer in a dream, he asked, "What's our current situation?"

Swinkle drew a heavy sigh, shaking his head. "Where do I begin?" Collecting his thoughts, he said, "The Scynthians have burned most of Arcadia. Bracken's army is fighting hard, but the creatures outnumber us almost two to one. The good news is that we know the terrain and every citizen of Arcadia has taken a stand to defeat the invaders."

Harrison absorbed the information. He then tried to stand, but instead began to wobble before dropping to one knee.

The young cleric caught his friend, keeping him upright. "You must stay with me," said Swinkle in a forceful tone. "Brendan told me to watch over you."

The young warrior glared at the holy man. "Do you really think that I want to stay here and not help our friends?"

"Of course not, but it would be unwise to leave."

Harrison dismissed the young cleric's last comment. "Where's my battle axe?"

Swinkle brought his gaze to the dining area. The weapon leaned against a chair, its blade glimmering in the sunlight shining through the window.

"Thank you," said Harrison. "Where are the men?"

"Everywhere," said Swinkle in a hushed tone, shaking his head in defeat.

"Stick with me," said the young warrior. "We need to help now."

Harrison approached the closed doorway and, as he did, noticed someone missing. "Where's Lance?"

"Last I saw him he was running with Murdock and Pondle."

"We need to find him, too." Swinkle nodded in agreement.

With no time to spare, the two men exited their temporary shelter and reentered the besieged city. Harrison took a moment to gauge his surroundings. Scynthians had set ablaze buildings that once housed residences and businesses. Smoke billowed from nearly every structure, hindering their breathing. Sounds of weapons clashing permeated the area, along with cries of anguish and horror.

Harrison motioned for Swinkle to follow him and the two diverted their course from a main street to an alleyway, which then connected with another thoroughfare. Peering around the corner of a building, the young warrior found five Arcadian soldiers running in their direction.

The young warrior leapt from his position, gaining the attention of the fighters. The startled men stopped in their tracks and struck a defensive posture, brandishing their swords in the direction of their new adversary. After a few tense seconds, one of the fighters lowered his weapon and took a step toward the young warrior.

Cocking his head, he asked, "Harrison Cross?"

The question surprised the Aegean. Narrowing his eyes, he said, "Yes, it's me." The rest of the Arcadians lowered their weapons upon hearing the answer.

The leader took purposeful steps toward the young warrior. "Thank the gods you're alive! Contingents of men are looking for you."

Harrison's eyebrows arched in surprise. "Why are you looking for me?"

"Word's spreading that you're dead." The lead soldier gestured with his hand. "Follow us."

Harrison peered back at Swinkle for a second before asking the men, "Where are we going?"

11

"To see Bracken and the others." The Arcadian gently grabbed the young warrior under the bicep, pulling him in his direction. "Come, time is of the essence." Harrison nodded, then gestured with his head for the young cleric to join them.

Harrison and Swinkle followed the Arcadians through a myriad of back alleys, clashes and screams emanating just beyond their reach. Harrison tailed the fighters with a keen eye to their tactics. These men know their city, he reasoned, and they're keeping us away from the enemy, an approach well understood at the Fighter's Guild. Brendan's voice echoed in his head, "Always use your terrain to your advantage."

The soldiers then made an abrupt stop, motioning for Harrison and Swinkle to do the same. "What's the problem?" asked the young warrior.

"Scynthians," said one of the men.

The young warrior snarled, his bicep tingling. "How many?"

"At least four," said the soldier, squinting. "There's a lot of smoke and commotion."

Harrison gazed back at Swinkle. "Remember, stay close." The young cleric nodded, praying to himself that he would not need to use his talents again anytime soon.

The young warrior then brought his attention back to the Arcadians, stepping to the forefront. "We take them by surprise," he ordered. "And remember, attack to kill. On my mark."

Harrison glanced over at Swinkle after his statement. The young cleric closed his eyes and nodded once, acquiescing his long standing position on fighting. The young warrior then turned a purposeful eye to the oncoming savages.

Waiting for the precise moment to launch their attack, he yelled, "Now!"

Harrison, battle axe poised and ready to strike, burst from the alleyway and charged toward the unsuspecting beasts. The soldiers followed his lead, their weapons eager for battle as well. Swinkle remained in the background, waiting for his chance to help from the safety of the passage.

The Aegean pounced on the Scynthian closest to him. The beast, oblivious to the oncoming human, barely had time to raise his weapon before Harrison's cold, steel blade entered his midsection. The creature buckled over in agony, blood pouring from his wound. Harrison's blow incapacitated the savage, exposing his side to the young warrior and leaving him vulnerable to another attack. The Aegean did not miss the opportunity, driving his axe deeper into the savage's torso. The Scynthian's innards spilled to the ground and he never rose again.

The Arcadians followed Harrison's lead, each one taking turns confronting their own enemy. Swords and maces clashed in the middle of the street, each being's survival mode dictating their actions. Harrison delivered a death blow to the Scynthian on his right, but the Arcadian in front of him could not avoid a vicious attack from his opponent. The Scynthian's mace shattered the young man's helmet, crushing his skull. His enemy slain, the beast recoiled his weapon, then turned his attention to Harrison.

The young warrior, adrenalin fueling the blood through his veins, readied himself for another round of battle. The creature burst toward the Aegean, swinging his mace twice at the startled human before recoiling to a defensive posture.

Harrison took advantage of the split second between strikes to find the Arcadians busy doing battle with their foes, leaving him to fend for himself. Without giving the creature a second chance to attack, the Aegean raised his blade, took a step toward the menacing beast, and swung his axe in its direction. The Scynthian avoided the assault and counterattacked, administering a forceful blow to Harrison's side. The young warrior's armor absorbed the hit, but he fell to the ground, the wind knocked from his lungs. Writhing in pain and gasping for air, Harrison strained to gather himself. The Scynthian, recognizing that he owned the upper hand in battle, loomed over the injured human, his mace ready to strike.

Before the beast could deliver the death blow, a bright flash blinded the Scynthian, halting his attack. Harrison, taking advantage of Swinkle's diversion, rolled away from his adversary. Collecting himself, the young warrior got to his knees and swung his battle axe at the beast's legs. His blade severed the creature's right limb, dropping the savage to the ground, writhing in pain.

13

The young warrior jumped to his feet and, channeling an inner strength, drove his battle axe deep into his enemy's chest. The Scynthian made one final gasp before the life left his body.

The young warrior, locking his eyes on the holy man, thanked him with a simple nod. His friend brought his gaze to the left and pointed. A final Scynthian remained locked in battle with two Arcadians.

Harrison took the cue to join the melee. The two fighters, upon seeing the young warrior enter the fray, pulled back from their enemy. The three warriors then positioned themselves in an equidistant triangular configuration around the Scynthian, halting their attack in order to determine the perfect time to strike. Without warning, an arrow whizzed between the men, lodging itself firmly in the creature's chest.

The Scynthian buckled and dropped to its knees. A second arrow hurtled through the air and penetrated the beast's forehead, splitting its skull, and scrambling its brain. The Scynthian dropped to the earth, dead before its body hit the ground.

The group of warriors panned in amazement, searching for the person who had fired the deadly weapon. The young warrior did not have to wait long to get his answer.

"It's about time you rejoined the war," said the leather-clad fighter.

"Murdock, where did you come from?" asked Harrison, as his friend headed toward him.

"From over there," said the ranger, pointing up the street. "You all made the intelligent decision to pick a fight in a wide open area. I could have picked you all off one at a time. Good thing the Scynthians don't possess the skills that I do."

Harrison cracked a smile. "Humble as ever!"

Murdock shook his head and shrugged. "Pondle's around the area, too."

"What about Lance?"

Before he could answer, the little dog came bounding out from one of the alleyways. "Lance!" exclaimed Harrison, as he dropped to one knee to greet his canine friend.

As Lance came closer he could not help but laugh at the dog's outfit. Before leaving Concur, Tara had insisted on protecting Harrison's friend. The young maiden had asked many of the Unified Army soldiers to help find suitable body armor for Lance, which they did, as well as a skull cap that boasted two little horns. She secured the pieces to the dog before sending him off to battle with the men.

Now, while he rubbed Lance's side, Harrison's thoughts drifted to Tara and he wondered if she were safe in Concur. He had convinced her to stay with Meredith and Thoragaard instead of marching with him to Arcadia and into harm's way. The Scynthians would have slaughtered her had they captured her, whereas a human army would have simply kept her as a trophy, neither scenario appealing. He longed to see her again, but knew they had more work to do and their reunion would have to wait for another day.

"I'm glad to see you, too," said Harrison as the little dog rubbed up against his master. While petting the pup, another nagging thought associated with Tara gnawed at the young warrior.

Lifting his eyes to meet Murdock's, he asked with concern, "Where's Gelderand?"

The ranger turned and jerked his thumb to the emptiness behind him. "He's right here," he said before furrowing his brow, a first wave of panic beginning to set in.

* * *

Gelderand chased after Murdock and Pondle through the dangerous streets; however he struggled trying to keep pace with the younger men. Moments ago, several Arcadian soldiers helped them fend off a pack of Scynthian warriors who had hindered their effort to reunite with Swinkle and Harrison in their makeshift safe haven.

The mage watched Murdock race ahead and even caught a glimpse of Lance scooting by the fleet-footed ranger as they rounded a corner. Up ahead, Pondle stopped in his tracks and waved Gelderand onward, encouraging the magician forward. Even though he ran a hundred feet behind the thief, the older man recognized Pondle's familiar look of concern.

15

The halfling squinted and cocked his head in an effort to hone in on an invisible target. Gelderand slowed, hearing a rumble emanating from the building next to him. Seconds later, Scynthian warriors burst from the doorway and flooded the street.

"Gelderand!" yelled Pondle, his eyes wide in shock. He took two steps toward the elder man before stopping in his tracks.

Five Scynthians sprinted past the magician who had frozen in place, incapable of casting a spell, let alone running to safety. Two huge beasts gripped the poor man by his arms and dragged him in the opposite direction from whence he came.

The remaining creatures surrounded Pondle. Outnumbered and overmatched, the thief sheathed his weapon and raised his hands in an act of surrender, knowing that attacking now would be akin to suicide. Two of the beasts grabbed the halfling in the same manner that they had Gelderand, hauling the two prisoners from the safety of the thoroughfare and herding them toward one of their strongholds.

* * *

"*Where* is he?" asked Harrison, his anxiety level rising.

Murdock's brow wrinkled, his tension elevating. "He was following me and Pondle." The ranger bolted back to the passageway he had traversed less than a minute ago. Finding nothing other than an empty street, he bent to one knee and inspected the ground, then peered deeper into the alley.

Harrison, Swinkle, and Lance chased after their friend. The remaining four Arcadians did likewise. Murdock examined the terrain in front of him, but even an amateur investigator could understand the clues presented before him.

"Scynthian tracks are everywhere!" said the bewildered ranger, panning in all directions. "Where did they come from?"

One of the Arcadian soldiers pointed out the obvious. Standing next to the open doorway in the passage, he said, "They came from here." The man stuck his head inside the door jam. "It was an ambush in the waiting."

Harrison had further concerns. Taking a hand to the wound on his head, he caressed the area while asking, "Where are the Scynthian strongholds in this city?"

"We're pretty much on the border," answered the decorated soldier. Motioning with his head toward the south and west, he continued with a scowl, "They control a large portion of Arcadia in that direction."

The young warrior knew that the city of Arcadia encompassed a large portion of the southern countryside. The Scynthians had invaded the metropolis from the southeast, stampeding from their fortresses in the Great Ridge of King Solaris, easily overtaking the little village of Ontario, the fishing villages of Polaris, Nordic, and Lars, and then the great city of Arcadia.

While Harrison and his noble allies had reunited the land in an effort to topple the walled city of Concur, the Scynthians laid in waiting until the formidable Arcadian army left to help in the cause. The thousand strong militia of savages brutalized the cultural center of the land, setting it ablaze, and severing the arms of every man, woman, and child they encountered. Bonfires raged as they sacrificed one human after another to their pagan gods.

The Great Hall of Arcadia housed many soldiers, who did their best to hold back the Scynthian onslaught. Yet they succumbed to the inevitable after a valiant two-week battle. Finding their situation hopeless towards the end of their failed campaign, a very young sentry who had the responsibility of caring for Arcadia's messenger falcon scribbled a frantic note and released the raptor. The bird of prey flew high into the sky, never to be seen again. Likewise, dignitaries from Nordic, Lars, and Polaris released their falcons with similar notes.

Upon receipt of the message, Harrison alerted his fellow leadership team stationed in Concur. Bracken Drake summoned his Arcadian army and left the metropolis that day. Brendan Brigade and the Forge Brothers followed several hours later, leaving a contingent of men behind in case of another Scynthian surprise attack on the newly liberated city. Lady Meredith acquiesced her request to tear down Concur's infamous walls for the time being, in case the beasts attempted the unthinkable.

17

Bracken led his army straight to Arcadia, bypassing the coastal villages, leaving them to the Unified Army to handle. Brendan, the Forge Brothers, Harrison and his friends, and scores of armored men tore through the small villages, beating back the Scynthian occupiers with ease, freeing the towns.

Though Polaris requested aid as well, the leaders had decided that Arcadia needed the assistance of the Unified Army first if it had any chance to retake the city. With Scynthians roaming the municipality, the Arcadians and Unified Army made their counterattack from the north and east in hopes of driving the beasts west, toward the harbor and the immoveable water barrier. After two months of battle, the same strategy still applied but victory had proven elusive.

Harrison glared in the same direction as the Arcadian soldier. The Scynthians still controlled all of the cityscape toward the harbor, as well as portions south and east. Worse yet, they occupied the Great Hall of Arcadia.

The young warrior's head ached and his blood began to simmer. Two of his good friends, one being his love's uncle and someone he swore to protect, now suffered at the hands of their enemy.

"This war has gone on long enough!" he yelled. "Gather all the men you can find! We hunt these beasts now!"

"Yes, sir!" exclaimed the soldier before running off to perform his duty.

Harrison turned his attention to Murdock and Swinkle. With conviction in his voice, he said, "Are you with me?"

Murdock grinned, waving his blade in front of him. "I'm always ready for battle!"

The young warrior took his gaze to Swinkle. "We're going to need you to help Gelderand and Pondle. I'm sure they'll have wounds from their abduction."

"I will be more than ready."

"Lance," called Harrison to his canine companion. The helmeted dog rushed to his master's side. "Stay near us at all times. Alright, boy?"

"Yes!" yapped the canine with a hop.

Harrison took his steely gaze to the alleyway where his friends had disappeared. Fresh tracks raced away from the immediate area; following them would not be hard.

Without another second to spare, he ordered, "Let's go!" The three men and dog then began their trek in earnest to save their friends.

Harrison raced ahead of the other two, Lance following close behind. Instead of being cautious and investigating what might lie ahead for them at the end of the alley, the young warrior rushed at full speed into the open roadway. In the distance he saw a pack of Scynthians running in the opposite direction.

The small platoon chased after the beasts, passing smoldering buildings, burning carts, and side-stepping dead bodies, human and savage alike. As the men closed the gap on the unsuspecting creatures, a pair of enemy warriors popped out from behind strewn carnage, blocking their advancement, clutching their bloody weapons, and ready for battle.

Harrison brandished his battle axe at his adversary, before swinging it at the Scynthian to the right, the one closest to him. The beast used his mace to thwart Harrison's attack but the young warrior's retaliation proved too much for his enemy. The Aegean spun, using the centripetal force in the maneuver to increase the speed of his weapon. The blade penetrated the Scynthian's side at such a high velocity that the beast slumped to the ground in almost two pieces.

The young warrior stepped on the creature's midsection, then jerked the battle axe out of its torso. Next, he brought his attention to the remaining Scynthian. Murdock had already engaged the beast in battle but Harrison's sheer determination changed the course of the fight.

In an unprecedented move, the young warrior shoved his friend out of the way, almost knocking him over. With eerie precision, Harrison swung his blade toward his enemy's head. The creature ducked. However the young warrior's axe severed the top of the monster's helmet, along with a fair amount of fur from its head.

Harrison was not through. In one smooth motion, he slung his battle axe over his shoulder, then took his knee and drove it into

19

the Scynthian's midsection, buckling him. Not finished with the pathetic soul, the young warrior reacquired his weapon, taking the butt of his axe and smacking the beast's exposed forehead, splitting it wide open. Blood poured from the gaping wound and the monster fell to the ground, dropping its club in the process.

Sweat pouring from his body, the young warrior locked his eyes on Swinkle's. "He's done!"

Glaring at the ranger, he yelled, "Follow me!" Murdock, surprised to see this side of his friend, dusted himself off and raced after Harrison.

The young warrior sprinted in the Scynthian convoy's direction, knowing he had little time to save his friends. The streets of Arcadia, the same ones that once sported vendors selling their wares, exquisite artwork and sculpture with a feeling of peace and harmony, now reeked of charred remains. Harrison's belly tightened and the scar around his bicep began to tingle; more battles would come today.

Harrison, leading the charge on the Scynthians, noticed a change in their tactics. Instead of continuing forward, the beasts had stopped their procession and dropped back into a defensive posture, presenting an unnerving foreground to the smoky decrepit buildings that lined both sides of the street. The armored-clad warriors now stood in the epicenter of four intersecting pathways, waiting.

"Harrison! Stop!" yelled Murdock from behind. The young warrior heeded his friend's command, ending his charge two hundred feet from his enemy's position.

The ranger caught up to the young warrior. Hunched, he said, "Slow down!" Between ragged breaths, he continued, "I want to slaughter these beasts as much as you, but we're outnumbered. Getting ourselves killed helps no one!"

Swinkle caught up to the two warriors. Straining to draw precious oxygen into his lungs, he said, "Murdock's right. We need reinforcements."

Harrison contemplated his predicament but a loud raucous roar bellowing from in front of the band of Scynthians more than broke his train of thought. Soldiers, both Arcadian and Unified Army alike, flooded the area from all directions, effectively stopping the Scynthians' forward progress. However, the number of men just about equaled the surrounded beasts. The platoons of human soldiers encircled the city's unwanted guests, halting thirty feet before them, holding their ground.

Both human and Scynthian armies glared at each other, neither side ready to make the first move. Amidst the crackling sound of burning buildings, an eerie silence enveloped the area while each group pondered their new situation. To the chagrin of the human forces, a Scynthian leader pointed his weapon at the enemy before him and let out a primal scream. His warriors acknowledged their leader's battle cry, rushing toward their adversaries, roaring in unison.

Fighters from both camps charged from all directions, engaging in battle, a myriad of weapons clashing. The once quaint Arcadian neighborhood had now become a hotbed of fallen fighters, blood spilling onto the pathways, staining them a deep red. Scynthians butchered the humans, severing their arms whenever possible, while the men followed their orders to kill any foreign invader in their path.

Murdock, taking his concentration away from the tumultuous battle before him, located Harrison, finding his eyes narrow and focused, his face red with rage. Grabbing the young warrior's forearm, he said, "Remember, we save Pondle and Gelderand first. Slaughtering those beasts is secondary." Harrison nodded once in affirmation.

The young warrior locked eyes with Swinkle. "Help our men any way possible."

"Of course." Also recognizing the young warrior's intensity, he said in a soothing tone, "Harrison, stay in control."

The Aegean glared at the holy man. "Don't worry about me! Let's save our friends!"

Out of the corner of his eye, the young cleric noticed Lance ready to follow his master into the melee. Pointing to the ground next to him, he said in a forceful voice, "Lance! Stay here!"

The small dog appeared confused at first, eyeing Harrison for approval, but the young warrior had already set his sights on battle.

"Now!" yelled Swinkle in the canine's direction. Lance dropped his helmeted head and reluctantly shuffled to the young cleric's side.

Harrison eyed the impending action with the fervor of a man possessed. Raising his battle axe, the Aegean rushed to the scene and launched himself into the melee, searching for Gelderand and Pondle in the process. Murdock flanked his friend to the right, his short sword in hand and ready to strike. Swinkle and Lance maintained their distance on the outskirts of the fighting, doing their best to keep a visual on their friends while staying away from the clashing weaponry.

Harrison took a split second to gauge his situation. Before him stood the back line of Scynthian warriors, four immediately in front of him with another twenty more battling at the forefront. Human soldiers attacked the mob from all angles, the majority of the fighting occurring in the middle of the Arcadian roadway.

The young warrior's battle instincts took over. Turning his attention to Murdock, he shouted, "Get ready to run if these cowards decide to retreat!"

The ranger peeked over his shoulder, finding only a rather nervous cleric and dog behind him. Returning his gaze forward, he caught his friend's eye and nodded. Pointing his sword at the group of Scynthians, he screamed, "Charge!"

Harrison prepared his weapon for battle and after three quick strides, swung his battle axe into the back of his unsuspecting enemy. The Scynthian howled in pain and buckled to the ground. "One down," said the young warrior.

Knowing that the beast's comrades would react to their fallen friend, the Aegean fighter took the offensive again, driving his blade into the side of his next victim. Murdock, taking Harrison's cue, attacked the Scynthian closest to him.

The ranger's blade sliced the creature's body, but did not incapacitate him. Growling in anger, the beast swung its mace at Murdock, striking the ranger in the chest, sending him reeling backwards.

Murdock's leather armor did a poor job cushioning the blow. Intense pain exuded from the ranger's chest, the strike knocking him almost senseless. Murdock tried to raise his weapon, but the throbbing sensation radiating from his sternum prevented him from attaining a proper defensive position.

The Scynthian, sensing his enemy's weakened state, took a purposeful step in Murdock's direction, readying his mace for the death blow. To his surprise, a small dog appeared near his feet, gnawing at his boots in a futile attempt to pull him away from the injured ranger. The strange sight of the armor-clad dog paused the Scynthian's attack just long enough for Swinkle to perform his task.

The young cleric threw his hands open in the creature's direction. A bright flash filled the area, blinding the Scynthian, causing him to instinctively cover his eyes with his glove-covered hands. Murdock, taking the opportunity at hand, rolled away from his distracted foe, safe for the time being.

Lance, exploiting the Scynthian's state of confusion, sunk his teeth deeper into the creature's leg. Disoriented, the beast tried to kick the little dog away, attempting to rid itself of the menacing canine. However, Lance persisted, intent on helping his masters. The warrior, his initial effort a failure, flailed its mace at the dog. Lance, anticipating the attack, teleported to safety just as the warrior's weapon smacked his own leg. The savage, infuriated, howled in pain, whipping into a crazed frenzy.

Taking advantage of the Scynthian's disillusioned state, Murdock hobbled over to the monster and drove his sword into its side. The creature wailed in agony, buckling to the ground. The ranger, not finished with his enemy yet, plunged his weapon into the savage's midsection again, killing the beast. The battle over, he tumbled backward, took a hand to his chest, and dropped to his knees.

Swinkle, knowing that he had precious little time to help his friend, grabbed the ranger and dragged him away from the melee. Lance, sensing the imminent danger, teleported to Swinkle's side, keeping a watchful eye on the chaotic fighting mere feet away.

"My chest hurts," said Murdock between painful breaths.

The young cleric assessed his friend's injury and with a scowl said, "You must remove your armor, otherwise my prayers will not work."

Murdock gave him an incredulous look. Pointing at the Scynthians who fought a short distance away, he yelled, "Not with them right there!"

Using a firm grip on the ranger's right arm, Swinkle began to pull him further away from the fighting and in the direction of an alleyway. "You're coming with me!" The young cleric glanced over to Harrison, finding him holding his own against his foes.

Before Murdock could protest, Swinkle had already led him toward the closest building. Lance scurried between the two humans and the battling Scynthians, ready to alert the men if the situation changed.

* * *

Harrison, sweat dripping from his brow, drove his battle axe into another Scynthian, dropping his enemy to the ground and adding to his internal count, six beasts down. The young warrior glanced over his shoulder, attempting to gauge Murdock's success rate. His heart raced harder when he saw no one behind him.

The young warrior frantically searched for his friends, panning in all directions while assessing the battle at the same time. A familiar bark eased his anxiety.

The Aegean focused on Lance's position, one hundred feet away. Beyond the dog he saw Swinkle attending to Murdock in the relative safety of the alley. No Scynthians close to them, good, he thought. He then brought his eyes back to the battlefront, realizing that he now stood alone.

Before him, the raucous band of Scynthians continued to fight, albeit with dwindling numbers. As Harrison contemplated his next move, a low rumble began to emanate above the din of clashing weapons. Utilizing his warrior training, he hyper focused on the new sound while remaining mindful of the melee at hand. Honing on the reverberation, he determined that it resonated from behind him. Jerking his head in that direction brought a wry smile to his face. Soldiers on horseback, adorned with red plumes and markings, galloped toward his position with weapons drawn.

The Scynthians halted their attack as the Arcadians rushed past Harrison, advancing deeper into their battle space. Their fighting position compromised, the creatures combatting in front of the young warrior turned and began to retreat in his direction. Harrison's eyes grew wide as fifteen beasts raced toward him.

Battle axe raised in a defensive posture, Harrison awaited the charging Scynthians, preparing for the onslaught. To his surprise, the savages sprinted past him, choosing to save themselves rather than continue the fight. The Arcadian horsemen chased the cowards, using their long, razor sharp lances to stab the creatures in their backs as they ran away. One by one, the men from the local army eliminated their enemy, dashing past Harrison and leaving him standing alone in the now deserted street. His enemy vanquished for the time being, the young warrior took the opportunity to regroup with his friends.

"What happened?" asked Harrison, shaking his head with concern, finding the ranger wincing in pain. Swinkle, sensitive to Murdock's injury, did his best to help him remove his leather armor.

"A mace hit me square in the chest," said Murdock through ragged breaths.

"You need to start wearing chain mail," said Harrison, a bit of agitation in his voice. Lance scurried beside his master, watching Swinkle work with anticipation, but still serving as protector to the men.

"Lean up against the wall," said Swinkle.

Harrison, in an effort to get Murdock into a sitting position, placed his hands underneath his armpits and lifted him up.

Murdock's eyes grew wide. "What are you doing?" he said, the pain evident in his voice. "Are you trying to kill me?"

"Stay still," said Swinkle. "I need to concentrate."

The young cleric positioned his hands over Murdock's injured area and began to pray. A soft white glow encompassed the ranger's chest for ten seconds before ceasing.

Murdock let out a sigh of relief. "I feel better already. What you did really took the edge off my pain."

"You are still going to need rest," said Swinkle, knowing Murdock's propensity for battling.

The ranger leaned over and grabbed his armor that lay on the ground. "We need to find Pondle and Gelderand, remember?" Murdock winced as he started to put on his body covering again.

Harrison focused on Murdock's comment. "I didn't see them after the Arcadians rode by," he said with worry in his voice.

The ranger rose to a standing position. "All the more reason to keep searching," he said, taking the lead and advancing into the now empty street. "Which way did they go?"

Harrison left the alley behind and surveyed the area as well. To their left he found five Arcadian horsemen holding their position three hundred feet away.

The young warrior pointed in their direction. "Follow me," he said, starting his trek toward the riders. "We need to talk with them."

Harrison led the small band of adventurers to the horsemen, but before he could address the lead soldier, the man exclaimed, "Sir! This is a miracle!"

The young warrior and his friends halted, surprised at the man's declaration. The rest of the riders maneuvered their horses to greet the platoon as well.

"We were sent to find all of you!" said the leader.

Harrison's brow crinkled. "You were? Who sent you looking for us?"

"Bracken himself," said the Arcadian. His expression then turned serious. "Sir, please don't think that we left you behind. We needed to handle those Scynthians first."

Harrison nodded and waved a hand toward the rider. "Understood. Have you captured any of the beasts?"

"They're all dead, per General Drake's orders."

The young warrior nodded once again, recalling how the Arcadian leader had placed a bounty on every marauding invader's head. "Where's Bracken and the rest of the leadership?"

"We'll take you to them," said the soldier.

"Wait!" lamented Murdock. "Where are Pondle and Gelderand?"

The young warrior's face dropped, having temporarily forgotten about their friends. "We chased after those beasts after they abducted them! We need to keep searching!"

The Arcadian smiled, raising a palm at the flustered Aegean. "We found your friends and brought them to a safe place for treatment. Follow us and we'll take you there."

Harrison let out a sigh of relief, then gazed over to his friends. Murdock wheezed with every breath he took and Swinkle's drawn expression meant that performing so many mental tasks in such a short period of time had taken its toll. The young warrior looked down at Lance. The little dog locked eyes on his master and wagged his tail in earnest. Harrison smirked. At least you're in good shape, he thought.

The young warrior addressed the man on horseback. "Lead us to our friends." The rider nodded, then led the small posse of tired and beaten warriors to regroup with their comrades.

27

CHAPTER 2

$\Box$

The five Arcadian riders led Harrison and his friends
away from the desolate streets and deeper into the city. While the
men ventured they noticed more of a human presence with many
additional soldiers patrolling the area, securing the streets and
alleyways. Fires that still blazed in the metropolis no longer raged
in this zone, and most of the landscape resembled charred
buildings instead of burning furnaces.

Harrison absorbed the sheer destruction. The Scynthians
had really sacked Arcadia, he thought, rationalizing that it would
take a miracle for the Arcadians to even salvage the city. Had they
not instituted the falcon messenger system they would never have
learned about Arcadia's fate for several more weeks, dooming the
land's former cultural center forever.

The horsemen led the men past hordes of injured soldiers
and townsfolk alike. The young warrior's belly tightened as the
wails of suffering people and the inconsolable cries of those who
had lost loved ones resonated throughout the area. The Scynthians
will pay for this, he promised.

Up ahead, Harrison noticed that the region took on more of
a militaristic zone. The warriors reached a checkpoint guarded by
a platoon of Arcadian soldiers, who allowed them to pass without
incidence. The young warrior quickly realized the mantra of the

28

Arcadian military; as long as you were not Scynthian, you would be allowed safe passage. The unmistakable stench of death clung in the air as Harrison ventured through the border crossing. Swinkle broke the young warrior out of his trance.

"There are so many people dying here," he said, panning the area, taking in the desolation. "I need to help."

Harrison nodded. "Do what you can, Swinkle." The young warrior scanned the immediate vicinity, searching for someone just out of sight. "I'm going to find Gelderand."

"And Pondle," added Murdock with conviction. "If he's hurt ..." he said through clenched teeth, his voice trailing off.

"I'm sure he's fine," said Harrison. "Make sure you find us when he appears and I'll do the same for Gelderand." Murdock agreed with a nod, then went off in search of the thief.

Harrison turned to speak to Swinkle, but the young cleric had already meandered over to a group of men addressing their wounds. The young warrior gazed down at his last friend. Lance sat next to his master, patiently waiting for their next move.

"Let's go, boy. Gelderand needs us."

Harrison and his canine companion began to roam the area, searching in earnest for their lost friend. Every few yards the young warrior would ask anyone who would listen if they had seen the elder magician. Each time he left unfulfilled.

The young warrior took a short break from his quest after fifteen minutes of unsuccessful investigation. Harrison used his down time to familiarize himself with Arcadia's basic roadway design. The Arcadians had fashioned the streets in a grid-like pattern with equidistant blocks that once housed residences and businesses. Today, barricades of charred logs and debris blocked all passages into this safe zone, preventing the Scynthians from charging into the compound unhindered.

Harrison brought his gaze down to Lance. "Not too promising, boy." The little dog cocked his head, unsure of his master's statement. "Let's keep moving."

Within minutes of their renewed search, Harrison and Lance ran into a familiar face. Swinkle, engaged in intense concentration, had hunched over a young man with bloody wounds. His efforts produced a white haze that encompassed the

29

fighter's injuries. After the light subsided, the young cleric sprinkled holy water on the lacerations, then bade the man farewell.

Harrison waited until his friend had finished performing his task before approaching him. "I see you have your fair share of good deeds to perform," he said with a smile.

Swinkle gazed back with weary eyes. "There are so many people to help and I am near exhaustion."

The young warrior placed a hand on the holy man's shoulder. "You can't save them all."

"But I must try." The young cleric fastened the cap on his vial of holy water, then said, "Gelderand?" Harrison shook his head without saying a word.

"He must be here somewhere," said Swinkle. "I will help you." Before the two young men restarted their search, Swinkle pointed to a pair of fighters taking inventory of their possessions.

"It's Murdock!" Harrison said, his voice full of excitement. "And he's with Pondle!"

The two men passed makeshift campfires and scores of soldiers before meeting up with their friends. Lance scurried to Pondle's side, wagging his tail. Harrison approached Murdock first, but quickly noticed the look of dejection on the ranger's face.

The young warrior, sensing something amiss, asked, "Are you two alright?"

"We're fine," said Pondle adjusting his backpack, putting Harrison at ease for the moment.

The young warrior brought his eyes to Murdock, his brow scrunched. "Then what?"

The ranger jerked his head back, signaling for Harrison to look behind him. Ten yards away, with men shuffling between them, sat Gelderand alone on the ground staring into nothingness, holding something in his hands.

Harrison's eyes widened. Without saying a word, he scooted past Murdock and Pondle and rushed to the magician's side. The young warrior's heart sank upon reaching him.

The elder man lifted his eyes to meet Harrison's worrisome gaze. "The Scynthians tossed him around like a toy," said the heartbroken mage, holding Rufus' motionless body in his hands.

30

"They didn't even treat him like a living creature." Lance made a cautious approach to Gelderand, rubbing his head on the still cat's back.

Unsure of what to say, Harrison feebly asked, "Is he dead?"

Gelderand pulled the animal close to his chest, sniffling. "I can't get him to awaken."

Swinkle approached the somber men. In a soothing tone, he said to the mage, "Will you let me pray over him? Pious adores all creatures, especially animals. He may have mercy on Rufus' soul."

Gelderand nodded, squeezed the feline a bit tighter, then released him to the young cleric. Swinkle took the cat from the mage's hands, caressing the tabby's orange fur. Rufus did not move. He then brought the animal's face close to his ear. Swinkle's expression turned hopeful.

"He's breathing," said the young cleric, a tinge of optimism in his voice.

Swinkle took care in placing Rufus on the ground, then laid his hands over the feline's frail body. The young cleric closed his eyes, concentrated, and prayed to his god, Pious. A soft white glow encompassed the cat's entire body. A moment later, the young cleric finished his prayer, ceasing the light.

All the men, along with Lance, waited in anticipation to see what would happen next. Rufus still did not move. Swinkle furrowed his brow, then took the cat into his arms. The young cleric, using his right hand while holding the animal in his left, fumbled for the elusive vial on his belt. Getting a firm grip on the bottle at last, he took the holy water and sprinkled it onto the cat's face.

"Pious, please show mercy for one of your creatures," said Swinkle. "Rufus should not leave this world at the hands of the Scynthians. In your name, I breathe life back into his lungs." Swinkle then blew warm air over the creature's furry face.

All eyes remained fixed on the pair. Harrison stared at the cat with anticipation, hopeful that Swinkle's prayers would work. However, with each passing second of inactivity, the group began to lose hope that Rufus would survive.

31

The young warrior walked over to Swinkle, placed a caring hand on the cat's little head, then approached the sorrowful mage. "I'm so sorry, Gelderand."

Before the elder magician had a chance to respond, Rufus let out a gasp, then meowed. The feline blinked twice and shook its head, trying to gather its bearings. Gelderand jumped to his feet upon hearing Rufus' cry.

"Rufus!" he exclaimed and reached for the cat.

"Wait!" said Swinkle, keeping his grip on the feline. "He is alive but hurt."

The magician lowered his hands, his brow crinkled with concern. "What are the extent of his injuries?"

The young cleric extended his arms in order to better examine Rufus' body. After a moment, Swinkle made a closer inspection of the cat's hind legs.

"I think he might have a problem with his back," he said, cradling Rufus, making him more comfortable. "His legs do not appear right to me."

Gelderand held out his hands. "Oh, Rufus, I'm so sorry I brought you to this desolate war zone."

"Be careful," said Swinkle, gently handing the feline to the wizard.

"I will keep you with me at all times, Rufus," said Gelderand, stroking the cat's little head. Rufus tried to purr, but his breaths were ragged and strained.

Swinkle took a closer look at the cat's backside while Gelderand held him close. "He is in pain, but he does not want anyone to know." The young cleric squeezed the cat's right leg and gave it a gentle tug. Rufus screeched, recoiled, and hissed at Swinkle.

"Rufus!" said Gelderand, surprised at the animal's outburst.

"He is in considerable pain," said Swinkle. "Please keep him still and I will pray over him again."

The mage did his best to maneuver the injured cat to expose his hindquarters. Swinkle then laid his hands over the feline's legs and prayed for Pious to alleviate Rufus' pain. A soft white glow encompassed the cat's injured parts. Rufus then snuggled deeper into his master's arms after Swinkle finished his task.

The young cleric patted Rufus on the head, then took his gaze to Gelderand. "He needs rest."

"I will give him all the rest he deserves."

Swinkle shook his head. "I don't think you understand what I mean. How old is he?"

The magician's eyes widened. "Fifteen? Sixteen? What are you saying?"

The young cleric pursed his lips. In a soothing tone, he said, "Gelderand, I think Rufus' time has come."

"No! You're wrong!" exclaimed the mage. "I will take care of him and make him comfortable! He's not dying today or any day soon!"

Swinkle raised his palms toward the elder man. "Alright, it is your decision. I just wanted you to know my thoughts."

Gelderand squinted and shook his head. "You prayed over him, he's fine now."

"Place him on the ground," said Swinkle. "Let him stretch his legs." The mage recognized Swinkle's tactic, forcing him to face realities that he did not want to acknowledge himself.

The mage turned his head away from Swinkle. "He's fine and he wants to be held."

"Gelderand, please put him on the ground," said the young cleric with a little more conviction. "We need to see how hurt he truly is."

Gelderand acquiesced, bending to one knee and placing the feline down with care. Rufus' hind legs buckled immediately, causing the cat to sprawl on the ground, letting out a whimper in the process.

The magician brought a hand to his face, understanding the gravity of Rufus' injury. Gelderand then took two steps back and bent down. Extending a hand, he said to the cat, "Come here, Rufus."

The feline stared at his master, but did not move. Rufus meowed in Gelderand's direction, but again stayed motionless. Lance left Harrison's side, intent on aiding Rufus. The little dog sensed the anxiety exuding from the creature and nudged him with his snout, encouraging the cat to move toward Gelderand.

Rufus meowed again and rubbed his little head against Lance. The tabby then channeled an inner strength, using his front legs to pull himself to Gelderand while his hind legs dragged behind. Upon reaching the wizard, the older man bent down and scooped his little friend back into his arms.

The mage gazed back at the men, his face long with sadness. "Swinkle, can you get him to at least walk again?"

The young cleric's shoulders slumped. Shaking his head, he said, "I don't know."

Harrison stepped forward. "Gelderand, I'm sure Swinkle will do all he can to help Rufus feel more comfortable." The young warrior locked eyes on his friend, who nodded in concurrence.

Gelderand held Rufus to his face. "Well, Rufus, it's official. You are retiring from adventuring and I will bring you back to stay with Tara."

Harrison made a subtle look to Swinkle, Murdock, and Pondle before saying, "I think that's an excellent idea. She'll be more than happy to take care of him and Rufus can stay out of areas like this for the rest of his life."

The magician took his weary gaze to his friends. "This is a hard day for me. Thanks for understanding."

The young warrior approached the mage and placed a caring hand on his shoulder. "We'll get Rufus to safety just as soon as we finish with our business here."

"What's our next move?" asked Murdock, taking the opportunity to change the subject.

Harrison, relieved by the ranger's question, said, "We need to find Bracken Drake."

"Any idea where he is?" asked the ranger.

The young warrior reexamined the immediate area. Most of the Arcadian military patrolled the vicinity, checking on the injured, keeping a watchful eye for any suspicious Scynthian activity. Though the enemy had set many of the buildings ablaze a short time ago, the structures in the neighborhood had withstood the worst conditions and survived. People utilized them to help shelter their battered lives and to somehow return to normalcy.

Soldiers congregated up one of the main arteries of the locale with a higher concentration a short way away. Harrison peered into the distance, noticing the change in the fortified area.

The young warrior pointed to a very heavily guarded section up ahead. "I'm willing to bet he's over there." The men glanced in the direction Harrison pointed. "Follow me."

The small group set their sights on a large, guarded tent erected fifty yards away from their position, protected from the makeshift camps of the countless injured souls. Harrison made a mental image of his surroundings as they strode up the street, finding that the oncoming grounds housed fewer townspeople and more of the healthier, able-bodied soldier types. The secured area rested in the middle of yet another Arcadian intersection with near-ruined buildings staring down from all angles.

Halfway to their destination loomed another checkpoint, where large spiked, wooden barricades prevented people from simply walking through to their leader's tent. Harrison surveyed the perimeter, finding that Bracken's sanctuary sat in the middle of a hundred-foot wide circle. The four-foot tall, spike-like pointed barriers left the Arcadian general in relative safety.

Upon reaching the guarded entranceway, the sentries recognized Harrison and his friends and, knowing that they posed no threat to their leader, allowed them to pass. The small group then walked unhindered to the entry.

Harrison made eye contact with the guards that flanked either side of the tent's opening. "We need to speak with Bracken."

"One moment, sir," said the Arcadian on the left, before he entered the tent. The sentry on the right gave Harrison a half smile.

"How's everyone holding out?" asked the young warrior.

"This city has seen better days, sir."

Harrison nodded. "That it has."

The first guard returned and held the tent's flap open for the men. "General Drake's eager to see you." The young warrior and his friends entered the sanctuary.

Bracken stood in the center of the tent and wasted no time in approaching the young warrior. Extending his hand, he said, "Harrison, it's good to see you alive." He took his eyes to the others. "All of you."

Harrison shook the Arcadian leader's hand. "It's good to see you again too, sir."

Bracken gestured toward a large table and chairs, a map of Arcadia sprawled on its surface. "Please, make yourselves comfortable." The men all found a seat, while Lance lay next to Harrison. Bracken took a seat at the head of the table.

The young warrior noticed a bed and sleeping area, a place for the Arcadian's armor and weaponry, and very little else. This man did not plan to stay here long, he surmised.

His assessment complete, Harrison asked, "What's the latest developments?" while his friends listened with intent.

Bracken tensed, drawing a deep exhale before answering. "These filthy beasts have done their best to ransack my city, but the tide's finally turning. We have a surprise for them coming soon."

Harrison leaned closer to Bracken. "What do you have in mind?"

"A major offensive," started the Arcadian. "We've stabilized all of our lines throughout the city. We haven't lost an outpost in over a week and have started making a dent in the Scynthian's main advantage."

The young warrior cocked his head. "Which advantage? They have many."

"Their sheer numbers," said Bracken. "The Unified Army has held the perimeter of the city, preventing them from getting reinforcements and supplies. It pains me to say this, but we needed to wait them out inside Arcadia, knowing that if we could trap them inside the city we would eventually defeat them."

"But there has to be thousands of Scynthians in the city," said Harrison, shaking his head. "And we've already slaughtered hundreds of them. How much longer is this war going to take?"

"The time is ripe, Harrison," said the Arcadian, with the coolness of an experienced leader. Panning slowly to each member of the group, he said, "They surprised us and wasted precious energy and resources defeating a limited army and simple townsfolk. Unfortunately, they entrenched themselves in my city and waited for the ultimate battle."

"And that battle is coming now?" asked the Aegean.

Bracken gave the young warrior a sly smile. "That it is."

Harrison's brain churned with potential military strategies. "What's the plan?"

Bracken waved the men closer to the detailed map of Arcadia. The adventurers leaned forward in their seats in order to get a better vantage point. Pointing to an area near the harbor, the general began, "We've pushed them to here and have held our ground." The Arcadian motioned to a zone that encompassed several blocks that ended with the harbor.

Harrison's eyes widened. "Are you sure about your strongholds? The Scynthians haven't breached them?"

Bracken smiled. "No."

The young warrior analyzed the ground the Scynthians held. "Is there anything of importance in that part of the city?"

The Arcadian grimaced. "Businesses, people's homes, and," he paused before adding, "the Great Hall of Arcadia."

Harrison understood the symbolic meaning of the Scynthians occupying the city's political and military building. Choosing his words carefully, he said, "Bracken, we'll root those savages out of that place and restore your city's dignity."

Bracken shook his head. "Now you're thinking like a Scynthian."

The general's comment surprised Harrison. With a crinkle of his brow and a shake of his head, he asked, "A Scynthian? What do you mean? The battle will be difficult, but we'll prevail."

"As far as I'm concerned, that land is stained. No Arcadian could stomach going back there in its current condition or after we eradicate them."

Harrison's brow furrowed. "What are you proposing?"

Bracken's face remained stone cold. "We burn it and use the Scynthians as kindling for the greatest bonfire this land has ever seen. A taste of their own medicine, so to speak."

The young warrior's face went blank, a myriad of thoughts running through his mind. He took his gaze to Murdock who gave him a subtle smile, agreeing with the general's strategy without saying a word.

Before Harrison could respond to Bracken's statement, the Arcadian continued, "How many limbs have they severed from

innocent men, women, and children? How many more did they
heave into raging infernos? While they were still alive?"

Harrison recalled having the same sentiments many times
in the past, even with Swinkle's constant resonating overtures.
Furthermore, his arm tingled, forcing him to recall his own grisly
encounter with the savages.

"If we go forward with this plan, the whole area will be
destroyed. You understand this?"

"I'd rather rebuild than to live in the stench of those
wretched beasts," said Bracken, his voice rising. "If I had it my
way, I'd burn the whole city to the ground, but that section of town
will do."

Harrison digested the information. He brought his gaze to
his friends, each one nodding, agreeing with the Arcadian leader.
With confidence, the young warrior said, "We stand by you on this
plan. It's high time we settle the score with these savages. When
were you planning the roasting?"

"Tomorrow."

Harrison's eyes widened. "Tomorrow! Is everyone on
board with this?" Images of Brendan Brigade and the Forge
Brothers flashed in his mind.

Bracken raised an eyebrow. "Do you really think they'd be
against it?"

It did not take much thought for Harrison. "Not really."

"They will be alerted tonight," said the Arcadian. Keeping
with the common battle theme, he continued, "Is there anything
you and your men need?"

"We could always use supplies," started the young warrior
before catching himself. "Where do we fit into your attack
strategy?"

"I'm glad you asked," said Bracken. "I would like you to
lead a platoon of men to the outskirts of the Scynthian
strongholds." The Arcadian paused. "We need to ready the area."

"Ready the area?" asked Harrison, not understanding
Bracken's train of thought.

"You need someone to prepare the fires," interjected
Pondle, sensing another covert mission was at hand.

"Precisely," said Bracken.

Murdock could barely contain his smile. "Things just got a little more interesting!"

Harrison raised his palms toward the Arcadian leader. "Wait a minute? How are we going to enter that part of the city without being attacked with every step we take?"

"I didn't say it would be easy, Harrison," started Bracken. "You'll need to position drums of oil in strategic places, douse other areas with the black liquid, and prevent the beasts from escaping the city when it ignites."

"And how are we going to light up the town, so to speak?"

Bracken had thought his plan through. Taking his gaze to Gelderand, he said, "Your attire leads me to believe that you're a magician of some sort, correct?"

The older man's brow furrowed. "Yes, I am. What does that matter?"

"You can cast spells of fire and the like, right?"

Gelderand nodded. "That would be true."

Without missing a beat, Bracken brought his gaze to Murdock and pointed at the ranger, saying, "And you're an expert bowman?"

Murdock lifted his eyebrows in surprise. "Well, yes, I am."

"You will have my archers at your disposal to hit their marks with flaming arrows," said Bracken. "I assure you, they won't miss."

The ranger folded his arms and sat back in his chair. "Works for me. We'll cook those bastards alive!"

Harrison still had more burning questions to ask. "How do we get the drums into the city? And, where are these strategic positions?"

Bracken smirked. "I'm assuming that you have nowhere better to be right now?"

The young warrior panned to his friends with a surprised look on his face. Taking his gaze back to Bracken, he said, "Well, no we don't."

"Good," said the Arcadian. "I'll summon my soldiers to get us some food and drink. We have some planning to do."

CHAPTER 3

Ｑ

Murdock and Pondle led the platoons of men to the outskirts of enemy territory as the daytime sky faded to twilight. Harrison took a hand to shade his eyes from the torches that illuminated the area. Panning the perimeter, he found more charred, two-story buildings littering the immediate landscape. Further investigation revealed wooden barricades blocking the main roads from passage. The Scynthians were not going anywhere, the young warrior concluded.

The Aegean reflected on Bracken's assessment of the Scynthian occupation, then evaluated his own predicament. The great harbor sat five blocks to the west, more Arcadian forces waited ten blocks to the east and the Unified Army amassed to the north. General Drake had recounted with pride how his army used the city's grid-like roadway pattern to push the Scynthians toward the immoveable waterway. He also gloated how his archers kept the savages at bay while soldiers and townsfolk alike constructed the roadway barriers.

Harrison stared at the wooden blockades. The Arcadians had used the remains of their burnt buildings to construct the obstacles, he deduced. Standing a good twenty feet wide and four feet tall, they resembled interlocking four-pointed barbs, with each spike three feet in length. The young warrior recognized the familiar pattern from Bracken's sanctuary, albeit in a smaller scale near the Arcadian's tent.

Murdock halted the convoy, noticing Harrison inspecting the obstructions. "Those beasts will impale themselves if they're stupid enough to try and get through these blockades." The ranger brought his attention to his leader. "We're here. What's next?"

Bracken's strategy continued to echo in the young warrior's mind, having studied the general's tactics to such a degree that one might think he had created the plan himself. "Have the Arcadians take three drums of oil to each intersection and tell them to wait for the signal."

Murdock hesitated just long enough for Harrison to notice. "And what about the other part of his plan?" he asked.

The young warrior shrugged. "This is his battle and we're going to do just what he wants us to do." Harrison stood tall. "Ready the Arcadians."

The ranger nodded, then he and Pondle relayed Harrison's orders. The young warrior peered back to Gelderand while the two men attended to their task.

"Don't wander too far away," said Harrison. The mage returned a single nod. "You have everything you need, right?"

"I will be ready to perform my task," answered the magician.

Harrison noticed a furry face sticking out of the wizard's pack. "How's Rufus?"

"Not good," said Gelderand with a grimace.

"I'll keep an eye on him," said Swinkle, reassuring the elder man. Gelderand closed his eyes, pursed his lips, and nodded, appreciating the holy man's concern toward his feline friend.

The young warrior returned to the task at hand upon seeing Murdock and Pondle coming back to their position. Harrison brought his focus to the ranger.

"Are you sure the Arcadians know where to position those drums?"

The ranger rolled his eyes. "For the last time, yes!" Murdock pointed to the building in front of him. "The Scynthians are one block away."

The Aegean felt his stomach tighten. Bracken had given him seven platoons of ten men each, with every man assigned a particular task. This did not include the archers who waited until

41

Harrison had established a safe perimeter. Still, the young warrior felt uneasy.

"The men understand the plan, right?" asked Harrison, knowing the answer already but needing to hear confirmation.

"Bracken would not send us into an unwinnable battle," responded Murdock. "Especially with his own men."

Harrison took his gaze to the buildings that loomed before him. Burned, charred, smoldering, but … quiet. Too quiet.

"Do we have any scouts over there?" asked the young warrior, motioning with his head toward the inevitable battle.

"No," answered Murdock.

The young warrior barked his final orders. "Swinkle, stay close to me," he said, staring at the young cleric. Swinkle nodded once in affirmation.

Looking down, he said to the helmeted dog, "Lance, you be careful. No adventures!"

The little dog yapped, "Yes!"

Harrison brought his gaze to Gelderand. "You must stay safe at all times. You're most critical to this operation."

"I understand my role and I will be ready when the time comes," assured the elder member of the group.

Harrison nodded again and again, mentally preparing himself for the upcoming fight. Turning to the Arcadian scout that stood a few feet away from him, he ordered, "Sound the horn!" adding, "Remember, one burst only!"

The young man nodded, placed the horn to his lips, then blew. The sound from the instrument reverberated throughout the area. Upon hearing the signal, everyone removed an article from their packs and placed it over their heads.

Harrison pivoted in Murdock's direction. The young warrior's blue eyes gazed at his friend through a blood-soaked, demon-faced mask. In the meantime, the flickering light from the torches cast haunting shadows over the army of devilish minions or so it seemed.

"Alright, Murdock, let's start this battle."

The ranger nodded once, his own skull mask staring at the young warrior. He then reached for a single arrow and doused it in oil. Motioning with his head, he summoned Gelderand. The mage knew just what to do. Mumbling a spell to himself, the wizard's hands began to radiate an orange glow before he placed them over the oil-drenched projectile. The heat from the man's hands ignited the arrow's tip and, once it did, the ranger drew back on his bow and let the arrow fly.

The projectile hurtled into the night, toward a two-story building in the distance, then struck the structure's roof, causing no real damage. However, the humans had sent their message. Upon seeing the signal, the Arcadians began dumping the oil alongside the buildings and, after they emptied the drums, the soldiers used torches to ignite the accelerant.

Harrison swiveled his demon face to the young soldier with the horn and nodded once. The Arcadian gazed back through a freshly oozing, blade scarred head covering and nodded back. Taking the horn to his lips, he gave it two quick bursts. Seconds later, the sound of death drums began to permeate the perimeter, their eerie cadence resonating off the structures in a hair-raising fashion.

Harrison watched his own army of minions perform their task, then lifted his eyes to the empty street before him. Within seconds, Scynthians flooded the area with weapons drawn, having observed the humans and planning their own counterattack.

The young warrior watched as the beasts halted their charge in lieu of the increasing flames and impassable barriers. Furthermore, he noticed the look of confusion on the Scynthians' faces as they gazed upon what appeared to be a demonic force. *Bracken, you're a genius,* Harrison thought, taking in the sight of the apprehensive expressions before him.

With the creatures across the blockade in check for the time being, Harrison turned his attention to Gelderand and, with a single nod, signaled for the mage to begin the next phase of their operation.

The magician, adorned with a horned demon mask of his own, took his cue and unfurled a long scroll that he had obtained as part of the Treasure of the Land. Swinkle, wearing an ogre face covering, came to his aid, helping to hold the parchment steady. Next, the mage started to recite the magical text.

43

The surrounding air stirred and, with each passing word, the breeze began to intensify. The men continued their task of igniting the area, the accompanying winds aiding their cause. The strong breeze fanned the flames, giving the fire much-needed oxygen that allowed it to consume the buildings in its path. Within minutes, the structures both to the left and right of Harrison's group became engulfed in flames. Furthermore, volleys of flaming arrows hurtled into the Scynthian-occupied area from all points beyond the barriers.

The young warrior took his line of sight to the beings on the opposite side of the barricades. For the first time in a very long while he recognized an unmistakable Scynthian emotion – fear.

The beasts quickly deduced the humans' strategy. Realizing the limitations of their own battle plans, they instead retreated from the flames and scampered deeper into their occupied neighborhoods. Lit projectiles rained on them at a greater frequency, lodging into the sides of buildings igniting them in the process.

Murdock rushed to Harrison's side. The young warrior raised a palm in the ranger's direction, ignoring the ever growing winds that began to swirl around him. "I know, they're running away! Be sure everyone stands their ground!"

The skull-covered ranger grabbed Harrison's forearm. Pointing behind him, he yelled, "Look!"

Harrison turned around, his jaw dropping inside his mask. Gelderand continued reciting his spell but two men, who Harrison could only assume were Swinkle and Pondle, now held him in place. Lance barked at a feverish clip, creating more anxiety to the chaotic situation.

"Murdock, we need to keep him grounded!" exclaimed Harrison as he dashed to the mage's position. He placed his hands around the older man's waist, while a small man in an ogre mask grounded one leg and a person in a hellhound covering grabbed the other.

"We need to keep Gelderand facing the burning buildings!" exclaimed Swinkle, keeping the mage's left leg planted on the earth.

"These swirling winds are making it difficult," came Pondle's voice from behind the demented canine mask.

"The spell will be broken if he stops reciting the text," said Swinkle.

Harrison and Murdock held the mage in place. The young warrior felt his mask flap in the erratic wind before he brought his gaze to the immediate area. The Arcadians continued their task of igniting the buildings, but the wind was becoming a nuisance. In the distance, flames grew taller with the help of the oxygen-rich gusts brought on by Gelderand's spell. The flaming arrows that lodged into the walls of the structures deeper in the occupied area began to take hold, creating an ever-growing inferno.

That is when the young warrior noticed the heat for the first time. Keeping Gelderand still had so preoccupied Harrison and his friends that they did not register the intensity of the flames. The combination of hotness and the young warrior's warm breath caused copious droplets of moisture to form on the inside of his mask. Moments later, he found his head soaked with sweat and beads of water flowed down his face.

His friends were experiencing the same phenomenon. "Harrison," yelled Murdock, "we need to get out of this place!"

"Gelderand must finish his spell," said the young warrior, not sure how much more the men could endure.

A muffled voice added, "I don't think we have to worry about that anymore." Pondle released his grip on Gelderand's leg.

Harrison felt the older man's body lift now that nothing held his right leg to the ground. "Pondle, what are you doing?" said the young warrior in bewilderment.

The thief pointed at the article in the magician's hands. "Look at the parchment!"

The young warrior did his best to get a glimpse at the scroll in Gelderand's hands. The increasing heat had started to ignite the dry paper and seconds later it burst into flames. The mage recoiled, dropping the burning scroll and cowering away from the growing embers.

The men instinctively maneuvered away from the sizzling parchment even though a firestorm raged about them. Gelderand's spell had created an inferno before their very eyes, the winds aiding the flames, pushing them deeper into the occupied territory. No sooner had the mage's spell completed than the next chain of events began.

Scynthian warriors flooded into the streets, trying their best to elude the burning buildings. In the distance, Harrison heard horns blowing, encouraging the archers to continue their hellish volleys. The young warrior witnessed creature after creature fall, impaled with a fiery projectile lodged in their body followed by blood-curdling screams.

A masked Arcadian pointed to the roadway in front of Harrison and his friends. "Here they come!"

The young warrior swiveled in the direction of the oncoming Scynthians. Twenty beasts braved the flames, taking their chances with the obstructions before them. The whittled barbs halted their progress, just as the humans had expected.

Harrison took his gaze to Murdock and nodded once. The ranger nodded back in concurrence and then ordered a simple command, having already assembled the Arcadian bowmen before Gelderand started his spell.

"Fire!"

Arrow after flaming arrow whistled through the air, easily hitting their marks, dropping one Scynthian after another. Harrison took his cue as well.

Pointing his battle axe toward the beasts, he yelled to his troops, "Prepare for battle! Don't let any Scynthians breach our barricade!"

Arcadian soldiers readied their shields and brandished their lances, daring their enemy to advance upon them. While they held their ground, Harrison panned to Gelderand.

The mage's body slumped and he dropped to one knee. Swinkle and Lance came to his aid, doing whatever they could to help. The young warrior gauged his situation. The troops held the Scynthians at bay, archers dropped their enemy at an alarming rate, and the area had become a raging inferno.

Knowing that they no longer needed the older man's services, Harrison called over to his friend. "Swinkle, take Gelderand away, his work here's done!" Noticing his canine friend protecting the incapacitated wizard, he added, "And take Lance with you!"

The young cleric helped the mage to his feet, then gestured his acknowledgement to Harrison. A moment later, Swinkle and Lance guided Gelderand away from the war zone and back toward the safe haven.

Harrison's mind felt more at ease knowing that the less combative members of his group had left the city's war torn area. Bringing his complete focus back to the battle at hand, the young warrior summoned a soldier.

"What do you need, sir?" asked the young fighter.

Harrison smirked behind his mask, pleased at the military training the Arcadians had displayed throughout the battle. "Take another sentry, survey the extent of battle and damage along these ten blocks, then report back to me." After pausing a second, he added, "Quickly!"

The fighter nodded and ran off to perform his duties. Harrison watched the sentry disappear into the throngs of men and enveloping darkness. Flames climbed higher into the night, its light casting ghoulish shadows of the men with their demonic, horned masks on the burning structures' walls. Screams of agony and distress emanated from the barricaded zone, and the smell of burning wood and death permeated the once cool, nighttime air.

Murdock approached the young warrior. "How long do we keep these beasts at bay?"

Harrison stared at the Scynthians flailing at the wooden barriers in the pathway in front of him. In a surprising cool tone, he answered, "Until they either breach the barricade or are all cooked alive."

The ranger allowed his stare to linger at Harrison but the young warrior never took his gaze away from the enemy standing a mere thirty yards away. Murdock detested the Scynthians but he did not expect that kind of response from Harrison.

"I'm with you one hundred percent," said the ranger.

Two sentries advancing to their position broke Harrison from his trance. "Sir," started the man under the wolf-faced mask, "the Scynthians are being held in check. None have breached any of the roadway barricades."

Harrison's demon face glared back at the Arcadian. "None have been breached?"

"No."

"How many did you see attacking the obstructions like these twenty or so are doing here?"

The sentry paused a moment. "Each avenue had about ten to twenty Scynthians attempting to break through the barriers."

Ten to twenty, thought Harrison, making a quick calculation in his mind. "Murdock, didn't Bracken say he thought there was anywhere from one to two thousand Scynthians in the occupied zone?"

"Yeah, he did," responded the ranger, in tune with his friend's line of thinking.

"Then where are the rest of them?" asked Harrison.

At that very moment a large explosion rocked the center of the occupied area. The force of the blast caused all the men to cower, everyone unsure of the new turn of events. The young warrior peered over to the roadway and saw the remaining Scynthians abandon their attempt to break through the barrier and run off in the blast's direction.

"What the hell was that?" exclaimed Murdock.

Harrison pointed to new flames climbing higher into the night. "The Scynthians last stand."

The ranger saw the growing pyre as well. "A bonfire? Typical!"

Pondle approached his two friends. "What are we to do now?"

"Bracken said to hold our ground and let the fires consume those vile creatures," said Murdock. The ranger gazed over to the young warrior. "Right, Harrison?"

The Aegean stared at the flames in the center of the dead zone, their fiery eyes flickering in the darkness. Harrison's mind churned. Something's not right here. Unbeknownst to his friends, his eyes widened behind his devilish mask.

"Murdock, did you say that they've lit a bonfire?"

The ranger looked at the growing flames. "It would appear so."

"Why do Scynthians construct bonfires?" asked the young warrior, his anxiety heightening and his heart pumping harder.

"Usually to make sacrifices to … their … gods," said the ranger, his voice trailing off.

"They have people in there!" said Harrison, the sudden panic evident in his voice.

Murdock shook his head. "Bracken said that there were no humans in that zone!"

The young warrior summoned the sentries over. Pointing to the Scynthian-controlled area, he commanded with authority, "Did any Arcadians enter the occupied zone to determine that there were definitely *no* humans in there?"

The two young men exchanged nervous glances behind their masks before they said in unison, "No."

Harrison tightened his grip on his battle axe. Murdock witnessed his friend's actions. "What are you thinking?" asked the ranger.

"You know what I'm thinking! We need to storm that area!"

The ranger stared into the inferno. "Harrison, it's like hell in there! If any people are alive, we'll never get to them in time!"

The young warrior glared at Murdock. "We're wasting time! Ready the men!" Turning to the sentries, he said, "Go to each roadway and tell the commanding officer to storm the zone. The Scynthians are going to sacrifice any remaining Arcadians!"

The two men held their ground, unsure what to do. Harrison did not hold back. "That's an order! Now, go!"

Upon hearing their leader's command, the two soldiers went off in different directions to execute his demand. Harrison then brought his attention to the assembled men.

"We're entering the occupied zone. The Scynthians have lit a bonfire and that means they plan on sacrificing innocent people. We won't let that happen!" The young warrior paused before continuing, allowing his comments to sink in. "The time has come to end this battle. Slaughter every Scynthian you see and prevent them from killing any more of us."

Harrison panned to the burning buildings and blockades. Pointing to the obstructions, he said, "Move these barriers! It's time to take back your city once and for all!"

The Arcadians cheered in unison and rushed to the barricades, oblivious of the heat. Moments later, the soldiers began to storm the Scynthian's stronghold.

Murdock bolted to Harrison's side. "Impressive speech, if I say so myself."

The young warrior smiled behind his mask. "Time to kill some Scynthians."

The next battle with the Scynthians finally underway, Harrison, Murdock, and Pondle charged toward the zone, following the Arcadian soldiers into the fiery blaze that was once the great city of Arcadia.

CHAPTER 4

◯

The heat wore on the men inside the occupied zone. Burning buildings surrounded Harrison and his friends with occasional explosions pushing flames higher into the nighttime sky. The young warrior maintained his focus, being wary of his enemy but more importantly, keeping an eye out for unfortunate townsfolk. His inspection did not take long to yield fruit. At an upcoming intersection, several Arcadian soldiers had engaged five Scynthian warriors in battle.

Harrison yelled over to Murdock and Pondle, "We need to head for the bonfire! That's where they're sacrificing people!"

"I'm with you," responded the ranger, "but first we have to tend to some business."

The three men approached the melee. Harrison made a quick sweep of the area, finding five enemy warriors engaging six Arcadians. Fine shops and eating establishments had once existed in the very spot where the skirmish now ensued. Flaming fingertips stretched for the stars, their heat inducing copious amounts of sweat over Harrison's body.

Evil faces squared off against each other, Scynthian and human-covered alike. Flaming arrows continued to rain down from the heavens and the constant thump of drums filled the air. We're truly in hell, thought Harrison.

Standing mere feet from the skirmish, the young warrior raised his battle axe into an offensive position, then made a quick glance to his left before engaging in the melee. From his vantage point, flames rose unusually high two blocks to the west. His blood simmered, knowing where he needed to go next.

The Aegean's right bicep started to tingle, the time ripe for combat. Harrison took a purposeful step toward the fighters to his immediate right. A Scynthian warrior had swung his mace at the Arcadian soldier, whacking the fighter's shield and rocking him backwards. The young warrior made the best of this new opening, attacking the creature, his weapon connecting with the beast's midsection.

The Scynthian held his ground, his thick leather armor absorbing the blow. Harrison peered into his enemy's green eyes, its cat-like orbs reflecting flickering flames. Mesmerized by the dancing lights, the young warrior failed to block a blow to his midsection. The Scynthian's mace struck Harrison's chain-mail armor, forcing the young warrior back, almost knocking him over.

The injured Arcadian came to his rescue, assuming Harrison's position in the melee and slicing the savage across its thigh, opening up a bloody wound. The Scynthian roared in pain, yet continued its charge. With a forceful parry, the creature struck the Arcadian in the middle of his chest, knocking the wind out of him and sending him to the ground. In one swift motion, the beast hammered the defenseless human's skull, smashing his helmet to bits, and splattering his brains. His enemy vanquished, the Scynthian then set his sights on Harrison again.

Horrified at witnessing the Arcadian's brutal death, the young warrior raised his blade in a defensive posture. The Scynthian was relentless. Oblivious to the heat, the fur-covered beast attacked Harrison with fervor, swinging his mace at the young warrior, only to have Harrison block his attack with his own weapon. The Scynthian countered with another blow toward the young warrior's leg. Harrison again blocked the creature's assault before counterattacking.

Raising his blade high, Harrison chopped at the monster's midsection, striking the Scynthian hard, reeling him backward. The Aegean did not let up; instead he took a step closer to his enemy, bringing their faces perilously close to one another. Gazing into the beast's eyes, Harrison jerked his weapon hard upwards, smacking the axe's hilt into his enemy's face. The Scynthian's forehead split open and blood began to pour from the fresh wound, covering both beast and human alike. His foe stunned, Harrison swung his weapon, cutting deep into the Scynthian's arm, a single frayed ligament keeping the beast's limb from falling to the earth.

The creature dropped its weapon and fell to the ground, howling in pain. Harrison continued his assault, brandishing his battle axe and severing the beast's arm. The monster wailed, clutched its stump, and writhed in agony. The young warrior, recalling his teachings at the Fighter's Guild, knew that an injured enemy had nothing to lose, making them the most dangerous of adversaries. With that thought in mind, he stomped hard on the monster's throat, crushing its windpipe with a disgusting pop. The Scynthian, its neck broken, went into convulsions. Seconds later, a vile white foam oozed from its mouth.

Harrison stared down at his defeated enemy. "Battle over," he said before taking his gaze to his friends. Murdock and Pondle, along with the Arcadians, had defeated their enemies as well and awaited their next assignment.

Chaos erupted all around the men, the streets becoming a violent war zone of hand-to-hand combat. Harrison took the initiative again.

Pointing to the pyre in the distance, he said, "We need to get over there. That's ground zero for the bonfire."

One of the Arcadians motioned in the same direction. Behind his demented goat-mimicking mask, he cried, "That's the Great Hall of Arcadia!"

All men swiveled their covered faces in the direction of the growing flames. "Those bastards are using the city's hallmark building for sacrifices!" exclaimed Murdock.

"All the reason to get over there as fast as possible!" said Harrison, breaking into a sprint. "Let's go!"

Harrison, Murdock, Pondle, and the five Arcadian soldiers headed west down the hectic roadway, toward the harbor and the once proud Arcadian landmark. All the while the young warrior kept an eye out for unmasked civilians. No more unnecessary deaths, Harrison promised himself, though he had not seen a single Arcadian townsperson yet.

A flaming projectile flew precariously close to the young warrior and lodged into the earth a foot from his position. A second hurtled through the air and impaled one of the Arcadian soldiers, stopping him in his tracks and dropping him to the ground. Pondle and Murdock rushed to the fighter's side and frantically patted the flames out, but their efforts proved fruitless. The arrow had torn through the warrior's body, rupturing organs, and draining his body of blood. The poor soul perished within seconds.

Murdock, his hands stained red with the fighter's blood, lifted his eyes to the young warrior. "Harrison, this is crazy!"

The young warrior gazed upward. More arrows had started their downward arc. "Run for cover!"

The platoon of seven men headed out of the unprotected roadway and to the uncertain safety of a nearby burning structure. Projectiles littered the street, some hitting the ground, others disappearing into scorching buildings.

The young warrior reassessed his situation. Scynthians and Arcadians clashed in the streets before them. The massive bonfire spewed flames a mere block away. His side hurt from the beating at the hands of a Scynthian and his body remained hot and sweaty. Amongst all of his trials and tribulations, Harrison discovered his true mission.

Squinting, he brought his focus to a small convoy that rushed in the direction of the sacrificial pyre, two hundred feet from their position. Scynthians shoved ten smaller figures into the road, then they disappeared around a corner that headed toward the Great Hall of Arcadia.

Harrison had no doubt about his next course of action. Turning to face his friends, he said, "The Scynthians are leading those people to the inferno!"

Without waiting for a response, the young warrior gripped his battle axe and entered the chaotic roadway once again, his friends and Arcadians following close behind. Harrison felt his anger rise with every step he took. Halfway to their intended target, a loud horn blast more than startled them. Roars and yelling began to flood the neighborhoods to the north and east of their position, while barricades burst free to their south. Harrison smiled for the rest of the armies had advanced into the Scynthian-occupied territory at last.

The young warrior did not let the sound of reinforcements hinder his advancement toward his hated enemy. Lives were at stake and he was not about to let those brutal creatures claim an ounce of victory.

Pointing forward with his axe, Harrison exclaimed, "Let the others battle the Scynthians! We need to save those people!" The rest of the men agreed without saying a word.

The Scynthians maneuvered the helpless humans around a corner, disappearing from the group's view. Harrison's brain churned with thoughts of horrific sacrificial rituals, knowing that every second he let the townspeople out of his sight could spell their doom.

"Catch up with them!" he exclaimed, but before he could lead his men around the same corner, a band of five Scynthian warriors confronted the small platoon. Seconds later, weapons clashed and blood began to spill again.

The young warrior used incredible skill to slay the beast before him, while the Arcadians' used their advanced battle tactics to overtake the two others. Their advantage gone, the remaining beasts turned and ran.

Murdock quickly sheathed his sword and readied his longbow. Using the skill of a marksman, he removed two arrows in succession from his quiver, planting them in the backs of the retreating savages, rendering moot their decision to flee.

Lowering his bow, the ranger said to Harrison, "Lead us on!"

The young warrior took charge once again and led the platoon around a smoky corner. The flickering flames and smoldering buildings made sight more difficult for the group than anticipated.

Harrison stopped in front of a war torn eatery, where columns of flames stretched into the street. Coughing, the young warrior said, "The Great Hall is only a block away!"

"Sir," yelled one of the Arcadians, "it's too hot! We'll bake before we get over there!"

55

"The Scynthians are covered in fur, yet they're persevering," said the Aegean. "We must as well."

"I'll lead the way," said the voice behind the hell hound mask. Though the dancing flames and thickening smoke hindered Pondle's infravision, the thief assumed his most comfortable position. "Follow me!"

Pondle took the small squad into the middle of the roadway, away from the infernos raging on either side of the street. Billowing smoke began to flood the area as the men approached what used to be the Great Hall of Arcadia.

As the thief forged the men closer to their destination, Harrison stopped in his tracks and absorbed the sight before him. The young warrior recalled the first time he had laid eyes on the Great Hall, how the impressive structure had taken his breath away. Now, he barely recognized the building.

Flames towered into the night, spewing out of the rooftop like an uncontrollable furnace. Fireballs burst from blown out windows, allowing built up heat and gas to escape into the nighttime sky. Smoke billowed everywhere, choking the area with a thick black fog.

The last of the Arcadians ran past him, breaking the young warrior from his stupor. Glaring in the inferno's direction, he recalled that the once-impressive building stood in the middle of a square, where the main pathways of the city converged. He also remembered that several long rows of stone steps rose away from the street, ending with a large double doorway. Running at full speed, he was thankful that his memories filled in the gaps that his sight had left behind.

Pondle led the men fifty yards from the entranceway, then halted in his tracks. What Harrison saw next horrified him, understanding the thief's rationale for stopping. Ten Scynthians manned the area, while several more held terrified humans down. Without mercy, five of the beasts started to methodically sever the arms of the victims. Men, women, and children alike wailed in agony.

Harrison had seen enough. "No!" he roared, then sprinted to the staircase. The Arcadians followed their leader.

Murdock held his ground. Being the expert bowman, the ranger held his anger in check and unloaded arrow after arrow from his quiver. Though his blood boiled with rage, his cool precision with the bow dropped seven of the wretched beasts. To his dismay, his triumph was short lived for more Scynthians scrambled from around the structure upon hearing their comrades' moans.

Harrison, ascending the staircase with visions of stopping the carnage, watched one beast after another fall to his friend's aerial attack. The direness of the situation came more into focus with each advancing step. The young warrior saw firsthand that the Scynthians had inflicted life-ending injuries to each townsperson that lay on the ground and, no matter how fast he ran, he could not stop the inevitable.

Halfway to the suffering townsfolk, the sight of two enemy warriors dashing to the immense entranceway heightened his cause for concern. The beasts grasped the door handles and swung open the huge, smoldering wooden portals. A rush of intense heat blew from the building, stopping the young warrior and his cadre of soldiers in their tracks. After a moment, Scynthian fighters gathered the wailing people and began tossing them into the Great Hall, creating the largest furnace the land had ever seen.

Harrison stood wide-eyed as the brutal beasts flung each helpless person into the burning building, adding more terror to the sacrificial pyre. The young warrior, horrified at the sight before him, could only imagine how many more humans had suffered a similar fate. With that thought in mind, he gritted his teeth and gripped his weapon with even more ferocity.

Raising his battle axe in the air, he bellowed, "Charge!" The Arcadians roared in unison, acknowledging the battle cry.

Harrison, along with the Arcadian soldiers, raced back up the stairs with weapons drawn and ready to attack. The beasts that had assembled near the entrance of the structure witnessed their actions and scurried to confront their shell-shocked enemy.

* * *

Murdock and Pondle watched the young warrior ascend the Great Hall's staircase from the luxury of their vantage point.

The thief grabbed his friend's arm, gaining his attention. "He's going to get himself killed!"

"Not if I can help it," said the ranger, raising his longbow for a second time. Murdock let his arrows fly again, hitting their marks with expert accuracy. Though many dropped, more creatures flooded the area.

Pondle's face fell behind his mask. "There's too many of them!"

* * *

The young warrior kept his focus on the beasts before him. A controlled rage fueled his muscles and his heart pumped at a feverish clip. Reaching the top step at the same time as a Scynthian warrior, the Aegean used cool precision to drive his battle axe into the beast's right thigh. The creature buckled and fell down the stairs. Two Arcadians awaited the savage's descent, chopping it to death with their weapons.

His first foe vanquished, Harrison pressed forward to the landing area. The intensity of the heat radiating from the open doorway started to singe his clothing the closer he got to the Great Hall's entryway. The high temperature notwithstanding, he pressed forward as disgusting images of twisted, smoldering, and freshly slain bodies churned in his brain.

Try as he might to remove those visions from his mind, he instead channeled the negative energy and used it to fuel his rage. An unlucky savage advanced on his position, failing to learn from his comrade's mistake. Harrison promised himself that this beast would feel his wrath.

The young warrior roared from behind his devilish mask, momentarily startling the Scynthian. Using the beast's hesitancy to his advantage, Harrison changed tactics. Instead of swinging his weapon at his enemy, which the Scynthian expected, he used both hands to thrust the axe's handle into the creature's chest. The unusual maneuver caused the beast to lose his balance and fall to the ground. His enemy down, Harrison gripped his weapon's hilt and chopped his blade deep into the Scynthian's chest cavity. The creature barely had time to realize it was dying.

Harrison brought his glare to the next wave of Scynthians. Three more rushed toward him, while many more started to emerge from around the building, flooding the area with chaotic weapon-wielding beasts. For a brief moment, the young warrior felt a pang of worry. That all changed after a projectile lodged itself in the chest of the Scynthian before him. A second arrow penetrated the skull of the next savage, and another impaled the third.

The young warrior smiled behind his mask, ready to give Murdock praise for his marksmanship when he heard several horns blow.

* * *

"Shoot every one of those bastards!" shouted Murdock to the Arcadian archers that stormed the sector. Arcadian soldiers flooded the square, advancing from the east, wielding razor-tipped lances, long swords, and battle axes.

Murdock continued volleying arrows until his quiver ran empty. Before he could address his new problem, Pondle tugged on his arm and pointed to the roadway to the east.

"Well, I'll be," said the ranger at the sight of the only man riding on horseback in the vicinity. Bracken Drake himself had returned to claim his city.

The eye-patched leader maneuvered his steed closer to the blazing inferno that once housed busts of Arcadia's hallowed warriors, Bracken included. Pointing his sword at the remaining Scynthians that lingered about the structure, he commanded, "Burn them!"

A roar erupted from the Arcadian soldiers who had invaded the area and seconds later a mass of red-clad soldiers stormed up the steps of the Great Hall.

* * *

Harrison welcomed the wave of ally soldiers, but his focus remained sharp. Recognizing fear and confusion on the Scynthians' faces, he turned toward his next victim. Already baffled by the demonic masks the humans had worn into combat, the added sight of the fighters running to engage them in battle was almost too much to comprehend. With nowhere to fall back, the remaining beasts stood their ground and did their best to fight.

The young warrior scanned the area. The hundred or so Scynthians were no match for the throngs of Arcadian soldiers that seemed to multiply as they rushed out of the smoke-filled roadways and into the ensuing battle. It took mere minutes for the Arcadians to overtake the beasts congregated on the Hall's main steps. Bracken's soldiers spared no mercy on the creatures that had invaded their city, slaughtering each and every one of them.

Harrison watched in amazement as the soldiers butchered the Scynthians one at a time. After one enemy fighter dropped to the ground, three Arcadians would lift the beast and take it to the Great Hall's grand entryway, where they tossed the still-living creature into the raging inferno.

Bracken's men had played out his strategy to perfection. Kindling they have become, said the young warrior to himself, hearing the Scynthians' horrified screams as the Arcadians hurled them one by one into the fire. Poetic justice for all the souls they've stolen, thought Harrison, smirking.

Now that the Arcadians controlled the area, Harrison brought his attention to the matter at hand—finding any remaining humans. The young warrior took his gaze down to the roadway below and found his friends helping with the Arcadian's fight.

"Murdock! Pondle!" yelled Harrison, gaining their attention. "Let the Arcadians battle the Scynthians. There's got to be more people holed up around here!"

"I agree, but where do we start?" asked the ranger, swiveling his head in search of people in need. The entire square felt like an oven, smoke billowed throughout, and the hot winds continued to fan the flames in every direction.

Pondle took the lead. Looking at a structure across the street from the Great Hall, he said, "Let's start over there. There aren't any flames shooting out of that building."

Harrison peered at the dilapidated shop. His focus became sharper and even though the area remained sweltering, a chill ran down his spine. "Yes, we must go there."

The thief waved Harrison and Murdock forward, leaving the fighting behind. The short trek from the steps of the landmark Arcadian structure to the general supply store took less than a minute. Pondle stopped his friends ten feet shy of the entranceway. Smoke wafted out of the rooftop, however nothing would impede them from entering the shop.

Pondle raised a palm to his friends, signaling for them to wait. "Is it me or does something not feel right?"

"I sense it, too," said Murdock. "Tread lightly."

The trio made a cautious approach to the doorway. Pondle pushed aside the damaged portal, then entered the establishment with Murdock and Harrison in tow. Harrison started to make a mental examination of the area before movement to his right grabbed his attention. Before he could make an accurate assessment of his situation, a large figure launched itself from the hazy surroundings.

Harrison barely blocked the Scynthian's attack, the beast's club grazing the young warrior's side. A second creature erupted from another part of the store, wielding a weapon of his own. Murdock and Pondle took a defensive posture as the next attacker advanced.

The Aegean decided to take matters into his own hands. However, as he tried to maneuver into an offensive stance to face his enemy, his right foot tripped on something that lay on the floor. Taking his gaze downward for a split second, he found a lifeless human corpse. The advancing Scynthian, coupled with the gruesome finding, sparked a new rage deep within his soul.

Sidestepping the dead body, Harrison swung his battle axe in the direction of the charging beast, connecting with its upper torso. The Scynthian's body armor protected him from the attack, however the beast reeled back from the force of the blow, tripping over a pallet containing bags of wheat and grain.

The young warrior took two quick steps, hovering over the fallen creature. Raising his blade to strike, he said through clenched teeth, "This is for that poor soul." He then chopped the axe deep into the Scynthian's chest cavity, snuffing out his life force.

Harrison did not waste time enjoying his victory, instead he turned and went to help his friends with their predicament. Murdock and Pondle teamed up to attack the Scynthian before them, slaying the beast without Harrison's assistance.

The young warrior squinted, trying his best to understand his surroundings without sufficient lighting and the ever-thickening smoke. Coughing, he said, "We need to get out of here."

Pondle pointed in front of him. "Take a look at this first."

The three men went down an aisle that once housed food supplies and found two more dead bodies. Harrison's blood boiled, for on the ground in front of him lay the smaller bodies of a female and her young child.

Murdock, brandishing his sword, continued down the row, making a turn at the end. "There's another body down here," came the ranger's voice through the smoke. "And his arms are gone."

"What possesses these beasts—" snarled Harrison through clenched teeth before a subtle noise from behind stopped him midsentence. Through the smoky haze he could identify the outline of a supply closet a few feet in front of him. Bringing a finger to his lips, he signaled for his friends to be quiet, then tiptoed to the closed portal. The others followed him, taking up offensive stances a few feet behind their leader.

Harrison gazed back to Murdock and Pondle, then slowly raised his weapon. Nodding to them before reaching for the door's handle, the young warrior made a mental count of three, then grabbed the latch and flung open the door. The young warrior's eyes widened and his heart sank upon finding the contents of the closet.

Cowering before him sat a terrified young girl, no older than five, curled in a ball, and staring wide-eyed at the demon face that glared back at her.

"Hey, Sweetie," said Harrison in a soothing voice, peeling off his mask, revealing his true face. "It's alright, we're here to save you."

The little girl did not move. Her big blue eyes stared at Harrison, unsure of the person that stood before her. Harrison noticed that blood stained the lass's clothing and that she began to shake with fear.

"Harrison," said Murdock in as calm of a voice he could muster, "we need to get out of this building. It's not safe." He and Pondle also removed their masks in an attempt to put the girl more at ease.

The young warrior knew that he needed to bring the child to safety. "We need to leave this place, alright?" he said, slowly stretching his hands toward the girl.

The child nodded, yet did not move from her spot. Harrison maneuvered closer to the closet, reached for the youngster, and pulled her toward his body.

"What's your name, honey?" asked Harrison, cradling the girl closer to his chest, still bent on one knee.

"Maisey," she said with a sniff. "Where's my mommy?"

"Harrison ..." said Murdock, trying to get his friend to resolve the situation quicker.

The young warrior knew he did not have much time. Gathering the dirty blanket the young girl had with her, he wrapped it around her tiny body.

"Your mommy is hurt, Maisey, but we need to get you out of here now," said Harrison. "I'm going to cover your head because of all the smoke. Alright?"

Maisey nodded and Harrison pulled the girl to his chest, covering her head in the process. The young warrior did not want the child to see the dismembered bodies of her family members, the gruesome scene rekindling past memories. As he walked through the damaged building and around the armless corpses, visions of his own parent's murder scene swirled inside his head—how the Scynthians had butchered them, severed their arms, and watched them bleed to death. For years he wished that he had travelled with his parents on that fateful day, knowing that his fighting skills could have saved them from the murderous beasts. However, he also understood that the savages would have killed him, too, since he was all of twelve years old at the time. Now, he vowed that Maisey would not see the blemishes on the wooden floor, stained red by her parent's blood. Though he could not save his loved ones all those years ago, he could save this little girl today.

The youngster leaned hard against Harrison's chest. "I want to go home," she said.

Harrison's heart sank further. Motioning with his head toward the doorway, he said to his friends, "Let's get out of here."

Pondle and Murdock exited the general store, Harrison and the child following. Outside, chaos continued to erupt everywhere. The Great Hall burned like a funeral pyre, flames and smoke spewing high into the nighttime sky. The surrounding neighborhood resembled a war zone—burning structures, clashing warriors, and scorching heat.

"We're leaving this place," yelled Harrison, clutching the young girl tighter. Motioning with his head to the thief, he said, "Find a way out of here, Pondle."

Turning to Murdock, he said, "You need to protect us."

"You can count on me," said the ranger, understanding that Harrison could not carry the child and wield a weapon at the same time. "Pondle, let's go!"

The thief utilized routes consisting of back alleys and unused roadways, steering clear of the heavy fighting and leading the small posse toward the human-held sectors. Within minutes, the small platoon followed a familiar roadway that led to the barricades where the Arcadians held their ground. Sentries moved the obstructions just enough for the men to cross the barrier, leaving the fighting and intense heat behind.

Harrison, mindful of the precious cargo he carried in his arms, swept his eyes about the area, finding it most unfit for a child. Calling to his friends, he said, "We need to get Maisey away from this place. Let's find Swinkle and Gelderand."

The young warrior followed Murdock and Pondle to their new destination, each step taking them further away from the raging Arcadian inferno and deeper into the safe zone.

"We're almost back to our camp," said Harrison in a calm voice, hoping to keep the child at ease.

"I want my mommy," said the young girl under the blanket, sniffling. Harrison did not say a word and kept moving forward.

After trekking for several blocks, the men reached a large camp where Arcadian soldiers protected scores of townsfolk.

"Swinkle and Gelderand are here somewhere," said Pondle, panning.

The men did not have to wait long to see a familiar sight. A small, helmeted dog came bounding in their direction, bringing a smile to the Aegean's face.

"I have someone for you to meet," Harrison said to Maisey as Lance rushed to his master's side. The young warrior removed the child's covering, revealing her to his canine friend. Lance yapped with excitement, his tail wagging at a feverish clip.

Maisey extended her arms, wishing to plant her feet on the ground. Harrison obliged and Maisey wasted no time grabbing the dog and giving him a big hug. Lance licked the little girl's face, her laughter lightening the mood in an otherwise desolate place.

"He's silly!" she exclaimed, scratching the dog on its side.

"Maisey, this is Lance, a very special friend of mine," said Harrison. As the two played, the young warrior motioned for Murdock to join him.

"We need someone to take care of her," he said in a hushed tone, not wanting the girl to hear.

"I understand," said the ranger. "Let me and Pondle poke around. Someone must know her and her family." Murdock glanced in the direction of two onlookers. "Here comes Swinkle and Gelderand now."

Harrison swiveled his head, finding his two cloaked friends approaching. "I'll be with them," he said, before facing the ranger again. "Let me know what you find."

Murdock nodded, then turned to Pondle. "Let's go." The two men then embarked on their quest to find anyone who knew the little girl.

Gelderand approached the young warrior first. "Who do we have here?" he asked, sounding every bit like a grandfather.

"This is Maisey," said Harrison. "We found her in the Scynthian's barricaded sector."

Swinkle's eyes widened. "People were still there?"

Harrison closed his eyes and nodded. In a hushed tone, he said, "It was horrific."

Gelderand understood the fragility of the conversation in front of the small child. "I'm sure Murdock and Pondle are searching for someone now."

"That they are," said Harrison. "In the meantime, we need to regroup and speak with Bracken, Brendan, and the Forge Brothers." Taking the conversation in another direction, the young warrior asked the mage, "How are you feeling?"

"Exhausted, but I will manage," said the elder man.

"I have done all I can to restore his strength," added the young cleric. "He needs a full day of rest."

"That he shall have," said Harrison.

The young warrior absorbed the activity of the surrounding area. People went about their daily chores as best as they could, in light of the ensuing battle that raged in the heart of their city. Soldiers patrolled the area, keeping the vicinity safe from unwanted Scynthian confrontations.

Harrison then thought back to the battle at hand. The unmistakable stench of burning buildings permeated the area and he swore that his nose could now differentiate between the smell of charred wood and searing flesh. With that thought in mind, he brought his gaze to the little girl who played with Lance, knowing that she would never see her parents alive again. He knew the story all too well and prayed that Murdock and Pondle would find a living relative for Maisey. Until that time, they would have no other choice than to wait.

"The battle's almost over," said Harrison, "We should take this time to regroup and wait until the armies return."

"And to make Maisey comfortable," said Gelderand. "Come, follow us and we will take her to a safe place."

Harrison nodded, then addressed Maisey. "We're going to go find somewhere to rest."

Maisey pointed to Lance. "Is he coming?"

The young warrior smiled. "Yes, he is." The little girl beamed as Harrison picked her up into his arms, Lance scurrying in front of the two. As they followed Gelderand and Swinkle to a more secure location, a feeling of calm overtook the young warrior, sensing that he finally had the situation under control.

"You're going to be safe, Maisey," said Harrison. The young girl snuggled in his arms, feeling more comfortable. "That I promise you."

CHAPTER 5

Ｑ

Lance kept Maisey occupied while the hellish battle raged inside Arcadia's innards. Thick smoke and orange flames continued to billow high into the nighttime sky, raging until the wee hours of the night. All the while, Harrison focused on the young child, knowing how her world had changed forever.

"So young, so innocent," said Gelderand, watching Maisey play with Lance. "She does not deserve to grow up without her parents."

"I know exactly how she feels," said Harrison.

Swinkle sighed. "I wish I could say a prayer that would make everything better for her again."

The young warrior faced his friend. "Any prayer will do." In the distance, Harrison noticed four figures heading in their direction. Gesturing with his head, he said, "Her prayers may be answered now."

All three members of the group turned to see Murdock and Pondle escorting a young couple toward them. As they approached, a woman ran to the child.

"Maisey!" she exclaimed, dropping to one knee and throwing open her arms.

The lass recognized the woman immediately. "Aunt Carrie!" Maisey left Lance behind and accepted her aunt's embrace.

"Thank the gods you're safe," said the woman's husband, taking a large hand and framing the little girl's face, caressing her soft cheek with his thumb.

Maisey's smile quickly vanished. "Where's my mommy, Uncle Jeffrey?"

The couple exchanged hesitant glances. "There's been a terrible accident, honey. Mommy and Daddy are gone now," said Carrie, tears forming in her eyes.

"Will they come back?" asked Maisey, her facing growing long.

Trying to keep her emotions in check, the woman said in a quivering voice, "No, baby, they're not." Carrie then pulled the girl closer to her.

"And, Robert?" came the next question from the distraught child.

"He's gone, too," said the woman with a sigh. Maisey finally reached her breaking point and began to cry.

"I want my mommy," she said between sobs. "I want my mommy!"

Carrie pulled the girl's little head into her chest in an effort to silence her cries. She then began to rock gently. "Shh, sweetie, you're going to stay with me and Uncle Jeffrey now."

Harrison's heart sank, realizing the pain people must have felt when they had to tell him his parents were never coming back either. Sensing eyes upon him, he turned, locking his gaze on the cold stare coming from the young man next to his wife.

Jeffrey took a step closer to the young warrior and, in a hushed tone asked, "Did you save her? Did you see her family?"

Harrison nodded. "Yes, we found Maisey in a building that the Scynthians occupied. She must have hidden in the closet while they attacked the other members of her family."

The man clenched his jaw, then asked, "What did they do to my brother?"

Harrison sighed. "They killed them all in their usual way."

Jeffrey took a deep breath and stared up into the night sky, clenching his fists and trying his best to keep his composure. Glaring at Harrison, he scowled, "Don't you let those bastards do this to anyone else. I don't care what it takes. I want to see them all dead!"

The young warrior approached Jeffrey, taking a hand to the man's back and leading him a couple of steps away from the crying woman and child.

"I understand how you feel and we're doing everything we can to eliminate these beasts from this world," said Harrison. "You have my word. We'll avenge your brother's death."

The young man nodded, satisfied with the Aegean's answer. "I hope you keep your promise." He then turned to face his wife and niece. "I need to take them to a safe place. It's going to be a long night."

Jeffrey went to Carrie's side and encouraged her to stand. The woman obliged, keeping a tight grip on the small girl in her arms. Before they left, Carrie approached Harrison a final time.

"Thank you for saving Maisey's life," she said. "You're a brave man."

"There's no need to thank me," said the young warrior. "Keep her safe and never stop loving her."

Carrie smiled even though tears streamed down her face. Jeffrey put an arm around his wife's shoulder and led her away from the warriors. Minutes later, the new family had disappeared into the night.

With the townsfolk gone, Murdock approached his friend. "This battle's not over yet."

The young warrior allowed his gaze to linger on the Arcadians a moment longer, before facing the ranger. "We need to consult with our leadership and see where we stand."

"The Scynthians better be burning alive," said Murdock, focusing on the orangey glow that emanated in the distance. "I think we should rejoin the battle."

Pondle, Gelderand, and Swinkle, who were listening in on the conversation, took greater interest in the fighters' discussion. "Are we going back?" asked the thief.

Harrison gathered his thoughts. "We need to find Brendan and I'm betting he's in the occupied zone."

"I'll lead the way," said Pondle, before putting on his mask once again. He then whistled for Lance, who followed the thief.

Murdock took his cue, put on his own mask, and followed his friend.

The young warrior had just about started to follow the ranger when he felt someone grab his arm. With an exasperated look on his face, Swinkle asked, "We're not going back in there, are we?"

"Like Murdock said, this battle's not over," said Harrison. "We need to defeat the Scynthians once and for all."

"Harrison, this is suicide," said the young cleric. "I understand the hatred we all have for the Scynthians, but we are merely tempting fate at this point."

"I have to agree with Swinkle," said Gelderand, Rufus' little face peeking out of his backpack. "Going back into that area is a risky maneuver."

The young warrior understood his friends' concerns. "This war needs to end — now." Harrison gazed at Murdock and Pondle, venturing further away. "You can stay here if you want, but I need to go."

Without saying another word the young warrior slipped on his head covering and began his trek toward the Scynthian stronghold. Lance, sensing the unrest, tailed his master.

Swinkle and Gelderand watched Harrison walk away. Taking his gaze to the older man, the young cleric said, "This is ridiculous."

"I agree," said the mage, "but we must follow him."

Swinkle sighed. "I know." Understanding their fate, the two men fumbled with their own head gear and reluctantly followed in their leader's footsteps.

* * *

The intense heat had begun to get the best of Harrison. The Aegean removed his mask and wiped the sweat from his brow, then fumbled with his tankard, sipping the last of his water. The young warrior and his friends had reentered the occupied territory an hour ago, finding that the Unified and Arcadian armies had pinned the Scynthians deep into the city's center. Hundreds of the beasts perished at the Great Hall of Arcadia, falling victim to their

71

own gruesome execution tactic. However, Harrison needed to know if all townsfolk had managed to escape the area and only Brendan knew the answer to that question.

The young warrior brought a hand to his eyes in an effort to shield them from the orange glow of the flames. Ten yards ahead, he saw Pondle in his hellhound covering waving him forward. Hastening his step, Harrison reached the thief, with Swinkle and Gelderand in tow.

"Brendan's leading the Unified Army over there," said Pondle in a muffled voice, pointing to a region where proud structures once stood. Now, the only visages of the buildings were their smoldering exterior walls.

"Take me to him," ordered the young warrior.

Pondle, along with Murdock, guided Harrison through the street cluttered with dead bodies — human and Scynthian alike. The young warrior made a mental examination of the vicinity, absorbing the utter destruction. Arcadia was gone, he concluded.

The thief interrupted his thought process. "He's over there, with the other warriors." Pondle motioned to a large platoon of soldiers on horseback that stood in the foreground of an intersection of smoldering buildings.

"Everyone, come with me," said Harrison as he took purposeful steps in the direction his friend had pointed. A moment later, he removed his demonic face covering and stood before his fellow Aegean leader. His friends took off their masks likewise.

Soldiers maneuvered their steeds out of the way in order for Harrison to find Brendan. The elder Aegean saw his prized pupil first and smiled. "I'm glad to see you and your friends are still alive."

Harrison nodded. "That we are." The young warrior held his gaze on his leader. "What's the Scynthians' status?"

Brendan's expression turned dour. "We have destroyed all the beasts in this area. They won't be hurting innocent townspeople anymore."

A burden seemed to lift from the young warrior's shoulders. "And all the townsfolk?"

The older warrior pursed his lips. "We've accounted for many, but a lot were lost."

Harrison lowered his head, nodding. "What do we do now?"

Brendan sat back in his saddle, thinking. "We'll leave the clean up to the Arcadians and some of the Unified soldiers. The Forge Brothers can lend some men, too." The Aegean leader leaned forward toward Harrison. "We must return to Concur and plan a strategy. This is but one battle in a much larger war."

The young warrior let his leader's words sink in. The Scynthians had launched a sneak attack, devastating a once proud city, and committing scores of atrocious acts. Brendan was right, he thought, we need to plan for whatever comes next.

Addressing his leader again, he asked, "When are we leaving?"

"As soon as we can." Brendan waved Harrison and his friends forward. "Follow us. We're going to regroup with Bracken and the Forge Brothers before leaving Arcadia."

Harrison nodded in agreement, then turned to face his friends. "You heard him, we're leaving this place."

"And not a moment too soon," said Murdock, shaking his head.

The young warrior took a moment to consider their next journey. He had not seen his love in over three months and a sudden feeling of joy coursed through his body. Harrison panned to Gelderand and Swinkle.

"We're going to see Tara soon," he said, beaming.

Gelderand smiled in return. "That we are." The mage swung his pack around in order to see his feline friend. "You are finally going home for good, Rufus." The cat meowed at the sound of his name.

Harrison watched the platoons of soldiers vacate the area. "Time to go," he said, as he and his friends followed Brendan's men and let the remaining soldiers tend to the burning city.

* * *

Brendan's scouts left the occupied zone and advanced through Arcadia's safe area, where Bracken Drake awaited their arrival. Harrison and his friends followed the soldiers to the

73

familiar Arcadian leader's tent. Upon seeing the leadership team, the two sentries who guarded the sanctuary's entrance lifted its canvas flap, allowing Brendan, Harrison, and the others to enter.

The young warrior followed his leader before finding the Arcadian general pacing, his head up in thought. Bracken then swiveled and glared at the men. "Have you seen what those beasts have done to my city?"

Brendan raised his palms, taking a cautious step toward the Arcadian. "Bracken, the destruction is legendary, but we have eradicated the vermin from Arcadia."

The eye-patched warrior allowed the Aegean's comment to linger. "Regardless, this city is destroyed. We must rebuild from the ground up." Bracken looked off into the distance, distraught.

Brendan approached the despondent leader, placing a caring hand on his equal's back. "Bracken, we will help you rebuild. All the villages will assist. We will not desert Arcadia."

The Arcadian nodded, accepting the Aegean's offer. "That is most gracious of you, but I'm not done with those beasts yet."

Brendan's brow cringed. "What are you saying, Bracken? We can't go after them now, no matter how desperately you want to."

"I understand," said the Arcadian leader, his tone cold and calculated, "but there will come a day when my army will set their homeland ablaze. That I promise you."

The elder Aegean nodded, hoping that that time would be in the distant future, when the land had time to regroup and heal their collective wounds.

Continuing the conversation, Brendan said, "We're going to convene the land's leadership in Concur. There's much to discuss considering the carnage that occurred here."

Bracken turned away from the men, placing his hands behind his back, hiding his scowl from the others. "You understand my position, don't you, Brendan?"

The seasoned warrior made a subtle glance over to Harrison before speaking. "Please reiterate your stance for all to hear."

Bracken wheeled around, but before he could speak, the canvas flap swung open, allowing two more men to enter the sanctuary. A wry smile graced the Arcadian's face. Recognizing the two fighters, he said, "Octavius, Caidan, glad you could join us."

The Forge Brothers nodded in response to Bracken's comment. Octavius planted a firm hand on Brendan's shoulder. "Good to see you again, old friend." He then panned to the other men. "All of you."

Brendan took the opportunity to bring the warriors up to speed with their current conversation. "We were just discussing the next course of events with Bracken."

"All Scynthians that had tortured this city are now dead," said Caidan, taking a step forward. "And we will destroy any that may have slipped through the cracks."

"My army has orders to kill any beast that they encounter with no remorse," added Bracken. "The Scynthians made a foolish decision attacking Arcadia."

"We are all in agreement on this," said Brendan, "however, we must return to Concur." The Aegean brought his gaze to meet the Forge Brothers. "Argos must be represented as well."

"We will accompany you," said Octavius, before turning his attention to the Arcadian leader, "and I shall leave a contingent of men behind to help with your efforts as well, Bracken."

"That would be much appreciated," said the eye-patched warrior.

Brendan addressed the Arcadian once again. "Are you coming with us?"

Bracken paused, pondering the request. "I can better serve my people staying here. The Scynthians crushed their morale and it would not be good for their leader to leave them again. Therefore, the answer is no."

The Aegean understood his equal's rationale. "Our discussions in Concur will be about dealing with the Scynthians. As the leader of Arcadia, what is your official position that you want us to relay to them?"

Bracken did not hesitate to answer. "Burn them as they burned us! The fires that will ripple through their land will make the inferno that engulfed our Great Hall look like a campfire! I don't want you to stop until their very civilization comes to a fiery end. Do I make myself clear?"

75

Brendan raised an eyebrow and swallowed subtly. "Our team will relay your position to the other towns. We will also leave some men behind to aid in the rebuilding effort as well."

"Thank you," said Bracken. "When are you leaving?"

"As soon as we regroup with our men and give them their assignments."

Bracken nodded, then said, "I'm counting on you," the Arcadian lifted his eyes to the rest of the group, "all of you to not hold back in dealing with the Scynthians. If I had it my way, I'd eradicate them from the land."

"We will certainly convey your point of view," said Brendan. He then motioned for the others to leave Bracken's tent. As the men began to depart, the Aegean said, "Good luck with your efforts. We'll send word of our next actions as soon as they are confirmed. And don't forget to utilize the falcon messenger system."

"Again, thank you," said Bracken. "Have a safe journey back to Concur." Brendan nodded, then left the Arcadian behind.

Outside, Harrison waited for his mentor to finish his business with Bracken. Seeing him now, he asked, "Is it wise to leave Arcadia in shambles?"

"We have no other choice," said Brendan, advancing to his awaiting steed while the Forge Brothers went in search of their men. "The Scynthians might be planning more surprise attacks. We need to be ready in case they do and that includes all the defenseless coastal villages."

The young warrior pondered the elder man's statement. Arcadia had a formidable army, yet the Scynthians took control of their city for a considerable amount of time. Harrison took in the sights of the smoldering buildings and the unmistakable aroma of charred wood and knew that his enemy would have run roughshod through the towns along the sea.

Harrison felt his belly tighten and he tried his best to stem the feelings of aggression that so wanted to course throughout his body. Sensing his friend's anxiety, Swinkle approached the young warrior and said, "The trip back to Concur will give us time to digest the happenings of the past three months."

The young warrior eased at hearing his friend's words. "I wouldn't bet on that."

"Harrison," said Swinkle in a soothing voice, "all I am saying is that it will be good to get away from all that has happened."

"That I can agree with," said the young warrior.

"Gather your men," said Brendan, before mounting his horse. "I'll need them to help lead the forces north."

"Will do," said Harrison, as Brendan departed to join the Forge Brothers and their soldiers.

Murdock and Pondle watched the elder Aegean leave, then joined Harrison and Swinkle with Gelderand and Lance following close behind. With all of them together, Harrison took the opportunity to address his friends.

"The plan is to return to Concur where we'll decide our next course of action," said the young warrior.

"You know how I feel," said the ranger. "What are we supposed to do now?"

Harrison gestured to Murdock and Pondle. "Brendan wants you to help lead the convoy back to Concur." The young warrior swiveled to Gelderand and Swinkle. "We'll journey with the rest of the soldiers."

"Fine with me," said Murdock before bringing his gaze to Pondle. "You?"

"I can't wait to get out of here. I'm ready to leave now," said the thief.

"Good, then let's go," said Harrison with a wave of his hand. Murdock and Pondle assumed the group's lead while Swinkle and Gelderand walked next to Harrison. Lance scurried to his master's side, happy to be leaving Arcadia behind in his own way.

Gelderand could sense Harrison's apprehension. "Put your mind at ease, son," said the mage. "Soon we will leave Arcadia and deal with the Scynthians on our terms. And," Gelderand smirked, "Tara will be very happy to see you."

The mention of his love's name warmed Harrison's heart. "I miss her so much."

"All the reason to get back as soon as possible," said the mage.

The young warrior nodded, agreeing with the older man. Harrison took a last look at the charred structures, digesting the gravity of destruction that occurred at the Scynthian's hands. He then pushed that image to the back of his consciousness and instead focused on Tara's beautiful face, which he kept in the forefront of his mind all the way back to Concur.

CHAPTER 6

☼

Foul weather forced Harrison and the armies to arrive a day later than expected to Concur. However, not even the pouring rain that fell from the midday sky could wipe the smile off the young warrior's face. Harrison figured that he had not seen Tara for over four months, but that would all end today.

The young warrior, along with his friends, entered Concur via the west gate. Walking up the main thoroughfare, Harrison could not help but notice repairs made to damaged buildings, the abundance of shops open for business, and the throngs of people in the streets. The sights brought a smile to his face, realizing that the Concurians had done a fine job cleaning up their city after the atrocities that their former ruler, Lord Nigel Hammer, bestowed upon them. However, townsfolk gave the peacekeeping army curious glances as they marched into the walled city, the scourge of battle still fresh on their minds.

Harrison gazed into the distance, his eyes stopping at the familiar structure that stood ahead of him. The Governor's mansion appeared exactly the same since the last time he had visited. On that fateful day, messenger falcons had alerted him and Tara that the Scynthians had sacked Arcadia, Lars, Nordic, and Polaris, and it was his duty to alert the leadership group.

Tara's tearful blue eyes had stared back at his and he recalled what she had said. "You're going to leave me again, aren't you?"

The young warrior had held her tight. "I must alert the others and join the battle in Arcadia."

How he had wished to take those words back and remain with his love, but both of them knew that never was an option. Today, he intended to make up for lost time.

The Governor's mansion loomed before the group. Before reaching the impressive structure, Brendan and the Forge Brothers dismounted their steeds, then instructed their men to enjoy the comforts of Concur, where they would remain for an extended period. The soldiers appeared relieved at their new orders, many of them scurrying away to find shelter from the rain, while others searched for a hot meal.

As the area thinned of fighters, Harrison and his friends took the opportunity to approach the leaders. "Has it really been four months since we were here?" asked the young warrior in Brendan's direction.

"That it has," said the elder Aegean, securing his horse's reins to a post. Before the men could continue their conversation, the sentries manning the main entrance of the mansion made an announcement.

The guardian on the right stood at attention, then bellowed, "All hail, Lady Meredith!"

Both men took hold of the portal's handles and swung the doors open wide. Inside the entryway stood Meredith, the ruler of Concur, adorned in a dark blue dress, the color contrasting her alabaster skin. She wore a sapphire necklace around her neck and a wide smile graced her face.

To her right stood Thoragaard, the illusionist wearing his customary dark hooded cloak and dour expression, while to her left a thin man tried his best to maneuver an umbrella in an ungraceful attempt to keep the rain from touching his superior.

Meredith took a step forward, Percival, her servant, by her side. She threw open her arms and exclaimed, "Welcome back to Concur! Now hurry and get out of this rain!"

Seeing Meredith brought a feeling of joy over Harrison, but the young warrior searched beyond her for someone just out of sight. A tap on his shoulder startled him.

"Where's Tara?" asked Gelderand, a hint of concern in his voice.

Harrison did his best to put the older man at ease. "I'm sure she's here."

The words had no sooner left his mouth when a smaller figure in a purple hooded cloak appeared in the doorway. The person stepped forward and pulled down her covering. Tara's eyes locked onto Harrison, her face hardly containing her smile.

Harrison's heart jumped at the sight of his love. "There she is!"

Gelderand gave the young man a slight shove. "What are you waiting for? Let's go!"

The young warrior waited for Brendan and the Forge Brothers to make the first move, and when they started to ascend the steps, he and his friends quickly followed. Lance, however, noticed Tara right away, yapped once, raced up the staircase past everyone else, and jumped at the young maiden with excitement. Tara bent to one knee to greet her canine friend, rubbing the dog's wet fur.

Harrison tried his best to climb the staircase while watching Tara in the process. However, when he reached the top steps, he found his eyes locking onto Meredith's. The Concurian leader greeted the elder soldiers first, then focused on the young warrior.

Harrison, unsure of how to greet the new governor of Concur, extended his hand and said, "It's good to be back, Meredith."

Meredith bypassed the young warrior's welcoming gesture and wrapped her arms around him, pulling him close. "You don't know how good it is to see you again." After a few more seconds of embracing, she kissed Harrison on the cheek and stepped aside.

"Someone has been waiting patiently a long time for you," said the dark-haired beauty.

By this time, Tara had finished her greeting with Lance and waited for Harrison to approach her. The young warrior brought his full focus to his love, taking a step in her direction, scooping the girl in his arms, lifting her clear off the ground, and spinning her around.

Tara giggled, then said, "I've missed you so much!"

"I've missed you more," said Harrison before the young couple engaged in a long kiss. Placing Tara back on the ground, he took hold of her hand and gestured to another person with his other.

"Someone else has missed you, too," said the young warrior.

"Tara," said Gelderand, his arms outstretched, reaching for his niece.

"Uncle," said the lass, her eyes glassy, accepting his hug. She then brought her focus to Murdock, Pondle, and Swinkle. "You all stayed away too long!"

"It is good to see you again, Tara," said the young cleric, while Murdock and Pondle waved in the girl's direction.

"Agreed," said the mage. "Let's hope we don't need to leave again anytime soon." The older man pulled away and kissed his niece on the cheek.

Tara smiled, then looked past Gelderand to the pack slung over his shoulder. "Where's Rufus?"

The magician exhaled, then swiveled his backpack around, revealing Rufus' furry little face. "He's right here."

Tara fumbled inside the pack and reached for the animal. As she placed her hands under his forelegs and lifted, the cat squirmed, then gave a loud screech. Tara's eyes went wide and she released her grip on Rufus.

"What's wrong with him?" she asked, her voice full of concern.

Her uncle furrowed his brow. "Tara, Rufus has had an accident and he is hurt."

"An accident?" said Tara, shaking her head, alternating her gaze between Harrison and Gelderand. "Did he fall?"

Gelderand dropped his head down, looking for the right words. When the mage did not answer right away, Swinkle said, "Scynthians ambushed your uncle and took Rufus. They hurt him very badly."

Tara's mouth lingered open upon hearing the sad news. She went back to Rufus and gently took hold of him under his front legs. In a slow deliberate motion, she lifted the cat out of the backpack and cradled him in her arms.

"What exactly is wrong with him?" she asked, her brow creased with concern.

"Those beasts tossed Rufus back and forth to each other," started Gelderand. "When he tried to run away, one of the Scynthians tried to stop him by stepping on his tail. Instead, he landed on his back legs." The mage shook his head, the emotion getting the better of him. "He might never walk again."

"I prayed over him many, many times," added Swinkle, hoping to put the girl at ease. "He is recovering."

Tara's eyes pooled as she brought her gaze down to the feline that rested in her arms. "I'll take care of him now. I'll make sure he gets better."

Her uncle nodded in concurrence. "His days of adventuring are over."

"And well they should be," said Tara, swaying the cat the way one does a baby.

Meredith, sensing that the greetings had come to an end, said, "Everyone, let's take today to settle in, find some warm clothes and hot meals, for tomorrow we'll have plenty of things to talk about."

"That sounds like a very good plan," said Brendan. "We need to apprise you on the Scynthian attacks and what it means for Concur and the rest of the land."

The Concurian woman agreed. "All the more reason to rest tonight."

Turning to his Argosian counterparts, Brendan said, "Shall we take the lady's advice?"

Octavius looked at Caidan, who nodded in affirmative. "You don't have to tell us twice to find good food and drink!" exclaimed the elder Forge before addressing Meredith again. "Thank you for your hospitality, milady. It has been a long and arduous journey indeed."

"We should brief our men," said Brendan, "and then we can partake in the comforts of Concur."

"Good idea," said Octavius. Extending a hand toward the main staircase, he said, "After you, Brendan."

The Aegean smirked. "Since when are you a diplomat?"

"I'm not," deadpanned the Argosian. "Let's go before I change my mind!"

Harrison listened to his superior's conversation and the thought of leaving Tara already started to gnaw at his insides.

Meredith noticed the young warrior's look of apprehension. "Harrison," she said, "why don't you and your friends stay with us for now? You can give me firsthand knowledge of the happenings in Arcadia."

The young warrior did a poor job trying to hide his smile. "Brendan, is it ..." he started before his leader cut him off in midsentence.

"Brief the governor," said the elder warrior with a wave of his hand. "We'll reconvene later tonight." The Aegean then began his descent down the staircase, the Forge brothers following.

Harrison felt the burden lift from his shoulders, flashing a wide smile in Tara's direction. Bringing his attention back to Meredith, he said, "We should discuss the battles we witnessed and start planning a war strategy."

The Governor of Concur showed her palms to Harrison. "Not now. You all have some catching up to do, as well as to get out of those wet, dirty clothes." Meredith gestured for her guests to enter the mansion. "Please make yourself at home."

Harrison led Tara back inside the building, followed by his friends. Meanwhile, Meredith continued, "Percival will show you to your quarters and direct my staff to help make your stay comfortable."

"Thank you, Meredith," said Harrison. "You have no idea what we've gone through."

Meredith placed a caring hand on the young warrior's arm. "I can only imagine. We'll talk shortly." She then left with Thoragaard, leaving the small band of adventurers to Percival.

With his superior departing, the mansion's lead servant took control of the situation. "Everyone has been here before. We've readied the same rooms for all of you, just as they were the day you left four months ago."

"That's most gracious of you, Percival," said Harrison. "We could use some rest after our journey."

The thin servant nodded, accepting the young warrior's gratitude. "Make yourselves at home. Dinner is in a few hours. I'll summon someone to fetch you when the time comes."

Percival then nodded before he too departed to continue with his daily chores. Harrison watched the skinny man disappear down the building's main corridor. Turning to his friends, he said, "We might as well take advantage of this time to relax."

"You don't have to tell me twice," said Murdock, already heading to the spiral staircase that led to their rooms upstairs. "You coming, Pondle?"

The thief followed his friend. "Of course I am. I'm exhausted after trekking in the rain for hours." The two then left their friends behind.

"The journey back to Concur has taken its toll," said Swinkle. "I am going to take this time to study and then take a nap. See you two later today." The young cleric then followed the ranger and the thief up the staircase.

"I could use some rest, too," said Gelderand. Gesturing to the animal in Tara's arms, he asked, "Are you going to take care of Rufus?"

The young maiden nodded. "Consider him my sole responsibility. I'll nurse him back to health."

The magician gazed at his niece, recalling the time when he presented Rufus as a kitten to the little blonde haired lass. Tara could hardly contain her smile as she reached out and accepted the orange fur ball. Now, his niece grown, he placed Rufus' care in the hands of a very capable young woman.

"I know you will," he said, pecking her on the cheek. "I'll see you both later today." The mage followed Swinkle's lead and ascended the staircase to a room of his own.

Her uncle now gone, Tara gazed at Harrison and said, "Shall we go upstairs, too? You're still wet."

The young warrior nodded. "I want to get out of these clothes as soon as I can."

Tara smirked. "We should probably wait until nighttime."

Harrison felt his face blush. "Oh, that's not what I meant, I …"

The young maiden giggled. "I know what you meant!" She then took a step toward Harrison and planted a soft kiss on his cheek. "But I have really missed you. Let's go."

Tara took the lead and headed toward the stairs, Lance scurrying ahead of her. Harrison, a smile on his face, could not follow the young girl fast enough.

Tara made a point to reach their room first where she gently placed Rufus on a large padded pillow, then went about lighting candles, providing a much needed soft glow to counteract the rainy day's gloom.

Lance scooted over to Rufus, rubbing his damp fur on the padding, then curled up against the feline to warm his weary bones. Harrison entered the room, placing his backpack and weaponry in an empty corner.

The young warrior appreciated the room's sights. Tara had arranged everything to perfection—the strategically placed candles provided ample lighting, the ornate bed covering and rows of fluffy pillows pleased the eye, and the aroma of freshly cut flowers placed in a glass vase offered a welcome scent to the air.

"You really have made a home here," said Harrison.

Tara came over to the young warrior, eager to help him out of his dank clothing. "Meredith made sure I felt comfortable while you all were away. She's a remarkable person."

"I'm happy to see that she took such good care of you," he said, unclasping his armor. "What else have you done to pass the time here?"

Tara continued to fiddle with Harrison's body covering. "I've been very busy with my studies. Thoragaard has taken me under his wing, so to speak."

The young maiden finished unhooking the last clasp and helped Harrison out of his armor. She then took off his wet undershirt, revealing his muscular upper torso.

Tara ran a soft hand over his chest. "I'm on my way to being a powerful mage," she said with a grin.

Harrison tried his best to focus on Tara's words, but her gentle touch more than distracted him. "You'll have to show me some of the tricks you've learned since I've been away."

"I'll have plenty of tricks to show you," she said, reaching up on her tiptoes to meet his lips, the two sharing a deep kiss.

Separating she said, "I'll draw you a warm bath while you take off the rest of your clothes." The young maiden then departed for the adjacent washroom.

Harrison watched her backside sway away before fumbling with his boots and pants. Noticing that he had nothing to cover his naked body with, he grabbed his damp shirt and wrapped it around his midsection.

"I look ridiculous," he muttered to himself, examining the makeshift covering that exposed his backside and left little imagination at what he tried to hide. Lance had even cocked his head, looking at his master in wonderment.

"Are you coming?" asked Tara from the bathroom.

"Yes," Harrison said feebly, then entered the room. Tara had arranged more candles to help illuminate the small room, the one window shedding little light on such a cloudy day. The young warrior held the shirt in front of himself as he approached the warm tub of water.

Tara pointed at the piece of clothing. "What are you doing?" she said with a laugh. "Don't be so shy!"

Harrison did not know what to say. "I felt a little funny just bursting in here naked." Lance scooted into the room, just to add more humility to the young warrior's scene.

"Relax, Harrison," said Tara, approaching the young warrior. "Drop the clothes and enter the tub."

Harrison did as she asked, feeling warm water touch his skin for the first time in what seemed an eternity. Tara sat herself down on a stool next to the bathtub, took a cloth, dunked it into the liquid, and began to wash his back.

"I figured that you would enjoy a warm bath after being away in battle for so long."

"This feels fantastic," he said. "Thank you."

"No need to thank me," she said, continuing with her washing.

"Please, tell me about your studies," said Harrison, closing his eyes and enjoying the feeling of Tara's soft hands caressing his tired back.

"Thoragaard had me practicing meditation, breathing exercises, and memorizing spells," she started. "We would spend several hours every day working on different things." Tara dunked the cloth again, dripping warm water on the back of Harrison's neck. "He says I'm ready for my next phase."

The young warrior's eyes remained closed. "And what would that be?"

Tara paused for a second before saying, "An adventure."

Harrison's eyes opened at Tara's last comment. Turning his head to face his love, he asked, "What kind of adventure?"

"Nothing big just something that would take me away from the confines of my studies and the city." The young maiden continued to clean Harrison, dabbing him as she spoke. "Maybe out in the wilderness for a few days, to get a feel of nature and such."

Harrison, intrigued, continued his interrogation. "Who would accompany you?"

"Thoragaard, most likely." Tara brought her face close to Harrison. "And I was hoping you would come too, of course." She then returned to her washing. "Lance would love to come along as well, I suppose." The little dog wagged his tail upon hearing his name.

Harrison felt more at ease after hearing Tara say that she wanted him to be part of the adventure team. "I would love to help you in any way, Tara."

The young maiden smiled, happy to hear Harrison's support. Changing the subject, she asked, "What was it like in Arcadia?" Tara noticed the young warrior's back muscles tighten after her question.

"Pure chaos," he said, trying to keep his anxiety in check. "The Scynthians are brutal beasts, Tara. They kill and destroy everything in their path."

"You beat them back, didn't you?"

Harrison chose his words carefully, not wanting to divulge the atrocities he witnessed. "We eliminated them from the city."

"Eliminated?" Tara stopped caressing the young warrior. "Are they all gone?"

"Yes. Bracken mandated that every Scynthian die and he succeeded on that mission."

Tara started dabbing Harrison's back again. "How many did you, they, kill?"

The young warrior clenched his jaw, then relaxed it before speaking. "Thousands."

Tara stopped her chore and leaned closer to Harrison's face from her seat on the stool. "You slaughtered thousands of Scynthians?" The young girl's gaze drifted away to a corner of the room. "How many people died?"

Harrison started to become uncomfortable with Tara's line of questioning, but knew that she had a right to know. His wet hand reached for Tara and he took one of hers to caress it with his thumb.

"Many, many people died in a brutal fashion, Tara," he started. "They surprised the city while the majority of Arcadia's army remained fighting here in Concur. Those monsters set the place ablaze, practically leveling the entire metropolis. Arcadia as we all knew it is gone."

Tara's eyes met Harrison's. "It's a miracle that you survived."

The young warrior had spoken enough about the horrors of war. "I promised you that I'd return. I love you so much, I couldn't bear the thought of leaving you alone in this world."

The young girl blushed, then leaned from her perch, her lips an inch from his. "I love you, too," she said before kissing him.

Harrison allowed his gaze to linger on Tara's beautiful face after their lips parted. The young maiden, noticing her love's stare, squinted and cocked her head. "What?"

"Why don't you join me?" he said with a mischievous grin.

Tara arched her eyebrows. "Join you where?" Harrison pointed to the tub. "In there?" The girl's face turned a deep red. "I can't!"

Harrison lay back, smirking. "Why not?"

The young maiden fumbled for words. "The water's dirty," she said. "And it's getting cool."

"It's not *that* dirty," Harrison said with a laugh. "And I'll keep you warm."

Tara lowered her voice. "Harrison, we don't have that much time."

"I've missed you the past four months. We'll make the time."

The young maiden thought for a moment, then stood from her seat next to the tub and slowly disrobed. Harrison watched Tara remove her clothes, his excitement level rising with every article of clothing that hit the floor. Fully nude, the young girl touched the water with her index finger.

Leaning her lips near Harrison's ear she whispered, "The water's cold."

The young warrior outstretched his arms. "I told you, I'm going to keep you warm."

Tara positioned her bottom on the side of the tub, then slowly submerged, laying on top of Harrison. With a shiver, she said, "Alright, it's time to make me warm."

The two then began maneuvering their bodies in every which way, splashing copious amounts of water out of the tub and onto the floor. Lance, tired of receiving the brunt end of his unintended bath, scooted out of the room while the lovers thrashed until the water became too cool to bear.

CHAPTER 7

¤

One of Meredith's servants arrived at Harrison and Tara's room, alerting them that the time had come to join Concur's new governor for dinner. The couple descended the staircase across from their chamber and strolled down the hallway to the grand dining room. Harrison recalled the times he had visited the mansion in the past, how he had to wield a weapon to guard against Nigel Hammer's physical threats, let alone defend himself against the former governor's condescending rhetoric toward his righteousness. Upon seeing the two approach, a member of the mansion's staff opened the doors to the chamber, allowing the pair to enter.

"Enjoy your meal," the woman said with a smile. The young warrior nodded, accepting her comment.

Harrison and Tara entered the ballroom hand in hand. The young warrior brought his gaze about the space with wide eyes. "This place is beautiful," he said.

"Meredith made sure that she rid the mansion of Lord Hammer's signature," said the young maiden. Taking her eyes to the back walls, she continued. "Meredith's house staff wove those tapestries for her, as a way to support her new rulership. They love her."

Gesturing with her head, she continued, "And do you see those plants over there?" Harrison took his gaze to the corners of the room, finding tall leafy trees with red blooms.

"The groundskeepers went into the countryside and specifically handpicked them for her," said Tara. "She loved them as a child and her servants wanted to do something extraordinary in appreciation of her hospitality."

The Aegean then glanced at the long wooden table that occupied the center of the space, finding their friends there chatting amongst themselves, making conversation while seated in plush chairs. Fine china, flatware, and chalices rested in front of each person. Beautiful cut flowers sprouted from ornate vases placed in strategic positions on the table.

Investigating further, Harrison found Meredith and Thoragaard at the head of the table, seated in two royal chairs opposite the main entryway. To the right of the illusionist sat Brendan, Octavius, and Caidan, in deep discussion. Gelderand, Swinkle, Murdock, and Pondle carried on conversations while filling the seats to Meredith's left.

Harrison noticed that two chairs remained open closest to her. Reading the apprehensive looks of the young couple entering the room, Concur's leader waved to get their attention.

"Harrison, Tara, please take a seat with us!" exclaimed Meredith, gesturing for them to occupy the chairs next to her. The young warrior acknowledged her request with a nod and the pair exchanged pleasantries with the others in the room as they walked to their place at the table. Harrison pulled Tara's chair out, allowing her to sit, before taking a seat of his own.

Meredith leaned toward the young warrior. "Did you get some much needed rest?"

"Yes," said Harrison. "Yes, we did."

"That's good," said the Concurian. "Journeying and battling can take its toll on the body."

"It certainly does," responded Harrison. "And we want to thank you again for your generosity."

"It's the least I could do after you helped save our city," she said with a flick of her wrist. "Not to mention that you also liberated Arcadia from those wretched beasts."

Before continuing their conversation, the two noticed three more figures enter the room. Harrison recognized the trio, but stared at them nonetheless.

Kymbra, the tall blonde warrior, and her two cohorts, Adrith and Marissa, approached the table. Everyone in the room had associated the three women with battle, only having seen them in their leather armor and wielding some sort of weaponry. Tonight, however, the women wore traditional clothing that showed their feminine side to the delight of the men seated around the table.

Harrison gazed over to Murdock, catching him glued to every step Kymbra made, his mouth slightly ajar. The young warrior chuckled when he saw Pondle poke his friend in the ribs, breaking him out of his trance.

Kymbra allowed her blue eyes to linger on Murdock, before sitting in the empty seat across from him. Adrith and Marissa flanked the tall blonde on either side, completing the dinner party.

Tara leaned over and whispered to Harrison. "They're stunning," she said. "I always thought they were pretty girls dressed in men's clothing, but tonight changes everything."

Harrison nodded, his eyes fixated on the ladies. "You can say that again."

Tara elbowed the young warrior in the side. Narrowing her eyes, she said to him with a scowl, "I'm sitting right here."

"Sorry, I didn't mean any disrespect," said the young warrior, fumbling for words. Tara maintained her glare for a moment longer before turning away.

Meredith stood and addressed the intimate gathering. "Now that everyone's here," she nodded toward the female warriors, "we can get started with our evening plans."

The Concurian glanced at Percival, who stood by a doorway, awaiting his superior's cue. Meredith gestured in his direction, signaling to her servant to commence with the party. Percival then flung open the kitchen portals and several waiters ushered through, carrying trays loaded with freshly cooked foods. Handmaidens followed with carafes of fine wine and pitchers of ale.

"Let it be said that Lady Meredith knows how to throw a party!" bellowed Octavius, raising his glass. Everyone at the table cheered and did likewise.

Meredith, still standing, took a goblet of her own and raised it in the air. "To all of you escaping the horrors of war," she said. "We will dine before we speak of anything else. No strategies, no battle stories, just good food and drink. Agreed?"

"Agreed!" everyone at the table said in unison. Servants placed hot plates in front of Meredith's guests, many of them not having tasted prepared meals for months.

Harrison, his stomach growling, tried not to devour his food in one bite. Tearing at a piece of warm bread, he gazed at Tara and said, "This is delicious!"

"The Concurians certainly know how to prepare food," said the young maiden, enjoying a dish of Cornish hen and vegetables. After a mouthful of leafy greens, she continued, "I feel a little ashamed that I dined on cuisine like this while you and everyone else had to scrounge for scraps."

The young warrior chewed some of the tasty meat before answering. "Consider yourself lucky," said Harrison, chasing his food with a swig of ale. "Things were difficult, but Meredith said no battle stories."

Harrison and Tara, along with the rest of the dinner guests, enjoyed the masterful feast without any talk of Scynthian atrocities. An hour later, after everyone had had their fill, Meredith felt the time had come to discuss the happenings in Arcadia.

Taking a spoon to her chalice, she repeatedly struck it, creating a clear clinking sound above the din of chatter. Everyone at the table halted their conversations and turned to face Meredith.

With the full attention of her dinner guests, she asked, "Who can provide details about their experiences in Arcadia?"

Brendan and the Forge brothers exchanged glances before the Aegean spoke. "I will, milady," said Brendan, as all eyes focused on the veteran warrior.

"As we all found out four months ago, the Scynthians coordinated a surprise attack against the towns of Nordic, Polaris, Lars, and Arcadia. The beasts destroyed the three smaller coastal villages and practically burned Arcadia to the ground.

"However, by the time we joined the Arcadians in the fight, the tide had already turned in our favor. The only problem we encountered was determining the best way to eradicate the Scynthians from the city."

Meredith creased her brow. "How did you rectify that?"

The Aegean scowled, then continued. "We," Brendan motioned with his hand to the men seated around the table, "had decided to take back the city block by block, killing every Scynthian in our path. Bracken, however, chose another strategy.

"The mere thought that Scynthians had occupied his city was too much for him to bear. Instead, he devised a plan to push the creatures toward the harbor before sealing them off several blocks from the water."

"So he planned to wait them out, until they ran out of food, water, and supplies," said Meredith, understanding battle tactics she had learned many years ago from her late father. "Then you would dictate the terms of surrender, right?"

Brendan made a subtle glance to Octavius, knowing that they both had discussed this exact strategy only to have Bracken overrule them. "The Arcadians deemed the land soiled and burned the rest of their city to the ground."

Meredith gasped, taking a hand to cover her open mouth. With wide eyes, she asked, "What happened to the Scynthians?"

"As Bracken had so eloquently stated, they used them as kindling for the epic blaze." Brendan maintained his stare on the Concurian, relaying with his eyes that he did not go along with Bracken's strategy.

Eyes still round, she asked in disbelief, "He burned them all alive?"

"He wants to rebuild his city without the stain of Scynthian fingerprints. He'll get his wish."

Meredith sat back in her seat, shocked at Brendan's revelation. A moment later, she leaned forward, asking the group, "What do we do now?"

Brendan brought his gaze to Octavius, who took the opportunity to speak. "This latest act by the Scynthians needs to be their last," started the Argosian leader. "We all know about the atrocities they perform on a daily basis to us humans. Many of their heinous crimes are orchestrated against random, unfortunate souls."

The warrior's comments resonated with Harrison all too well. His bicep started to tingle, knowing that his parents and their friends were innocent souls caught in a random, horrific act.

Octavius continued. "Now they planned and executed a surprise attack against one of the largest cities in the land. This is an act of war and we must stop them — now."

"Are you suggesting a full out war between the humans and the Scynthians?" asked Meredith, knowing the historic ramifications of the answer she awaited.

The Argosian leader did not hesitate. "Yes. We hit them back ten times harder than they hit us." Meredith again sat back in her chair, contemplating this latest revelation.

While the governor remained deep in thought, Harrison felt it time to speak his mind. With a subtle glance toward Swinkle, he said, "Battling the Scynthians will result in hundreds, if not thousands, of human lives. Can we sustain that?"

"The better question," interjected Murdock, "is exactly how many Scynthians are still out there?"

Brendan and the Forge brothers exchanged anxious glances. "As far as we know," started the Aegean, "there are probably ten thousand beasts scattered throughout the land. As for how many live in the Empire Mountains ..." Brendan shook his head and raised his palms to the sky.

"Answering your question," Octavius pointed to Harrison, "we have no other choice but to fight. We can't just sit back and wait for another Scynthian onslaught."

Harrison spread his arms wide. "We could defend our towns and villages by patrolling the outskirts of our lands," said the young warrior, attempting to save lives before heading to war. "Sentries can report back if they see any significant Scynthian movements. They're not the best tacticians, you know."

"Tell that to the Arcadians," responded Brendan, a scowl on his face. "Humanity must band together to rid these beasts of the land."

"There may be another option," said Gelderand, who had patiently waited for an opportune moment to speak. All eyes focused on the magician.

"Many years ago, I ventured with a group in search of the Ancient Scrolls of Arcadia. The scriptures, it is alleged, contain prophecies about the land, ancient and future rulers, battles and wars, and the fate of humanity."

"I'm familiar with the scrolls," said Brendan. "It's part of the teachings at the Fighter's Guild. However, I don't see how uncovering them will do us any good."

"Maybe they already state who'll be victorious in a future war," suggested Harrison, his brain churning. "Knowing that outcome could help us create battle plans to our advantage."

Caidan nodded in agreement. "I like the sound of that."

Gelderand waved his palms toward the group, shaking his head as well. "No, no, no. That is not what I am trying to convey. Again, it is alleged, there exists a parchment contained within the Scrolls of Arcadia that, if read, can eradicate an entire race from the world. We call it the Genocide Scroll."

Octavius' eyes opened wide. "We could wipe them out entirely without losing a single soldier!" The Argosian could barely contain his excitement, his head reeling with possibilities. "We need to start looking for these scriptures now!"

Brendan raised a hand. "Now hold on a moment." Taking his gaze to the elder mage, he asked, "You mentioned that you ventured for the scrolls. Did you ever *find* them?"

Gelderand shook his head. "No."

"Where are they laid to rest?" asked Meredith, her interest piqued by the new course of events.

"All my studies have led me to believe that they are hidden somewhere in the Dark Forest," said Gelderand.

"The Dark Forest?" said Harrison, his brow crinkling, understanding that the immense forest and Arcadia rested on opposite sides of the countryside. "Then why are they called the Scrolls of Arcadia?"

"Supposedly the creator hailed from Arcadia at the time," said Thoragaard, adding to the conversation. Taking his gaze to Gelderand, he continued. "I too have studied this topic."

"We should share our knowledge," said Gelderand. Thoragaard closed his eyes and nodded once, agreeing. "And I also suggest speaking with my mentor for more clarity on the situation."

Harrison thought for a moment before the visage of an elderly man sprung to mind. "Are you speaking of Martinaeous?"

The mage nodded. "That I am."

Murdock waved a hand at the mage. "You're talking about that old man who barely recognized your face the last time we were there," said the ranger, shaking his head. "He's hardly competent."

Gelderand crossed his arms across his chest and sat back in his chair, glaring at the bowman. "Did he not help us with clues in finding the Talisman of Unification?"

"Maybe so," said Murdock, "but it took him three days to recover from gazing at a crystal ball!"

The mage leaned forward again. "I admit that he is old, but he sent me on my first assignment and that was to find the Scrolls of Arcadia." Gelderand slowly panned the faces at the table. "He has more knowledge about those parchments than any of us in this room."

"Did you go back to this Martinaeous after you failed in finding the scrolls?" asked Brendan.

Gelderand took a deep breath. After exhaling, he said, "I had issues within my family that needed tending." After a pause, he added, "I never went back."

"Where does Martinaeous live?" asked the elder Aegean.

"Valkala," said Gelderand, "which is a short detour on the way to the Dark Forest."

Brendan brought his gaze to the Forge Brothers, both men shrugging with indifference. "Seek your mentor," said the Aegean, "and get the finer details of the scrolls' resting place."

Meredith had waited for the men to finish their discussion before adding her concerns. "Are we really talking about erasing a species from this world?" The Concurian's eyes were sharp and focused, assuring that her reservations were known to the group.

"It will save lives," said Brendan.

"Our warriors won't need to battle a brutal enemy on a daily basis ever again," added Octavius.

Murdock leaned forward in Meredith's direction, resting his weight on his forearm. "Have you actually seen what these beasts do? This world would be a much better place without them."

After the ranger's comment, the table erupted in arguments for and against discovering and using the Genocide Scroll on the Scynthians. As the heated debate continued, Tara tugged on Harrison's sleeve.

Her blue eyes filled with concern, she asked, "What do you think?"

The young warrior took a moment to gather his thoughts. He gazed about the room, watching his mentors and friends whip themselves into a frenzy about the touchy topic.

"I think we should find the scroll," said Harrison. "And at that time we'll decide if we should use it."

Tara arched her eyebrows, surprised at his answer. The young warrior swiveled in his chair to face the young maiden. Sensing her concern, he took her hand in his and gave it a light caress.

"Maybe we'll be able to beat them back without destroying them or come up with a truce that satisfies us all. Either way, having the scroll in our possession enables us to make an ultimate decision."

The lass shook her head. "I'm afraid of who might get their hands on that piece of paper," said Tara, worried. "You can't trust everybody."

As Harrison contemplated the young maiden's comment, he noticed a figure rise from his seat. The robed person outstretched his arms and waved his hands, trying to gain everyone's attention.

"Everyone! Quiet, please!" exclaimed Swinkle. The young cleric's antics did not go unnoticed and, a moment later, all eyes in the room focused on him, awaiting his speech.

Having garnered everyone's attention, Swinkle took a moment to gather his thoughts. He exhaled, then began speaking. "I think we all have forgotten something very important. Aside from the Scynthian's unspeakable acts, we are not the ones to decide the fate of an entire race. We are all quick to assume that every Scynthian is evil."

Swinkle turned and faced Harrison. "Did we not encounter a juvenile named Naa'il who at least showed signs of reason? Eradicating him in one fell swoop would be deemed an inexcusable mistake."

"Swinkle," said Harrison, "I think we need to at least uncover this relic, as a last resort."

"An artifact such as the Genocide Scroll contains too much power — for any man." Many of the leaders averted their eyes upon Swinkle's last statement. "Furthermore, this is not only a decision the human race should make. Other beings should be involved."

Brendan furrowed his brow. "Like who?"

"The elves of the Dark Forest, for one," said Swinkle.

Harrison's eyes grew wide. "The ancient kings instructed us to seek them!"

Swinkle smiled and nodded. "Exactly. We must visit with them before proceeding."

Octavius threw up his hands. "Now wait just one second!" he exclaimed. "We can't take an army into the Dark Forest and leave the rest of the villages unprotected. That's inviting the Scynthians to run roughshod over us again!"

Harrison's mind raced. "I agree," he said, rising to his feet. "Taking an army would be foolish. We should send a smaller team." The young warrior made eye contact with Murdock, who started to understand his friend's line of reasoning.

"We visited the elves with Marcus and a small group of adventurers and they were very hospitable."

"And a smaller team works better together," added the ranger, encouraging his friend.

"Plus it leaves the rest of the men behind to protect against another large scale Scynthian attack," finished the young warrior.

"Visiting the elves to get their input is not a bad idea," said Brendan, trying to temper Harrison's enthusiasm. "And you're going to have to fill me in on these ancient kings later. Until then, who do you suggest will comprise this team?"

Harrison tried to hold back his smile. "Obviously me and my friends," he said.

"You'll need more support than that," said Octavius.

"We'll join you as well," said Kymbra, to the surprise of the group. "We've exhausted our talents here." She gazed over to Marissa and Adrith, who nodded their approval.

"And you will have my support, too," came a monotone voice.

Meredith swiveled her head in the illusionist's direction, her brow furrowed with surprise. "Thoragaard?" said the Concurian leader, taken aback by the illusionist's inclusion to the party.

"These people will need my help. It is a noble cause."

"What about Concur? Our rebuilding plans?" Meredith brought a hand to her chest, unsure at the sudden change of events.

"Meredith, your citizens adore you," said Thoragaard. "Your soldiers are loyal to you and the reconstruction effort is an ongoing success. You will be fine on your own for a short time."

"We will see to it that no one comes close to Concur," added Brendan, allaying the Concurian woman's doubts. "You have our word."

Meredith allowed the Aegean leader's words to sink in, nodding in agreement even though she had her reservations.

Tara, patiently waiting for her turn to speak, felt the time was right to voice her opinion. "I'm going as well!"

Harrison turned and stared at Tara, trying to conceal his surprise at the young maiden's outburst. "I'm not sure this is the kind of adventure Thoragaard had in mind for you."

"In actuality, it is," said the magician to the young warrior's disbelief.

"Thoragaard, it's dangerous in the wilderness," he said in a most unconvincing tone.

"She is not joining us as a showpiece, but as a mage."

The young warrior focused on his mate. Tara placed her arms across her chest, returning a hard stare of her own.

"Tara, are your skills that polished?" asked Harrison.

"I've studied very hard and done everything Thoragaard has asked of me," she said. "I passed every test!"

"Harrison, she will be an asset, not a liability," said the illusionist with conviction.

The young warrior maintained his stare on Tara, trying to get a better sense of how important being part of the adventuring

101

team meant to her. The young girl did not waver; instead she kept her stare on Harrison, saying with her eyes all he needed to hear.

At that moment, Harrison knew deep down that continuing the debate would be fruitless. Hearing Thoragaard's assessment made him feel better about the situation as well. With that thought in mind, a slight smile graced his face, coming to the realization that he would not have to leave his love behind again.

"Welcome to the team."

Tara's eyes widened a bit more and she arched her eyebrows, a little surprised that Harrison would actually agree to her membership to the group. With a wide smile, she hugged the young warrior hard, showing her appreciation to him before turning to face Gelderand. The young maiden knew how her uncle felt about her and wanted his approval, too. To her surprise, a beaming smile graced his face as well.

"Uncle?" asked Tara, her brows lifted. "Are you alright?"

"I'm getting older, Tara, and I don't know how many times I can leave you and promise that I will return," said the mage. "I'm glad you are joining us and I look forward to helping you with your apprenticeship."

"It's settled then," said Brendan, rising from his chair. Reaching down for his chalice and raising it in the air, he continued. "Let it be known that today you will set forth to return the Scrolls of Arcadia and all that they entail. We'll discuss the parameters of your mission in detail later but let us enjoy the rest of tonight."

Everyone stood from their seats and raised a glass, toasting the formation of the new group. Harrison brought the drink to his lips, then turned to face Tara, finding her gazing back at him.

"What?" he asked.

"You're going to be very proud of me," she said. "Just wait and see." Tara then took a sip of the sweet liquid from her chalice.

"This isn't going to be all fun and games," said Harrison, turning serious. "There are many situations that can turn dangerous at a moment's notice. I'll be there to protect you."

Tara crinkled her brow. "You think that I need your protection? Thanks, but I can do fine on my own. You'll see."

The young warrior had started to become accustomed to saying the wrong thing. "What I meant to say is that I'm happy that you'll be joining me on this adventure and I'll be there for you if you need me."

"That's better," said Tara with a wink, taking another sip of her wine.

The young maiden, sensing another set of eyes on her, peered past Harrison's loving gaze and found Meredith staring in their direction. Catching the young warrior's eye, she lifted her eyebrows and cocked her head in the governor's direction.

Harrison noticed Tara's subtle head gesture, then felt a hand squeeze his forearm. Swiveling in his seat, he faced Meredith, who sported an apprehensive look on her face.

Creasing his brow in concern, he leaned toward the woman and asked under his breath, "Meredith, is something wrong?"

The governor pulled back her hand and pursed her lips, thinking before speaking. "You need to add someone to your group that's heading to the Dark Forest."

Harrison made a quick scan of the people seated around the long table. He knew all of them well and looked forward to journeying with them. Intrigued, he asked with a shake of his head, "Who else did you have in mind?"

Meredith, her lips still pursed, pointed a finger in the air. "Hold that thought." She stared in the direction of one of her servants and, having caught the person's eye, waved him over.

"What is your wish, milady?" asked the young man.

"Please fetch Percival and have him bring up our last guest," said Meredith. "He'll know what I'm talking about." The servant nodded once, then departed to start his chore.

The governor locked eyes with Harrison. "Please have an open mind. Promise?"

Harrison's brow remained furrowed. "Sure, but can you give me a hint at who this person may be?"

Meredith shook her head no. "It's better to see for yourself than to have me tell you."

Harrison gazed at Tara, who had managed to overhear their conversation. Bringing his attention back to Meredith, he said, "Alright."

Moments later, the grand ballroom's doors swung open. Everyone stopped their conversations and all heads turned to the entranceway. Percival entered first, followed by a Concurian guard and a person with their hands bound.

Harrison recognized the woman immediately. The auburn-haired beauty locked her green eyes on the young warrior, flashing a sheepish smile.

The Aegean swiveled to meet Meredith's anxious gaze. "Fallyn Tierany?"

"I know what you must think of her, but she's made an amazing transformation," gushed the governor.

"Meredith, this woman conspired with Gareth Tyne to go behind our backs and ally themselves with Nigel Hammer!" Harrison's eyes remained round.

The Concurian leader averted her eyes, saying, "I understand that, but she also came to our rescue at a most opportune time."

Harrison recalled how Fallyn's metamorphosis into a raven had distracted Lord Hammer, allowing Tara to blind him with a spell. The young warrior still had reservations, however.

"That might be true, but I'm still not sure I completely trust her," said Harrison, trying to make his point.

Before the two could continue their conversation, another voice bellowed from across the table. "Why is one of Aegeus' deposed elders standing in this room with us?" Brendan alternated his stoic gaze between Meredith, Harrison, and Fallyn.

"Brendan," started Meredith, "I was just telling Harrison how Fallyn has taken responsibility for her actions and wants to help our cause."

"Might I be allowed to speak?" asked the bound woman.

"By all means," said Brendan, staring at the disgraced town official. "We're all dying to hear what you have to say."

Fallyn hung her head and exhaled. Taking her gaze back to the room full of people, she began, "I'm sorry for the actions that led to so many innocent deaths in Concur. I should never had allowed Gareth to influence me the way that he did. He was wrong and I was wrong to follow him.

"I cannot take back my actions of the past. I understood the ramifications of my deeds before Nigel Hammer crushed the rebellion. I could have fled Concur, flown off to the countryside, and never resurfaced again. However, I decided to right the wrongs I had made and intervened in Lord Hammer's plans. I accepted my prison sentence and did my time in the hopes that Meredith would see that I am truly sorry for my actions."

"How long did you serve?" asked Brendan with a scowl.

"Thirty days."

"Thirty days?" said the Aegean leader, eyebrows arched in surprise. "That short amount of time is justification for your heinous actions?" Brendan spread his arms wide, glaring at Fallyn.

"Brendan," interjected Meredith, "Fallyn has repented. She has accepted her mistakes and has helped us," the governor circled her finger around pointing to Thoragaard, Tara, and herself, "in aiding in Concur's rebirth. She's willing to help us in any way."

The Aegean leader took his gaze from Meredith back to Fallyn. The woman had cast her eyes downward, appearing ashamed at what she had done, but Brendan knew better than to put his stock into someone who had spent a minimal amount of time in prison.

Bringing his focus back to the governor, he asked, "How can she help Harrison on his journey?"

Meredith stared at the veteran fighter. "A doppelganger is good to have at your disposal."

Brendan's eyes widened a bit and he sat a little higher in his chair. "That is true." The decorated fighter swiveled in Harrison's direction. "This is your call, Harrison. If you believe that you can trust her, then by all means, take her with you on your journey."

All eyes turned to the young warrior. Harrison knew he had a checkered past with Fallyn, with her teaming against him and his friends, and siding with Nigel Hammer, of all people. He also remembered that she distracted the evil Lord at just the right moment, probably saving his life in the process.

Known for trying to understand all parameters of a situation before making a final decision, he turned to Tara and asked, "What can you tell me of Fallyn's actions while you've stayed in Concur?"

Harrison's question surprised the young maiden. Sitting up in her chair, she said, "Well, um, she has helped with the city's reconstruction effort, providing counsel to Meredith, and being an advisor of sorts." Tara gazed at Fallyn, then continued, "I think she's really sorry for what she did and wants to make up for it."

Harrison brought his gaze to the red-haired shape shifter. "We have room for another traveler, but let me say this. If you ever cross us again, you'll never see the light of day from your prison cell."

Fallyn nodded in agreement. "You needn't worry about me crossing you again. I've learned my lesson and wish nothing more than to help our cause."

The young warrior pursed his lips, then said, "Very well. Consider yourself part of the team." Harrison turned to face Meredith. "Can someone fetch her a chair so that she might sit with us now?"

Meredith smiled. "By all means." She signaled to one of her servants, who retrieved the piece of furniture for her superior, placing the chair next to Marissa.

Harrison extended his arm toward the chair. "Have a seat." Fallyn turned to the guardian, who released her bonds, then took her place at the table.

"Thank you," said the woman to Harrison. "I will not disappoint you." Harrison nodded in acknowledgement.

The group then spent the rest of the evening talking about their upcoming adventure and their various expectations.

CHAPTER 8

◘

The posse of eleven humans and one dog set their sights on Valkala three days after meeting with Meredith and the land's military leaders. Harrison took the lead role, assigning marching orders, calculating travel routes, and making the final decision in cases where many inputs could not yield a satisfactory result. Brendan and his previous mentor Marcus Braxton had prepared the young warrior well for this day and no one raised any leadership concerns about his latest mission.

Murdock and Pondle, along with Lance, assumed their usual role as the lead trackers on the trip, trekking twenty yards ahead of the others. The trio guided the party from Concur using a well-traveled path toward Argos. The large inland bay sat less than a quarter mile to the west, providing a cool breeze for their journey. Rolling hills and knee-high grass littered the Concurian countryside.

Harrison and Kymbra agreed that she, Adrith, and Marissa would create a triangular defense around the non-weapon wielding party members, with Kymbra taking the point, Adrith to the left, and Marissa to the right. Each warrior maintained a ten yard perimeter from Swinkle, Gelderand, Tara, Fallyn, and Thoragaard. Harrison, the last lone fighter, assigned himself to protect the three mages, one cleric, and shape shifter in case enemies tried to breach their military configuration.

Although he would never admit it, the setup also allowed Harrison to venture close to Tara, enabling him to protect her if the situation arose. Though he would rather have the young maiden out of harm's way, the simple fact that she joined them on their quest allowed the two to be together, albeit with the rest of the group. On a certain level that outweighed any negative feelings he had felt about leaving her behind yet again.

After several hours of uneventful travel, the young warrior caught a glimpse of Kymbra gesturing for the group to halt. Heeding the warrior's command, the smaller contingent of adventurers stopped their trek.

"Is there a problem?" asked Tara, doing her best to not appear anxious.

Harrison took his gaze to the horizon, noticing that the sky had begun to darken. "If I had to venture a guess, I think we'll be stopping for the day." Seconds later, Murdock and Pondle appeared from behind a rolling hill with Lance sprinting in their direction. The little dog saw his master and bolted to his side.

"Find anything interesting, boy!" exclaimed the young warrior, the dog leaning against his leg, and his tail wagging at a feverish pace.

"Looks like someone's happy to be back with the group," said Tara with a smile. "Is he always like this?"

"Usually," said Harrison. "And he also knows it's almost feeding time."

Kymbra and her cohorts collapsed their position, joining Harrison and the others, while Murdock and Pondle completed a sweep of the immediate area.

"No signs of anything," said Murdock. "This looks like as good a place as any to set up camp for the night."

Kymbra glared at Murdock. "How far did you survey the area?" she asked in a direct tone.

"Far enough." Murdock arced his hand across the landscape. "Nothing's out there."

"Where's Pondle?" asked the female warrior, continuing her interrogation. "Does he concur?"

The ranger huffed, looked down, and placed his sword in its scabbard. "Look, let's get something straight right now," he said, staring Kymbra down. "We always do a thorough search.

You don't need to ask me if we surveyed the area because the answer is always going to be yes. Got it?"

"I won't have my throat slit in the middle of the night because you didn't do your job correctly." Kymbra folded her arms across her chest, cocking her head to one side.

"Then I'd sleep with one eye open," said Murdock. "Right, Pondle." The ranger turned and looked behind him. No one was there.

Kymbra noticed the subtle look of apprehension sweep across Murdock's face. Gripping the hilt of her weapon, she demanded, "Where is he?"

"He was right behind me," said the ranger, panning the area.

Harrison noticed the sudden turn of events. "Go find him. Now!"

Kymbra pointed her sword, motioning to Adrith and Marissa. "Stay with them!" The women fighters joined Harrison to create a small perimeter of protection around the others.

Before a full panic set in, the thief appeared from behind a small incline, waving the group forward. Harrison knew what Pondle's antics meant.

"He's found something," said the young warrior to the rest of the group. "Everyone, proceed with caution."

Harrison, with his weapon drawn, worked with Adrith and Marissa to guide the robed party members toward Pondle's position. In less than fifty yards, the group reached the small incline and peered over the crest.

Harrison let out a sigh, lowering his weapon. A hundred feet away rested a burnt cart and three charred bodies. Pondle and Murdock had already started to sift through the wreckage while Kymbra surveyed the scene.

Gelderand, Fallyn, and Swinkle continued past Harrison and Tara to help identify the cause of the accident. The two other females took up scouting positions at the crest of the hill to avoid a sneak attack.

"What do you think it is?" asked Tara, staring at the burned cart.

"A sign of things to come," said Thoragaard, remaining by her side.

Harrison brought his focus to the illusionist, then said, "I'm going to assist with the examination. Watch our backs."

Tara took a step forward. "I'll help." The young warrior started to say something but stopped when Thoragaard placed a hand on her shoulder.

"Let them do their job, Tara," he said. "We will only impede their progress." Harrison gave Tara a nod, then left to help his friends.

The young warrior approached the destroyed vehicle intent on helping Murdock and Pondle rummage through the debris.

Pondle, eyeing Harrison's approach, said, "Three dead humans, no belongings of value."

The young warrior hated to ask his next question. "Do they still have their arms?"

"No," said Murdock, rising from a bent knee. Taking his sword, he pushed the bodies with his weapon. "But something's not right here."

"What do you mean?" asked Harrison.

"Scynthians would definitely butcher these people but they wouldn't light them on fire."

The young warrior crinkled his brow, perplexed. "Don't they sever the arms of their victims, then hurl them into a bonfire?"

Murdock spread his arms wide. "Do you see remnants of a bonfire?"

Harrison panned the general vicinity, finding only the charred corpses. "No, but maybe they didn't have time to build one."

Kymbra, her own examination complete, joined in the conversation. "He's right. This was made to look like a Scynthian slaughter, but it's not."

"Why would someone do this?" asked Harrison to no one in particular. His friends shrugged and shook their heads.

"We need to keep an eye out for anything else unusual," said Kymbra. She then brought her glare to Murdock and Pondle. "That goes for you two leading the pack."

The ranger brushed off her comment with a nod, knowing full well how to advance in the countryside while keeping a watchful eye. Pondle, however, intensified his inspection of the scene.

Waving the small group away from the cart and bodies, he said, "I found some tracks." Pointing to the tall grasses, he continued. "They're human, not Scynthian."

"What?" exclaimed Harrison, surprised at the thief's assessment. "Are you sure?"

"Positive," said Pondle, bending to one knee. "Beings wearing boots, possibly soldiers, made these markings but they aren't as big and heavy as a Scynthian."

"Probably just a bunch of looters," said Murdock. "Nothing to worry about."

"Pondle said soldiers made the imprints," said Harrison. "And they purposely made it look like the Scynthians did this."

"I said possibly," responded Pondle, clarifying his assessment.

"Whoever killed these people wants us to blame the Scynthians for their crimes, not them," said Murdock. "We'll steer clear of these 'soldiers'. Don't we hold rank with the armies of the land now anyway? No soldier's going to attack us. Those bodies are a few days old already and whoever killed them is long gone. I'm not worried about them."

The ranger took his gaze to the surrounding landscape and its relative safety, as well as recognizing the rapid loss of sunlight. "We might as well set up camp a little way from here."

"We'll be sure to coordinate rotations come nightfall," added Kymbra. "Everything will be fine."

A nagging feeling gnawed at the young warrior, telling him that this encounter meant more than it seemed. Reluctantly, he agreed with his friends and after a short trek the group settled in for the night.

Adrith and Marissa kept the first watch while Pondle took on the task of building a campfire. The rest of the group had already settled their belongings in a tight perimeter to keep surprises at a minimum.

Swinkle joined Harrison and Tara around the fire, taking a seat next to the young maiden. Lance scampered to the young cleric's side. Gelderand, Thoragaard, and Fallyn joined the group, followed a few moments later by Murdock, Pondle, and Kymbra.

"How are you enjoying our excursion?" asked Swinkle to Tara.

"I like it so far," she said with a smile. "Can you tell me a little about the elves we're going to meet?"

"Has Harrison told you about the terrain?" interrupted Murdock. "That's more important than the elves."

Tara scrunched her brow and glanced at the young warrior before answering the ranger. "No, he hasn't. Is it something to worry about?"

Murdock took a bite of dried meat, then rolled his eyes. In between chews, he said, "It's called the Dark Forest for a reason. The trees are huge and block out the sun. And the place is overrun with Scynthians."

The young maiden tried not to show fear and maintained her stare on Murdock without saying a word. Sensing her uncomfortable state, Harrison said, "Murdock's right about the darkness but we'll be fine when it comes to the Scynthians."

"Tara, the elves have a wonderful, peaceful complex," said Swinkle, attempting to allay her concerns.

"In the middle of a Scynthian stronghold," added Kymbra, glancing toward Murdock with a smirk. "We need to stay vigilant and expect the unexpected."

"What does that even mean?" asked Tara, her brow crinkled.

"It means keep your eyes open," said Kymbra. "You'll be putting your new skills to work for sure."

"The elves have kept the Scynthians at bay a long time," said Swinkle. "All will be well once we find their encampment."

"Find?" said Tara, cocking her head, eyebrows arched. "You don't know how to get there?" Swinkle sat back, his gaze directed to Harrison.

"The elves found us the last time we were in the forest," said Harrison, matter-of-factly.

Tara panned to Gelderand. "Uncle?"

The magician shook his head. "Don't ask me. I was not with them the first time they visited the complex."

The young maiden panned the group, asking, "Does *anyone* know how to get to the elves' compound?"

Swinkle alternated his glances to the people that he had accompanied on the trip, allowing someone else to answer the question. Murdock fiddled with his food and Pondle pretended to survey the area from his seat. Harrison, figuring that his friends felt he should address his love's question, broke the uncomfortable silence.

"When we set out to uncover the Treasure of the Land, Marcus had told us that we needed to travel toward the center of the Dark Forest," he explained. "A platoon of elves found us while we camped for an evening."

"Platoon?" said Tara with surprise in her voice, the images in her head of fairies frolicking in the woods replaced with those of weapon wielding beings. "These elves are fighters?"

"Very good fighters," said Harrison.

"Possibly better than we humans," said Fallyn.

"With strong magical capabilities," added Thoragaard. "An asset we must have."

"I agree," said Harrison. "Their allegiance is very important."

Swinkle had taken the time to mumble a quick prayer before tearing a piece of meat and tossing it over his shoulder. Lance darted to the discarded food, gobbling it up.

"The Talisman of Unification directs us to seek the elves," said the young cleric, his ritual complete. "Things will get clearer once we meet with them."

"Keep in mind that we are venturing to find the Ancient Scrolls of Arcadia," said Gelderand, placing the group's immediate plans to the forefront. "Meeting the elves comes later."

"Can Martinaeous help with finding the elves, too?" asked Harrison.

"Possibly," said Gelderand, "but no guarantees." The mage faced his niece. "I am sure we will have a better understanding of our route when the time comes to seek the elves."

Tara nibbled at her food, shaking her head. "I hope you're all sure of yourselves."

Harrison rested a caring hand on her knee. "I know it all sounds a bit choppy, but we'll be fine."

Tara flashed the young warrior a worrisome smile. "I'm just trying to understand our mission better, that's all." Harrison smirked, recalling those same words he had uttered to Marcus long ago.

The young warrior then brought his gaze to two figures approaching the campsite. Marissa took the lead, saying, "Our watch is up and we're hungry! Who's next?"

Kymbra started to rise from her seat but stopped when Murdock clutched her forearm, signaling for her to stay put. "We'll take the next rotation," said the ranger, jerking his thumb in Pondle's direction. "You stay with your friends and protect the camp."

"I'm perfectly capable of standing guard," said the woman, yanking her arm out of the ranger's grip.

"I know, but you're not this time," said Murdock. "We got this. Let's go, Pondle."

The thief rose from his seat and headed away from the glowing flames. Murdock leaned over to Kymbra, saying, "I'll see you after my rotation."

Kymbra scowled and crossed her arms across her chest. Murdock smirked, leaving the woman and his friends behind. The rest of the group remained around the small fire, enjoying the clear cool night, finishing their meals, and talking about their upcoming encounter with the elves.

* * *

Two armored men maneuvered in the darkness, the light of the moon their only means of sight.

"What do you think?" said the fighter to his comrade.

"There are a lot of them, but we can handle that."

The second man focused on the campsite from their position in the tall grass. "I see several women. No need to count them." He squinted to get a better read on the rest of the campers.

"Looks like a couple of warriors and a few men in robes. Typical bunch of travelers."

The first man turned and faced his friend. "I think we've seen enough. Let's go back and alert the others."

The two figures then proceeded to vacate the area and disappeared into the Concurian countryside.

C H A P T E R   9

◘

Harrison and his friends remained seated around the campfire, making small talk while discussing the finer points of their journey. The young warrior enjoyed the philosophical talk that Thoragaard, Swinkle, and Gelderand professed, while taking the opportunity to stay by Tara's side.

"Pious does not discourage magic, per se," started the young cleric, "he just does not condone its use in regards to hurting other beings."

"So, what you're telling me," said Kymbra, "is this god of yours is fine with everything in this world except for fighting?" The woman placed her elbow on her knee and leaned forward, awaiting an answer.

Swinkle cocked his head from side to side, then said, "I suppose you could interpret his actions that way."

"Not all magic is learned with the intent for violence," added Thoragaard. "I for one rarely use my talents to inflict harm on others."

"And I only do so if the situation calls for drastic measures," said Gelderand.

Kymbra leaned back and crossed her arms across her chest. Tilting her head, she said, "If what you say is true, then Pious must be pretty upset with all the fighting this group does on a routine basis."

Swinkle closed his eyes and pursed his lips. As he opened them again, he said, "As long as the cause is noble, then Pious understands our occasional vicious deeds."

The woman let out a single laugh. "That's very convenient."

As the debate continued for a while longer, Tara leaned closer to Harrison and whispered, "So this is what you do on your adventures?"

The young warrior smiled. "Exciting, isn't it?" The two then laughed as the young maiden rested her head against Harrison's chest. The young warrior began to softly stroke her blonde hair when he noticed Lance's head pop up.

Harrison knew what Lance's actions meant. The little dog began to sniff the nighttime air in earnest, sensing something outside the reach of the campground.

The young warrior made a subtle sweep of the area with his eyes. The female warriors, along with Fallyn and the cloaked men, joined Harrison and Tara in a neat circle around the fire, their intense discussion continuing nevertheless. Kymbra, Adrith, and Marissa had weapons by their sides and daggers on their belt, while the young warrior's battle axe rested near his feet. Murdock and Pondle were nowhere in sight, presumably keeping watch in the darkness.

Lance jumped to his feet at the same time Harrison noticed two figures emerge from the shadows from behind the women's position. The little dog began to bark, halting all conversations and alerting the group to the unwanted presence.

Tara jerked her head from Harrison's chest while the young warrior reached for his weapon.

"Everyone stay where you are!" yelled an armed fighter. "No one makes any moves or the halfling's dead!"

Harrison left his weapon on the ground, knowing full well he could snatch it in an instant if the situation turned. The young warrior fixed his eyes on Pondle, a knife pressed to his neck and his hands raised in front of him in a gesture of surrender. However, the young warrior read his friend's face, finding him calm and rather unfazed by his predicament. A little too calm, he noted to himself.

The young warrior made eye contact with Pondle, who made two subtle nods in his direction. Harrison almost smiled, for if on cue two more fighters wielding bows and arrows emerged from the shadows, their weapons trained on the young warrior.

"Stay calm," said Harrison under his breath in Tara's direction. The young warrior then glanced to Kymbra and found her and her cohorts ready to fight.

"Shut that dog up!" yelled the man accosting Pondle. Lance, oblivious to the command, continued to bark.

Harrison raised his hands and started to rise from his seat. "Lance, quiet!" he ordered, the little dog stopping his barking upon hearing his master's command. "What do you want from us?"

"Sit back down!" ordered the fighter with the dagger, pressing it harder against the thief's neck.

"Alright," said Harrison in a soothing tone, returning slowly to the ground. Continuing his mental examination of the situation, he found the three men appeared no older than him. "Again, what do you want with us?"

"Your valuables!" shouted the dagger-wielding warrior. "All your gold, jewels, anything of worth!"

"That's fine," said the young warrior, "just take the knife away from his neck."

"Just do as I say," barked the young man. "I make the decision here. Understood!"

"Yes, you do, I'm sorry," said Harrison, showing his empty palms to the fighter. "Just please be careful."

"Your women, too," said the warrior.

Harrison squinted, his demeanor starting to change. "What?"

The young man flashed a devilish grin. "We're taking your women."

The young warrior heard Tara take a quick breath, surprised at the latest command. "You can have the gold and treasures, but the women stay." Harrison's tone was stern and to the point.

"You're going to find yourself dead, warrior," said the young man. He then gestured with his head to one of the archers who maneuvered closer to Harrison with his arrow targeted at the young warrior's heart.

"It's okay, Harrison," said Kymbra, raising her hands in surrender. The blonde warrior spun her head around to gaze at her soon to be captor, making eye contact.

In a weak voice, she asked, "Will you free the rest of them if we go with you?" Kymbra used her sad, blue eyes to her advantage.

"I'll think about it," said the young man, letting his eyes wander all over the lithe warrior's body.

Motioning to the other women in the camp, Kymbra said, "Do what they say and our men will be spared." She slowly rose from her seat, as did Adrith, Fallyn, and Marissa.

"Go with them," whispered Harrison to Tara. The young maiden's eyes grew round with surprise, her mouth falling agape. "Go," said the Aegean again. Tara, more than apprehensive, rose from her seat as well and began to follow the other girls.

Kymbra took her time getting to her feet. All the while the young man watched as the woman seemed to grow in front of him, finally standing a few inches taller than he.

"I like strong women," he said, a sly smile gracing his face.

"You won't be able to handle me," said Kymbra, failing at keeping her emotions in check.

"Stand over there!" ordered the fighter, gesturing with his head for the ladies to position themselves behind his comrades. "All of you go with her!" Adrith, Marissa, Fallyn, and Tara walked over to where Kymbra now stood.

"What gives you the right to rob innocent passersby?" asked Harrison, his eyes canvassing the immediate area and his brain churning with strategies.

"With Lord Hammer no longer in control of the countryside, we can take what we want without worrying about his soldiers." The man removed the dagger from Pondle's neck and he pushed the thief in Harrison's direction.

"Now that we have what we really want, we'll divide your belongings after you're all dead."

As the man raised his hand to his archer friends, two arrows whizzed from the darkness, hitting their marks squarely in the chest of each bowman. The archers fell to the ground writhing in pain, their blood staining the earth red.

At the same time, Kymbra removed a knife from her belt and drove it deep into the back of the shocked intruder. The man had no reaction, dropping his own weapon and falling to the ground, howling in pain. The female warrior showed no mercy, flipping the young man over and dropping to one knee over his body.

Taking her face closer to the fallen attacker, she said with a hiss, "I don't like weak men." She then drove her dagger through the man's chest. The fighter gasped and coughed blood. A moment later, he was gone.

The immediate threat extinguished, the blonde warrior wheeled around and glared in Murdock's direction. "And what the hell took you so long?" she shouted, enraged.

Raising his palms to the agitated fighter, he said, "Hey, we saw them coming and let them 'ambush' you! We had everything under control!"

Kymbra brought her glare to Pondle. "You were involved in this stupid plot?"

"Those kids wouldn't have hurt us," said Pondle. "Anyway, they were too far into their plan to stop them. If we had, they might have started firing arrows at all of you, which would have resulted in a much worse situation."

Kymbra pointed at Harrison. "They trained arrows at him!" Maintaining her glare on the thief, she continued, "One arrow in the chest and he's gone!"

Murdock approached the woman. "Listen, we've been operating like this way before you and your friends showed up! We know what we're doing!"

The female warrior panned the group of men, saying, "I can't believe you're not all dead by now."

Harrison had seen enough. Rising from his seat on the ground, he said, "Alright, that's enough! Things might not have gone perfectly, but we're all still alive."

Outstretching his hand toward Murdock and Pondle, he said, "They've never let us down in the past and they won't in the future. You'll have to get used to our style of venturing."

"Three boys are dead," said Kymbra, pointing to the latest casualty at her feet. "I can stomach slaughtering Scynthians or enemy warriors, but kids?"

"They came into our camp unannounced, threatened to rob us of valuables, and take you and the other women away," said Harrison, his voice rising. "Those boys sealed their own fate."

The young warrior thrust a finger in Kymbra's direction. "*This* is how we protect ourselves, and *this* is how we're going to continue from here on in. If you don't like it, I suggest you gather your belongings and leave now!"

Kymbra's face turned beet red, but before she could further her tirade, Thoragaard rose from his seated position. "This stops now," he said in forceful, yet still monotone voice. Bringing his gaze to Kymbra, the illusionist said, "You are on this mission because *I* am on this mission. You will heed the orders of Harrison and his friends."

The female gestured to the fallen thieves, but the mage cut her off before she could speak. "That is all, Kymbra. You will listen to them."

"Fine!" said the tall blonde, flustered and repositioning her dagger into her belt. "I just hope things go more smoothly from this point forward."

"They will," said Harrison. "You need to trust us." The young warrior then addressed the whole group. "We all must stick together as a team. This incident will pale in comparison to what could happen if we don't trust each other."

Harrison faced his close friend. "Swinkle, can you prepare a burial ceremony for these robbers?" The young cleric nodded in affirmation.

The young warrior locked his gaze on the ranger. "Murdock, can you, Kymbra, and the others help with the graves?"

"What?" said the bowman, his brow scrunched, and an incredulous look on his face. "Why don't you let them dig the graves?" The ranger jerked his thumb at Kymbra and her cohorts.

"I'm asking you to take the lead, Murdock," said Harrison, narrowing his focus and driving his point home.

The ranger, though reluctant to accept his latest task, understood Harrison's rationale. "Fine." Turning to the women, he said, "Gather your shovels, ladies."

Kymbra was about to protest, but instead she found Thoragaard staring her down. Without saying a word, the female warrior found her pack and went about preparing for her chore. Adrith, Marissa, and Fallyn followed her lead.

Harrison, sensing the tide turning in his favor, continued with his orders. "Pondle, take Lance and secure the perimeter. Be sure to alert us sooner if you sense something out of the ordinary."

"You got it," responded the thief. Pondle found the group's canine companion seated next to his master. Patting the side of his leg, he said, "Let's go, Lance!" The little dog scurried over to Pondle, then the two dispersed into the darkness beyond the camp.

The group had one more thing to handle. "Gelderand and Thoragaard, will you help me move these bodies away from our camp?"

"Of course," said Gelderand, not wanting to go against his leader's wishes. Thoragaard nodded his approval as well.

"Thank you," said the young warrior. "I'll assist you in a moment."

Before tackling their chore, Tara came to Harrison's side. "What do you need me to do? I feel foolish not having a chore like everyone else."

"They'll need markers near their graves," said Harrison. "Can you search for something appropriate?"

"Of course," said the young maiden. Tara moved a step closer to Harrison. Lowering her voice, she said, "You did the right thing here. Don't feel bad about anything."

"I don't feel bad, Tara. This is what I'm trained to do." Smiling at his love, he added, "See, we don't always just sit around the campfire and talk about things."

Tara let out a little laugh of her own. "I think I prefer the small talk around a warm fire over the surprise attacks." The young girl gave Harrison a peck on the cheek, then went about tackling her chore.

Harrison watched Tara venture away, pondering the unpredictable horrors that could happen at any moment. This situation had resolved itself without anyone in their party being harmed, but he knew better than to expect that outcome every time. He then recited a silent prayer to himself, hoping that he would be able to protect his love from the atrocities that may lie ahead.

The young warrior noticed Gelderand and Thoragaard waiting to start their assignment. Without saying a word, he joined them and the three men began to maneuver the poor souls away from their camp.

* * *

Murdock surveyed the campsite's perimeter, in search of a suitable place to begin their grave digging. Adrith, Marissa, and Fallyn had wandered ahead, while Kymbra rummaged close to the ranger. Her actions conveyed a high level of disinterest in her current task.

The ranger, sensing her humility at the recent course of events, decided to approach the tall woman. "Hey," he said, walking closer to Kymbra.

"What do you want?" said the lithe fighter, not bothering to look back at Murdock.

"Are you alright?" asked the ranger. He outstretched his arm toward to the woman before pulling it back, thinking better of touching her at this moment.

Kymbra wheeled around, locking her gaze on his. "Alright? Everyone gangs up on me and you ask if I'm alright?" The blonde girl did not wait for an answer. "You attacked me! You!"

"Gang up on you?" said Murdock, his eyes wide. The ranger took another step toward the warrior. "That's nothing! I was just making my point!"

"I don't appreciate being singled out, especially when you were wrong." Kymbra pointed at Murdock with emphasis.

"Wrong?" The ranger shook his head. "I told you, this is how we operate and you need to get used to it. I don't care if you think our actions were wrong. We're all still alive and that's all that matters." Kymbra crossed her arms, shook her head, and looked away.

Murdock took another step in Kymbra's direction, now standing directly in front of her. Lowering his voice, he said, "You need to stop being so angry and let some things slide." Kymbra's eyes briefly met the ranger's before glancing away again.

"I know about your past," continued Murdock, "and I know how badly you were hurt. It's time to move forward."

The tall woman squinted at Murdock, her arms still folded. Leaning toward him, she said, "Easy for you to say."

"You're a great fighter, but you need to relax," said the ranger. "Why can't you be more like that night in Concur?"

Kymbra's eyes returned to meet Murdock's longing gaze. The woman's stoic stare softened and she let out a little laugh. "Too much alcohol will do that to a girl."

"I liked that girl very much that night," said the ranger, grinning.

"I bet you did," said Kymbra, her face turning a shade of red, recalling the exploits between the two. "That was a fun evening."

"And there can be more of them, but you need to let your guard down from time to time," said Murdock. "Your defenses are always at high alert."

"It's just the way I am," said Kymbra.

Murdock smirked. "That's what I like about you, but you make it so damn hard sometimes!"

"I'll try to change, but don't expect miracles."

"I'm only asking you to relax a little more," said Murdock. "I'm not asking you to change." The ranger's last comment brought a smile to Kymbra's face.

"See, it's working already," said the bowman. "But it's time to clean up our little mess." Murdock arched an eyebrow. "We can relax later?"

Kymbra smirked. "Not with all these people around!" The woman then leaned closer to the ranger and, in a suggestive voice, said, "Just be ready for the next time we find ourselves alone."

The warrior then rummaged through her backpack for a shovel. Finding one, she continued, "That thought should keep you busy for a while."

Kymbra turned away from the ranger and began searching for a place to bury the fallen villains, while Murdock's brain churned with a myriad of thoughts.

CHAPTER 10

Ⱉ

The small group of adventurers buried the three unfortunate souls before embarking on an uneventful weeklong travel to the small village of Valkala. Murdock and Pondle led the travelers alongside the Guard's River before picking up the well-travelled path that led into the town.

Gelderand had enjoyed his last trip to his mentor's homestead, but feelings of uncertainty coursed through his body today. Tara sensed her uncle's apprehension.

"Is everything alright, Uncle?" asked the lass.

The magician snapped out of his trance, the question startling him. "With me? Yes," he said.

Tara waited for more and when her uncle stopped speaking, she asked, "Is there anything we need to know?"

"Martinaeous has gotten old, Tara," sighed the mage, taking his gaze to his niece as they entered the town. "I hope he still has his wits about him."

The young maiden pursed her lips and took hold of her uncle's arm, pulling him close. "I'm sure he's fine."

Gelderand smiled, recalling how the same girl would pull on his limb in a similar fashion as a youngster. Patting her head, he said, "I hope you are right, child."

Murdock halted the procession when the group approached the first set of homes. Pointing to a dilapidated building, he yelled, "It's this one, right?"

The magician cast his eyes about the unkempt home, its overgrown shrubbery, and lack of maintenance. With yet another sigh, he said, "Yes, it is." The elder mage then took the lead. "I will approach the house first."

Taking purposeful steps, Gelderand crossed the overgrown lawn and reached the main doorway, followed by Tara, Harrison, Swinkle, Lance, and the rest. The magician paused at the doorway, hesitating to knock.

Harrison, sensing Gelderand's uncertainty, tapped him on the shoulder. The magician raised a finger. "Wait one second," said the mage before turning to face his friends.

Gelderand outstretched his arm in Harrison, Tara, and Swinkle's direction. "Let us go in first," he said to the gathering crowd of adventurers. "We don't want to startle the old man."

The portal opened a crack just as the rest of the platoon started to back away from the residence. Gelderand noticed the door's sudden movement, finding an old face glaring back at him. An unfamiliar old face.

"What do you want?" barked an elderly woman, her cold gray eyes piercing the intruder. "We have nothing of worth in here."

Gelderand furrowed his brow in confusion, unsure of the person at the door. "Excuse me, Ma'am, but we are looking for Martinaeous. Would he be home?"

The old woman maintained her glare from behind the doorway. "Are you family?"

The elder magician cast a curious glance in Harrison, Swinkle, and Tara's direction, then answered, "In a way, yes. Martinaeous was my mentor many years ago." Gelderand focused hard on the woman. "Is he alright?"

The woman let out a deep sigh, then opened the door. "I suppose that's close enough," she said. "Please come in and try to make yourself comfortable. And be quiet."

Harrison motioned for the others to remain outside before the four people and little dog entered the residence. Once inside, the young warrior recognized the old man's place. Just as in his first visit, dust and cobwebs littered the main room, and plates and discarded meals lay strewn about the kitchen area. A lingering

127

smell of rotting food hung in the air, enough to bring a hand over the young warrior's nose and mouth.

"It stinks in here," he whispered to Tara, the young girl also covering her face.

"I know," she said. "I don't like the looks of this."

Swinkle noticed the couple's actions. "We might have additional work to do here again," he said under his breath, recalling the three days of cleaning it took to make the old man's home look respectable during their last visit.

Gelderand decided not to address the immediate reactions of the younger people; instead he focused on a more important issue. "Ma'am," he started, before the woman cut him off.

"My name is Melinda and I'm Martinaeous' caretaker," she said.

The magician gazed at the old woman, her disheveled appearance, knotted gray hair, tattered clothing, and shuffling gait, and wondered why someone was not taking care of her as well.

"Melinda," Gelderand began, "where is Martinaeous?"

"He's asleep," she said, searching for a chair. Finding one at the kitchen table, she sat down and motioned for the others to do likewise, which they did. Lance scampered around the furniture and sat next to Harrison.

"Asleep?" asked the mage. "It's midday."

Melinda focused on the magician. "What's your name?"

"I am sorry, my name is Gelderand," he said, then motioned with his hand, "and this is Tara, Harrison, and Swinkle." The young people nodded upon hearing their names.

"Gelderand," started Melinda, "your mentor is very ill. I'm sorry to say, but he's nearing the end."

The mage stood up tall in his chair, knowing that Martinaeous had appeared weathered the last time they met and had secretly wondered if the old man would survive much longer.

"He is an elderly man," said Gelderand. "I am very sorry to hear this." Searching for words, he continued, "What is the matter with him?"

Melinda threw her hands in the air and looked away. "Old age, I suppose. People in town started to wonder where he was when he stopped coming into town for food and supplies." The old woman gazed at the doorway to the bedroom. "I found him in bed, mumbling. He was hungry and needed water. That was about a month ago."

The woman shook her head. "I wasn't intending to come see him, but I was walking by the house and I got this odd feeling. You know that sensation you get when you know you should do something, even when you don't want to? Something dragged me into his home and that's when I found him. Been here ever since."

Gelderand reached across the table and took hold of the lady's hand, squeezing it in the process. "You very well might have saved his life, Melinda." The woman cocked her head, semi-nodding in acceptance.

The mage pressed for more information. "Is he conscious? Can he recognize people and things?"

"From time to time," she said. "When was the last time he saw you?"

Gelderand looked over to Harrison and Swinkle, then said, "Several months ago."

"He helped heal me," said the young warrior, raising his limb and revealing the scar encircling his bicep. "Without his help I wouldn't have any use of this arm."

"That operation may well have been the last trick he'll ever perform," said Melinda. The old woman rose from her seat. "Let's take a look at him."

Melinda shuffled toward the bedroom with the adventurers in tow. Lance scooted ahead of his master, reaching the room first. The five people and dog then entered the dark bedroom. Melinda found a candle and lit it, bringing a soft yellow glow to the chamber.

The young warrior brought his gaze about the place, finding the old man asleep in his bed. The rest of the sleeping quarters appeared untouched and the faint smell of body odor clung in the air.

"This is how I find him most of the time," whispered the lady, approaching the bed. She then lightly shook the old man. "Martinaeous?" The man remained sleeping, his chest rising with every inhale.

Melinda shook him a little harder. "Martinaeous, you have visitors."

The elderly man stopped snoring and caught his breath, his eyes opening wide. "Who's there?" he said, his eyes darting, trying to get a fix on his situation. "I might be an old man but I'm armed!"

His mentor's last comment brought a smile to Gelderand's face. The magician moved closer to the bed, leaning nearer to the elderly man. "Where do you hide your sword, Martinaeous?"

The man's eyes started to focus on the familiar face. Seconds later, Martinaeous smiled and said, "Gelderand? Is that really you?"

The mage found his mentor's hand and he clasped it tightly. "Yes, it is I. How are you feeling?"

Martinaeous smiled for a moment more before sighing. "Time is catching up with me, my friend."

"Nonsense," said Gelderand, trying to raise the man's spirits. "You're just a little more tired than usual."

The elder magician smiled again. "You always knew how to say the right things."

"Martinaeous, I want you to meet somebody." Gelderand waved Tara over, the girl obliging. "This is my niece, Tara. Remember her?"

Tara leaned closer to the man in the bed. "Hello, Martinaeous. I've heard a lot about you."

Martinaeous gazed at the heavenly body hovering above him. "I feel like I'm looking into the eyes of an angel, my sweet girl." A wide smile stretched across the magician's face. "You are very beautiful."

Tara blushed in the shadows. "Thank you, sir. It's a pleasure to meet you."

"Likewise," said Martinaeous.

Harrison joined Tara by the bed. "Do you remember me? You healed my arm not too long ago."

The old man took a hard look at the young warrior, his brow scrunched, trying to recollect the young man that stood before him. "Harold, isn't it?"

The young warrior smiled. "Close, it's Harrison."

The man's eyes sparkled, hearing the familiar name. "Harrison! That's it! How's your arm?"

"Good as new," said the Aegean, lifting his limb in the air. "As if I had never injured it."

"That's good to hear. Do you still have that dog of yours?"

Harrison patted his leg and Lance scooted to his side. "Lance is here as well."

Martinaeous rolled to his side and gazed down. Lance jumped and placed his paws on the mattress, finding the man's face and giving it a hearty lick.

Martinaeous, startled by the dog's antics, lay back down and waved his hands in front of his face. He then started heaving in his bed.

The five people leaned even closer, concerned for the old man's well-being. "Martinaeous," said Gelderand. "Are you alright?"

The older magician placed his arms by his side and started to laugh so hard that tears started rolling down his cheeks. "That little dog scared the daylights out of me!"

"He's lucky he didn't give you a heart attack," said Melinda. She then swatted Lance's paws from the bed, causing the dog to land on the ground. "Don't scare old people!"

Tara cradled Lance around the belly, scratching him on the side in the process. "He didn't mean any harm. He was just being friendly."

"Be that as it may," said the old lady, "but you can't go around spooking folks like that."

Martinaeous took a moment to collect himself and after his laughing fit had finished, he peered over to Gelderand and asked, "Why have you stopped in Valkala? Surely not to meet with an old man."

"We are searching for an artifact and I think you might be able to provide us with our best lead," said the man's former protégé.

Martinaeous wiggled himself up while Melinda positioned a pillow behind his back. In a more comfortable position to speak, the man asked, "Tell me, did you find what you were searching for since our last meeting?"

"We did," said the mage. "And then some."

"Then my crystal ball really works!" exclaimed Martinaeous with a smile. "Maybe we can use it again." Gelderand nodded, agreeing with the old man.

"Tell me," continued the elder mage. "What do you seek this time?"

The younger wizard focused on his mentor. "The Ancient Scrolls of Arcadia."

Martinaeous' demeanor turned dour. "Why do you seek them?"

Gelderand made a subtle glance toward Harrison before speaking. "We are very curious about their contents."

The old man grimaced, staring off to a dark corner of his bedroom. Returning his gaze to Gelderand, he said, "I need to get out of this bed." He then began to remove the covers and wiggle to its side.

"You're not going anywhere!" yelled Melinda, grabbing the blankets and trying her best to cover the old man's shuffling body.

Martinaeous slapped the woman's hand. "Nonsense! I want to get up!"

Melinda furrowed her brow, gripping the coverings tighter. "No, you don't!"

The elderly man's face began to redden, his agitation rising. "Yes, I do!"

Gelderand shook his head and waved his hands in front of himself. "Melinda, please let the man try to get up."

The old woman squinted and pointed a finger in the magician's face. "Don't think you can just show up and start telling Martinaeous what he can or cannot do!"

While the woman scolded his old friend, Martinaeous wiggled his legs free from the blankets and swung them over the side of the bed. Sounding more like a child than an adult, he said, "I'm getting up!"

A second later, the elderly man's legs dropped to the floor and he stood for the first time in a while. Wobbly, Martinaeous placed a hand on the bed to stabilize himself.

Feeling secure with his body, the mage held his head high and said, "Let us meet in the kitchen." He then turned his attention to his unsuspecting maid. "Melinda, please find my guests some good drink. I'm sure they're thirsty."

The woman squinted one eye and pointed a finger at the man, then thought better of arguing further. Mumbling something inaudible under her breath, the old woman exited the bedroom and headed into the kitchen area.

The rest of the people followed Melinda's lead and entered the cluttered room. Harrison, remembering that his friends remained outside, said to Martinaeous, "There are others with us. Is it alright if they come inside, too?"

"More?" Martinaeous' eyebrows arched high on his forehead. "By all means, let them in!"

The young warrior then went to the doorway, opened it, and waved his friends forward. Martinaeous' eyes remained wide as he watched the rest of the adventurers enter his home. He paid particular attention to the female warriors as they strutted by, each one more fetching than the next.

"Please, make yourselves comfortable," said the elderly man.

Kymbra, who stood next to Murdock, leaned closer to the ranger and said under her breath, "You weren't kidding about this place."

Melinda walked into the cramped area carrying a tray with three mugs of water. Her eyes round, she said, "I don't have enough drink for everyone!"

"That's quite all right," said Harrison. "We have more than enough of our own." The young warrior then turned his attention to Martinaeous. "I know there are a lot of people here today but we'll be gone soon enough."

Martinaeous found a chair at his kitchen table and made himself comfortable. Gazing at Gelderand, he said, "I like your odds a little bit better now."

"Our odds?" said the mage, his brow scrunched. "Why do you say that? The scrolls are hidden, not guarded. We just have not located them yet."

The old man sighed and took his gaze to the table. "I have something I must confess to you, my good friend." He kept his eyes fixed on the wooden surface.

After a few uncomfortable seconds, using a tone a parent would employ on a misbehaving child, Gelderand asked, "Martinaeous, do you have something to tell me?"

The man lifted his head, his eyes locking on his protégé. "That I do," he started. "When you first came to me, I knew that you were going to be a very powerful magician some day and I took it upon myself to teach you all that I had learned throughout the years. However, I did not care for the group you had aligned yourself with." Gelderand nodded, taking in the old man's confession while everyone else in the room remained riveted on Martinaeous' words.

Continuing, the old mage said, "Especially that Allard character. You did not see it at the time, but I knew he was full of malicious intent."

Harrison recognized the man's name immediately as Lord Nigel Hammer's lead magician, the same person responsible for so much destruction in Concur and the main reason the evil lord escaped the walled city several months ago.

"What does he have to do with the Ancient Scrolls of Arcadia?" asked Gelderand.

"Twenty years or so ago," said Martinaeous, "you and your friends at the time assembled here, not unlike the group that stands before me today. At that moment, I knew you were ready to find the scrolls and, you would have, had I sent you in the right direction."

Gelderand clenched his hands into two tightly wound fists. Closing his eyes, the magician took a deep inhale before releasing his grip and taking a cleansing breath. In a direct, yet soothing tone, he asked, "How far out of our way did you send us?"

Martinaeous fidgeted in his seat, wringing his hands. "Not too far."

"We traveled into the Dark Forest," started the magician in a deliberate tone. "We fought countless Scynthians, had no sense of day or night due to the whims of the forest, and wandered lost for weeks. Are you telling me we were way off base?"

The older mage nodded once. "You searched the wrong forest for the prize."

Gelderand furrowed his brow, pursed his lips, slanted his eyes, and glared in Harrison's direction, realizing now that the better part of his adventuring life had all been for naught. The mage felt his stomach churn as he tried to hold back the anger he felt toward his old mentor. Taking his gaze back to Martinaeous, he found the old man's drawn face staring at him, begging for forgiveness.

"Gelderand," started Martinaeous, "the place where these secrets are held is merciless."

"We're going there now," said the mage in a firm voice. "Tell me where the scrolls are hidden and do not deceive me again."

Martinaeous panned the group that stood in his home, all of them glaring back at him, repressing their anger, and waiting for an answer that had alluded one of their friends for decades. With a sigh, the old man started his tale.

"As you know, the scriptures detail the prophecy of this land and along with that are several sacred parchments. This is what you seek and this will seal your doom."

Gelderand did not waver. "Martinaeous, I have heard this speech before. Where are the scrolls hidden?"

Martinaeous swallowed hard. "Rovere Moro."

Gelderand's eyes widened and he sat back in his seat. "Rovere Moro," he said in a hushed tone, more to himself than the group. Martinaeous closed his eyes and nodded once.

Harrison allowed the gravity of the situation to sink in before placing a hand on Gelderand's shoulder. "What and where is Rovere Moro?"

The magician exhaled slowly and took his gaze to an empty part of his mentor's home. "Oh, it is not far away," said Gelderand. "As a matter of fact, we are on the doorstep of the wretched land as we speak."

Harrison knitted his brow, confused. "I still don't understand."

Martinaeous continued the conversation. "Rovere Moro is commonly known as Troll's Hell and it resides at the center of the Valkaline forest."

"Troll's Hell!" Murdock exclaimed, his eyes wide with shock. Panning to Harrison he said, "Do you know what this means?"

The young warrior's shoulders slumped, the burden of the words weighing him down. "I only hear stories of atrocities when people talk about that place."

Swinkle did not care for the obvious sidestepping of critical information. "What are you not telling us?" asked the young cleric, taking his nervous gaze between the people seated around the table.

"It's not called Troll's Hell for nothing," said Murdock. "Those monsters control that portion of the forest."

"Trolls?" reiterated Swinkle, concern in his voice.

"And I'm sure they're guarding the scrolls," added Harrison.

"No!" exclaimed Martinaeous. "They are not guarding anything. These beasts are exactly that—beasts. They have no loyalty to the scroll's creators nor do they know what resides in their land. All they crave is flesh of any kind, including human. Though they do not guard the parchments, they provide protection nonetheless."

"Then we must not take them lightly," said Gelderand. "If we wish to find this sacred treasure, then we must vanquish the trolls that will stand in our way."

Harrison took exception to the elder man's statement. "Gelderand, do you understand how dangerous trolls are?" The young warrior tried his best to temper his anxiety, not wanting Tara or any other members in his party to fear. "These beasts have no intelligence, just an unbridled desire to consume flesh."

"Oh, and they can regenerate if they happen to lose a limb or two," added Murdock for good measure.

"I am well aware of that," said the magician. "Then I propose another question. Do we even bother searching for this treasure?"

Another voice of reason stepped forward. "We must," said Thoragaard with a pause. "Gelderand, Tara, Fallyn, and I can keep these creatures at bay with our magical capabilities. What we need to know is where the Scrolls of Arcadia reside."

All heads turned toward Martinaeous. "Venture to the center of the Valkaline Forest. There you will find a path that leads deeper into the belly of the woods. Take that path and pray."

"Find a path that leads deeper into the woods?" mimicked Murdock, unpleased with the man's answer. "That's a bit vague to me."

"Let me tell you this," started Martinaeous with unnerving clarity and an edge to his voice. "The pathway descends into a bone chilling abyss. You will be in the right area when you wade through a hazy fog. From there, you are on your own."

Harrison had another question to ask. "How do you know of this mystical resting place of the Scrolls of Arcadia and the path in the middle of the forest?"

The elderly man locked eyes with the young warrior. "Because I was the only member of my party to escape unscathed from that hell. The area is appropriately named. I hope that you change your mind and decide not to venture to that desolate place."

Martinaeous dropped his head and sighed. "I'm feeling a bit weak all of a sudden. I need to rest."

Harrison rushed to the old man's side. "Let us get you back to bed."

"I will follow you," said Swinkle. "I might have some medicinal herbs that can help him."

Melinda placed a hand under Martinaeous' armpit. "Help me hoist him out of this chair."

The young warrior did just that and used his strength to guide the old man back to his bedroom. He and Melinda then placed Martinaeous into his bed, allowing the old soul to rest.

"Why don't you join the others," said Swinkle, searching for some concoctions he had in his pack. "I will remain with Martinaeous and give him a proper thorough examination." Harrison looked over to Melinda, who nodded in agreement.

The two then departed the bedroom and rejoined the rest of the group in the kitchen where they debated the perils of searching for the hidden treasure while the old man fell into a deep sleep.

CHAPTER 11

Ơ

Martinaeous remained in bed the whole day as well as the following morning. Around noon, Gelderand, Harrison, Tara, and Swinkle followed Melinda to the old man's bedroom, finding him still fast asleep.

Melinda pulled the covers to the man's neck. "He's like this more often than not," she said.

Gelderand approached the bed, searching for his mentor's frail hand outside of the blankets. "This might be the last time we meet, old friend."

"Let me wake him for this," said the older woman. Lightly shaking the wizard, she said, "Martinaeous, get up." Martinaeous' eyes flittered before he awoke from his slumber. "Your friends want to say goodbye."

The elderly man found five faces staring at him, just as he had the other day. "Have we not done this once before?" A smile graced his weathered face.

"That we have," said Gelderand. "We are off to uncover the Scrolls of Arcadia and wanted to wish you well."

"Thank you, Gelderand, you have always been a good friend and an even better student." The old man shifted in his bed, trying to sit up.

His protégé held him in place. "Do not waste any more energy than you need. Lay still."

Martinaeous heeded Gelderand's words. "Please be careful venturing into Troll's Hell. Those beasts must be shredded and boiled in acid for them to truly be destroyed." The elderly man held his stare on his former student. "Boiled in acid, Gelderand!"

The magician nodded. "I know. Let us worry about that, but in the meantime you rest. We will return with the scrolls and check in on you in the not too distant future."

"Don't wait too long, old friend," said Martinaeous, searching for Gelderand's eyes.

The mage pursed his lips and gripped his mentor's hand tighter. "I will be back, that I promise you." Martinaeous closed his eyes and nodded, then drifted off into sleep once again.

Gelderand held his gaze on his mentor a moment longer before releasing his grip. Turning to Melinda, he said, "Please, take good care of him."

"I will," said the old woman. "Be careful on your journey," she said to Gelderand before lifting her eyes and panning the whole group. "All of you."

"We will," said Gelderand.

"Come, let me lead you outside," said Melinda with a wave of her hand. The woman led the small group to the doorway, then bade them farewell. A few moments later, the small party left Martinaeous' home and congregated in his front yard along with the rest of the adventurers.

Harrison could sense the inner turmoil that haunted Gelderand's soul. "Are you alright?"

The mage nodded. "I fear that today will be the last time that I see my mentor alive."

The young warrior placed a caring hand on the magician's shoulder. "Don't think that way, Gelderand."

"Thanks for your concern, but I am fine," said the mage. "Martinaeous is a great man and has taught me many things. I will help recover the scrolls in his honor."

Tara approached her uncle, taking his arm and giving it a heartfelt squeeze. "All will work out fine, Uncle."

"I know it will," he said, kissing the top of her head. Taking his gaze to Harrison, he said, "It's time to plan our journey."

The young warrior took his cue and gathered the adventurers. With everyone huddled together, he began, "We all heard Martinaeous' story about the location of the scrolls. He also said that to completely destroy the trolls we need to either chop them to pieces or boil them in acid."

After allowing his last comment to linger, he took his line of sight to Murdock and Pondle. "Do you know what direction we should head in?"

Pondle took the lead. "He said to hike toward the forest's center. I've ventured into those woods in the past but never toward the middle. There's a sense emanating from there. We kept away from that area."

"Can you lead us toward the center?" asked the young warrior.

"Of course."

Murdock had additional concerns. Waving his hands in front of himself while shaking his head, he said, "Can someone humor me on how we're going to boil trolls in acid?"

"The old man is correct," said Thoragaard in his usual monotone voice. "Unless you obliterate the creature, the only other option to truly kill it would be to boil the monster in acid."

The ranger concurred. "I got that, but how do we *do* it?"

"I'm with him," said Harrison, jerking his thumb in Murdock's direction. "We don't have vats of acid just lying around."

"Can we purchase any corrosive liquids here?" asked Gelderand in Murdock and Pondle's direction.

"In this town?" said Murdock with a laugh. "We'd be lucky to find enough water for our journey, let alone acid."

"Gelderand, can you conjure something up?" asked Harrison.

The magician thought, then shook his head. "Transforming water into an acidic liquid with the potency to boil a beast is a hard trick indeed. I do not have the ingredients nor have I ever tried to perform a spell as this. I am afraid the answer to your question is no."

"How about you?" asked Murdock in Thoragaard's direction.

"I am in agreement with Gelderand," he started. "Acid is a hard thing to create. However, I might have a different trick up my sleeve, so to speak."

"Please," said the ranger, cocking his head and folding his arms across his chest, "elaborate."

"If we can give the illusion of destroying these beasts in acid, to deceive them, confuse them, then we might be able to attain our goal."

"Trick a pack of wild trolls?" said Murdock, exasperation in his voice. "What if they don't fall for your little deception?"

"Then I suggest honing your battle skills," responded Thoragaard. The ranger's mouth fell open, surprised at the wizard's statement, searching for words to say. Nothing came out.

"I am sure that magic will work against them," added Gelderand, trying to put the group at ease. "I have an array of spells that I can employ."

"We're going to need everything you have," said Harrison. Panning the group, he added, "We'll need *all* of our skills."

"Enough talk then," said Murdock. "We never turned our back on a challenge and we're not going to start now."

"I agree," said the young warrior. "I suggest that we venture toward Rovere Moro and strategize along the way."

"Sounds good to me," said the ranger. "Usual marching order?"

"Yes," said Harrison. "Let's be extra careful, though."

"Aren't we always?" said Murdock with his signature smile. "Pondle, let's lead the way."

"Don't forget about us!" exclaimed Kymbra. "Adrith, Marissa, let's set our formation." The female warriors formed their triangular pattern around Harrison, Tara, Gelderand, Swinkle, Fallyn, and Thoragaard.

"Ready when you are!" yelled Kymbra to Murdock and Pondle. The two trackers waved the group forward as they led everyone away from the little village of Valkala and toward the forest that loomed ahead.

* * *

Pondle and Murdock guided the group through the wooded landscape for the better part of two days. On the second day, an overcast sky with darkening clouds turned into a light rain.

141

"I always hate when the weather becomes foul," said Swinkle, journeying alongside Harrison and Tara.

"At least it's not a downpour," said Tara.

"Give it time," added Harrison. "Rain only brings soggy clothes, slow travel, and," the young warrior noticed Lance bounding in their direction, "a wet dog!"

Lance reached his master and began to yap. "Here! Here!"

Harrison dropped to one knee to greet his canine friend, patting him on the head before his demeanor turned dour. "He says we're here."

"Troll's Hell?" asked Tara, her blue eyes round with concern.

Before the young warrior could answer, Murdock and Pondle appeared over a small crest, trekking back to their position. "It would seem so," said Harrison, noticing his friends' advancement.

"Did Lance fill you in?" asked Murdock, trying to lighten the increasingly sullen mood.

"Yes," said Harrison. By this time, the rest of the group congregated together with the female warriors, maintaining their perimeter position but still in earshot of the ongoing conversations.

"What have you found?" continued the young warrior.

The ranger did not hesitate with his assessment. Pointing from whence he came, he said, "We're standing at the top of a little hill. After you descend about two hundred feet, the area flattens out a bit before you come to the path."

Harrison squinted. "The path?"

Murdock took a deep breath. "You need to see this for yourself."

The young warrior panned his party, assessing their condition. He found obvious signs of concern from each and every member, including the normally stoic Thoragaard and Kymbra.

"Lead us there," said Harrison to the ranger. Looking at everyone else, he added, "Let's all ready our weapons and use extreme caution." Murdock and Pondle guided the adventurers over the slight crest and down the backside of the hill.

Harrison swept his eyes about the general area from his spot in the lightly wooded forest, the sound of precipitation splattering on the ground. The young warrior squinted due to the lack of adequate lighting, homing in on a pathway that led deeper into the woods. Aside from the ominous predictions from Martinaeous, all seemed normal otherwise.

The group halted their procession at the beginning of a trail that led further into the Valkaline Forest. "I think this is the place Martinaeous alluded to," said Murdock. Kymbra came to the ranger's side, staring at the path that lay before them.

"I feel cold all of a sudden," said the tall female. "And not from the rain."

"I do, too," responded the ranger, while the rest of the party joined the two at the trail's opening.

"Swinkle, can you sense anything out of the ordinary?" asked Harrison, never removing his gaze from the pathway. Unbeknownst to him, he reached back and found Tara's hand, giving it a firm squeeze. The young maiden maneuvered next to the Aegean, not wanting to leave his side.

"I will say a prayer," said the young cleric before pressing his hands firmly together, closing his eyes, and mumbling to himself. A few moments later, Swinkle calmly unclasped his hands and opened his eyes wide.

Harrison, noticing the strange look on his friend's face, asked, "What's wrong, Swinkle?"

"I sense an evil like no other I have ever felt," said the young cleric. "This is a very dangerous place, Harrison."

The young warrior brought his free hand to his face, caressing his cheeks as he thought about what he needed to say to the people waiting on his next words.

Standing firm, he started. "The fate of our people may lie in our hands. Who knows what the Scynthians are planning next and we need to be one step ahead of them." The young warrior scanned the group, finding them riveted on his speech.

"Trolls lie ahead of us. Swinkle has pretty much assured us of that. However, so does a great treasure, something that can tip the scales in our favor against those beasts that ransacked our cities. Therefore, we must proceed, no matter the consequences."

The group pondered Harrison's words, the pattering of raindrops filling the silent void. After a brief moment, Thoragaard took the opportunity to speak.

"These monsters will be a menace. Stay close to each other and do not get separated from the group." The illusionist paused for effect. "Separation will result in certain death."

"How do we proceed?" asked Kymbra, standing tall, ready to take on the challenge.

"Murdock, how wide is that trail?" asked Harrison. All eyes shifted to the pathway that descended to an unknown depth.

The ranger made his best calculation. "Looks like we can comfortably fit three people side by side."

Harrison's brain churned, recalling battle tactics from the Fighter's Guild. The young warrior took a step forward, taking in the sight before him. The dirt path led downward at a forty-five degree angle with leafy trees arching over it from fifteen feet above, while a dark abyss awaited them at the bottom of the seemingly endless walkway.

Turning toward Gelderand and Thoragaard, the young warrior asked, "Trolls can inhabit trees, can't they?"

Both wizards nodded. "I believe so," said Gelderand.

Harrison peered down the path once again. His mind told him that venturing forward with the current group would be challenging at best, a debacle at worst. He also knew that everyone leaned on him for guidance, waiting in anticipation for their orders.

Still forming a strategy, he asked the elder members of the group another question. "What do you know of this treasure?"

"I think we have already discussed that, Harrison," said Gelderand.

The young warrior showed his palms to the mage. "No, where are these scrolls resting?" he asked. "I mean, are they encased in anything, lodged between boulders, in an elaborate tunnel system? Where?"

Gelderand locked eyes with Thoragaard. The illusionist raised his eyebrows, unsure. "No one truly knows, save the people who hid them," said Gelderand.

"If I had to venture a guess," added Thoragaard, "I would have to believe that they are not placed in anything that needed a long time to create. Menacing trolls would tend to cause one to hurry."

Harrison nodded. "My thoughts exactly."

"What are you getting at?" asked Murdock, folding his arms across his chest.

"I don't think we'll need to search very hard to find them," said the young warrior. "Unless the people who hid the scrolls had kept the trolls at bay, I can't imagine that they took a lot of time in concealing them."

"If your reasoning's true, wouldn't someone have uncovered them by now?" asked the ranger.

"With wicked beasts patrolling the area?" said Harrison, his eyebrows arched. "Who would want to spend time searching for hidden artifacts with monsters attacking you?"

"Us," deadpanned the ranger.

Harrison smirked. "That would be true, I suppose." The young warrior addressed the group again. "Let's descend down this path carefully and be ready for anything."

"Wait!" exclaimed Kymbra, who had remained uncharacteristically quiet until now. "How do you suggest we attack these creatures?"

Harrison brought his focus to the robed figures. "Gelderand, Thoragaard, and Tara have spells that should confuse the beasts. And Swinkle," the young warrior swiveled to face his friend, "I'm sure you have prayers that can do something similar." The four party members gazed at each other, agreeing with nods.

"That's fine and dandy," said Kymbra, "but what do *we* do?"

"Hack those trolls to pieces," said Harrison. "These monsters will regenerate quickly. The more pieces that they're in, the longer it takes for them to reconstitute themselves."

The tall female warrior drew a deep breath, agreeing with the young warrior without saying a word. Harrison slowly panned the group before him, sensing that they had agreed with his strategy.

"Alright, I think it's time to enter the trail," said Harrison.

"How should we march?" asked Murdock, knowing that they had to proceed with extreme caution.

"Might I recommend an order?" suggested Thoragaard. The magician's monotone voice caught the young warrior by surprise. Harrison extended an arm in his direction, giving the illusionist the opportunity to speak.

"Gelderand, Swinkle, Tara, and I will form a diamond, me at the point, Gelderand behind, and Swinkle and Tara on either side.

"Murdock and Pondle will lead as usual, Harrison and Kymbra will bring up the rear. Adrith and Marissa will be next to Swinkle and Tara. By marching this way, we who possess magical and spiritual capabilities will be able to cast spells and recite prayers from safety. Those wielding weapons will then hack the fallen trolls."

"What about me?" asked Fallyn. "I have skills that are useful as well."

Thoragaard stroked his beard. "True, though I have not seen you in action. You shall venture in the middle of our diamond." The mage circled his finger around the robed members of the group. Fallyn, understanding her unusual role in the group, nodded in compliance.

Harrison understood the illusionist's rationale. "This is a sound strategy, Thoragaard. I think it'll work. Murdock?"

The ranger nodded as he thought. "Sounds good to me."

"I agree," said Harrison. "Let's set up our order."

Murdock and Pondle assumed their usual position at the head of the group. Thoragaard stood twenty feet behind the trackers, with Swinkle off to the left of him and Tara to the right. Both stood no more than ten feet behind the illusionist. Gelderand then centered himself ten feet after Tara and Swinkle. Fallyn assumed her position in the formation once the others had maneuvered into their designated spots.

Harrison flanked to the right with Kymbra to the left, both of them ten feet behind the cloaked members of the group. The young warrior then gazed down to the little dog that sat next to him.

Bending to one knee, he brought his face to Lance and said, "You trek between me and Kymbra," he said. Lance looked up at the blonde woman, then scooted nearer to her. Harrison pointed to Fallyn. "When we start fighting, you go next to her. Alright, boy?"

Harrison's canine friend yapped once. "Yes!"

After giving instructions to Lance, the young warrior approached Tara. The young maiden's expression did little to hide her apprehension. "You'll be fine, Tara."

"I know. Thoragaard taught me well," she said, glancing at the others at the same time, sensing their eyes. In a hushed tone, she said, "Go back in formation. You're embarrassing me."

Harrison smiled, knowing that his love was ready for the trip. Positioning himself near Kymbra, the young warrior shouted to Murdock and Pondle. "Lead us on!"

After the simple command, the eleven adventurers and one dog began their trek toward the horrors of Rovere Moro.

CHAPTER 12

Ｏ

The icy winds blew hard against the frozen wooden structure, the construction doing little to prevent drafts from spreading throughout the living quarters. King Holleris sat in his favorite chair, having spent the morning pondering his next move, but now he needed something to warm his bones. Rising from his seat, he ventured over to the hearth, finding a kettle next to the fire. Taking a cloth to protect his hand, he grasped the handle and poured hot tea into his mug, warming the liquid that had chilled over the past hour.

A door leading from the workshop flung open. Finius, sporting his customary disheveled appearance, entered the room, closing the portal behind him. He took two steps toward the king before stopping, holding his ground.

King Holleris locked eyes on the wizard, then took a sip of his tea. Lowering his drink, he asked, "What's the status of our creation?"

The warlock cast his eyes downward, then shuffled toward the king. "They're progressing as expected," he hissed. Lifting his gaze to meet Holleris', he continued, "But they need time to mature."

The regal man did not flinch. "The beasts succeeded on their first mission. They're ready for their next."

Finius rocked back and forth. "Succeed, yes, but what you ask for is much more difficult." The ancient warlock shook his head. "Dragons take centuries to mature, not weeks!"

"Did you not accelerate their growth cycle?" asked the king in a simplistic tone, like one would use when questioning the ingredients of a chef's recipe.

"Of course!" lamented Finius, "but physical maturity is one thing. Experience is another. These beasts can live for a thousand years."

"I don't have the luxury of time!" exclaimed the king. "Now that I'm no longer immortal, we must speed up our process!"

Finius nodded, growing tired of hearing the king moan about his shorter lifespan. Slanting his eyes, he said with a scowl, "You knew the ramifications of me healing you, then taking you away from Dragon's Lair."

King Holleris took a hand and rubbed above his collar bone, the thick, jagged scars encircling his neck visible to the eye and touch. "Did you expect me to live forever with my head detached from my body?"

"That would make for a rather wasteful immortality, wouldn't it?" hissed the warlock. "Remember, we are tied to each other. Your mortal life is now draining *me*."

The king squinted. "The past thousand years have been hard on you, Finius. However, you can thank me now for extending the time that you have."

The warlock gritted his teeth and took a deep breath. Pointing a bony finger toward the royal man, he grimaced and said, "Our creation is what I'm thankful for. I created them in a way that will allow us to live even longer. Our blood and their blood are one. As they grow stronger, so shall we."

The king closed his eyes and took inventory of his body. He felt a resurgence in his health ever since the dragons hatched and began to develop. Every day the creatures grew stronger, faster, and smarter, enhancing his own physical being in the process.

King Holleris flashed a wicked smile. "I feel stronger already." He then took another sip of his tea.

"Don't get ahead of yourself, Holleris. You are a middle-aged man and will never be truly young again."

"But I *feel* young!" said the king with a glint in his eye. "I've waited a millennium to put my plan into action and I finally have the strength to succeed. Our dragons will see to this!

"I've outlived my fellow lords and I'm ready to unleash our creation upon the populace. Every race will bow to my sovereignty and every leader will recognize one throne in the land, and I shall be the one sitting on it!"

"My king," said the wizard, "please, give the creatures more time to mature. Let's not act in haste."

"I'm through waiting!" bellowed the king. "We shall begin our trek westward in two weeks. The time is now and we will vanquish everyone that stands in our way."

Finius slumped his shoulders, defeated. "As you wish, my king. I shall ready the beasts for their journey over the next few days." The warlock then turned to leave.

"Finius," said the king, stopping the magician in his tracks. "You're a good man and have done an amazing job for me throughout the years. However, the time for us has come and I will not let another minute go to waste. You have two weeks."

Finius, sensing the king had finished his speech, nodded once and headed out the door, not bothering to look back at his superior.

King Holleris sat back in his chair, facing the warm fireplace. He took another sip of his warm tea and smiled, knowing that his long awaited plan was about to commence.

* * *

Harrison kept watch from the back of the group while they followed the trail that descended deeper into the Valkaline Forest. The ground felt cold and muddy, the trees draping thick leaves over the darkening walkway. Even the cool rain started to dissipate due to the thickness of the vegetation. Though he could not see any beasts, his gut told him otherwise.

The young warrior gazed over to Kymbra. The woman maintained a firm grip on her sword, surveying the surrounding woods for any sign of the vile creatures that lurked just out of sight.

"It's getting dark," said Harrison, "we're going to need to light torches soon."

"That's a bad idea," said Kymbra, looking away from Harrison. "The flames will act like a beacon in the night for the trolls."

"Maybe so, but those monsters hate fire almost as much as we hate them."

"Point taken," said the female fighter. "Let's wait a little longer before we light anything."

The small group continued down the dank path for a short time, continuing their downward trek before the trail started to level. Harrison peered upward, noticing that the thick leafy vegetation had given way to barren branches.

Pointing at the bare trees, he said to Kymbra, "I don't like the looks of this."

The woman trained her sword toward something up ahead in the distance. "Or that either."

The young warrior swiveled his head in the direction the woman pointed, his brow scrunching. Squinting at the anomaly, he asked, "What is that?"

"The beginnings of a very thick mist."

Murdock raised a hand from up ahead, signaling for the group to halt their procession. "Martinaeous spoke of a fog, didn't he?" said the ranger, walking toward his friends.

"That he did." Gelderand recalled his mentor's tale. "I believe that we are standing on the outskirts of Rovere Moro."

Harrison felt the cool mist sting his warm cheeks. The light rain had covered his body in dampness, chilling him to the bone. The sight before him only intensified his unsettling feeling.

"I think we're safe as long as we don't enter the mist," he began. "Once we're inside, all hell will break loose."

"Shall we light our torches?" asked Thoragaard.

"And risk those trolls seeing us?" exclaimed Murdock in exasperation, raising his palms to the sky.

"Believe me when I say this, they will find us with or without the torches," said the illusionist. "Trolls possess infravision capabilities similar to Pondle. They will see us just as clearly whether we ignite the torches or not. However, our sight will become limited as it darkens."

"Thoragaard is right," said Gelderand. "We need to see or they will surprise us at every turn, which could lead to very bad circumstances for us."

"Very well," said Harrison. "Everyone, light your torches." A moment later, ten beacons of light illuminated the immediate area. Pondle, the only member of the group able to see in the darkness, chose not to ignite his light source.

The young warrior issued his usual command now that the torches had enhanced the group's vision capabilities. "Murdock, Pondle, lead us through the mist."

The trackers took their cue from their leader and began their trek into the thickening fog. Harrison, bringing up the rear, scanned the area, searching for the beasts that he knew lurked in the shadows.

The path remained murky and dank, the fog's thickness increasing with every step he took. The young warrior gazed to his left, finding Kymbra making a thorough examination of the immediate area. However, when Harrison turned in Tara's direction, he could barely make out her body's outline. Though she ventured a mere ten feet in front of him, her bobbing torch was the only real sign that she existed at all.

Murdock and Pondle guided the group another two hundred feet deeper into the forest before the fog started to lift. Moments later, the two trackers halted, leaving the mist behind them altogether.

"The fog's gone," said Harrison in Kymbra's direction.

"We're inside now," said the tall female warrior, clutching her sword a bit tighter.

The young warrior continued to survey the landscape. The land inside the mystical fog appeared even darker. The trees loomed taller, their branches longer yet still bare. Even though this part of the forest lacked a leafy canopy, high above the trees' thick branches reached across the pathway, intermingling with their neighbors, not allowing light to reach the floor and keeping the area devoid of illumination. Perfect for trolls, thought Harrison, squinting beyond the soft glow of his torch and into the ensuing darkness.

The adventurers continued to take measured steps for another fifteen minutes, no one daring to make a sound, their anxieties running high. From up ahead, Harrison noticed that Gelderand's group had stopped their procession. With a glance toward Kymbra, the young warrior approached the five robed people just ahead of him.

Sidling next to Tara, the young warrior asked. "Why have we stopped?"

"I think Pondle's found something," said the young maiden, doing her best to stay calm.

Harrison placed his hand on her forearm. "How are you doing?"

"I'm nervous, but I'll be fine," said the young girl.

The young warrior nodded. "Stay here. I'm going to see what's going on." Glancing back toward Kymbra, he said, "Watch our backs." The female warrior nodded once, obeying her leader's command.

Harrison walked past his friends with Lance joining his master. Reaching Murdock, he asked the ranger in a hushed tone, "What have you found?"

Leaning close to the young warrior, Murdock also spoke softly, saying, "You're not going to like this." The ranger motioned with his head for Harrison to follow.

The young warrior took a few steps and found the thief hunched over a dark mass. Harrison inched toward Pondle, lowering his torch closer to the object to get a better view.

"What is that?" asked Harrison, furrowing his brow, unsure of what the thief had found.

"A deer carcass."

Harrison leaned closer, getting a better view of the dead animal. A strong odor of decay wafted over him causing him to cover his mouth with his forearm, his torch precariously close to his head.

"Oh, that stinks!" he exclaimed, turning his head away in disgust.

"You need to take a closer look," said Pondle.

153

The young warrior approached the thief, crouching to better examine the animal. His eyes grew wide as his brain began to process the information that lay before him.

The deer's head rested next to the carcass, severed from the torso, which had deep gashes all about the midsection. Harrison brought his examination to the animal's limbs, which begged another question.

"Pondle, where are the deer's legs?"

"Torn off," said the thief, staring at the shredded animal.

By that time, the rest of the group had taken it upon themselves to come closer to the scene. Tara maneuvered next to Harrison and peered at the carcass from behind him.

The young maiden took a hand to her open mouth, her eyes wide. "What happened to this deer?"

"Trolls attacked it," said Harrison, shaking his head. In a firmer and louder voice, he said to everyone, "We need to stay vigilant. These beasts are close by."

Murdock approached the young warrior. "What's our next move?"

Harrison pondered the situation for a moment. "Let's keep pushing forward. I don't like staying still for too long."

"Should we move off the trail?" asked Murdock. "These creatures are probably trolling this path for travelers like us."

The Aegean took the ranger's comment into consideration before answering. "No, we stay on the path. If they're in the darkness we won't see them but they'll see us. I don't want to give them any more of an advantage than they already have."

"There's more room to fight in the pathway," added Kymbra, keeping her eyes on the landscape.

"That's true, too," said Harrison. "Let's venture for another hour, then we'll need to think about camping for the night." The young warrior knew they had trekked for a long time since leaving Martinaeous' house and the group had started to tire. "Lead us away from here." The adventurers assumed their positions, then followed Murdock and Pondle deeper into the Valkaline Forest.

The next hour went by quicker than Harrison anticipated, but what really worried him was the lack of activity from the forest. Aside from the carcass they had left behind, Pondle had not witnessed any signs of life—human, animal, or troll alike. Fatigue beginning to get the better of them, Harrison ordered the group to halt and set up a perimeter for the night.

Pondle and Murdock surveyed the immediate area and found a place that appeared safe for the time being. A grand oak rested in the middle of their camp, its large branches splaying almost down to the ground.

"We'll need to set up a watch schedule," said Pondle. "And I suggest we keep guard in pairs."

"Good idea," said Harrison. "Two hour shifts. We need to stay vigilant but also get as much rest as possible."

"Why haven't we seen anything yet?" asked Murdock to no one in particular. "Is it just me or does anyone else find this odd?"

"I was wondering the same," added Harrison, removing his pack and placing it on the ground. "Martinaeous wouldn't have led us astray. We'll find what we seek, eventually."

"That old man better not have sent us on another bogus treasure hunt," said the ranger, glaring in Gelderand's direction.

"My mentor was very forthcoming," said the mage. "I am confident that he would not have sent us in the wrong direction, especially into such a dangerous part of the land."

"Let's settle in," said Harrison. "Keep your torches lit, but let's not make a campfire. I don't want too much light coming from us."

The group of adventurers heeded their leader's wishes and prepared for the night. Murdock and Pondle, along with Lance, took up positions a short distance away from the group, their eyes riveted to the ensuing landscape, looking for any movement.

Harrison and the others did their best to get something to eat and rest. The young warrior sat next to Tara, his battle axe by his side and ready for use in a moment's notice.

"You're holding up well," he said, trying to allay any fears she might have.

"I don't like this place, Harrison," said the young maiden, not bothering to hide her emotions. "I have a bad feeling about this whole journey here."

Harrison nodded. "You're right, there's nothing good about Troll's Hell but we must persevere and keep searching for the scrolls."

Tara huffed and shook her head. "I hope we find what we're looking for soon."

The rest of the party members had taken seats near the couple in an effort to all stay close together. Gelderand had heard his niece's anxious words.

"Something tells me that we are closer to our destination than we think," he said, taking a bite of dried meat after speaking.

"However, the lack of beasts is disturbing," said Thoragaard. "I, too, had expected to encounter them by now."

"Then where are they all?" asked Tara, exasperated. "If this is Troll's Hell, shouldn't these monsters be running around trying to kill us?"

"She's right," said Kymbra, standing and gazing into the darkness. "I don't like this. I feel like there's something out there watching us, waiting and calculating."

"Trolls are not that sophisticated," said Thoragaard. "They have no real intelligence, just brutal killing instincts."

"Thanks, that makes me feel a whole lot better," said the female warrior in a snide tone. "How many do you think are out there?"

The illusionist shook his head. "No idea."

Harrison, keeping an ear on the conversation, took a second to peer over at Swinkle, who had kept his head down, remaining out of the conversation. Concerned, he asked, "Swinkle, is everything alright?"

The young cleric lifted his eyes to meet his friend's. His shoulders slumped as he said, "I've recited several prayers along our way in this forest and each one has revealed the most evil presence I have ever felt."

Harrison swallowed hard, knowing that his friend's faith was unshakable. "We'll get through this," he assured Swinkle before scanning the rest of the group.

"Remember why we're doing this. To save humanity from the wretched beasts that are trying to overrun our lands. This journey that we're on is a test of our resolve and, if we're worthy, all people in the land will prevail. We must succeed."

Everyone took the young warrior's words to heart, knowing that the outcome of their adventure could very well determine the fate of humanity.

Tara took hold of Harrison's hand. "I believe in you and our mission. We'll make it out alive."

Harrison smiled at his love. "I'll make sure of that." The group then continued their meals in silence, each one pondering their leader's words and wondering what secrets the dank woodlands harbored.

CHAPTER 13

O

Morning arrived with no sign of trouble. All those who had kept watch throughout the night reported that they had neither seen nor heard anything out of the ordinary the entire evening. Though the lack of activity concerned Harrison, after finishing their morning meal, he ordered everyone to break camp and assemble in their usual marching order. After a final status check, the young warrior commanded the adventurers to continue their trek deeper into Troll's Hell. They encountered their first oddity less than an hour into their trip.

Murdock and Pondle, as they usually did, had allowed Lance to scamper ahead of their position; however this time the canine's feverish barks more than startled them. Anxiety coursing through their veins, the two trackers rushed toward the dog's location with weapons drawn.

Pondle reached Lance first. The thief let out a sign of relief and sheathed his sword upon finding the root of Lance's commotion. With the constant thought of vicious trolls attacking and devouring their group fresh in his mind, the halfling dropped to one knee and began his inspection in earnest. Lance circled the area, his nose pressed to the earth, sniffing the ground. Murdock arrived seconds later and stood in awe at the scene before him.

Harrison and the rest of the crew rushed to their position. "What's going on?" asked the young warrior, his concern level rising. His eyes darted in every direction, on constant lookout for menacing beasts.

"Take a look for yourself," said Murdock, stretching his arm toward Pondle, still taking in the gravity of the situation.

The young warrior peered in the ranger's direction. Before him, Pondle continued his examination of tracks that littered the immediate landscape. Then he saw the bodies.

"What the hell happened here?" said Harrison, his eyes wide in shock.

Tara maneuvered next to the young warrior in an effort to better see what lay on the ground. Upon registering the carnage, her eyes grew round and she gasped, covering her mouth with a quivering hand. Swinkle did his best to keep his emotions in check and started to pray to Pious in earnest.

Harrison focused on the remains of men that lay before the group. Panning, he found body parts littering the area, with limbs snapped in jagged edges, flesh torn completely off the bones.

"Look at the ground," said Pondle, motioning with his short sword before him.

Harrison gazed at the muddy landscape, his brow scrunching. "There must be hundreds of footprints here," he said, his voice trailing off. The young warrior took a few steps closer to the markings in order to make a better examination.

"I'm no ranger, but even I can tell that these are human tracks running off in every direction." Harrison shook his head in disgust. "Those creatures must have terrorized these people, forcing them to run anywhere in an effort to escape."

Kymbra shook her head, her face flush with anger. "These beasts are nothing more than wild killing machines," she said. "Take a look at this!"

The tall female warrior pointed beyond Marissa and Adrith to a set of non-human footprints. The young warrior followed her lead with intent.

Harrison focused on the larger prints that ran roughshod throughout the area, imagining trolls chasing their hysterical prey. Finding one set of particular interest, the young warrior bent to one knee to give it a closer examination. Large claw marks protruded from the top of the impression that measured about a foot and a half in length.

Gesturing toward the footprint, he asked Pondle, "How large a creature do you think made this print?"

"This one," said the thief, cocking his head from side to side as he made a mental calculation. "I'd guess ten feet tall."

Harrison closed his eyes and pursed his lips, understanding full well the destruction a monster of that size could do. "Where do these markings lead?"

Pondle gazed about the area. Aside from the dismembered bodies, the footprints ran in every direction. "I'm not sure. We need to take some time and do a thorough investigation." He brought a steady stare to Harrison. "I don't want to run into these things without having an idea where they came from or where they're going."

The young warrior nodded in understanding. "Do what you must," he said, then added, "quickly." Pondle and Murdock then went about handling their task.

Harrison peered over to the women fighters, saying, "Help them in any way you can." Kymbra nodded once, caught the attention of her friends, and motioned with her head for them to follow her. The lithe blonde then led them in the trackers' direction.

Tara and Swinkle waited until Harrison had finished his conversation with the women before approaching him. "I do not have to remind you of the intense evil I have felt in this area," started Swinkle, "but it is something that we cannot underestimate."

The young warrior agreed. "I might not possess your capabilities, but I've felt a heaviness ever since we entered this forest."

Tara came to Harrison's side. "I have, too, and I don't like it one bit."

"We need to stay strong and, more importantly, alert," said the young warrior.

Gelderand, Thoragaard, and Fallyn, finished with their own examination of the gruesome scene, joined the trio. "It is in our best interest to find what we seek, then leave this desolate place," said the illusionist.

"Thoragaard is right," said Gelderand. "I am unsure if magic will keep these monsters at bay for very long."

Harrison nodded in concurrence. "I don't want to spend a second more in this awful place than we have to."

A few moments later, the rest of the group returned with their assessment. "You're not going to like what we have to say," said Murdock in his usual dour demeanor.

"Let's hear it," said Harrison, shaking his head in disgust.

The ranger gave way to Pondle, who said, "All of the bodies are old, the decay telling me that they've lain here for months or longer."

Harrison's spirits lifted a bit. "That means the trolls aren't around here now, right?"

Pondle raised a palm in the young warrior's direction. "I didn't say that. The prints from the monsters ran everywhere, but I think I have an idea where they went."

"Again, that's good!" exclaimed Harrison. "We can steer clear of them now!"

The thief shook his head. "No, you don't get it. We need to *follow* them."

"What?" said Harrison, his brow scrunched with an incredulous look. "Isn't that the *last* thing we want to do?"

"I think I understand Pondle's rationale," interjected Gelderand. "The trolls are guarding something, just like Martinaeous said."

Harrison's eyes widened, understanding. "The trolls are guarding the scriptures." His shoulders slumped with the realization.

"It only makes sense, son," said the mage.

"Gelderand's right," said Murdock. "And we think we know which way to go."

The young warrior took in the information, coming to grips with his friends' assessment. Drawing a heavy sigh, he said, "We must do what we must do. Pondle, lead us onward."

The thief gave his leader a reluctant nod, then started his trek once again from the point position. The rest of the adventurers followed, their weapons firmly in hand and eyes scouring the landscape.

Tara sidled next to Harrison. "What should I do when we find these monsters?"

The young warrior had thought long and hard about that very question. Every ounce of his being told him to be her personal guardian, not allowing anything to touch her golden locks. On the other hand, he knew he needed to portray the skills of a leader, not putting one person's needs above the whole group, even if that person was his true love.

"Stay away from them if at all possible," he started, "but if the creatures start attacking us, blind them."

The young maiden nodded. "I can do that."

Harrison stared into her eyes. "After you steal the beast's sight — run."

Tara's eyes widened. "Run where?"

"Anywhere. Just get as far away from them as possible." The young lass digested Harrison's answer and trekked beside him, remaining speechless the rest of the way.

* * *

Pondle and Murdock led the team deeper into Troll's Hell, the landscape transforming into a series of hills, abundant with tall trees that sported long, spindly branches. Heavy tracks littered both sides of the path that the group followed, heading to and from the underbrush. After another twenty minutes of trekking, the adventurers came to an abrupt stop.

Harrison, who had travelled more to the rear of the group, approached Murdock and Pondle's position. The two trackers stood motionless, staring into the distance.

The young warrior peered in the same direction. Squinting slightly, he asked, "What is that?"

Murdock, maintaining his gaze, said, "I think we're about to find out."

By this time, Tara, Swinkle, and the rest of the group followed Harrison's lead and gazed at a structure that emerged from out of the wilderness.

Gelderand maneuvered closer to the young warrior. "We have found what we are looking for."

Harrison stared at the building that loomed a hundred yards away, neatly tucked in an area surrounded by the tall trees. "We need to take extreme caution."

"That goes without saying," said the mage.

"How do you want us to proceed, Harrison?" asked Pondle, reluctant to continue without a firm plan in place, knowing that he would be the one leading the way.

The young warrior took a moment longer to gaze at the structure in the distance. From his vantage point, the edifice resembled a temple that sported white columns in a rectangular orientation. However, he remained too far away to make an accurate assessment.

"I say that we split into two groups and flank either side," started the young warrior. "We'll make a more thorough investigation once we get closer. Of course, we'll have to make a cautious approach to the building. If we're going to get surprised, I'd rather it happens before we enter the structure."

"What about the trolls?" asked Murdock.

"Keep your guard up," said Harrison before scanning the rest of the group members, "they're here and they're waiting for us."

"I suggest we march another fifty yards, then split from there," said Pondle.

"That's fine," said Harrison, before addressing each member of the party. "When we get to that point, I want to divide the group as evenly as possible, so that we all have a fair chance to survive any battle we might encounter."

Pointing at his friend, he said, "Murdock, you take Kymbra, Marissa, Adrith, and Thoragaard with your team." Gesturing in the thief's direction, he said, "Pondle, Gelderand, Swinkle, Fallyn, Tara, and I will make up the other team."

"You don't have enough fighters," said Murdock.

"Gelderand will torch as many of the beasts that he can," said the young warrior. "That evens things out a bit." He then looked down at the dog sitting by his side. "And we got Lance."

163

The ranger regarded Harrison's last comment, thought for a second, then nodded in concurrence.

"Pondle, lead us forward," said Harrison.

The thief did as commanded and led their procession to the agreed upon halfway point. "We're fifty yards away," he said, fixing his gaze on the temple-like structure. Pondle focused on the columns that surrounded the perimeter, sure that monsters lay in wait, ready to attack.

Harrison gazed into the distance as well, before taking his line of sight to the ground. Finding familiar markings, he said, "These tracks run everywhere."

"It appears that way, but if you take a closer look, they lead to the structure," said Pondle. Everyone followed the chaotic clawed tracks, recognizing that the thief had made the correct assessment.

Uncertainty coursing through his veins, Harrison gripped the hilt of his battle axe tighter. "Ready your weapons." All non-cloaked party members did as commanded and waited for the young warrior's next order.

"Murdock, take your team and investigate that side of the structure," said the young warrior, motioning to the left. "We'll check out this side."

"What do we do after that?" asked the ranger, clutching his sword.

Harrison gazed at the edifice. "With all those columns, I'm thinking it's an open air structure. We'll meet in the middle."

"That's a bit too easy for me," said Pondle. "Those trolls are somewhere. Keep your eyes open."

The young warrior nodded, then said, "It's time to get moving. Be ready for anything and, most of all, be careful." With their discussion over, the groups parted ways.

Harrison watched his friends leave, then turned to address his team. "Alright, Pondle you lead the way and if these trolls attack, don't hesitate to kill them."

"Harrison," said Swinkle, "we do not have any weapons. How can we defeat these beasts?"

"Use your prayers and spells," said the young warrior. "Leave the fighting to me and Pondle."

"It is not as simple as you think to conjure a spell while under duress," added Gelderand.

"I understand," said Harrison, "but it's our only means to survive." The young warrior gazed at his friends, reading the apprehension on their faces. "It's time to go. The others need us. Pondle, lead us forward."

The young warrior motioned for his friends to follow the thief. Lance scooted ahead, being mindful to stay only a short distance from his leader. Harrison assumed the point behind the halfling, while Swinkle, Fallyn, Tara, and Gelderand followed, left to right.

The woods began to clear and the structure became more visible with every step they took. Harrison could make out rows of twenty foot tall white stone columns, their brilliance dulled with dirt, vines, and overgrowth. The flooring mimicked the architecture, the marble stones covered in soil and mud.

Taking cautious steps to the building, Harrison followed ten paces behind Pondle as the thief angled the team to the right, losing sight of Murdock, Kymbra, and the others in the process. While pondering his next move, the young warrior heard a soft, nervous voice from behind.

"What do you see?" asked Tara.

In a quiet tone, Harrison said, "It looks like a temple. The inside is a bit dark. We need to get closer."

"Look down," said Swinkle.

The young warrior gazed at the dirt and found that large, clawed footprints littered the area. "They're here somewhere," said Harrison. Lance sniffed the tracks, then gazed up at his master and whimpered.

Pondle raised a hand from up ahead, signaling them all to stop. Cocking his head and squinting, he said, "Do you hear that?"

Everyone listened with intent, hoping to hone in on the sound. "Is that running water?" asked Tara to no one in particular.

"That's what I'm guessing," said Pondle. He then gestured for them to follow him again, taking them closer to the right side of the temple.

Moments later, Harrison's group positioned themselves almost at the center of the shrine. Gazing head on to the edifice,

165

they could see with clarity that the columns graced the perimeter of the rectangular temple and that more stone statues stood inside. All the while, the sound of flowing water filled the area.

"We need to go inside the temple," said Harrison.

"Where are the others?" asked Swinkle, doing his best to calm his nerves.

"I'm sure they're on the other side," said the young warrior. "I'm going to go with Pondle. Everyone else stay back and ready your spells and prayers."

Harrison exhaled, slowly releasing the built-up nervous energy from his body, then he gripped his axe tighter and nodded in Pondle's direction. The halfling took his cue and the two began their trek toward the temple.

Leaving the confines of the underbrush behind, Harrison knew that walking the twenty feet to the building left him exposed to whatever waited for him from inside. Lance took guarded steps as well, keeping pace with his master.

The young warrior made a cautious approach toward the temple, knowing full well that unpredictable beasts loomed somewhere in the vicinity. Upon reaching the structure, Harrison hid behind a vine-covered marble column, resting his back on the pillar. Lance joined him, waiting for his master's next move. His heart pounding, the young warrior counted to three, then peeked around the column, peering into the building's depths.

Harking back to his warrior training yet again, Harrison utilized his skills in making a quick examination. His eyes focused on a large, rectangular basin resting in the structure's center, while his ears understood that the temple's marble construction provided the perfect acoustical backdrop for the splashing water, making it sound as if the water ran everywhere.

Continuing his assessment, he brought his warrior gaze to the interior walls, noticing that, as on the outside, equidistant tall columns surrounded the perimeter. However, the existence of massive gargoyle-like statues took his breath away. Before he could further his investigation, he saw out of the corner of his eye a shadowy figure that grabbed his attention.

"Harrison," whispered a female voice amidst the murmur of hushed speaking.

The young warrior squinted, recognizing Adrith's lithe outline. "Where's everybody else?" answered Harrison in a soft voice.

The female warrior came nearer, her weapon drawn and ready to strike. "We're inside the temple," she said. "Gather the others and join us."

Harrison nodded in her direction, then called to his friends who had remained hidden in the underbrush. Waving, he said in a low voice, "Come on over! We're going inside." Seconds later, four nervous robed people joined the young warrior.

"I need you to say a prayer over that basin," said Harrison in Swinkle's direction. "I find running water in a deserted temple to be a bit odd, don't you?"

"I would say so," said the young cleric. "I will follow you."

"What's inside?" asked a soft, anxious voice.

Harrison gazed back at Tara, trying to hide his look of worry. "You'll see."

The young warrior escorted his friends toward the temple's interior, Lance dashing ahead to continue his own examination of the area. Once inside, Harrison found several familiar figures hovering around the central basin.

"What do you make of this place?" asked the young warrior to the man on the other side of the stone container.

"Typical temple structure," said Murdock. "Pondle's searching for traps as we speak."

Harrison panned the building. If a twenty foot long by ten foot wide by three foot deep water basin did not pique his interest, then the stone monsters that encircled the perimeter certainly did.

The young warrior stood from his position near the liquid phenomenon and peered upwards at the ten foot tall gargoyles. Harrison brought a lingering gaze to each of the statues that encircled the perimeter, finding four stone monsters perched on pedestals along the length of the temple walls and two each at the opposite ends of the basin, making ten figures in all. The beasts hovered over the people below, their long snouts presenting sharp teeth and their clawed hands ready to strike. A tug on his sleeve interrupted his investigation.

"Harrison," said Tara, "I don't like the looks of these carvings."

The young warrior stared at the menacing faces that glared back at him. "I don't care for them either." Turning to his friend, he called, "Swinkle, can you pray over the water and the area as a whole?"

"Yes, I can," said the young cleric, pressing his hands together, closing his eyes, and beginning to pray. A short moment later, he opened his eyes wide.

Harrison saw the anxious look on Swinkle's face. "Well?"

The young cleric shook his head. "Pure evil," he said, swallowing hard. "I suggest we leave as soon as possible."

"Not until we find the scrolls," said Harrison.

"Oh, that's not going to be hard to do," said Murdock, pointing into the stone container of water. "They're right there."

Everyone hurried to the basin, resting their hands on the side and peering into the watery depths. Sure enough, just as the ranger had said, the artifacts appeared to be submerged a foot below the liquid's surface.

Harrison stared at the parchment, finding them just out of his grasp. "Gelderand, can you detect magic?"

"There is no need to cast a spell," said the mage. "Strong magic exists in this place." Motioning with his head toward the scroll, he said, "Need I say more?"

"What's our next move?" asked Murdock, keeping his eye on the prize.

"Obviously, we need to get those scrolls," said Harrison. Before he could speak again, Lance began to bark at the feet of one of the statues.

Harrison jerked his head in the dog's direction. "Lance, what is it, boy?"

The little dog gazed at the stone gargoyle, then barked again. "Bad monster."

The young warrior brushed off the canine's fear. "Yes, we know they're bad monsters, Lance." Still, the dog growled at the stony figure.

Turning his attention back to the matter at hand, Harrison said, "Pondle, did you find anything of importance?" The young warrior kept his eyes fixated on the parchment.

"Nothing aside from this neat magic trick," said the thief. "But there's got to be something we're missing."

"Like the flesh eating trolls?" said Kymbra, her voice thick with sarcasm. "They're here somewhere, you know. We need to leave this place now."

"Not before we get those scrolls," said Harrison, mesmerized by the ripples of water that shimmied over the parchment. The soft waves seemed to draw him in and, unbeknownst to himself, he started to reach for the scriptures. A hand grabbed his forearm, snapping him out of his trance.

"Harrison, no!" said Swinkle. "This place radiates dark magic. We must be careful!"

The young warrior shook the cobwebs from his head. "Agreed," he said, before Lance's growls startled him again. This time Tara came to the little dog's side.

"Lance, it's alright," she said. "They're only statues." The canine whimpered, then stared back up at the stationary monster.

Tara gazed at the menacing gargoyle, too. The young maiden swallowed with fear, sensing something amiss. "Let's go, Lance," she said, keeping a wary eye on the figure in front of her. "Come over here with everyone else."

"Pondle," said Harrison while Tara approached him from behind, "are there any sign of the trolls?"

The thief spread his arms wide. "Their tracks run everywhere—inside the temple, outside in the forest—but I haven't found any shred of their existence."

"Nothing?" asked Harrison, shaking his head, incredulous.

"I figured that we'd find skin, blood, bones, anything that proves these beasts are here," said Pondle with a shrug. "But I can tell you that I've found nothing."

The young warrior placed both hands on the basin's rim and gazed into the water while he digested the thief's information. Turning to the robed members of the group, he asked, "Do any of you have anything to add?"

"This place is protected," started Thoragaard in his usual monotone demeanor. "These trolls exist and reside somewhere close by."

"I have already felt their presence," said Swinkle. "I agree with Thoragaard, they are here."

Fallyn shook her head. "Something's amiss."

Harrison peered over to Gelderand, who closed his eyes and nodded in agreement with his fellow sorcerers. "We have come a long way, Harrison," said the mage. "Martinaeous led us here and the scrolls lie before us. We must take them but all the while remain vigilant."

The young warrior let their thoughts swirl in his head. He gazed over at Tara, reading the anxiety on her face, waiting for him to make a decision. Whatever the outcome, there was one thing he knew for sure; he would not let anyone or anything harm his love. With that final thought in mind, he turned and faced the group.

"This is what I'm thinking," said the young warrior. "The scrolls are in this pool, we can see them. I have to believe that something is going to happen as soon as we touch the water.

"I want to form a perimeter around the basin. I'll reach for the scrolls, but everyone else needs to protect me."

"What exactly are you proposing?" asked Murdock. "Give us more about this perimeter defense."

Harrison gazed about the water container, working calculations in his mind. "Alright," he began, "Murdock and Pondle will guard me as I reach for the scrolls." Addressing the magicians, he continued, "Gelderand and Thoragaard," Harrison then used both hands to point at the shorter widths of the basin, "I want you both stationed on opposite sides and ready to use a magical attack."

The young warrior brought his attention to the female warriors. "Kymbra, you, Adrith, and Marissa will fan out and create a triangle around the container. Protect us from anything entering the temple."

"How far away do you want us?" asked Kymbra.

"No more than twenty feet," said Harrison. Kymbra nodded in concurrence.

The young warrior then addressed Swinkle, Fallyn, and Tara. "Swinkle and Tara, I need both of you to ready blinding spells or prayers, something to distract these beasts if they decide to show up." Focusing on Fallyn, he continued, "And I need you to also create a distraction, if at all possible." The redhead nodded, understanding her role.

"Where shall we stand?" asked Tara.

"You and Fallyn go with Gelderand," Harrison said to the women, before looking at Swinkle. "And you stand with Thoragaard."

Harrison then bent down to one knee. "Lance, you stay by my side." The little dog yapped once in affirmation, then maneuvered beside his master.

The young warrior rose again and addressed the entire group one last time. "Are we all in agreement?" Everyone nodded, no one saying a word.

Harrison, satisfied with his plan, readied his team. "Positions, everyone." All members of the party went off to their assigned posts. Thirty seconds later, each adventurer stood in his or her place, ready for action.

The young warrior focused on the scrolls, lying harmlessly in the water, taunting him to snatch them from their watery grave. Before commencing the operation, he said one last thing. "Be ready for anything."

Tara stood by her uncle, her heart pounding and breath short. As Harrison started to reach his hand toward the basin, the young maiden glanced at the stone beast that stood across from her. She stared into its hollow eyes, again sensing something amiss. To her surprise, the statue's eyes shifted in her direction, then darted back toward the young warrior.

Tara's eyes went round and she screamed, "Wait!"

Harrison recoiled his arm and everyone else glared in the girl's direction. The young warrior, his heart pounding and voice full of concern, said, "What's the matter, Tara?"

The lass pointed to the frozen beast. "Its eyes moved!"

The adventurers broke formation and rushed to the gargoyle that Tara had in her sights. Harrison stared into the beast's eyes, waiting for them to shift. After a long minute, he sighed and said, "I don't see anything out of the ordinary, Tara."

The young maiden remained adamant. "I'm telling you, that thing's eyes moved!"

Pondle, ever the investigator, took it upon himself to examine the sculpture in closer detail. Placing a hand on the piece, he found it cold and constructed of solid stone. He gazed into its eyes as well, but found no movement.

Still focusing on the beast, he said, "I still don't find anything—" but a subtle shift in the statue's eyes startled him as well.

Taking a step back, he exclaimed, "Did you see that?"

Kymbra took a step forward, her sword gripped tight at the hilt. "I certainly did! These things are alive!" Everyone took two guarded steps back, moving away from the figurines, weapons drawn.

"We need to rethink our strategy," said Murdock in Harrison's direction.

"I think you're right," said the young warrior, his eyes locking on figure after figure, trying to see their shifting eyes. After several tense moments, the group's anxiety abated at the sculptures' relative inactivity.

With the group pondering their predicament in silence, Thoragaard walked back over to the stone figure. He inspected it closely, looking at the platform it stood on, the intricate details of the monster's muscles, claws, and teeth, and the position it housed inside the temple. The illusionist then brought his gaze to the other statues, his brain churning in thought.

After a few minutes of watching Thoragaard's examination, Harrison asked, "What are you thinking?"

"These beasts are in an altered state right now," he said.

The young warrior cocked his head. Lifting an eyebrow, he said, "An altered state?"

"I believe that given the correct trigger, these gargoyles will spring to life."

Harrison's eyes widened. "Trigger? What kind of trigger?"

Thoragaard shook his head. "That is something we must determine."

Pondle again took it upon himself to reexamine the figurines. It took him much less time to agree with the illusionist. "He's right," said the thief, jerking his thumb at the massive stone monsters. "These are your trolls."

The young warrior understood his friends' rationale, but his brain yearned for more. "What can this trigger be?"

Thoragaard raised his palms to the young warrior. "You are missing the point. We must know how to defeat these creatures once they come alive or we will suffer the fate of those that came before us."

"I agree with Thoragaard," said Gelderand. "Anything that we do might activate these things. Being careful is of the utmost importance."

"They're going to wake up," added Murdock. "Our job is to get the scrolls and I bet their job is to guard them." The ranger looked into the basin. "If we grab those parchments, they're coming to get us."

Harrison let Murdock's comments sink in. "I'm betting you're right." He then panned the group. "How do we defeat trolls again?"

"Fire," said Thoragaard.

"Acid," added Pondle. "And we have limited supply of both."

"What are you talking about?" said Murdock in a snide tone. "We have *no* acid." Pointing at Gelderand, Thoragaard, and Swinkle, he said, "Can any of you conjure up a vat of this stuff?" All three men traded surprised looks, shaking their heads no in unison. "That's what I figured."

"Harrison, didn't you say that trolls can regenerate?" asked Kymbra.

The young warrior nodded. "Yes."

"Then we must hack them to pieces," continued the tall blonde warrior, "and burn them with our torches."

Murdock threw his hands up in the air. "Just like that! Just hack away at them!" The ranger then pointed at each ten-foot tall statue while counting out loud, stopping when he reached ten. "Ten trolls! You think we can smash them *all* to bits!"

"Do you have a better idea?" shouted Kymbra, her glare burning a hole in Murdock's forehead.

"Actually, I do," said Thoragaard. All eyes turned to the illusionist. "As Kymbra has stated, we must smash them to bits."

Harrison concurred with the mage's line of reasoning, but needed to hear more. "Thoragaard, these statues are made out of solid stone and our weapons are basically blades. How can we smash them?"

"Blades are useless, I agree," started the illusionist. "However, we can knock them from their perch and allow gravity and momentum to do the work."

Pondle did not wait to hear the rest of the conversation, instead he rushed to the closest sculpture. He made a brief inspection, then said, "He's right! Each one of these figures is standing on its own platform. We should be able to knock them over, though I bet they're very heavy."

Murdock and Kymbra rushed to the thief's side, examining the monster's pedestal. The ranger placed a cautious hand on the side of the stone gargoyle and gave it a push. The figurine did not budge.

Murdock removed his hand. "Heavy is an understatement. It's going to take all of our combined strength to move these one at a time."

"Maybe not," said Thoragaard. The illusionist brought his focus to Gelderand, Swinkle, and Tara. "Do any of you possess the ability to push objects?"

Harrison's eyes lit up upon hearing the magician's comment. The young warrior raised his left hand and stared at the ruby-colored stone set in his ring. "I can move objects with my ring!"

Swinkle chimed in, his voice excited. "That's right! I helped Harrison work on transporting objects with that ring! It can be done!"

"I, too, have a spell that can jolt things," added Gelderand. "More in the way of making a shockwave, which could help further break apart these statues."

Thoragaard brought his eyes to the young maiden. "Tara, do you recall your studies? Remember the activities we worked on?"

The girl thought back to her time in Concur with the illusionist. "I do! We studied a dispersal spell where objects can be hurled away from a common center."

"Excellent," said Thoragaard with an uncharacteristic smile. "Harrison, I think we now know what we must do."

"I agree!" said the young warrior, excitement in his voice for the first time since entering the desolate forest. Gesturing to his robed friends, he said, "Why don't we take a closer look at the basin while you," he then motioned to his comrades, "make a better examination of the gargoyles."

"Sounds good to me," said the ranger. Adrith and Marissa accompanied Murdock, Pondle, and Kymbra as they all began to examine the creatures' pedestals. Meanwhile, Harrison and the others took a closer look at the watery basin.

Harrison gazed at the parchment that appeared to float just below the water's surface. "Will those scrolls be soaked after we reach for them?"

"I doubt it," said Gelderand. "The magical signature on the parchments will keep them dry."

"What is of more concern is keeping the stone trolls away from the basin," said Thoragaard. "We must direct them away from the water so that they will not destroy the container."

"Why is that?" asked the young warrior.

"It is best not to tempt fate on so many levels," said the illusionist. "Crushing the stone giants, though a sound strategy, might also trigger something we have not thought about."

Harrison's mind churned with images of trolls springing to life and decimating him and his friends, uncertainty being the only sure thing about their current situation.

"Hey," said Murdock, approaching Harrison with Pondle and the female warriors in tow. "I think this wizard's plan just might work."

"Elaborate, please," said the young warrior.

The ranger pointed at one of the stone monsters. "Each one of these creatures is standing on a pedestal and all of them are made of stone. But they're not connected to the columns."

"They're freestanding," said Pondle, following his friend's line of reasoning.

Harrison took the information a step further. "So, we can knock these sculptures down like dominoes?"

Murdock cocked his head, then nodded. "I would say yes. They're heavy, but if we push them over at the right angle, they should fall right into each other."

Thoragaard raised a palm to the adventurers. "Let us prepare our spells before you try anything."

"We'll get into position," said Harrison. As the cloaked members of the group maneuvered away from the rest, the young warrior sought out his love.

"Tara, do as Thoragaard, Gelderand, and Swinkle say," he started. "I have the feeling you're going to do great things!"

The young maiden maintained her anxious disposition. "I just hope this all works out."

Harrison nodded to reassure her. "It will." Gazing over to his friends, he said, "I'll be right over there." The lass pursed her lips and left to take her position next to her uncle.

The Aegean then joined the warriors of the group. Regarding the statue that stood before them, he said, "What do you think?"

Pondle gestured to the row of four stone creatures erected closest to him. "We need to push this one," the thief pointed to the sculpture at the end, "into the one next to it and hope that they all fall down."

"And shatter," added Kymbra. "What do we do if they don't break apart like we think they will?"

Harrison jerked his thumb to the people across from them. "That's why we have them. I'm sure they can conjure something up." The young warrior examined the sculptures that stood before him one last time.

Placing a hand on one of the stone monsters, Harrison said, "It's time to smash these things. Let's all get behind this pedestal."

The young warrior positioned himself in the middle of the object, resting his hands on the cool, hard surface. Murdock and Pondle flanked him on either side, while Kymbra, Adrith, and Marissa, leaned against each side as well.

Harrison, with his head down, called to the other members of his group. "We're going to push this statue over! Be ready with your spells!" Panning the faces around him, he added, "On a count of three, we start pushing."

Everyone readied themselves for the countdown. "One … two … three!" exclaimed the young warrior, and on the final command everyone pushed the stony gargoyle with all of their might. At first the figure did not budge, but as they tried harder, the structure began to tip.

"It's working!" exclaimed Harrison. "Keep pushing!"

Seconds later, the sculpture began to tilt past its breakeven point. The three men and three women, sensing the sculpture's impending demise, dug deeper to find the remaining strength to topple the pedestal. With a resounding thud, the rock hard figure smashed into the one standing next to it, falling over and breaking into several large chunks. However, it did not have enough momentum to shatter the figurine adjacent to it, only chipping part of the frozen creature's arm.

"Great!" said Murdock. "Now what?"

Harrison did not skip a beat. "We do the same for each and every statue that's standing in this temple."

"That's what I thought you'd say," said the ranger, hunching over, placing his hands on his knees. "Why can't they perform some kind of magic so we don't die of exhaustion during this task?"

"Because we can't risk destroying the water basin," said the young warrior. "If we did, who knows what would happen to the scrolls."

Murdock did not respond, instead he readied himself against the next stone beast. The warriors performed the same physical task on each standing figure. Sweat covered their bodies and their muscles ached but one by one the statues came crashing down onto the temple flooring. After thirty minutes of physical exertion, all that remained of the menacing gargoyles were piles of crumpled stone.

Harrison, his breathing heavy, wiped the sweat from his brow. Gazing at his party's robed figures he said, "Your turn."

Thoragaard and Gelderand maneuvered near the piles of broken statues. Both mumbled to themselves before spreading their arms wide. In an instant, a rumble emanated throughout the temple, rippling the water in the basin, but more importantly, making the stone creatures reverberate on the floor.

As the shockwaves intensified, more and more of the sculptures turned into rubble. Tara had waited for the older men to begin with their spells, and when she felt the time was right, she unleashed her own.

The young maiden outstretched her arms as if she were pushing a heavy object and, like marbles on a smooth surface, the smaller stones dispersed to all corners of the temple, spacing the rocks further apart.

Swinkle approached the young warrior while the magicians continued with their conjuring. "Harrison, it is time to utilize your ring."

The young warrior proceeded to the opposite side of the basin, intent on using his ring's powers. First, he focused on a large chunk from one of the shattered statues. Next, he outstretched his right arm and concentrated on the stone piece. The rock started to levitate. Harrison then raised his hand toward the ceiling in a slow deliberate motion before throwing it down fast when the broken piece of gargoyle reached a height of ten feet. The fragmented statue smashed hard into the ground, shattering into even smaller pieces.

"Did you see that?" he said, his voice filled with excitement.

"You did well," said Swinkle, trying to temper his friend's enthusiasm. "There are many more to go."

Tara, her job finished away from Harrison, approached him and Swinkle to begin casting another dispersal spell. As the young warrior slammed large chunks to the floor, the lass's magic pushed them farther away from each other. Twenty minutes later, the scattered rubble became the only visual remnants of the statues that had stood in the entire temple area.

Harrison wiped the sweat from his brow and panned the stone flooring, admiring their handiwork. "I think we've crushed these monsters as much as we possibly can. It's time to retrieve the scrolls."

The young warrior walked over to the basin, again placing both his hands on its stony ledge. The scrolls remained just under the surface, taunting him.

"One last time, what do we think will happen after I grab these scrolls?" he asked his team.

"More than likely, these creatures will come to life," said Gelderand.

Harrison maintained his gaze on the parchments, agreeing with the magician without saying a word. Keeping his stare on the water, he said, "Ready your weapons and prepare to run."

"Run where?" asked Murdock.

"Back from where we came," said Harrison. "The less battling we have to do, the better."

"Harrison, we travelled a few miles," said the ranger.

The young warrior swung his head in his friend's direction. "Then you better pace yourself," he said, his face hard and serious. "Are we ready?"

Harrison panned the group, receiving an anxious nod in the affirmative from each member. Satisfied, he returned his gaze to the prize. After a mental count to three, he plunged his hand into the cool water, grabbed the scrolls, and removed them as fast as he could. To no one's surprise, he found that as the chill of the water dissipated, the parchments remained dry.

The young warrior brought the Ancient Scrolls of Arcadia closer to his face. Making a closer examination, he determined that a scribe had used a fine crisp pen to etch the writings onto the parchment; however he could not decipher the text. Magically encrypted, he thought to himself, figuring that an ancient wizard must have penned the symbols.

Without warning, things in the temple began to change. The clear water in the basin begin to bubble and a split second later the color turned a blood red.

"What's happening?" exclaimed Tara, her nervous voice echoing in the chamber.

Harrison's eyes grew wide. "I don't know," he said, as he and everyone else watched the water's metamorphosis.

Seconds later the red liquid began to spill over the sides of the basin, splattering onto the floor, and travelling down four equidistant small gullies that masons had carved between the stone slabs of the flooring.

Harrison watched in horror as the transformed water exited the basin on each side and began flowing in the direction of the fallen statues. To the group's amazement, the fluid rushed toward its destination in the same manner water flowed in an aqueduct.

Even though they had smashed the stone creatures to bits, the watery concoction began to stray from its destination and headed toward the destroyed figures. Simultaneously, all of the trolls' hard exteriors soaked in its life force and started to take on a more fleshy appearance.

The young warrior quickly rolled the papers in his hand and passed them to Swinkle. The young cleric, his eyes fixated on the scene unfolding before him, grabbed the scrolls and stuffed them into his backpack. Harrison swung his battle axe around, gripping the hilt as tight as possible. The hunks of flesh that lay strewn on the temple floor then started to jiggle as they absorbed blood into their fragmented systems. Then the individual pieces began to merge at a most disturbing rate.

Harrison rushed toward the bits of flesh that tried to reconstitute themselves and began hacking at them. Not bothering to look back at his friends, he screamed at the top of his lungs, "Run!"

Tara rushed to his side, wary of his blade. "Harrison, we must go!"

The young warrior jerked his head, his face cold and serious. "This is not open for debate! Run!"

The young maiden hesitated, surprised at Harrison's stern tone, before someone grabbed her arm hard from behind. Swinkle did not say a word. Instead he pulled the girl with him as the two began to run out of the temple, Fallyn following close behind.

Harrison went back to his task of splattering the fleshy pieces that tried their best to become whole. As he did, he noticed

Lance's frantic barking, the dog using a paw to hold down the small bits of flesh, before tearing at them with his teeth.

"Lance!" shouted his master. "Go with Swinkle and Tara! Now!" The dog obeyed his master and, an instant later, he teleported away from the chaotic scene.

The young warrior's blade continued to crash to the floor, severing small pieces of flesh into even tinier portions. Without warning, a huge orange glow engulfed the area to his right. Taking his eyes to the light, Harrison saw Gelderand's outstretched arms, fireballs blazing from his fingertips. The fiery orbs smashed into the flesh strewn on the ground, sizzling and charring them, while many other pieces started to burn. Harrison had barely registered the scene before him when a similar explosion caused his head to jerk to the left. Thoragaard had duplicated Gelderand's feat, scorching more jiggling portions of troll flesh.

Harrison harkened back to his warrior training and took a split second to assess his situation. Two mages had begun to torch the area while the other warriors performed a similar action as he, smashing anything that moved into bits. However, he realized that their noble fight would not keep up with the trolls' will to regenerate. Out of the corner of his eye he found that even the charred pieces of flesh had started to reconstitute faster than they could hack them.

Knowing that time was against them, the young warrior slashed at a large mass of flesh before him, splitting it in two, then slung his weapon over his shoulder and yelled, "Everyone! Run!"

Heeding their leader's command, the remaining members of his team halted their noble quest of destroying the monsters and sprinted out of the temple. Harrison had already run ten yards from the structure's entrance before he stopped to check on his friends' advancement. To his satisfaction, everyone had obeyed his command and now scrambled out of the temple.

Murdock and Pondle, accompanied by Adrith and Marissa, rushed to the young warrior's position. Before he could ask any questions, two large explosions rocked the area, producing huge fiery plumes inside the temple. Seconds later, Gelderand and Thoragaard exited the building with Kymbra in tow.

Harrison turned to Murdock and Pondle. "Keep going! I'm bringing up the rear!"

"We'll get those magicians out of here," said Murdock. Without missing a beat, he and Pondle grabbed hold of Thoragaard and Gelderand, encouraging them forward as Adrith and Marissa gave them not so gentle pushes on their backs.

Kymbra paused as the smaller group sprinted away from the ensuing chaos, before feeling someone grab her forearm from behind. Harrison, his focus laser sharp, stared into her blue eyes. "I need you back here with me."

The female warrior leered at the fiery temple, then swallowed hard. She locked her eyes on Harrison and nodded once in affirmative. The two then turned and ran after their friends, all the while knowing that a gruesome scene was about to unfold.

CHAPTER 14

✺

Lance darted ahead of Swinkle and Tara, making a point to look back every ten yards to be sure that the two did not lag too far behind. The young maiden ran through the unforgiving landscape with Swinkle a step behind her.

"What's happening back there?" she asked, continuing to press forward.

"I don't know," said Swinkle, knowing that ensuring Tara's safety had become as paramount as finding the Arcadian Scrolls. "Harrison will be joining us before too long."

Tara lurched forward, ducking under a low hanging branch. "Can we help them?"

"No," said the young cleric with emphasis. "Harrison would only try to protect you, which would cause him to lower his guard." Swinkle sidestepped a large root, then added, "That will get him killed."

The young maiden knew Swinkle spoke the truth. She knew how deeply Harrison loved her, as she loved him, but the situation they now found themselves in required immediate, calculated actions without emotional attachment. The best way to convey her love would be to stay out of his way. Maneuvering around another old oak tree, the young girl hastened her step and followed the little dog farther away from the temple.

* * *

"Come on, you two!" barked Murdock, agitated at the older mages' slow pace. "Those trolls are twice as fast as us!"

The ranger had taken up position behind Thoragaard and Gelderand, allowing Pondle, Adrith, Marissa, and Fallyn to lead the group away from the stone structure.

Murdock ran with his sword in hand, but he knew it would take only a second to switch to his weapon of choice. The temple stood beyond his field of vision now, the trees of the forest obscuring his view. He listened for the sounds of howls and screams, yet heard nothing. Good, he thought, Harrison and Kymbra have a chance. He took another second to stare behind him before returning to the task at hand.

"Keep running and don't look back!" yelled the ranger, all the while hoping that the unmistakable mist would soon come into view.

*　*　*

Harrison left the jiggling lumps of flesh behind, gesturing for Kymbra to follow the same path that their friends had taken only minutes ago.

Kymbra's gait exceeded that of the young warrior, allowing her to take a slight lead. "Anything following us?" she managed to ask while maintaining her forward stare.

Harrison glanced back at the temple, not seeing anything out of the ordinary. "No, not yet," he said. Just as the words left his mouth, an odd shape appeared in the structure's entrance and seemed to slither in their direction.

With eyes wide, he yelled, "Check that, yes!"

Trying his best to both maintain his forward progress while glancing back, the young warrior spotted several figures leaving the temple. Even his jostling eyes could not deny that the exiting shapes had the appearance of fleshy globs and did not resemble trolls. Whatever had left the ancient structure was not running on hind legs, he concluded, at least not yet.

"Something's heading our way!" he yelled again, still moving forward.

Not bothering to stop, the female warrior shouted back to Harrison, "Should we stop to fight?"

The young warrior was about to answer when he witnessed a most disturbing sight. Harrison slowed his pace, unsure of what he saw next.

The lithe warrior continued onward, and when she did not receive an answer to her question, she yelled, "Well?"

Harrison stopped and gazed back at the eerie structure. "Wait!" he shouted, his heart pumping and his anxiety level rising.

Kymbra jerked her head around, finding the young warrior standing motionless and staring at the temple. She too halted and squinted in the same direction as Harrison. Walking back to him, her eyes grew round and her heart skipped a beat.

Standing beside the young warrior, she swallowed hard and gripped her sword tighter, then said, "Am I seeing what I'm seeing?"

Harrison nodded, maintaining his stare on the regenerating trolls. "Yes, you are." The two warriors watched helplessly as the dismembered beasts began to split into more creatures, far outnumbering the initial ten monsters that they had encountered in the temple.

The young warrior scanned the area, his brain churning, registering the new information. The larger trolls had spawned smaller ones, each one resembling the original beast. Harrison stopped counting when he reached twenty.

"What do we do now?" asked Kymbra, sweat beading on her forehead, stress coursing through her veins. She watched in horror as the trolls' hobbled and slithered in their direction while she awaited Harrison's response.

The young warrior's eyes remained riveted in disbelief at the scene before him. Knowing that they had no other option, he ordered, "Run as fast as you can!"

The two warriors pivoted and sprinted down the pathway, following their friends' footsteps. Behind them, the trolls' dispersed body parts began to regenerate, combining into complete living monsters much quicker than the group had anticipated. After only ten minutes removed from being crushed stone pieces, the beasts had become whole again and they appeared very, very hungry.

Harrison, his breathing short and his heart hammering, figured that they had run for thirty seconds when the demonic sounds began. Grunting and panting echoed off the lifeless trees, casting the illusion that the trolls were everywhere.

Without warning, a single, hellish howl bellowed through the leafless forest, reverberating off the small inclines and hard oaks, bringing a shiver throughout the young warrior's body. Kymbra and Harrison stopped in their tracks and gazed behind them, their breathing ragged, horror all but overtaking them.

"What the hell was that?" said Kymbra, her voice quivering.

The young warrior looked over to the woman and read the unmistakable signs of panic and fear on her face. The usually impenetrable fighter trembled; her weapon shook in her right hand. He needed to snap her out of her state of shock at this very moment, knowing the two would face certain death otherwise.

"We both know what that was!" Harrison exclaimed. "Get ready to fight!" Seconds later, breaking tree limbs and crunching underbrush resonated right behind the adventurers.

Before Harrison could react, three smaller trolls advanced upon Kymbra, snarling and hissing, baring their teeth and claws. The female warrior, with her eyes wide, started to swipe at the monsters as they attacked her from every direction.

"Kymbra!" yelled the young warrior, before two trolls mounted their attack on him, preventing his aiding her. Harrison raised his battle axe and prepared to take on the being closest to him. A troll, standing a good eight feet tall, howled at the puny human, lunging at him with sharp claws and teeth ready to bite.

Harrison had studied trolls, albeit briefly, at the Fighter's Guild and knew that they would continue to attack until they were either destroyed or succeeded in devouring their victim. The young warrior preferred the first option. What the beasts lacked in armor and weaponry they made up for with tenacity.

The monster, its black eyes devoid of intelligence, tried to claw the smaller human. Harrison blocked the beast's attack with ease and, when the opportunity presented itself, he swung his axe at its midsection. The blade cut deep into the troll's unguarded torso, splitting its skin, and opening a profound gash. The creature wailed in pain, its high-pitched screech shaking the trees around them.

* * *

All members of Murdock's group halted in their tracks. The ranger stared into the forest's depths, sensing something horribly wrong. Squinting, he searched for Harrison and Kymbra, yet found nothing. Pondle noticed his friend's change in demeanor.

"Harrison and Kymbra are under attack!" shouted the thief.

"We need to help them," said Murdock, straining to get a glimpse of the two fighters.

Adrith overhead the two men. "We must keep going!" she exclaimed. "Those were Harrison's orders!"

Murdock understood the young warrior's plan, but his instincts told him otherwise. Panning the group, he made a quick calculation, then said, "I'm going back to help. They're outnumbered!"

"Not without me!" said Pondle, taking a step toward his friend.

"What?" exclaimed Adrith, eyebrows arched in surprise. "You're going to violate your leader's primary order?"

"You got that right," retorted Murdock, taking a step away from the group. Pointing to Adrith and Marissa, he said, "You two need to get Gelderand, Thoragaard, and Fallyn out of this forest. Now!"

Adrith brought a nervous gaze over to the three people, unsure if she should disobey Harrison's command. Marissa joined her, also unsure of Murdock and Pondle's makeshift plan.

"Murdock, lead the trolls this way," said Gelderand. "Do not try to fight them alone. You will lose."

Murdock spread his arms wide, exasperated. "What do you plan on doing?"

"Lead them this way," reiterated the mage. "Thoragaard and I will be ready for them." Gelderand pointed in the direction of the temple. "Go! All of you! Our friends need your help!"

"Hold on a second," said the ranger. "We're not leaving you unprotected. Adrith and Marissa stay with you."

Gelderand knew that they had precious time to lose. Raising a palm to Murdock, he acquiesced saying, "Fine, but leave now. We do not have the luxury of time."

Murdock, satisfied with the mage's response, glanced over to Pondle and cocked his head. The thief took his friend's cue and started to scamper away.

"Be careful and don't do anything stupid," said the ranger, before turning and following his friend.

Gelderand allowed the two men to get a head start. When they had raced twenty yards away, he peered over to the two female warriors and said, "What are you waiting for? Follow them!"

Both women glanced at each other, stunned at the mage's order. "Didn't you hear Murdock tell us to stay and protect you?" questioned Adrith, cocking her head.

"That I did," said Gelderand. "We will be fine, but your friends are fighting for their lives. Go!"

The female warrior pointed her sword at Fallyn. "What about her?"

"I have a few tricks up my sleeve," said the woman. "I'll follow you shortly."

Adrith pursed her lips, unhappy with the fact that she was about to disobey two orders in the span of five minutes. However, one look over to Marissa reaffirmed her intuition. Marissa gestured with her head to follow Murdock and Pondle's lead.

"Don't get yourselves killed," said Adrith. Gazing at her colleague, she said, "Let's go." The women gripped their swords tighter, then dashed down the pathway.

Gelderand watched the four fighters race back toward the temple. As they did, Thoragaard stepped forward and joined his fellow magician.

"What do you have in mind?" asked the illusionist, keeping his eyes fixed on the fleeing people.

Gelderand gazed at Thoragaard with a smirk. "Oh, I think you know."

The illusionist turned his attention to Fallyn. "And you?"

The auburn beauty smiled. "I'm going to help our friends." In an instant, the human female transformed into a large, black bat sporting green eyes. It circled over the two mages, then headed down the path, flying over Adrith and Marissa as it proceeded toward the temple area.

* * *

Harrison slashed at the creature again, this time severing its hand, which fell to the ground with a thud. The beast howled in pain, using its other hand to cradle its injured arm. Gritting its teeth, the troll lunged at Harrison. As it drew closer, the monster opened its mouth wide, revealing jagged, chipped fangs.

The young warrior timed his attack well. Waiting until the troll had extended itself to the point of no return, Harrison sidestepped the beast and with one swift swing, lopped off the monster's head. The troll's body crashed to the ground, its head rolling away.

Harrison had no time to gloat for the creature's severed body parts began to wiggle and search for their familiar corpse. The young warrior knew all too well about the trolls' regeneration process but he still stared in amazement at the sight unfolding before him. A loud grunt snapped him from his trance. Ten feet away, Kymbra hacked at another blood thirsty troll.

The young warrior watched the female fighter's sword slash across the monster's chest, slicing the beast, spilling its dark blood onto the ground. Infuriated, the creature stumbled back, gathered itself, and lunged again with purpose. Harrison, intent on helping his fellow fighter, took a step in Kymbra's direction before two more trolls intercepted him.

The young warrior took on a defensive posture, placing his battle axe between himself and the beasts. Analyzing the smaller creatures that flailed before him, he figured that he had a good chance to defeat them. However, to his dismay, the creature that he had apparently slayed moments ago had completed its regeneration process and, within seconds, all three trolls commenced their attack.

Knowing that the monsters had no real sense of fighting ability, Harrison allowed them to approach him with their arms flailing and teeth ready to bite. One creature advanced to his right, its hideous mouth opened wide.

The creature's foul breath wafted over Harrison, the stench forcing him to turn his head away for a brief second. The slight hesitation threw off the young warrior's timing and his axe missed its mark, allowing the troll a clear avenue to Harrison's exposed limb. The beast's jaws clamped down on the young warrior's right forearm, crushing it with all its might.

Harrison's eyes widened with terror, realizing the monumental mistake he had just made. The young warrior felt the muscles in his forearm tighten, his chain-mail stopping the troll's bite, for now. Harrison, with his right arm compromised, used his left to grab his weapon. The Aegean mentally thanked his mentors at the Fighter's Guild for instilling in him the importance to learn how to fight with either hand, the dexterity of that task coming to fruition at this very moment. Using his opposite hand, Harrison swung his axe at the monster's head, smacking it with the side of his blade. The troll resisted. The young warrior attempted the same attack, yielding the same result.

The other two trolls, sensing a meal was close at hand, joined the melee. Harrison raised his blade to block his new enemies' attack, while the first monster chomped harder on his arm. The young warrior knew the seriousness of his situation would only get worse if he did not free his limb from the troll's clutches. The first monster took its massive hands and clamped down on Harrison's forearm in an attempt to bite the young warrior's arm off.

Harrison's brain churned with battle sequences. Nothing made sense, aside from the shooting pain that radiated from his limb. Before all was lost, something clicked in the young warrior's mind. Using his left hand, Harrison pushed his weapon against the trolls in front of him, forcing them back. With the trolls at bay for the moment, he dropped his battle axe and, in one smooth motion, reached for a dagger on his belt. Slicing down, the young warrior drove the blade into the back of the monster's skull that had locked onto his arm.

The beast released its evil grip with a blood-curdling shriek. Harrison drove the blade deeper into its head, then viciously wiggled it from side to side. Blood poured out of the gaping wound, the young warrior's antics scrambling whatever semblance of a brain the creature had. Seconds later, the monster dropped to the ground. His immediate foe vanquished, he returned his attention to the trolls standing in front of him.

Harrison, his arm throbbing with intense pain, knew he could not defeat the trolls with a dagger alone. The young warrior thought back to his training on how to defeat an enemy without his primary weapon. Incorporating the first step in those teachings, he readied himself in a defensive posture. One of the creatures took a step in his direction, then inexplicably dropped to its knees, shrieking in horror.

Confused, the young warrior witnessed the second monster fall to the ground with a thud. Kymbra placed a boot on the creature's backside for support, then removed her sword from its torso. Making eye contact with Harrison, she reached for the young warrior's battle axe and tossed it to him.

The two warriors, without saying a word, knew exactly what they needed to do next. Both took their weapons and slashed at the fallen monsters, severing body parts, dark blood splattering the terrain. The trolls wailed, flooding the area with screams of agony and pain, but the two fighters paid their shrieks no heed, continuing their arduous task of dismembering the creatures.

Harrison and Kymbra did not stop their attack until they had butchered the trolls into mounds of bloody flesh. Out of breath and near exhaustion, both fighters stared at each other in silence, knowing that their fight had only just begun. In that instant, Harrison took inventory of his counterpart's face and body, finding her left cheek slashed and bloody, her armor scratched and torn. To his dismay, out of the corner of his eye he saw that the dismembered bodies began to wiggle on the ground.

"Let's go!" said Harrison through ragged breaths.

Kymbra grabbed his arm and pointed in the temple's direction. Her chest heaving as she tried to gulp more air into her lungs, she said with round eyes, "They're everywhere!"

Harrison panned the immediate area, his battle axe poised and ready to strike. Kymbra gripped her sword tighter and took a step back. The two fighters now stood back-to-back, waiting for the surrounding monsters to attack. The young warrior looked on in horror as trolls, large and small alike, encircled the trapped humans.

The female warrior, understanding the desperation of their situation, shouted, "What's your plan now?"

Harrison, his eyes darting in every direction, said, "Keep chopping and don't stop."

Kymbra's voice wavered. "There's too many of them." The trolls took a step inward, tightening the small circle, coordinating their attack.

"I'm not going down without a fight," said the young warrior. "Are you ready?"

The lithe fighter swallowed. "Ready as I'll ever be."

"Good." Harrison took a deep breath, then bellowed, "Now!"

Both humans roared, then began their assault on the menacing trolls. Harrison swung his battle axe at the creatures before him, slicing their exposed hands and severing their limbs. The young warrior did not allow the monsters to regroup, rather he flailed at the next beast that entered the fray. Kymbra did likewise, slashing at the closest troll with her sword, drawing blood and exhorting screams of anguish.

The trolls were relentless. With each monster that the young warrior hacked to bits another took its place, eerily reminiscent of the minotaurs that continued to attack him and his friends in the Sacred Seven Rooms a lifetime ago. Sweat dripped from his brow and his muscles strained with each blow he delivered. Though the beasts outnumbered him, he managed to hold his own. However, he noticed Kymbra not fairing as well.

Harrison took a split second to gauge her situation. The woman possessed excellent fighting skills but the trolls had worn her down. Three monsters clawed at her and snapped their spike-filled jaws toward her exposed skin, hoping to savor their first taste of human blood and satiate their hunger.

The Aegean took a step in Kymbra's direction before buckling to his knees. To his dismay, a troll had maneuvered behind the young warrior and lunged at his backside. During the creature's attack, its claws stuck in the links of his chain-mail and forced him to the ground. Then, all the trolls pounced.

Harrison lay on his stomach, his weapon trapped under him. Trolls clawed at his backside, tearing his covering and grating his armor, the hideous sound of scraping metal ringing in his ears. The young warrior covered his head with his hands in an effort to protect himself. Finding his left hand exposed, one of the monsters bit clear through his leather gauntlet, puncturing the soft skin underneath. Harrison hollered in agony as shooting pain radiated from the open wound. Seconds later he felt warmness gushing from the gash. The trolls smelled the blood and, sensing that they had the upper hand, seized the opportunity, setting off into a relentless feeding frenzy, their attacks appearing never ending.

Harrison understood that he needed to somehow flip over and use his weapon, but now the beasts had compromised his fighting skills. Battle tactics flashed though his mind while he lay helpless on the ground. Amid the myriad of defense strategies his brain presented to him, fangs tore into the back of his right thigh, drawing blood yet again. Instincts getting the better of him, he flipped over, let out another guttural scream, and gripped his weapon with both hands.

Grotesque faces glared back at him, their black soulless eyes penetrating his inner being. Shooting pains ran from his left hand and continued down the length of his arm. Using his right hand, he lifted the battle axe off his chest and drove it toward the monsters in an effort to thwart their assault. However, his weakened left hand gave and he dropped the hilt of his axe onto his chest. A beast followed the injured body part, bringing its jaws perilously close to Harrison's head. The troll lunged, chomping at the young warrior. The Aegean swiveled away from the attack in the nick of time, leaving the monster snapping at air. Harrison's cheek now lay flat on the ground and, to his horror, he saw Kymbra's still body between the shuffling trolls' legs, the monsters taking turns clawing and biting her.

Harrison understood the gravity of his situation. Kymbra lay incapacitated and unable to help the young warrior. Beasts snarled and snapped their jaws close to Harrison's head, and they had severely injured his extremities. Claws scraped deep into his armor, denting and chinking his chain-mail one link at a time. The dampness on the back of his leg meant that his own blood had pooled on the ground and started to soak his clothing. Fatigue had overtaken his body and only pure adrenalin had managed to keep his weapon in place long enough to prevent the trolls from tearing into his face.

Gazing upward from the earth, Harrison recognized that the larger of the creatures had maneuvered to get a better attack angle. A dark shadow flew past the monster's head, its leathery wings fluttering around its skull. The troll, sensing another presence, threw its clawed limbs into the air, trying to hit the moving target. The bat zipped past the beast again. Infuriated, the monster slashed at the animal, roaring in frustration at not striking the creature.

Still trying to gauge his new predicament, the young warrior heard a thwack, then felt the weight of the troll's body slamming down on him, pinning him to the ground. Before he could register the new situation, a second and third thump followed the first, both hitting their marks, dropping two more beasts to the earth. The young warrior replayed the incident in his head, identifying the unmistakable sound of an arrow entering an unarmored body.

"Kymbra!" screamed Murdock, drawing back his bow and unleashing his wrath on the creatures that hovered over the fallen woman's body.

Harrison took advantage of the unforeseen break in action to push the injured monsters off him. As he did, a flash of humans rushed past his position. Harrison pivoted to locate Murdock, knowing very well that only a marksman as he could deliver such precision attacks. Another arrow flew by him and hit its mark, this time entering a troll's forehead and exiting out the back of its skull. The beast's head exploded like a watermelon thrown to the ground, halting its advance. Then, he felt a hand grip his forearm.

"Get up!" shouted Marissa, her face hard and fearful, a small sword in her right hand.

The young warrior tried to rise to his feet, but the injury to his leg forced him down to one knee. "I can't!"

Marissa did not care for his answer. "You must!"

The female fighter lifted the young warrior under his armpit and threw his left arm over her shoulder. Harrison allowed the weight of his body to fall on the smaller person, his right leg dragging and useless, his empty hand bleeding and hurt. Furthermore, it took all his might to keep his battle axe clutched in his right hand.

Marissa, knowing that time was of the essence, began her trek from whence she came, gripping her sword and ready to strike whatever beast crossed their path.

Harrison, his leg dragging, watched in horror as the wild trolls attacked his friends. Murdock had finished using his longbow and switched to his sword, hacking at the beasts hovering around Kymbra. The same bat circled around the melee, doing its best to distract the trolls and their quest for food. A brief flash illuminated the area, startling the human fighters and nearby creatures alike.

Panning, the young warrior identified the light source. Pondle had ignited his torch and pressed it into the troll's body closest to him. The monster's hide caught fire and began to burn. The troll bellowed in pain and ran off into the darkness. The thief did the same to another as he forged his way toward Kymbra.

Marissa, witnessing Pondle's actions, said, "That's a good idea." She sheathed her sword and removed Harrison's arm from around her shoulder.

The young warrior's eyes grew round. Unprotected at this very moment, Harrison understood the woman's mistake all too well.

"What are you doing?" he exclaimed, but it was too late.

Marissa took an extra second fumbling for her torch and, finding it at last, held the unlit base in her hand. Before she could ignite her light source, one of the larger trolls pounced from out of the darkness. The beast snarled and swiped a clawed hand at the woman, splitting the torch in half, sending its tip hurtling into the ensuing melee.

The female warrior reached for her sword but instead felt the full brunt of the monster's fury. The troll lunged at the fighter, its jaws locking onto her right shoulder, piercing through her leather armor. The petite warrior screamed in terror and cried for help. The troll bit down harder, this time drawing blood and bringing tears to the woman's eyes.

"Help me!" cried Marissa, dropping her weapon and planting her hands on the beast's chest in an effort to push it off her. The monster did not budge.

Harrison, bent on one knee and all too close to the melee, gripped his axe tighter with his good hand and swung it at the creature's legs. The blade hit its mark, driving a deep gash into the monster's calf. The troll unhinged its jaws from Marissa's shoulder and wailed in agony.

Marissa took the opportunity to backpedal from the creature, holding her bloody shoulder and applying pressure to her wound. Terrorized, she regained her senses and picked up her sword, forcing ragged breaths while pain swarmed throughout her body.

The young warrior, knowing that the battle had just begun, recoiled his weapon and flailed again, hitting the monster in the same spot. The troll's calf exploded and the beast came crashing to the ground roaring in pain. A dark object flew around the fallen creature, distracting it from going after the humans again.

Harrison took the break in fighting to join Marissa. "Are you alright?" he asked, knowing full well the seriousness of her injury.

"I can't stop the bleeding!" she screamed on the verge of hyperventilating. "This hurts!"

"We need to find the others," said Harrison, searching for any semblance of his party. Ten yards from their position he saw an orange glow.

"Pondle!" yelled the young warrior, knowing that they could not fight their way out of this battle. "Pondle!"

The thief heard his name and scampered to join his injured friends. "We're not going to make it," said the halfling, his eyes darting, waiting for the next creature to attack.

"Yes, we will!" exclaimed Harrison. The young warrior thrust his torch in Pondle's direction. "Light it!" The thief did as commanded. "Hers, too!"

Pondle scurried over to Marissa, finding the injured fighter pale and badly hurt. "Where's your torch?"

The girl's glazed green eyes stared back at the thief. "Broken."

Pondle made a quick examination of the surrounding area, finding the two severed pieces. Reaching into his pack, he removed another torch, ignited it, and handed it to the woman. Marissa gladly accepted her new weapon.

The thief helped the female warrior to her feet and with conviction in his voice said, "Burn everything you see."

Marissa cocked her head. "You mean the trolls?"

Pondle shook his head. "No, *everything!*" The thief turned and went to help Harrison, knowing that his leader remained incapacitated. Marissa followed, cradling her right arm against her chest, gritting her teeth through the pain.

Harrison, with torch in hand, started scouring the area again for his next target. To his surprise, Pondle grabbed his chain-mail armor and, in a not so subtle way, attempted to push him forward. The young warrior winced, his hamstring throbbing and bleeding, trying his best to hold onto his only light source.

"We have to get out of here," said Harrison, amidst the chaos.

"That's the plan," said Pondle, maneuvering Harrison into a standing position with the young warrior's arm around his shoulder. "Hold your torch out and I'll do the same." The young warrior complied, outstretching his arm, forming what looked like one body holding two heat sources.

Still unsettled about their current situation, Pondle called back to Marissa nevertheless. "Start setting this place on fire!"

The female warrior nodded, ready to follow Pondle's command, but two trolls forced them to alter their plans. Harrison and Pondle waved their torches at the beast before them, keeping it at bay, while Marissa did the same to the smaller troll that had taken up position behind the trio.

Harrison looked into the beast's black eyes. The monster waved its claws and lunged with its gaping jaws. The young warrior thrust his torch at the creature, which recoiled from the flame. This just might work, he thought, finding that the trolls appeared to avoid the fire at all costs.

Behind the men, another troll pounced on Marissa. Lacking maneuverability due to her injury, the woman tried in vain to turn away from her attacker. The monster sliced her face, leaving three deep claw marks that drew blood. Her shoulder already compromised and now her face cut, the woman fell to her knees and waited for the inevitable. The troll, sensing a meal at hand, lunged at Marissa with jaws agape. In a last gasp effort, the female warrior shoved her torch into the monster's chest, igniting its hide. The beast burst into flames, howled, and ran off. Marissa dropped her torch and fell to the ground.

Unbeknownst to the battle that had just occurred behind them, Harrison and Pondle continued their melee with the troll closest to them. The creature bobbed and weaved at the men, doing its best to avoid the flames, trying to find an opening to attack.

"Draw it in," said Harrison to Pondle. "I'll light the bastard on fire when it gets too close."

Pondle understood Harrison's rationale. The thief waved his torch at the beast, then lowered it toward the ground, dropping his head and feigned cowering. The monster tried to exploit the fake opening and lunged at Pondle. Harrison took his cue to drive his torch into the creature's side, scorching its skin, causing it to burn. As with the others, the troll's hide started to blister and backed away to address its injury.

With a break in the action, Harrison swiveled and found the woman motionless on the ground. "Marissa!"

The men came to her aid, shielding her from the beasts. "Marissa?" said Harrison, lowering his head to her level. The woman did not answer; however, he heard soft moans.

The young warrior made eye contact with Pondle. "We have to get out of here!" Before the thief could respond, the familiar bat flew near the men, hovering over them. A second later, the animal morphed into a recognizable person.

Harrison scrunched his brow in surprise. "Fallyn?"

The woman rushed to the fighters. Almost out of breath, she asked in a panicked voice, "Are you two alright?"

Pondle shook his head. "No." Gesturing with his head, he said, "Look around you!"

Fallyn, her breathing heavy, scanned the vicinity. Chaos erupted at every turn. "I'm going to distract as many of these horrible monsters as I can. Get out of here as fast as possible!"

"Easy for you to say!" exclaimed the thief.

Harrison focused on the shape shifter. "Go and do what you can. We'll fight our way out of this."

Fallyn cocked her head, her face full of concern. "Harrison …"

"Go!" said the young warrior, cutting her off in midsentence. Fallyn pursed her lips, then transformed into the familiar bat, hovering over the men again. Moments later, the animal flew off to find its next target.

The thief panned the vicinity, forgetting about Fallyn for the time being and addressing the monsters that occupied the land close to them. Shaking his head, he said, "Harrison, they're everywhere!"

The young warrior scanned the landscape. Monsters scampered all around the perimeter, flames erupted in the darkness, people screamed in pain, and ghoulish shadows danced along the tree trunks. Throw in the myriad of injuries to him and his friends, and their situation had become more than dire.

"Where are Murdock and the others?" asked Harrison, trying to formulate a plan.

Pondle pointed to his left. Harrison followed the thief's line of sight and located the ranger hacking at two trolls, Adrith by his side doing the same. Kymbra lay at their feet, motionless.

Harrison's heart dropped at the sight and, for a brief moment, a feeling of hopelessness overtook him. Advancing trolls snapped him out of his trance. Glaring at Pondle, he said, "We fight our way out of this!"

Pondle nodded once and raised his torch. Harrison did the same, the two of them huddling close to Marissa in an effort to keep her safe. The young warrior, though he had the will to continue, swallowed hard when he counted five beasts converge on their position. He drew a deep breath, then fell into a defensive posture.

Without warning, an orange glow hurtled past them, striking a large oak tree, creating a massive explosion. The tree burst into flames, consuming the dry wood, and igniting the area. Harrison's eyes grew round with surprise as the new fire crackled and popped.

The young warrior recoiled as a second explosion rocked the immediate area, torching two more trees. Shrieks of terror swirled around him, the trolls burning in the night, abandoning their attacks for the time being.

Pondle pointed his torch in the direction of the escaping pathway. "They came from down there!"

Harrison peered in the direction the thief pointed. Some fifty yards away he thought he saw two robed figures. However, before his brain could process the new information, two more orange fireballs accelerated toward their position. Harrison and Pondle instinctively ducked as the fiery projectiles struck their targets.

The young warrior watched the burning missiles strike midway up a large tree behind him. The objects exploded yet again, the force of their blast cracking a huge limb, sending it crashing to the ground. The branch leveled three trolls, smashing them and sending body parts in all directions.

Harrison watched in horror as the severed pieces started to jiggle, their regeneration process already kicking in. With his hand and hamstring still throbbing in pain, the young warrior tried to maneuver away from the destruction. His body did not allow him.

"Pondle, we need to get Marissa away from here," he said, "but I'm having trouble moving myself."

The thief jerked his head to the left, then smiled. "Here come reinforcements."

Harrison lifted his eyes, finding two recognizable faces amidst the dancing flames that cast ghoulish shadows throughout the burning landscape.

"What are you doing here?" he lamented, finding Gelderand and Thoragaard positioning themselves in the muddy path, gauging the dire situation.

"We're going to end this madness," said Gelderand, his expression focused and stoic.

"Where's Swinkle and Tara?" asked Harrison, panning the area but not finding his love or best friend.

"Lance is leading them to safety," said the mage. "Stay down and watch out."

Harrison and Pondle huddled over Marissa, awaiting the cloaked man's next trick. The young warrior stared down the pathway littered with trolls, having a good idea at what would happen next. Turning to the mage, he watched him crush a dust-like substance in his hands, mumbling to himself as he did. Gelderand then threw his hands out and released the ingredients into the air. The mage's spell worked to perfection as another huge orange fireball hurtled down the trail. As it did, Thoragaard recited a spell of his own that intensified the glow and heat of the projectile.

The fiery orb crashed into more of the surrounding trees and overhanging limbs, creating a third enormous explosion that set the woods further ablaze. Harrison heard howls of terror echoing in the vicinity, the creatures igniting and perishing before his very eyes. Thoragaard waved his hands, casting another spell, pointing them toward the ever growing blaze. The fires appeared to rise and multiply, separating the trolls from the men and women.

A smile graced Harrison's face as he realized the extent of the damage. "The fire's going to consume them!"

"And they're afraid of the fake flames!" added Pondle as the remaining beasts were hesitant to approach the pyre that had taken up residence in the woods.

"That is the plan," said Gelderand, satisfied with their work. "However, we must leave now."

201

The mage maneuvered past the young warrior, dropping to one knee to examine Marissa while Thoragaard rushed by them to aid Kymbra and the rest.

Gelderand lowered his head to the injured girl's level and listened. A couple of seconds passed before his eyebrows arched. "She's alive, but injured badly."

The mage took care in raising the female warrior's body, lifting her from the ground and placing her uninjured arm around his shoulder. Marissa moaned in pain, her speech unintelligible.

"Time to go," he said to Harrison and Pondle.

Pondle, maneuvering Harrison in a similar position, started to lead the small group away from the raging inferno. The flames intensified around them, though the pathway remained clear enough to pass.

The young warrior, pain radiating throughout his entire body, gazed ahead. Only another twenty yards and we'll be away from this hell, he thought.

Without warning, a loud crack came from above and with it a massive tree limb fell from the sky. Pondle and Harrison both looked up at the same time, then leaped in opposite directions to avoid the falling branch. Pondle eluded the object but Harrison was not as fortunate. The fiery limb struck the Aegean, slamming him to the earth, knocking him out cold.

"Harrison!" yelled Pondle, gathering himself from the ground and rushing to the fallen fighter's position. Gelderand witnessed the act and, gently placing Marissa back on the ground, accompanied the thief.

"Is he alive?" asked Gelderand, noticing more blood around the young warrior's skull.

Pondle hovered over his friend. Nodding, he said, "Yes, but I need your help."

"I must tend to Marissa," said the mage, gesturing to the motionless female.

The thief grimaced, temporarily forgetting about the warrior. "I'll take Harrison and you get her."

The magician nodded once, then proceeded to carefully lift Harrison from the ground with Pondle's help. The thief propped the young warrior up, allowing his body weight to lean on him.

He then slung one of the young warrior's arms around his shoulder, allowing Harrison's legs to drag behind him.

Gelderand, finding that Pondle had his situation under control, took hold of Marissa in the same manner, again being sure to not injure her further.

Locking eyes with Pondle, he said, "Ready."

Pondle motioned with his head toward the muddy pathway. "That way."

The two men, their injured friends in tow, started their quest in earnest to leave the horrors of Rovere Moro behind.

CHAPTER 15

Ⓞ

A huge explosion halted Swinkle, Tara, and Lance's procession out of the forest. The young maiden whirled in the direction of the reverberating echo that enveloped the woods.

"What was that?" she exclaimed, her eyes wide, thoughts of despair racing through her head.

Swinkle, huffing from their trek, approached Tara. "I have to believe Gelderand and Thoragaard had something to do with that." The young cleric placed a caring hand on her forearm, giving her a gentle tug in the opposite direction. "Tara, we must continue."

The lass, her eyes glassy and her heart filled with worry, nodded. "I know," she said, her voice trailing. Lance, sensing the girl's pain, rubbed his nose against her leg, then nudged her toward Swinkle, telling her to continue in his own way.

"Let's go," she said. Lance scampered ahead with Swinkle and Tara following close behind. A few minutes later, the little dog began to bark in earnest.

Tara pointed at the phenomenon that loomed just ahead of them. "Look, it's the foggy barrier!"

Swinkle almost smiled, trudging forward. "We're almost there!"

Moments later, Swinkle led Tara through the thick mist and away from the path that they had travelled. Venturing fifty yards into the woods, the young cleric found a level spot near a large tree with overhanging branches that provided a decent amount of coverage. Not being an adventurer on par with Harrison, Murdock, and Pondle, the religious man did his best to conceal Tara from the elements of the forest.

Tara placed her pack on the ground next to the base of the tree. Lance curled up around her. "Where are they?" she asked, staring at the heavy mist that shrouded the land before her.

Swinkle strode over and took a seat next to her, his eyes locked in the same direction. "Still in Troll's Hell," he said, doing his best to keep her spirits up. "We had a significant head start. They will be coming soon."

The young maiden agreed with Swinkle with a simple nod, though her anxiety did not wane. The couple waited thirty long minutes before Lance sprung to his feet. The little dog began barking, his tail stiff, and ears pricked.

Swinkle searched for Tara's hand and took it, then helped the girl to her feet. At that moment, the young man wished he had a weapon to protect the lass, something out of character for a person of his stature.

Lance stopped barking and growled, knowing that something stirred just beyond the mist. Seconds later, his agitation turned to happiness as several familiar figures emerged from the fog. The little dog scampered to their side, his tail wagging.

Tara recognized the man exiting the cloudy barricade. "Uncle!" she exclaimed with a tinge of relief in her voice upon seeing the magician emerge from the mist. In an instant, her emotions changed from elation to concern, realizing that the person Gelderand had slung his arm around appeared seriously injured. She ran from her position with Swinkle rushing close behind.

"What happened to Marissa?" she asked, taking the weight of the young girl's body, relieving Gelderand of his task.

The older man took a moment to catch his breath before answering. The mage, his cloak singed and head sweaty, said, "The trolls got to her before we could help." Gelderand then hunched over, placing his hands on his knees, trying to get more air into his lungs.

Swinkle examined the girl in Tara's arms. "She's lost a lot of blood," he said, finding the female warrior's skin cool and gray in color. "I must tend to her immediately."

205

"What can I do?" asked Tara.

The young cleric placed his hands around Marissa's shoulders. "Help me guide her to the ground." The two slowly maneuvered the injured fighter to the forest floor, where Swinkle held her wrist and gazed into her eyes.

"Her heartbeat is weak and she's not very responsive," he said with a grimace. "Hold her hand and talk to her. I need to retrieve some items."

Tara bent down to Marissa's level. Taking her hand, she stroked the girl's bloody hair away from her eyes. "You're safe now, Marissa. Everything will be alright."

The injured fighter looked at the lass and mumbled something inaudible. Tara did her best to stay strong for the girl but knew her life held in the balance at this very moment. The young maiden inspected Marissa's body, finding deep scratches on her face and vicious bite marks on her extremities. With each breath the girl took, more blood oozed out of her shoulder's open wound.

Swinkle, his holy water retrieved from his pack, began to pray over the girl's body. As he did, he took the vial and sprinkled the sacred liquid over her deepest wounds. Once he completed that chore, he placed his hands around Marissa's head and shoulders, then recited another prayer. A soft white glow enveloped the warrior's injuries, closing some of them in the process.

"Is it working?" asked Tara, hopeful to see the girl recover now.

"Time will tell," said Swinkle. "I have another trick."

The young cleric removed another small vial from his pouch, this one containing a blue liquid. He tilted the girl's head upwards and placed the flask to her lips. Marissa instinctively swallowed the container's contents, drinking the potion without knowing its intent. Swinkle then laid her back on the ground.

"She will need a lot of rest," said the holy man.

Tara nodded and took hold of the fighter's hand, agreeing with the young cleric's assessment. Lance's frantic barking more than startled the group. Tara lifted her eyes to the eerie mist, finding two cloudy figures wading through the fog. Her eyes grew round.

"Harrison!" she exclaimed, recognizing the injured fighter along with Pondle. Tara made haste in placing Marissa's hand by her side before rushing to her love. The young maiden maneuvered under Harrison's unaided shoulder, helping Pondle with his heavy burden.

"What happened to him?" she asked, panic in her voice.

"Trolls," said Pondle, motioning with his head to continue further away from the mist. The thief took a couple more steps before lowering the young warrior toward the ground next to Marissa. Tara assisted in placing Harrison down as well, then fell to her knees to get a closer look at him.

The young maiden brought gentle fingers to Harrison's scalp, examining the deep wound on his head. She then brushed aside the hair from his closed eyes.

"Oh, Harrison," she said, tears forming in her eyes. "I should have stayed with you."

"Nonsense," said Gelderand, hovering next to his niece. "The trolls would have killed you."

"I could have helped," she said between sobs. "I should have been with him."

Swinkle crouched next to his friend. "Please give me some space to work," he said, assessing the young warrior's injuries.

While the holy man looked over Harrison, Pondle added, "The trolls bit his forearm and hand, and gashed his leg." The thief pointed to the Aegean's head. "A huge falling branch caused this."

"That is what knocked him unconscious, but I am more worried about the loss of blood," said Swinkle.

"And the onset of disease," added Gelderand. "Trolls are dirty, filthy beasts."

Swinkle nodded, concurring. "My praying can only help so much." The young cleric made a quick glance in Tara's direction, finding her preoccupied with Harrison, then said to Gelderand in a hushed tone, "It will not stop anything foreign from spreading."

"I, too, have limited supplies," answered the mage. Gazing to the injured woman on the ground, he added, "And Marissa is a long way from being healed as well."

Tara's ears pricked up after hearing her uncle's last comment. "As well as who?" she asked with round eyes. "Harrison?"

Gelderand maneuvered next to his niece and placed a gentle hand on her forearm. "The trolls hurt him badly, Tara. We must accept this."

The young maiden squinted, then said with conviction, "Then we will heal him."

"It is not as simple as you think," said the magician, but before he could continue, four more figures staggered from the misty boundary.

The alert group members watched as Thoragaard emerged from the fog dragging Murdock with him, while Adrith labored with Kymbra. Both Murdock and Kymbra did not move, their bodies stained with blood, their armor slashed and torn.

Pondle rushed to Thoragaard's side, helping to ease his burden. Likewise, Swinkle and Gelderand hurried to Adrith's aid.

"What happened to him?" exclaimed Pondle, pointing to Murdock. "He was keeping the trolls at bay when we left him!"

"Things changed," said the illusionist, almost out of breath. "Those monsters attacked someone he cares for."

"Lay them over here, next to Harrison and Marissa," said Swinkle, guiding the tall female to the earth with care. Pondle and Thoragaard laid the ranger next to Kymbra. Everyone stepped back to assess their situation. Lance scurried between the injured fighters, taking particular interest in Harrison, then whimpered and plopped himself next to his master.

"This is bad!" exclaimed Pondle. "All of our fighters are hurt and, look," the thief pointed to his injured friends, "we've laid them in line like corpses on a battlefield!"

Adrith brought a nervous gaze to the robed people. "You must save them now!"

Thoragaard, Gelderand, and Swinkle attended to each person, checking their vital signs and assessing each one's condition. Swinkle laid his hands over each fighter's most debilitating injury, a soft white glow lighting the area for a brief moment each time. After completing that task, he removed bandages from his backpack, sprinkled holy water over their bodies, and covered open wounds.

Thoragaard attended to Kymbra first, finding her hurt the most and clinging to life. The trolls had mercilessly slashed at her body, tearing her leather armor to shreds, and scratching almost all of her exposed skin. The illusionist concluded that her body covering was the only thing that stopped the beasts from devouring her flesh.

Gelderand's examination revealed that Murdock's back had sustained the brunt of the trolls' attacks. Inspecting the slashes to his armor, he asked, "Why did the creatures attack only his backside?"

"He laid on top of Kymbra so that the trolls could not harm her anymore," said Thoragaard. "He saved her life."

"Well, they're all going to die if we don't do something more," said Pondle, agitated that he had nothing to offer the group in regards to healing their friends.

Swinkle, taking a moment to gather himself after praying over the injured, said, "There is not much more we can do. I only have so much healing power and most of their wounds are grave."

Tara did not accept the young cleric's assessment. "Then you must do more," she said, refusing to let go of Harrison's hand. "These are our friends! We can't sit idly by while they deteriorate!"

"I understand," said Swinkle, sensitive to Tara's emotional state with Harrison unmoving by her side. "We all will work harder, but you must realize that the healing process can be a long one."

"We're in the wilderness," said Pondle, outstretching his arms for emphasis. "We're vulnerable to everything that's out here."

"Then you must stay alert," said Thoragaard. Pointing to Adrith, he said, "You, too."

"We need to make a plan," said the female fighter. "Or we're going to die."

"Waking our friends up and assessing their total physical *and* mental states are the first thing we need to do," said Gelderand. "The trolls' attacks have traumatized them all, including us."

Swinkle, examining Marissa during Gelderand's statements, said, "Her gashes are deep and the trolls bit into her skin." He then gestured toward the rest of the fallen warriors. "All of them have sustained grievous injuries at the hands of those beasts. I am confident that they will all heal eventually from their wounds, but I am most worried about the potential for disease."

"You can cure them if they develop something, right?" asked Tara, hope in her voice.

The young cleric shook his head. "No, I cannot."

"You must have something!" lamented the young maiden, throwing up her hands, not ready to accept Swinkle's response.

"I do have some medicinal herbs but nothing to stave off a troll-contracted illness."

Pondle walked close to the three robed men. "Then what do we do?" The thief took a moment to gaze at the people who lay on the forest's floor, taking in their injuries. "All of them are going to get sick."

The thief took his eyes to Gelderand, who then looked at Thoragaard. The illusionist shook his head and looked down. Pondle's anxiety level, already way beyond high, jumped up another notch.

"How long before disease sets in and symptoms occur?" asked the thief.

Gelderand shook his head. "Days? Weeks? I do not really know." The mage bent to one knee to get a closer look at Kymbra's injuries. Shaking his head, he said, "Everyone will react differently and have their own timeframes."

"I say we head back to Concur," said Pondle with a scowl. "Immediately."

"I agree," said Adrith. "We need to get out of the woods as quickly as possible."

"Concur will provide little in the way of healing their wounds," said Thoragaard. "Lord Hammer maintained tight control over those who could heal and perform magic."

Pondle spread his arms wide in exasperation again. "Then what?"

Swinkle had remained quiet while the others conversed about courses of action. Taking advantage of the break in their discussion, he said, "We must visit the elves. Only they can save our friends before sickness sets in. Furthermore, we needed to meet with them anyway at some point. It might as well be now."

Pondle's eyes lit up with a glimmer of hope. "Yes! They could definitely help us and they're not too far away from our current position!"

Gelderand and Thoragaard had reservations. "Can we trust them?" asked the mage.

"I believe so," said Swinkle. "They helped us traverse the Dark Forest and led us to the entrance of the Morgue, as they called it."

"And fought side by side with us against the Scynthians," added Pondle. "I can lead us to them."

Tara rose from her position next to Harrison. "Uncle," she said, tears glistening in her eyes, "they're our only hope."

Gelderand pursed his lips, knowing that Tara was right. With a nod, he said, "It is settled then. We embark for the Dark Forest in the morning. In the meantime we must do all that we can to aid our friends and make them comfortable."

Lance sprung to his feet and maneuvered in front of Harrison, then began to bark at a feverish rate. Everyone focused on the little dog.

"What is it, Lance?" asked Tara, her voice wavering.

The canine stared at the mist, barking. Moments later, a majestic hawk exited the fog and headed for the group. The bird hovered above the people for a second, then landed on the ground. Next, it transformed into Fallyn Tierany. The woman buckled, then dropped to her knees, panting.

"Fallyn!" exclaimed the young maiden, hurrying to her side. "We'd all but forgotten you!"

"Those monsters won't come this way," she said through breaths. "They can't escape the fog."

Swinkle rushed to the shape shifter. "Are you alright? Have you been injured?"

"I'm fine," said Fallyn, still breathing hard. "I just need rest." The woman lifted her head, then rose to one knee. The young cleric held out his hand and aided the woman to her feet, then led her next to the injured party members, where she took a seat on the ground. Swinkle offered her a tankard of water, which she gladly accepted.

"Adrith," said Pondle to the lithe fighter, "even though Fallyn believes that the trolls can't exit the mist, it's still up to us to stand guard all night. Lance will help, too." The female warrior nodded in affirmation, gripping the hilt of her sword.

"Pondle, are we safe here?" asked Gelderand.

The thief panned the immediate area, finding the mist far enough away from their position and the path close proximity if they needed to leave in a rush.

"Yes, we should be as safe here as anywhere else."

"Then let's settle in for the night," continued the mage. "The rest of us will take care of one person each." Gelderand pointed to Tara first. "You monitor Harrison," he said before gesturing to Swinkle, "and you handle Marissa." Taking his eyes to the illusionist, he said, "Watch over Kymbra and I will work on Murdock. Is everyone in agreement?"

All party members gazed at one another for a moment before nodding in unison, accepting Gelderand's strategy. With a plan in place, they then went about the arduous task of helping their friends with their multitude of injuries throughout the course of the night.

CHAPTER 16

О

Harrison fluttered his eyes, allowing a blurred white glow to enter his consciousness. Then came the pounding headache. The young warrior stirred and attempted to rise, but halted when shooting pain ripped through his hamstring and fire radiated from his forearm. He sensed a small furry body wiggling against his side, then the unmistakable slobber of a warm, sloppy tongue across his face. The young warrior knew those feelings meant only one thing.

"Lance," said Harrison, his throat parched. "Where am I?"

The little dog barked once. "Awake!"

The young warrior stayed flat on his back, unable to move without pain, his head ready to explode from the constant thumping. A blurry image passed in front of his eyes while soft hands caressed either side of his face.

"Harrison?" said the sweetest voice he had ever heard. Next, soft lips pressed against his own and a tear dropped onto his cheek. "Oh, Harrison."

"Tara?" asked the young warrior, straining to see. Seconds later, Tara's angelic face came into focus, hovering inches above his own. "What happened?"

"Swinkle!" shouted the young maiden before turning her full attention back to Harrison. "Thank the gods you're awake!"

The young warrior, still in a state of confusion, again tried to get up. Tara placed her small hands on his chest, stopping his upward momentum. "Stay still. Swinkle's on his way."

"What happened?" reiterated Harrison. "Where's everybody else?"

"The trolls injured you, Murdock, Marissa, and Kymbra," said the girl, doing her best to stop from sobbing. "We've suffered terrible losses."

Harrison's heart dropped, knowing full well that the group's safety was his utmost responsibility. "Did we lose anyone to those savage beasts?"

Tara shook her head. "No, but the damage was done."

Swinkle approached the injured Aegean, bending to one knee and looking into his eyes. "Harrison, it's Swinkle. How do you feel?"

"Awful," said the young warrior.

"Where does it hurt?"

"The back of my leg, forearm, hand, and my head's pounding," said Harrison. "And I feel nauseous."

The holy man smiled. "Actually, that is good. It is exactly how you should feel."

"Can I get up?"

Swinkle nodded. "Tara and I will try to prop you up, but please move slowly."

The young cleric gestured to the girl, each one grabbing Harrison under his armpits. The two of them hoisted him to a seated position, Tara resting her hand on his back in an effort to keep him upright.

"You need a lot of rest," said Swinkle. "And that is not up for debate." The young cleric placed his hands on either side of Harrison' head, then mumbled a prayer.

A soft, white glow clouded the Aegean's vision. Harrison's headache subsided by the time Swinkle removed his hands from his head. The holy man then held his friend's face in his hands, stabilizing him as he gazed into his eyes.

Harrison noticed apprehension in Swinkle's face. "What's wrong?"

"Your pupils," said the young cleric. "They are not right."

A range of emotions coursed through the young warrior's body. "How so?"

"You have suffered internal injuries that will heal over time," said Swinkle. "Until then, no activity except eating and sleeping."

"You can't be serious," said Harrison, pushing Swinkle's hands away as he tried to get up.

The young cleric took both his hands to Harrison's shoulders and forced him down, sending him to the ground. With a stern look, he said, "I am totally serious. If you were not so injured, I would never be able to move you, let alone push you to the ground."

"He's right, Harrison," said Tara, taking her hands and holding the young warrior's cheeks. "I won't leave your side until you're better." She turned to Swinkle and said, "I'm going to take care of him myself, don't worry."

The young cleric smiled. "I know you will, Tara." He then focused on his friend. "I mean it, no activity."

"Or you'll push me around again?" said Harrison with a laugh.

Swinkle chuckled. "You can count on it!" Looking to Tara, he said, "Give him some food and water. I need to check on the others."

Harrison waited for Swinkle to leave before asking Tara, "Please tell me what happened to everyone?"

"You don't remember?" questioned the girl, shaking her head. "Look around you. Those savage beasts almost killed you, Kymbra, Murdock, and Marissa."

The young warrior panned the campsite. Pondle sat with Murdock, addressing his wounds while the ranger sat up and tried to gather his bearings. To their left, Swinkle and Thoragaard worked on Kymbra, who lay flat on the ground. Next to her, Fallyn helped Marissa sit up as Gelderand adjusted a makeshift sling that kept her bloody shoulder in place.

Tara took a moist cloth and dabbed it with water from her tankard, then began to wash away the caked blood from Harrison's face. The lass's soft touch felt good on the young warrior's otherwise damaged body.

"The last thing I remember, Pondle and I stood back to back, trying to ward off the trolls with our torches." Harrison shook his head. "Then all went black."

"Pondle said a huge tree limb hit you on the head," said Tara, dabbing a spot on his face. She then pulled back, tears filling her eyes. "When I saw Pondle dragging you out of the mist, I thought ..." Tara swallowed, then continued. "I thought you were dead." Tears rolled unfettered down her cheeks.

Harrison maneuvered in an effort to comfort her, but shooting pain from the back of his leg forced him to stop. He reached out with his left hand and caressed her cheek, taking a thumb to dry her tears. Tara leaned hard into his strong hand.

"I'm not ready to leave you yet, Tara," said Harrison.

Sniffling, she said, "Is this how it's going to be all the time?"

The young warrior chose his words carefully. "Battles are unpredictable. I should hope not."

"I don't know if I can get used to seeing you return from battles like this or worse," said the young maiden. Gathering herself, she sat tall, took a deep breath, and started removing the blood from Harrison's face again. "But I'm grateful you're back with me now."

Harrison lightly held her hand, preventing her from washing him. "I'm not going to take unnecessary chances in battle. I'll always come back to you."

Tara lowered her head. "I want to believe that so much, but ..." The young maiden shook her head and looked away, sniffling.

"You have to trust me," said Harrison. "I'm not going anywhere."

The girl looked deep into the young warrior's unwavering eyes, knowing that he believed every word he spoke. Nodding, she said, "I believe you, Harrison. Just promise me you'll be careful." She then waved toward his damaged body. "More careful than this!"

"I'll do my best, that's all I can promise." He leaned over and pressed his lips to hers, ignoring the shooting pain radiating from his leg. Pulling away, he said. "I love you."

Tara smiled. "I love you, too." She then started dabbing his face again. "Now that I'm watching over you, it's time to get you better."

Harrison smirked. "I might just enjoy being injured."

Tara raised an eyebrow. "Don't get used to this. Once you're better, you're going to take care of me!"

The young warrior smiled back. "Deal!"

Gelderand and Thoragaard approached the two, ending the couple's intimate conversation. "I'll leave you all for a bit," said Tara, rising to join Swinkle and the others. "I'll be back soon."

Both magicians nodded to the young maiden, then bent down to Harrison's level to better assess his situation.

"How are you feeling, son?" asked Gelderand.

"I've been better," he said, shaking his head. "My brain is thumping, my leg and hand hurts, and my forearm aches. Aside from that, everything else is fine."

The mage let out a little laugh. "At least you still have your sense of humor."

"We are worried more about the possibility of an illness than your physical injuries," deadpanned Thoragaard. "The others are in worse shape than you, particularly Kymbra and Marissa."

Harrison's smile disappeared from his face. "How bad are they?"

"They need immediate medical assistance," said Gelderand, "for which there is none."

The young warrior's brain churned in thought before a sudden thought sprung to his mind. "What if we visited the ..."

"Elves," said Gelderand, finishing Harrison's statement. "That is our current plan."

Harrison recalled his time with the woodland creatures, their king, Moradoril, and their beautiful queen, Brianna. His thoughts then turned dour. "Even if they could help us, we could never venture to them in our condition."

Gelderand nodded in agreement. "Therein lies the problem."

"Maybe a couple of us could venture to their complex," said Thoragaard. "We would leave the injured here and return with reinforcements."

217

Harrison shook his head. "Too dangerous. There are Scynthians in that forest and, most likely, bands of those beasts around here."

Gelderand took a deep breath and sat up straight. "What do you propose?"

The young warrior took a moment to ponder the question, then said, "We camp here another day. We'll have a better idea how everyone is faring after that."

The magicians nodded in concurrence. "Very well," said Thoragaard, "but keep in mind that whatever disease those trolls might have carried will incubate in you and the others." The illusionist rose to his feet. "I need to check on Kymbra." He then left the men behind.

Harrison watched Thoragaard walk away. Concerned, he asked, "Is there something festering inside me?"

Gelderand patted the young man on the knee before rising to his feet. "I hope not, but we will not know for a few days. All the reason to seek help as soon as possible. Rest now and mull over our travel options." He then left the young warrior behind to check on the other injured fighters.

Harrison gazed past the mage and to his friends littered around the makeshift campsite. People assisted Murdock, Kymbra, and Marissa, administering food and drink while addressing their wounds. Fallyn did her best to help, but even she appeared worn and tired from her escapades. As he watched them, Lance bounded over to his master and rubbed his snout in Harrison's torso.

"I'm alive, boy!" he said, scratching the little dog behind his ears. "Hurt but alive."

Lance pulled back and stared at Harrison. Barking once, he said, "Leave!"

Harrison furrowed his brow. "Leave?"

The canine grumbled and barked once again. "Leave!"

The young warrior shook his head. "We can't leave yet, Lance. We're not ready." Lance huffed, then snuggled up to his master again.

Harrison rubbed the dog's belly. "I'll figure this out, Lance, but right now my head hurts and my body aches." The young warrior yawned and lay back on the ground, making himself comfortable. The little dog curled up in a ball, keeping his master warm.

Harrison yawned again. "We're going to leave soon, Lance. I promise you." Moments later, the young warrior fell into a deep sleep, all the while thinking about how to get his friends to safety.

* * *

The young warrior's eyes popped open. Without thought he tried to rise from his position on the ground but shooting pain throughout his body thwarted his attempt. Allaying his discomfort, he maneuvered into an upright position, then used his good arm to push his body upwards to reach one knee. His head pounded and his right hamstring ached, but his determination allowed him to stand on one leg. Moving like a zombie with one limb dragging behind him, Harrison approached the makeshift infirmary.

Before him rested his injured comrades, while robed figures administered medicinal herbs and adjusted bloody bandages. Lance caught sight of his master first, bounding over to him and barking. Tara's head swiveled, anxious to find what had made the canine so excited.

Eyes wide, she shouted, "Harrison! You're not to be up!"

Disregarding his love's exclamation, he asked a general question to all party members, "Where are the scrolls?"

Tara shook her head. "The scrolls? I don't know."

"I have them," said Swinkle, coming to the young warrior's side. "You need to sit down and rest."

"No!" said Harrison, determined. "We need to look at those scrolls now."

Tara positioned her small body under Harrison's shoulder, giving him some much needed support. "You need to sit down first."

Harrison huffed. "Swinkle, please get those scrolls!" The young warrior, with Tara's help, carefully lowered himself to a sitting position on the forest's floor.

Tara examined the young warrior's dressings while Lance rushed to his master's side, protecting him. "What's so important about those parchments that you need to see them at this very minute?" asked the young maiden.

"I have a hunch," he said.

Swinkle approached the couple with his backpack in tow. Placing his hand inside, he fished out the sacred scriptures and handed them to Harrison.

"What are you thinking, Harrison?" asked the young cleric.

By this time, the young warrior's antics caught the attention of the other members of the group. Gelderand, Thoragaard, and Fallyn joined the three, while Murdock, Kymbra, and Marissa remained lying on the ground.

"I'm willing to bet that there's an escape plan in these papers," said Harrison, unfurling the scrolls. To no one's surprise, the Ancient Scrolls of Arcadia were comprised of more than one piece of parchment.

The young warrior took a closer look at the inscriptions, then frowned. "I can't say that I'm surprised about this." Harrison turned the documents around for all to see.

Tara's eyes wandered all over the scripture. "I can't understand a single word!"

Thoragaard placed a hand on the young girl's shoulder. "Take a closer look. What do you see?"

The young maiden focused on the text, then her eyes lit up. "It's magical!"

The illusionist cocked his head once and nodded in affirmation. "What needs to be done now?"

"We cast a spell to read the magical text," said Tara, positive in her answer.

"Very good," said Thoragaard. "Who shall read it?"

"I can!" said Tara, excited. "I've studied about these situations in Concur. I can do this!"

The magician shook his head. "No."

Tara crinkled her brow. "Why not?"

"I'm sure that the magic performed on these important documents is very strong and something we should not take lightly," said Thoragaard before turning to Gelderand. "One of us should read the text."

"Better yet," said Gelderand, "we will need someone to transcribe what we read. I am sure the wording will disappear shortly after we cast our spell."

"Very good point," said Thoragaard before peering at Tara.

The young maiden's eyes opened wide. "I'll take notes!"

"I will help you as well," said Swinkle. "I have plenty of parchment that we can share." Bringing his focus to Fallyn, he said, "One of us should stay here and help Pondle tend to the wounded."

"It's alright, Swinkle. I'll stay here. You go," said the auburn haired woman, waving the young cleric away.

Harrison allowed the robed people to converse, waiting for the opportune time to speak. "Wait a minute," he said. "What am I going to do?"

"Rest and wait for us to finish our task," said Gelderand. "This will take some time."

The young warrior huffed again, perturbed with his lack of knowledge in all things magic as well as his physical state. "Fine," he said tersely. "Let me know what you find as soon as you're done."

"We will," said Gelderand. The mage pointed to an area away from the campsite, close to a large tree. "Let us read these scrolls over there, away from everyone else."

Harrison squinted. "Why?"

Gelderand flashed him a sly smile. "Just in case something goes wrong." The magician motioned for his friends to follow him to the outskirts of the camp.

Tara bent down and gave Harrison a peck on the cheek. "It's my turn to help the group," she said. "I'll let you know as soon as we decipher the text."

"Be careful," said Harrison.

"I'll be as careful as you," responded Tara.

The young warrior grabbed her arm as she tried to rise. "That's not too comforting," he said with concern in his voice.

Tara leaned over and kissed him again, shaking her arm from his grip. "Trust me, Harrison, all will be fine." She then left the young warrior behind to help with the group's task.

Harrison watched her walk away and smiled, admiring her will to help with the task at hand, regardless of the consequences. His pride then turned to worry, knowing full well the dangers that had to do with anything magical. He huffed again, cursing his incapacitated state under his breath and doing the one thing he hated the most—waiting for others to complete a task that did not involve him.

Lance scurried alongside his master and rubbed his snout against the young warrior's body, his tail wagging feverishly. Harrison gave the dog rough scratches all over his torso, getting his little friend to wag so much it appeared he would tip from excitement.

"Just me and you again," said the young warrior. "Like old times." Lance's tongue hung from his snout, too enthralled with Harrison's petting.

While the Aegean fighter continued pleasing his canine friend, he brought his gaze to the small congregation of magicians and clerics on the other side of their encampment. Harrison watched as Tara conversed with her uncle, using her hands to drive home her point. The young warrior smiled, pleased that Tara had accompanied them on their journey and had become an important member of the group.

Harrison stopped rubbing Lance and pulled him to his chest, offering the little dog a place to lie. "We're going to be alright, boy," he said. "Tara will make sure of that." Lance gazed over to the young maiden and seemed to agree without making a sound.

The young warrior drew a heavy sigh, wincing as he maneuvered into a more comfortable position. "Now we wait," he said aloud, doing his best to relax while his friends went about deciphering the ancient scriptures.

C H A P T E R 17

⬡

Tara felt a bit uncomfortable, leaving Harrison alone while she helped the group. The young maiden peeked at the warrior, finding him playing with Lance. Good, she thought. Now it's my turn to really prove my worth. She followed Swinkle, Gelderand, and Thoragaard to the outskirts of their camp. When they found a spot that they deemed safe from the others, Swinkle unfurled the Ancient Scrolls of Arcadia.

"Who shall read these scriptures?" asked the young cleric to his colleagues.

Gelderand and Thoragaard exchanged glances. "I will read the first one," said Gelderand. "I deciphered the book that contained the clues to finding the Talisman of Unification. I am confident that I can do the same for these."

"You understand the potential consequences, right?" said Thoragaard, his face hard and focused.

The mage nodded. "If something goes horribly wrong, I leave behind an arduous task for three capable wizards."

"Don't talk like that!" exclaimed Tara. "Uncle, if these parchments are too dangerous maybe we should just let them be."

Gelderand smiled at his niece. "Oh, I assure you they are dangerous." He then wagged a finger in her direction. "If they are not handled the right way."

"And what would that be?" asked Swinkle. "We have been very fortunate during our adventures across the land."

"I agree, Swinkle," said Gelderand, "However, now is not the time to quit. The fate of the land might hinge on what we have in our very hands."

"It is also not the time to be overly cautious," added Thoragaard. "Careful, yes, but our friends need us to be bold."

Everyone panned to the injured fighters, finding them all in various stages of pain and agony. Four sets of eyes returned determined stares, all agreeing with Thoragaard without anyone saying a word.

Swinkle handed the first scroll to Gelderand. "There are three in total. I suggest that we read them in sequence."

"That would make sense," said the mage, accepting the magical parchment. Gelderand unfurled the scroll and examined the encrypted text, focusing on the ancient runes that did not resemble the customary alphabet.

Taking his eyes to Thoragaard, he said, "As expected."

"Do you need a place to set the scripture down in order to cast your spell?" asked the illusionist.

"I do," said the magician. Bending to the earth, he splayed the scroll out, then looked to Tara and Swinkle. "Can both of you hold the scroll down so that it will not curl back up?"

The two youngsters heeded the elder mage's request and stretched the parchment out inches above the ground while Gelderand removed a small pouch from his backpack. He then took a couple pinches of a purple grain and sprinkled it over the parchment. As he did, he closed his eyes and mumbled undecipherable words.

Tara watched with wide eyes. The sand-like ingredients bounced on the taut parchment but as soon as Gelderand began his chant they started to swirl about the page.

"I don't understand any of this text," lamented the young maiden.

"That makes sense," said Swinkle. "Gelderand is casting the spell. He will be able to read it." Tara pursed her lips and nodded, upset at herself for not realizing that simple fact.

Gelderand chanted for another minute, then lifted his eyes. The magician canvassed the scripture before a wide smile graced his face.

"I can understand the text!" he exclaimed. "Quick, stand up and hold the scroll in front of my face!" Swinkle and Tara rose from their position and did as the mage commanded.

Gelderand did not hesitate in reading the parchment, knowing full well magic had its mysteries and intricacies. *"Behold, the Ancient Scrolls of Arcadia,"* started the mage. *"You have proven your worth by holding these scriptures in your very hands and in the moments to come you will understand the mysteries of the land.*

"No one is safe, nothing is as it seems, and all will end." Gelderand lifted his eyes, finding the others hanging on his every word. *"Battles are yet to be fought and enemies are surfacing. Before the Great Battle, an unlikely alliance will be forged. Without the contributions of the combined armies, the war will surely be lost. Death will come to the lucky ones and anguish to the unfortunate. Be vigilant, for the war to end all wars is coming. Time is no longer on your side."*

Gelderand paused. "That's all this one says."

"Ominous prognostications of war are nothing new," said Thoragaard, unfazed by the scripture's warnings.

"This doesn't tell us anything!" lamented Tara. "There must be more!"

Gelderand flipped the parchment over, finding a blank page. He then turned to the second scroll, finding more encrypted text. The runes, bound under Gelderand's spell, transformed into words.

"I can understand this text as well," said the mage, his excitement level rising. Focusing on the first line, he said, *"Summer, Year 27 after the formation of The Kingdom ..."*

Gelderand stopped speaking upon witnessing the magical text swirl on the page. Seconds later, a hologram illuminated the area, surrounding everyone including the injured fighters.

"What's happening?" asked Tara, panning the encampment. Everyone scanned the area with wide eyes, finding that a chamber's image had intersected with their woodland camp.

Harrison witnessed the event as well, stopping his playful antics with Lance and focusing on a particular figure. Trying to rise, the young warrior locked his eyes on the holographic image of a knight adorned in plate-mail armor.

225

"That's Sir Jacob!" he shouted, getting up halfway before his bad hamstring prevented him from rising further.

All eyes turned to Harrison, surprised at his outburst. Swinkle and Tara rushed to his side, aiding him to a standing position. Pondle also scampered from the outskirts of the woods, leaving his lookout post to join in the commotion.

"What's happening?" asked Pondle, taking over for Tara and helping Harrison stand.

"Take me closer!" said the young warrior. "Hurry!"

Harrison never removed his stare from the scene unfolding before his eyes. The images took on a bluish hue with just enough detail to see a lead knight and three of his henchmen. The fighters stood on the opposite side of a long table where a man adorned in a hooded robe sat. Upon further examination, the young warrior realized that the figures did not remain motionless. Rather they seemed to be waiting for the Aegean to position himself to get a better view, as if the scene was meant specifically for him.

Pondle and Swinkle escorted Harrison in front of the translucent images, giving him a straight on view of the action. As if on cue, the man Harrison identified as Sir Jacob began to speak.

* * *

"This madness has to stop!" shouted Sir Jacob at the seated man. "This kingdom is in shambles and it is all because of your king!"

The hooded figure turned his head to face the decorated knight and spoke in measure tones. "My king is the rightful heir to the throne. He is alive and is fully capable to rule."

Sir Jacob thrust a finger at the man, his eyes glaring. "Your king exiled his equals to another realm in order to sit upon the royal chair alone! He is not fit to lead anyone ever again."

The seated person did not respond; instead he took his hands and slowly pulled down his hood. Harrison, riveted to the scene, allowed his eyes to study this person's face, reading his features, and storing them into the recesses of his mind.

The young warrior did not recognize him from any of the visions he had while reading Philius' ancient scriptures including the manuscript the old wizard had handed him before searching for the Treasure of the Land. This man appeared young, maybe ten years older than Harrison himself, and had sharp, handsome features. Dark, mysterious eyes sat atop high cheekbones and nary a scar graced his clean-shaven face.

"King Holleris is alive and well," said the man in an even tone. "His throne room on Dragon's Lair is appropriate for his rulership."

"He orchestrated a coup that overthrew the rightful rulers!" said Sir Jacob, furious. "And you, Finius Boulware, was his right hand man!" The knight glared at his men. "Seize him!"

The three henchmen unsheathed their swords and took purposeful steps toward the man in the chair. Finius raised his hands, showing the men his palms. "There is no need for weapons, I am unarmed."

"You are a dangerous wizard," said Sir Jacob. "Bind him!"

As the men converged on the magician, Finius pulled back his hands, mumbled something under his breath, then thrust his palms forward. The soldiers reeled back, tumbling head over heels and out of the holographic perimeter.

Finius lowered his hands, placed them on the table, and gazed at the bewildered knight. "Really, Jacob, is this all necessary? Can we not just get down to business?"

Sir Jacob pointed at the wizard. "We are not through yet," he said, never taking his eyes off the man. With reluctance, he pulled out a chair and took a seat at the table. "You will pay for your sins."

Finius leaned forward, grinning. "Not today." The wizard reached into a pack beside his chair and removed parchment, a quilled pen, and ink. "We both need each other, like it or not."

Sir Jacob scowled, knowing that Finius spoke the truth. "You will not deviate from what I say."

The magician shook his head. "I gave you my word," said Finius. "What transpires here today is bigger than both of us."

The knight drew a heavy sigh. "That it is. Very well," said Sir Jacob, gazing upward and stroking his orange beard. "What I have to say comes straight from Maligor the Red, recited to me many years ago before his untimely death."

Finius lowered his pen and glared at the knight in front of him. "Maligor died almost ten years ago! You have kept this information to yourself all this time? What if you had died, too?"

"The time was never right. It's still not today; yet I have no choice now," said Sir Jacob. "Ready?" Finius raised his pen and cocked his head once.

"King Ballesteros is the one with the regal lineage," started the knight. "From his family will the heirs of the throne come."

"When will these heirs arrive?" asked Finius, continuing to write.

"That is undetermined," said Sir Jacob with a scowl.

The magician stopped writing and lifted his eyes. "No timeframe?" he asked, raising an eyebrow.

The knight shook his head. "No. Denote this in your scripture."

"Continue," said Finius.

"Maligor indicated that the heirs will be brothers who will unite an army and bring together the people of the land."

"Did he relay any names?"

Again, Sir Jacob shook his head. "No, he did not."

"What precipitates the brothers' ascension?"

"The uprising of an evil the likes the land has never seen."

Finius stopped and gazed at Sir Jacob. "A doomsday scenario?"

"So to speak," answered the knight. "Unnamed beasts will troll the land, destroy villages and cities in a single day, and wreak havoc on all races."

The magician pressed for more. "Any description of these creatures?"

"Only that they will be large."

Finius frowned. "That does not help our descendants much, now does it?"

Sir Jacob waved his hands in frustration. "Maligor was old and tired, and his visions were not always clear."

Finius put down his pen, leaned back, and tented his fingers in front of himself. "So you mean to tell me that I'm transcribing the visions of a weak, elderly man?"

The knight raised a palm in Finius' direction. "I would not put it that way," he said. "Though his visions came and went. I collected this information over a three month period and I believe he had his wits about himself."

The magician allowed his gaze to linger a moment longer before leaning forward and grasping his pen. "Anything else?"

Jacob focused on the mage, his stare intense. "Maligor instructed me to relay the need to create a death scroll."

Finius shook his head and furrowed his brow. "Death scroll? What's a death scroll?"

The knight paused. "The great mage said a strong wizard could create something to eradicate a whole race by uttering a single word." Sir Jacob kept his stare on Finius as he digested the information.

The magician scowled and cocked his head, unsure how to take the news he had just heard. "Eradicate a whole race? A genocide scroll?"

Sir Jacob nodded once. "Yes."

Finius threw his arms open wide and sat back. "Do you understand the ramifications of a genocide scroll?"

The knight drew a heavy sigh. "I do, but ..."

"No buts!" exclaimed Finius. "You're not being asked to conjure up such a parchment!" The magician folded his arms and glared at Sir Jacob. "What you ask for is too powerful."

"Can you do it?"

Finius took his eyes to a dark corner of the room and contemplated this man's request. Bringing his gaze back to the knight, he hissed, "Yes."

Sir Jacob's shoulder's dropped in relief, as if the wizard's answer had lifted a heavy burden. "Will you do it?"

"That's the real question here, isn't it?" said Finius, leaning forward and placing his interlocking hands on the table in front of himself. "Did Maligor relate to you what phrase should be written in the scroll?"

Sir Jacob did not blink when he said, "A single word, not a phrase."

"You're joking, right?" said Finius. "A single word?" Sir Jacob nodded once in affirmation. The mage pursed his lips in anger, taking his gaze once again to the same dark corner.

"This is reckless!" he shouted, swiveling his head and glaring at Sir Jacob. "One word leaves too much room for mistakes!"

"How so?" asked the knight.

Finius flashed a sly smile. "Let's say the scroll's reader is having a difficult time as of late and when he reads it decides that the answer to the eradication question is humanity? Hmm?" The wizard raised a closed hand, then splayed his fingers wide, saying, "Poof! All humans instantly disappear from the globe. How does that sound to you now?"

Sir Jacob understood the gravity of the question, his shoulders slumping from its weight. "You raise a good point; however this is Maligor's command and we should honor it."

Finius closed his eyes and shook his head. Opening them again, he said, "So be it, but I swear to you, this will come back to haunt us some day."

"We will be long gone before it does," said the brave knight. "I hope our descendants will have the restraint that you say they might lack."

The wizard continued with his notes, not bothering to look up. A minute later, he rested his pen on the table and leaned back in his chair. "I have everything I need to create the scrolls. What shall we name them and where shall they be hidden?"

Sir Jacob looked up in thought. "I have pondered this question for years but I think I know what we should do. First, they will be known as the Scrolls of Arcadia."

"Arcadia?" said the magician, creasing his brow. "Why there? We are nowhere near that city."

"Precisely," said the knight. "A bit of deception on our part. These scriptures are not to be found by the faint of heart."

Nodding, Finius said, "Fine. Where do you suggest we hide them?"

"We will take them to Rovere Moro where you will create a sanctuary to house them."

"I will?" asked the mage with concern in his voice. "What happened to we?"

"You are the wizard, are you not?" said Sir Jacob, arching his brows. "I'm sure you can dream something up."

Finius cocked his head once, concurring. "I'm assuming that you want these scrolls guarded."

"But of course," said the knight. "Finding these artifacts should not be an impossible task, however it should not be easy either."

"I have something in mind," said the magician, jotting down some notes.

"How long until we can put this plan into action?"

"What's the rush?" asked the wizard. "You've sat on this information for almost ten years!"

"I know, but now is the time," said the knight. "I will assist in any construction, just as I did with Maligor, when you are finished creating the scrolls."

Finius rolled up his parchments and placed them, along with his pen and ink, into his backpack. "Give me a few days, then I will seek you."

The two men held their gaze on each other for a few seconds before the hologram ended, its bluish hue disappearing from view and the campsite returning to normal.

* * *

"What the hell was that all about?" asked Pondle, his eyes still wide, mouth agape.

"You just witnessed the creation of the Ancient Scrolls of Arcadia," said Gelderand, still staring in the direction where the hologram had existed.

"The more pertinent question is, what have we learned from this?" said Thoragaard.

"I'm familiar with Sir Jacob, Maligor the Red's faithful knight," said Harrison. "But I never heard of Finius Boulware. Has anyone else?"

"That name does not ring a bell," said Gelderand. "Thoragaard, have you heard of him?"

The illusionist shook his head. "I have not, though I must believe he is an important part of our history's past, based on the scene we just witnessed."

"I am sure his importance will surface if and when the time is right," added Gelderand.

Harrison kept his gaze forward, deep in thought. "Brothers will unite the land," he said, his voice trailing.

Swinkle took a step toward his friend, resting a caring hand on his back. "I am convinced that these men spoke of you and Troy."

The young warrior maintained his forward stare. "That's my thinking, too." Harrison turned and faced his friends. "But my brother is gone now."

"Prophecies are a tricky thing, Harrison," said Thoragaard. "Many prognostications must be interpreted and not taken as absolute truth."

"He is right, Harrison," said Swinkle. "Troy's death might have caused a fracture in the prophecy, but it does not mean it is dead."

Tara took hold of the young warrior's hand, intertwining her fingers with his. "You're going to unite this land."

"How is that possible without my brother?" answered Harrison, shaking his head in disbelief.

The young maiden gazed into her lover's eyes. "With our help," she said, extending her other hand toward the people gathered around them. "All of us."

"Harrison," said Swinkle, "we cannot take the place of your brother, but our combined strengths will offset his loss."

The Aegean took a moment to read the many faces that stared back at him. With a smile, he said, "How can we not succeed? I'm humbled to be put in this position but honored to have all of you by my side."

"There is a long way to go," said Gelderand, still clutching the sacred parchments and flipping through the pages until he stopped at the one with remaining encrypted runes.

Holding the paper up for all to see, he said, "This page here is your Genocide Scroll."

Pondle took a step forward and addressed the group. "We could eradicate the Scynthians right now if we so choose."

"Wait one minute," said Harrison, thrusting his palm in the thief's direction. "This decision is too big for us to make. We must convene a session of the Legion of Knighthood and let them make the call."

Pondle pressed the issue. "We can stop all unnecessary deaths at the hands of our hated enemies right now. Right now!"

The young warrior understood Pondle's rationale. "Pondle, this is too big."

"Regardless of what either of you say," intervened Gelderand, "I will not read this scroll."

"Nor shall I," added Thoragaard.

Pondle pivoted, taking his incredulous stare between both magicians. "What? Why not?"

"Harrison is right," said Thoragaard. "This decision cannot be taken lightly. The land's leadership must decide."

"You also heard Sir Jacob mention large creatures," said Harrison. "Who knows what he was talking about. You never know, the Scynthians might be the least of our worries."

"I agree one hundred percent," said Swinkle. "I think everyone knows my feelings about this." The young cleric had further thoughts. "We are also forgetting another important thing," he continued, pointing in the direction of Murdock, Kymbra, and Marissa. "Our friends need help immediately. This discussion must wait."

Harrison nodded in agreement, albeit reluctantly. "Swinkle's right, we need to heal before we do anything rash." He then gestured toward the scriptures in Gelderand's hand. "Does it say anything about leaving this place?"

The magician, his brow creased in concentration, fumbled through the scrolls, alternating between each parchment, flipping them front side to back.

Shaking his head, he said, "There does not seem to be any escape route from Rovere Moro."

Harrison pursed his lips, agitated. "I can't believe that the scrolls' creators would leave us with no way of getting out of this forest."

"Harrison," said Thoragaard, "we *are* out of Troll's Hell." The illusionist pointed to the eerie mist, a mere fifty yards away.

The young warrior gazed in the direction of the fog. His shoulders wilted, realizing their dire predicament. "If there's no escape route, then we'll have to trek to the Dark Forest in our current condition."

Pondle raised his hand. "Not a good idea," he said. "Take a good look at us, at yourself. We're in no shape to venture."

"We can't stay here!" exclaimed the young warrior, his frustrations mounting. "How do we get to the elves in one piece?"

Swinkle approached his friend, placing a caring hand on his forearm. "Harrison, we must handle one crisis at a time. Let's not forget about the ramifications from the trolls' attacks."

"The seeds of disease are festering in all of you," said Gelderand, motioning with his hand in a slow arc that encompassed the group. "This must be stopped first."

Harrison shook his head. "How?"

An unlikely voice chimed in with her thoughts. "We must collect the troll's blood."

The young warrior swiveled in the young maiden's direction. "Collect their blood? Why?"

Tara thought before continuing. "I'm assuming that those beasts don't get sick from the very disease that they spread, right?" The lass looked at Gelderand, Swinkle, and Thoragaard for support. All three men exchanged hesitant glances, shrugging their shoulders.

Gelderand stepped forward. "That seems reasonable to conclude, but I am not sure how that helps us."

"Follow me on this," said Tara, narrowing her thought process. "If the trolls are immune to the diseases they inflict, then their blood has immunities to protect them." The young girl raised an eyebrow. "Which means if we can collect their blood, we can create a serum to cure their affliction on us."

The magician waved his palms at his niece. "Wait a minute," he said, shaking his head, too. "You are making a very valid point; however I think you are taking liberties with your hypothesis."

"She might be right," said Swinkle, agreeing with Tara. "The blood from those vile creatures just might be able to save our friends."

"Even if it could," said Gelderand, "how do we create such a concoction?"

"The elves would know," added Thoragaard, staring at Tara with an approving grin. "Good work, Tara."

The young maiden beamed. "I figured that we would need additional magic, something that the three of us could not perform to perfection. The elves are the natural choice."

"As I recall," said Swinkle, "Lady Brianna possessed considerable powers. And," he pivoted in Harrison's direction, "she took a special liking to you." All eyes focused on the young warrior.

Harrison flashed a sheepish smile. "I suppose so," he said before changing the subject. "If what Tara says is true, how do we get the troll's blood?"

"We must go back into Rovere Moro, slice one of these beasts, and collect its life force," said Thoragaard, matter-of-factly.

"Go back and collect it?" said Harrison, his eyebrows arched with surprise. "Who's going back in there? Other than Pondle and Adrith, all of our fighters are hurt!"

"I suggest that Pondle escorts us," the illusionist gestured toward the robed members of the group, "and we will return with the blood."

"Absolutely not!" exclaimed the young warrior, glaring at Tara in particular. "Those beasts will tear you all apart! Look what it did to us and we're seasoned fighters!"

"Gelderand and I saved you all," said Thoragaard, not wavering in spite of the Aegean's defiance. "You must learn to trust us, Harrison."

The young warrior shook his head. "I don't like being in this position. I'm the one who's supposed to lead us."

"You are incapacitated," said Gelderand. "We can more than pick up the slack."

Swinkle approached the young warrior. "You cannot do everything, Harrison. It is our turn to take the lead in this part of our journey."

The young warrior swiveled to each robed member of the group. Stopping at the young maiden, he pleaded, "Tara, please don't go! It's too dangerous!"

The young girl sidled up to Harrison, placing a hand on his chest. "Harrison, they need me and I'm not going to let them down. I'll take all necessary precautions."

The young warrior shook his head. "You saw those monsters, what they can do."

Tara nodded, trying to forget the images of death and destruction. "You never waiver when called upon. Now it's my turn."

"But Tara ..." Harrison realized that nothing he could say would stop his love from joining the small team.

In a soft voice, she said, "I need to do this." The young warrior, with nothing more to say, lowered his head, defeated.

"I'm going with them," said Pondle, breaking the couple's tension. "Adrith is more than capable to stand watch over the group."

Harrison shook his head again in an effort to collect his thoughts. "You're going to need all the tricks you've learned over the years to escape Troll's Hell."

"That we will," said the young cleric. "I suggest we leave soon."

"Take Lance with you," said Harrison. "If things get out of hand, send him back to alert us of your situation."

Swinkle nodded. "That is a good idea."

Harrison gazed over to Pondle. "Find Adrith and inform her of your latest mission. You can leave within the hour."

"We have enough daylight, for now," said the thief gazing upwards at the cloud shrouded sun. "I'll be back in a minute." Pondle left the group in search of the female scout keeping watch.

Harrison turned his attention to the robed members standing around him. "Do you have something to collect the troll's blood?"

"I have a few vials of holy water," said Swinkle. "I will use the liquid to subdue the trolls, then utilize the empty containers for their blood."

Harrison, though satisfied with the answers, still did not care for the actions that his friends needed to perform. "I still don't like this one bit."

Tara took hold of her love's arm, pulling him close to her. "Harrison, we can do this." She then motioned with her head in Murdock's direction. "Look at him. He needs our help now." Harrison gazed at the ranger, finding him sitting up, coughing, withdrawn.

"He's sick," continued Tara. "And so are Kymbra, Marissa … and you."

The young warrior fixed his eyes on Tara's. "I'm not sick yet."

"And I won't let you get ill, but we must leave now."

At that moment, Pondle returned to the group with Adrith by his side. "We're ready."

"Pondle's told me about your plans," said the female warrior. "I'll protect us while they're gone."

"I know you will, Adrith," said Harrison. The young warrior then addressed his friends. "Do what you must but don't take any unnecessary chances with those beasts. And, please, be careful."

"We will, Harrison," said Swinkle, placing a hand on his friend's shoulder. "We will be back before you know it."

The young warrior nodded, still with reservations of the upcoming operation. Gazing into Tara's eyes, he said, "Don't do anything foolish."

Tara gave Harrison a peck on the cheek. "We won't, you have my word."

The young warrior allowed his gaze to linger a second longer before saying to the others, "I'll let you work out your strategy." Turning to Adrith, he said, "Please help me to my injured partners."

Adrith approached Harrison and took his arm, Tara still clutching his other one. The young warrior gazed down at her angelic face, then gave her a passionate kiss.

Separating, he said, "Don't stay in Troll's Hell a second longer than you have to."

"You don't have to convince me about that," said Tara.

"Go," he said, with a grimace.

The young maiden let go of his arm and headed toward her uncle and the others. Harrison turned to Adrith. "Hold on one more second." The Aegean whistled for his canine companion, who scampered to his master.

"Stay by Tara's side," said Harrison.

The little dog looked over to Tara, then yapped once, "Yes!" Lance then darted next to the young girl.

Harrison, knowing that his part of the plan was over, said to Adrith, "Alright, let's go."

The female warrior threw Harrison's arm around her shoulder and helped him walk over to his injured friends, allowing the others to put the finishing touches on their most delicate of missions.

C H A P T E R 18

Ｏ

Pondle led the anxious group to the fringe of the
mysterious mist. The thief gazed at the aura, mystified that he
would venture into Rovere Moro under his own will for a second
time.

"Here we are again," he said, taking his gaze to the nervous
cloaked members of his party. "I'm assuming that we light torches
and enter the mist."

"Fire is our ally," said Thoragaard. The five people
removed torches from their packs, allowing Pondle to light them
one at a time.

With a soft glow illuminating the area, Pondle said, "I'll
lead the way, but I'm sure the trolls are starving and ready to
pounce. I wouldn't be surprised if they're on the other side of the
fog waiting for us as we speak."

Tara gazed into the haze and shuddered at the thought.
Lance sat by her side, feeding off her anxiety. "How are we going
to subdue the trolls in order to draw their blood?"

Pondle shrugged and brought his focus to Gelderand,
Swinkle, and Thoragaard. "The best thing we can hope for is to
capture one and incapacitate it enough to hold it down," said
Gelderand. Pointing at the thief, he continued, "From there, you
can slice the beast and make it bleed."

"I have prayers that can hold an evil presence," said
Swinkle, "but I cannot be overwhelmed or it will not work."

"How would you be overwhelmed with maniacal trolls running around?" said Pondle, rolling his eyes.

"You know what I mean," said the young cleric.

"Our torches will keep them at bay," said Thoragaard. "But will also attract them."

Pondle waited for more and when he realized the illusionist had finished his statement, he said, "That's it? Prayers and torches will keep these monsters at bay?"

"Our magic will work," said Gelderand. "It must."

"This is less of a plan and more of a suicide mission," said Pondle, shaking his head in disgust. "I'm not comfortable with this at all."

"I have to agree with him," said Tara, with a slight quiver in her voice. "Look what they did to Harrison and the rest."

"We all possess spells that can keep the beasts away from us," said Gelderand. "Thoragaard is an illusionist who can confuse the trolls, Swinkle has holy prayers to combat evil, and you," he said, pointing to Tara, "can create blinding flashes to impair the monsters' vision."

"We still have to capture one," added Pondle, realizing that the magician left out an important component of their return trip to Troll's Hell.

"Subdue, not capture," said Gelderand with conviction. "That makes all the matter in the world."

Pondle, though not thrilled with the answers he heard, nevertheless agreed with the robed men. "Let's get this over with, then," he said, removing a small sword from its sheath. "I'll lead us forward, but you all must be ready to perform your magic as soon as you spot the first troll."

"Agreed," said Gelderand, gazing at his counterparts for approval. Swinkle, Tara, and Thoragaard all responded with anxious nods. Satisfied, he said to the thief, "Whenever you are ready."

Pondle turned his attention to the thick fog, searching for any signs of life. He saw none but knew better than to trust his vision for he believed with all certainty that the trolls awaited them beyond the mist.

His torch outstretched in front of himself with one hand and his sword clutched in the other, he took a step forward and said, "Follow me and make sure we all stay together. If we get separated, we're dead."

One by one, each party member followed the thief into the eerie haze. Tara's heart pounded with every step she took. Lance journeyed by her side, keeping his master's promise. The fog began to dissipate only minutes into their trek, revealing the leafless forest once again.

Though not a tracker, even the young maiden discovered a myriad of footprints leading in every direction. To her horror, she also found bloodstained earth along with markings that suggested someone was dragged through the terrain. Harrison and the others, she thought to herself, trying to keep her fear in check.

Moments later, Pondle held his sword toward the group, gesturing for them to halt their procession, while maintaining a forward stare. Tara squinted down the dark path. Something loomed in the distance. Lance sensed it too, growling under his breath and moving closer to the young maiden.

"What's out there, Lance?" asked Tara with concern in her voice. The canine's answer came in the form of a continuous growl.

"Something's moving up ahead," said Pondle, keeping his eye locked on the target.

Thoragaard stepped to the forefront, maneuvering next to the thief. "I shall handle this."

Pondle, his brow creased with confusion, asked "What are you planning to do?"

"Provide a distraction," said the illusionist as he waved his hands in front of himself. Seconds later, a small orange, sphere-like object formed before him, hovering four feet above the ground. He then raised his arms to chest level with his palms parallel to the ground before thrusting them hard downward in a pushing motion.

The sphere slammed into the forest's floor without a sound, creating an orangey river that left Thoragaard's position and flowed toward the image in the distance. As it did, fiery tributaries jutted from the main artery and poured into the surrounding landscape, illuminating the otherwise dark terrain with a series of jagged glowing streams. From the river-like phenomenon, smoke rose into the air and, along with it, the appearance of orange flashes that sparked in all directions. The cloud thickened and began to cover more ground, leaving the pathway and entering the surrounding woods. Flames started to erupt from the smoldering haze, casting the illusion of a forest fire.

Pondle watched with wide eyes. "How are we going to trap one of those trolls? We can't walk through fire!"

Thoragaard smirked. "Apparently my trick is already working."

The thief shook his head. "Stop speaking in riddles! We need to address this situation now!"

Thoragaard cocked his head. "The fire is not real," he said, "however it is a very convincing rendition of an inferno."

Pondle watched the blaze engulf the area. However, he did not feel the flame's intensity, something that he knew he should perceive by now. "You're right! There's no heat!"

"Let us surprise these beasts before they also figure that out."

The thief waved the group forward, rounding up Swinkle, Gelderand, and Tara. "Everyone, follow me and be sure to stay close together." Focusing on Swinkle in particular, he added, "I need you to hold down one of the trolls."

Swinkle's eyes widened in surprise. "Me? I'm not strong enough!"

"All I need you to do is incapacitate the creature so that it won't attack me," said Pondle. "Can you do that?"

The young cleric thought for a split second before a wide smile graced his face. "I know just the thing."

"Good," said the thief, raising his eyes to the rest of the group. "Follow me!" The anxious band of adventurers set forth from their position and followed the main flaming vein.

Pondle clenched both his torch and sword tight, knowing each would be used in his next battle. Though Thoragaard's spell interfered with his infravision, he used his other senses to locate his enemy. Moans and howls emanated directly in front of him, signaling that the beasts loomed near.

Peering down, the thief found troll markings leading in all directions. "Fresh tracks," he said to no one in particular. Then, to his surprise, he tripped over a large object.

Pondle dropped his torch, but quickly scurried to his feet and regained his light source. Bringing the flame to ground level to see better, he made a surprising discovery.

"It's a dead troll," said the thief, waving the torch back and forth over the corpse to examine it better. Furrowing his brow, he said, "If I didn't know better, I'd say that another troll had killed this one."

"How do you know?" asked Swinkle, his eyes darting in every direction, waiting for the creatures to spring forth from the darkness.

Pondle used his torch to point at gashes across the troll's midsection. "Claw marks," he said, then added, "and chunks of flesh torn from the body."

"They ripped the meat right off the bones?" asked Tara, shocked.

"No, it was bitten off," said Pondle. "These beasts are so hungry that they're resorting to cannibalism."

"And they're all around us," said Tara, her voice quivering as she scanned the area for the monsters that she knew lurked just beyond her sight.

Pondle brought his focus back to the carcass that lay on the earth. "Can we extract blood from this one? If so, we can draw it and get out of here in no time."

"I'm afraid not," said Gelderand. "The being must be alive in order to create a viable serum."

The thief shook his head in disgust. "Figures." Bringing his gaze to the ever growing imaginary blaze, he said, "Let's find one of the trolls fast."

Pondle forged forward, wading through the heatless orange embers and increasing smoky fog. Further ahead he heard the sounds of creatures scampering away, trying to flee from the area. Having traversed the terrain a short time ago, he knew that the temple sat a little way ahead of them and that it was the most logical destination for the menacing beasts.

Quickening his pace, Pondle urged the others forward. Fifty yards further down the pathway, the terrain opened up, revealing the familiar temple structure. Thoragaard's illusion continued forward with the river of flames leading to the building.

Pondle raised a hand to the group, signaling for them to stop. The thief scanned the area, sensing something amiss. Where are these beasts, he lamented to himself.

Tara, sensing his apprehension, asked, "What's wrong?"

"Where are they?" said Pondle, continuing with his examination of the area.

"I was thinking the same thing," added Swinkle.

"It appears we must enter the temple again," said Gelderand. "The trolls must have trekked back there after we left."

Pondle heard the comments but something gnawed at his stomach. His brain agreed with the magician, however his instincts told him otherwise.

"Everyone, stay here," said the thief. "I'm going to investigate the area further."

"Harrison instructed us to stay together," said Swinkle. "I do not think that it's wise to separate now."

"Harrison's not here," said Pondle. "He'd say the same thing as me. I'm going to investigate while you all remain here."

Tara gazed down at Lance. "Go with him," she said to the little dog. Lance cocked his head, unsure of the lass's command. Tara repeatedly pointed toward the thief, saying, "Go with Pondle."

Lance followed her finger, stopping when his line of sight reached the thief. The canine gazed back at Tara and whimpered.

"I know what Harrison told you," said Tara, "but I'm telling you to go with Pondle now." She thrust her finger toward the thief. "Go!" Lance let out a huff before obeying the girl's command.

Pondle, still surveying the landscape, noticed the small dog by his side. With a wry smile, he said, "Me and you again, Lance." The thief then turned his attention to the others. "We're going into the temple. Stay low and be ready for anything."

The halfling waved Lance forward and the two began their move to the building. Pondle clutched his torch and thrust it in front of himself, not to see but to burn any unlucky troll that attempted to make a meal out of him. The temple loomed up ahead. To his left, the thief heard rustling leaves in the underbrush.

Lance let out a whimper, staring in the same direction as Pondle. The thief maneuvered his torch in the sound's vicinity. "Stay right by my side, Lance."

Twenty steps more and the two arrived at the entrance of the structure. Pondle planted his back on a column near the entryway, then peeked around the pillar. His initial examination took his breath away. Littered on the floor lay mangled corpses, troll body parts, and gallons of blood.

"What happened here, Lance?" asked the thief, knowing the dog would not answer.

Waving his sword-wielding hand, he gestured for Lance to follow him into the edifice. As before, the large basin sat in the middle of the temple, but this time it remained empty. A few steps away a bloodied arm rested harmlessly on the ground. Pondle took care in approaching it, knowing full well that trolls regenerate and the limb might spring to life at a second's notice.

Lance cocked his own little head, unsure of what lay before him. He took two small steps to it, then sniffed the limb. It did not move. Pondle, finding the lack of movement disturbing, brought his torch to the severed arm, allowing its heat to radiate over the appendage. Then, it started to burn.

Pondle watched the wrinkled skin begin to blister, the acrid stench of burning flesh wafting over him. The limb suddenly sprung to life and jumped from the flooring, using sharp claws to dig into Pondle's flesh, gripping the thief's leg.

Lance teleported backward to avoid the attack, while the thief shrieked more in surprise than pain. Pondle plunged his torch onto the troll's exposed arm, keeping it on the skin and allowing it to catch fire and burn. Seconds later the clawed hand released its grip and dropped to the ground where it had seizures before the flames consumed it completely, rendering it dead.

Pondle took his hand to his leg, finding it bleeding, staining his fingers with his own blood. The thief scowled. Add me to the list of potential disease victims, he thought.

Lance scurried to the halfling's side, finding the threat of danger gone. Pondle gazed down at the dog, saying, "They're not all completely dead, boy. Let's be more careful."

Pondle, his senses on full alert, continued deeper into the temple, arriving at the empty basin. Peering over its side, he found remnants of the red liquid at the bottom of the container that had housed the troll's life force. However, he found no trace of a living creature.

He brought his focus to the pedestals, but no monsters rested upon them. Bewildered, the thief shook his head, unsure what had happened to the beasts that ran roughshod throughout the forest, attacked so many of his friends, and rendered them unable to fight. As he contemplated the situation, a smoky fog began to enter the temple, bringing with it flashes of orange embers and heatless flames.

Thoragaard entered first followed by Tara, Swinkle, and Gelderand. Lance bolted to the young maiden's side, taking up a defensive posture with his tail straight in the air.

Pondle glared at the small team. "I told you to wait for me!"

"We heard you yell and decided to investigate," said the illusionist. Thoragaard gazed at the thief's bloody leg. "Are you hurt?"

"I'll survive," said Pondle. Panning the temple's interior, he said, "The trolls haven't returned to their perches."

"There are body parts everywhere," said Swinkle, taking his eyes all about the room, finding bits and pieces of the wretched beasts in all corners of the temple.

"Have you found any living creatures?" asked Gelderand, a hint of concern in his voice.

Pondle shook his head. "No."

Tara, gazing at the carnage as well, asked, "Can we draw blood from these parts?"

"We should be able to," said Pondle. "One of those severed limbs launched itself at me. That's what cut my leg."

"On the contrary, we cannot use them," said Gelderand, quashing the thief's hope. "We need a living, breathing troll."

"What?" exclaimed the thief. "Why?"

"A beating heart guarantees living, oxygen-rich blood flow," explained Gelderand. "The life force in these appendages are more dead than alive. We cannot take the chance of drawing tainted blood from these things."

"Well, I don't see any living trolls running around," said Pondle, spreading his arms wide. "Do you?"

"No, I do not," said the magician.

Swinkle had meandered over to the basin while the men discussed their predicament. Peering at the shallow puddles of red liquid, he said, pointing at the bottom of the well, "What if we used this?"

The others rushed to Swinkle's side, peeked over the edge of the container, and looked at the final remnants. "As I recall, the red liquid provided the stone creatures their life force," said the young cleric. "I think it acts as good as blood."

Thoragaard took a hand to his chin, caressing it while he thought. "You might be correct with your assumption, Swinkle. This liquid was indeed the key to them springing to life."

"Let's take some while we can," said Tara, anxiety in her voice. "I don't like staying here too long."

Thoragaard took his gaze to Gelderand, who thought for a moment before giving the illusionist a single nod. "Collect as much of the solution as you can. Quickly," said the mage.

Swinkle placed his backpack on the ground and fumbled for vials of holy water. Finding three, he removed two and left one in his pack. He then uncorked both of them and dumped the water on the ground, the liquid making a splashing sound as it struck the stone flooring.

After emptying the containers, the young cleric positioned himself next to the basin's wall and leaned over its side. The liquid lay in a shallow puddle in one of the corners, a little out of his reach.

Swinkle fell back, hopping to his feet once again. "The liquid is harder to get to than I thought," he said. "Can you two," he pointed to Gelderand and Thoragaard, "hold my legs as I lean deeper into the well?"

The older men obliged and positioned themselves on either side of the holy man. Swinkle then went about leaning over the container's wall once again. This time his feet lifted off the ground and flailed in the air, while the two mages held him in place, preventing him from crashing headfirst into the bottom of the basin.

Tara placed her hands on the well's siding and observed the young cleric coax the liquid toward the vial's opening. Pondle took in the scene as well, oblivious to the increasing fog that wafted into the temple, Thoragaard's illusion working to perfection. A hideous roar all but ruined the group's noble combined efforts to fill Swinkle's vials with the elusive liquid life force.

All eyes shifted from Swinkle's labors to the beast that strode toward them from between two columns. Pondle, the only true fighter in the group, took a split second to gauge their predicament. Clearly, this monster was the cause for all of the carnage, rationalized the thief.

The eight foot tall monster loomed a mere twenty feet away from the group, standing on the exact opposite side of the well. Meanwhile, Tara stood at the basin between the monster and the two wizards, who were holding Swinkle in a most vulnerable position. The troll roared again, showing its teeth and raising its clawed hands. Next, it took two steps toward the magicians.

"Hey!" yelled the thief, waving his torch from side to side, trying to gain the troll's full attention and distracting it from the non-fighters of the group. "Hey! Over here!"

The beast stared at Pondle and roared a second time, its shriek reverberating throughout the temple, shaking the people to their core. Gelderand and Thoragaard released their grip on the young cleric's legs, tumbling Swinkle into the container. The two then rushed in front of Tara and pushed her toward Pondle and away from the menacing monster. Lance leaped forward, zipping around the corner, confronting the troll, barking all the while.

The creature did not halt its forward progress. Rather it fixed its cold black eyes on Pondle's waving torch and proceeded to race around the well, toward the thief.

Pondle used his sword-wielding hand to signal to his friends to get behind him, which they did. He swallowed hard as the beast rounded the corner and rambled a few steps away. Before it could take a swipe at the distracting illuminous object, the troll felt jaws clamp onto its leg just above the ankle. Lance's teeth sunk into the monster's soft flesh, drawing fresh blood. The troll glared at the dog attached to its limb and, taking a swipe with its strong hand, smacked the canine, sending poor Lance careening into the basin's stone siding. The small dog whimpered and rolled into a ball next to the container's wall. He did not move.

The troll, rid of its annoyance, turned its full attention to Pondle once again. The thief held his ground, his torch the only thing between him and the oncoming monster. As the creature lunged toward Pondle, a bright flash lit the area, blinding the monster. The troll screeched and brought its hands to its eyes in a vain attempt to stop the light.

All eyes turned to the unlikely source of the luminary distraction. Tara, her eyes round and breathing coming in quick bursts, said, "Don't stare at me! Do something about that thing!"

Pondle heeded the young maiden's advice and planted his torch into the troll's midsection. Gelderand mumbled a spell to himself, then threw out his hands. The flames quadrupled in size and intensity, dropping the beast to its knees, howling in pain.

Swinkle, standing up from the relative safety of the basin, clasped his hands together and mumbled to himself. Throwing his hands in the troll's direction, he exclaimed, "Stay!"

The monster dropped to the stone flooring, unable to move, burning all the while. "Put those flames out!" yelled Swinkle. "We can't let it die!"

Pondle swiveled his head in the young cleric's direction. "What? This thing is about to tear us apart!"

"We need its blood!"

Swinkle hopped over the well's siding and rushed to the incapacitated creature. Removing water from his tankard, he spilled it over the troll's burning flesh, extinguishing the flames. He then fumbled for his last vial of holy water, thanking Pious that he had not emptied all of his bottles of the sacred liquid.

The holy man crouched down, bringing his head close to the hissing troll. As he maneuvered nearer, the monster tried to lunge at the young cleric. However, Swinkle's prayer held the beast in check. Instead, all it could muster was snapping its jaws in the young cleric's direction.

Knowing that his prayer proved successful, Swinkle slowly lowered his head in the beast's direction, staring into its black eyes. Uncorking the vial of holy water, he raised the bottle up, allowing the troll to see it clearly, then spilled a small amount of the liquid on the troll's chest. The water hit the monster's flesh and began to bubble as if it were acid, scorching the troll's midsection, and causing it to howl in pain.

Swinkle, his hand still raised and holding the holy water, stopped its painful flow. A few seconds later the troll stopped screeching in agony, realizing that the young cleric had ended its torture. The holy man maintained his stare, being sure that the troll locked eyes on him. When it did, Swinkle cocked his head and raised an eyebrow, tilting the vial to the point of spilling the water again. The troll tensed its body, waiting for more pain. It did not come.

The young cleric, with reasonable confidence that the troll understood its predicament, called to Pondle. "Bring a dagger and draw the blood. Now!"

The thief, still shocked at the turn of events, approached the troll, removing a blade from his belt. "I need vials."

Thoragaard, having retrieved the containers from the basin after figuring out Swinkle's impromptu plan, handed them to Pondle. "Here they are."

The thief accepted the bottles from Thoragaard, then went over to the incapacitated beast. Finding a bulging vein in the monster's arm, Pondle sliced its flesh and drew blood. The red liquid trickled down its limb and into the strategically placed vial. When that one was all but filled, Pondle took the second one and positioned it accordingly. Moments later, the thief corked the two blood-filled vials.

"Done!" he exclaimed.

"Everyone, slowly back up and leave the area," said Swinkle, never removing his stare from the troll.

"What about you?" asked Pondle with genuine concern.

"I'll be right behind you," he answered. "Go!"

Pondle gestured for the group to do as Swinkle commanded. The thief went over to Tara's side and collected Lance in his arms, the little dog dazed but alive. After the small group had backpedaled out of the temple, they began to run back down the pathway.

Swinkle, knowing that his friends were safe, allowed his stare to linger a few seconds longer on the monster. He then raised the vial up again, showing it to the beast. The troll shuddered. Swinkle took the cork and secured the vial, then slowly showcased it through the air, all the while allowing the troll to watch him place it in his backpack. When done with that task, he rose to a standing position. The beast never removed its glare from the young cleric.

Knowing that his prayer to hold the troll in place neared its end, Swinkle backpedaled away from the creature and, when he felt he had allowed enough separation between the troll and himself, he turned and ran out of the temple.

CHAPTER 19

Ο

The small group of adventurers waded through Thoragaard's fog, tripping on body parts, and doing their best to flee the temple area. Tara, running for her life, caught up to Pondle, the injured dog in his arms slowing his retreat.

"Is Swinkle going to be alright?" asked the young maiden between ragged breaths.

"I haven't heard any screams yet," he said, ducking below an overhanging branch. "I'll take that as a good sign."

The small cadre took another twenty steps before a hideous roar all but stopped them in their tracks. Tara glared toward the temple with wide eyes.

"Swinkle!" she screamed, halting her forward progress. Panning to the men in the group, she pleaded, "We must go back!"

Pondle did not hesitate, placing Lance on the ground and withdrawing his sword. "We never leave our friends behind!"

"Wait!" said Gelderand, stopping the thief from doing something irrational. "That creature will slaughter you without a sound plan!"

"What do you have in mind?" said Pondle, spreading his arms wide in exasperation. "Think! Quickly!"

"Lure the troll toward us," said Gelderand. "Thoragaard and I will roast him."

Pondle nodded. "I'm going after Swinkle. Be ready." The thief turned and left the group behind, scampering back to the structure.

Tara, on the verge of tears, said, "What do we do now?"

"Stay calm," said Gelderand, raising a palm to his niece. "First, take care of Lance." Turning to Thoragaard, he said, "Shall we get into position?"

The illusionist nodded, knowing exactly what Gelderand had in mind. Tara, unsure of her role, asked, "What about me?"

Gelderand took a step toward the young maiden. "Listen, and listen to me good," he started in a stern, direct tone. "We have only one chance at this."

* * *

Pondle, brandishing his sword before him, identified Swinkle's body outline. Before the young cleric ran into him, Pondle shouted, "Swinkle! It's me!"

Swinkle slowed his pace, squinting into the ensuing darkness, searching for the thief. "Pondle, it's coming!"

The halfling retrieved a torch from his pack, lit it, and handed it to Swinkle. The young cleric accepted the light source with wide eyes. "You just alerted that beast to our position!"

"Then I suggest we run," said the thief, grabbing Swinkle by his forearm and jerking him in the other direction. A thunderous roar erupted from the temple, some two hundred feet from their position. "Now!"

The two men turned and ran in the opposite direction as fast as their legs would take them.

* * *

"I heard it again!" lamented Tara, visions of the troll dismembering her friends racing though her mind.

"Maintain your position, Tara," said Thoragaard in his monotone voice. "You are our first line of defense."

The young maiden nodded nervously, trying to keep her fears at bay. Lance, still dazed from whacking his head on the stone basin, lay on the ground a few feet from her. Tara now stood in the middle of the muddy pathway with Gelderand and Thoragaard flanked on either side of her, slightly off the road.

253

Stay on task, stay on task, she repeated to herself, knowing their plan would fail if she faltered. The girl closed her eyes tight, ushering out negative thoughts while reciting the words to her spell over and over in her mind. I must not fail!

Tara opened her eyes and found a small fiery object bobbing in the distance, heading in her direction. Another roar erupted, echoing throughout the dank forest. Trembling, the young maiden focused on the temple, finding a large, shadowy figure rushing out of the structure.

"Swinkle and Pondle," she said under her breath. "Please, hurry!"

* * *

Pondle knew that Swinkle heard the bellow as well, thus the reason why he raced past the thief. Utilizing his infravision, Pondle recognized the curves of a woman standing in the distance, awaiting their return. Tara? Thunderous steps advanced from behind, the thief knowing full well what chased them without needing to look back.

His mind racing with battle tactics, Pondle did the best he could to pan the immediate area, though the jostling from sprinting hindered his vision. Where are Gelderand and Thoragaard, he lamented to himself, not finding either magician in his field of vision. Crunching sticks and heavy footsteps broke him from his trance.

Pondle peeked over his shoulder, finding the hideous beast a mere twenty steps behind him and closing fast. Taking his focus to the forefront again, he found the young maiden holding firm in her position.

The blinding light surprised everyone in the pathway, including Swinkle and Pondle. Both humans stumbled, blinded by Tara's spell, but managed to maintain their footing.

Pondle, his sight compromised, knew to maneuver off the trail and hoped that Swinkle thought to do the same. Next, he heard clawed feet making a sudden halt, then the unmistakable roar of an infuriated beast that had lost its sight. Even though he could not see, his eyes registered the change in luminosity as three glowing orbs whooshed by his position and struck their target.

Explosions rocked the area. Pondle, still trying to gather his bearings, thought he heard the objects hit a soft, fleshy target, then the unmistakable sound of dismembered body parts thudding to the ground. The smell of charred flesh began to permeate the area.

Pondle called out into the darkness, sensing that their adversary had sustained a mortal injury. "Swinkle! Can you hear me?"

"Yes," said the young cleric in a shallow voice, trying his best to conceal his position. "I'm over here!"

Pondle homed in on the voice, figuring that he had exited the pathway on the opposite side. "Stay where you are and don't move."

Swinkle remained motionless and quiet, signaling to Pondle that he had heeded his command. The thief rose from the ground but shuffling sounds close to his position forced him to stop in his tracks. Before he could raise his blade in a defensive posture, he felt something grasp his forearm, forcing his weapon downward in a controlled movement.

"Pondle, it is me, Thoragaard," came the familiar voice.

The thief let out a sigh of relief. "Am I glad to see you!"

"See?" said the illusionist, his monotone voice thick with sarcasm. "I believe you mean to say that you are glad to hear me."

"Indeed!" exclaimed the thief. Pondle's mood turned dour, recalling their predicament mere seconds ago. "Is the troll incapacitated?"

"Obliterated," said Thoragaard. "And no longer a threat." Pulling the thief gently into the road, he continued, "Let us gather Swinkle."

The mage guided Pondle across the trail and headed for the cowering holy man. Swinkle, oblivious to the fact that he had crouched down and hid behind nothing more than a shrub, sensed their presence.

"Pondle?" he called out. "Is that you?"

"It is," said the thief. "Thoragaard's with us."

"I shall escort you both back to our position," said the illusionist, grabbing the young man's outstretched hand, lifting him up. "You did good work back there, Swinkle."

The young cleric flashed a sheepish smile. "I only did what had to be done."

"Be that as it may, we now have the necessary ingredients to save our friends," said Thoragaard.

The illusionist bent his arms out at the elbows. "Both of you, hook your arms around mine and we will walk up the path together." Swinkle and Pondle did as commanded and the three men started their trek back to Tara and Gelderand's location.

* * *

Tara saw the three men approaching. "They're safe!" she exclaimed in her uncle's direction.

The young maiden had watched in horror as the magicians' spells incinerated the beast that had haunted them from the temple. However, she could not determine with any certainty if their magic had killed their friends by mistake due to the combination of the fireball's speed and its majestic explosion.

Tara rushed toward Thoragaard, taking Swinkle's arm, assisting him. The illusionist maintained his grip on Pondle, leading him to a safe patch of land as well.

"Are you both alright?" asked the nervous lass, giving the two a quick visual examination, searching for obvious injuries.

"Aside from our inability to see, I feel we fared well," said Swinkle, outstretching his arms in search of the ground. Finding dirt at last, he planted himself down. Pondle, with Thoragaard's assistance, did likewise.

"How long before our sight comes back?" asked the thief, not one to enjoy any vulnerabilities while in a hostile environment.

"No more than ten minutes," said another familiar voice, followed by the sound of scampering feet. "Tara's spell was key to our whole operation."

Pondle instinctively swiveled in the direction of Gelderand's voice. As he did, Lance jumped into the thief's lap and licked his face. Pushing the dog away, he said, "Nice to see you too, Lance!"

"Tara," called Swinkle, searching for the young maiden. The girl placed a soft hand on his shoulder. Looking in what he believed was her direction, the young cleric continued, "You did a great job today and you will be commended."

Tara blushed. "I'm still shaking!" she said, letting out a nervous laugh. "Thank you."

"Gelderand," said Pondle, "we should leave right away. I find it hard to believe that one troll is all that remains from the chaos we witnessed a short time ago."

"I could not agree more," said the mage, gripping Pondle's bicep, encouraging him back to his feet. "We will be your eyes for now. I assume that all we need to do is follow this path out of Rovere Moro?"

"Yes," said the thief. "Straight as an arrow."

The young maiden helped Swinkle rise from his seat on the ground as well. "I'll handle Swinkle." The young man smiled and nodded in the girl's direction.

"Then it is time to move," said Thoragaard. "Come, Lance, we shall lead the way."

The little dog, recognizing his name, obeyed the illusionist's gesture to move forward. The precious cargo of troll's blood secured, the small group began their trek out of Rovere Moro for what they hoped would be the last time.

CHAPTER 20

Ω

Harrison thought he heard howls and screams in the distance. Adrith, standing watch over the injured party members, recognized her leader's apprehension.

"I'm sure they know what they're doing," said the female warrior, never taking her stare away from the mystical fog.

The young warrior maintained his glare on the mist. "I wouldn't be too sure of that." He planted a hand on the ground in an effort to lift himself from the forest's floor. "Please help me get up."

"You really should rest, you know," said the green-eyed woman, assisting him to his feet anyway.

"Everybody keeps telling me that," Harrison muttered under his breath as he placed his arm around the warrior's shoulder. The smaller woman did her best to hold the Aegean upright.

Harrison nodded to the pathway that led to Troll's Hell. "Let's go over there."

Adrith panned to the others, finding them incapacitated on the ground. "We shouldn't leave them."

The young warrior gazed over his shoulder. "They'll be fine. We'll be right over there." Harrison motioned to the trail that lay only a few yards away.

"It's your call," said the warrior, who helped guide the Aegean away from their encampment to get a better look down the pathway.

From Harrison's vantage point, aside from the fog that loomed a short distance ahead of them, all that he could see were the bare trees that lined the road, their leafless limbs entangling above the surface.

The young warrior focused on the mysterious haze, searching for any sign of movement. Harrison's eyes widened.

"Look!" he exclaimed, pointing into the distance. "Is that a light?"

Adrith stared in the same direction, also spotting a soft, bobbing glow emanating from the forest's depths. "I see it!"

"Trolls don't carry torches!" said Harrison. "Hurry, let's get down there!"

The small female did her best to trudge both of them down the trail and closer to the light source. Halfway to their destination, a small group of figures exited the fog. A little animal darted toward them as well.

"Lance!" exclaimed Harrison as his canine friend sprinted to his master, jumping on his legs, yipping with delight.

Gazing down at the dog, he asked, "Where is everybody?"

Lance stopped his welcoming act and pivoted toward the shuffling figures. By this time, a second set of wanderers came into focus. The little dog rushed to the people, then turned and dashed back to Harrison and Adrith.

"It's them!" said Adrith, a wide smile gracing her face. "They've all returned!"

Harrison squinted, sensing something amiss. "Why does it look like they're assisting people?" The young warrior's mind churned, wondering if something had happened to Tara.

"Let's go find out," said Adrith, pressing forward, encouraging the young warrior to move with her. Lance darted back and forth, unable to contain his excitement at the inevitable reunion.

Willing himself forward, Harrison, with Adrith's assistance, finally reached the small group of adventurers. The young warrior removed his arm from the female fighter's shoulder and balanced on one leg. At the same time, Adrith hurried to Tara's side and gently took Swinkle's arm, guiding him while he remained blind.

Tara, confident in Adrith's ability to assist the young cleric, rushed to Harrison's side and maneuvered her body next to his, allowing him to place his arm over her shoulder for support. After the young warrior regained solid footing, he leaned over and planted a hard kiss on her forehead.

"I worried every second you were away," said Harrison.

"Now you know how it feels," said Tara with a smirk. "Come on, we have lots of work to do."

The young maiden moved her weight forward, encouraging Harrison to follow. The young warrior grinned, finding the sudden role reversal amusing.

"That we do," he said. Gazing back at his other friends, he found Swinkle and Pondle more than a bit incapacitated. "What happened to them?"

"I blinded them," said Tara, matter-of-factly. "It was either that or have the troll kill us all."

Harrison arched his eyebrows in surprise. "Did you get the monster's blood?"

"Yes, we did," said Tara, pressing onward toward their encampment. Moments later, all party members congregated around the makeshift campsite.

Adrith and Gelderand assisted Swinkle and Pondle, finding them seats on the forest's floor. Next to them, Murdock, Kymbra, and Marissa nursed their broken bodies. Fallyn sat up, almost back to full strength after her shape shifting adventures.

"Swinkle, Pondle, how are you two doing?" asked Harrison.

"I am fine," said the young cleric. "Tara did a wonderful job today."

"I'm starting to see hazy shapes," added Pondle. "Tara did great but we need to leave this place soon."

The young warrior panned to the injured fighters. "They're still in no shape to travel." Harrison also contemplated his own injuries, coming to grips with how badly the attacking trolls had compromised their group.

"Harrison, we're sitting ducks," said Pondle. Alluding to the incapacitated group members, he asked, "When was the last time they even moved around?"

The Aegean gazed at his hurt friends before answering. He knew the seriousness of their injuries and the toll trekking through a hostile forest could have. They did not have the luxury of time.

"A few hours ago," said the young warrior. "We can't leave until daybreak anyway."

"I can see the outline of my hand," said Pondle, waving it in front of his face. "I'll be ready to venture in the morning."

"How do you propose we get them travel ready?" asked Gelderand. "Harrison, they are badly hurt. They can't even walk."

"We must think of something!" said the young warrior with a huff. "The longer we stay here, the better the chance that someone with bad intentions comes along."

"And let us not forget the contamination potential," added Thoragaard. "Reaching the elves is paramount."

"Again," said Gelderand, this time posing his question to the whole group. "What do you propose?"

Harrison pondered the question again. The elves resided in the depths of the Dark Forest, quite a distance from their current location. Trekking there with healthy bodies would take a week, maybe more, he knew. In their current condition, the young warrior speculated a minimum of two weeks, which depended upon no Scynthian entanglements. Then came the prospect of disease rendered by the trolls. No one knew how fast or to what extent the illness would spread, but all concurred that symptoms would start showing sooner rather than later.

Harrison stared at the magician with a blank expression. "I honestly don't know."

Gelderand drew a heavy sigh. "We should take the night to think through scenarios." Panning the group, he added, "All of us."

The young warrior nodded. "Agreed." Making a mental inventory of the group's condition, he added, "Let's get some rest tonight so that we can start our new journey tomorrow."

"I'll be ready for guard rotation soon," said Pondle. "My sight's returning."

"Pondle, I can offer sentry assistance as well," said Fallyn. "I'm feeling much better."

The thief scrunched his brow in surprise. "That's nice of you to offer but you don't wield a weapon. I'd have my concerns about you walking the campsite's perimeter unarmed."

Fallyn smirked. "I said assist in guard duties. You'll see."

Pondle shrugged. "Alright by me. The more eyes the better."

"And I will go about laying my hands on everyone shortly as well," said Swinkle.

"Gelderand and I will assist you, Swinkle," said Thoragaard. "Though our healing powers are much less than yours." The young cleric nodded in agreement.

"I'll return to my post," said Adrith, removing her short sword from its hilt. "Pondle, you can relieve me when you're ready." The female warrior left the campfire and ventured to her sentry position.

"I'll watch over everyone individually," said Tara to Harrison. "I don't have the powers to heal, but I can at least lend a hand."

"You're stronger than you know," said Harrison, leaning over and kissing her on the cheek. "I'll be back to normal in no time."

Tara gazed at her mate. "Maybe your leg," she started, biting her lower lip. "But what about the troll infection?"

Harrison pursed his lips before answering. "One thing at a time. I need to be physically ready to fight at a moment's notice." Tara nodded and looked away, pushing future disease-riddled atrocities out of her mind for the time being.

"Let's eat and ready ourselves for the evening," said Tara, changing the subject. "Like you said, you need to get your strength back."

The young maiden, along with the others, then went about eating, resting, and thinking about ways to alleviate their predicament for the remainder of the evening.

CHAPTER 21

⌀

Lance romped through the terrain away from the camp, helping Pondle keep watch over his master and the others. The pale moonlight offered little to aid his sight, but his sense of smell matched no others. The dog scratched at something on the ground, giving it a good sniff before determining the plant was inedible. A louder than usual hoot startled him.

The little dog's ears pricked up and he swiveled in the direction of the sound. Another hoot and the canine pinpointed his target. High above him, an owl rested on a thick branch. The bird's large, round eyes stared at the dog from its perch.

Lance whimpered, doing his best to refrain from barking. The owl bobbed its head and hooted again. The small dog kept its stare on the bird of prey, watching its every move. The owl, satisfied with its examination of the canine lookout, lurched from the branch and flew deeper into the forest and out of Lance's sight.

The watchdog focused into the distance and, with the threat gone, scurried back to the campsite, finding the humans asleep. Lance sought his master, finding his body next to Tara's, and curled up against the young couple. Harrison felt the dog sidle up to him and plopped his arm over Lance while still asleep. The canine lowered his head to the ground and waited for the intruder's return.

* * *

Shards of sunlight woke Harrison from a sound sleep. Tara lay snuggled against him in an effort to stay warm. The young warrior pulled her close, kissing her blonde head. The girl wiggled closer to the Aegean, not ready to awaken.

Harrison, his leg and forearm aching still, maneuvered ever so slowly away from the young maiden, not wanting to disturb her slumber. Tara clutched her blanket tighter in an effort to maintain her warmth.

The young warrior, free from his partner, gazed about the campsite. His injured friends remained sleeping, along with Pondle and Swinkle. He did not see Adrith or Fallyn and assumed that they had left for their lookout posts. However, he found Gelderand and Thoragaard huddled together, peering at a book in the magician's hand. Being careful not to put too much pressure on his leg, the young warrior lumbered over to the mages.

Gelderand lifted his eyes from the scripture when he saw Harrison approach. "Good morning, son. How do you feel?"

"Sore," said the young warrior. "My wounds are kind of itching and I have a funny feeling in my mouth."

The magician crinkled his brow. "What kind of funny feeling?"

Harrison cocked his head in thought. "It's hard to describe. I'd say it feels like biting down on a chewy ball, like there's something in my mouth."

Gelderand and Thoragaard exchanged anxious glances. "It is happening already," said the illusionist to the mage.

Harrison furrowed his brow in concern. "What's already happening?"

"You are exhibiting symptoms," said Gelderand, his face drawn at the revelation. "We had hoped that any indications of disease would not show themselves so soon."

Harrison's eyes widen in understanding. "You think this is from the trolls?" Both wizards nodded in unison.

"That we do," said Gelderand. "That is why we are studying our spell books."

The young warrior took a vested interest in the mage's statement. Maneuvering next to the older men, Harrison took a seat beside Gelderand and peered over his shoulder at the book's text.

"What are you looking for?" he asked.

Gelderand glanced at the young man who sat uncomfortably close, then said as he looked at the open page, "Um, something that can counteract vicious inflictions."

Harrison scanned the text, seeing titles such as "A Frog's Remedy" and "Snake Venom Stew." Brow creased, he pointed to the writings and asked, "What kind of spells are these?"

Gelderand pursed his lips before answering. After a deep sigh, he said, "We are looking for anything that can alleviate your pain as well as to slow down the acceleration of the illness that festers inside you and the others."

"Only slow down," said Harrison, recognizing that the older man did not use the word cure in his statement.

"Until we meet with the elves," said Thoragaard, adding to the conversation. "They have immunities we humans do not possess."

Harrison's pulse quickened. "How long do we have? And what if we're left untreated."

Gelderand and Thoragaard exchanged glances again, with the illusionist shrugging. "We do not know the answer to either question," said Thoragaard.

The young warrior looked to the heavens in thought. "The Dark Forest is a ten-day hike under normal circumstances," he started. "With all the injuries …" Harrison stopped and panned to his incapacitated friends, shaking his head in disgust.

"We must venture onward," said Thoragaard.

"Let's gather everyone together," said Harrison, feeling the time was overdue for a group conference. "Now. Awaken those asleep."

Gelderand closed his spell book and, along with Thoragaard, rose to his feet to commence with his leader's task. Harrison shuffled his injured self to the center of the encampment and took a seat next to the extinguished fire pit.

Mumbles and groans permeated the camp as the magicians gathered the adventurers. Lance bounded to his master's side while Tara approached the young warrior, yawning as she sat next to him. Snuggling her head into his chest, she asked, "What's so important?"

Harrison panned the group, watching his friends make themselves comfortable around their leader. "Everything."

A moment later, the small group of adventurers sat facing the young warrior, eager to hear what he had to say. Harrison remained seated, unable to stand due to his injury.

"As you can see," started Harrison, making a wide arc with his hand, "we can't trek through the forest in our current condition. I can barely stand without shooting pains. I'm sure that you're all hurting as well."

"What gave you that impression?" said Murdock, sarcasm thick in his voice. After coughing twice, he said, "We can't stay here."

"I know," said Harrison, nodding. "I'm here to lay out our options." All eyes remained fixed on the young warrior. "Gelderand and Thoragaard have informed me that everyone that the trolls bit or gouged are infected with some kind of disease. My wounds itch and I don't feel quite right."

"My whole body hurts," mumbled Kymbra, her wounds deep. "And I itch, too. I can barely move."

"My shoulder's a mess," said Marissa. "I can still feel that monster's jaws clamping down on me." The female warrior took a hand to her shoulder, lightly touching her wound.

"We need the elves' help," said Harrison. "But we can't get to them like this."

Pondle waited for his leader to finish his statement, then said, "The elves live in the Dark Forest. I could trek there myself and ask them for help."

Harrison focused on his friend. "That's noble of you, Pondle, but we need you with us." The young warrior continued.

"Gelderand and Thoragaard," he said, pointing in the mages' direction, "are working on slowing down the onset of disease. They'll continue with that."

"That's all fine and dandy," said Murdock, "but that keeps us here."

"I'm not finished," said Harrison. "Pondle, can you and Adrith construct some kind of stretcher, something that we can use to drag the injured members of the group?"

Pondle arched his eyebrows and said, "I have a small axe, twine, and there are plenty of trees, but …" The thief shook his head, his voice trailing off.

"Can you do it?" asked Harrison again.

Pondle shrugged. "I suppose, but it won't be a work of art."

"We're not looking for quality, just something that we can use to transport Murdock, Kymbra, and Marissa."

"Leave us here," said Murdock. "We'll be a burden to the rest of the group."

Harrison glared at the ranger. "Forget about it! All of you are part of our team and we won't leave anyone behind."

"We can't fight, we can't travel, and we'll slow everyone down," said Murdock. "You're better off leaving without us."

"You're right, we are," said the young warrior. "But that's not going to happen, so let's just change the subject and continue with our plan."

"Which is?" Murdock knew before he even spoke that Harrison would not grant his request.

"They," said the young warrior, pointing at the uninjured members of the group, starting with Swinkle and arcing to Pondle, "will drag you through the terrain."

Murdock, Kymbra, and Marissa all turned to their friends with wide eyes and furrowed brows. "Seriously?" said Murdock, exasperated. "Do you know how long it's going to take dragging us through the forest?"

"A very long time," said Harrison, nodding. "That's why Gelderand and Thoragaard have spent the evening trying to figure out how to slow down the onset of disease."

"*Disease*?" said the ranger with emphasis. "What are you talking about?"

Gelderand pivoted in his seat to address Murdock, Kymbra, and Marissa. "The trolls bit and clawed you quite badly and their filth-ridden attacks have certainly contaminated you." The magician paused, allowing the fighters to digest the new information.

"Thoragaard and I have no doubt that you all will develop some sort of infection," continued the mage, "and the elves are the only ones who can help us combat that."

Lance, who had laid by his master's feet, raised his head and looked beyond the campsite. The little dog rose to his feet and bounded over to the camp's perimeter. Harrison watched his furry friend depart but paid him no attention, keeping his focus on the ongoing conversation.

"When will the disease begin to spread?" asked Murdock with concern in his voice.

"It already has," said Harrison before Gelderand could speak again. "My wounds are itchy and the inside of my mouth feels funny."

"I feel the same way," added Kymbra, pushing her tongue against the roof of her mouth, then swallowing. "I can't pinpoint the feeling, though."

"So do I," said Marissa. "My shoulder's burning and I'm trying not to scratch it."

Murdock absorbed the information from the injured fighters. "I thought it was only me," he said, making a mental examination of his ailments. He then opened his mouth and moved his jaw from side to side. "My mouth feels ... like I'm chewing on something that's not there."

"Yes!" exclaimed Harrison. "That's exactly how I described it to Gelderand!"

"What happens next?" asked the ranger in Gelderand's direction. The mage lifted his palms to the sky and shook his head.

Harrison started to speak but stopped when he heard Lance growling. Seconds later, the little dog barked at a feverish clip, herding a smaller animal out of the underbrush.

The young warrior squinted, trying to get a better fix on the unraveling situation. Pondle grabbed his sword and rose from his seat, taking two steps toward Lance's position. As he did, a rabbit with large green eyes hopped from the forest scrub, entering the campsite.

Thoragaard did not let the peculiar turn of events go unnoticed. Rising from his seat on the ground, he said, "Everyone stay where they are!"

Murdock glared at the illusionist. "What are you afraid of? A bunny?" The ranger peered at the rodent, finding its nose twitching, staring at the humans.

The magician, avoiding eye contact with the ranger, said, "That's no bunny."

"Sure looks like one to me," said Murdock, shaking his head. Meanwhile, Lance continued to bark at the rabbit, who disregarded the dog's antics.

Thoragaard stared at the intruder. "Fallyn!"

Harrison, as with everyone else, alternated his glances from Thoragaard to the furry creature, unsure of the transpiring events. After several uncomfortable seconds, the harmless rabbit morphed into a radiant, red-headed woman, with beautiful green eyes and cloak.

"I hope I didn't startle you," said Fallyn to the surprise of everyone in the group. "I was just patrolling the area."

Harrison's eyes opened wide after recognizing the trespasser. "We didn't expect you to reappear as a rabbit."

"It's better to blend into the background than to be easily spotted," said Fallyn. "I'm just doing my part to help the group."

The young warrior shuffled in his seat, leaning forward. "Thank you. Your efforts are appreciated, especially with most of us incapacitated." Harrison extended his hand. "Take a seat and join us." The woman obliged, finding a place to sit with the rest of the adventurers.

Thoragaard stared at the red-headed woman, his brain churning in thought. "Can you elaborate more on the abilities you possess?" asked the illusionist, changing the subject.

Fallyn nodded once in concurrence. "I'm a shape shifter and can assume any animal form, including their abilities."

The illusionist raised an eyebrow. "For how long?" he asked, cocking his head.

"That depends on what animal and the intensity of its capabilities," said Fallyn.

"Then it would reason that you could take on the appearance of a bird or bat and fly, like you did the other day."

"Yes, that would be a true statement."

Thoragaard crossed his arms across his chest. "Let's say you shifted into an eagle. How far could you go?"

"That is hard to say," said the red-haired beauty. "Many miles at a time."

"Can you travel for days in animal form?"

"No," said Fallyn, shaking her head. "I would need to revert to human form and rest. The farther I fly, the longer the waiting period."

Thoragaard nodded, bringing his hand to his chin in thought. Satisfied with the woman's answers, he said, "She is going to fly to the elves stronghold and alert them to our needs."

Harrison arched his eyebrows in surprise, then a wide smile spread across his face. "That would be perfect!" he said, almost unable to control his excitement. The young warrior, trying to temper his enthusiasm, asked, "Do you believe she can make it that far?"

"Harrison, she's our only hope," said Thoragaard. "Her arrival at the elves' compound will be days or weeks before we could get there. We need her to attempt this trip."

"Harrison, Thoragaard's right," said Murdock. "She's our only hope."

"I can do this," said Fallyn. "No one else can make the journey in the same timeframe."

Harrison stared at Fallyn, deep in thought. "You're positive you can make it that far by yourself and arrive unscathed?" asked the young warrior, worried at the prospect of sending a member of his party alone on such a long and dangerous journey.

"I'll break up my trip into smaller legs," said the woman. "I'll be able to spot safe places to rest. All I'll need to do is to map out the most direct route to the elves' compound."

Harrison pondered Fallyn's request, though he had reservations about sending her on a solo trip. Scanning his small group, he knew without a doubt that the trolls had more than hindered their mission, they had almost put it to an end. No one ever questioned the young warrior's heart nor his conviction to his friends and cause, but he knew the decision he needed to make would shape his destiny from this day forward.

Pushing doubt aside, he said, "Work with Pondle on your travel route and ready yourself for your journey. We'll be trekking at a slower pace to start our trip while you head for the elves' compound. We all need you to succeed."

Fallyn brought her focus to the thief, nodding once at him. Bringing her gaze back to Harrison, she said with a smile, "I will find the elves and get them to help us." She then spread her arms wide and asked in a caring tone, "What can I do to help now?"

Thoragaard took the lead. "Gelderand and I are working on tempering the onset of disease to our injured people. Do you possess any other unforeseen powers?"

"Not powers like the ones you possess, no," she said, shaking her head. "However, I do have limited magical abilities."

The illusionist nodded. "Good," he said. "I suggest that you work with Gelderand, Swinkle, Tara, and myself while the others construct stretchers."

Fallyn nodded once in agreement. "Anything to help."

"How long before you can begin your journey to the Dark Forest?" asked Harrison before the groups could separate.

"Give me a day or so to rest, get plenty of food and water, and to chart my course," said the shape shifter. "I will need to make many stops along the way to rejuvenate my body."

Harrison absorbed all the information. "Very well," he said. "Let's go about our chores and ready ourselves for travel from this forest in a day's time."

All members of the group appeared satisfied with the young warrior's direction. They then went about readying themselves for their tasks, leaving the confines of the campfire and joining their assigned circles.

Tara, who had remained by Harrison's side, took a moment before going off to begin her assignment. Her big blue eyes focusing on the young warrior, she asked in private, "Harrison, are you sure about this?"

The young warrior pursed his lips and exhaled. "No, but we don't have many options."

"The Dark Forest is a long way and an unforgiving place, from what I've been told," said the young maiden, in a hushed tone.

"I've been there. It's dangerous."

"Exactly," said Tara, keeping her eyes locked on Harrison's. "Can Fallyn really locate the elves' complex?"

Harrison shrugged. "I'm putting my trust in her to do just that. She must succeed."

"That's what worries me the most. A singular point of failure."

The young warrior brought his focus to a tree in the distance, thinking about what Tara had said. "I know what you mean, but right now we don't have any better options."

Tara cast her eyes downward, pressing her lips. "I suppose you're right," she said. "I'm just worried about this mission."

"As you should be. I am as well." Harrison smiled. "Why don't you let me worry about Fallyn's logistics? No need for you to get worked up about what might or might not happen."

Tara smiled back, then wiggled over to give him a peck on the cheek. "I need to go help my uncle and the others, and to get you healed up faster."

"I'm all for that!" said Harrison.

"I'll be back later," said the young maiden. "Have fun making stretchers!" A wide smile graced her face before she turned and went with the others.

Harrison watched her leave, then brought his focus to the red-haired woman who sat with the cloaked members of his group. He watched Fallyn converse with the men, providing input while also taking in their strategy. The conversation with Tara fresh in his mind, the young warrior pledged to make their journey a success, knowing that failure was not an option.

Having a doppelganger at his disposal had indeed proven to be a very valuable commodity, recalling Brendan's sentiments at their meeting in Concur where the leaders discussed the ramifications of Fallyn joining the team. Keeping an eye on his unexpected asset, he gathered himself and joined Pondle, Adrith, and his other injured friends as they began to tackle their mundane task.

CHAPTER 22

〇

The group of adventurers had spent the previous day and night readying themselves for their respective journeys. The overcast day began with Harrison convening the group during their breakfast meal.

The young warrior rummaged through his pack for dried meats. As he did, he said to the assembled people, "We made great progress yesterday, enough so that we can leave this place today."

"And not a moment too soon," added Murdock, eager to leave the lifeless forest.

"Pondle," said Harrison, "are the stretchers ready for travel?"

The thief glanced over to Adrith, who gave him a single nod. "We're good to go," said the halfling. "We'll get a better feel of their construction once we start trekking."

The young warrior nodded his approval, then panned over to the robed members of the group. "Do you all have everything you need?"

All eyes focused on Gelderand first. Darting his eyes to the members of the group, he said, "Why is everybody looking at me? To answer your question, yes, I have all the supplies necessary for the journey."

"I am supplied as well," added Thoragaard.

Swinkle tore a piece of bread, mumbled to himself, then tossed it over his shoulder. "I, too, am ready to leave," he said while Lance gobbled up his sacrifice.

Harrison focused on their party's most crucial member. "Fallyn, have you charted your course?"

The woman placed her plate of food on her lap, then answered, "I've consulted with Gelderand, Thoragaard, and Pondle in regards to the most direct route to the elves' compound. I've also determined rest stops along the way. To the best of my knowledge, I'm ready to go."

"Have you ever visited the elves in the past?"

"No," said the red-haired beauty, "but after having spoken with Swinkle, I now know the names of their king and queen, as well as some of their warriors." Fallyn looked at Swinkle and smiled.

The young cleric acknowledged Fallyn's comment with a nod. "She has the basic understanding of their compound and way of life," said Swinkle. "Hopefully, the elves honor our request for help."

"I hope so, too," said Harrison. Addressing Fallyn again, he asked, "How long until you reach the elves?"

"I'm planning to use my abilities to travel in the form of an eagle, flying high above the forest and well away from enemies," said the woman. "However, morphing into this type of creature takes more energy, which means more rest time."

Harrison nodded in agreement. "That's understandable, but how long?"

Fallyn made another mental calculation, same as she had done so many times the night before. "My best guess is ten days, less if the weather is good and if I have access to ample food and rest."

"A little over a week then?" said the young warrior.

Fallyn nodded. "That sounds about right."

Harrison digested the group's information. After a moment of reflection, he said, "It's best we get started then. Everything seems to be in order, so to speak."

The young warrior brought his gaze to the four makeshift stretchers that lay on the ground, knowing that Pondle and Adrith would be strapping him into one of them soon. With reservations, he asked, "Pondle, are those things strong enough to trek all the way to the Dark Forest?"

The thief shrugged. "I'd do my best to heal before then."

Harrison pursed his lips. "Comforting," he said, maintaining his stare on the objects. Turning his attention back to Fallyn, he said, "I suggest you ready yourself for your journey. We'll be breaking camp soon."

The shape shifter nodded. "I'll be ready to leave within the hour."

"We need to administer medicine to the group before we depart," added Gelderand.

"Of course," said Harrison. Panning the group, he continued, "Let's finish our meals, then break down this campsite. It's time to leave."

Everyone went about finishing their breakfast and gathering their belongings. Pondle and Adrith surveyed the perimeter and deemed it safe for travel. They then dragged the stretchers over to the injured warriors. Before they could start placing people onto the gurneys, Harrison addressed the group a final time.

"Fallyn, it's time to go," said the young warrior.

"I have my travel route and I'm ready for action," said the woman.

"Very well," said Harrison. "Let's hope that we see you and the elves in the very near future."

"I pray for that, too," said Fallyn. Without saying another word, the red-haired woman morphed into an eagle with brown feathers and striking green eyes.

The sudden metamorphosis took Harrison and the others by surprise, as they all watched the majestic bird of prey use her talons to grip her backpack, then flap her wings and rise through the trees. A minute later, the beautiful bird flew away and headed east toward the Dark Forest.

The young warrior maintained his upward stare, watching Fallyn leave their encampment. "Are you sure she's going to make it?" asked Murdock, looking skywards as well from his seat on the ground.

"I sure hope so," said Harrison, waiting until he lost sight of the eagle before bringing his attention back to the group. Searching for Gelderand, he asked, "What do you have for us?"

The magician fumbled with his pack, retrieving two vials of liquids, handing one to Harrison and the other to Murdock. "Both of you, drink these," he said. "Thoragaard, Swinkle, and I have mixed some of the troll's blood with medicinal herbs that our spell books say will delay the onset of infectious disease."

"This will cure us?" asked Harrison.

"No," said the mage, flatly. "The hope is that this concoction will slow the spread of whatever is coursing through your bodies."

"Hope?" said Murdock, noticing the magician's lack of complete faith in his experiment.

"Nothing is guaranteed when magic is involved."

"Isn't that the truth," said the ranger, uncorking his vial. Placing the container to his lips, he took a big swig of the liquid. Seconds after hitting his tongue, Murdock closed his eyes and scrunched his face, forcing the potion down his throat. "That's disgusting!"

Swinkle glanced at the mage. "I told you putting some fruit juice in the mixture would sweeten the taste."

"I was not going to deviate from the spell's ingredients list," said Gelderand, defending his decision.

Murdock, a tear rolling from his eye, motioned to Harrison. "Go ahead, your turn."

The young warrior uncorked his vial, then held the container away from his face, having witnessed Murdock's reaction only seconds ago. Shaking his head once, he took the container to his lips and gulped the solution down. Just like Murdock, the young warrior's face contorted like someone biting into a lemon.

"Oh, you're not kidding!" he exclaimed. "This is awful!"

"Be that as it may," said Gelderand, wagging a finger at the warriors the way a parent does to a misbehaving child, "you must finish it all. And, we'll repeat this process every two days."

"What?" cried the ranger. "We have to drink this garbage more than once?"

"Yes," said the mage. "Every two days."

Thoragaard approached the men, placing his hand in his knapsack and pulling out two apples. "These will sweeten your palette," he said with a smile.

The two fighters took the fruit and immediately bit into them, trying to rid their mouths of the vile taste.

"Swinkle, Tara," said Gelderand, "please help me administer the elixir to the women."

Tara nodded and looked over to Kymbra and Marissa who lay on the forest floor. Before she started her task, she came over to Harrison. "I hope you start to feel better right away."

"Me too," said the young warrior, taking another bite of Thoragaard's apple. "That's the worst thing I've ever tasted," he said, his mouth still full of fruit.

Tara placed a caring hand on his arm, giving it a loving squeeze. With a smile, she said, "I'll be back soon." The young maiden left Harrison and went off to help her uncle and Swinkle.

Harrison, his eyes still fixated on the girl, did not see Pondle approach. "Ready to get strapped in?"

The young warrior swung his head in the thief's direction. "I, I suppose," he said.

The thief dragged a stretcher by Harrison's side, positioning it next to him. "You're the least injured of them all," said Pondle. "Do your best to lie flat on the gurney, then I'll tie you in."

Harrison examined Pondle's handiwork. The thief, with Adrith's help, had gathered several sturdy tree limbs and hacked them into custom-fitted stretchers. The main poles on the young warrior's gurney were about six feet in length with five smaller sticks tied horizontally for support. They then covered the exposed wood with blankets, preventing the warriors from having to lay directly on the rough surface.

"Not bad, Pondle," said Harrison, as he took care in sliding onto the stretcher. The young warrior rested his hurt leg against the hidden wood, being careful not to place all of his weight down just yet. When he felt comfortable with his injured limb in place, the young warrior allowed the rest of his body to come in contact with the gurney. Pieces of the wooden brackets dug into his back, the slats not flat due to the knots and rigidness of the tree limbs. Though not a perfect solution, Pondle's creation proved to be more than useful.

Comfortable for the time being, the young warrior shimmied his body into place. Looking up, he saw Pondle hovering over him with a rope dangling in his hands.

"What's that for?" he asked, eyes wide.

"I'm going to secure you to the stretcher, so that you won't fall out after we prop you up."

Harrison shook his head. "No, you're not! I don't want to be tied up with no way to escape if something goes wrong."

"Harrison, there's a good chance that you'll fall out of the gurney," said Pondle.

"I'll take my chances," said the young warrior, folding his arms across his chest in defiance.

"Have it your way," said the thief, winding the slack around his forearm. "Don't think I'm picking you up all the way to the Dark Forest."

"You won't have to," said Harrison.

Pondle motioned with his head toward the others. "I'm going to help Adrith with the girls. I'm sure Murdock's response will be just like yours."

"Do you even have to ask?" said Harrison, smiling.

Pondle grinned back. "I'd love to see him tied up for the duration myself," he said with a laugh. Turning serious again, the thief added, "We should be ready to leave in no time."

Harrison nodded from his position on the ground, then watched his friend go off to secure the others to their stretchers.

* * *

The small group of adventurers traversed the Valkaline Forest in single file for several hours. Swinkle led the way while Thoragaard dragged Kymbra, Gelderand followed with Murdock, Adrith trudged Marissa along, and Pondle struggled with Harrison. Lance darted back and forth from his position at the head of the procession, checking for any signs of danger. Tara, positioned at the back of the group, smiled at Harrison.

The young warrior, his body growing weary of the constant jostling while Pondle dragged him through the rough terrain, gazed at the young maiden.

"What's so funny?" he asked.

"You," she said, flashing him a flirtatious smile.

"How so?"

"The big strong warrior is being pulled through the woods, while the frail maiden must protect him," she said with a laugh.

Harrison crinkled his brow, agitated. "Those trolls could have slaughtered all of us! We're lucky to escape alive!"

Tara flicked her wrist at the fighter. "Oh, Harrison, I'm just teasing you! Do you really think I'd feel any differently?"

The young warrior took a second to know his answer. "No, I know you don't. I just hate being in this position."

"Well, I don't think you should've let those beasts get the best of you," came Pondle's voice from the other side of the stretcher, apparently eavesdropping on the young couple's conversation. "I ought to drop you right here in the woods and keep going without you!" The thief started to laugh, shaking Harrison's contraption, jostling the young warrior from side to side.

"Hey!" exclaimed Harrison. "I might fall out of this thing!"

Tara brought a hand to her face, giggling. "Now that would be funny!" Something caught the young maiden's eye, causing her brow to crinkle with concern.

Harrison noticed the subtle shift in her expression. "What's the matter?" he asked, his anxiety rising a tad.

The lass opened her mouth slightly and was about to speak when Lance began barking at Pondle. Tara kept her focus on the frantic little dog while Harrison maintained his stare on his love's face.

"Why's Lance repeating stop, stop, stop?" asked Harrison, becoming more nervous by the second. Tara shrugged and shook her head, her golden locks swaying back and forth.

The young warrior then felt Pondle stop their procession. "Pondle! What's happening?"

The thief took care in placing Harrison on the ground. "Something's wrong up ahead with the others. I'll be right back." Pondle removed the sword from his scabbard and ventured off.

Harrison rolled on his side to get a better view of the commotion, while Tara knelt beside him.

279

The couple gazed ahead, watching Adrith, Gelderand, and Thoragaard rest their gurneys on the ground as well. Harrison saw Swinkle rush over to Kymbra and lay his hands on her torso. Seconds later, a bright white flash encompassed her body.

"Oh, no," said Tara, sadness in her voice. She locked her gaze on Harrison. "I'm going to see what happened." The young warrior nodded, then gripped the hilt of his battle axe that he had kept close to him. Lance remained by his master's side, protecting him from whatever might spring from the woods.

Harrison, not one to sit idly by, maneuvered himself out of the stretcher, rolling onto the ground. The young warrior winced, as shooting pain radiated from his hamstring. He then rose to one knee, before standing and limping to the rest of his party who had congregated around the injured woman. Lance accompanied his master.

"What happened?" asked Harrison, joining the circle around Kymbra.

Swinkle had remained bent over, examining the warrior. "She's burning up," he said. "We need to stop for a while."

The young warrior gazed down at the defenseless woman. The usually stoic fighter now lay on her gurney, her face pale and long blonde hair matted with sweat. Perspiration bled through her clothing.

"What's happening to her?" asked Murdock, his voice full of concern.

"It's the trolls' infection," said Swinkle, rising to his feet. "Whatever those creatures carried, they passed on to her."

Harrison allowed his friend's comment to sink in. "Is she going to be alright?"

Swinkle shrugged. "I have no idea." The young cleric fumbled in his pack, taking out a cloth. Bending down toward Kymbra again, he dotted her forehead with the fabric, absorbing her sweat. "We'll need to administer more of our elixir."

"We cannot," said Thoragaard. "It is too soon since her last round of medication."

Murdock swiveled, locking his eyes on the illusionist. "I don't care!" he shouted. "Give her more medicine!"

"Giving her more now will be fruitless," said Thoragaard. "Her body has not completely processed her previous dosage."

"So we just watch her die!" said the ranger. Murdock bent down next to Swinkle and took hold of Kymbra's hand. "She's on fire!"

The young cleric removed a tankard of water from his belt and pressed the tip to the woman's mouth, encouraging her to sip. Kymbra mumbled something unintelligible, then accepted the cool liquid. After several gulps, she began to cough.

Murdock maneuvered near her head, craning his neck toward her. "Take it easy, Kymbra," he said, grabbing the rag from Swinkle and dabbing her forehead and cheeks. "I'm here for you."

The female warrior's eyes darted to meet Murdock's. She coughed again, then flashed him a weak smile. The ranger's eyes lit up. "You see! You're going to be fine!"

Swinkle leaned back, creating space between him and the couple. "We are going to make sure she recovers. I will continue to pray for her and all those infected." The young cleric brought a worrisome gaze over to Harrison after his comment, unsure if he could deliver on his promise.

Harrison stood as strong as he could on his injured leg, trying his best to minimize his injury. However, he took his friend's comment as a warning about what might come to be in the future. Gazing down at Kymbra he understood that he could be in her situation sooner than later.

Tara felt her mate's apprehension and came to his side. Hugging him tightly, she said, "We'll see the elves long before this ever happens to you."

The young warrior said nothing, instead he maintained his stare on the sick woman and prayed that Tara's words would prove prophetic.

CHAPTER 23

Ò

Kymbra's fever broke two days after the team had stopped to address her situation. In the meantime, Murdock and Marissa began to exhibit signs of infection—runny nose, itchy eyes, a slight fever followed by chills—but had managed to overcome the symptoms without becoming sicker.

Harrison's wounds continued to itch, but he felt nothing more than a recurring headache, the result of the fallen tree limb. As with the others, he continued to drink Gelderand's concoction twice a day, just as the magician had ordered.

The young warrior, having commanded the group to break camp, rose from his seated position and placed more weight on his injured leg. Though stiff and still painful, he felt that he had put the worse of his aches behind him.

Pondle approached his leader, awaiting his next command. "Are you ready to venture again or do you still need me to drag you through the forest?" he asked with a wry smile.

Harrison grimaced, trying to place even more of his body weight on his injured leg. With a huff, he said, "I'll be ready tomorrow," before cocking his head and looking upward. "Maybe the day after."

The thief jerked his thumb toward the other members breaking down the encampment. "Kymbra's doing better," he said, bringing his gaze to the blonde warrior.

Harrison looked in her direction, finding the lithe fighter gathering her belongings and maneuvering onto her gurney unaided. "That's a very good sign."

"The others are showing signs of recovery, too," said Pondle, trying to sound hopeful.

"How long since Fallyn left?" asked the Aegean.

"Six days? A week?" answered the thief with a shrug. "Maybe a little longer."

"Where do you think she is in relation to our position?"

Pondle shook his head and raised his palms to the sky. "I have no idea. We're probably another day or two from the end of these woods. Fallyn, I have to believe, has already reached the Dark Forest."

A flicker of hope warmed Harrison's heart. "Maybe she'll be back sooner than expected."

"If she comes back at all," said Pondle, staring at Harrison, awaiting his response.

"What makes you say that?" asked the young warrior. "You've been talking to Murdock for too long."

"Maybe so, but I also find something else disturbing," said the thief.

Harrison crinkled his brow. "Which is?"

Taking a step closer to Harrison, he asked, "Where are the Scynthians?" Pondle kept his voice low. "We haven't seen them at all on this journey and, furthermore, I haven't seen a single track."

"No tracks?" asked Harrison, pondering the statement. The young warrior reflected on their time in the forest and, aside from the battles with the trolls, they had seen nothing else.

"Not one," said Pondle with conviction. "And that bothers me."

"Maybe they gathered all their forces when they attacked Arcadia," said the young warrior, trying to convince himself in the process. "That would make sense, right?"

Pondle shook his head. "Actually, no. The Scynthian's strongholds are in the Empire Mountains, further north and east of here," he said, panning the immediate vicinity. "I'd expect to see more of their activity the longer we venture in their direction."

Harrison digested his friend's assessment. Where were his race's arch nemesis? Pondle had made a good point, something to keep in the back of their minds.

"We need to keep pressing forward," said the young warrior. "But let's take note of what we see, or don't see, on the way to the elves."

Pondle gave his leader a single nod. "Understood." Gesturing to the stretcher, he said, "Shall I strap you in?"

Harrison gave him a scowl. "I'm never going to let you strap me in!" With a laugh, he continued, "You're lucky that I even let you drag me through this terrain!"

"It's no picnic for me either!" said the thief with a smile. The two shared a laugh before Harrison assumed his position. A short time later, the small pack of adventurers continued their journey.

* * *

In less than two days, Pondle announced to the group that they had finally reached the end of the Valkaline Forest. The thief, with Adrith's support, found an area on the outskirts of the woodlands to set up camp for the night.

"We'll stay here for the evening," said Pondle. Pointing to the east, he continued, "A small clearing over there leads to a bridge that crosses the Guard's River. We'll enter the Gammorian Forest tomorrow."

"We're so far behind schedule," lamented Murdock.

"We make our own schedule," said Harrison. "No one's expecting us to return any time soon."

"And we won't at this pace," added the ranger with a huff.

"Let's just set up camp," said Harrison, agitated.

The group heeded his wishes with Pondle and Adrith surveying the perimeter with Lance. Gelderand and Thoragaard administered more of their elixir to Murdock, Kymbra, and Marissa, while Swinkle prayed over their injured parts. Harrison, satisfied with their new encampment, limped over to Tara, who was assisting the magicians.

"Want to go for a walk?" he asked, extending his hand.

"A walk?" said Tara, placing her hands on her hips. "More like a shuffle, don't you think?"

Harrison forced a smile, not happy with his body's continued injured state. "I'd still rather call it a walk."

Tara smiled and accepted his hand. "Sure. Where are we going?"

Harrison gestured with his head to an area beyond the campsite. "Towards the river, away from everybody else."

The young maiden raised an eyebrow. "What do you have in mind?" she asked, flashing him a mischievous smile.

"You'll see," he said. "And, I need to keep moving or my leg will stiffen up again."

Tara allowed Harrison to take the lead and, after a few minutes, the young couple had left their friends behind and entered a clearing. The churning water of the Guard's River created the acoustical backdrop to a beautiful landscape. Tara leaned into Harrison, clutching his hand tightly.

The young maiden allowed her eyes to wander upward. "Look at all the stars," she said, gazing into the clear blackness, not a cloud in the sky and only a sliver of a moon.

"It's very pretty over here," said Harrison, guiding the pair through the wetlands filled with tall reeds, venturing closer to the waterway.

The marsh vegetation gave way to a rocky shore with plenty of places to sit. Tara pointed to a structure to their left. "Is that the bridge?"

Harrison looked over to the wooden construction in the foreground, the outline of the Saturnian Mountains in the distance. "Yes, it connects the Valkaline and Gammorian forests." Pointing away from the bridge, he said, "Let's go over there."

The young couple found a flat rock formation large enough to fit both of them. Harrison lay on his back, his feet dangling over the side of the stone. Tara lay next to him, both young people gazing upward at the heavens.

"It's so peaceful," said Tara, the rushing water drowning out everything around them. "I could stay here with you forever."

"So could I," said the young warrior. "But we need to press forward. And we need everyone healthy again."

Tara continued to gaze at the stars, placing a hand on Harrison's chest. "All in due time. Until then, let's enjoy the time we have."

The young maiden rolled over, kissing Harrison's cheek. She then pressed her body closer to his, craning her neck in an effort to reach his lips. Harrison accepted her kiss, rolling on his side in order to embrace his mate.

The young warrior pulled away from Tara after the passionate moment. "We need to be careful," he said with eyes darting, his warrior instincts taking over. "There's no one here protecting us."

Tara smiled. "Look around," she said. "It's only us. We're safe."

Though he knew better than to let his guard down, he allowed Tara's soft hand to turn his head and receive another long kiss from her. Giving in to the inevitable, the young man pulled the girl closer. The soft sound of scraping stones snapped them out of their passionate embrace.

"Young love has led to the demise of many a man," said a voice, mere steps from the young couple's position.

Harrison released his grip on Tara's torso, flipping over to face the intruder, spreading his arms wide to shield the young maiden in the process. The young warrior stared at the being. Though the lack of lighting hindered his examination, he recognized a key feature of the silhouette standing before him. The being had pointed ears. Bringing his focus to the item slung over its shoulder, he determined this person carried a quiver filled with several feather-tipped arrows.

The elf extended his hand toward the young warrior. "Rise," he said.

Harrison, still surprised at the sudden turn of events, accepted the being's hand, aiding him to a standing position. Tara scurried from her spot on the rock and took safety behind the young warrior, peering around his muscular torso at the trespasser.

"Who are you?" asked Harrison. Out of the corner of his eye, several figures started crossing the bridge, marching in unison with horse-drawn carts in tow.

"You do not recognize me?" said the elf.

"I …," stammered Harrison, squinting at the shadowy face. "I can't see in the dark!"

"A deficiency you humans have," said the being. Seconds later, the elf removed a small orb from a sack attached to his belt, illuminating the area with a soft blue-white hue.

Harrison allowed his eyes to adjust to the new light source, then gazed back at the figure before him. The being was most certainly an elf, the young warrior surmised, and a familiar one at that. Still, the name escaped him.

"It is I, Liagol," he said with a smile. "I assisted you and your friends when you arrived in the Dark Forest a short time ago. Floriad and Gaelos have joined me on our journey as well."

The young warrior took a moment to digest the elf's information. A smile stretched across his face as he recalled his adventure in the Dark Forest, how the elves had found them, and their role in leading them to the entrance of The Morgue.

"I do remember you!" exclaimed the young warrior with elation. "It's so good to see you!" Feeling a tug on his clothing, he turned his head to find Tara gazing back with wide eyes. "Forgive me, this is Tara, a friend of mine." The young warrior felt his face cringe after the words left his mouth.

"I think more than a friend," said Liagol, maneuvering past the young warrior and to the girl's side. Extending a hand, he said, "A pleasure to meet you. Come, be not afraid." Tara accepted his hand and ventured out from behind Harrison's shadow.

"How long have you been here?" asked Harrison.

"Not long," said Liagol. "Let's meet with your group and I'll provide an explanation to everyone all at once." Harrison nodded and led them away from the river.

"Friend of mine?" said Tara under her breath, raising an eyebrow and squinting in the young warrior's direction. Harrison closed his eyes and raised a palm toward the girl, signaling that they would talk at a more appropriate time. He reached for her hand but she politely brushed it aside.

By the time Harrison and Tara had led Liagol away from the river and back to the encampment, a contingent of elves had already encircled the camp to the astonishment of the other adventurers.

Pondle and Adrith had placed a hand on the hilt of their weapons, the only line of defense between their injured friends and the intruders. The robed members of the group sat on the ground sporting anxious stares.

A pair of elven archers parted, allowing Harrison, Tara, and Liagol into the encampment. "I see you've met our guests," said the young warrior, motioning for Adrith and Pondle to release the grip on their weapons.

"I'm glad to see their leader found you two unharmed," said Murdock from his seat on the ground, his tone thick with sarcasm.

"There was never a threat to us or any of you," said Harrison, trying his best to defend his actions.

"I'm glad you see it that way," responded Murdock, agitated.

Harrison raised his palms to the ranger, halting their conversation for the time being. "This is Liagol," he said, extending his hand toward the lead elf. "He and his men are here to help us." Lance bounded to the elf who stood in the small encampment.

Bending to one knee, the leader patted the small dog on the head. "I do remember you," he said with a smile. "Lance, correct?" The dog barked once in affirmation.

Liagol rose once again, then gestured to two of his counterparts. "I believe you remember Gaelos and Floriad?" The two elves nodded upon hearing their names.

"That I do!" exclaimed Harrison. The young warrior could hardly contain his excitement at seeing twenty proven warriors at their site. "Are we all happy to see you!" Harrison introduced the rest of his party to the elves, with Liagol extending the same pleasantries.

Taking his gaze back to Harrison, Liagol continued. "Brianna urged us to find you immediately, based on what Fallyn said."

Hearing the name of the elven queen warmed Harrison's heart. Brianna had taken a liking to the young warrior and his cause when they met many months ago, and she vowed to help him whenever possible.

"Thank the gods Fallyn found you," said Harrison with a sigh of relief. "How is she?"

"Exhausted but in excellent health," said the elf with a smile. "She's going to recover from her journey in no time."

"That's good to hear," said the young warrior, happy to know that the elves' would handle Fallyn's recovery. Changing the subject, he said, "We're in dire need of your services."

"We will certainly help," said Liagol. "Fallyn has a strong will and speaks highly of you, Harrison." Panning the rest of the group, he added, "All of you."

"We've been through a lot," said the young warrior. "Troll's Hell's inhabitants wreaked havoc with our group."

"The trolls of Rovere Moro are a formidable test for any warrior," said Liagol. Bringing his focus to the injured fighters who sat on the ground, he asked, "Did you lose any members of your team?"

Harrison shook his head. "No."

"You are most fortunate," said the elf, his brow slightly raised with surprise. "However, Fallyn tells us some of you are sick."

"Yes," said Harrison, his hopes rising that the elves had brought with them a cure to their afflictions. "Can you help us?"

Liagol nodded. "We can certainly make your journey more comfortable; however only Brianna can heal you."

"Then I suggest we leave immediately!" exclaimed Harrison, knowing full well the longer they stay, the better the chance of serious illness.

Liagol stood firm. "Let us assess your situation, then we can make a better determination for a course of action."

Harrison nodded several times, saying, "Of course, of course."

"Please allow my team to secure a camp for the night," said Liagol. "We will attend to your needs when we are finished with that task."

"By all means," said Harrison, feeling better about his group's situation with every passing second. "We're not going anywhere."

Liagol addressed his men, who heeded their leader's command and commenced with erecting their campsite. Less than an hour later, the three elves and several of their counterparts joined Harrison and his friends.

Gelderand noticed the elven leader rummaging through his backpack. "Might I be of any service to you?"

Liagol looked up with a smile. "It would be very helpful to know the extent of everyone's injuries and the remedies you have tried." Thoragaard and Swinkle joined the mage in the discussion.

"Four of our fighters—Harrison, Murdock, Kymbra, and Marissa—were hurt during the melee with the trolls," started the magician. "The women are injured the worst, but they are making a slow recovery.

"We have used a combination of healing spells, prayers, and an elixir that we created using troll's blood to slow the onset of disease. The remedy appears to be working, though Kymbra just had a bout with fever and chills."

The elf creased his brow. "Troll's blood?"

"We," said Thoragaard, pointing to Gelderand, Tara, and Swinkle, "went back to extract blood from one of the creatures. Our thought being if the trolls had immunity to disease, their blood might possess a way to stave off infection in humans. So far, it has worked."

The elf leader leaned toward the illusionist. "That was ingenious," he said. "You definitely saved their lives. However, your antidote will not cure them."

"That we know," added Swinkle. "Getting to your people was the only true hope we had."

"Time is not on our side, though," said Liagol. "Our compound is quite a distance away and we cannot travel fast with sick people."

Harrison interjected into the conversation. "I saw that you brought carts."

"Their sole purpose is to transport your wounded to our compound."

"That should make the trip go faster, right?"

Liagol flashed a sly smile. "For humans, perhaps. For us, it has slowed us down dramatically."

The young warrior understood the elf's logic. The elven race was known throughout the land for their quickness, speed, and agility. Horse-drawn carts did not factor into that equation.

"At least it will help us," said Harrison.

Liagol nodded. "Time to look at your wounded, starting with you."

The elves fanned out and proceeded to examine Harrison, Murdock, Kymbra, and Marissa. Liagol gave the young warrior a piece of a tasteless, bread-like food substance first, which he ate. The energy source immediately filled his belly.

"This bread is full of nutrients and will aid in the healing process," said the elf. Removing a flask from his backpack, he handed it to Harrison and said, "Drink this next."

"More medicine?" questioned the young warrior.

Liagol shook his head back and forth. "In a manner of speaking, yes. More minerals and nutrients, something we elves take to recover from battle."

Harrison gazed at the pink liquid that stared back at him from the container before taking a sip. The young warrior raised his eyebrows, surprised. "This is super sweet!"

"Drink it all," said Liagol, not bothering to notice the warrior's expression, instead he rummaged for something else. A second later, he removed a small pouch.

Harrison chugged the rest of the sugary elixir, licking his lips when finished. Handing the flask back to the elf leader, he looked at the small sack and asked, "What's that?"

"A topical solution that we will spread on your wounds," said the elf. "This will kill whatever germs remain on or in your slashed skin. Please remove your armor."

Harrison peeked at the rest of the injured team, finding Murdock, Kymbra, and Marissa going through the same routine. The young warrior removed his body protection, then revealed his slashed skin.

Liagol grimaced. "Sharp claws and fangs."

"Lucky to be alive," answered the young warrior.

Liagol rubbed the thick brown solution into Harrison's forearm and hand, then he had the young man flip on his stomach to address his damaged leg. The cream had an immediate effect on the young warrior. His skin tingled at first, but then felt warm as the healing ingredients entered his skin.

"I feel better already!" exclaimed the young warrior.

"Superficial wounds will heal faster," said Liagol. "However, your insides are still sick."

Harrison nodded, knowing full well that nothing heals immediately, not even the elves' remedies. Feeling much better, he asked, "Do we leave in the morning?"

"At first light," said Liagol. "I suggest you rest tonight and leave watch to us." The elf leader gazed over to his friends. "I am going to assist the others. They appear more damaged than you."

Harrison nodded and watched Liagol tend to his other friends. In the meantime, Tara and Lance joined him, Gelderand, Thoragaard, and Swinkle.

"How are you feeling?" asked the young maiden.

"Much, much better," said Harrison with a smile. "I'm starting to think I'll be ready to walk by the morning."

"Don't get ahead of yourself," said Gelderand, raising a palm to the young warrior. "Allow the elves' medicine to work."

"I'll be ready," said Harrison, brimming with confidence.

"I expected that answer," said the mage. "Now that our camp is secure, I suggest that we get our belongings together so that we can break camp as soon as possible."

"That is a very good idea," said Swinkle. "I could use a night's rest without expending energy healing people."

"And I shall go back to my studies," added Thoragaard.

"Tara," said Gelderand, "make sure Harrison does not get any delusions of grandeur now that he is feeling better."

"Oh, don't worry about that," said the young girl, crossing her arms across her chest and staring at the fighter.

The mage smiled. "Good," he said. "See you both in the morning." The three robed men then left the young couple alone.

After the men ranged out of earshot, Harrison said, "I'm sorry that …"

"Silence!" she said, cutting him off, leaning closer to him, arms still crossed, and brows pinned down. The young warrior closed his mouth, his eyes wide in surprise.

"I am NOT your *friend*, I am NOT your *girl*, I am your equal, your lover, and your mate," started Tara. Harrison swallowed, knowing that interrupting the young maiden at this time would not be wise. "Until I tell *you* that I am not any of those things."

"I understand …"

"Silence!" Tara maintained her glare. "I love you and you will let everyone know that you love *me*. Understood?"

"Absolutely."

Tara continued to stare at Harrison, enjoying her dominance over him at this particular moment. Arms still crossed, she sat down on the log that Harrison had used to lean against.

"Tonight, you will address your wounds, cover yourself, and lay next to me." With a smirk, she added, "And if you're lucky, I'll let you kiss me again."

Harrison's eyes remained wide. "If I'm lucky?"

Tara leaned closer. "If. You. Are. Lucky." The young maiden motioned with her head toward Harrison's body. "Let the elves' medicine do its magic before covering up. I'm going to get something to eat and I'll meet you back here later. *Friend.*"

The young warrior nodded, not wishing to add another word to the one-sided conversation. Tara rose from her seat and called to Lance. "Come on, boy. Let's get some food."

Lance, sensing that listening to Tara would be the best course of action, sprung to his feet and followed the girl. Harrison watched the young maiden's petite frame walk away.

"My friend," he said to himself, shaking his head in disgust. "What an idiot!"

His personal lecture over, the young warrior waited a little while longer before heeding Tara's command, covering his wounds and dressing himself, all the while knowing that they would lay in relative safety tonight.

293

CHAPTER 24

Ⓠ

The first shards of sunlight gleamed through the forest, waking the young couple, and signaling the start of their new journey. Harrison, Tara snuggled close to him for warmth, raised his head to gaze about the camp. The elves had already assembled their horse-drawn cart and broken down their portion of the campsite. The young warrior panned his own encampment, finding Pondle and Adrith securing Kymbra, Marissa, and Murdock's belongings, while Lance darted between the two.

Harrison leaned his head close to his mate's ear. "Tara," he whispered, doing his best to not startle the girl. "Time to wake up."

The young maiden heard the warrior's voice and proceeded to pull her blanket over her head. "It's too early," she said, her voice groggy.

"Liagol and his team are ready and waiting for us," said Harrison.

Tara tossed the blanket aside and popped her head up. Sure enough, the elves were milling about the camp, waiting for their human counterparts.

"Did they even go to sleep?" she wondered aloud, gathering herself, wiping the sleep from her eyes.

Harrison furrowed his brow. "That's a very good question. I'll have to ask Pondle." Changing the subject, he asked, "Should we get breakfast?"

"I'm still mad at you," said the girl, not missing a beat, realizing that her slumber was all but over for the night.

The young warrior drew a heavy sigh. "I can only say I'm sorry so many times."

"I know," said Tara, rummaging through her pack for some bread and berries. "I'll be fine over time."

Harrison wanted to give her a loving kiss and warm embrace, but thought better of that for now. Hoping to gain her approval again, he started a new conversation. "Have I told you about the elves' compound?"

"You've mentioned it in the past," said Tara, eating a bit of food, "but not in much detail."

Harrison found some dry meat of his own and handed them to Tara. "You're going to love their place!" he said, as she took some of his food.

"They live amongst the trees," said the young warrior with wide eyes, like a child recalling his favorite adventure. "Swinkle and I slept in a loft high upon the treetops. It was amazing!"

"I'm looking forward to seeing it myself," said Tara, envisioning a magical place.

"You'll meet Moradoril, the elven king, and his queen Brianna," said Harrison. "She's a wonderful and beautiful person."

"I can't wait!" said Tara, as she noticed people heading their way.

The elves, led by Liagol, Floriad, and Gaelos, rounded up their men and proceeded to place the injured members of Harrison's party onto the cart. With Murdock, Marissa, and Kymbra secured, Liagol approached the young warrior with a proposition.

"I suggest you ride on the wagon for a couple of days," he said in his most convincing voice. "That way you will give your body extra time to heal."

Harrison shook his head. "No, I can march with the others. I'm fine."

Liagol frowned, doing a bad job trying to hide his disappointment. "I would rather you ride."

Tara, knowing all too well about her mate's stubbornness, came to the elf's aid. "Harrison, listen to Liagol. The sooner you heal, the faster you can lead our team."

"But I feel good now," lamented the Aegean, sounding more like a child than a seasoned warrior. "I can do it!"

Tara placed her hands on her hips. "I'm not denying that you can do it, but wouldn't you want to walk through the front door of the elves' compound instead of being wheeled in on a cart?"

"Of course I would."

"Then do as Liagol says. Get on the cart, rest for a couple of more days, then lead us to their homeland."

Harrison pursed his lips, knowing that Tara was right. "Fine. But only for two days!"

Tara smiled, then gave Liagol a wink. She approached Harrison, took his arm, then started to lead him toward the awaiting wagon. "Come, let me help get you situated."

The young couple walked over to the cart to find Murdock, Kymbra, and Marissa safely stowed away. Surrounding the wagon stood Pondle, Gelderand, Swinkle, Thoragaard, and Adrith, awaiting their assignments. Lance sidled up next to his master.

Harrison placed his backpack and battle axe on the cart, then sat down and shimmied back, his feet dangling off the end. Murdock locked his gaze on the young warrior.

"It took Tara for you to smarten up, I see," he said with a smirk.

"I can march if I had to," said the young warrior, trying his best to hide the fact that he remained injured.

"I'm sure you could." Murdock reached for his longbow and held it high in his hand. "I'll be taking shots at anything that looks suspicious from here."

"Good to know," said Harrison. The young warrior noticed Liagol, Floriad, and Gaelos approaching the wagon.

"Harrison," said Liagol, "we're ready to leave whenever you are."

The young warrior raised a finger to the lead elf. "Give me two minutes to talk to my team."

Liagol nodded, then backpedaled a few steps, leaving the people to discuss their next course of action.

"Pondle," started the young warrior, "take Adrith and Lance, and venture ahead with the scouts." Turning to the robed members of the group, he said, "Swinkle, Gelderand, and Thoragaard, you can march alongside the cart. The elves will protect us from all sides." He then looked over to Tara.

"Tara, you march behind the cart, keeping an eye on all of us, and making sure that everyone continues to get better."

The young warrior panned the group of adventurers. "Is everyone in agreement over this strategy?"

All members nodded in concurrence. "Good." Locking his eyes on Liagol, he said, "My team's ready to leave. Lead us to your compound."

The elven leader nodded once and took his cue to start the procession to the Dark Forest. Pondle and Adrith brought Lance with them as they marched with the scouts. Floriad and Gaelos picked up the horses' reins and urged the beasts forward.

Harrison heard the horses grunt and the cart's wheels creak, then felt the gentle tug of the wagon lurching forward. Swinkle, Gelderand, and Thoragaard began walking next to the cart, while Tara eyed the young warrior from behind.

The Aegean focused on the young maiden, finding her smiling back at him. He then brought his gaze to the elves and the surrounding forest. Letting out a deep sigh of relief, the realization that their long journey to Rovere Moro was over finally hit him. Holding his head high, he bid the desolate forest goodbye and looked forward to visiting the elves' compound once again.

* * *

A long ten days had passed before the convoy reached its destination deep within the Dark Forest's depths. Now, Harrison stood alongside Liagol and his counterparts, making good on his promise that he would walk through their compound's gates unscathed. The young warrior let his eyes wander, taking in the tall trees, the enormous coverage of the coniferous forest, and the perfectly built wall structure that stood before him.

Harrison knew that the elves' home rested in the middle of a hostile environment with the Scynthians a constant presence in and around their encampment. However, the group had not seen any activity from them during the course of their journey, which surprised and alarmed both humans and elves alike.

"Shall we enter?" asked Liagol, extending a hand toward the huge wooden gate.

"We've journeyed a long time to get here," said Harrison. "Let's go and get our people healed."

The elf smiled, then gestured toward the two gatekeepers who sat perched atop the massive wall. Moments later, the doors slid open without making a sound.

"How did they do that?" asked Tara, standing by Harrison's side.

Harrison maintained his forward stare, looking into the complex. "They're an amazing race, Tara. You'll see."

Liagol waved the people onward, encouraging them to enter the relative safety of the compound. Harrison walked hand-in-hand with Tara, taking in the sights, recalling the beauty from the last time he had visited. In front of them stood tall trees on either side of the elegant pathway. The young warrior pointed out to Tara how the elves had hollowed out the trunks, creating living spaces for their families. They marveled at the elven writings that accompanied every trunk, identifying each residence, with carved out holes serving as windows. A lit candle adorned each ledge, casting a soft glow to the area.

Up ahead, Harrison noticed a small cadre of elven archers heading in their direction. The young warrior's eyes lit up upon seeing who marched behind them.

Leaning over to Tara, he said under his breath, "Here comes their king and queen." Tara craned her neck, hoping for a better view.

Liagol stopped their procession, allowing the convoy to approach. The eight archers halted, then broke off four to a side. In one smooth motion, they pivoted, then stood tall, creating passage for the elven royalty.

The lead elf extended a hand in the royal couple's direction. "May I introduce to you our king and queen, Moradoril and

Brianna." All the warrior elves bowed upon hearing their leaders' names.

Harrison, having taken on the lead position for him and his friends, bowed as well, Tara and the others following suit.

"Rise, Harrison," said Moradoril. "Enough with the formalities."

The young warrior stood tall once again. "You remembered my name?"

The elf king smiled widely. "How could I forget the man who is so instrumental in bringing his people together?" Moradoril extended his hand, receiving a firm shake from the young warrior.

"I'm honored, sir," said Harrison.

"And you remember my queen Brianna," said the king, brimming with delight, smitten with his wife.

"I could never forget you, milady," said the young warrior, bowing and taking her hand.

"It is good to see you again, Harrison," said Brianna. "I have watched you from afar and am pleased with what I have seen."

"Thank you," said Harrison, delighted to see the beautiful women again, but at the same time unsure of her statement's meaning.

Extending a hand to the people behind him, he said, "We have a few new members since we last met." The young warrior then introduced all of the people in his party, saving Tara for last. "And this is Tara, the love of my life and a very talented magician."

Brianna allowed her stare to remain on the young maiden. Taking a step in Tara's direction, she took hold of the girl's hands and gazed into her eyes, offering a thin smile.

"My dear, you have completed this fine young man," said the elven queen, staring into her indigo pools. "You will provide him with many years of happiness. That I can see." Brianna allowed her gaze to linger a moment longer before releasing the girl's hands and stepping back to Moradoril.

Addressing the rest of the adventurers, she said, "I hear that some of you are in need of my help." Brianna swiveled her head, calling back to someone just out of sight. "Come, my dear!"

A familiar figure appeared from one of the adjacent trees. Fallyn, adorned in a green cloak and flowers in her red hair, approached the king and queen.

"Fallyn has informed me of your unfortunate battle with the trolls," said Brianna. "We shall fix those who are sick."

Harrison gazed at Fallyn, the auburn-haired beauty locking eyes with him. The young warrior gave her a single nod of approval, recognizing her efforts to the group. Fallyn smiled back in acceptance.

Brianna continued. "However, for now we shall take you to your quarters, bring you some food and drink, and allow you to rest from your long journey."

"Liagol," said Moradoril, "take these people to their shelter. I shall speak with Harrison alone." The elf soldier did as commanded, gesturing for the rest of Harrison's friends to follow him, leaving the young warrior behind.

Tara gazed at Harrison before turning to leave. "My dear," said Brianna, "we wish for you to join us as well." The young maiden's eyes widened.

The elven queen smiled. "You are more important than you can possibly know, child," said Brianna, approaching the young girl, intertwining her arm with Tara's. "Time will reveal your true calling soon enough."

Turning to address Fallyn, she said, "Come with us. Let us leave the men alone." Fallyn joined Brianna and Tara, the trio wandering deeper into the elves' compound.

Moradoril placed a hand on Harrison's back, encouraging him to walk with him. "Fallyn informed us that you were among the ones afflicted."

The young warrior nodded. "I was. We underestimated the speed of the trolls' attacks, as well as the quickness in their regeneration abilities."

"No ordinary trolls," said Moradoril, as the two leaders enjoyed a stroll through the soft-lit complex. "I am sure that a wizard or two enhanced the monsters with some sort of magic. Normal trolls are a bit heavy of foot and regenerate at a slower pace."

"Troll's Hell appeared different to all of us," said Harrison.

"Once you entered the fog of Rovere Moro, you were at the mercy of dark magic."

"Yet, we all survived."

"Barely," said Moradoril, stopping in his tracks. "Brianna can work miracles, but there are limitations to her powers." A grimace overtook the king's face. "I noticed Marcus and some others are no longer accompanying you."

Harrison's heart sank at the mention of his lost leader. Visions of him, along with Jason and Aidan, flashed across his mind. "Marcus taught me so much, and my other friends left me with enduring memories."

"Memories are not the same as the living flesh," said Moradoril. "You must take precautions at all times. Death is around every corner."

The young warrior took the king's words to heart. "We always try to do what's right, especially avoiding death."

"Be that as it may, Brianna will restore your health." The king cocked his head. "Is there another reason you are here?"

"There is," said Harrison, "but I'd like the rest of my friends with me before we start that conversation."

Moradoril smiled. "It seems that we have much more to discuss than just healing humans. Come, let us join the others and get you better first and foremost." The two men continued their stroll, each one pondering the discussion to come.

CHAPTER 25

◻

Harrison and Moradoril meandered through the complex, talking about many topics, including the current state of human and Scynthian affairs. Upon completion of their stroll, the two found themselves in front of an immense tree that sported a large trunk.

The young warrior looked skyward at the oak's huge branches and never-ending climb to the heavens. Harrison smiled, recognizing the location he, Marcus, and the rest of his friends had visited the first time they entered the elven compound. As he recalled, it was also the first time he had met Brianna.

Moradoril entered the massive trunk, leading Harrison up a long spiral staircase. "My soldiers have escorted your other injured friends here. Brianna should be helping them as we speak."

Moments later, the two men entered a larger room, finding many familiar faces. The first person he saw brought a wide smile to his face. Tara locked her eyes on Harrison's and beamed. The young warrior's heart felt as if it grew in size, seeing his love adorned with small white flowers in her hair, which she had braided to mimic the elven women.

"Do you like the way I look?" she said with a sly smile.

"Absolutely!" exclaimed the young warrior.

"Brianna and her handmaidens helped with my hair," said the young girl. "I think I'm going to keep it this way until we leave."

"You'll get no objections from me," said Harrison. Looking past his love, he found Liagol, Floriad, and Gaelos administering concoctions to his friends. Murdock, Kymbra, and Marissa sat in comfortable chairs, conversing with their elven counterparts.

"Everyone's getting better," said Tara, unable to contain her smile. "I love it here!"

Harrison leaned forward and kissed her on the forehead. "Let's enjoy our stay, alright?"

The young maiden understood the perils of their journey and took Harrison's message to heart. "We will."

Harrison felt a tug on his arm. "Come," said Moradoril, "let Brianna have a look at you."

Tara stepped aside to allow Harrison to pass, winking at him in the process. The king led the young warrior to a chair next to his friends. "I am going to leave you in the good hands of my men and queen. Later, we all will share a meal together and discuss the other things that we spoke about." Moradoril gave Harrison a single nod, then departed.

No sooner had the king left, Brianna appeared before the Aegean, holding a small, gold chalice. "How are you feeling today?"

"Much better," said Harrison. "The food and medicine that you had your men give us seems to be working quite well."

Brianna smiled. "Good. However, that only helped heal your superficial wounds. The troll's disease runs deep inside your body." The queen presented the chalice to Harrison. "Drink this."

Harrison accepted the cup. "What is it?"

"Using the troll's blood that you brought to us, I created an elixir that will attack and kill the germs that are festering in your system."

The young warrior raised the goblet toward his mouth, stopping to ask, "I'll be rid of all of the beast's infliction after drinking this?"

Brianna slowly cocked her head. "Almost."

Harrison squinted. "Almost?"

"The concoction will neutralize the spread of disease from overtaking your body." Brianna paused. "But with everything in this world, you will be left with remnants. Good remnants."

"Remnants?" asked the young warrior, narrowing his eyebrows.

The elven queen smiled, panning the room, looking at all the humans afflicted by the monsters. "All of you will gain some of the troll's ability to regenerate, however at a much slower rate."

"Seriously?" said Harrison, his eyes wide and eyebrows arched upwards, envisioning severed arms growing back.

"At a much slower rate," reiterated Brianna. "Come, take a look." The queen strolled over to Murdock, who had already drunk the potion before Harrison had entered the room.

Brianna held out her hand in Liagol's direction, the elf placing a sharp dagger in her palm. Using uncanny poise and precision, she grabbed Murdock's forearm, slicing it with the knife. The ranger opened his mouth to protest, but the elf had already drawn blood, her quickness surprising the human.

All eyes focused on the bleeding wound. Blood stained the ranger's arm, but seconds later the hemorrhaging stopped and the skin began to heal. Murdock's wound closed less than a minute later.

The ranger stared at Harrison with wide eyes. "That's unbelievable!"

"I gave you little more than a scratch," said Brianna. "Thus the reason your wound healed so fast. Do not expect the same results in battle, but if you are patient, your injuries will heal."

Harrison, his chalice still in hand, gulped down the elixir, then placed the cup on the table. "How long until I can heal my own wounds, too?"

"Not long at all," said Brianna with a cunning smile.

"Just what's in this concoction?" asked the young warrior, still more than intrigued about his newfound power.

"Ground medicinal herbs that only we elves grow, roots from select trees, the troll's blood, and some old fashioned magic," said the queen, not revealing the particulars of the therapeutic recipe. "Suffice it to say, aside from the regeneration process, all of my people benefit from these healing powers, as well."

Harrison, speaking on behalf of the group, said, "We all thank you for your care and generosity." Changing the subject, he asked, "What should we do now?"

"Simple rest is actually the best medicine." Brianna began to collect some of her things and headed toward the doorway. "We will be gathering soon. Enjoy your stay and I will see you at the assembly."

The elven queen, along with a couple of soldiers, exited the room, leaving Harrison and his friends to mingle with Liagol, Gaelos, and Floriad.

"Where and when will this meeting take place?" asked Harrison, directing his question to Liagol.

"My counterparts will prepare this room for later tonight," said the lead elf. "Moradoril has asked us to escort you to your dwellings, then retrieve you for the festivities. You will have a couple of hours to settle in before the talk."

Harrison nodded in concurrence. "Are the rest of my friends already situated?"

"That they are," said Liagol. "Your dog is with Swinkle." The lead elf gestured to his counterparts. "We will escort you to your quarters now."

The humans rose from their seats, with Harrison taking Tara's hand, and followed their elven guides out of the massive tree and deeper into the complex.

Tara leaned on Harrison's arm as they strolled through the enchanting landscape. Towering trees used for housing spread as far as the eye could see, with illumination fixtures hanging high in the trees, providing a soft light that contrasted the darkness of the forest's interior.

"This feels like a dream," said the young maiden in total bliss.

Harrison smiled and kissed the top of her blonde head, knowing all too well the dangers that existed beyond the compound's walls. For now, he kept that knowledge to himself, not raining on Tara's happiness.

Liagol stopped their procession in front of an immense individual tree that sprouted three huge trunks. "Your friends are here," said the elf, extending a hand toward the vegetation.

Harrison gazed upwards, figuring that their rooms rested two stories above the forest floor. "This is beautiful, Liagol. How do we get to our quarters?"

"Each trunk has a spiral staircase, similar to the one in the main tree that we just left behind." The elf pointed to the leftmost trunk. "Harrison, that one is yours. The rest of your friends will be in the adjacent trunks."

"I'm sure they'll be more than adequate," said the Aegean. "When shall we reconvene?"

"Two hours," said the elf. "We will come get you at that time. For now, relax."

The young warrior peered back to Murdock, Kymbra, and Marissa. "You heard Liagol, take advantage of some down time. We'll have an important meeting soon enough."

Murdock took a step toward Harrison. "I'm feeling better already." The ranger made a subtle shift of his eyes toward the women. "A lot better," he said with a sly grin.

The young warrior smirked. "Be ready in two hours, alright?"

The ranger cocked his head. "See you at the meeting." Gesturing with his head toward Harrison's residence, he added, "Rest up."

Murdock extended his hand toward the center trunk and gazed at the women. "Ladies." Kymbra and Marissa followed the ranger's lead to the tree, disappearing into its massive body with Murdock trailing.

"Our turn," said Harrison. Addressing the elf, he said, "We'll be awaiting your return." Liagol nodded, then turned on his heel, gathered his counterparts, and left the couple behind.

Harrison motioned with his hand, similar to Murdock. "After you, milady," he said with a smile.

"Such the gentleman," responded Tara, as she sashayed to the tree and climbed the staircase. After a minute of ascension, the young couple reached their chamber.

Tara entered the open space to find soft lit candles illuminating the domicile, the aroma of freshly baked breads and cakes, and a bowl of colorful fruit resting on a table. The young maiden's eyes grew wide, like a child who had just received an unexpected gift.

"This place is wonderful!" she exclaimed, admiring the fine tapestries that hung on the wall, as well as the ornate décor of the room. She hopped over to a large bed that rested against the far wall, plopping herself on the down covers.

"This blanket is so soft!" she said with a wide smile.

Harrison kissed her on the cheek, then stepped forward to an open terrace that led away from the chamber. The deck sat high above the ground, giving the young warrior an incredible view of the elves' compound. Tara rushed outside as well, darting over to the other side and resting her hands on the railing.

"This keeps getting better and better!" she exclaimed, taking in the sights. While she held her gaze on the surrounding landscape, Harrison sneaked up from behind and pulled her close to his body.

Whispering in her ear, he said, "Why don't you come back inside with me?" He then nibbled her earlobe.

Tara, still in the young warrior's grasp, said in a hushed tone, "Harrison, it's too quiet here! Everybody will know what we're doing!"

"Then we'll make it a game."

Tara raised an eyebrow, swiveling her head in her lover's direction. "A game?"

"If we make too much noise, we lose."

The young girl furrowed her brow. "And if we don't? Who wins?"

Harrison did not have to ponder the question. "I think we win either way, don't you?"

Tara giggled. "I suppose you're right." The young maiden spun around from Harrison's grip, facing him. "Promise to be quiet?"

The Aegean nodded, not saying a word, then cocked his head and arched his eyebrows, as if to say, "See."

The young maiden laughed under her breath. "I'm still mad at you." She paused. "A little."

Harrison pulled back to stare down at Tara. "I introduced you to elven royalty as my lover, did I not?"

Tara glanced away. "Well, you did do that." She then locked her eyes on his. "Let's go! But we only have two hours."

"More than enough time," said Harrison. In one smooth motion, the young warrior lifted Tara into his arms. The girl, surprised by the warrior's quick action, wrapped her arms around his neck.

"My hero," she mocked, giving him a kiss on the lips, as Harrison carried the young maiden to their chamber for a much needed break.

* * *

Precisely two hours later, Liagol arrived at Harrison and Tara's quarters to escort them to their most important assembly. "Floriad and Gaelos have gone to fetch your friends," said the elven warrior.

"We can't thank you enough for your hospitality," said Harrison. "It almost makes us want to stay here forever."

"If only the world were as safe as it is here," said Liagol.

Harrison glanced over at Tara, who was just about ready to leave. Turning his attention to his elven escort, he asked, "What makes this place so secure?"

"Constant monitoring of our surroundings, teaching our youth the finer points of archery and sword play, and learning the good powers of magic," said Liagol. "Nothing can harm us with such a solid foundation under our collective belts."

The young warrior raised a brow. "Nothing? What about a ferocious dragon spewing fire throughout the forest?"

"Our preparation would be our advantage against an enemy of that caliber," said the elf. "I would like our odds."

"So, you're admitting that nothing's guaranteed?"

Liagol flashed a wry smile. "No, nothing is guaranteed." Tara, finished arranging flowers in her hair, approached the two men.

"I'm ready to go," said the young maiden.

The elf extended his hand toward the doorway. "After you, milady."

"Thank you," said the girl, departing the room. Harrison walked right behind her, leaving Liagol to bring up the rear. After a short stroll through the elves' compound, the young couple found themselves entering the large tree in the complex's middle, arriving at the meeting.

Tara entered the large room before stepping aside to allow Harrison passage. The young warrior found Moradoril and Brianna seated on one side of a large, circular oak table, flanked by four elven warriors on either side. The king's servants had arranged eleven seats on the opposite side of the table for Harrison's group.

The young warrior panned the room, in awe at how the elves transformed their meeting space from a triage for him and his injured friends to a majestic conference room. Flowers and dinnerware adorned the table where bandages and medical supplies had once lain. Gold chalices awaited their guests' arrival. Candlelight gave the area a comfortable glow, as the smells of freshly cooked foods wafted throughout the chamber.

Moradoril and the elven warriors rose from their seats. The king gestured toward chairs directly opposite the royal couple. "Please, take a seat while we await the rest of your team."

Two of Moradoril's men pulled out chairs, allowing the couple to sit. "How did you find your quarters?" asked the elven king.

"Words cannot describe the generosity we feel toward you and your people," said Harrison.

"The view is breathtaking," added Tara.

"We are happy to hear that you liked your space," said Moradoril.

After a few seconds of silence, Brianna gazed at the young maiden, locking eyes on hers. "Our compound is a most sacred and fertile place," she started, almost unable to contain her smile. "Only good can come from things that happen within our walls."

Tara cocked her head slightly and crinkled her brow. "Alright," she said in a meek voice, not quite understanding the queen's comment.

"Your actions here will yield the richest of fruits," continued the queen. "Remember that."

Tara felt her belly tighten, nerves getting the better of her. *She knows what Harrison and I did!* Brianna's stare lingered as a voice entered the young maiden's mind. *Your role within this group is far more important than you can ever fathom.* Tara's eyes widened just a bit before noticing a subtle tilt of Brianna's head,

309

acknowledging the young girl's mental exclamation without uttering a word.

Several familiar faces entered the conference room, breaking Tara's train of thought and leaving her to ponder Brianna's actions. Murdock, feeling and looking much better, led the rest of his team to their side of the table.

Taking a seat next to Harrison, the ranger said in a low voice, "Whatever they're giving us is remarkable." He made a subtle glance toward Kymbra and Marissa and with a sly smile added, "I feel like a kid again."

"That's good," said the young warrior, "but we're here for an important meeting."

"Oh, I'm on board. Don't worry about that!"

Moments later, elven sentries escorted the remaining members of Harrison's crew to the assembly, each person filling an empty seat. After everyone had taken their place at the table, Moradoril rose from his chair to speak.

"I am glad to see that you all look well-rested. Over the centuries, the elves and humans have shared a unique bond throughout this land and I hope that we can continue for the foreseeable future."

The elven king gestured to his servants who took their cue and began serving their guests food and drink. "More refreshments before we start our discussion."

The elven wait staff filled the adventurers' plates with fresh meats and vegetables, along with loaves of tasty breads. Other servers poured wine into chalices placed in front of each person.

The king sat back down and allowed the servers to finish their chore. When they completed their task, he gazed at Harrison and asked, "Aside from your grave injuries, were there any other reasons for you to venture to our compound?"

The young warrior nodded. "Yes, there is. First, thank you once again for your hospitality and for helping our warriors heal," started the Aegean. "As for the reason for our journey, a short time ago we opened a gateway and spoke to the Ancient Kings, and they directed us to find you and your people."

The elven king furrowed his brow in confusion. "How could you possibly have met with them? The warlock who cast that spell used powerful dark magic. Something so sinister that even experienced wizards would have a hard time breaking."

"There's no doubt in what you say," Harrison agreed, "but after we uncovered the Treasure of the Land, we also found a faded manuscript that instructed us to find the Talisman of Unification."

"Talisman of Unification?" repeated Moradoril, unfamiliar with the term.

"The Talisman turned out to be more of a treasure hunt, taking us to all corners of the land to find specific jewels and artifacts. In the end, when we placed them all together in a magical cradle, it created a gateway that led us to the Kings."

"Have you heard the name Maligor the Red in your travels?" interrupted Brianna.

"Yes!" exclaimed Harrison. "I've seen his name and image in many manuscripts that I've read."

The queen glanced to her king. "There is your mystery man."

The king patted his wife's hand, acknowledging her statement with a smile. Narrowing his focus on the young warrior, he asked, "Did Ballesteros instruct you to meet with us?"

Harrison's eyes widened. Leaning forward, he said, "Yes, he did. How could you know that?"

Moradoril drew a heavy sigh. "I knew Ballesteros, Nicodemus, and Solaris. We fought battles together in the distant past. That is, until they disappeared." The king leaned forward, resting his forearms on the table and interlocking his fingers. "How did they look?"

"The kings?" Harrison spread his arms wide, palms to the ceiling, shaking his head. "As if they hadn't aged a day past their fiftieth birthday."

Moradoril gazed at his wife, the woman giving him a nod. "Suspended in time." Taking his focus back to Harrison, he said, "Ingenious."

"How could you have known about their disappearance?" asked Harrison, skeptical. The young warrior had studied elven heritage at the Fighter's Guild, but hearing about their longevity now still took him aback.

"The elves did not always live in the Dark Forest," said Moradoril. "In the Good Times, we shared the land with humans, fought Scynthian insurgencies together, and helped to maintain order. All that ended when they vanished."

Anger welled throughout Harrison's body. "It was King Holleris' fault!" erupted the young warrior. "My twin brother Troy and I confronted him on Dragon's Lair. Troy severed his head. The king is dead."

Moradoril shook his head. "No, he is immortal as long as he remains on that island."

Harrison scrunched his brow, confused. "How can he be immortal if his head is detached from his body?"

The king flashed a wry smile. "Dark magic."

The young warrior's face went blank with understanding. "Then he's not dead? We didn't kill him?"

"No," said the king, shaking his head again. "Incapacitated, but not dead."

"What do we do now?" asked Harrison, his stomach nauseous.

"That's for another day," said Moradoril, "but evil has a way to perpetuate. We must be vigilant."

Harrison returned the king's stare, recalling the pain of losing his twin brother. "We will."

Leaning back in his chair, the elven king said, "Back to the matters at hand. What is so important that your Ancient Kings told you to seek out the elves?"

"I'm not sure. That's what they told us we needed to do in order to reunite humanity."

"Reunite humanity?" said Moradoril, furrowing his brow. "We are not human, nor do we succumb to your laws or way of life. How can this meeting start you on your journey to reunite your fractured race?"

Harrison drew a heavy sigh. "We had hoped that you'd know. The Kings did give us an artifact that we're supposed to show you."

"An artifact?" asked Moradoril, a glimmer of suspicion in his eye.

"A part of a silver ring or something," said Harrison, matter-of-factly.

The king gestured with his fingers. "Let us have a look at this artifact."

The young warrior gazed over to Swinkle, seated next to Tara. The young cleric fumbled through his backpack before finding the object he had sought. With the silver piece in hand, he leaned past Tara and handed the metallic object to Harrison.

The Aegean held the curved piece of silver in front of him, allowing everyone to see. "Behold, the Talisman of Unification."

Moradoril and Brianna gasped as they stared wide eyed at the artifact. Harrison noticed that the rest of the elves had become uncomfortable, the subtle mood in the room taking a turn away from peaceful to apprehension.

The elven king extended his hand. "Might I have a closer look at that, Harrison?"

"By all means," said the young warrior.

Moradoril gestured to one of his guards, who in turn fetched the artifact from the Aegean and gave it to his king. The elven ruler made a meticulous examination of the curved piece of metal, in the same manner someone might search for clues at the scene of a crime. After his inspection, he handed the shiny object to his queen, who in turn assessed the relic in her hand. She returned the silver artifact to Moradoril after her mental examination.

Harrison waited patiently for the royal couple to complete their task. "Do you know what this Talisman is for?"

"No, not completely," said Moradoril. "However, I believe you when you say that your Kings directed you to visit us with this object."

The young warrior crinkled his brow. "I don't understand."

"Ballesteros sent a courier many years ago," started the elven king, "with a message that we should take action if we ever saw this piece." Moradoril raised his hand, showing all in the room the silver artifact. "I, too, now understand why he sent his scout."

Harrison's mind churned in wonderment, unsure what the elf's story meant. "So you know of this object?"

"Not this one in particular," Moradoril reached back and handed the relic to his soldier, who returned it to Harrison. "But one like it."

The young warrior's eyes grew round, his eyebrows arching high on his forehead. "You have one like it?"

Moradoril glanced at his queen. Brianna slipped a slender hand into a pouch secured to her belt, removing its contents, and handing it to her husband. The king raised his hand again, showing all in the room what Brianna had given him.

Harrison pointed to an identical piece of metal, just like the one he held in his hand. "They're the same!"

The elven king nodded. "They appear to be."

The young warrior shook his head. "Why in the world do you possess something identical to what took us so long to find?"

Moradoril shook his head as well. "I don't know," he said, before pausing.

Harrison noticed the king's subtle hesitation. "What is it?"

The elven leader drew a heavy sigh. "Ballesteros' sentry also gave us another request."

"Which was?"

"He told me that we all," Moradoril swept his finger in a circle, encompassing everyone in the room, "need to enlist the help of the dwarves upon uniting the Talisman."

Harrison digested the new information, then gazed at his friends. All sported looks of confusion, unsure of what Moradoril's statement meant.

"That's news to us," said the Aegean. "Did this sentry provide more direction?"

Moradoril gazed to Brianna, who smiled back at him. "Come here, Harrison," said the elven queen. "And bring your treasure with you."

The young warrior did not hesitate to do what Brianna asked, hurrying to the royal couple's side. The queen placed her relic on the table in front of her.

"Place your object next to mine," said Brianna.

Harrison obliged, leaning between the royal couple and setting the silver slab of metal to the right of the elves' piece.

314

Almost immediately, the two curved sections combined into one, semicircular artifact.

"Did you see that?" exclaimed the young warrior.

Brianna reached for the newly minted Talisman, raising it for all to see. "It seems that we have a new treasure."

The young warrior continued to stare at the silver object when something caught his attention. Pointing to the metallic relic, he exclaimed, "Look!" Everyone at the table strained to see what Harrison saw.

Brianna's eyes widened ever so slightly. Taking the piece in her hand again, she brought the object closer to her face for inspection. "It appears that Dwarvish runes have graced the surface."

Harrison shook his head. "I'm confused. What does any of this mean?"

"All signs point to the dwarves," said Moradoril.

The young warrior spread his arms wide. "What dwarves? Aren't all of them extinct?"

Moradoril and Brianna exchanged anxious glances. "That's the story that has been told for centuries," said the king. "It might not be totally true."

A monotone voice interjected his thoughts. "Ancient scripture mentions a battle between the elves and dwarves," said Thoragaard, raising an eyebrow and gazing at the royal couple.

"My studies at the Fighter's Guild mentioned that the Salinian Dwarves disappeared during a battle with the Scynthians, not elves," said Harrison, bringing his focus to the illusionist.

Thoragaard, maintaining his focus on the two elven leaders, asked, "The Scynthians do not possess such powers."

"No, they do not," said Moradoril, locking eyes with Thoragaard.

The illusionist maintained his stare. "But you do."

The king sat taller in his seat. "What are you insinuating?"

"Is it possible that your people, with your magical abilities, eradicated the Salinian Dwarves?"

Moradoril leaned forward from his throne and said, emphatically, "No." Brianna, recognizing her husband's growing agitation, took her hand and squeezed his forearm.

"Eradicate is the wrong word," said Brianna in a calm voice.

"What word would you use?" asked Harrison, coming to grips that a serious occurrence happened many centuries ago.

"Suspended," said the queen. "For their own safety."

"Brianna," said Moradoril, swiveling his head to stare at his mate.

The elven queen flicked her wrist toward the humans who surrounded the table. "The time is now, Moradoril," she said, trying to calm her king. "The very people who set this whole game in motion instructed Harrison and his friends to seek us. There is no turning back now."

Harrison, fed up with all the cryptic talk, said, "I think it's time for answers. Why did the Ancient Kings send us here?"

Moradoril grimaced. "Your ancient leaders babbled about ruling the land a thousand years ago," started the king. "My people did not care to control the world like humanity. Not like your kings did back then nor the way you want to today."

"We don't wish to rule the land, just reunite our people," said Harrison.

"Humans cannot rule without getting intoxicated with power," said the elven king. "It happened to the old kings and it will happen to you."

"That's not true!" said the young warrior. "We want to make the world better for us all."

"That is noble of you, Harrison," said Brianna. "However, your race's history is not on your side."

The young warrior felt his belly tighten again, doing his best to stay in control. "We are not the old kings," said Harrison with firmness to his voice. "I feel that we deserve the chance to make things right. To make things better."

Moradoril gazed at the Aegean. Sensing a deep sincerity radiating from the young man's soul, he said, "There is something about you, son. I cannot explain it, but I do not doubt your intentions."

"Then give us a chance," said Harrison. "Haven't we passed countless tests to stand before you today?"

"You have," said the king with reluctance.

"Then why are you hesitating with your answers?"

Moradoril held his gaze on the young warrior. "For today starts a new direction for this world. Ours and yours."

"Do you know what's to come?" asked the Aegean.

"I do not and that is what worries me."

Harrison extended a hand toward his friends. "We are here to help and to bring back what's right for us all."

Moradoril smirked. "Don't get ahead of yourself, Harrison. All of you can die tomorrow, just like any of us. Hard times are ahead."

"Understood," said the young warrior. "Can we get back to the dwarves and what this artifact that we both possess means?"

"We placed the dwarves in hibernation," said Brianna, taking the lead. "They are frozen in the Empire Mountains."

"Empire Mountains?" said Harrison, his brow crinkled with surprise. "That's Scynthian territory."

"All the better to propagate the story that the Scynthians caused the dwarves' disappearance," said the elven queen.

"How do you release them?" asked the young warrior.

"I have no idea," said Brianna.

"What?" said Harrison, shaking his head. "How can you not know?

"Your kings asked us for a monumental favor, which we obliged. They, in turn, took it from there."

"Perhaps that piece of metal is needed," said the Aegean.

"I am sure it has much more importance than its rudimentary appearance," said Brianna.

Harrison took a moment to digest all of the new information. "Then I guess our next move is to go to the Empire Mountains."

"That it is," said Moradoril. "The terrain is cold and brutal, best suited for beings with thick fur coverings, not fragile skin. We will accompany you, but we will need to prepare furs, food, and provision for the trip."

"How long will that take?"

"A few days," said Moradoril.

"We'll be ready," said Harrison.

317

"Will you?" asked the king, an eyebrow raised. "Gather your belongings as well. My soldiers will provide you all with the necessities to trek to the mountainous region."

The young warrior nodded. "Thank you again, Moradoril. My friends and I look forward to venturing with you to help solve this mystery."

Moradoril rose from his seat. "My soldiers will escort you back to your dwellings. Feel free to roam our complex and treat it as if it were your own. You are all our honored guests."

"That's most generous of you," said Harrison. The young warrior then gestured to his group to rise from their seats. "Please let us know if there is anything we can do to prepare for this trip."

"There will be ample opportunities to help," said the king. Moradoril turned to his queen. "Come, Brianna, it is time to go."

The queen rose from her seat and followed her king out of the room. Several soldiers trailed the royal couple before Harrison and his team made their departure. Swinkle, who had sat two seats away from Harrison, maneuvered closer to his leader.

Leaning toward the young warrior, he whispered, "We need to talk."

"Oh, that we do," answered Harrison in a hushed tone. "About a great many things."

The young warrior then led his party away from the elves' grand meeting room, knowing that their discussions for the night were far from over.

CHAPTER 26

Ｏ

Harrison did not utter a word as he led his team of adventurers away from the massive tree structure and to a more secluded area of the compound. The young warrior panned the vicinity, finding tall trees set aglow with soft candles in their limbs, providing ample lighting for the humans.

The young warrior huddled his friends together. "This should be safe enough," said the Aegean.

Murdock stepped forward. "Safe enough for what?"

"To take a closer look at the Scrolls of Arcadia."

The ranger held his palms to the sky. "What more are you expecting to find?"

The young warrior held his gaze on his friend. "Insights." Without shifting his eyes away from Murdock, he continued, "Swinkle, let's have a look at those scriptures."

Gelderand maneuvered next to the ranger. "Harrison, I have to agree with Murdock. What are you looking for?"

Harrison did not hesitate. "Look, I respect and trust Moradoril and Brianna, but they're holding something back. We need to find out what that is."

Murdock panned from side to side. "It's not safe here, Harrison. They can hear us."

"I'm not worried about that," said the young warrior. "It wouldn't surprise them if we delved deeper into their secrets, now would it?"

The ranger arched his eyebrows. "I suppose not. If I were them, I'd do the same."

"Exactly," said Harrison with a smile, noticing that Swinkle had unfurled the first scroll. "Swinkle?"

The young cleric's eyes scanned the parchment. "There are many things written on a variety of subjects."

"Anything about the elves?"

Swinkle continued with his examination, stopping several seconds later on a paragraph of interest. "This might be something."

Harrison approached his friend. "What have you found? Tell us!"

"This does not mention the elves by name but it could allude to them," said the holy man. "The section states, *'Before the Great Battle, an unlikely alliance will be forged. Without the contributions of the combined armies, the war will surely be lost.'*"

"Unlikely alliance?" muttered Harrison, looking skyward in thought.

"It must mean the elves and dwarves," said Swinkle.

"I'm confused," said the young warrior. "What makes these races an implausible team? Our Kings instructed us to seek the elves, which we did, and they in turn tell us to find the dwarves. This seems more like an expected alliance than not."

"The elves and dwarves do not like one another," said Gelderand. "The histories between each other are tarnished at best."

"Can you give us some understandings into their past?" asked Harrison.

The mage shook his head, exhaling deeply. "There's much to say." Holding his chin in his hand to ponder the question a moment longer, he said, "The two races have fundamentally different beliefs. The dwarves crave treasure, particularly gems, and mine for them day after day. The elves are more in harmony with nature and the land, possess magical abilities, and seek not treasures.

"They differ even more when it comes to fighting. The dwarves are stubborn, noisy, and headstrong in battle, whereas the elves are quick, stealthy, and prefer well-coordinated battle plans. The two races could not be any more different."

"Do you think Moradoril knows of this unlikely alliance?" asked Harrison.

Gelderand shook his head. "That I don't know."

"There has to be more to this," interjected Murdock. "The Salinian Dwarves are no more and we know that the elves had something to do with that."

"Why would our Ancient Kings ask the elves to place the dwarves in suspended animation?" asked the young warrior.

"To fight in a future battle," said Thoragaard, adding to the conversation. "Dwarves age more like humans. Who knows, they might have died off on their own accord at any point in history, rendering this conversation today moot."

"Interesting hypothesis," said Harrison, taking Thoragaard's assessment to heart. "The elves are taking us to the dwarves with the chance of creating this unlikely alliance. I wonder just what the future has in store for us all."

"All very good questions," said Gelderand. "Might I say something more?"

"Of course," said the young warrior.

"I think we should tell them about the Genocide Scroll, as well as the other prophecies we've uncovered."

"Why in the world would we do that?" exclaimed Murdock, spreading his arms wide in exasperation. "Don't you think we should keep some things to ourselves?"

"I have to agree with Murdock, Gelderand," said the young warrior. "It might be in our best interest to keep this a secret for now."

The mage nodded in understanding. "I can see your point; however, if the elves are such a great ally of ours, they should be entitled to some important information, especially when that means we have the capability to eradicate an entire race."

"And what of the prophecy?" asked Harrison. "Do we tell them that brothers will reunite the land?"

"We tell them everything," said Gelderand. "They might know more than we do as it is."

Harrison pondered the magician's request. Generations of humans understood, even longed for, the elves' longevity. The fact that they might know the history of their world even better than the humans themselves made disclosure easier to digest.

"We have a few days before we leave for the Empire Mountains," said Harrison. "That should give us ample time to chat with our new friends as well as to establish marching orders to the region."

The young warrior panned the group, finding many nodding in agreement without any dissent. "Let's regroup, determine a plan for ourselves, and try to figure what to expect on this trip. We also need to take a closer look at the Talisman and what those markings mean."

With nothing left to discuss, the small group of adventurers headed back to their dwellings to ponder the next leg of their journey.

Swinkle caught up to Harrison, Tara, and Lance as they trekked toward their hollowed tree dwelling. "Harrison, would you mind if I came up with you for a little while?"

The young warrior glanced at Tara, the girl shrugging. "Sure. Is there anything wrong?"

"No," said the young cleric. "I wanted to study the Talisman and figured that the both of you might be able to lend some insights."

Harrison smiled. "That sounds like a good plan. Let's head on up." Lance scooted ahead of Tara, Swinkle, and Harrison, entering the spacious room first.

The young warrior extended his hand toward a table and vacant chair. "Make yourself comfortable."

"Thanks," said Swinkle, taking a seat.

"If you both don't mind," said Tara, "I'd like to sit in on the conversation as well."

"By all means," beamed Harrison.

The young maiden nodded, then took her seat at the table. Their elven hosts had restocked their room with freshly baked cakes and fresh fruits. Tara tore a piece of warm bread and began to nibble on it while Harrison gathered another chair, placing it next to his mate.

"Can we take a look at the Talisman?" asked the young warrior.

Swinkle fumbled through his backpack, retrieving the elusive silver object. "Here it is," he said, holding it for all to see.

"It's such a simple piece of metal," said Tara, gazing at the glimmering artifact. "How can this possibly be so important for our mission to reunite humanity?"

"The Ancient Kings were very cryptic," said Harrison, reaching for the object and taking it in his hands. The young warrior ran his thumb over the smooth surface, feeling the subtle scrapes of raised markings. "But I'm sure these runes are very important."

"What are runes?" asked Tara, crinkling her brow.

"Runes are ancient symbols that the dwarves used in the past," said Swinkle. "History states that they contain some kind of code."

"A code for what?" asked the young maiden.

"That is a very good question," said the holy man. "One that holds the key to this whole mystery."

"Have you studied Dwarvish runes before?" asked Harrison, inspecting the symbols he held in his hand.

"Not to any great depth," said Swinkle. "I'm wishing that I had. How about you?"

Harrison handed the semi-circular ring back to Swinkle. "We did at the Fighter's Guild, but like you, we didn't delve into them very much. With the dwarves extinct, the elders didn't think it was very important to study their ancient language."

"But it must mean something," said Swinkle in a low voice, taking the artifact close to his face, examining the symbols. Raising an eyebrow, he continued, "I am willing to bet that there are more symbols on the other part of this piece."

"What makes you say that?" asked Harrison.

"Look," said the young cleric, placing the metal object on the table in front of the couple. Pointing at the symbols starting from the left and continuing to the right, he said, "See how these symbols here appear to be cut." Swinkle rested his finger on the rightmost rune.

"This one seems to be split in two," said Tara.

"Correct," said Swinkle. "There must be more on the next piece."

"Do you think the dwarves have that section?" asked Harrison.

"We humans had the first section and the elves had the next part," started Swinkle. "It would be reasonable to assume that the dwarves possess the subsequent sector."

Harrison and Tara nodded, agreeing with Swinkle's assessment. "If that's true," said Tara, "who has the fourth piece?"

The two young men traded curious glances. "I have no idea," said Harrison, his eyes wide and brain churning in thought.

"We are far from solving this mystery," said the young cleric. "However, I am sure that the dwarves will shed more light on our cause." Swinkle pushed his chair back from the table. "If it is alright with you, I am going to take this object back to my room with me and study it further."

"Go ahead," said Harrison. "Take it and let us know what you find, if anything."

Swinkle rose from his chair. "I will. See you later." The young cleric then exited the treetop dwelling, leaving Harrison and Tara behind.

"What do you make of that artifact?" asked Tara, crossing her arms.

"I honestly don't know," said the young warrior. "I'm guessing that things will get clearer when we reach the dwarves."

"I suppose," said Tara. Thinking about their upcoming mission, she added, "It's going to be cold in the mountains, isn't it?"

"Bitter cold," said Harrison, nodding. "Moradoril's men will equip us with everything we need. But yes, it's going to be cold."

"I hate frigid temperatures," said the girl with a huff. "I'd rather be in the warm weather."

"I couldn't agree more," said Harrison. "Let's get some rest. I want to talk to Moradoril and Brianna about the scrolls in our possession sooner rather than later."

Tara leaned over and kissed Harrison on the cheek, before rising from the table. "I agree. Let's lie down for a while. I'm sure there won't be much down time trekking in the mountains."

Harrison followed his love to their bed, all the time wondering if their meeting with the royal couple will go as smooth as he hoped.

* * *

"When were you going to enlighten us about your revelations?" questioned Moradoril with a scowl.

Harrison, along with his friends, had allowed a couple of days to pass before broaching the subject with the elven king. Now, the two groups of humans and elves awaited their departure to the Empire Mountains and the continuation of their quest.

"There really wasn't a good time to discuss the writing in the Scrolls of Arcadia," said Harrison.

"How about at our initial meeting?" said Moradoril, agitation evident in his voice. "Withholding information on a scripture that can wipe out an entire race is of paramount importance. What other secrets are you harboring?"

"None, I promise," said the young warrior. "To be honest, we're not sure how to use the Genocide Scroll at all."

"Use?" said the elven king, cocking his head, his brow creased with anger. "Harrison, be careful what you say next."

Before the young warrior could speak again, a voice of reason broke the tension. "Moradoril, I do not believe the young man has evil intentions," said Brianna. Facing the Aegean, she continued, "Do you?"

"Absolutely not," said Harrison. "We've spoken at great length with our leadership and discussed what we should do if we even discovered the scroll. Now that we have it in our possession, the question of what to do with it is of utmost importance."

"May I ask what you and your leaders discussed?" pressed the queen.

Harrison glanced over to Swinkle, who gave him a nod of encouragement. "I'm sure that you're well aware of the Scynthian's brutal attacks on several of our towns and villages," started the young warrior. "If we possessed the Genocide Scroll, we could use it as a deterrent against future aggression."

"Harrison, the eradication of an entire race makes the assumption that all beings of that race are evil," said Brianna. "A very short sighted rationalization."

The young warrior exhaled deeply, Brianna and Swinkle's comments echoing in his head. "That's the same argument that many people brought up at our council."

"My queen is correct," said Moradoril. "This scripture that you possess is very powerful." The elven king gazed past the young warrior and to the robed members of his group. "And you have people capable of reading its magical text."

Harrison raised his palms toward the elves. "All the more reason to disclose this information now."

Moradoril cast his gaze away from the Aegean, staring at the ground. Shaking his head, he said, "This changes everything, Harrison."

"How so?"

"Who is to say that you won't use this power against us?" The king glared at the young warrior. "I am the leader of the elves. I must look out for all of my people's best interest."

Harrison gazed back at his friends, finding blank expressions. "What do *you* propose we do?"

Moradoril stood tall. "Give us the parchment to hold. We have more restraint than you do."

The young warrior did not waver with his answer. "I cannot do that. But I promise that we don't and never will intend to use the scroll's power against the elven race."

"I believe you," said the king. "However, *you* cannot read the magical text. You need to convince me that your entire *race* will not use the scripture's powers against us."

"Moradoril," said Harrison, circling his finger at the band of adventurers that stood behind him, "we possess the scroll, no one else. I trust all of the people who are with me and I promise you that no one will read that text. After we complete our mission, my hope is that you'll come with us to discuss this matter in more detail with our leadership. You can trust me."

The elven king took a deep breath, holding his gaze on the young warrior. He then peered past Harrison to his friends, finding them agreeing with their leader.

Exhaling, the king said, "You make a strong case, Harrison." He then made a subtle glance to his queen, who nodded her approval. "The elves will fulfill their part of the mission and lead you to the dwarves. When that is complete, we will take you up on your offer to discuss this matter further with your superiors."

Harrison could feel the tension lift. "Then we're good to start our travels?"

"Is there anything else we should know?" asked the elven king, eyebrows arched, waiting for the young warrior's response.

"There is one more thing," said the Aegean. "The Scrolls of Arcadia mentioned a prophecy that brothers will reunite humanity. I'm still on that quest, but my twin brother died in battle a short time ago. Do you know what this means?"

Brianna stepped forward. "Perhaps your prophecy is shattered now that your brother is dead." The queen lifted an eyebrow. "Or, maybe you are not part of the brother tandem that you believe you are."

The queen's answer took Harrison aback. Upon learning of the prophecy, he had always assumed that it pertained to him and Troy. Brianna's revelation suddenly changed all of that.

"I hadn't thought of that in those terms," said the young warrior.

Brianna walked over to the young man, taking hold of his arm. "Just another thing to ponder on our way to the northern mountain range." Looking over her shoulder to her king, she asked, "Shall we depart?"

Moradoril pressed his lips. "It appears that we are done with our discussions for the day. Let us venture forward." The elven king waved his hand, his soldiers breaking into their marching formation.

Harrison watched as the elves positioned themselves for their journey. "We will speak often, Harrison," said Brianna. Peeking at Tara, she added, "Take extra special care of her. She is more precious to you than you can possibly understand."

The elven queen released her grip on the young warrior and strolled back to her king, preparing herself for the long journey. Harrison took the opportunity to gather his friends.

"Let's break into the marching order that we discussed earlier," said the young warrior as the group of adventurers did as Harrison asked. However, before Tara could find her spot, the young warrior made a point to address her.

"Tara," said Harrison.

The young maiden turned to face her love. Before she could say a word, he hugged her, bringing the girl tight to his chest and planting a kiss on her forehead.

"What was that for?" asked the young maiden.

"Just to say I love you," said Harrison. "I'll never be far from you at any moment on this trip."

Tara smiled. "That's good to know. I love you too, Harrison." She then slipped out of his grasp and assumed her position in the group.

Harrison allowed his gaze to linger on the young maiden a moment longer before falling into line. With everyone set, the elves began their march out of their complex with the humans taking up position alongside them. As they departed, Brianna's words resonated in the young warrior's mind and he promised himself to never let his love out of his sight.

CHAPTER 27

Ɵ

The large squadron of human and elven adventurers trekked through the Dark Forest for several days before reaching the shores of Lake Alessandra, a large inland body of water that rested east of the woodlands and south of the Empire Mountains.

Harrison and the others took their elven counterparts' advice and started to don their furs and boots, the temperature plummeting by the minute. The young warrior, taking advantage of the break in their journey, sought out his mate, finding her fastening a clasp around her neck and binding a fur covering across her chest. She then pulled a large, furry hood over her head, hiding most of her face.

"Hello? Is anybody in there?" chided Harrison, bringing his face close to the hood's opening.

"I think this outfit is too big for me," said Tara, pulling back her hood to reveal her face.

The young warrior let his eyes wander about the girl's body. Raising an eyebrow, he said, "Furs look good on you."

"I'm glad you like it," said Tara in a mocking tone. "I'm sweating in here."

Harrison brought his gaze to the north, finding the snowcap-covered mountain range looming before them. "Not for long you won't."

"Do you think it's going to be cold?"

Harrison held his stare on a large peak in the distance. "Very cold."

Tara trudged over to the young warrior, trying to familiarize herself with the heavier boots. "How long until we get to our destination?"

The young warrior shook his head. "I'm not sure, three days, four."

Tara looked off into the distance as well, finding gray, cloudy skies. "How high up are we climbing?"

"It's not how high, but how deep into the mountain that we need to trek," said Harrison. "Dwarves are gem miners and the jewels they seek lie buried deep in the mountains."

Tara took another step and tripped, grabbing hold of Harrison's arm to break her fall. The young warrior caught the girl and propped her back up. "Hey, be careful or you're going to hurt yourself."

The young maiden shook her head. "It's these boots. I'm not used to walking in them."

Harrison once again admired her fur-lined foot coverings. "They're practical, but still look cute on you."

Tara rolled her eyes. "I'd rather be sitting on the shore of a stream with my bare feet dangling in the cool water while feeling the warm sun on my face."

Harrison gazed at the young maiden covered head to toe in furs with just her head poking out of her parka and envisioned the scene she just described.

Taking her in his arms, he said, "I'll take you there after this journey and we'll spend a lot of time together, just me and you."

"Promise?"

The young warrior gave her a loving kiss on her forehead. "Promise."

Tara smiled, then noticed Swinkle approaching the two. The young cleric sported heavy fur coverings, just like his friends. "We are leaving now. Murdock wanted me to come get you."

"We're ready," reassured Harrison. "The sooner we start our trek, the faster we'll get to our destination." The young warrior noticed a look of concern on his friend's face. Creasing his brow, he asked, "What's the matter, Swinkle?"

The young cleric shook his head. "Aside from the trolls, things have gone too smoothly."

Harrison cocked his head. "How so?"

"Where are the Scynthians?" asked Swinkle. "Why haven't we seen a trace of them?"

"I have to agree," added Tara. "We forced the action with the trolls, but I expected to witness a lot of battles with the Scynthians based on what you've told me in the past."

"They're here," said Harrison. "Remember, they ambushed our civilization not too long ago. They're regrouping and we need to be ready for them."

Swinkle shook his head. "That is what conventional wisdom states, but I still feel that something is not right."

"I appreciate your concern, Swinkle, but trust me they're out there, waiting."

The young cleric lifted his palms to the sky. "Just expressing my concerns. We should go."

"Yes, let's fall into line. All of us." The three young people left to join their counterparts for the next leg of their journey, all the while wondering about the whereabouts of their hated enemy.

* * *

Harrison marched behind the elves' caravan, trekking deeper into the frigid mountain range. The young warrior swore that the temperature dropped a degree with every step he took as steam spewed from his mouth, the cold biting his extremities. Taking his eyes to the furs covering his body, he thanked his marching counterparts for the lifesaving apparel.

Lance scurried to his master from up ahead. The young warrior could not help but chuckle upon seeing the thick furs that covered his faithful companion's body.

"I don't know how you're making it, Lance," said Harrison. "I guess all your darting around keeps you warm." The little dog barked once in affirmation, his tail wagging feverishly. The canine then dashed away in Tara's direction. Harrison watched the animal's antics, figuring Lance wanted to check on Tara's wellbeing, as well as to keep moving in order to stay warm.

The young warrior then took his gaze ahead to the snow-filled trail. Evergreen trees, their strong limbs shouldering thick snow, lined the pathway, forcing the convoy to march in a virtual straight line. Harrison, positioned toward the back of the pack, strained to locate Tara but alas the young maiden trekked out of his view. He cursed under his breath, wishing that he could travel closer to her in order to fulfill his promise of protection. A shout from behind broke his train of thought.

"Harrison!" yelled Floriad. "How are you holding out?" The elf quickly advanced to the young warrior's position.

"Freezing, but alright," said the Aegean. "You?"

"Cold as well," said the archer, marching side by side with his human counterpart.

"These mountains are much colder than the forest. How can you stand the contrast?" asked the young warrior.

"The Scynthians have kept us on our toes for years," said Floriad. "Many times we had to push them back into the mountains. Thus the reason we have so many furs and coverings. We're used to this terrain."

Floriad's last comment piqued Harrison's interest. "Speaking of the Scynthians," he said, "where are they?"

The elf's face went blank for a second. "I have wondered the same. It is not like them to be out of view for so long."

"My people are assuming that they're regrouping. They attacked Arcadia and we beat them back soundly. I believe they're licking their wounds and waiting to attack again."

"Perhaps, but I think you're giving them too much credit."

The young warrior creased his brow. "How so?"

"The Scynthians are stupid," said Floriad flatly. "They have no real concept of battle plans and count on their physical strength and sheer numbers to win their skirmishes." The elf pushed away a low hanging branch before continuing.

"Their sneak attack on your city was surprising. It took planning and coordination, something they lack. I give them credit for their success, though their acts were heinous."

"We beat them back and regained control of the city," reassured Harrison. "They must be planning a counterattack; it only makes sense."

"Normally I would agree, however the utter lack of their presence disturbs me."

Harrison gazed ahead, agreeing with Floriad's assessment. "I'm still under the assumption that they're going to try and surprise us again. We must remain vigilant." The elf nodded once, concurring.

Changing the subject, the young warrior asked, "Do you have any insights to share about where we're going?"

"The dwarves have a vast empire in the heart of the mountainside," said the elf. "Their lust for gems and jewels has confined them to their own little world."

"Did you know about the plot to suspend them in hibernation?" asked Harrison, moving the conversation in another direction. "We learned at the Fighter's Guild that the Scynthians had done this."

"As you heard, that's not one hundred percent true," said Floriad. "Moradoril briefed our people a long time ago. We all accepted his wisdom for the betterment of our race."

Harrison noticed his counterpart's subtle inflection. "Floriad, is there something more to the Salinian Dwarves' story?"

"The Salinian Dwarves and our people have a history," said the elf. "One that goes back thousands of years."

"Care to elaborate?"

Floriad cocked his head. "Let's just say there was no love lost when they disappeared."

Harrison needed to know the truth. "Is there a different version of this story? Something other than what your leadership told us?"

"I'm not at liberty to make statements of what did or did not happen in the past," said the elf, maintaining his forward stare. "However, once we reach our destination," Floriad stopped and stared into Harrison's eyes, "question everything." The elf grabbed Harrison's arm and nodded once, being sure the human understood the gravity of his statement.

The young warrior's eyes widened a bit, sensing that he just received a vital piece of information. Floriad motioned with his head. "Let's go. It is getting dark and we don't want to get too far behind."

Harrison nodded, not saying a word. The two men then continued their hike in silence.

* * *

The trek through the mountains did not come without its fair share of peril. A massive snowstorm forced the whole convoy to hunker down for a week on the side of a huge mountain. The young warrior and his friends witnessed harsh, frigid, merciless winds that lashed at the group, swirling snow that created a nauseating spinning effect.

Harrison huddled with Tara in their tent in an effort to stay warm, their shelter thrashing day and night, trying to keep the bitter wind at bay. The young warrior, his nerves wearing thin, gazed over at Tara, finding her bundled up in furs and blankets. Lance's little head protruded out from under her layers, doing his best to keep warm under the circumstances.

The young warrior heard familiar shuffling beyond the canvas and drew a slight smile. Moments later, the flap opened wide, aided by the howling wind, allowing fresh cold air into the sanctuary. Two figures scurried inside, doing their best to secure the flap again before the weather tore it from its posts.

The beings lowered their hoods, revealing their frigid faces to Harrison and Tara. Murdock tossed a sack in the young warrior's direction. "I never thought I'd eat so much elven bread."

Harrison grabbed the pouch and held it close. Cocking his head toward the tent's opening, he asked, "Is the storm subsiding?"

"Believe it or not, yes," answered Pondle.

Murdock took a second to brush ice from his moustache. "The sky's lightening up and the winds are slowing down. But it's still bitter cold out there."

"Are you done with your rounds?" asked the young warrior.

"You're the last tent," said Pondle.

Harrison motioned for his friends to sit. "You might as well warm up a bit. Have you eaten?"

Murdock nodded, accepting a seat on the ground. Pondle did likewise. "We ate before we headed outside," said the ranger.

"How's everybody else doing?" asked Tara. The young maiden had not ventured out of the tent for two days and all of the waiting had started to take its toll.

"They're surviving," said Murdock. "The elves want to push forward as soon as the weather improves."

"I'm all for that," said Harrison, tearing a piece of bread and handing it to Tara. The young maiden gladly accepted the food, taking a morsel to her mouth. She then gave a small amount to Lance who gobbled it up whole.

"We need to get out of this place," said Harrison between bites.

"You don't have to tell me twice," said the ranger. "Have you heard anything new?"

Every day Harrison had attended counsel sessions with Moradoril and his advisors, who kept him apprised of their situation. "Nothing since the last time we spoke. The king says we're only a few days away from the dwarves' main entrance."

"I'm willing to bet there's not a big welcome mat laying in front of the doorway," said Murdock.

Harrison looked off to a far corner of the tent. "I'd have to agree."

The ranger took interest in his leader's aloofness. "Is there something wrong, Harrison?"

Turning to face his friend, he asked, "How far away do the Scynthians live?"

Murdock and Pondle exchanged glances, neither sure of the answer. "Their civilization rests in these mountains but where exactly ..." said the ranger, shaking his head.

"Don't you think we should have run into them already?" asked Harrison. "Somewhere? Even if it were only trails or markings?"

"Definitely," said Pondle. "Something's not right with this whole situation."

Harrison felt his belly tighten. Facing his friends, he said with conviction, "Be ready for anything. I don't trust the Scynthians and I don't want to fall into another trap like Arcadia."

"We'll be sure to give you updates," said Murdock. The ranger lifted his sack of elven bread. "Time to secure these rations

335

for another day. Let's go, Pondle." The two men exited the tent, leaving Harrison, Tara, and Lance behind.

"I have a very uneasy feeling, Harrison," said the young maiden. "And I can tell that you do, too."

"Maybe the weather's keeping them at bay," said Harrison in a not too convincing tone. "Either way, we must be ready for them."

"Did the Scynthians really not have anything to do with the dwarves' disappearance?"

Harrison pursed his lips. "We'll see about that, too."

* * *

The convoy of elves and humans continued their trek up the mountainside for two more days. By then, the storm had subsided and blue skies greeted the adventurers for the first time in a week. The terrain leveled out a bit, enough to walk on a horizontal plane instead of a steady upward climb.

Harrison, though the weather remained bitter cold, lowered his hood to take in the gorgeous view. Panning the panoramic landscape, he found snow-covered peaks with evergreens for as far as the eye could see. Way to the south, he barely could make out the deep green shades of the Dark Forest as well as the sun's faint reflections off Lake Alessandra.

"You're a brave one," exclaimed a voice from behind. "Your ears will freeze!" Gaelos caught up to his human counterpart.

Harrison pulled the hood back over his head. "I had to take in the scenery. It's beautiful."

"I'm glad you like it," said the elf. "Because we're here."

"We're here?"

"The dwarves' stronghold," said Gaelos, pointing to the mountainside up ahead. "The entrance is less than a quarter mile away."

Harrison swiveled in the direction that the elf pointed. In the distance, a large, snowy area devoid of trees loomed ahead. "Is that where it is?"

"Yes, buried under the snow."

The young warrior's heart sank, figuring a good ten to fifteen feet of freshly packed snow covered the vicinity. Trying to cheer up, he said, "At least all of this exercise will keep us warm."

"That and the fact that we have so many men," said Gaelos. "We will clear the area in no time."

"What do you expect to find?"

"A massive doorway," said the elf. "I have seen it before."

"Have you gone inside?" asked the young warrior, his excitement level akin to that of a child who had listened to countless fascinating tales spun by his elders.

"No, I remained outside to stand guard."

The young warrior fixed his gaze on the snow mound. "I guess we'll find out this mountain's secrets soon enough."

"That we will. Let's go!" The two men continued their trek toward the buried entranceway, meeting up with the rest of the adventurers a short time later.

Before Harrison loomed a massive mound of snow, covering a ledge that sat back roughly two hundred feet from the edge of the mountainous trail. The elves had begun surveying the perimeter of the snow-filled area, while his team awaited commands.

Harrison trudged through the thick snow and advanced to Murdock's position. Shielding his eyes from the glare, he said, "I guess this is the place."

"It appears to be," said the ranger, while the rest of the group huddled close together to stay warm.

"Let's find Moradoril and see about his strategy," said the young warrior. Pivoting to the rest of his team, he said, "Everyone else wait here. We'll let you know the plan soon." Harrison and Murdock plodded forward, advancing to the elven king's position.

"Welcome to Almandine's Cradle," said Moradoril. "The gateway to the Salinian Dwarves' empire."

Harrison focused on the white mass that loomed before them. "Buried under the snow, I presume."

"Frozen away for many, many years," said the elven king. "It is time to open their doors once again."

337

"How do we do that?" asked Harrison, performing a quick mental calculation. "The snow's piled up at least twenty feet high and we're a few hundred feet away from the entrance."

Moradoril smiled. "We shovel our way through. The task will keep us busy for a while."

The young warrior nodded. "That it will. How would you like us to proceed?"

The king surveyed the area, taking into account the number of elf and human workers he had at his disposal. Moradoril pointed to the middle of the massive snow bank. "There's a large doorway situated in the center of the mountain wall. We must dig a trench that leads us there."

"We'll ready our shovels," said Harrison.

"As will we," said the elven king. "I will get my men to commence with the chore. Have your people start clearing behind them."

"I'll let them know."

Harrison and Murdock returned to their frozen party members. "The elves are going to start clearing a passage," said the young warrior. "We'll help them once they get started."

"That's an awful lot of snow," said Kymbra, resting her hands on her hips.

"Can't you two conjure up some snow removal spell," said Murdock, gesturing to Gelderand and Thoragaard.

"I'm glad you are feeling better," said Gelderand with a smirk. "To answer your question, no."

"Sometimes good old fashioned hard work is the best remedy," said Thoragaard, brandishing a shovel before him. "I suggest we help our friends in order to hasten this project."

The adventurers followed the illusionist's lead, albeit with huffs and grumbles, retrieving their shovels and readying themselves for the task ahead while the elves began the arduous task of clearing the accumulated snow. The two groups worked in unison, meticulously inching forward while shoveling snow away from their ever-growing path to the doorway. After several hours of their mundane task, a shout from the lead elf raised everybody's spirits.

"We're here!" exclaimed one of Moradoril's men.

The elf took his shovel and cleared more snow away from the base of the wall, exposing a non-natural object. Using the end of his spade, he tapped the metal door, eliciting an audible reverberation that everyone heard.

Elf and human alike rushed forward as far as the narrow trench would allow, hoping to get a glimpse of the elusive portal. Harrison, situated toward the back of the mob, could not see the doorway but he did hear the unmistakable thud of metal on metal.

"Everyone, clear away the area in front of the portal!" exclaimed Moradoril.

Shovels dug into the snowy embankment, eliminating the substance that had impeded their progress. A short while later, the team of elves and humans had removed the remaining snow, enabling everyone to see the massive door before them.

Harrison gazed at the large metal doorway. "That's one big portal," said the young warrior, marveling at the entrance's size.

Tara sidled up next to him. "How do we get inside?"

The young warrior strained to get a good look at the entranceway, but the amount of people crowded into the small area made that task difficult. "I'm not sure. I don't think there's a simple knob or latch that'll just let us in."

"On the contrary," said Gelderand, overhearing the young couple's conversation and approaching from behind. "There's probably a code that we need to use in order to open the portal."

"Code?" asked Harrison. "What code?"

"I am willing to bet that there are runes that we need to manipulate."

Harrison shook his head, perplexed. "Where do we find them?"

"I believe the Talisman had runes on it, did it not?" said the mage.

The young warrior's eyes widened. "It does!"

"Let's get a better look at this portal before we do anything hasty," said the magician.

"Good idea," said Harrison. "Everyone, follow me."

The young warrior led his group through the elven lines, reaching the cleared area in front of the massive doorway.

Moradoril and Brianna had started to inspect the entry, using their bare hands to feel symbols etched into the metallic door.

"What have you found?" asked Harrison to the royal couple.

"A bit of a mystery," said Brianna. "There are many runes carved throughout the portal."

"Didn't you visit this place before? In the past?" asked Harrison. "How did you get in then?"

"The door was already open at that time," said Brianna. "When we left, it closed from behind and never opened again."

Moradoril approached the two. "The Talisman you possess contains runes, does it not?"

"Yes, it does," said Harrison, "and we were just about to compare the symbols on it to the ones etched in the portal."

"I think that is a wise decision," said the elven king.

Harrison gazed over to his friend. "Swinkle, can you bring the Talisman here?"

The young cleric rummaged through his sack, found the silver object, and handed it to Harrison. The young warrior focused on the raised markings, not understanding their meaning.

With a huff, he said, "I have no idea what to make of this."

Swinkle took the opportunity to make a closer examination of the portal's runes. Recalling Maligor the Red's magical signatures, he said in confidence, "Harrison, these runes are Dwarvish and not made by humans."

"Are you sure?"

"I am positive. Nothing here reflects Maligor's handiwork."

"That should not surprise you," said Moradoril, joining the two young men. "However, we are better versed in the ways of the dwarves. Allow me to take a look?"

Harrison and Swinkle stepped aside, giving Moradoril and his queen ample space to conduct their examination. Harrison watched the two mouth words to themselves, in an apparent attempt to read the ancient language. The young warrior paid particular attention to Brianna's actions, how she touched the cold metal-etched runes with elongated fingers as she read the symbols to herself. After several minutes of inspection, the royal couple turned to present their findings.

Moradoril nodded to his queen, giving her the floor. Brianna extended her hand in Harrison's direction. "May I have the Talisman?"

The young warrior did not hesitate, relinquishing his race's sacred gift to the elven queen. Brianna accepted the piece of metal, alternating her gaze from the relic to the portal.

Satisfied with her assessment, she said, "I believe the clues that we need are contained in this artifact. However, we must manipulate the access key with some level of certainty."

Harrison crinkled his brow. "I don't understand."

Moradoril stepped forward, outstretching his hand to the massive entryway. "The runes that are etched here are similar to the ones carved into the Talisman. That is the good news," he started. "What we need to decipher is the combination to enter the Dwarves' realm."

"That only makes sense," said Swinkle. The young cleric recalled his past experience with magical combinations, particularly in the Sacred Seven Rooms. "However, invalid sequences can lead to dire results."

"That is very true," said Brianna. "We must be careful."

"What do you propose we do?" asked Harrison.

"Come closer and I will show you," said the elven queen, gesturing for the humans to approach the doorway. Pointing to the runes before her, she continued, "These symbols here correspond to the runes on the artifact."

Harrison focused on the portal, counting twenty symbols. Upon closer examination, he realized that the runes on the door were identical to the ones found on the Talisman.

"They're the same!" exclaimed Harrison.

"Yes, they are." Waving the young warrior closer, Brianna said, "Look harder."

The young warrior brought his focus to the ancient text. Squinting, he found small slits just below each rune. Pointing to the anomaly, he said, "That's not natural."

"No, it is not," answered the queen.

Swinkle, having listened to the conversation, stepped forward. "I think I know what they are!"

Everyone turned to face the holy man. "I have a guess as well, but I would like to hear your hypothesis first," said Brianna.

The young cleric took a moment to clarify his thoughts, then said, "From my experience, we need to match up the symbols." Swinkle pointed to the Talisman in Brianna's hand. "All four of the runes on the artifact are listed in this row of symbols." Everyone gazed back to the entranceway, finding the same runes.

Swinkle pointed to the razor thin slits in the portal. "The openings under the characters lead me to believe that something gets placed into the slot. That would be the artifact." The young cleric paused, collecting his thoughts again. "And we need to push the relic into the slot until it meets the same symbol."

"That's sound judgement, Swinkle," said Harrison. "But the Talisman's curved and we'd risk breaking it if we tried to force it into the slot."

The young cleric smiled, as if he knew something the others did not. "Harrison, I have seen more than my fair share of strangeness on this adventure and this situation is no different.

"We possess a magical object that contains the same symbols that exist on a magically shut door. I am willing to bet something will happen when we place the Talisman into one of the slits."

Swinkle panned to Brianna. "Shall we try?"

The elven queen exchanged glances with her husband, then said. "Though your rationale is sound and thought through, magic can still be a tricky thing." Brianna smiled. "However, I had come to the same conclusion as you."

The queen strode back to the portal, finding the first symbol from the line of runes. Raising the curved piece of the Talisman to the etching, she found that the third symbol matched the rune on the door. She then used her finger to examine the slit, finding it just a bit wider than the thickness of the artifact she held in her hand.

After pondering her next move, Brianna placed the edge of the curved Talisman into the awaiting slot, which fit perfectly. Then, to everyone's surprise, the silver relic straightened and stayed stuck in the slit, while the rune above it glowed white, as if illuminated from behind the wall.

"Now, this makes more sense," said Brianna. The elven queen inspected the straightened piece of metal, finding that all four runes now rested equidistant from each other.

"The third symbol is exactly the same as the one glowing," she said. "I am going to push this into the doorway until the two meet."

Brianna felt no resistance as the silver relic slid deeper into the portal. She stopped upon reaching the matching rune. As soon as the two symbols touched, the white light changed to a glowing, blood red. The queen then removed the Talisman from the opening and repeated her steps with the next symbol to the right, finding that it started out glowing white but then changed to red upon the runes meeting.

"I am going to complete the process," said Brianna, removing and inserting the Talisman under each symbol in the sequence. When finished, the twenty runes glowed red.

Harrison had stood by like everyone else and watched the queen complete her task. Now that she was done, he said, "What happens next?"

Before the woman could answer, a low rumble permeated from behind the portal. Everyone took a step back as the massive door unlocked and slowly cracked open about a foot before stopping.

Moradoril waved the legion of men and elves over. "Come! We must push it in from here!"

The mass of elves and humans positioned themselves along the doorway and after a count of three pushed the portal inward with all their might. The massive hinges creaked, having remained stationary for a thousand years. Moments later, the doorway to Almandine's Cradle stood open.

Murdock and Pondle sidled next to the young warrior. "We're going in with the elves," said the ranger.

"Good idea," said Harrison. "Take Lance with you." The little dog heard his name and rushed to his master's side.

Murdock and Pondle unsheathed their swords. "Let's go, Pondle," said the ranger as the two men and dog followed the elven scouts.

Harrison gazed back at his remaining friends. "Ready your torches, I'm sure it's going to be dark in there." The young warrior sought Kymbra, making eye contact with her.

"Kymbra," said Harrison, "you, Adrith, and Marissa form a tight perimeter around the rest of the team. We'll all proceed forward with Moradoril and Brianna." The young warrior then locked his eyes on Tara, giving her reassurance without uttering a word.

Harrison assumed the lead position, then waved his friends forward. With his people situated, he slung his weapon into his hands, relishing the feel of his axe's hilt. For the first time in a long while, he actually yearned for battle, his blade having rested far too long.

The young warrior allowed eight elven sentries to surround their royal leaders and, moments later, the contingent of men and elves stood on the precipice of the entryway.

Moradoril addressed the assembled mob. "The dwarves' empire resides deep inside the mountain; however, we have no idea what to expect along the way. Keep your weapons in hand and be ready for battle."

The king turned his attention to his sentries. "Scouts! Lead the way!"

Floriad, Gaelos, and Liagol had assumed their position with five other sentries, while Murdock and Pondle rounded out the team of ten. Lance scurried to the forefront, eager to begin his task as well. Their marching order set, the reconnaissance team began their trek into the bowels of the mountain.

Moradoril, satisfied with the start of their next journey, summoned a squadron of his soldiers. Ten elven fighters approached their king.

"Remain here at the portal's entrance," said the elven leader. "Protect us from anything that might try to enter through the open doorway. If you do not hear from us in three days, send half of your team to search for us." The elves nodded in unison, then dropped back to take up their new position.

Moradoril beckoned Harrison. "Your group will advance with us and we will locate the dwarves together."

The young warrior heeded the king's command, gesturing for his friends to step forward. The eight elven soldiers assumed positions in front of their leader and began their march, while others dropped back to protect the rear.

Harrison turned to face his friends, finding ready but anxious eyes gazing back at him. With a single nod, he and his friends crossed the portal's threshold and stepped into the ensuing darkness, beginning their trek into the inner depths of Almandine's Cradle.

CHAPTER 28

Ͼ

The adventurers' hand-held torches cast eerie shadows along the stone walls of the passageway. Harrison strained to see how far ahead Murdock, Pondle, and the lead elves ventured from their position. Instead of seeing his friends' bobbing torches, ever thickening spider webs kept clouding his vision.

The sheer size of the corridor surprised the young warrior. The walls consisted of solid rock, carved out of the mountain itself, twenty feet high by twenty feet wide with a dirt flooring remarkably level and easy to traverse. Great engineers, he thought.

Before venturing further into the mountain's dark depths, the young warrior's fighter instincts harked for him to evaluate his surroundings. The elves appear to know where they're going, he thought, and a subtle glance to his left and right allayed any worries. The dwarves did not have any secret passageways branching off the main trail, and nothing could penetrate the solid stone walls, eliminating a sneak attack on the convoy.

Harrison continued his assessment. Elven sentries provided tight security around Moradoril and Brianna. Peeking over his shoulder, his friends clutched torches and advanced at a nice even pace with more elves bringing up the rear. So far, so good.

The cadre of beings continued their march for another hour before stopping. Harrison counted ten bobbing torches advancing back to their position from up ahead. Moments later, familiar faces greeted them, along with one happy canine.

"The passage starts taking a turn downward fifty yards ahead," said Murdock, as Lance bounded toward Harrison and Tara, happy to be reunited with his master.

"That makes sense," said Moradoril. "The dwarves mine deep inside the mountain. Almandine's Cradle is still further."

"What exactly is Almandine's Cradle?" asked Harrison, having heard the term many times since arriving at the main entrance to the passage.

"It is where the dwarves keep their treasures," said the king. "An elaborate mining system filled with gems, jewels, and precious stones."

Harrison's mind drifted, imagining rare gems and perfectly polished stones piled as high as the eye could see. Pushing that image aside, he honed in on a topic that had gnawed at his gut since their meeting with the elves. Baiting the king, he asked, "Will they mind us entering their realm?"

Moradoril glanced to Brianna, then said, "They will not mind at all."

The young warrior raised an eyebrow. Pressing the elven king, he said, "Why is that? I'd be very concerned if someone showed up to my sacred mines unannounced." The rest of Harrison's team inched closer, wanting to hear the conversation and, more importantly, the king's answers.

"They are not here, Harrison," said Moradoril in a guarded tone. "In a manner of speaking."

Harrison shook his head, recalling that Floriad had told him to question everything not too long ago. "Can you please elaborate? Something doesn't feel right about this suspended animation you mentioned at your complex."

"It is best that you see for yourself," said the king. "We are almost there."

"No!" said Harrison with emphasis. "You're hiding something and I want to know now instead of being surprised later."

Unaccustomed to being refused, Moradoril's brow creased and his lip curled, signaling his disapproval at the young warrior's latest remark. The elven king glared at the Aegean fighter. "My people are not hiding anything. I told you what we did."

347

"I want to know more, Moradoril, and I want you to tell me." The young warrior did not waver, returning his own glare toward his counterpart. "We have come a long way and I want answers before anything unusual happens."

"Tell him," said a calm voice behind the king. "He deserves to know." Brianna's request softened the king's stance.

Moradoril sighed, shaking his head. "They are all frozen," he said. "Each and every single one of them."

Harrison's eyes grew wide, surprised at the king's statement. "All of the dwarves are frozen solid?"

Moradoril cocked his head from side to side. "I would not say frozen like a block of ice, more like a person placed into a deep sleep. Their bodies are cooled to the point where they are suspended in time and completely safe, just like I have told you many times already."

Each answer struck Harrison harder than the previous one. "I still don't understand the ramifications of why you'd place an entire race in hibernation?"

Moradoril thrusted a finger at the young warrior. "Your people gave us those orders."

Harrison spread his arms wide, his voice rising. "You keep telling us that, but what's the real reason why?"

"That, I don't know," shouted the king. "And I don't want to speculate!"

Harrison took a moment to gather his thoughts. Why would his human ancestors order the elves to place the Salinian Dwarves in stasis? Something did not make sense to this warrior.

"Everything you've said leads me to believe that we're not understanding something," said the Aegean, taking a finger and circling it around the members of his group. "Please relate the facts of the past again."

Moradoril had grown tired of all the explanations but acquiesced nonetheless. Drawing a heavy sigh, he said, "Your King Ballesteros sought us and asked to provide him a favor to the human race," started the elven king. "A very complex and controversial favor."

"I've always sensed there was something more to this plan. What did he ask?" said the young warrior.

"Your people had a division of power and the three kings knew that their days had come to an end," continued the elf. "They wanted to be sure that an army would be ready to fight when the time came."

"A Dwarvish army, right?" asked Harrison, cocking his head.

"Yes, as well as elven soldiers."

"Why are the dwarves suspended in time?" Harrison knew the answer but he needed to hear the words spoken from Moradoril's mouth to be certain.

The king sighed again. "They were not keen to Ballesteros' plan," he said. "They balked at his grandiose battle strategy."

The young warrior's eyes narrowed, his anger increasing. "Let me get this straight," said Harrison. "You entombed an entire race against their will?"

Moradoril nodded once with a slight slump to his shoulders. "Time was not on our side."

"Because the kings knew that King Holleris would banish them," said Harrison.

"Yes."

"Then why do we need them now?" asked the young warrior, trying desperately to piece together the land's sordid tale.

"That I do not know," said the king. "Your kings told us long ago to wait for an heir to the throne to arrive before enacting anything."

"Why didn't you say this to Marcus when we arrived several months ago?" asked Harrison, recalling his visit to the elves compound with his deceased leader, Marcus Braxton. "You had the opportunity then."

"He did not possess the Talisman at that time," said Moradoril, hammering his point home. "That is the key to everything."

Harrison took another moment to digest the information. No matter how much he thought on the matter, something still did not feel right. "Just because we arrived with an obscure piece of silver means that we're all preparing for war?"

Moradoril maintained his stare on Harrison. "It would seem to be."

"A battle for what?" asked the young warrior.

"Again, that is something I do not know."

Harrison recalled a passage in the Ancient Scrolls of Arcadia that mentioned an improbable alliance. "The scrolls we uncovered talked about an unlikely partnership. I'm assuming that means you and the dwarves?"

"It makes sense," said the elven king. "There is no love lost between our peoples."

"Even less now, knowing that you froze them against their will!" exclaimed the young warrior. "How exactly did you manage to do that?"

"Harrison," said Brianna, stepping forward, "we possess strong magical capabilities. Our magic has bound them and only we can set them free."

"How are they bound?" asked the young warrior.

"It is best you see for yourself," said the elven queen. "The entombed army is not that far away from our current position."

"I suggest we continue our trek then," said Harrison. "The sooner we resolve this matter, the better."

The royal couple nodded in silent concurrence. Moradoril motioned to his sentries to press forward, which they did, along with Murdock, Pondle, and Lance.

Harrison assumed his position in the procession, trekking deeper into the mountain's depths, all the while trying to understand how he came to his current predicament. Some fifty yards later, the passageway started to pitch downward, just like Murdock had said. Sweat began to collect on the young warrior's forehead, his fur coverings no longer needed to protect him from the bitter cold. Torches bobbed in the distance, indicating that nothing was impeding their forward progress.

From the corner of his eye, Harrison noticed more cobwebs lining the stone hallway, his hand-held flame illuminating them as an eerie white lattice. Old relics left behind from another time, reasoned the young warrior. However, as the soldiers trekked deeper into the mountainside, more webs appeared, growing thicker with each passing step.

"Swinkle," called Harrison to the holy man on his right. "What do you make of these spider webs?"

The young cleric gazed upwards, finding the sticky substance littering the ceiling of the passageway. Crinkling his brow, he said, "That is odd. I know this corridor is very old and has not been used in years. I would expect to see cobwebs, but these appear much thicker."

"And relatively new," said Harrison, taking more of an interest in the stringy material.

"Where there's cobwebs, there's …" said Swinkle before Harrison cut him off.

"Spiders!" Harrison pointed his torch straight into the air. The young warrior brought his focus to the ceiling, finding that it undulated in a most disturbing way. Thick, stubby torsos that sprouted eight legs apiece scurried as one from high above.

Everyone in the general area heard the young warrior's exclamation and saw his subsequent gaze to the ceiling. As if on cue, spiders dropped from the heavens on sticky strands, their spindly legs searching for their awaiting prey below. Tara shrieked, shocked and frightened at the arrival of the unwanted beasts.

Harrison heard his love's screams and focused his eyes on the closest spider. However, before he could flail his weapon, elven archers used incredible quickness to train their bows on the unsuspecting menaces, filling one after another with arrows, dropping them to the floor. One of the spiders fell in front of the young warrior, who then sliced the three foot wide arachnid in two with his battle axe, the dismembered creature's legs still twitching.

The immediate threat neutralized, the young warrior frantically searched for Tara. The young maiden, torch clutched in her hand, cowered several feet in front of his position.

"Tara, use your torch to keep them at bay!" shouted Harrison.

A spider dropped from the ceiling landing beside the lass. Heeding Harrison's command, she waved her torch at the beast that hovered just over her head. The spider stopped its descent, not wanting Tara's flame to burn its underbelly. The monster reached with its many legs, trying its best to avoid the flame while attempting to grab the terrified girl at the same time.

As she kept the spider at bay, an archer planted an arrow between the monster's eyes, halting its attack and dropping it to the floor. On its way down, its bloody abdomen smacked Tara's head, smearing the young maiden with a gooey substance, along with sticky strands of webbing.

Tara wailed, horrified. In an act of desperation, she planted her torch against the spider's body, igniting it in the process, insuring the monster's death. The dying beast's limbs began to spasm and, as they did, smacked against the girl's leg. The young maiden's eyes widen in shock, her breath sucked from her lungs. Disgusted by the unwelcome touching, she brushed the unwanted limb aside in one smooth motion, using her torch to push the severed torso away from her for good.

"Tara!" exclaimed Harrison, reaching the young girl. "Are you alright?"

Finally catching her breath, she clenched her teeth and cried, "I hate spiders!"

"Then you're going to be in for a long afternoon!" said Harrison.

The ghastly creatures continued to drop from the dark ceiling, grabbing elves and humans alike. Arrows whizzed through the air, while swords and axes clashed in fighting, everyone doing their best to repel the disgusting beasts. A sudden flash startled everyone in the immediate area.

Harrison stopped hacking at the spiders, spinning to see what had created the new light source. Several yards ahead of him, Brianna held her arms toward the heavens. A greenish-yellow glow sprung from her fingertips, producing an impenetrable shield, stopping the spiders' descent onto the fighters.

"Gelderand! Thoragaard!" exclaimed Moradoril. "Torch the beasts!"

The two men heeded the elven king's command. Mumbling to themselves, the mages angled their hands toward the ceiling. Seconds later, bright orange flashes sprung from their fingertips. The projectiles penetrated the shield and rocketed toward the ceiling, incinerating the cobwebs and spiders. The creatures shrieked in agony as burning bodies fell from the top of the passageway to the magical buffer zone. Below, the men thrashed at

the spiders trapped under Brianna's shield spell, severing an
untold number of limbs, splattering goo and sticky strands
throughout the ranks.

"This is horrible!" squealed Tara, her clothing smattered
with gelatinous matter.

Harrison, sweat flowing from his brow, continued to hack
at the grotesque beasts, slaying all those in his way. After several
exhausting minutes of fighting, Brianna ended her spell, the
protective shield disappearing from sight. Burned body parts fell
onto the adventurers, the smell of charred flesh permeating the
area.

The young warrior, eyes wide and senses heightened,
panned the vicinity. The spiders' sudden attack was over and none
of the creatures remained. Kymbra, Adrith, and Marissa stood
close by, their weapons still drawn. Gelderand and Thoragaard
had their hands up and ready to cast another spell, if needed.
Swinkle and Fallyn readied themselves to heal those bitten by the
spiders, while Tara did her best to compose herself. However,
people were missing.

"Where's Murdock and Pondle?" asked the young warrior,
his concern rising.

"They were up ahead with the elven scouts," said Kymbra,
worried about the unaccounted group members.

"Lance is with them, too," said Tara.

"We need to press forward!" exclaimed Harrison. "They're
in trouble!" The young warrior took the lead, bypassing Moradoril
and Brianna in the process. Turning to the elven couple, he said,
"We're going to need more of your magic!"

Harrison headed down the pitched corridor, sidestepping
spider carcasses along the way. Each step brought him closer to
ever-thickening cobwebs, while a sickening feeling brewed in his
stomach. Straining in the low light, the young warrior identified
the vague outline of someone bent on one knee. His heart
pounding, he quickened his pace until he reached the person.

Halting, he said with trepidation, "Murdock?"

The ranger remained hunched over and did not
acknowledge his friend. A second later he heaved, vomiting onto
the dirt passageway. Harrison took a step back, shocked.

"Murdock," he called again in a guarded tone. "What's the matter?"

The ranger groaned, catching his breath. "Be prepared for what you see when you go in there." Murdock pointed down the hallway, not bothering to look back at his friend.

Harrison swallowed hard, staring in the direction his friend pointed. In a feeble voice, he asked, "What am I going to see?"

"Words cannot describe it," said the ranger. "You must see for yourself."

By that time, the rest of the party had reached Harrison's position. Swinkle approached the young warrior first. "Is he alright?" asked the young cleric, staring with apprehension toward Murdock.

"No," said Harrison. "He's sick. Please tend to him." The young warrior turned and faced the rest of the party. "Kymbra, I need you, Adrith, and Marissa to come with me. Everyone else, remain here."

Moradoril stepped forward. "We will accompany you." Motioning for five of his soldiers to follow him, he said, "We have men down this passage, too."

Harrison took his focus down the corridor, finding a soft light emanating from a chamber about fifty yards away. Pointing to the light source, he said, "We need to go there."

The small convoy took cautious steps while approaching the awaiting chamber. Harrison, clutching his battle axe's hilt with a tight grip, maintained his forward focus. To his amazement, he found a familiar being bounding in his direction.

"Lance?" he said with surprise in his voice. "What's going on in there?"

"Bad monster!" yapped the little dog, circling the people. "Monster!"

Harrison craned his head in Kymbra's direction. "He says there's a monster in the chamber. Be ready." The tall blonde warrior nodded, her cohorts hearing Harrison's interpretation of Lance's barks as well. Moradoril and his men readied their weapons, anticipating a battle.

The young warrior continued his trek toward the lit sanctuary. The passageway's slight pitch leveled off, allowing the

354

group secure footing heading into the room. Harrison kept his eyes wide, taking in his surroundings.

Craning his neck again, he said, "There's a larger room in front of us."

"Looks like it goes to the left and right as well," said Kymbra, analyzing the new phenomenon from her position.

"Keep on the lookout for this monster," added the young warrior.

The ten people and one dog reached the end of the corridor. Instead of a big open space, another passage spanning to the left and right, just like Kymbra had suspected, loomed in front of them.

Harrison and the others entered the new passageway. The young warrior gazed overhead, solving the mystery of the light source.

"Torches," said Harrison, motioning with his head at the wall-mounted lighting that spanned the hallway in both directions. "They're about ten yards apart."

"And magically lit," added Moradoril. "An oil-based torch would never still be burning after a thousand years."

The young warrior gazed at the torches, finding no obvious source for their continued burning after such a long time. "Be ready for anything."

"Indeed," replied the elven king.

After Harrison and the small group entered the new passage, an elf scout trained his bow on a figure running toward them from their left. "Look!" he shouted.

"It's Pondle!" exclaimed the young warrior. Lance bolted at the halfling upon seeing him. The thief ran past the dog without acknowledging him. As he got closer, Harrison noticed a very anxious expression on his friend's face.

"Where's Murdock?" asked Pondle, gasping for air.

"He's back there and he's sick," said Harrison, jerking his thumb to the corridor behind them. The young warrior took a closer look at his friend. Pondle appeared disheveled, his hair matted with sweat and his clothing covered in goo and thick strands of webbing.

"Pondle," said Harrison in a steady tone, "what's over there?"

The thief lifted his eyes to meet his leader's stare. "Spiders are everywhere and they're … they're …" Pondle stuttered, a blank expression on his face.

Harrison crinkled his brow, confused. "They're what?"

The thief's face dropped. "They're eating the dwarves," he said in a meek voice, part of him still shocked at what he had seen.

The young warrior's eyes grew round. "Eating the dwarves!" Gasps permeated throughout the small group. With all eyes turning to Moradoril, Harrison asked, "Why are spiders making a meal out of the dwarves?"

For the first time, Harrison saw a blank stare flash across the elven king's face. Eyes wide as well, Moradoril slowly shook his head and said, "I have no idea."

The young warrior took a purposeful step toward the king, recalling Floriad's words about questioning everything. "Didn't you tell us that your people suspended the dwarves in animation? Keeping them alive until we arrived?"

Moradoril, his mind churning, focused on the Aegean. "That had always been the plan, to keep the dwarves in hibernation until the time came."

Harrison again tried to wrap his mind around the elven king's cryptic facts. "You said that the Ancient Kings had plans for the Salinian Dwarves and now they're dead!"

"They're not all dead," said Pondle, still trying in vain to erase the images he had seen from his brain. "Some are still alive now."

"We must save them!" exclaimed Harrison. Pointing at Moradoril, he shouted, "You need to make this right!"

Moradoril raised his palms to the angered warrior. "Calm down, Harrison! We need to think this through before we go charging into a trap!"

"What do you propose then?" asked the young warrior, his patience wearing thin.

The elven king approached Pondle, placing a hand on his back. The thief tensed upon feeling Moradoril's touch. "Pondle, give us a detailed description of what is down the corridor."

The thief's shoulders slumped before turning to face the small group. "This corridor goes on for quite a way," started the halfling. "The deeper into the mountain you go, the more Dwarven soldiers you'll find frozen in the walls, in some kind of stand-up coffin filled with ice."

"Yes, that's true," said Moradoril in a calm voice, nodding in agreement. "That is how we left them."

Pondle shook his head. "Except the spiders have broken into the frozen sarcophaguses and began making meals of the dwarves."

The king shook his head, disagreeing with the thief's assessment. "That's not possible! We magically sealed their tombs. The spiders could not possibly shatter the ice through conventional ways."

"There's only one answer then," said Harrison, all eyes turning to the Aegean. "The spiders aren't using predictable tactics."

Moradoril spun on his heel, defiant. "Impossible! Spiders are unintelligent creatures and live on pure instinct. They cannot negate magic."

"Maybe they had some help," said the young warrior. Moradoril stood with mouth agape, trying to figure out how that scenario was remotely possible.

"Either way," added Pondle, "we're going to need more men. A lot more men."

The elven king turned to one of his soldiers. "Gaelos, fetch everyone else! Now!"

The sentry ran off to complete his task while the rest of the people contemplated their next move. Minutes later, the entire contingent of humans and elves congregated in the passageway.

Harrison glanced at the elven king, then addressed the group. "Just to let everyone know, what stands before us is a horrific scene. I haven't ventured down these passageways yet, but gauging by Murdock and Pondle's reactions, we're in for a challenging time. Spiders are everywhere and we must slaughter them."

Anxious stares remained fixed on the young warrior as he trained his eyes on his own party. "Tara and Fallyn, you'll remain here. I don't want either of you involved in the fighting." Focusing on two of the female warriors, he continued. "Adrith, Marissa, you hang back with them. Lance will come with us and I'll send him back if we need you to fight."

Before anyone could protest, Moradoril added, "Floriad and Gaelos will accompany your people, in case these spiders get crafty and attack from another direction." The two sentries maneuvered away from their fellow elves and stood beside their human counterparts.

The elven king turned to his partner. "Though I would rather have you stay behind, you know as well as I that I need you with us."

Brianna nodded. "You need not worry, my king."

Harrison, sensing the time for battle had come, said, "Everyone, ready your weapons." Making eye contact with Gelderand and Thoragaard, he added, "Be ready to torch the living hell out of these monsters." Turning to Moradoril, he continued, "We're ready."

Moradoril pointed his sword down the corridor. "Onward!" he bellowed, signaling to his sentries to take the lead.

The elven scouts inched forward with their bows ready to fire. Harrison and his crew followed close behind, their weapons ready to strike. The young warrior, along with Moradoril and Brianna, trailed a few steps behind Murdock and Pondle, with Lance scurrying between the two groups. Thoragaard, Gelderand, and Swinkle took cautious steps behind the young warrior, while Kymbra brought up the rear, along with the rest of the elven soldiers.

From the young warrior's vantage point, the lit torches allowed ample lighting in the general area. Peeking upwards, some twenty feet above his head he saw the beginnings of webbing, thickening with every step forward he made. His belly churned when he noticed the ceiling's grotesque undulation, realizing that many creatures were moving *en masse*. Up ahead, the corridor began to bend to the right, emulating a circular pattern.

Harrison's eyes darted everywhere, the cobwebs growing thicker and descending closer and closer to the passage flooring. Noticing something unusual, he squinted to find intertwined in the webbing several tightly wound sacks high in the webs. Upon further examination he determined that the spiders tended to these objects more than anything else.

Pondle spun his head back. "Be ready, we're almost there."

Harrison nodded, eyes glued forward. Ready for what, he asked himself. The corridor continued its circular bend before the group encountered the first burial chamber. The young warrior gazed upon what was supposed to be a dwarf frozen in ice, but instead nothing more than an empty coffin awaited them. Shards of broken glass took the place of the frozen liquid, the jagged edges stained dark red. Sticky strands of webbing cascaded all around the opening.

A few of the elven sentries moved forward, then held their position, allowing their superiors to investigate. The archers trained their bows in every direction, keeping a careful eye on the gyrating ceiling.

Pondle sheathed his sword and approached the compromised tomb. Having seen this coffin before, he pointed to the chamber's insides and said, "Look here." The thief motioned toward the crypt's innards. "If I had to venture a guess, I'd say something forcefully extracted the being from inside this tomb."

Harrison peered into the sanctuary. Blood stained the stone surfaces and hardened webbing clung to the walls. The young warrior's stomach churned as he thought of what might have happened.

"Do you think the spiders pulled out one of the dwarves?" he asked, hoping his assessment was false.

"That's the most plausible conclusion," said Pondle. "I'm thinking that those creatures shattered the glass and snuffed out the poor soul."

"That dwarf was trapped with nowhere to run," said Murdock, his face pale. "What if he were somehow awake before the attack? Imagine the horror of knowing that a hungry spider kept slamming into the clear covering with no way to fight back or escape. Eventually, the monsters broke into the coffin and ..." the ranger's voice trailed off, not needing to state the obvious.

Harrison gripped his axe tighter, then turned to Moradoril. "Why is this glass and not ice?" he asked through clenched teeth.

"I assure you," said the elven king, staring deep into Harrison's eyes, "that we sealed every one of these tombs in a cold, life supporting liquid. The dwarves rested in perfect hibernation for a millennium."

The young warrior grabbed a shard of the clear substance and snapped it off the casing. "How can you say that when this is nothing but thin glass!" Harrison threw the broken sliver to the ground, shattering it to pieces.

"I am telling you, Harrison, foul play has happened here," replied Moradoril with conviction. "You don't really believe that we would have sentenced an entire race to a horrifying death, do you?"

The young warrior shook his head, disgusted and confused. "No, I don't. But how did this happen?"

"We must investigate further," said Moradoril.

"Then be prepared for what's up ahead," said Pondle. "What you see here is just the tip of the iceberg."

The thief waved the small group forward, the elven archers advancing next to him, ready to fire their weapons. Harrison and the others followed close behind, waiting for something to happen. The young warrior panned either side of the corridor, finding more broken tombs and streaks of old, caked blood. The sight of thickening webbing began to work on his nerves.

Each step down the curving passageway led the group deeper into the dwarves' domain, along with bringing more anguish and pain. Ripped clothing and torn armor hung from shards of broken casings. Harrison could only imagine the horrors these beings endured. The next step the young warrior took changed everything.

From the corridor's ceiling dropped spider after spider, each one on their own sticky strand. Hovering mere feet over the men, the monsters attacked with their long legs and lunged with their fangs. The young warrior did his best to fend off the creatures with his axe, the close quarters limiting his fighting ability.

The archers fired arrow after arrow, each one hitting their mark but barely halting the attack. In one smooth, coordinated effort two of the creatures teamed up to clutch one of the elves, grabbing him with its front legs and yanking the poor soul upward toward the ceiling. Harrison heard the sentry's screams from above, bringing his worrisome gaze to the corridor's upper limit, watching in disgust as the monsters bit the archer, paralyzing him in the process. After the soldier stopped thrashing, the spiders spun the elf in a cocoon, encasing him. They then left him in one of the myriad of cobwebs, storing him away for another time. The beasts then descended on their threads for another meal.

Harrison flailed wildly at the falling creatures, severing legs in the process, but scarcely stopping their advancement. As sweat broke on his brow, he yelled back to his friends, "Gelderand, Thoragaard! Torch them!" To his dismay, he heard nothing.

The young warrior spun his head, finding that the two magicians had no room to maneuver, let alone time to concentrate on such an intense spell.

A hard push on his back broke him from his trance. Two furry legs leaned against the young warrior, the spider doing its best to maneuver Harrison closer to its jaws. The young warrior slashed at the spider, but soon realized that his battle axe proved more cumbersome than a sword, each attempt to hit the creature leaving him open to an attack. To his surprise, the spider leaned forward, exposing itself. Harrison did not miss his opportunity to strike the beast, slicing the creature and severing its head. The monster's legs twitched as it slid to the floor.

"You owe me!" exclaimed Murdock, removing his sword from the spider's back.

"There's too many of them!" lamented Harrison.

The young warrior raised his blade again, thwarting another attack from above. By this time, spiders dropped like rain from the heavens. Sticky webbing started to entomb the area, preventing him from using his primary weapon. The more he fought, the more he knew that the spiders were winning the battle. He kept repeating to himself a rule he learned at the Fighter's Guild: the enemy will always have the upper hand in their own territory; you must take away that advantage. Scanning the vicinity in a controlled panic, Harrison realized that he and his friends had failed to secure the area and they were now paying the price for that mistake.

A flash of light erupted from behind the young warrior's position, halting the monsters from encasing the group with their thick webs. Spiders scurried back up their sticky twine, evacuating the area. Harrison turned and trained his eyes on a smaller figure near Moradoril, finding Brianna waving her hands, producing even more blinding light.

The young warrior brought a hand to shield his eyes, the area turning a bright white, preventing him from seeing anything at all. Even though the whiteout rendered his sight useless, he felt an intense heat radiating near his position. Orange blurs rushed skyward, exploding upon contact with the chamber's upper limit. Instead of screams of pain, gooey severed body parts and sticky webbing pelted the adventurers from above.

The young warrior instinctively covered his head from the raining debris, not realizing that a fiery orange glow had replaced the blinding light. Taking his gaze upwards, the ceiling burned as fire enveloped the webbing, using it as kindling to continue its blaze. Crispy spiders scurried to get away from the unwanted inferno, giving Harrison's group a chance to move onward.

The Aegean glanced back, finding Gelderand and Thoragaard awaiting his next move. He gestured with his head for them to follow, then turned to Murdock and Pondle, ordering, "Keep moving forward!"

The men pressed on, along with the elven scouts, thickening cobwebs choking the passageway. The young warrior took a few more steps before a new set of circumstances presented itself.

"Are these coffins frozen?" asked Harrison, making a closer inspection at the entombed beings in the walls.

Moradoril took great interest in the new finding, scrutinizing the casing and running his hands on the surface in order to look deeper into the chamber.

"Look! This dwarf is in perfect hibernation!" exclaimed the elven king.

Harrison and the others rushed to Moradoril's side. "Are you sure?" asked the young warrior.

"See for yourself," said the king. "The spiders have not compromised this one."

The young warrior placed his hand on the outer casing, feeling the smooth ice surface, sensing its coldness. Taking his sleeve, he rubbed away the fog on the tomb's exterior. To his surprise, a set of eyes gazed back at him.

Harrison jumped back. "There's someone in there!"

"And in perfect hibernation," reiterated Moradoril. "This is how we left them a millennium ago."

The young warrior pointed deeper into the cavern. "The spiders disturbed a lot more tombs."

"Let's get to king's room before we make any final assessments," said the elven leader. "It is where we laid Drogut to rest."

"Drogut?" said Harrison, creasing his brow, unfamiliar with the name.

"Drogut is the dwarf king," said Moradoril with a hint of disgust. "A very stubborn, staunch, unruly, dwarf king."

Harrison shook his head. "There's so much I still don't know."

"Let's continue onward."

The group resumed their trek down the corridor, finding more compromised chambers, blood, and debris. Harrison lifted his anxious eyes upward, seeing movement in the ceiling, but nothing dropping down on him and the men for now. He also noticed untouched chambers sprinkled throughout the array of tombs, unsure why some dwarves had escaped the horror of certain death. A loud crash broke his concentration.

"What was that?" he yelled to no one in particular. Before anyone answered, a loud shriek bellowed from down the hallway, followed by horror-filled screams.

Harrison's instincts took over and he started to rush forward. "Someone needs our help!" he exclaimed, the elves, Murdock, and Pondle chasing after him. Lance raced past the people, then stopped short. The small dog began to bark at a feverish clip, standing in an attack position with his tail stiff.

The young warrior looked on in disgust as three spiders descended on a damaged coffin. One of the spiders flicked away broken shards of glass and reached inside the tomb with its hairy legs. Stubby fists punched at the intruder while the occupant screeched at the top of its lungs. Moments later, the second spider lunged into the encasing, its fangs puncturing something soft. The yelling subsided as the spiders continued their gruesome extraction task.

Harrison watched the scene unfold, shocked and horrified. The two spiders worked in unison to yank the paralyzed dwarf through the casing, the sharp glass edges ripping the being's flesh, pouring blood all over the chamber and flooring. The third spider hovered from above on its twine, teetering for its opportunity. After the other spiders had removed the hapless soul from its coffin, the arachnid latched onto the dwarf and ascended to the ceiling where it began to encase the paralyzed being in webbing.

The young warrior stood dumbfounded, not believing what he had just seen. However, the spiders were not finished hunting for food. Using their legs to feel the tomb next to the previous one, they quickly determined that it too lacked coldness. The three beasts started pounding the casing with their legs in an attempt to get to their next meal.

In the distance, Harrison heard more shattering glass and horrified wails. *This stops NOW*, he lamented to himself. As the next casing began to crack under the duress of the spider's attack, the young warrior took his battle axe and rushed from his position, pushing a couple of stunned elven sentries from his path.

Harrison brought his axe over his head and, with a mighty chop, severed the body of the creature closest to him. The carcass fell to the floor, its legs twitching in uncontrollable spasms. Anger coursing through his veins, he took aim at the next spider. The monster saw the young warrior's actions and stopped pounding the casing to tend to its new enemy. Harrison recoiled his weapon and readied himself for another attack.

The spider, still dangling, raised its front legs in the young warrior's direction, trying to feel its way to its adversary. Harrison found himself entranced by the creature's many eyes, almost unaware that its jaws opened, showing two large fangs. Its prey mesmerized, the spider lunged at Harrison, striking his chest with his forelegs, pushing the human back. The young warrior shook his head, breaking the beast's spell, and chopped at it with his axe. The blade found its mark cutting into the spider's front legs.

Injured, the monster pulled itself upward, hovering ten feet over the young warrior's head.

A second spider made a rapid descent from the ceiling, whizzing past the first arachnid, and dangled right above the young warrior's head. Lunging from its position, the creature tried to sink its fangs into the Aegean's shoulder. Harrison's fur coat and body armor prevented the beast from biting through his skin. Shocked at the monster's sudden attack, the young warrior flailed his battle axe at the spider, pushing it away. The arachnid lunged again; however, it halted its approach after an arrow pierced its head. The projectile burst whatever skull casing it had possessed, sending goo and body parts to the floor. The remaining torso dropped to the ground, where Harrison hacked it to bits.

The young warrior turned to face the men, finding Murdock lowering his bow. "That's two you owe me," said the ranger.

Harrison was about to respond when screams and hollers from deeper in the cavern stopped him. "You see what they're doing," said the young warrior. "We have to stop them!" A sudden thumping from inside the coffin startled Harrison and the others.

The young warrior turned his attention to the tomb, examining the cracks on the casing, the result of the spider's constant pounding. By this time, many of the team had surrounded the burial chamber.

Harrison, unable to see the person inside the coffin due to copious amounts of sticky webbing and spider innards, used his sleeve to wipe away the debris. To his surprise a dwarf stared back at him with eyes wide and terrified, screaming at the top of his lungs.

The young warrior, understanding the trauma this person had just suffered, took the butt of his axe and began breaking the fragile glass. After a few taps, the flimsy covering broke free, falling to the floor and shattering. To his surprise, the being continued hollering at the top of his lungs, terrified.

"Hey," said Harrison, trying to put the dwarf at ease. "We're going to save you." The young warrior's words did nothing to comfort the poor soul. Instead, he just shrieked with no signs of stopping.

Moradoril and Brianna took a vested interest in the new situation. Standing next to Harrison, the elven king said, "This person is beyond terrified."

"He has gone mad," added Brianna.

Harrison gazed into the dwarf's eyes, finding them vacuous and clear. Nowhere did he see any signs of comprehension, only sheer madness.

"I think you're right," said the young warrior, maintaining his focus on the being. "What do we do now?"

Moradoril focused down the corridor toward the Dwarven king's room. Thick cobwebs littered the area and horrified shouts and screams cascaded off the passageway's stone walls.

"We must get to Drogut's room," said the king. "Immediately!"

"What about him?" asked Harrison.

"Leave him," said Moradoril. "He's already gone."

The young warrior felt a pang of doubt at leaving the maniacal soul behind but understood the ramifications if spiders had comprised Drogut's lair. With reluctance, he turned to Murdock and Pondle.

"Lead us further down the passage," said Harrison.

The duo, along with the elven scouts, chopped at the scattered webbing in the same manner someone would hack their way through a jungle thick with vines. An orange flash and subsequent explosion rocked the upper area in front of the group.

Good job, Gelderand, thought Harrison, the magician lobbing another fireball to disperse the vile creatures away from their passageway. During their short trek, the Aegean noticed that more and more chambers no longer housed dwarves in suspended animation. Instead, the pathetic souls screamed in terror, their voices muffled behind the glass casing.

After a few more steps forward, Harrison noticed an anomaly up ahead. Directing his next question to Murdock and Pondle, he asked, "Is the corridor opening to another chamber?"

"Must be the king's room," said Murdock, doing his best to keep his forward focus. Another fireball forced several spiders to vacate their lofty position on the ceiling, lest they become the fire's next ignition source.

Harrison followed his friends, passing tombs sealed in solid ice, as well as those swathed with thin glass. Depending on the encasement, the occupant either continued to live in hibernation or glare at the passersby with horror in their eyes. Furthermore, just as many blood stained coffins had succumbed to the spiders' endless quest for food.

Several yards in front of them, a bright white glow emanated from a corridor that extended to the right. Murdock and Pondle made a cautious approach to the new passageway while elven archers trained their weapons on anything that might pop out from around the corner. Pondle peeked his head inside the corridor, then turned to address his friends.

"It's the king's room, alright," said the halfling. "Follow me!"

Harrison watched his friend turn the corner, followed by Murdock and the elven sentries. With each step the young warrior made toward the bend, the brighter the light grew. Things came into better focus after he stepped foot in the passageway. To his surprise, a bright light shown down from the ceiling, illuminating a thick block of ice. Upon further examination, Harrison identified a body suspended in the middle of the immense cube.

Swiveling his head back to Moradoril, he asked, "Drogut?"

"It is," responded the elven king with a nod.

The small group took guarded steps toward the frozen block. "Pondle, check for traps and anything else unusual," said Harrison, knowing what loomed before him had obvious magical signatures.

"You mean something other than a dwarf frozen in a giant block of ice?" said the thief, his voice thick with sarcasm.

Everyone stood back while Pondle investigated the rectangular structure. After several minutes of examination, the thief said, "All clear."

Relieved for the moment, Harrison took the opportunity to make his own inspection. Standing next to the solid block, he brought a hand within inches of the smooth surface, the ice's coldness radiating from the cube. Inside the six foot tall block, Drogut lay flat, clutching an immense battle axe that made the young warrior's own weapon look like a child's. The dwarf

367

appeared peaceful, eyes closed, and in perfect hibernation. Harrison backed away from the phenomenon and swept his eyes around the room, finding nothing more than perfectly carved solid rock walls.

Satisfied with his examination, the young warrior asked to no one in particular, "He's been asleep for a thousand years?"

"Give or take a few," answered Moradoril.

Harrison turned to face the elven royal couple, then crinkled his brow. "How do we get him out?"

"That is where the Talisman comes into play," said Brianna. "The Ancient Kings had tasked us with encasing the dwarves, which is what we did."

"With no way of getting them out?" asked the young warrior, dumbfounded at the apparent short sightedness of the assignment.

Brianna took a step toward Harrison, placing a hand on his forearm. Locking eyes with his, she said, "Your kings sent you to us, which then led us to the dwarves. The key to all of this is the Talisman, literally."

Harrison digested the queen's comment, then turned to Swinkle. "Can you hand me the artifact?"

The young cleric fished the object out of his backpack and handed it to his friend. Harrison brought the metallic relic to his face for a closer look, once again feeling its smooth, semi-circular surface etched with runes.

"If what you say is true," started the young warrior, "then this artifact should rescue the king."

"I would have to agree," concurred Brianna.

"But how do we use it?"

"That is what we must determine." The queen spread her arms wide. "Everyone, fan out and examine the immediate area. Search for ways that this Talisman might be used. We will investigate all suggestions."

Harrison teamed with Swinkle, Gelderand, and Thoragaard, while Murdock, Pondle, and Kymbra went off in another direction. The young warrior chose to examine the area around the frozen king, hoping for a breakthrough.

Swinkle, finding his friend preoccupied in thought, asked, "What are you thinking, Harrison?"

The young warrior shook his head. Holding the Talisman in front of him, he said, "This thin piece of silver must hold the key."

Swinkle approached his friend, looking over the relic in Harrison's hand. "Brianna used the symbols to open the gateway in the mountainside," started the young cleric. "There must be a place to utilize the Talisman here as well."

"I agree, but how?" asked Harrison. Swinkle shrugged.

"I think you might have answered your own question," said Gelderand, overhearing their conversation.

"How so?" asked Harrison, furrowing his brow.

"You said the word 'key'," said the magician. "I am willing to bet this artifact works in the same manner."

"Like a key?"

"Yes."

"Then we should look for a keyhole?" asked Harrison, panning for a place that would fit the Talisman.

"In a manner of speaking, yes," said the mage.

Murdock rushed over to Harrison's group, oblivious to his friends' conversation. "I think we found something on the other side of this block of ice. Follow me!"

The three men followed the ranger's lead and looped around to the back of the cold tomb. Harrison brought his eyes to the frozen block, finding nothing different.

"It's still a big hunk of ice," said Harrison, extending his hand toward the solid cube.

"Not there," said Murdock, pointing to the immense cube. The ranger then extended his arm toward Pondle, standing next to the far wall, some twenty feet away from the others. "There!"

Harrison swiveled his head in the thief's direction. At first glance it appeared that someone had carved symbols into the wall next to where Pondle stood. The group hovered around the halfling, along with Moradoril, Brianna, and their sentries.

"What is that?" asked Harrison, pointing at the engraving.

369

"Look closer," said Pondle, before gesturing to the piece of silver in Harrison's hand. "I think you put the Talisman into this thing."

The young warrior took a step toward the stone wall in an effort to better analyze the anomaly. Two vertical slits, one above the other, existed in the surface with a rune symbol carved to the right of each one. What he needed to do next seemed obvious to Harrison.

"I think you're right, Pondle," said the young warrior. "This piece will fit in the slots perfectly."

"Line up the runes," added the thief.

Harrison nodded, then examined the details of the artifact. Just like Pondle had said, the ancient symbols engraved on the Talisman appeared to line up with the markings on the wall. The young warrior aligned the relic with the slits in the same manner Brianna had done with the mountain's massive doorway. The action also yielded the same result as the curved piece of metal straightened when Harrison placed it next to the openings. Without any more time to waste, the young warrior pushed the Talisman into the slots, stopping when the runes on the artifact matched the exact symbols on the wall.

The young warrior stopped penetrating the casing when the markings glowed red. Seconds later, the light that shone on the frozen tomb turned from a bright white to an orangey-red. Harrison also realized another significant change.

"That light's warm," said the young warrior. The rest of the group also felt the effects of the newfound heat source.

"This place is getting hot fast," added Murdock.

Pondle pointed to the cube. "Look! It's melting!"

Everyone panned to the frozen block. Sure enough, the ice had started to melt, wetness collecting around the base of the tomb.

Moradoril, piecing together the turn of events, dashed outside the king's room and toward one of the frozen coffins. Taking a hand to the ice, he found that the room's sudden increase in temperature had begun to change the consistency of the casing.

"The ice is melting on this coffin as well," said the elven king.

Harrison took a moment to assess his new predicament, looking at the Talisman still inserted into the wall, then panning to the melting block near Moradoril's position.

With the chamber's sudden warmth obvious to all, he exclaimed, "Everything's melting! It's going to set the dwarves free!"

The elven king inspected the frozen tombs, then went over to Drogut's resting place to examine the icy surface. His assessment complete, he said, "That is exactly what is going to happen. However, this process is going to take some time. You do not want to rush coming out of hibernation. The dwarves' biological processes need to start up again and slowly at that."

"What do we do in the meantime?" asked the young warrior.

"Wait," said Moradoril, "and monitor the frozen coffins. It is up to us to make sure every dwarf comes out of suspended animation alive."

"What about the ones the spiders' attacked?"

The elf grimaced. "We will handle that as it happens." Moradoril then spread his arms wide. "First we need someone to fetch the rest of the group," he started, referring to the party they had left behind at the end of the passageway. "Then we need to monitor all of the tombs."

Harrison stepped forward. "Pondle can escort Tara and the others back here." The young warrior gazed over to the thief, who nodded in agreement. "And let's not forget about any remaining spiders." Many of the group members turned their worried eyes upward, finding no arachnids at the moment, but knowing that they were not far away.

"Good," said Moradoril. "Let's fan out and start monitoring the melting process."

As Pondle dashed away to find his separated party members, the rest of the squad broke off in different directions to begin the mundane process of monitoring the progress of the encased dwarves.

CHAPTER 29

O

The congregation of humans and elves waited almost seven hours for the melting process to complete. Harrison, along with the others, encircled the area where a thick block of ice had once encased Drogut the Dwarf king for almost a thousand years. Now, the stubby king's sleeping body hovered over the ground, waiting to be awaken.

"Is he alive?" asked Harrison.

Moradoril glanced at his wife, who approached the levitating body. Brianna examined the dwarf, feeling his wrist for a pulse, then placing careful fingers on his jugular vein. Continuing her inspection, she lightly lifted the king's left eyelid and gazed deep into his eye. Satisfied, she stepped back and addressed the adventurers.

"He's in perfect hibernation," said the queen. "It's time to wake him up." Brianna gestured for the men to come closer. Pointing to the sleeping dwarf, she said, "His body is going to fall to the floor after I perform my spell. I will need you to hold him up."

Harrison stepped forward. Murdock and Pondle did likewise, taking their leader's cue. Brianna turned to two of her sentries. "Floriad, Gaelos, assist Harrison and his men." The two elves rushed into position upon hearing their queen's request.

Brianna, satisfied that Drogut's body would not come crashing to the floor after her antics, approached the dwarf once again. She removed a small sack from her gold belt and poured a fine, white powder into her right hand. The queen sprinkled the substance over the sleeping being's body, ending with his head.

The elf hovered over the king and placed her hand inches from his face. She then made a subtle glance to the men in position, conveying the message to ready themselves to catch the dwarf upon his awakening.

Finding everything to her liking, she spoke in a loud, forceful voice, "I command thee to awaken from your slumber!" She blew the powder from her hand onto Drogut's face, then backed away.

All eyes remained fixed on the dwarf king. Seconds after Brianna completed her spell, Drogut gasped for air. At the same time, his body dropped from its position. Harrison and the others caught him midair, preventing the king from smacking into the hard ground.

Drogut's eyes opened and grew round, darting in every direction, unsure of his surroundings, desperately trying to get a fix on his situation. Finding strangers supporting him, he sprung to his feet and clutched the hilt of his axe, raising it in a defensive posture.

"Who are you?" exclaimed the king.

Brianna stepped forward. Upon seeing the elven queen, the dwarf's face softened and his brow crinkled. "Brianna?" Drogut looked past the woman, finding the elven king.

In an angrier voice, he bellowed, "Moradoril!"

"Drogut," said the king, raising his palms. "There's no need for your weapon."

"Where are my people!" demanded the dwarf, refraining from lowering his axe.

Moradoril drew a heavy sigh. "In hibernation. Brianna is going to awaken them as she did to you."

"You have a lot to explain, Moradoril," said Drogut, maintaining a defensive posture. Taking his gaze to Harrison, he said, "Who are you?"

"My name is Harrison Cross," said the young warrior. "My friends and I are from Aegeus and we summoned the elves to take us to you."

"Aegeus?" questioned Drogut, cocking his head, squinting. "Where's Ballesteros, Nicodemus, and Solaris?"

Harrison turned and faced Moradoril, his face blank, unsure of his answer. "They are gone, my friend," said Moradoril. "Times are different now."

Weapon still raised, Drogut asked, "How so?"

"For one, a thousand years have passed since you last awoken," said the elven king. "The Ancient Kings you alluded to are gone."

Drogut's eyes widened, his eyebrows arched. Lowering his axe, he said, "A thousand years?"

"I am afraid so," said Moradoril. "There is much to talk about."

The dwarf's expression quickly changed from shock to anger. Raising his blade once again, he took a step toward Moradoril and said, "This is your doing! I want answers now!"

The elven king raised his palms to Drogut, hoping to calm him down. "We put you into hibernation at the request of the humans."

Moradoril's comment hit the dwarf like a mighty blow to the body. Shaking his head in disbelief, he said, "Ballesteros told you to entomb us? I don't believe you!" Drogut swiveled and locked eyes on Harrison. "Is this true?"

The young warrior shook his head, unsure. "That's what they told me," he said, in reference to the elves. "Moradoril has all the answers."

"Now wait, Harrison," started the elven king. "Your kings commanded you to seek us."

"And they told you to give us a part of the Talisman," rebutted the young warrior.

"Talisman?" said Drogut, his ears perking up upon hearing the word. "Ballesteros spoke of a Talisman."

"Moradoril," said Harrison. "The Ancient Kings also told us to find the dwarves."

"That they did," said the elf leader. "They also said that the dwarves would possess part of the puzzle."

All eyes focused on the dwarf king. Skeptical, Drogut said, "Ballesteros gave me something with special instructions."

"Which were?" pushed Harrison, knowing this man held an important clue to the Talisman mystery.

"To hand over an artifact when the time was right," said Drogut.

"I believe the time is right," said Harrison. The young warrior fished for something in his backpack and, when he found it, he held it in front of himself for all to see. "Did Ballesteros give you something like this?"

Drogut focused on the curved piece of silver with wide eyes, before setting his axe by his side and placing his hand in a sack attached to his belt.

Having found what he searched for, he said, "I would say it does." The dwarf king held a similar curved piece of metal in his stubby hand and showcased it to everyone.

"It's another part of the Talisman!" exclaimed Harrison upon seeing the relic. "We need to put them together!" The young warrior took a step in the dwarf's direction.

Drogut pulled his share of the Talisman close to his chest. "Not so fast!" Harrison stopped in his tracks, his brow furrowed in surprise.

"What do you mean?" said the young warrior. "That section must be joined with ours!"

"Not until I have my people with me," said the king. "Just in case something *happens*."

"What's going to happen?" asked Harrison, shaking his head, puzzled at the question.

"Any number of things can occur," said Drogut. "I'd rather address them *en masse* and not alone. Understood?"

"Harrison," said Brianna, hoping to smooth the conversation. "It is only right that I awaken his kin." The young warrior, nodded, conceding his argument for the time being.

"Drogut," said Moradoril. "There is something you need to know before we start this process."

The dwarf king cocked his head. "What is that, elf?" he asked in a snide tone.

"Something terrible has occurred in Almandine's Cradle since we put you into suspended animation," said Moradoril. "A most horrible happenstance indeed and something I'm not sure you will handle very well."

"What have you done, Moradoril?" said the dwarf, his eyes cold and dark, locked on the elven king. "Did I not state my objections clearly enough for you a millennium ago?"

"There is no easy way to say this," said the elven king. "You must see for yourself." Moradoril stepped aside and extended his arm toward the main passageway.

Drogut maintained his glare on the king, then proceeded to advance in the direction Moradoril indicated. Everyone in the small party gave the anxious dwarf a wide berth, knowing full well what he was about to see.

The dwarf king, axe firmly in hand, exited his chamber and entered the hallway. The sight of cobwebs, blood, and shattered glass brought a look of shock to his face. Harrison watched Drogut glance back toward the group before heading further down the passage.

The stubby leader reached the first casing, finding one of his kind still asleep, the ice melted away and the being hovering harmlessly in the center of the tomb. The next sarcophagus proved the same, however the shards of glass that littered the following coffin brought a look of horror to his face. Drogut wailed, his eyes bulging from his skull.

"What have you done?" he screamed and took his axe to break away the remaining glass. The dwarf panned to the awaiting crowd, his face pale.

Harrison, his eyes transfixed on the horrendous scene, felt Moradoril grip his forearm. The elf motioned with his head for the young warrior to follow him as the two approached the distraught dwarf leader.

When they reached the king, Drogut spun, dropped his axe, and grabbed Moradoril by the chest, clutching his leather armor in tightly held fists. "What have you done?" he screamed again through clenched teeth.

The elven king, taken aback by Drogut's sudden actions, stammered, "Our magic is not the problem here! Something else has interfered with our hibernation process!"

Brianna, who had trailed the men, approached Drogut and placed a caring hand on his tense forearm. "Please, Drogut, release Moradoril. This is not his doing."

The dwarf king turned and gazed into Brianna's sad, blue eyes. His own eyes welled up as he released his equal. Moradoril, free from Drogut's grip, stood tall and smoothed out his armor, regaining his composure.

Drogut, in a sad, melancholy voice, asked the queen, "I need to know what has happened here." Taking his gaze down the corridor and finding many more instances of broken glass, he pleaded, "Where are all of my people?"

Brianna swallowed ever so subtly, then said, "My dear king, someone negated our magic, allowing vile creatures to infiltrate your hibernation chambers.

"We had successfully placed your entire race into suspended animation, just as you were, and left everyone here in a peaceful slumber over a thousand years ago. All those that have endured the melting process are still alive but those that had their sarcophaguses compromised ..."

Drogut did not wait for Brianna to finish. Instead he rushed down the passageway, mumbling, "My brothers! My brothers!"

Blood and broken shards littered the corridor. Drogut passed one after another destroyed coffin before stopping at a specific tomb. Inside, a dwarf hovered, still in a blissful sleep state.

"Rogur!" exclaimed the king with joy. Turning to Brianna, he ordered, "Awaken him!"

Brianna acquiesced, using her magical powder serum to rouse the sleeping dwarf. Rogur stirred for a moment before opening his eyes. A profound look of surprise graced his face upon finding so many people staring back at him. A familiar person reached in and grabbed him.

"Rogur!" yelled the king again, pulling him from the tomb. "You're alive!" Drogut hugged him with all his might.

The dwarf, still in a mild state of shock, said, "That I am, big brother!" Narrowing his eyes, he focused on his elder sibling, and asked, "Who are these people? Why are they here? What's happening?"

"Many questions to ponder," said Drogut, "but there's more work to be done. Come with me!"

Harrison followed the two dwarves, stopping a couple of tombs down. Drogut glared into the empty, blood stained coffin, then dropped to his knees. Wailing, he cried, "What has happened to Thorum?"

Rogur, his brow creased and eyes narrowed, asked, "This is Thorum's tomb?"

"Yes," said the dwarf king between sobs. "He's gone, Rogur!"

The king's brother, trying his best to understand the gravity of the situation, spun on his heel, clutching his weapon in hand. Glaring at Moradoril, he exclaimed, "Where is my other brother?"

"Spiders infiltrated the tombs, Rogur ..." The elven king shook his head, unable to utter another word.

Rogur, as his brother before him, panned wildly, finding cobwebs, blood, and shattered glass. "Are you saying that spiders *ate* our people?"

Moradoril swallowed hard. "Yes."

The dwarf's face went blank, his brother's cries reverberating off the stone walls. "Thorum is dead?"

The elf nodded, unable to make eye contact. "Yes."

Rogur turned and placed a hand on his brother's shoulder, pulling him hard in order to face him. "We must find Gromrimm!" The dwarf king rose to his feet, wiping a tear from his eye.

Both men continued down the pathway, each bloodied tomb churning their empty stomachs. They stopped a short distance from their missing brother's casing, both staring at the sarcophagus.

Harrison, unsure why the dwarves had not tried to pull their brother out of the coffin, maneuvered to get a closer look. From his vantage point, he could see that whatever covered the tomb's opening had remained intact. Odd, he thought, since the rise in temperature had melted all of the ice from the encasements. Upon further examination, the surface appeared smooth, almost like ... glass.

Drogut pointed to the being inside the tomb. "He's alive!"

Rogur peered deeper into the makeshift coffin. "Something's wrong, Drogut."

Harrison, along with Moradoril and Brianna, took a couple of steps closer to the tomb. The young warrior gazed into the casing and found a pair of wide eyes staring back out. However, the dwarf's head appeared to twitch back and forth, and his mouth moved rapidly, like he was saying something. The unbroken glass prevented any sound from escaping the coffin.

Drogut, exasperated from the moment Brianna had awoken him, took the butt of his weapon and tapped the covering. The glass cracked. The dwarf king hit it a bit harder, this time breaking the casing, dropping several shards to the floor. A continuous drone of gibberish filled the hallway with the opening now compromised.

"Get him out of there!" exclaimed Rogur, lunging toward the sarcophagus, grabbing pieces of glass, pulling them away. Blood ran from the cuts he sustained while gripping the sharp edges. Moments later, they had set free the third Dwarven family member; however, he continued to speak nonsense, his eyes darting everywhere.

Drogut pulled his trembling brother close, doing his best to remain calm. "Gromrimm," started the king. "It is I, your brother, Drogut."

"And me, Rogur," said the other dwarf. Gromrimm swiveled his head in his brothers' direction, but he continued uttering nonsensical phrases. "What's wrong with him?"

Brianna sighed. "If I had to venture a guess, I would say that he remained awake for the whole time and watched as the spiders devoured those around him."

"What?" exclaimed Rogur, his eyes round, shaking his head in disbelief.

"He has gone mad," said Brianna.

Both Drogut and Rogur gazed into their youngest brother's vacuous eyes, finding no semblance of sanity. The poor dwarf stared into nothingness, mumbling something over and over.

While the dwarves pondered their brother's predicament, Swinkle approached Harrison and tugged at his sleeve.

"What is it?" asked the young warrior in a hushed tone.

"It is the phrase the dwarf keeps repeating. I think it is the same."

Harrison swiveled his head back to the dwarves. Concentrating on the constant gibberish, he too found a similar pattern. "I think you're right, Swinkle. But what's he saying?"

Swinkle focused on the maniacal being. Honing in on the sound, he said, "Bow where? Boo where?"

Harrison listened more closely, trying his best to differentiate the words. "It does sound like boo where, but what the heck does that mean?" The young warrior shook his head. "Swinkle, he's gone crazy. This means nothing."

The young cleric pursed his lips and shook his head. "I don't know, Harrison. It could mean something."

Rogur and Drogut, unaware of Swinkle's conversation, tried to understand their brother's gibberish. "What's he saying?" asked Rogur.

The Dwarven king shook his head. "Boolair? Boowhere? It makes no sense!"

Moradoril overheard the two dwarves conversing, trying to make sense of their assessment. The dwarf's constant gibberish sparked a memory in his brain. A bad memory. Standing tall, the elven king said with disdain, "Boulware."

Brianna spun her head in his direction upon hearing the uttered name. "It cannot be!" she exclaimed in a rare emotional outburst.

"Think about it, Brianna," said Moradoril. "It only makes sense!"

By this time, Drogut and Rogur, as well as Harrison and his friends, started to take a vested interest in the elves' conversation. "You understand what he's saying?" asked Drogut while Gromrimm continued his jabbering.

Moradoril's expression dropped with his eyes narrowing, jaw clenching, and focus cold. "He is repeating the name Boulware."

"Finius Boulware?" exclaimed Harrison, familiar with the name.

"Yes," said Moradoril with a scowl. "That same ruthless, dark warlock we spoke of before. He aligned himself with King

Holleris a long time ago." The elven king shook his head in disgust. "Only a wretch like he could negate our magic."

"Even if he did do this," sneered Drogut, "I'm sure the bastard's dead by now. Too bad, I would've enjoyed killing him with my bare hands!"

"That's not necessarily true," said the elven king. "He was well-crafted in the inner secrets of dark magic. Anything's possible."

"No human," Drogut panned his finger to Harrison and his friends, "can live a thousand years. No human."

Moradoril raised his palms to the dwarf king. "I am just saying that it is not out of the realm of possibility. Doubtful, but not impossible."

"Well if he is still alive," said Drogut, "consider him a marked man." The elven king nodded once in agreement.

Drogut turned his attention back to his crazed brother. "What can we do about him? Can you save him?" The dwarf king took his hopeful gaze to Brianna.

"There are a few things that I can try," she said. "However, I am not very optimistic." The queen took a moment to gaze down the passageway before addressing Drogut again. "First, I must release the rest of your people."

Drogut nodded. "Thank you, milady."

Brianna brought her focus to Floriad, Gaelos, and Liagol. "Please bring me their food."

The three sentries heeded their queen's command and brought forward sacks of elven bread. Brianna broke two small pieces from one of the loaves and handed a portion to Drogut and Rogur.

"Eat this now," she said. "The bread will fill your bellies and give you strength. Drink plenty of water as well." She then gestured toward her soldiers. "Come, join me in waking the rest of Drogut's people."

Brianna, along with Moradoril and her sentries, headed down the corridor and began the process of waking all dwarves who had survived the hibernation process. However, they skipped all tombs that housed maniacal dwarves.

Harrison and his friends remained behind with Drogut and his brothers. Being the leader of the group, the young warrior felt compelled to speak with the king.

"I'm truly sorry for your loss," he said.

Drogut lifted his sorrow-filled eyes to the Aegean. "Your people are partly to blame."

"Forgive me, Drogut, but I don't understand what happened in the past between our peoples."

"Your King Ballesteros came to Almandine's Cradle many years ago," started the dwarf king. "He said he needed an army."

"An army for what?" asked Harrison, having heard the need for a militia too many times.

"A great war. He said all good beings would be called to join the war to end all wars."

"Then why the Talisman of Unification? Why all the secrecy?"

Drogut shook his head. "The Talisman? Probably to prove your worth." The king gazed at his lost brother, his heart sinking lower. "The secrecy to prevent others from knowing our actions."

"Who are these 'others'?" asked the young warrior, still baffled.

"That I don't know," said Drogut. "Whoever they are, they must be formidable since the dwarves, elves, and humans are now all in the mix, at the same time."

Harrison wracked his brain, trying to figure out the logic, but only a single thought came to mind. Removing his part of the Talisman from a pouch on his belt, the young warrior asked, "Do you want to join your piece with ours? It might provide more answers than just guessing."

Drogut pondered the request for a moment, before handing his axe to his brother. Retrieving the small piece of metal, the dwarf king held it before him and said, "Let's see what this thing's all about."

Harrison brought his semi-circular piece of metal close to Drogut's. When the objects spanned a few inches from each other, the dwarf's section leapt from his hand and joined Harrison's, forming a single C-shaped object.

The young warrior's eyes grew round as he held the strange artifact in his hand before noticing another change in the Talisman. Pointing at the silver surface, he said, "Look! The runes are gone and replaced with letters!"

Everyone leaned in closer to the young warrior, straining to get a better look at the object.

"What does it say?" asked Murdock.

Harrison brought the relic up close to examine it and could easily make out the letters. Reading clockwise, he said, "E T H A." Everyone remained standing, eagerly waiting for more.

"That's it? E T H A?" said the ranger. "That doesn't spell anything!"

"It's obviously part of a whole word that must be on the last section," said Harrison. All eyes turned to the dwarf king. "Did the Ancient Kings give you any more instructions?"

Drogut shook his head. "All they said was to prepare for battle. Then the elves froze us in the mountainside for a millennium."

"Harrison, this makes no sense!" lamented Murdock, throwing his arms wide in disgust. "Why come this far only to be left at a dead end?"

The young warrior shook his head, exasperated. "I don't know. We need to think about this a lot more."

"You can think," said Drogut. "I have people to save." The dwarf king turned to Rogur and Gromrimm, encouraging them to follow him down the long passageway.

Harrison felt his friends' stares. "I know what you must be thinking," he said. "I'm frustrated, too. Let's just take some time to try and figure this riddle out."

The young warrior led his friends back to the king's throne room where they settled in for a long night of doubt and debate.

CHAPTER 30

◻

Hile Moradoril and Brianna went about reviving Drogut's people, Harrison and company spent time trying to decipher their latest riddle. The team congregated in Drogut's throne room, everyone surrounding Harrison as they focused on the item in the young warrior's hand.

"What do you think those letters mean?" asked Tara.

Harrison massaged his temple with his other hand, answering, "I've been racking my brain over this problem, just like everyone else, and still have nothing."

"It's got to mean something," said Murdock, frustrated. "Or else this whole trip was a waste of time."

"E T H A," mumbled Harrison aloud, reciting the letters on the Talisman.

"It doesn't even spell a word," said Kymbra, rolling her eyes. "Can we add letters to the ones we have?"

"That would not be a good idea," said Gelderand. "Making assumptions might lead us to unwanted trouble."

"Wait, it does spell HATE," said Murdock, raising an eyebrow.

The magician showed his palms to the ranger. "Again, don't make assumptions without all of the clues."

Murdock shook his head. "The word HATE seems to make the most sense right about now."

The young warrior gazed over to Murdock, agreeing without saying a word. "Swinkle," he said, turning to his other friend, "do the Ancient Scrolls of Arcadia mention anything about this?"

Swinkle unfurled the scriptures and glossed over them. "Nothing is jumping out at me."

"Can you reiterate the highlights?"

The young cleric scanned the parchment again. "There's the mention of brothers reuniting the land," he said, pausing to continue reading. A few seconds later, he lifted his head and said, "Hmm."

Harrison focused on his friend. "What is it, Swinkle?"

"It is the scrolls alluding to an unlikely alliance of necessity," he said. "I have to believe it is pertaining to the elves and dwarves."

"We've already established that," said Murdock, having witnessed their contentiousness firsthand. "They don't like each other, that's for sure."

"Then it's probable that the writings refer to them," said Harrison. "Isn't that right, Gelderand?"

The mage raised his palms to the sky and shook his head. "I am not well versed in the history between the elves and dwarves but it only makes sense that they are who the scriptures are talking about."

"Or it could be something different altogether," added Thoragaard. "Prophecies are tricky, Harrison. The one about brothers reuniting the land is already fractured and, since it is, all other prognostications may be effected in regards to those scrolls." The illusionist paused. "And the assumption that you and your brother are the ones related to the prophecy might be invalid."

Harrison pursed his lips. "I hadn't thought of that. I just assumed it meant us." Bringing his focus back to Swinkle, he asked, "Is there any mention of the Talisman and the letters we've found?"

The young cleric scanned the document again. Frowning, he said, "I'm afraid not."

"We just discovered this new phenomenon," said Gelderand. "We need to let this situation play out. Prophecies cannot be rushed."

"I've never heard about any of this during my time on the Aegean council," added Fallyn. "To me, it's a great mystery."

"So, we came all this way to find dwarves devoured by spiders, the elves' magic compromised, and a few letters that sound like gibberish," said Murdock, throwing his hands up in frustration. "Wonderful."

"I'm not happy about it either," said Harrison, "But Gelderand and Thoragaard are right. We need to let things evolve."

The ranger shook his head, resigning himself to the fact that this current mystery would remain unsolved for the time being. "Don't forget that someone else has the fourth piece to the Talisman or has everyone forgotten about that little tidbit, too." Murdock drew a heavy sigh, then asked, "What's our next move?"

"Talk to Moradoril and Drogut, find out their plans," said Harrison. "I got a feeling the dwarves are in rough shape."

"You think? When spiders suck the life out of over half your population, you have more than your fair share of problems." Advancing shadows halted Murdock's thick sarcasm.

Moments later, Moradoril, Brianna, and the rest of the elves joined Harrison and his team. The young warrior placed the Talisman back in his pouch before addressing the elven king.

"How's Drogut and his brothers?"

"Beyond distraught," said the elf, his face long with shock and sorrow. "The spiders killed seventy-five percent of their race and the half who remain have gone insane. He's inconsolable."

Harrison covered his face in his hands, then dragged them down his cheeks. "What does that mean for us now?"

"We have done our part," said Moradoril. "The dwarves are out of hibernation and ready for whatever task lies ahead for them."

"But what *is* that task?" asked Harrison, his frustration boiling over all of the unknowns.

"Your kings told Drogut to prepare for a battle," said Moradoril. "That is what I would focus on."

Harrison shook his head, not pleased with the answer. "What about you? Where do you stand now that your part of the mission is over?"

"I am not sure that we are finished with our purpose just yet," said the elf. "If there is a major battle on the horizon, I am sure we will be involved. As for now, we are going back to our compound in the Dark Forest."

A dark mass of silhouettes began to grow from the passageway around the corner from the dwarf king's chamber. Drogut, followed by a throng of Dwarven warriors, emerged from the shadows.

Harrison read their leader's face. From the time they met, the current situation had stressed Drogut to no end. Dark, focused eyes glared back at the small group of elves and humans, and the young warrior knew Drogut was not pleased.

"One hundred and forty-four," bellowed the king. "That's how many of my people remain alive after this hibernation fiasco." Drogut allowed that figure to sink in before exclaiming, "One hundred and forty-four!"

Harrison had not encountered a situation like this before in his life. A horrified and shocked race of beings, all with weapons in hand, stared down the much smaller group before them. The young warrior needed to say something bold, and he needed to do it now.

"We all mourn with you, Drogut," started the Aegean. "Though I'm still trying to figure out what all of this means, one thing is for sure. Your people did not deserve to end up this way."

"There are no words that can console us, Harrison!" Drogut took a step in the young warrior's direction. "Our future is gone!"

"No, it's not," said the young warrior. "You're all devastated, clearly, but you're still here. All my studies indicated that the dwarves are steadfast fighters, willing to overcome the worst of obstacles. Isn't now one of those situations?"

"That's easy for you to say! Your people count in the thousands!"

"And we will help you in any way possible to make it through this horrific situation," said Harrison.

"That's very diplomatic of you," said Drogut with a scowl. "You want to make it up to us? Find Finius Boulware and bring him to me. He's a dead man!"

"Will you honor your debt you made with our Ancient Kings and fight when the time comes?"

Drogut pointed at Harrison with emphasis. "You bring Boulware to us and we'll fight until none of us are left."

"Deal," said the young warrior. "Now we just need to figure out when this battle is supposed to happen."

"Harrison," said a soft, familiar voice, breaking the tension between the men. Brianna continued, "Do not search for the battle. It will come to you."

The young warrior drew a heavy sigh. "I suppose you're right." Fumbling in his pack, he removed the Talisman and held it out for all to see. "And what about the final piece to this?"

Brianna smiled. "In due time, you will find the last part of the puzzle, just as you have the other pieces. And at that time, you will finally have all of your answers."

Harrison placed the artifact back in his pack. Panning the group, he asked, "So what do we all do now?"

"I'm tending to my people's needs," said Drogut, his brother Rogur standing defiantly beside him. "We need food and water. The elves' bread will only last so long." Gazing at the people before him, he added, "After we settle in and get back to some sense of normalcy, then, and only then, will we entertain battle plans."

"As I said before," said Moradoril, "our portion of this mission is complete. We will head to our compound and await our next move."

Harrison listened to the other leaders before adding, "Then I suppose we'll head back to Concur to confer with our leadership group and discuss the Scrolls of Arcadia." The young warrior swiveled to his friends, who nodded their silent concurrence.

Knowing their journey had come to an end for now, he looked over to Moradoril and said, "We'll follow you back to your complex, then venture for our home from there, if that's alright with you."

The elf king smiled. "I would have it no other way."

Harrison addressed Drogut one final time. "Don't hesitate to ask if you need our help. We'll do whatever we can."

The dwarf king remained stoic. "Bring me Boulware." Drogut turned to face his followers, then raising his hands in the air he waved for them to leave down the passageway. The dwarves heeded his signal and began to depart the area.

Facing Harrison a final time, he said, "We'll meet again." He then turned and followed his people out of the chamber.

The young warrior took a moment to watch the battered race of beings leave before addressing his friends. "Let's gather our things and get out of here." Moradoril gestured to his people to depart as well.

Murdock approached Harrison, placing a hand on his shoulder. Shaking his head, he said, "I have no idea where to go next."

Harrison dropped his head. "Neither do I." Hoisting his pack onto his back and gripping his weapon, he said to the ranger, "Lead us on."

Pondle joined Murdock and headed to the front of the group with the elven sentries. Lance scurried to be at the head of the pack as well, while the rest of Harrison's friends fell into their marching order.

Tara, feeling that the time was right, sidled up next to Harrison, looping her arm around his. She went on her tiptoes and whispered, "I'm glad we're going home."

"So am I," said Harrison with a smile before bending down and giving the young maiden a peck on the cheek. The two were about to start their trek when they found someone blocking their path.

Brianna approached the young couple and, staring into Harrison's eyes, said, "Be sure to protect her at all times."

The young warrior, taken aback by Brianna's comment, said, "Of course I will. I always have."

The elven queen remained focused. "I mean all the time. Do not let her out of your sight." Brianna raised an eyebrow and cocked her head, then left to rejoin her people.

The young couple exchanged curious glances, confused. "What was that all about?" asked Tara, her brow furrowed.

Harrison shook his head. "I don't know, but you know I'll never leave you to fend for yourself."

Tara smiled. "I know you won't." She then unhooked her arm from his and took her spot in their procession. "Let's go home."

The young warrior smiled back at her, then said to his friends, "Let's get out of this place. We're going back to Concur."

The small contingent of humans and elves left the king's chamber, beginning their trek out of the mountainside and back into the cold, snowy wilderness.

CHAPTER 31

 Q

The elven complex stood tall in the middle of the Dark Forest, a symbol of peace in an otherwise harsh environment. Several sentries patrolled the front wall that housed the compound's main gate. Sunshine struggled to reach the forest's floor on a clear day, but today it seemed that darkness had fallen early.

"There must be a storm on the way," said one archer to his comrade. "The forest has gotten darker sooner than expected."

The second sentry heard his equal's remark but instead gazed into the ensuing woodlands, trying to hone in on an invisible target. "Something tells me this is not a natural phenomenon."

The first elf cocked his head. "I have not sensed anything unusual."

"Nor have I," said the second. "Yet, I have an unsettling feeling."

The first archer turned his gaze to the woodlands again. Moments later he hunched over, pulling his chin to his sternum. Closing his eyes tight, he shook his head and said, "I just felt a sharp pain."

The second elf glared at his comrade. "Where?"

With concern in his eyes, the first answered, "In my head."

Three fireballs hurtled from the forest's depths, striking the elves' hallowed walls, exploding on contact. Both archers, the sudden violence surprising them, fell back, dropping twenty feet to the complex's dirt floor.

Shaken, the two sentries struggled to regain their senses. "What in the world was that?" exclaimed the first sentry.

The second, injured from the fall, groaned, "I don't know. Alert the others!"

The first archer rose from the ground and hobbled away from his friend, intent on sounding the alarm to his people. The second elf, his leg badly hurt, tried to stand but could not, falling back to the ground. Unsheathing his sword, he waited. Horns blew, alerting the compound of the new threat if they had not already known.

The fallen archer kept his eyes fixed on the complex's doors, the sound of thunderous footsteps approaching from outside the compound's walls. The noise stopped just beyond the massive wooden gates, the area becoming eerily quiet. The sentry kept his weapon drawn, knowing some sort of enemy loomed just outside the complex. A hideous shriek echoed throughout the woods, forcing the elf to drop his sword and cover his ears. To his dismay, the entranceway doors flew open, as if they had been unlocked all along.

Filling the entire doorway stood a massive, two-headed dragon. The elf's eyes grew wide in terror, focusing on the bobbing heads atop two long, muscular necks. The sentry stared at the undulating body parts, its rhythmic motion mesmerizing him. Shaking his head, the elf reached for his fallen weapon, clutching it firmly in hand. Though he knew he was no match for the monster that stood before him, he nonetheless pointed his blade at the beast.

The dragon's heads stopped their dance and stood tall. Glaring at the lesser being with their deep black eyes, the creature focused all its mental energy on the terrified archer. The elf felt his skull warm and his cranium began to ache. The sentry shook the cobwebs from his head before the monster could unleash the full power of its mental intensity, ridding himself of the beast's psychic attack. Released from the creature's invisible grip, the elf welcomed the soft sounds of approaching feet from behind.

Twenty of his counterparts rushed ahead of their injured comrade and dropped to one knee, forming a straight line of archers. In one smooth motion, they drew arrows from their quivers and readied their bows. Each marksman trained on one of the monster's heads.

Preempting another attack, the lead sentry yelled, "Fire!" Projectiles flew from the ground and hurtled through the air.

Each arrow hit their target. Some bounced off the dragon's thick scales, while others barely stuck into its hide. The first volley over, the monster shook both of its heads, then raised them up high. Both necks dropped down and forward, opening their mouths wide, releasing a blood-curdling screech.

The elves reloaded and let fly a second volley. Just as the first, the projectiles could not penetrate the dragon's thick hide deep enough to hurt the beast. To their horror, if their current weapons had appeared useless, the sight of a second, then a third monster demoralized the elves even further.

"Fall back!" ordered the elven squad leader, sensing the futility in attempting to defend their home. All three beasts shrieked again, shaking the walls from their foundation.

The fallen archer, his sword still in hand, submitted to two of his comrades grabbing him under his armpits, lifting him off the ground, and dragging him behind them as they ran in the opposite direction. Unbeknownst to the running elves, the injured sentry had an unintended clear view of the forthcoming atrocities.

The dragons' six heads started to take turns spewing fire from their mouths, igniting everything in their path. Within seconds, the elves' complex turned from a peaceful encampment to a raging inferno. Though his counterparts dragged him further away from the ensuing chaos, the elf maintained his horrified glare at the compromised entrance. With his brain still reeling from the destructive imagery, something even odder caught his eye. Squinting, he swore he saw two smaller figures enter through the gateway, their bodies hard to identify, the rising heat blurring his vision.

The archer narrowed his eyes, doing his best to identify the new intruders. Before he could make an assessment, three smaller projectiles flew from the doorway, exploding near his feet and sending him and his comrades flying into the air. The sentry fell to the ground, landing on his head. His right arm dangled in an awkward angle, broken, and his legs burned. To either side of him lay his motionless companions.

The elf, unable to move without excruciating pain, slumped over, panting. Taking his focus back to the entranceway, he observed the monsters lumbering deeper into his compound, while two humanoids ventured in his direction. The archer, on the verge of full panic, came to the realization that he could not move, let alone escape his predicament. In a quick decision, the injured sentry feigned death, the only thing not difficult for him to do at this time.

The sentinel did his best to stay stationary. Holding his breath as the two people advanced closer, the elf determined that the pair were indeed humans. Avoiding eye contact at all costs, the fighter stayed as still as could be, allowing the beasts' masters to walk by, hoping they did not notice that he was alive. Fortunately for him, the two figures shuffled past, paying the fallen fighter no heed.

Relieved for the time being, the sentry began the arduous task of determining the extent of his injuries. Grimacing at the smallest of movements, the elf barely had started his examination when more eruptions occurred.

Thunderous booms echoed throughout the encampment as mighty trees snapped and fell to the ground. Explosions uprooted smaller vegetation, destroying the elves' homeland. Hellish screeches filled the air, coinciding with more deafening blasts. Crackling fire and the stench of burning wood followed.

The sentry stopped his personal assessment and strained to turn his head in the direction opposite the main gate. His mouth fell open, horrified at the utter destruction of his homeland. Huge beasts took turns spewing flames, while their masters looked on with contentment.

The elf swiveled his head back to its original position, alleviating some of his physical pain. However, his mental anguish endured. With all hope lost, he tried to suppress his sobs while tears slowly rolled down his face.

* * *

Cold winds whipped through the Empire Mountains as a vicious storm refused to release its grip on the mountainside. Harrison and the others hunkered down to ride out the harsh weather for the third time in the past five days.

From the safety of his tent, the young warrior shared a meal with Tara, Lance curled up on the ground next to the girl. "When's this storm going to end?" asked Tara, wrapping a blanket tighter around her cold body.

Harrison heard her question; however, he did not answer, staring off into a corner of the shelter. Tara, crinkling her brow, said, "Hey, did you hear me?"

The young warrior shook the cobwebs from his head. "Oh, sorry, I was just in deep thought."

"About what?" asked the young maiden. "Hopefully somewhere warmer than this place." Harrison smiled but remained distracted.

Tara took exception to his lack of attention. "Is everything alright?"

Harrison gazed at his mate, his brow furrowed. Shaking his head, he said, "Something's not right. I just have a feeling."

"How so?" asked Tara, her concern level rising.

The young warrior shook his head again. "I can't put my finger on it." He looked away again, before returning his gaze to Tara. "I think we need to talk to Brianna."

Tara's eyes grew wide, surprised at Harrison's statement. "Right now?"

Harrison started to rise from his seat. "Yes, right now."

The young maiden did likewise, dropping her blanket and closing her fur coverings around herself. Harrison led her and Lance out of the tent and the three of them braved the elements in order to reach the elven royalty.

Floriad and Gaelos, who stood guard in front of Moradoril and Brianna's shelter, saw the trio approaching. "Harrison, isn't it a little cold for a stroll?" asked Floriad in jest.

"Just a bit," said the young warrior with a smirk. "I need to speak with Brianna."

"Let me see if she's in condition to receive guests," said the elf before departing. Gaelos shifted from his position to guard the entranceway.

"What's so important that you need to find her during a storm?" asked the sentry, snow swirling about the vicinity.

"I need to ask her a question," answered Harrison, not willing to reveal his true concern.

Floriad appeared, waving them forward. "Come on in."

Harrison allowed Tara and Lance to enter before him. Inside, the young warrior found the royal couple awaiting their arrival. Moradoril gestured toward a covered spot on the ground.

"Please, take a seat," said the elven king. After the young couple found a place on the flooring, he asked, "Tell me what brings you two out of your shelter to visit us on such an awful day?"

"I'm sensing something out of the ordinary," said the young warrior. "I can't explain it."

Brianna leaned forward, her face serious. "You are not alone, Harrison. We both have felt unnerving. Something's not quite right." The queen's face softened. "I am surprised that you would sense anything. Most humans do not feel nature's undercurrents as we do."

Harrison felt relieved at hearing Brianna's admission. "Is there anything we should do?"

Moradoril shook his head. "No. We must get home first, to see if there is truly anything to worry about."

"But there might be," said the young warrior, raising his brows high on his forehead.

Brianna smiled. "Every day brings its fair share of peril. Hopefully, our feelings will be just that, feelings. However, we should prepare for anything."

Harrison shook his head. "I suggest we take care while venturing home. I've never felt an uneasiness like this."

"Your instincts are keen, Harrison," said Moradoril. "I would not simply dismiss them."

The young warrior felt better about interrupting the elves' daily routine, understanding that the world might be trying to tell him something. "How long until we reach your complex?"

"A week, if this storm decides to break," said the elven king. "I suggest that you both get your rest and be ready to trek again in the morning."

"That's probably a good idea," agreed Harrison. The young warrior rose from his seat on the ground, then offered his hand to Tara in order to help her up as well.

"How do you feel, dear?" asked Brianna to the girl.

The young maiden flashed the queen a smile. "Fine as usual," said Tara, a little confused at why Brianna would ask about her wellbeing.

"That's good. Get plenty of rest." Brianna smiled back at the girl.

"I'll be sure to do just that," said Tara.

"We'll regroup in the morning. Thanks for talking to us this afternoon," said Harrison.

"Our pleasure," said Moradoril as Harrison, Tara, and Lance exited the tent.

After the trio departed the shelter, Moradoril turned to his queen. "They don't know?"

Brianna smiled, her gaze fixed on the tent's entrance. "No, not yet."

CHAPTER 32

Ọ

The smell of charred wood and burning structures hung heavy in the air. Pondle, having investigated the obvious, approached Harrison to make his report.

"Harrison, whatever did this destroyed ..." The young warrior raised a hand to the thief, signaling for him to stop. Pondle gazed past Harrison, finding Moradoril attempting to console his grieving wife.

The young warrior placed a hand on the back of Pondle's shoulder, guiding him away from the sober couple. In a hushed tone, he asked, "What have you found?"

The thief raised his eyebrows and drew a heavy sigh. "Massive beasts rolled through the complex," started Pondle. Gazing at the scorched trees and burning embers, he continued, "They smashed everything in sight."

Harrison had an inkling of what kind of monster could serve such utter devastation, but he needed to hear for himself. "What do you think did this?"

"If I had to guess? Dragons." Pondle waved his arm deeper into the elven compound. "And take a look at what they did."

The young warrior panned the vicinity, absorbing the destruction. Before him once stood the massive tree structure that held Moradoril's meetings, the same one that he had visited more than once in the recent past. Beyond the burning tree sat crumpled vegetation that once housed their lofty residences, where he and Tara had shared a special moment only weeks ago.

"These creatures didn't just wander through this compound to wreak havoc," said Harrison. "They wanted to obliterate the elves' very existence."

From the corner of his eye, the young warrior saw five figures advancing toward him. Murdock, along with Kymbra, Adrith, Marissa, and Fallyn joined their friends.

"Bodies are everywhere," said the ranger, speaking low, his eyes darting. "We need to have Swinkle give them all a proper burial."

"Did you find any survivors?" asked Harrison.

Murdock closed his eyes and shook his head. "Very few," he said, tears welling in his eyes.

"Where are the others?" The young warrior strained to look beyond the small group of humans standing before him.

"Searching for any signs of life," said Murdock. "Tara's with them, too."

Harrison's anxiety level began to rise upon hearing his love's name, making the decision to seek her an easy one. "Help Moradoril's men with their dead. I'm going to find Tara and Swinkle." The young warrior started to walk away before adding, "And be sensitive to their state of mind right now."

The young warrior left his friends behind and ventured deeper into the obliterated complex. The stench of burned carnage permeated the area, adding to the gloom that clung in the air. Up ahead, Harrison found Swinkle bent on one knee, examining a figure that lay on the ground. Tara kneeled alongside of him.

The young warrior squatted next to the two, gazing at the dead body. "Swinkle, what happened here?"

The young cleric sighed. "I cannot be sure how this sentry died."

Harrison crinkled his brow and shot Tara a quizzical look before turning his attention back to Swinkle. "Isn't it obvious?" The young warrior pointed to the elf's broken body. "He's bruised and bleeding, and I'm sure many of his bones are broken."

"Those are the noticeable injuries," said the young cleric. "Which I'm sure attributed to his demise. But see here," Swinkle circled his index finger in the air around the archer's ear, "there is blood."

Harrison nodded, again assuming the obvious. "He probably whacked his head in battle, injuring his brain, and causing it to bleed."

Swinkle gripped his chin with his right hand, thinking. "Possible."

"What are your thoughts?" asked the young warrior, curious.

"Something else caused this," said Tara before Swinkle could speak. "He wasn't hit in the head."

The young warrior brought his focus to Tara. "What makes you say that?"

Tara pointed to the elf's head gear. "His helmet isn't cracked. As a matter of fact, it appears pretty much intact."

Harrison brought his gaze to the elf's head covering. Sure enough, it appeared dirty and smudged, but not damaged. The young warrior smiled. "Good observation." Turning to Swinkle, he asked, "So where does this leave us?"

"My thought is he suffered some kind of psychic attack, something that jarred his brain from the inside," said the young cleric. Pointing to the elf's broken body, "Everything else is superficial to make it look like a physical confrontation."

Harrison arched his eyebrows and exhaled deeply, taking in the new assessment. "Not that I don't believe you, but I'd like to run that by Gelderand and Thoragaard, just to hear their thoughts."

Swinkle nodded once. "By all means."

The young warrior rose from his position and scanned the immediate area, finding the two magicians several yards away, helping elven sentries tend to their dead. Excusing himself, he went over to the men and asked them to look at what Swinkle had discovered. The young cleric recited his findings to the elder men, just as he had to Harrison.

After hearing Swinkle's assessment, Gelderand bent down to take a closer look at the fallen fighter. Cocking his head, he gazed at Swinkle and said, "A very astute observation."

"So, do you agree with it being a psychic attack?" asked the young cleric.

"I would not rule it out," said the mage.

"We should look for these symptoms on all the dead," added Thoragaard. "Only then can we rule in favor or not."

"How about Moradoril and Brianna?" asked Harrison. "Should we tell them of our finding?"

"That is a good idea," said Gelderand. "Maybe they can shed some light."

The young warrior located the mourning couple tending to their fallen comrades. Brianna had bent over an injured fighter, administering aid. Trying his best to not disturb her, the young warrior made eye contact with Moradoril.

"I think we've discovered something but we'd like to hear your thoughts," said Harrison.

Moradoril nodded once and approached the young warrior. Placing a hand on his back and turning him away from Brianna, he asked, "What have you found?"

"Swinkle was examining one of your men and found something out of place," said Harrison. "He believes that one of your sentries died from a psychic attack, masked by physical injuries."

Moradoril stood tall, defiant. "Elves cannot succumb to mental tactics. We can block out the most formidable attempts at accessing our minds."

Harrison nodded, not wanting to press the issue at such a delicate time. "I didn't know that your race had such a high tolerance to psychic attacks. Forgive me."

"What exactly did your cleric friend find?" asked a soft voice. Both men turned, finding Brianna standing before them, her disposition focused and determined.

"Bleeding from the ears without any sign of head trauma," said Harrison. "The archer's helmet had sustained no damage nor did his head or face."

Brianna stared at Moradoril. Harrison thought he saw her brow crease ever so slightly with concern. "It is a possibility," said the queen.

"Nonsense!" barked Moradoril, the destruction of his homeland and shock of the situation getting the better of him.

"Elves *do not* succumb to these attacks! We are a strong and proud race, Brianna!"

The elven queen approached her king, placing a caring hand on his forearm in an effort to calm him. "That we are, Moradoril. However, look at the destruction that took place here. Were our people not surprised?"

Harrison had studied elven history at the Fighter's Guild and learned that a surprise attack against them was more than a rare occurrence. The elves prided themselves at being one with nature, learning patience and restraint, to monitor their enemies, then allow them to make the first move, which gave them an advantage in battle more often than not. He agreed with Brianna's statement in silence.

"It is the only explanation for the carnage," agreed Moradoril. "However, I still cannot fathom that an enemy had manipulated their brains."

Brianna sighed. "If our bodies break down first, the threshold to attack us mentally lowers, especially if the enemy has strong magical capabilities."

Moradoril stared into his queen's eyes with concern. "Who or what possesses magic like this?"

"Finius Boulware," said Brianna, her shoulders slumping and her eyes hollow.

"Finius Boulware?" said Harrison. "The same warlock who nearly wiped out the dwarves?"

"One and the same," said Moradoril.

The young warrior's mind raced upon hearing the old wizard's name. "What's this magician's agenda? First the dwarves and now your people?"

Brianna and Moradoril allowed the young warrior's own statement to sink in. A moment later, Harrison's eyes widened. "He's coming after us next!"

"I would not be surprised at all if he has now targeted the human race," said Moradoril.

"But why?" exclaimed the young warrior, but before anyone could answer, the trio heard excited shouts coming from the main entrance area.

All people in the vicinity rushed to the two sentries who hovered over something on the ground. Harrison, Moradoril, and Brianna joined elves and humans alike to see what had caused all the commotion.

Harrison reached the fallen elf along with the others. Floriad and Gaelos knelt before their fellow comrade, while Liagol held his hand. Brianna stepped to the forefront.

"My child, what has happened to you?" asked the elven queen, squatting to the archer's level, gently touching his forehead. The sentry's head was warm and sweaty.

The injured being gritted his teeth, not wanting to disappoint his queen. "Queen Brianna, they burst through the gates and set the complex ablaze," said the sentry, quivering. "We tried to stop them, but the monsters were too large. Our arrows did not faze them one bit."

Brianna nodded as the archer told his story. "Who did you try to stop?"

Tears welled in the elf's eyes. "Two headed dragons. They stood two stories high and breathed fire throughout the compound. Their green scaly hides were too thick for our arrows to penetrate. I'm sorry we failed you."

"Don't say things like that!" exclaimed Brianna. "You did not possess the appropriate weaponry to fight against those monsters." Continuing her interrogation, she asked, "How many dragons did you see?"

"One to begin with," started the sentry, doing his best to recall every minute detail of the attack. "Then several more entered the complex. Somehow our gates flew open. We did not hear or sense them. They appeared from the depths of the woods and rattled our walls with fiery explosions."

One of the archer's comments piqued Brianna's interest. "Our gates flew open?"

The elf squirmed and took a deep breath before continuing. "Yes. After a fireball rocked the outside of the structure, the portals burst free. We did not allow them in."

Brianna gazed up at Moradoril from her lowered position. "Our doors are sealed. No one can enter from the outside unless we open the gates."

The king nodded once. "Only an evil wizard can negate our powerful magic."

Harrison waited for a lull, then said, "Finius Boulware?"

Moradoril drew a heavy sigh while Brianna cast her eyes to the ground. "He is the only one that could have done this," said the king, distraught.

"Milady," said the elf on the ground. "I did see two humanoid figures enter our sanctuary after the dragons rumbled through the entranceway."

Brianna took great interest in the elf's new information. "Go on, what did they look like?"

The sentinel closed his eyes, trying to recall the scene in his head before relaying it to his queen. "Two old men, one ancient, looking more like a skeleton with a thin layer of wrinkled skin covering his bones. This one had an eye that looked like a solid white mass."

"That would be Finius, the warlock," said Moradoril in Harrison's direction.

"What about the other man?" pressed Brianna. "Can you remember what he looked like?"

"Younger than the wizard, but older than the people who stand before us," said the elf. "He was dressed in black, had a beard with white flecks."

Harrison heard the sentry's description and an image popped into his mind. Stepping forward, he asked, "Did this man have any noticeable physical qualities?"

The elf turned his focus to Harrison. "How so?"

"Did he have any scars around his neck or have trouble turning his head?"

"Not that I noticed," said the archer. "They shuffled by me and I was in too much pain to move."

The young warrior nodded. "Thank you." Harrison stepped back, then made eye contact with Murdock and Pondle.

Brianna stroked the injured elf's hair. "You did well. We are going to heal you very soon." She then rose from her position and joined the other men.

Harrison had already started an intense discussion before the elven queen arrived. "The person walking with this wizard is King Holleris," said the young warrior.

"What?" exclaimed Murdock, sporting a look of astonishment. "You were there with all of us. Troy lopped his head off!"

"I agree," said the young warrior. "I vividly remember his head falling to the ground and his shouts of anguish as we left his decapitated body in the throne room on Dragon's Lair." Harrison's eyes narrowed. "But who else would want vengeance on us?"

"Harrison, he's dead," said the ranger, outstretching his arms while making his point. "No one survives their head getting chopped off!"

"No, Philius instilled in me the fact that he would remain immortal as long as he stayed on Dragon's Lair," said the young warrior, recalling the story told to him by the elderly Aegean magician. Harrison paused to think. "He was alive when we left him."

"Then how did he get here," said Murdock, pointing to the ground. "A headless body doesn't just wander from the island to the mainland without being noticed."

"And, he'd die instantly if he left the island," said Pondle. "He'd bleed out if his head and body had remained detached."

"Unless he had help," said Brianna, who had patiently listened to the two men argue.

"Milady," said Murdock, "who would help him?"

Brianna remained focused. "The same person who orchestrated the destruction of our home."

"Finius Boulware?" asked Harrison.

"Has to be," added Moradoril. "His name is becoming a common thread to this mystery."

"Why would this warlock be involved with King Holleris?" asked the young warrior.

"Holleris was a mere man without any outstanding capabilities," started Brianna. "A talented fighter, yes, but not someone who could render himself immortal. Only a powerful mage could do that."

"And only a great magician could reverse a spell of immortality," said Moradoril. "One who could piece together a broken body and make it whole again."

"Alright," said Harrison, "let's suppose these two men are together now. Why are they doing what they're doing?"

"Your Ancient Kings were good men," said Brianna. "I met them, talked with them, fought beside them, and respected them. However, they eventually grew apart."

"Enough to send the land into disarray?" asked Harrison, his brow furrowed in disbelief.

"Your race's lust for power is its biggest downfall," said Moradoril. "It created a wedge between them. One that still exists today."

"Then why cause all of this destruction?" asked Harrison, still trying to piece together the storyline.

Moradoril shrugged, lifting his palms to the sky. His eyes narrowed, he said, "Ask yourselves that question. Our people did not deserve this."

The young warrior felt the sting of the king's comment. In a moment of clarity, he said, "He wants to finish what he started a thousand years ago. To rule the land as he sees fit, without having to deal with his equals."

"That would be my guess," said the elven king. "And he's taking his fury out on all of us—elves, dwarves, and humans alike."

"We must stop him," said Harrison, realizing now that King Holleris would target his people next.

Moradoril shook his head. "You are on your own. We need to gather our people, pick up the pieces, and relocate our home."

"I understand," said the young warrior, "but we're going to need help fighting these wicked men and their beasts. Your magical capabilities are vital to the cause!"

Moradoril took a step in Harrison's direction. "Whose cause? Not ours."

Harrison knew that he needed the elves' support if his race were to take on these two headed dragons. Recalling events from the recent past, he said, "Didn't you align yourself with our kings a thousand years ago?"

"Yes, we did."

"And didn't you suspend an entire race in hibernation in order to have them ready to fight at a point in the distant future?"

The elven king raised his palms to the young warrior. "Circumstances have changed, Harrison."

"Not the way I see it," said the Aegean. "King Holleris and his henchmen have brought two races to the brink of extinction and I'm sure we're his next target. We need your help." Harrison paused for emphasis, before adding in a direct tone, "The *land* needs your help."

Moradoril glanced to Brianna, finding her staring back at him, beckoning for her king to make the right choice. "As the leader of the elves I am not going to allow these heathens to rule the land. Our forces are now small, but we will help with your crusade."

Harrison nodded once, smiling. "Thank you, Moradoril."

"Just let it be known that we expect a seat at your leader's table after this conflict," said the elven king.

"We can work out the details later," said the young warrior. "Right now, we need to help you regroup, then devise a strategy."

Harrison and his friends went about helping the elves tend to their injured and dead, as well as salvage what they could from the burning complex.

CHAPTER 33

О

The adventurers suffered through hours of caring for severe injuries and mangled elven bodies. Harrison panned the carnage, compiling a complete understanding of the utter destruction at the hands of King Holleris and his wicked mage.

Tara sidled up to her love. Eyes downcast, she said, "My heart breaks for these people."

Harrison felt his own blood simmer as well. "As bad as this is, we'll be in the same situation if we don't stop these monsters now."

"What are we going to do?"

The young warrior gazed at the young maiden, having formulated a crude plan the better part of the afternoon. "I have an idea," he said, then bent down and planted a kiss on her forehead. "And I think it just might work. Come with me."

The couple wandered through the remnants of the compound and regrouped with their friends. Having everyone accounted for, the young warrior started, "I don't have to tell you all how bad this situation is but it's about to get much worse.

"King Holleris is going to seek vengeance on my brother Troy's betrayal. In his mind, my brother left him for dead after all his years of training and caring for Troy. I'm sure he didn't like that."

"That might be true," said Murdock, folding his arms across his chest. "But what's your plan?"

Harrison smirked. "The king doesn't know that Troy's dead."

The ranger's eyes widened a tad. "No, he doesn't," he said, his brain churning. "He just might be looking for him."

"What are you up to, Harrison?" asked Pondle, sensing the young warrior had more to say.

"Troy and I were twins," said Harrison. "I'm thinking that I," the young warrior brought his focus to Fallyn, "or someone else could pose as him when the time's right."

Fallyn's eyes grew wide after Harrison's statement. "Are you suggesting that I impersonate your brother?"

The young warrior nodded. "Can you? You're able to shape shift into other animals, why not a human, too?"

The woman gazed to the ground in thought, spreading her arms wide, shaking her head. "I suppose so, but impersonating someone is a lot different than morphing into an animal."

"I can help you with Troy's mannerisms and the way he did things," said the Aegean, bolstering his case. "This could work."

"That is a very risky game, Harrison," interjected Gelderand. "This king sounds evil and unpredictable. I am sure that he would want to kill Troy for his disloyalty. You are making Fallyn and yourself targets."

The young warrior nodded, accepting the mage's assessment. "Aren't we all doomed if we do nothing?" Harrison gestured at the chaos around them. "Take a look at what they did to the elves. These people never saw them coming and they're the stealthiest beings in the world. And don't forget the massacre of the dwarves over the centuries. He must be stopped!"

Murdock let out a heavy sigh. "You've obviously been thinking about this," he said. "What else do you have in mind?"

Harrison raised his palms to his friends. "First, we need to get word to our people about what's heading in their direction. The messenger falcons need to be deployed."

"Why not send Fallyn?" asked Murdock. "Like she flew off to find the elves?"

"I thought the same thing but I figured that her trip there and back would take too long, and I'll need her services here," said

Harrison. "Our enemies are close by and we need to work fast." The ranger cocked his head in acceptance.

The young warrior continued. "Next, we seek King Holleris and his dragon army. We need to know their plan in order to stop them."

"Are you crazy?" exclaimed the ranger. "You said it yourself, look what they did here! How can a small band of warriors take on these creatures?"

"We can't," said Harrison. "All we need to do is figure out how to stop them, then we can report back to the leaders to formulate a master plan."

Murdock began to understand Harrison's rationale. "I'm assuming that you want to split up our group, right?"

Harrison nodded. "Yes." Everyone took a vested interest in what their leader said next. The young warrior pointed toward the female warriors. "Adrith and Marissa will escort Thoragaard back to Concur, where they'll alert Brendan and the Forge brothers of the oncoming army.

"The rest of us will venture deeper into the woods and catch up to these beasts. I'm sure Pondle can track these monsters with ease."

"This'll be the easiest tracking job I've ever had," said the thief, leering at the path of destruction leading out of the elves' complex.

Gelderand raised a hand in protest. "I feel that Tara should return to Concur with the others." The mage gazed at her niece. "A battlefield is no place for you."

"Normally I would agree," said Harrison. "But Brianna made it clear to me that I should not let her out of my sight and I intend to honor that advice."

"Harrison," pleaded Gelderand. "This is the wrong decision!"

"Uncle, I choose to trek with you and the group," said Tara. "If we're going to die, I'd rather that it be all together."

Gelderand took a step toward his niece to push a strand of hair away from her face. "Why must you be so much like your mother? I am just doing what I feel is right to protect you."

Tara took her uncle's hand and pressed it against her cheek. "I know you are, but there's no place that I'd rather be than with you and Harrison, no matter how dangerous the circumstances."

"You are brave. I will give you that," said the magician with a huff. Turning to face the group, he said, "We must all look out for one another. This journey will be the most perilous one that we have ever made."

"That we will," said Harrison. "Our goal is to determine how to stop these beasts. Only then can we formulate a plan to defeat them."

"It is best that we leave at once," said Thoragaard, bringing his focus to Adrith and Marissa. "We shall move as swiftly as possible to reach Concur and alert the other villages and towns." The illusionist turned his attention back to Harrison. "Be sure to create a thorough plan in regards to Fallyn before confronting the king and his warlock. They will not be fooled as easily as you think."

"I agree one hundred percent," said the young warrior. "Do what you must to prepare, as will we. I need to speak with Moradoril and Brianna before we depart." Taking his gaze to Murdock and Pondle, he asked, "How long before we can leave?"

Pondle looked skyward, trying to get a fix on the time of day. "Less than an hour, there's nothing more for us to do here. I can't get an exact reading on how much sunlight we'll have, but we need to venture until it gets dark anyway."

"Go talk to the elves," said Murdock, motioning with his head in the royal couple's direction. "We'll be ready when you return."

Harrison gave the ranger a single nod, then turned to Tara. "Come with me." The young maiden nodded her head yes and walked beside the Aegean.

The young couple found the elves administering aid to several wounded sentries. Soft white glows, similar to Swinkle's healing practices, enveloped their hands as they touched injured body parts. Brianna lifted her eyes, spotting the two approaching. She finished her work on an archer, then rose to her feet.

"Our task is daunting, but we shall overcome the atrocities of this day," said the queen in a defiant tone.

"We're so sorry for your losses, Brianna," said Harrison, wishing that he had more to say. "Is there anything else we can do to help?"

"You have done what you can here," said Brianna. "Finding the beings responsible for these heinous acts would be your greatest contribution."

"We intend to do just that," said the young warrior. "Unfortunately, that means leaving you now. We must alert our people."

Brianna nodded in understanding. "That is the prudent course of action."

"Is there any way you can join us?" asked Harrison, knowing full well the formidable task that lie ahead of them. "We can use all the help we can get."

Brianna cocked her head and panned the area with her eyes. "Not now, Harrison. Our commitment must stay with our own people first." At that time, Moradoril completed his tasks and accompanied the small group.

"On the contrary, milady," said Moradoril. "We will fight these marauders with them. No one shall create such devastation and not pay the price."

"Then you'll help us?" asked Harrison, hopeful.

"Yes, but as Brianna stated, we must tend to ourselves first," said the king. "We will join you in battle at a later date."

The young warrior felt his spirits lift. Gazing around the compound, he found only a small number of elves remaining. With concern in his voice, he asked, "How many people do you have left?"

"Here?" said Moradoril. "Less than fifty. However, this is not our only compound. We have many more scattered throughout the land."

Harrison crinkled his brow. "Really? This is the only place that we've ever known about."

The king's lips curled in a slight smile. "It would not be wise for a race to house all their people in one place. Who do you take us for? The dwarves?"

"On the contrary," said Harrison. "I shouldn't be surprised to hear that your people are dispersed all over the countryside."

Moradoril extended his hand. "Go, son. Alert your people and hunt these beings down. We will not be too far behind." Harrison accepted the king's hand and gave it a firm shake.

The elven king turned his attention to Tara. "Stay safe, lass. Your importance has not reared its head yet."

Tara flashed a meek smile, unsure of the king's comment. "I will. Thank you."

Brianna approached the girl, taking hold of both her hands. Focusing on the young maiden, she said, "Do not underestimate your powers. You are stronger than you know and you harbor something deep inside that will alter the future of this land."

The queen leaned over and kissed Tara on the cheek, then let go of her hands. "Go and be safe," said Brianna.

Harrison nodded to the royal couple. "We will. And we'll see you again, very soon." The two then left the elves behind to regroup with their friends.

"Are they joining us?" asked Murdock, motioning toward the elves.

"Eventually," said Harrison. "As for us, we need to make our move now." The young warrior turned his focus to Thoragaard and his female escorts. "Are you three ready to leave?"

"We have enough food and water for now," said Adrith, taking the lead. "We'll make double time across the countryside."

"Lady Meredith will be alerted before the monsters step foot in the Valkaline Forest," added Thoragaard. "I have a few tricks that should allow us to avoid detection."

"Good," said Harrison with a nod. "We're counting on you to alert the people of the coast."

Adrith gazed at Marissa and Thoragaard. "If there's nothing more to add, we're good to go." Neither Thoragaard nor Marissa had anything else to say. "Alright then, we'll see you in Concur."

"Be careful," said the young warrior. "And steer clear of danger."

"We will," said Thoragaard. Taking his eyes to Tara, he added, "Remember your studies, Tara, and all will be fine."

"I've recalled everything we did together," said the young maiden. "I'm ready for anything."

Thoragaard nodded his approval, then motioned with his hand for Adrith and Marissa to take the lead. Without another word, the trio left their friends behind, departed the elven complex, and headed for Concur.

Harrison, having watched three of his friends venture into the wilderness, knew that the time had come for them to do the same. Collecting their belongings, the young warrior instructed Murdock and Pondle to lead the smaller group in the direction of King Holleris' beasts. Swinkle, Gelderand, Fallyn, and Tara marched together, flanked by Kymbra on the left and Harrison to the right. Lance darted between the travelers, ensuring that everyone was safe. The small contingent left the elves' complex behind and traveled in silence, each one harboring their own fears about the great unknown enemy that loomed somewhere ahead of them.

C H A P T E R 34

Ophrase

Pondle and Murdock led the adventurers deeper into the gloomy depths of the Dark Forest. The massive trees blocked out most of the sunlight, forcing the group to resort to torches. Harrison, realizing that his own body began to tire, called for the group to halt for the night.

"Is this place safe?" asked the young warrior in Murdock and Pondle's direction.

The ranger shrugged. "As good as anywhere," he said. "I'll grab Pondle and we'll survey the vicinity. Don't wander too far, we'll be right back." The two men scampered away to make their reconnaissance run.

"These torches are going to attract unwanted attention," said Kymbra, panning the area over and over again.

"Understood," said Harrison. "Tara and Swinkle will keep theirs lit. Everyone else, douse your flames."

The group did as their leader commanded and, a few minutes later, the two trackers returned to the group. "There's a better cluster of trees a hundred yards ahead of us that we can use to our advantage," said Pondle.

"Very well," said Harrison. "Did you notice anything out of the ordinary?"

"No," said Murdock. "And that's what bothers me." The ranger, like Kymbra before him, panned the vicinity. "We didn't find any Scynthian tracks, just the dragons' markings, and even theirs have become spotty."

Harrison crinkled his brow in confusion. "How so?"

"My assumption's that they're walking and flying from point to point," said Pondle. "These trees are too thick to fly between, especially if they're as big as the elves said they were."

The young warrior's eye lit up. "Maybe they're having difficulty navigating through the forest."

"A distinct possibility," said Pondle.

"That could buy Thoragaard's group some time," said Harrison. "We need every spare minute we can get."

Pondle led the adventurers to the cluster of small trees that they would use to shelter the team. Everyone removed their packs and began to settle in, taking advantage of resting their weary bodies. Harrison gathered food from his backpack, handing some dry meats to Lance, who happily gobbled them up. The rest of the team members formed a circle, removing their own meals, and taking a seat on the ground.

The young warrior gazed at his friends congregated around him. Two torches provided just enough light for everyone to see each other. "It's been a long time since we ate together," said Harrison, recalling that inclement weather and unexpected atrocities at the dwarves' and elves' compounds had taken center stage for the group.

"I like it better this way," said Murdock, tearing at a piece of bread. "Like the old days when we just searched for treasures and clues."

"More important things are at stake now," said Harrison, secretly wishing for simpler days as well. Directing his next statement to Pondle, he said, "We can't be too far behind them now."

"We're not," said the thief, munching on his meal. "Their tracks continue that way." Pondle pointed to his left. "Due west."

"In Concur's direction," said the young warrior.

"And Aegeus, and Argos, and Robus," added Murdock. "All human outposts for that matter."

Harrison let the ranger's comments sink in, picturing the faces of innocent men, women, and children who had no idea that a menacing army of two-headed dragons stormed their way.

Taking the conversation in a different direction, he asked, "What do those creatures eat anyway?"

"They are carnivorous," said Gelderand. "They prefer meat like deer or horses, something large to sustain them."

Harrison crinkled his brow. "Is there enough food in this forest to satisfy them?"

"A very good question indeed," said the mage. "This forest is huge and has a lot of animals living in it, but I am not sure there is enough."

The young warrior's brain churned in thought. "What if they're not getting enough to eat?"

"They'd get very mad," chimed in Murdock, not bothering to lift his eyes from his food.

"Maybe they are getting a different food source," said Swinkle. "I can create food, albeit in small quantities for myself. If Finius is with them, he probably can make much more than I."

"If this warlock is all powerful, then that might be an accurate assumption," said Gelderand.

"All the more reason to stay cautious," said Harrison. A high pitched screech echoed in the distance, halting the discussion.

"What was that?" asked Tara, her voice filled with apprehension.

Pondle rose from his seat on the ground and glared in the direction of the new sound. "I have an idea but we need to investigate. Murdock, let's go!" The ranger followed his friend's lead, the two men scampering off into the woods. Lance yapped once in Harrison's direction, then sprinted after the trackers.

"Everyone," said Harrison. "Gather your belongings and be prepared to move." The rest of the party members heeded their leader's command, their break for the evening over before it could even start.

After securing her things, Tara approached Harrison. "What do we do when we finally reach these creatures?"

More screeches filled the air, everyone scanning the area with anxious eyes and heightened concern. "Don't allow them to see us, for one," said Harrison. "We need to know how many of them are lurking in this forest, where they're going, and how to stop them."

417

"What about the evil people they're with?" asked the young maiden.

"We'll make an assessment on them as well," said the Aegean.

Lance bolted back into the makeshift camp, running straight to Harrison. The little dog started yipping at his master, "Monster! Monster!"

The young warrior bent to one knee to be at the dog's level. "Yes, Lance, we expected to find monsters," he said, petting the canine on the head. Moments later, Pondle and Murdock emerged from the darkness.

"Three hundred yards ahead," said the ranger.

"Huge beasts with two long necks, just like that elf said," added Pondle.

"Did you see Finius or Holleris?" asked the young warrior.

"No," said Murdock, "but we weren't making a full investigation, just trying to locate the dragons and see which direction they were heading."

Harrison nodded, thinking all the while. "We need more information," he said. "How many dragons did you see?"

"Only two, but there's got be more of them out there," said Pondle.

An explosion, followed by a burst of energy, erupted from the dragons' last known position. Everyone in the group cowered at the sound, all heads turning in that direction.

Pondle pointed down the path he had just taken. "Look! Fire!" Sure enough, a large blaze had started to consume several trees in the distance.

"What are they doing?" asked Harrison to no one in particular.

"We have to make a proper assessment," said Murdock with emphasis, driving home his point. "We don't have all the facts yet and we can't make any assumptions."

"How do we do this without getting ourselves killed?" asked the young warrior.

"We'll give them a wide berth," said Pondle. "Loop around them in big circles, then tighten the gap between them and us. It'll take longer but also keep us out of harm's way."

"What's the best plan for positioning everyone?" asked the group's leader.

Pondle thought for a moment, then looked over to Murdock. "Pondle and I will take the lead," started the ranger. "Then branch off to the left and right of the dragons' position. Kymbra will flank to the left with me and you'll bring up the rear with the rest of the group."

"Why are we staying further behind?" asked Harrison.

"In case they change direction," said Murdock. "If they do, you'll get a better visual on them."

"Let's do this," said Harrison, agreeing with his friend's reconnaissance suggestion. "However, keep in mind that we want to gather as much information about what we see without engaging the beasts. We can't defeat them without an army and I'm not thrilled about having a wicked warlock in our midst."

"That's the plan," said Murdock before taking his gaze at the fire erupting in the forest ahead of them. "Pondle, lead the way."

The thief took his friend's cue and led the small group of nervous people forward. Flames intensified and shrieks flooded the woodlands. After trekking a hundred yards, Pondle motioned for Murdock and Kymbra to sweep left while he began his loop to the right.

Harrison raised his hand, signaling for his group to stop. "We'll let them get into position," said the young warrior to his squad.

"Is there anything specific we should be doing?" asked Swinkle, unsure of their duties.

The Aegean peered at his fellow adventurers, realizing that he had to protect them at all times. "Not yet," said Harrison. "Let's see what the others find first." Thinking about the young cleric's question, he added, "Stay low and out of sight."

The young warrior gazed into the distance, eventually losing sight of Murdock, Pondle, and Kymbra. To his right, a large coniferous tree stood tall with a base ten feet wide.

Pointing to the grand pine, he said, "Let's stay over there." The young warrior led his friends to the tree.

Another screech echoed from up ahead. Tara, nervous already, asked, "What happens if the dragons head this way?"

Harrison, knowing that lying to appease his mate would be wrong, said, "Follow me as fast as you can."

* * *

"How close are you going to get to them?" asked Kymbra, more than a hint of concern in her voice.

"As close as I can," said Murdock. Each warrior continued forward, running from tree trunk to tree trunk in an effort to conceal themselves from the menacing beasts.

The ranger, sweat on his brow more from nerves than physical exertion, leaned his back against a tree. Kymbra stood right beside him. "They're close," she said.

"I know," said the ranger. "We need to get a good visual on them and be able to describe their characteristics to Harrison and the others."

Kymbra cocked her head and in a sarcastic tone, said, "Well, they're big."

The warrior's comment caused Murdock to reflect on his own manner of speaking, feeling a sense of commonality with the way others felt when he spoke.

"No kidding, they're big!" exclaimed the ranger. "I meant more subtle features."

Kymbra peeked her head around the tree, seeing one of the dragons in the forest's depths. "Alright, they're green as well."

Murdock squinted in disgust. "I should just leave you here in the woods by yourself."

The blonde warrior flashed a slight smile. "What's the matter? Did the warrior girl upset the mighty bowman?"

"Not now, Kymbra!" said Murdock. "We need to finish this mission."

"That I agree with," said the female warrior. "And we're doing it all wrong."

Murdock's shoulders slumped. "Oh, really?" he said, his voice thick with equal sarcasm. "Enlighten me, then."

Kymbra gazed around the trunk again. "We need to get in front of the creatures in order to see the humans venturing with them."

"I'd rather follow from behind," said Murdock. "They don't have eyes on the backs of their head … or heads."

"True, but we're wasting our time back here," said Kymbra. "We need to advance faster."

"Fine!" said Murdock, taking his glare away from Kymbra and panning the forest in front of them. Focusing on a rather large tree trunk, he said, "The big tree, twenty yards ahead. See it?"

Kymbra peered around the trunk. "Yes."

"Let's make a break for it."

"What about the flames?"

Murdock raised an eyebrow. "Avoid them?" Peeking around the tree trunk again, he said, "Let's go!"

Without looking back, the ranger bolted from his position and headed to their new lookout point. Kymbra followed close behind. The two arrived at the tree, avoiding the fire just as Murdock had stated.

"This is a better view," said the ranger. "I see three dragons, how about you?"

Kymbra focused on the monsters that lumbered ahead of them in the forest. "Yes, three."

"I'm sensing more, though," said Murdock. An explosion further ahead more than startled the couple.

"That wasn't from one of these monsters," said Kymbra.

"Make that at least four then," said Murdock. Poking his head around the tree, he added, "I see thick, dark green scales, with a lighter green underbelly. Massive wings and two heads as well."

Kymbra nodded in concurrence. "I agree, with the beasts able to spew fire."

"Typical dragons, save for the second head," quipped the ranger. "And no way to defeat them using the weapons we possess."

The female warrior shook her head, raising her long sword. "Nope, not with this."

Murdock gazed into the distance, trying to gauge his next reconnaissance point. Making a sweeping arc to the left, he said,

"Alright, we're going to make a wide loop that way. I figure we can be ahead of them in a quarter of a mile."

Kymbra looked in the same direction and agreed with his assessment. "Remember, we have no defense against these beasts."

"Don't remind me," retorted the ranger. "Let's go!" The two then scurried off to position themselves in front of the lumbering creatures.

* * *

Harrison did not enjoy waiting for action, rather he liked to initiate his battles. Standing back and awaiting his friend's reconnaissance mission gnawed at his warrior pride.

"Harrison," said Swinkle, approaching his friend, breaking his train of thought. "How do you propose defeating these creatures?"

The young warrior gazed at the battle axe in his hand, then shook his head. "I could hack away at one of those dragons for days with this axe and never penetrate its scales." Harrison sighed. "I honestly don't know."

"I think I have an idea," said the young cleric.

Lifting an eyebrow, Harrison said, "Oh, really?"

"We possess a scroll that can eradicate them from the earth," said Swinkle, a slight smile gracing his face. Tara, Fallyn, and Gelderand overheard the young cleric's comment and, along with Lance, came over to join the two.

"We could read the scroll right now and destroy them!" exclaimed Harrison with excitement in his voice. A thought crossed his mind. "Doesn't this go against your core beliefs? Eradicating a race?"

Swinkle shook his head. "No. Wicked people created these monsters with the intent to cause great harm. Wiping them out of existence would be a benefit to all living creatures."

"I hate to dampen your spirits, but we have a major obstacle to overcome," added Gelderand, patiently waiting to add his thoughts to the conversation.

"I know, we need to consult with the leadership team," said Harrison. "I've thought of that as well."

The mage shook his head. "Oh, it's much simpler than that."

The young warrior crinkled his brow. "What do you mean?"

"The scroll states that the race specified by the reader will vanish from the face of the earth."

"I understand that," said Harrison, not putting the pieces together.

"What's the name of the dragon's race?" asked Tara, understanding her uncle's reasoning.

The young warrior opened his mouth to speak but said nothing. Shaking the cobwebs from his head, he asked, "They're a race of two headed dragons, right?"

"Yes," said Gelderand, "but what is their *specific* name?"

Harrison shook his head. "I haven't the foggiest idea. Can't we just state that we want to wipe out all two-headed dragons?"

"That action would go against my core beliefs," said Swinkle. "Blindly eliminating an entire race of beings is bad enough but using such a broad stroke to include these specific creatures is wrong."

"How do we find out their name?" asked Fallyn, unsure of the answer just like the others.

"I suspect that only two people in this world know what these monsters are called," said Gelderand.

"King Holleris and Finius Boulware," said Harrison in disgust, coming to grips about the gravity of their problem.

"Extract the name from them and I'll read the scroll," said Gelderand.

Harrison let out a heavy sigh. "They'd die before telling us anything."

"There is always another way," added Swinkle. "We just have not made that determination yet."

"We might as well continue trying to find a weakness in those beasts until we capture those two wicked men," said Harrison, knowing that their plight had just become much more difficult. "Let's see what Murdock, Pondle, and Kymbra have uncovered."

The young warrior motioned for his friends to venture onward, all the while contemplating how they could extract the dragon's name from the minds of two evil human beings.

CHAPTER 35

Ⴍ

"You're getting too close!" muttered Kymbra in Murdock's direction.

The couple had trekked ahead of the large beasts, making a wide loop, ending up in front of the creatures. Now, hiding behind a large tree trunk, the inferior humans saw firsthand the enormity of their adversaries.

The ranger pointed to two older men walking in the midst of the dragons. "King Holleris and his wicked warlock."

Kymbra's eyes remained locked on the approaching monsters. Her breath coming in short bursts, she said, "Seven, no eight! Eight dragons!" She clutched Murdock's shoulder, garnering his full attention. "We need to leave now!"

Murdock started to say something sarcastic, but noticed the sheer look of panic on Kymbra's face. The woman's eyes stayed round and fixed, her face pale, and her brow covered with sweat.

"Alright, we head back to Harrison and the others," said the ranger.

Before starting their return trek, he took another peek at the looming beasts. To his surprise they had halted their procession.

Murdock leaned harder into the tree's base, squinting into the distance. "What are they doing?"

Kymbra shook her head, frantic. "I don't care! Let's go before they smell us!"

The ranger held up a hand. "Wait," he said as he watched the dragons form a circle around the humans. Kymbra's eyes stayed glued to the scene as well.

Murdock and Kymbra watched Finius walk into the middle of the beasts. The creatures lowered their heads and hunched their bodies down, waiting for their master to perform some kind of trick.

"What's he doing?" asked Kymbra, her voice a whisper.

"I think we're about to find out."

Finius lowered a sack to the ground, then rummaged through it, removing nine fleshy objects. The dragons leaned closer in anticipation.

"What are those things?" blurted the female warrior, not really expecting a response.

Murdock shook his head. "Let it unfold, Kymbra."

The warlock removed fine grain from a pouch on his belt and sprinkled it all over the blobs. Next, he bellowed something inaudible, then walked away from the beasts, leaving the objects behind. The dragons creeped closer, each one bobbing a head toward the lumps that sat on the ground, sniffing them, then quickly pulling away.

Finius walked over to stand next to King Holleris, both people outside the circle of creatures. Picking a staff up from the ground, the warlock pointed it at the meaty globes.

"Life!" screamed the wizard. A bolt of electricity shot from the tip of the wooden staff after the magician's command.

The current penetrated every object, jolting each one off the ground. When they landed, the pieces transformed into large, oversized war horses. Within seconds, the dragons roared and lunged at the animals, grabbing the unsuspecting steeds and tearing them to pieces.

Kymbra, her eyes round in shock, gasped and covered her mouth. Her eyes remained riveted to the horrific scene as body parts flew in all directions, the sound of bones crunching and flesh tearing filling the air. The female warrior felt her belly churn, hunched over, and wretched her stomach's contents to the ground.

Murdock, his eyes glued to the diabolical scene, slowly backed away from the tree and reached for Kymbra's hand.

426

"Let's get out of here," he said, his voice barely a whisper. Kymbra clutched his hand and squeezed hard, surprising the ranger. Swiveling his head, he found the female warrior's eyes filled with tears.

Murdock grabbed Kymbra's arms, giving her a firm shake to try and break her from her trance. Using a forceful voice, he said, "We're leaving now. Follow me."

Kymbra nodded repeatedly, though her eyes remained fixed on the feeding frenzy. Murdock tugged her arm, snapping her from her stupor, starting their trek back to Harrison and the others.

* * *

Lance held his ground, his ears pricked up and tail stiff. "Coming," he growled, showing his teeth.

Harrison heard his little friend's remark and gripped his battle axe tighter. "Something's out there," he said to the rest of his group, motioning for them to get low and take cover. Seconds later, Murdock and Kymbra emerged from the underbrush. Lance darted over to greet the warriors.

Exhaling a sigh of relief, the young warrior lowered his weapon and engaged his two friends. "It's been awhile. What did you find?"

"Nothing good," said Murdock. Panning, he noticed someone missing. "Where's Pondle?"

"He went with you," said Harrison, his anxiety level beginning to rise.

Murdock turned to look back from where he came. "We went on different reconnaissance routes, but I expected him back by now."

Something in the thickets stirred, springing Lance back into action. The little dog did not have to venture far to greet the group's missing party member.

"Thanks for leaving me behind!" said Pondle, patting the canine on his head.

"I figured you'd come back this way," said Murdock in defense. "Did you see what happened out there?"

"If you're talking about the feeding frenzy, then yes," said the thief.

Harrison's brow crinkled at the thief's comment. "Feeding frenzy? Tell us what happened out there!" The rest of the adventurers closed ranks to hear what the scouting team had uncovered.

Murdock began. "Ahead of us are eight dragons …"

"Nine," interrupted Pondle.

"Nine?" said Kymbra, a single eyebrow raised. "I counted eight."

"Trust me," said the thief, "there are nine."

"Fine," said Murdock. "Ahead of us are *nine* dragons with a very healthy appetite. The king's magician created oversized horses out of lifeless clumps of flesh, then fed them to the monsters."

Harrison's eyes arched high on his brow. "He fed them to the dragons?"

"It was horrific," said Kymbra, recalling the merciless slaughter. "They lowered their necks down to the defenseless horses, then tore them apart with their razor sharp teeth. It was gruesome."

"So much blood," said Pondle, shaking his head. "So much pain."

Harrison digested the information before an idea sprung into his mind. "If we can capture Finius, we can halt their food production."

"Good luck with that," said Murdock.

"What's wrong with that idea?" asked the young warrior.

"Dragons aren't stupid," said the ranger. "They know that this wizard generates their meals for them. They won't let anyone near him."

Harrison turned his head toward Gelderand and Swinkle. "If we can't capture Finius, then our only recourse is to read that scroll."

"Why haven't we done that yet?" asked Murdock, raising his palms to the sky.

"No one knows the name of the dragon's race," said Harrison.

"Magic?" said the ranger with a shake of his head. "More a waste of time than what it's worth."

"Then what's our next course of action?" asked Pondle.

Harrison pondered the question. "Maybe we can follow these beasts, eavesdrop on the king and Finius, listen for them to utter the name."

"I could morph into a small creature," said Fallyn, a hint of reluctance in her voice. "Maybe a mouse or squirrel, something that wouldn't draw suspicion."

"Out of the question," said Kymbra before Harrison could respond. "I wouldn't take any chances with those monsters. They'll destroy us all before too long. We need to get away from them."

"Harrison, she is right," said Swinkle. "I studied dragons at our seminary and they possess a myriad of abilities. One being that you can never sneak up on them."

"These are not ordinary dragons," said Gelderand. "That warlock created them; they were not born the traditional way."

Swinkle raised an eyebrow. "Then it is possible that they do not possess all the characteristics of a typical dragon."

"True," said the mage. "However, there are many subspecies of dragons, all having different characteristics and abilities."

"Forget it!" exclaimed Murdock, waving his hands. "We're not going to risk any of us just to listen for a special phrase that those maniacs may or may not utter. Think of something else."

"The Scrolls of Arcadia don't mention these monsters?" asked Harrison, despair in his voice.

"I will check them again, but I do not recall reading anything about a two-headed dragon race," said Swinkle.

"There might only be one option left," said Harrison. "We need to get back to Concur and ready ourselves for the fight of a lifetime."

"That might be the prudent course of action," said Gelderand. "These creatures have destroyed the elves civilization and Finius took it upon himself to severely incapacitate the dwarves. We are next."

Harrison shook his head and raised his weapon. "Not if I have anything to say about it!" He panned his friends, reading their faces that awaited a decision.

"Pondle," said the young warrior, "lead us to Concur and keep us well away from those beings."

The thief nodded. "You have no problem convincing me of that. However, it's getting late and we should hunker down for the evening. I'll find us a place nowhere near those monsters."

Harrison and the others followed Pondle through the underbrush in the opposite direction of King Holleris' dragon army. After twenty minutes of trekking, the small group found a natural configuration to their liking and settled in for the evening.

Murdock, Pondle, and Kymbra debated on their guard rotation, while Harrison and the others settled in for the night. Tara placed her pack next to Harrison's and lay next to him on the ground.

"Will we make it safely back to Concur?" she asked, a hint of anxiety in her voice.

"I'm sure we will," said Harrison, leaning over and planting a soft kiss on her lips. "No one's going to harm us, I promise you that."

"How can you be so sure?"

"I have faith in Murdock and Pondle. They'll guide us on a track far away from those beasts," said the young warrior, allaying the girl's fears. "Once we're in Concur, we'll discuss our options with the leaders."

"Can we defeat those dragons?"

Harrison thought for a moment, then yanked Tara's blanket up over her chest in order to keep her warm. Pulling her small body closer to his, he said in his most convincing voice, "We have to."

CHAPTER 36

○

The sudden feeling of a hand covering his mouth woke Harrison from a blissful slumber. Before he could regain his senses, he felt the unmistakable chill of a cold blade against his neck.

"Get up slowly and don't make a sound," whispered the voice in his ear. Harrison's eyes opened wide and he immediately tried to gather his bearings. Tara lay no more than a foot away, her back facing away from the young warrior. Good, she's safe, he thought.

The young warrior took his time lifting himself up from the forest's floor, not wanting to startle the intruder and thereby getting his throat slit. Rising slowly from the ground, his eyes darted in search of Lance but found him nowhere near the campsite. Must be on patrol with Murdock or Pondle, he rationalized.

Coming to a standing position, he craned his neck in an attempt to see his adversary. Instead, he felt a sharp jab to the back of his neck, forcing his head down.

"Move," said the voice in a harsh whisper.

Harrison allowed the prowler to guide him away from the camp. As he did, the young warrior did his best to pan the vicinity, finding his friends fast asleep.

"What do you want?" said Harrison through clenched teeth. "We're simple adventurers. We have nothing of worth."

Another forceful jab to the back of his neck. "Shut up and keep moving!"

Harrison did as commanded, though his warrior training screamed for him to do more. Knowing that his battle axe remained at the campground, he began to formulate a plan utilizing his dagger, which he kept on his person at all times.

While continuing in the direction the thief led him, he subtly panned to either side of his body in an effort to size up this person. Maybe it was the darkness of the forest or the position the intruder had placed himself in, but Harrison could not see any body parts nor make out any distinguishable features. After trekking some two hundred feet from his original position, the man grabbed Harrison's shirt at the base of his neck.

"Stop! This is far enough," he said.

Harrison stopped in his tracks, then felt the person spin him around to face him. To the young warrior's surprise, he saw no one standing before him.

"You seem surprised, Harrison," came the voice out of nowhere.

The young warrior's brow crinkled. "How do you know my name? Who are you?"

"Oh, I think you know, boy," said the person in a mocking tone.

The young warrior's eyes widened, recognizing the term. "It can't be you!"

"Oh, but it is," said the man. Seconds later a very familiar figure materialized before Harrison.

"Nigel!" exclaimed the Aegean.

Lord Nigel Hammer's expression turned dour, pointing a dagger in the young warrior's direction. "Keep your voice down!"

A myriad of feelings coursed throughout Harrison's body, most of them being different shades of anger and surprise. "How did you escape Concur?"

Nigel smirked. "A ring that turns one invisible is a very handy weapon, don't you think?" Lord Hammer slipped the ring on his finger and disappeared. Seconds later, he reappeared, showing the young warrior the gold ring with a red stone.

"I basically walked out of my city while the rest of you searched frantically for me," he said, keeping a smug look on his face. "The only problem I can see is that it makes me very hungry if I choose to wear it for prolonged periods. I can live with that."

Harrison squinted, balling his fists by his sides. "What's stopping me from calling for my friends?"

Nigel shook his head, drawing a long exhale. "So predictable, Harrison. You remember my friend, Allard, don't you? He's lurking in the shadows wearing a similar ring and standing right beside your precious Tara." Lord Hammer smiled. "You try to hurt me and Allard slits her pretty little throat. No one will know she's dead for a few hours, not until they wake up for the next day. Is that what you really want?"

Harrison seethed. He knew Nigel Hammer's history as a ruthless dictator and did not question the possibility of him commanding the heinous act. With anger evident in his voice, he said, "What do you want?"

Nigel raised his palms and shrugged. "I want a lot of things but I'm not here for that. I'm here to broker a deal."

Harrison raised an eyebrow. "A deal? You're a free man for now. What more could you want?"

"We'll discuss that later," said Nigel. "However, I know what you're up against and I can tell you that you'll fail."

"Oh, really?" said Harrison with a little laugh. "Just what am I up to?"

Nigel's demeanor turned serious. His eyes focused on Harrison as he said, "You cannot defeat them."

The young warrior cocked his head. "The dragons? We're working on a plan." Harrison motioned with his head in Nigel's direction. "Why would you even care?"

Nigel pointed a finger at the young warrior. "Look, I could care less about you, your friends, and all the peasants who fill up this countryside," he said with a snarl. "But these things ..." Lord Hammer shook his head, then continued. "These monsters are brutal and will destroy everything, even their makers."

"So you want to help?" asked Harrison with surprise in his voice.

Nigel raised his palms to Harrison. "Help defeat the dragons? Yes. From there, we'll continue to have our differences."

Harrison allowed Nigel's comment to linger, amazed at his offer of assistance. The young warrior knew better than to take Lord Hammer at his word and, with reservations, he asked, "How do you envision beating these things?"

Nigel smirked. "I have a plan, boy, but you'll have to trust me for now."

"Trust you?" Harrison laughed. "Why in the world would I ever trust you?"

"Because the beings I'm involved with only want to deal with you," said Lord Hammer. "The only reason I'm still alive today is that I convinced them that I could find you." Nigel spread his arms wide. "And here we are."

The young warrior still had a hard time believing the set of circumstances that the former governor of Concur had brought before him. He knew the Unified army, Arcadians, elves, and dwarves would all rally to try and defeat the dragon army, for the good of all races. However, a pang of doubt had always hung over him, knowing that destroying these beasts would take unlimited resources, something he might not have, and the fact that the two evil men would just create more menacing creatures. Now, his greatest adversary stood before him with a deal.

Narrowing his eyes, Harrison asked, "Who are these people you're working with?"

Nigel shook his head. "You don't get that information from me so easily. You must trust me."

"That's the problem, Nigel, I don't trust you!" Both men swiveled their heads, hearing shuffling in the proximity.

"That's one of my friends on patrol," said Harrison in a low whisper.

Nigel again pointed a finger at Harrison. "Flush those monsters out of the forest and into the countryside south of the Gammorian Forest. We'll be waiting for you, ready to fight."

"Who'll be waiting?" asked Harrison, spreading his arms wide, shaking his head in disbelief.

The shuffling came closer. "Just do it," said Nigel, glaring at the younger man. In one smooth motion, he placed the gold ring back on his finger and disappeared from Harrison's view.

"Nigel," called the young warrior in a hushed tone, but Lord Hammer did not answer.

"Harrison?" came the female voice from behind. The young warrior turned around to find Kymbra advancing, her sword firmly clutched in her hand. "What are you doing out here?"

"I thought I heard something and went to investigate," said the young warrior.

Kymbra panned the area, looking for an intruder. When she found nothing, she glanced at Harrison with a look of surprise. "You left camp without your weapon?"

Harrison's eyes darted as he thought of a lie. "I guess so," he said, shaking his head. "I woke from a deep sleep and must have just wandered out here."

Kymbra approached Harrison, lightly taking hold of his arm. "Let's get you back to the campsite, alright?"

Harrison nodded. "Sure." The young warrior turned and headed back to the encampment with Kymbra, all the while looking for any sign of the man he had left behind.

* * *

"You're seriously considering listening to him!" scolded Murdock after hearing Harrison's story. The ranger removed a dagger from his belt and threw it into the ground in disgust, its blade penetrating the soft earth.

"And you didn't think of alerting us?" added Murdock.

"He had me in a compromised position," defended Harrison, knowing that he would not have done anything to bring harm to Tara or any other member of the team.

The young warrior had awoken his friends soon after his encounter with Nigel, and now they all huddled together in the late night darkness.

"He says he has an army?" asked Pondle, more than concerned that a hated enemy breached their camp unnoticed.

"He didn't say that," said Harrison.

"Only an army's going to defeat those monsters," said Murdock, reaching for his blade and securing it back in his belt. "Maybe."

"He wants us to flush out the dragons and get them into an open area, correct?" asked Gelderand.

The young warrior swiveled to the older man. "That's right."

"You do not lure large, menacing beasts into the open without significant force to handle them," said the mage. "I would have to believe that he has an army waiting."

"Even if he does, is that enough?" asked Murdock, still unconvinced about anything Lord Hammer might have said to his friend.

Harrison pondered the question before answering, formulating a raw plan. "What if he does have men ready for battle? If we can bait the dragons into the open, then maybe we have a chance."

"About the same chance as me being king," remarked Murdock in a sarcastic tone.

"We'll still need fighters from all corners of the land, including the elves and dwarves," said Harrison.

"What if they don't want to fight these beasts?" asked the ranger.

"Then we're all doomed," said Harrison. "I'd rather go out in a fight. Wouldn't you?"

Murdock smirked, having heard himself say that same phrase countless times. "Of course I would, but this is almost suicide."

"Not if we plan it right," said the young warrior.

"Alright, I'm game," said Murdock. "What's your plan?"

Harrison smiled. "Something dangerous and unconventional. I think you're going to like it." The young warrior focused on Fallyn. "We're going to revisit you impersonating Troy. We need this to work."

The auburn-haired woman slowly shook her head. "Harrison, it's not that I don't want to help, but I'm not sure this can be done."

"You said yourself that you can transform into a human, right?" said Harrison, his brows almost touching his hairline.

"Yes, that might be true, but I'm *not* Troy," said Fallyn. "Even with hours and days of practice, I still don't know his backstory. I hope you understand."

"Harrison, this isn't dangerous or unconventional," said Murdock. "It's just plain stupid!"

The young warrior raised his palms to his friends. "Hold on one second! I understand this'll be difficult to pull off, but it's our only hope."

"Agreeing with Nigel Hammer is unfathomable, yet we're doing it," said the ranger. "Putting Fallyn in a position of failure is worse."

"I didn't say I'd fail," said Fallyn, directing her comments to Murdock. "I'm just saying that this will be a difficult task."

"Where did Troy train when he was eight years old?" asked Murdock, cocking his head and raising his eyebrows.

Fallyn shrugged. "I have no idea."

"Exactly," said the ranger. Swiveling to Harrison, he asked, "How about you? Do you know where he trained?"

"Of course not!" exclaimed the Aegean. "We're not going to know everything about his past!"

"Let's hold on a second," said Gelderand, trying to ease the situation. "Maybe we can come to some common ground."

"I'm with Murdock," said Kymbra, jerking her thumb toward the ranger. "This won't work."

"Again," said the mage, raising his palms toward the naysayers. "Let's talk this out." Taking his gaze to Harrison, he asked, "Suppose you give Fallyn enough background information and you both practice what your confrontation may be like, how do you intend to get close enough to the king?"

Harrison nodded. "That's where flushing the dragons into the countryside comes into play," started the young warrior. "Nigel's men need to preoccupy the beasts long enough for us to confront the king. We," Harrison circled his finger around everyone seated before him, "will sneak past the dragons' position and approach King Holleris. Once we get him alone, Fallyn and I will challenge the king."

Murdock threw his hands up into the air. "Just like that? Lure the dragons from their master, then tiptoe to the king and his madman mage? Sounds like an easy task to me!"

"I can get you to the king," said Pondle, going against his friend's tirade. "You get those dragons far enough away from their masters and I'll pinpoint Holleris' position."

"Are you kidding me?" exclaimed Murdock, staring at his best friend. "You're going along with this?"

Pondle held his gaze on Murdock for a second, then refocused on Harrison. "What are you two going to do when you approach the king alone?"

Harrison tried to conceal his smile, sensing the tide turning. "Distract King Holleris long enough in order to kill him and Finius."

Murdock shook his head. "How do you plan on killing him?"

"You could fire an arrow through his heart," said Harrison.

"What about Finius?" asked Kymbra. "He'll be more difficult to take down."

"Leave him to me," interjected Gelderand. "Only a mage as myself can defeat a warlock like Finius."

"I have prayers that can protect us from an evil presence," added Swinkle. "It might not be much but it can help."

"Uncle, are you sure about this?" asked Tara, worry evident in her voice.

"No, I am not," said the mage. "However, the only way to destroy those beasts is to extract their name from the men who know it, and if that doesn't work, cut off their food supply."

"Defeating Finius," said Harrison. Bringing his gaze back to Fallyn, he said, "Which brings us back to you. Can you do this?"

Fallyn drew a deep breath, then sat tall. "I would certainly call this plan dangerous and unconventional, but I will do my part." The woman nodded once. "Yes, I believe I can do this."

"I can't believe this is really happening," said Murdock, shaking his head.

"We're all in agreement," said Harrison. "We have to."

"Oh, I'm not disagreeing," said the ranger, "I'm just saying this is crazy."

"I told you it would be," said the young warrior, the smile disappearing from his face. "First and foremost, we catch up to the dragons."

"They're a good day's trek ahead of us," said Pondle. "Far enough along that they might already be out of the forest."

"In a way, that might be better for us," said Harrison. "If they're already in the steppes of Gammoria, we'll be able to spot and follow them easily."

"Same goes for them," said Pondle.

"Let's hope it doesn't get to that," said Harrison. "I'd bet my life that Holleris has his sights on Concur, Aegeus, and Arcadia. He's going to arrive and have his monsters flex their muscles."

"Harrison," said Gelderand, "those dragons can fly. I am worried about them torching cities and townsfolk from above."

The young warrior nodded in agreement. "Like we've discussed, that's a very strong probability." Turning to Pondle, he asked, "When should we leave?"

"How about right now?"

"In the middle of the night?" responded Harrison, a little surprised at the thief's answer.

"You said it yourself," said Pondle, "those beasts might already be out of the forest. I say let's light our torches and go."

The young warrior pondered his friend's rationale. Nodding, he said, "Alright."

"Enough talk then," said Murdock. "Let's get moving!"

Harrison fastened the straps on his backpack, then took his battle axe in hand. "I'm with you. Everyone, light your torches and assume marching positions." Bringing his attention to Pondle, he said, "Lead us out of this desolate forest."

"As you wish," said the thief. "Come on, Lance, you're with us!" The little dog bounded to Pondle's side and the two started to lead the procession of adventurers.

Murdock approached Harrison, slapping a hand on his shoulder. "This is a brave and bold strategy. I never thought you were crazy."

"Sometimes you need to choose the least favorite option," said the young warrior.

The ranger removed his hand from his friend's body. "That you did. I just hope you know what you're doing. We'll keep you posted." Murdock then left and took his position at the head of the group.

Harrison swiveled to make eye contact with Kymbra. "You protect the left."

The lithe warrior nodded. "You got the right."

The young warrior brought his focus to Gelderand, Swinkle, Fallyn, and Tara. "We trek as usual. Be ready for anything."

Swinkle took a step closer to his friend. "Harrison, we don't have to do this."

"I know how you feel, but this is the only way we can succeed."

"This is very risky."

"Understood," said Harrison. Motioning with his weapon, he said, "We need to start moving."

The young cleric nodded once and took his position without saying another word. Gelderand sidled up next to him and Fallyn, while Tara came to Harrison's side.

"Brave doesn't begin to describe your plan," said the young maiden.

"That's a word they'll use only if we succeed."

"And what word will they use if we don't?"

Harrison's face dropped. "Suicide."

C H A P T E R 37

❑

Pondle led the group through the Dark Forest, easily following the menacing beasts' tracks. Murdock and Pondle had given Harrison their best estimation on King Holleris and his dragon army's heading, and now the time had come for the young warrior to make his decision.

Harrison gazed into the distance, finding the trees thinning, signaling that they stood close to the forest's end. Murdock halted the procession and approached his friend.

With a bit of apprehension, the ranger asked, "What's it going to be?"

Harrison had pondered that simple question the whole night, running many scenarios through his head. He knew teaming with Fallyn to try and con the king was risky at best, possibly a disaster waiting to happen. Just before dawn he entertained another approach and was ready to reveal it to his friends.

"We need to draw those monsters away from King Holleris in order to apprehend him," reiterated the young warrior, before adding an alternative strategy. "To be honest, I'd really like to face him alone."

"You're out of your mind!" exclaimed Murdock. "That was never part of any discussions that we had!"

"Harrison," said Swinkle, hoping to take a softer approach. "This man is evil. He cares only for himself and won't listen to anything you say, however rational your words might be."

"It's suicide," said Murdock. "And I won't let you do it."

"I understand your feelings," said the young warrior. "I honestly believe if I talk with him, get him to understand that we don't have any quarrels with him, that we can reach an agreement of some sorts."

Gelderand, being the elder member of the group, spoke next. "Harrison," he started in a fatherly tone, "your heart is in the right place and what you propose is very noble; however, you are not dealing with a sane man." The magician spread his arms wide. "We all want to avoid conflict but the truth of the matter is King Holleris has nine dragons at his disposal."

"Eighteen if you count two heads per dragon," added Kymbra.

"He unleashed these beasts on the elves and I must believe he will do the same to our settlements in the very near future," continued Gelderand.

Harrison huffed, understanding the mage's manner of thinking. "You make valid points," said the young warrior. "But we must talk with him. We need to try and stop him from destroying everything."

"Harrison, the plan you outlined last night can work," said Fallyn, adding to the discussion. "We need to practice Troy's mannerisms and understand his history. I have faith that we'll succeed."

"Harrison, we don't know his master plan," said Murdock, dismissing Fallyn's optimism. "We won't get close enough to speak to him. Not with dragons surrounding him."

"Then let's make a plan to get them away from King Holleris," said Kymbra. "Like we spoke about last night."

Harrison recalled their discussion from the previous evening, how they concluded that drawing the dragons into the open in hopes that Nigel Hammer's army would be waiting.

With that thought in mind, he said, "Alright, let's lure these monsters into the countryside."

Murdock smiled. "That's better. You can talk to the king and his crazy warlock buddy after we've captured them."

"Deal," said the young warrior. Changing his tone to a more militaristic one, he continued the conversation. "Pondle, where do you believe the dragons are now?"

The thief panned to the forest's end where it opened up to the Gammorian plains. "The tracks suggest that they left the woods less than twelve hours ago. I have to believe the dragons have taken flight at some point in their journey."

"Makes sense," said Harrison. "However, Holleris and Finius are walking."

"Unless they're hitching a ride on one of the beasts," quipped Murdock.

"I doubt it," said Gelderand. "Those men are old and I must imagine that riding atop of a dragon is a much younger man's game."

"Let's assume they're walking," said Harrison. "That means some of the dragons are with them for protection. Only makes sense."

"Agreed," said Murdock. "What are you getting at?"

"These are the dragons that we must lure out in the open, toward Lord Hammer's position," said the young warrior.

"Which is where, exactly?" asked Pondle.

"Nigel said to flush them into the countryside south of the Gammorian Forest," said Harrison. "They'll be there."

"The countryside's pretty big, Harrison," said Murdock with a shake of his head. "Can you give us a better location?"

Harrison thought hard, recalling his geography. Pointing out of the forest, he said, "The Gammorian Forest abuts the plains. I wouldn't bring an army of men into such an open space, especially with fire breathing dragons that can attack from the skies."

"There are hills that extend south of that forest, before the plains," said Pondle.

Harrison nodded. "That's right. I'd hide my men under the cover of the trees, then storm out over the hills and into the countryside."

"Assuming that's where Nigel's taking cover, how do we lure these monsters away?" asked Murdock.

Harrison turned his attention to Gelderand and Swinkle. "I was hoping that either of you might be able to conjure up something."

Both men's eyes widened in unison. "Harrison, what are you proposing?" asked Swinkle.

Before the young warrior could reply, Gelderand offered an answer of his own. "You want us to provide a means of attracting a dragon, correct?"

The young warrior nodded. "Exactly."

"Like what?" asked the young cleric, very unsure how he could provide any help in the matter.

Gelderand looked up in thought. Tapping a finger against his nose, he said aloud to himself, "What would grab the attention of giant beasts?"

"Murdock and I witnessed a grotesque feeding frenzy not too long ago," said Kymbra, answering the mage's question. "They seem to be very food oriented."

"That makes sense," said Swinkle. "Due to their large size, it would take great quantities of food to sustain them."

Harrison pointed in Gelderand and Swinkle's direction. "Can you two create a food source the same way that evil warlock did?"

The two robed men exchanged anxious glances. "I can only create small amounts of food," said Swinkle. "Barely enough for myself, let alone a dragon."

"I can only duplicate what Swinkle creates," said Gelderand. "Nothing near the quantities that we would need."

The young warrior shook his head. "How are we going to do this?" he questioned aloud.

"You mentioned that Allard is still with Nigel Hammer," said Gelderand with a grimace. "He is more adept in the realm of dark magic."

Harrison pondered the mage's comment. Was it not bad enough that in order to defeat the dragons he had to depend on his hated adversary, Lord Hammer? Just the thought of working with his mage went against his core beliefs.

"I don't like the path we're heading down," said the young warrior. "My trust threshold for either one of them is low."

"That goes without saying," said the elder man. "However, our choices are limited."

"Could we go back to the elves?" asked Harrison. "They definitely would help."

"They're dealing with the aftermath of a catastrophe," said Gelderand. "I cannot imagine that they would be in the mood to help us again quite so soon."

The young warrior nodded in agreement. "I suppose so."

"There might be another option," said Swinkle, before he set his pack down and began rummaging in earnest. "I remember reading something in these scrolls ..."

"What are you talking about?" asked Harrison. "Which scrolls?"

The young cleric pulled out several parchments, still searching. "I brought along several scrolls we uncovered with the Treasure of the Land," he said. "One in particular might help." Swinkle unfurled then rerolled several scriptures before a wide smile flashed across his face.

"This one!" cried the young cleric.

"Swinkle, what do you have?" asked Harrison in anticipation.

Swinkle's eyes glossed over the parchment that he outstretched in front of him. Nodding, he said, "This just might work." The young cleric lifted his gaze, making eye contact with the many sets of eyes that stared back at him.

"Gelderand, Tara, and I found scores of scrolls and books as part of the large hoard, but this one always touched me," started the holy man. "I always believed the scripture's creator had a soft spot for humanity."

"Swinkle, we're losing time!" exclaimed Murdock, losing patience. "Out with it!"

The young cleric held up the piece of paper. "It is called a Scroll of Abundance. In hard times when farmers cannot grow large crop quantities, a magician can recite these words over a pile of produce and increase it tenfold.

"If Gelderand and I can produce a small quantity of food, then recite this scroll, we would have a much larger pile of food."

"Enough to attract a dragon?" asked Harrison.

Swinkle shrugged. "I do not know that answer." The young cleric brought his gaze to Gelderand.

The mage held his chin in his hand. "We need to create a protein source."

"I can do that," said Swinkle.

"Then I can duplicate some of that using a spell of my own," said the mage. Wagging a finger in Swinkle's direction, he continued, "After that, I can read the scroll and multiply what we have."

"Will that be enough to attract the beasts?" asked Harrison again.

Both robed men shrugged in unison. "It is the only option we have right now and, like Murdock stated, we are losing time," said Gelderand.

Harrison quickly agreed. "Alright, we need to head toward the Gammorian Forest before it's too late."

"Follow me," said Pondle, "and I'll lead us deeper into the Gammorian countryside."

Murdock flung his arms wide. "Is this really going to work? We're going to trust Nigel Hammer and battle dragons with him?" lamented the ranger. "This is crazy!"

Harrison cocked his head. "All we need to do is lure one dragon, the rest will follow. Nigel's situation will resolve itself."

The ranger let out a heavy sigh. "I'm not one hundred percent sold on this approach, but it's better than waiting around."

The young warrior flashed a sly smile, then said to Pondle, "Lead us on."

The small group of adventurers gathered their gear and made haste to enter the Gammorian countryside in order to put their plan into action.

* * *

King Holleris walked alongside Finius, both of them enjoying the shade the dragons provided as they flew overhead. Holleris removed a tankard from his belt, uncorked the top, and took a deep sip. The liquid was ice cold, providing instant relief to his old and weary body.

"This elixir makes me feel like a young man again," said the king with a smile, taking another sip.

446

"You only need small quantities," hissed the ancient warlock. "Conserve."

"Why?" said Holleris with a smile. "You'll just conjure me some more."

Finius continued to stare straight ahead, not bothering to reiterate his magical limits to the king once again. Changing the subject, he gazed skyward and said, "It is time for their next mission."

Holleris looked to the heavens as well. "Which target?"

Finius, still looking upwards, said, "Argos."

"How many do we send?"

"Seven," said the warlock, bringing his gaze to the king. "Two remain behind for protection."

King Holleris hated looking into the white mass that Finius called his left eye. Trying not to stare at the abnormality, he said, "No one can harm us while we're near our creation."

"Don't get overconfident," hissed the ancient wizard. "All creations have flaws."

Holleris glared at Finius. "Not these dragons. You produced a superior race of creatures."

"Thank you, my king," said Finius with a slight bow. "Shall I summon them for their mission?"

Holleris gazed upward, taking a hand to shield them from the sun. "Do it!"

Finius stopped his trek and clutched his hands together. The wizard concentrated, closing his eyes hard, mumbling to himself.

Holleris peered into the distance, finding nine figures flying high above the ground. Without warning, all of the creatures stopped their forward progression and looped back toward the two men.

The king smiled. "Argos won't know what hit them," he said, laughing aloud.

* * *

Octavius and Caidan Forge had gathered fifteen hundred men from their city of Argos, heeding the call to battle once again.

Two days earlier they had received a messenger falcon from Concur, calling for an emergency meeting of the Legion of Knighthood. Now, they traveled on horseback while their men marched toward the walled city.

Octavius surveyed the landscape ahead of him. The day could not have been more perfect. Large puffy, white clouds provided ample shade from the afternoon sun, making their trek much more enjoyable, from a weather standpoint. Gazing eastward into the distance, he noticed several dots in the sky. Squinting, they began to get larger with every passing second.

"Caidan!" called the elder Forge, directing his exclamation toward his younger brother who rode ten yards ahead.

Caidan looked back, noticing Octavius pointing in the distance. The younger Forge brought a hand to shield his eyes, then found the objects heading toward their position. At first he did not recognize the aerial shapes, but as they drew closer, a hollow feeling began to course throughout his body. A minute later, his eyes grew round in shock.

"Dragons!" he yelled, fear evident in his voice.

Octavius knew the ramifications of that one single word. The Argosian leader panned the area, finding lightly wooded terrain on either side of the well-worn path. Nowhere to hide.

"Sound the horn!" barked the elder Forge in the direction of his squire. Yelling at the top of his lungs, he screamed, "Take cover! Hide!"

His squire frantically blew into his instrument, sending the signal to all who could hear him. The call for retreat was too late. Seven two-headed monsters swooped from the heavens and lit the forest ablaze. Soldiers screamed in terror, while horses bucked and stampeded in a panic. The beasts screeched from above, wreaking havoc on the defenseless humans below.

Octavius secured his weapon and jumped off his horse, knowing that the ravenous beasts would not pass up a meal as they terrorized his men. Trees burned and fell to the forest floor, the vicinity's temperature rising at an alarming rate.

The elder Forge knew the battle was over before it had even started. "Seek cover! Save yourselves!" exclaimed the Argosian leader. His men ran in vain, trying to escape the chaos. Dragons seemed to litter every corner of the sky, making one attack run after another. Flames hurtled down from the heavens, hitting the earth, splaying in all directions.

Octavius' survival instincts kicked in. As he ran for cover, only one thought occupied his mind — find his brother. "Caidan!" he yelled, his voice barely a whisper above the din of pandemonium. "Caidan!"

Octavius scurried in the direction he had seen his brother last. Fires erupted everywhere. A monster flew way overhead, above the billowing smoke clouds, searching for another target. Men screamed and cried, horses neighed in terror, trying to avoid the flames and dragons' jaws.

"Caidan!" hollered Octavius and for the first time he began to lose hope. The creatures had more than neutralized his army; they had defeated it in less than fifteen minutes. His men scattered in all directions, not bothering to fight, rather they just tried to stay alive.

The Argosian leader stumbled forward, smoke stinging his eyes and blurring his vision. Three of his men came into view, running toward him.

"Where's Caidan?" he yelled in desperation.

The soldiers stopped upon encountering their leader. "Last we saw him, he had fallen from his steed and was seeking shelter."

Octavius grabbed the man by his arms, pinning them to his side. Glaring at him, he bellowed, "Where!"

The soldier pointed from whence he came. "Back that way!"

The elder Forge peered past the fighter, then ordered his men, "Lead me to him!" A terrifying shriek from above caused them all to cower, covering theirs heads in the process.

After the threat passed, Octavius spun the man around, yelling, "Now!"

The soldier's face dropped, not wanting to follow the order but realizing that he had no choice. Octavius pushed him forward with one hand while clutching his sword with the other. The Argosian turned to bark orders to the remaining two men but instead he found them running away. Gritting his teeth in anger, he pressed the fighter forward.

Octavius followed the soldier through the burning forest, sidestepping flaming underbrush and staying away from trees set ablaze. "He was over here!" exclaimed the fighter, pointing to a small clearing.

The elder Forge wandered into the open space, doing his best to avoid the charred corpses that littered the area. Men and horses by the score lay dead, not a soul moving. Octavius ventured further into the opening, searching for anything he could recognize. A screech from above stopped him in his tracks. He turned to locate the fighter who had accompanied him, but instead found him fleeing back into the fiery forest upon hearing the dragon's next hideous call. Octavius now stood alone.

Smoke obscured his view of the heavens and he silently gave thanks to his god for the thin veil of coverage. The Argosian leader scoured the corpses, ignoring the heat and the smoke induced burning sensations in his lungs. He needed to find his brother and nothing would stop him from accomplishing his task.

Several minutes passed without finding Caidan. In that time, the smoldering dissipated, allowing pockets of blue sky to peek through the haze. Trekking deeper into the clearing, Octavius heard the heavy panting of disabled animals. Two horses had fallen to the ground, their bodies badly burned and their legs broken. The Argosian leader left a pang of sorrow in his heart, knowing that these very steeds had led him and his men into battle countless times. Now, they suffered with death not coming soon enough.

Octavius approached the first horse and gazed into its eyes. The horse's breathing came in quick bursts. Taking his blade, he sliced the animal's throat, taking it out of its misery, allowing the stallion to die a noble death. With a heavy heart, he knew he had to do the same for the next horse. As he approached the steed with his bloody blade, he recognized its familiar markings.

"Caidan!" he wailed, realizing the fallen animal was his brother's horse. Octavius frantically panned the vicinity, searching for his lost sibling. "Caidan!" he yelled again at the top of his lungs.

The elder Forge's eyes darted from corpse to corpse, searching for his brother. Moments later, he focused on a most recognizable body. Octavius sprinted to the lifeless soul, bending to one knee to get a closer look at the dead man who lay face down on the earth. With a lump in his throat, he spun the soldier over, revealing his brother's face.

"Caidan," lamented Octavius, tears welling in his eyes. Dropping to his knees, he lifted his brother's body into his arms, pulling him close to his chest. Knowing his brother was gone, he sobbed while softly muttering his sibling's name over and over again.

In the midst of his sorrow, a large shadow cast over him, the whooshing of leathery wings emanating from overhead. Octavius did not have to cast his eyes upwards to know what flew above him. Caidan's horse, still alive and terrified, neighed and tried to rise, but to no avail.

The two-headed monster screeched from the heavens and swooped down toward its next meal. Octavius swiveled his head toward the sky and watched as the scaly green beast hovered over the ground a mere ten yards away from him.

Terrified, the elder Forge tried not to move but he sensed an evil presence glaring in his direction. Octavius pivoted his head slightly, peeking at the monster from the corner of his eye. One of the heads stared right at him, acknowledging that he was still alive.

The Argosian leader felt an undying desire to flee, however he knew the futile ramifications of that action. Mustering all the courage he had, he turned his head in the dragon's direction. One head bobbed at the defenseless horse, while the other continued its stare, boring a hole in the human's mind.

Octavius' breaths came in short gasps, afraid to make even the smallest of maneuvers. A warmth began to encompass his brain, the same feeling one gets when standing directly under a summer sun without protection, only this came from the inside. The soldier shook his head, clearing his mind, ceasing the heat sensation. Its trance broken, the dragon's eyes widened in anger.

The elder Forge knew what might happen next. The dragon's chest began to expand as it sucked in a heavy dose of air, its neck straightening, preparing to strike. Octavius thought no more; instead he dropped his brother's body, jumped up from the ground, and began to run away.

451

A hellish sound permeated the area, followed by spewing flames. The dragon's breath hit the ground where Caidan lay, incinerating the body and torching everything in the immediate area. The blaze reached Octavius, igniting his clothes and charring his armor. The horrified human dropped to the ground and rolled, trying desperately to extinguish the flames. Glancing back at the two-headed monster, he saw the beast readying itself for another fire-filled breath when a second dragon entered the arena.

Swooping from the sky, the creature used its large claws to pick up the helpless steed, lifting it off the ground, then continuing its rise back to the heavens. Infuriated at losing its meal, the first dragon ignored Octavius and flew after its fellow creature.

Dazed and bewildered, the Argosian leader peered back to where his brother's body had lain, only to find the area engulfed in flames. Knowing the futileness of returning to the inferno to retrieve Caidan's body, Octavius harkened back to his survival training skills. Panning the vicinity, he found utter destruction and death with little room to escape. Fires grew with nothing to stop their expansion.

Octavius thought hard, recalling the last scenes before the dragon's horrific attack. He and Caidan had led their men from Argos and headed toward Concur. They had traversed through some lightly wooded areas, climbing small rolling hills.

The hills, thought Octavius. I must get to the hills!

The Argosian turned his eyes upward, finding the sun. The heavenly body had crossed its midpoint, meaning that it now pointed toward the west, Argos' direction. Octavius did his best to scurry around the flames, dashing in and out of the once lush forest, finding the base of a small hill.

Fires climbed up the incline with Octavius, spewing smoke and heat higher and higher. The elder Forge withstood the flame's intensity, knowing that he needed to reach the summit. Looking ahead, he found an opening that led to the top where blue sky peeked through the smoldering blaze.

Octavius, clear of the trees, reached the peak at last. Gazing to the west, he found the inland sea that separated Argos and Concur. His heart nearly stopped beating when he focused on his hometown. Billowing smoke rose from the buildings and orange

452

flames burst from all corners of the city. Flying monsters continued to circle Argos, spewing flames from high above.

A tear rolled down the warrior's cheek as he imagined the horror that his fellow townsfolk were enduring at this very moment. The only saving grace for him was that he could not hear the screams of anguish from such a great distance. The nauseous feeling that churned in his stomach slowly gave way to a focused anger. Clutching his sword as tight as possible, the Argosian gritted his teeth, allowing the oncoming wave of rage to consume him.

"No one does this to my people!" he yelled, his eyes glaring at his burning city. "I shall have vengeance for them! I shall have vengeance for Caidan!"

Octavius roared at the top of his lungs, then began his trek out of the localized inferno to search for survivors, while keeping his pledge of retribution in the forefront of his mind.

C H A P T E R 38

Ω

For the next six days, Pondle led the small group of
adventurers across the Gammorian countryside, veering north
toward the foothills of the Saturnian Mountains. Harrison knew he
had taken a huge gamble depending on Nigel Hammer, a man who
had constantly tried to thwart him in the past, but the task at hand
called for desperate measures. That and a gut feeling that Nigel
meant what he said this time.

The young warrior gazed ahead, hoping that his adversary
turned ally waited for them. Tara, sensing no imminent danger,
sidled up to Harrison.

Looking at the looming mountains, she said, "Such a
breathtaking view."

Harrison maintained his stare. "They are, but I'm more
worried about who lurks in the woods."

Tara frowned. "You mean that wicked Nigel Hammer."

"Yes," said Harrison. "He must keep his word or he'll
doom all of humanity."

"Harrison, he's evil," said Tara, shaking her head. "I'm not
sure we can trust him."

The young warrior's expression remained stoic. "We have
to."

"Where is he?" asked the young maiden, gazing into the
upcoming forest.

"He has to be in the woods, not too deep," said Harrison,
adding, "make that, he better be."

"We'll find out soon enough, right?"

Harrison flashed a wry smile. "For better or worse." Pondle's actions up ahead caught his attention. "Let's see what Pondle has to say."

The thief, along with Murdock, returned to the group. Lance scampered back to join his masters. Pondle gazed upwards before speaking.

"The sun's setting soon, we should camp out for the night."

Harrison panned the area. At the present moment they stood in the countryside about a quarter mile from the foothills that led to the forest. The young warrior focused on the woodlands, a short trek away.

"We need to see this army as soon as possible," said Harrison. "Can you lead us to the forest before dark?"

"Sure, we'd be there within the hour," said the thief.

"I'd feel more comfortable in some coverage as well," said Harrison.

The small group took advantage of the encroaching twilight to reach the forest's edge by nightfall. Pondle halted the procession before entering the woods.

"How deep into the forest do you think they are?" asked the thief.

"Less than a quarter mile," said the young warrior, harking his warrior training. "Deep enough to be hidden from the plains but not too far to strike quickly if called upon."

"I'm against using torches then," said Pondle. "I'd rather stumble upon them instead of vice versa."

"We won't be able to see," said Harrison.

"Maybe not you, but I will," said the halfling, knowing that his vision allowed him to see short distances in the darkness as if it were day.

"I have something that should help us," said Swinkle. The young cleric fumbled with his pack, removing a small orb, which glowed a soft blue hue.

"Tara and I also have orbs," said Gelderand. The two did as Swinkle, finding the spheres and providing a subtle lighting to the area. "We will be able to see ten feet in front of us without generating too much attention."

"Great," said Pondle. Turning to Harrison, he asked, "Which way do you want to proceed?"

The young warrior pointed to the forest's depths. "Straight ahead," he said, then added, "and remember, it's Nigel Hammer we're dealing with. Proceed with caution and alert us of anything unusual."

"Got it," said the thief. "Lance! Come with me!" The little dog jumped at hearing his name and joined Pondle at the head of the group. Murdock followed his friend as well.

"Where are you going?" asked Pondle. Jerking his thumb, he said, "Get back with the others."

"What?" said the ranger, pinning his brows. "We always track together."

"Not when you can't see. Stay back and provide extra protection."

"What about him?" asked Murdock, pointing at Lance. "He can't see that well either!"

"His night vision is better than you think and his sense of smell is superior to ours," said Pondle. "Plus, he listens to orders."

Murdock narrowed his eyes. "Don't do anything foolish, alright?"

"Don't worry," said the halfling. "We need to get moving."

The ranger nodded with reluctance, then headed back to join Harrison and the others. Pondle motioned for Lance to lead the way, which the little dog did, placing his nose to the ground and heading deeper into the woods. The thief followed Lance and he, too, disappeared from the group's view.

A moment later, Harrison signaled for the rest of the party to move forward. Swinkle, Tara, and Gelderand's hand held orbs provided enough light so that no one tripped on broken limbs or jutting stumps.

Murdock took position next to Harrison. Under his breath, he asked, "How soon until we run into this army?"

"Sooner than you think."

* * *

Pondle trekked a good fifty yards ahead of Harrison and the rest. Gazing back, he found three bobbing orbs in a typical marching formation. Lance sniffed and scampered not too far ahead of him. Nothing to worry about so far.

A few feet away, a small indentation caught the halfling's eye. Pondle allowed his eyes to linger on the track. A boot print. A very large boot print. The thief's heart began to pound a bit faster as he bent to one knee to investigate further. Panning to his left and right, he found several more tracks heading away from his position and deeper into the forest's depths. Lance darted to his right, then held his position, his tail up and ears pricked. The little dog stared into the darkness and started to growl.

Pondle slowly rose from his bent knee position and focused in the dog's direction, searching for something just out of sight. Subtle shuffling ahead of their location caught the halfling's attention. The thief tried to hone in on the target but the sounds appeared to come from several directions.

Confused, the thief brought his focus back to his friends, finding them proceeding as normal, oblivious to his apprehension. Then, Lance began to bark with a fervor.

Pondle saw the large figures advance from the darkness, running toward him and Lance. The little dog barked repeatedly, then scampered to Pondle. The halfling's eyes widened with surprise as the beings converged on them.

"Scynthians!" shouted Pondle at the top of his lungs, hoping to alert his friends. Four creatures, wielding clubs and maces, surrounded the halfling, preventing him from running away.

Pondle held his ground, knowing that he was no match against four savage beasts. To his surprise, three of the beings converged on him and, instead of using their weapons, they attempted to apprehend the thief. Pondle slashed at his adversaries with his small sword, striking the beasts but unable to penetrate their thick chain-mail armor. The fourth Scynthian chased after the barking dog, unable to come close to the elusive canine.

A very large gauntlet-covered fist struck Pondle on the side of his head, dropping him to the ground. Incapacitated by the punch, the thief tried to regain his senses but to no avail. The two other creatures pounced on Pondle, grabbing him with their large hands, preventing him from continuing to fight.

The thief, dazed and his arms pinned to his side by his captors, felt his body bounce with every step the Scynthian took. Completely at the mercy of his Scynthian abductor, Pondle did his best to assess his surroundings. He heard Lance barking but could not pinpoint his location. Though his head jostled, he managed to peer in the opposite direction. All the glowing orbs had dispersed as more enemy savages rushed past him and headed toward Harrison and the others.

* * *

This couldn't be happening! Harrison leveled his battle axe in the direction of the closest savage, missing but managing to keep them at bay. Tara shuddered, trying her best to keep close to the young warrior while being wary of his swinging blade.

The Aegean panned in disbelief, trying his best to identify the number of Scynthians who now occupied the area. Swinkle and Gelderand had either run or the savage beasts had abducted them since their soft light no longer illuminated the woods. Tara's orb continued to glow but provided little relief for him to clearly see the many dark masses that converged on their position. Fallyn, Murdock, and Kymbra were nowhere to be seen.

A Scynthian advanced from the shadows, standing in front of Harrison with his mace held across his body in a defensive posture. Seconds later, two more beasts closed in on the young warrior.

"Tara!" yelled Harrison. "Get next to me!"

The young warrior clutched his axe in his left hand while he used his right to corral the young girl, pulling her to his body. Gripping his weapon with two hands again, both of them stood back to back, awaiting the beasts' next move.

"Bring them with the others!" bellowed a deep voice in the darkness.

Harrison darted his eyes in every direction, trying to get a better fix on his situation. Three Scynthians surrounded him and

Tara, while his other friends remained out of his field of vision. A dog barked in close proximity, giving the young warrior some solace that Lance had eluded the creatures for the time being.

The savage in front of him took a step forward. "Drop your weapon!"

The Scynthian's demand took him aback. "Why? So you can kill us? Never!"

The beast raised his mace a little higher, bringing it to an attack position. "Drop it!"

Harrison gripped his weapon's hilt tighter, knowing the Scynthian's mode of operation all too well. If captured, they would imprison, torture, and kill them all in a gruesome ceremony that included hacking off their arms before sacrificing everyone to their pagan gods. Not the way he chose to die and certainly not the way for Tara's life to end either.

"Harrison," said Tara, her voice filled with terror and apprehension. "What's happening?"

"Stay with me," said Harrison, trying to formulate a plan.

The Scynthian took another step nearer, getting dangerously close to the young warrior and his mate. "This is the last time I'm telling you, human! Drop your weapon!"

Harrison stared into the savage's green, cat-like eyes, finding them cold and filled with hate. The young warrior then felt a smack on the side of his head followed by a burning sensation. Dizzy and losing his balance, Harrison tumbled over, the echoes of Tara's shriek ringing in his ears. A second later, everything went black.

* * *

The young warrior opened his eyes, his head throbbing yet again on this burdensome journey. A small fire illuminated the forest where he sat on the ground, rope binding his hands behind his back.

"Harrison," called a familiar voice.

The young warrior turned his head to the right, finding Murdock bound in a similar manner. "Scynthians?" asked the Aegean, groggy.

"We're in trouble," said the ranger, not hiding his anxiety. "They confiscated our packs and weapons."

Harrison figured as much, doing his best to concentrate in spite of his painful, throbbing head. A thought jumped to the forefront of his mind. "Tara!" he called, then began swiveling his head in search of the young maiden.

"I'm right behind you," she said, her voice trembling. "Are you alright?"

"Yes," he lied. "Are you?"

"As good as everyone else," said the girl.

Harrison brought his focus to the group. The Scynthians had secured them all and sat them in a circular formation, facing away from each other. Panning to his right he found Murdock beside him with Pondle by the ranger's side. To his left sat Swinkle and Gelderand after him. Try as he might, he could not turn his head back far enough to see Tara, Kymbra, or Fallyn.

"Kymbra?" asked the young warrior.

"Right behind you with Tara," she said. "We're unharmed."

"How about Fallyn?"

"Gone," said the female warrior. "We're assuming she morphed into something and is somewhere close by."

Harrison agreed with Kymbra's assessment, before breathing a sigh of relief. His group intact, he made a sweep of his surroundings. The Scynthians had taken them to an unknown location in the forest, arranged them next to the fire, and had two armored guards watching over them.

His head still swimming, he continued his evaluation. Savages milled about the area, all covered from head to toe in body armor with weapons by their sides. To his dismay, there were too many beasts to count. Bringing his focus to the forefront, he found Lance laying on the ground, unbound, and staring back at him. Odd, he thought. The Scynthians should have captured or killed him as well.

"Lance," he called in a hushed tone.

The dog's ears pricked up and he jumped to his feet. A second later, the canine teleported to his master, placed his paws on his chest, and began licking his face.

"Down, boy," said Harrison in a stern tone, worried that the guards would pounce on the dog for his actions. Instead, they allowed Lance to continue with his greeting.

"Murdock, something's not right," said Harrison out of the side of his mouth.

"You think?" said the ranger. "I can't figure out their game plan."

"We should be dead," said the young warrior.

"They might just be delaying the inevitable."

Harrison let the ranger's comment sink in. He had witnessed his fair share of Scynthian rituals, including having his arm severed at the hands of the wretched beasts. However, something felt different now. The clanging of metal chains broke his concentration.

Two Scynthian guards led a shackled man toward him and his friends. The young warrior noticed another savage trudging behind the trio, most likely their leader, he supposed. The unlucky soul's face became visible as he plodded past the campfire. It was Lord Hammer!

The two sentry's stopped Nigel a few feet before the adventurers' circular group, then shuffled aside, allowing their leader to step forward.

Pointing to the people on the ground, the chief Scynthian barked, "Any of them Harrison?" The young warrior's eyes widened with surprise upon hearing his name uttered from this beast's mouth.

Nigel, his hands cuffed in front of him, locked his gaze onto Harrison's. With a nod of his head, he said, "That's him."

The guard to his right stepped forward, placed his hand under the young warrior's armpit, and hoisted him to his feet. The lead Scynthian approached Harrison, standing a foot from his chest. The young warrior gazed up at the savage, unsure of his intentions.

"Are you Harrison Cross?" barked the leader, unflinching.

Harrison shifted his eyes to Nigel, the chained man keeping his head down and not looking at the young warrior. Taking his gaze upwards once again, he said, "That I am."

The head Scynthian brought his focus to Lord Hammer. "This one tells the truth. Unchain him!"

The two sentries jumped at the order, gripping Nigel by the forearms, unlocking his cuffs. The shackles fell to the ground. Lord Hammer looked over to Harrison, rubbing his wrists.

"I told you I'd find him," snarled Nigel. "I didn't need to be treated this way!"

The main Scynthian pivoted to face Lord Hammer. "Bark at me again and you're dead."

Nigel did not chance upsetting the savage any further. Showing his palms to the beast, he asked, "Now what?"

The chieftain turned his attention to Harrison. "Our orders are to listen to this man and do what he commands." The leader gestured to his sentries. "Release all of them from their bindings."

Lord Hammer spread his arms wide, exclaiming, "What?"

The lead savage pointed a glove-covered finger in his face. "Don't test me, human!"

Harrison stared at the lead Scynthian, shocked at his statement. At the same time, the two guards unbound each of his friends. When finished with that task, the young warrior's colleagues rose from their position on the ground and stood behind Harrison, just as confused as their own leader.

"Why's everyone searching for me?" asked the young warrior, skeptical.

Facing the Aegean, the lead Scynthian snarled, "Not my decision. Our new leader convinced us you would help."

Harrison still did not follow this being's rationale. "Your leader?" he asked aloud, shaking his head in wonderment. "I don't know your leader. How can he even know who I am?"

"You know him," said the chief. "You showed him mercy."

Try as he might, Harrison could not follow the Scynthian's line of reasoning. Throughout his adventure, he had nothing but hatred toward this savage's race. Had they not slaughtered his kinsfolk, sacked Arcadia, and killed hundreds of innocent souls? Then, a thought sprung to his mind.

With wide eyes, he said, "Naa'il?" The Scynthian confirmed his question with a single nod. "Naa'il's your leader?"

462

"Yes," said the lead Scynthian. "He survived the Great Disaster."

Harrison did not understand. "What's the Great Disaster?"

"Winged serpents demolished Mahalanobis," he said. "Naa'il saved many, led them to safety. Convinced our people to seek you."

"Dragons," said Harrison, taking his gaze to Lord Hammer. Nigel nodded in concurrence. Bringing his focus back to the Scynthian, he asked, "Your homeland is destroyed?" The savage nodded again.

The young warrior, though he despised the being who stood before him, felt a pang of sorrow. Part of him felt nothing, glad that these monsters had felt the dragons' wrath, but another part of him felt compelled to help. He hated this side of himself at times, especially at this very moment.

Standing taller, he asked, "Can you take me to see Naa'il?"

The leader shook his head no. "He's not here."

Harrison cocked his head, surprised. "He's not here? Where did he go?"

"Back to Mahalanobis. To retrieve a sacred treasure."

Harrison shook his head, incredulous. "I don't understand. What's so important about this artifact that he went back to a destroyed city to retrieve it?"

The chieftain stood tall, proud. "Alabaar instructed us to only retrieve the gift as a last resort. That is now."

Harrison squinted. "You called it a gift. Why?"

The Scynthian narrowed his eyes. "We give it to you."

The Scynthians have a *gift* for us, thought the young warrior. The lead beast's story just confused him more. "When will Naa'il be back?"

Again, the savage shook his head. "Don't know."

"Harrison, let's all meet alone," interjected Nigel. "We humans that is."

The young warrior felt the same. Gazing at the leader once again, he said, "He's right, we need to discuss matters amongst ourselves."

The Scynthian motioned toward the group of standing people. "We will protect you until Naa'il returns." The leader turned to walk away.

"Wait!" said Harrison. "Do I interact with only you until then?"

The chieftain nodded. "Me only."

"Alright, but what's your name?"

The Scynthian hesitated. No human had ever asked him his name before. Standing tall, he declared, "Rashaa."

"Thank you, Rashaa," said Harrison. "I'll seek you very soon."

Rashaa stared at the Aegean, then turned to his sentries. "Watch them. Don't let them go," he said, before leaving the adventurers behind.

"Hey!" shouted Lord Hammer. "What about my friend?"

"I will have him returned to you." The Scynthian continued on his way.

Harrison glanced over to Nigel. "What friend?"

"Allard," said Lord Hammer. "He's in rough shape."

Murdock took a step toward Lord Hammer. "You just keep popping up out of the blue, don't you?"

Nigel glared at the ranger. Rolling his eyes, he said, "You again." In a sarcastic tone, he added, "You don't care much for me, do you?"

"No," said Murdock. "No, I don't."

"Then you must love the fact that we must work together in order to save the world as we know it," said Nigel, full of smugness.

Murdock thrust a finger in Nigel's face. "I don't know how you figure into all of this, but if I have a chance to take you out, I will."

Lord Hammer frowned. "Idle threats, all the time." Narrowing his eyes, he said, "Do you really think I want to be here with you?" Panning the rest of the group, he added, "All of you?"

Harrison interrupted the argument. "Look, like it or not, we're all in this together." Gazing toward Nigel, he asked, "Why are we here?"

The black-clad warrior let out a deep sigh. "I told you already, these beasts captured Allard and me, and the only way we could bargain for our lives was to tell them that we would find you."

"Well, you have," said Harrison. "Do you have a plan?"

Nigel cocked his head. "Sort of. It's obvious they wanted you. They got you now."

"Fine," said the young warrior. "We'll be held hostage until Naa'il returns. What about us drawing the dragons into the countryside?"

"That's also part of the plan," said Nigel. "We need to get in the open so that we'll have a chance to defeat them."

"Any ideas how?" asked Harrison.

"There's over a thousand of these savages milling about the woods," said Nigel. "They'll fight to the death knowing that these monsters were responsible for torching their homeland."

The young warrior pondered the scenario. "Even if we could ground one of the beasts, and the Scynthians attacked the dragon over and over again, there's still eight more after that."

"And the downed dragon's friends would come to its rescue," said Murdock.

"Look, we'll kill one at a time," said Nigel, his agitation rising in dealing with people he felt were below him. "Nothing's invincible."

"That might be true," said Harrison. "We've also formulated a plan using magical scrolls and multiplying food sources."

Lord Hammer shook his head. "What's that going to do for us?"

"We've watched these monsters," said Harrison. "They need a lot of food to survive and that's what drives them. Our mages have a way to create something appealing to the dragons."

"So the food attracts the dragons?" asked Nigel, intrigued.

"Yes," said the young warrior. "This is where your army comes in."

"My army?" said Nigel, his eyebrows rising. With a laugh he added, "What makes you think I'm in control of these savages?"

"You're with them, aren't you?"

465

"*They ... captured ... me,*" said Lord Hammer with emphasis. "If I had it my way I'd be done with all of this."

Harrison smirked. "Funny, they capture you in order to find me and, when they do, they don't harm any of us."

"You're a regular golden boy, aren't you," hissed Nigel. "Let's work more on this plan, alright?"

The young warrior left the smirk on his face, glad to see that he had the upper hand on Lord Hammer, for now. "Fine by me. I'm sure the Scynthians are going to have ideas of their own."

Harrison motioned for Nigel to join his group. More than uncomfortable, Lord Hammer reluctantly accepted the younger man's invitation, stepping closer to the adventurers. As the night wore on, they put their ideological differences aside and formulated a most convincing strategy.

CHAPTER 39

○

"I think this just might work," said Harrison, reflecting on the plan his group and Lord Hammer had ironed out.

"It's more solid than I thought it would be," said Nigel in a snide tone, surprised at the outcome. During the night he had secretly hoped that the group's ideas would fail and that his proposal would be the one of choice. Instead, he responded, "Now we just need the Scynthians to buy into it as well."

"I can handle that," said the young warrior. Before he could add to his statement, three figures approaching the group gained his attention. "Looks like our 'friends' have captured someone else." All eyes shifted to where Harrison stared.

Nigel pointed to the man in shackles. "That's Allard!"

Two guards escorted the magician to the group of humans. Unlike the others, the Scynthians had shackled Allard's wrists and kept them bound close together. Each sentry placed a large hand under the mage's armpit, more than helping him reach his destination.

Without saying a word, the savages stopped in front of Harrison and the others, placing Allard down. One of the Scynthians unlocked the magician's cuffs, allowing them to spring open, releasing him of his bindings. Allard rotated his wrists in a clockwise manner, loosening them, and relieving some of his pain. The two savages turned and left the humans behind, while several other Scynthians watched over the group from afar.

Nigel stepped forward, placing a firm hand on the magician's shoulder. "Are you alright?"

The mage's pale, drawn face met Nigel's gaze. "How do you think I feel?" hissed the magician, dark and sarcastic.

"I understand," said Lord Hammer, feigning real concern. Extending his arm toward Harrison and his party, the armor-clad warrior continued, "We have a plan."

Allard raised an eyebrow, then gazed over at the group of men and women that stood before him. His eyes scanned each member, coming to a halt at Gelderand.

Glaring at his fellow mage, he scowled. "You did this to me!"

Gelderand's eyebrows arched. Raising his palms to Allard, he asked, "What are you accusing me of doing?"

Allard maintained his laser focus on Gelderand, pulling his cloak down with his right hand, exposing his chest. Puncture wounds from the base of his neck down his torso had pitted his skin.

"Does this spark your memory?"

Gelderand knew exactly what the magician meant. Pointing a finger at his counterpart, he explained his past action, saying, "I gave you every chance to do the right thing! You insisted on creating a vortex that would have destroyed Concur and killed hundreds, if not thousands, of innocent lives!"

Allard released his grip on his cloak, covering his chest again. Pointing to the staff in Gelderand's hand, he said, "Those porcupine quills impaled me! I should be dead!"

Gelderand stood tall. "You brought that upon yourself. I do not regret my actions from that day."

The dark mage narrowed his eyes. "And now I am supposed to join forces with you?"

Harrison stepped forward in an effort to diffuse the escalating situation. "Allard, we all had different agendas that day. Gelderand did what he felt he had to do. Now, our world is in trouble of falling into the hands of an evil man and his legion of dragons."

Allard shifted his eyes in Harrison's direction. "Why should I care what happens to this godforsaken world?"

The young warrior chose his words carefully, knowing that he needed this man's talents in order to have any chance of defeating the dragon army.

"Allard, King Holleris is a wicked man. He's already destroyed the elves', dwarves', and Scynthians' strongholds, and now he's setting his sights on our towns and cities. If we don't stop him, the world is lost for us and future generations."

The magician held his gaze on Harrison. "That is a nice story, young man, but how can I help anymore?" Allard spread his arms wide. "Look at me! I am weak and battered, and my body aches all the time. I can barely concentrate on getting enough food every day, let alone conjure up sorcery to defeat fire-breathing monsters."

"You have to at least try," said Harrison with conviction. "You can't stand there, look me in the eye, and say you give up."

Allard squinted. "Why do you really care?" asked the mage. Waving toward Lord Hammer, he continued, "We tried to stop you and will continue to do so when we have the chance again." The mage gazed at Nigel, who remained stoic, unmoving.

Focusing again on the younger man, he reiterated, "*Why do you care?*"

Harrison stood tall, waiting for this moment, ready to answer this particular question. "It's the *right* thing to do. It's what we *must* do. I was born to help people, to lead them if they needed me. Now, with the crisis this world faces, I can't think of anything else more righteous than to fight the evil that's rising or at least die trying to defeat it."

Allard smirked, somewhat inspired by Harrison's statement. "Righteousness flows in your veins, young man, that is obvious. Misguided, but obvious." Drawing a deep breath, he continued. "I'll tell you what I am going to do. I will employ my services to your cause in exchange for what we want." Allard jerked his thumb in Lord Hammer's direction.

Harrison alternated his gaze between Nigel and Allard. Shaking his head, he asked, "Which is?"

"Full immunity from any crimes and imprisonment," barked Lord Hammer. "When this ordeal is over, we walk away without fear of persecution."

469

Harrison's eyes widened in bewilderment. Showing his palms to the men, he said, "I'm not in any position to grant this request! That comes from our leadership and must be brought up with the Legion of Knighthood."

"Then there's no deal," said Allard.

"Think about this, boy," said Nigel, narrowing his eyes. The former governor of Concur extended his arm in a wide arc. "Take a look at all these beasts just waiting to avenge the destruction of their homeland. *I* can lead them, not you!"

Harrison's mind churned with scenarios, all not good. Gazing over to his friends, he found Murdock shaking his head no, while the others sported blank expressions. Tara, her eyes round, waited in anticipation for his decision. The young warrior allowed his focus to linger on his love, realizing that being a leader included having to make hard decisions at times.

"This is what I'll offer," said Harrison. Pointing at Allard, he said, "You will work with Gelderand on a strategy to defeat the dragons." Directing his finger at Lord Hammer, he continued, "And you will lead the Scynthian army against those monsters.

"In exchange for these services, I promise not to hunt you down or bring you to justice. You'll be free men. However, you're not to step foot in the Concurian countryside, let alone enter any of the coastal cities. I won't order your arrest, but I also won't stop people from extracting a bounty for your capture. You're on your own. Deal?"

Nigel did not look at Allard for confirmation. "Deal."

"Furthermore, if you renege on helping us in any way, this deal becomes null and void. Understood."

"Don't worry about us, boy," snarled Lord Hammer, thrusting a finger in Harrison's direction. "I always keep my word!"

"We'll see about that," said the young warrior. "Now that we've settled that, let's fill in Allard on our strategy and get ready to inform the Scynthians."

The uncomfortable group took the next hour to find a place to congregate, talk about battle plans, and how to best present their ideas to a race of savages.

* * *

Rashaa and his guardians listened to Harrison and the magicians. Shaking his head, the lead Scynthian said, "This is not good. Too risky."

The young warrior had expected pushback on their plans, if for just being humans. "What don't you like about it?"

Rashaa peered at his comrades, then said, "The dragons are too strong. This won't work."

Harrison tried to allay the savage's fears. "How many soldiers do you have?"

The Scynthian shrugged. "Many, not sure."

"A thousand? Two thousand?"

The beast cocked his head. "Sure, maybe more."

"You don't think that two thousand Scynthians can defeat one dragon?"

"We will kill this one dragon!" bellowed the beast. "It is the other ones I'm worried about."

Harrison shook his head. "How so?"

Rashaa wagged a finger at the humans before him. "My people will slay this dragon, but we will lose many." Training his finger on Harrison, he said, "What will you do?" The Scynthian slowly arced his gloved digit across the awaiting people.

"We'll capture their masters," said Harrison. "Without them, those monsters will die."

The Scynthian leader rested his hands on his knees, thinking. Shaking his head, he said, "Still not sure."

"What more do you need from us?" said Harrison, incredulous. "We're going to incapacitate the dragons, the same ones that destroyed your homeland, the same ones that will help in overtaking the world as we know it." The young warrior leaned forward, focusing on Rashaa's cat-like eyes.

"If we don't take this opportunity now, we're condemning the world to an unspeakable death and the Scynthian race will no longer exist." Harrison paused, then drew a heavy sigh. "We all need to come together, starting now."

Rashaa allowed Harrison's words to sink in. After a moment of contemplation, he panned to his sentries, finding them eagerly awaiting his answer. Huffing, he declared, "You lure the dragons and we kill them. When the war is over, we will discuss future arrangements between our peoples."

"Agreed," said the young warrior, sensing that the tide had turned in his favor, however he had one more additional concern. "Will Naa'il agree to this strategy when he arrives?"

"I speak for the Scynthian army," barked Rashaa, puffing his chest out. "Naa'il granted me authority for all strategies. He will agree." Changing the subject, he asked, "When do we leave?"

"Whenever you're ready."

"I will gather my soldiers," said Rashaa. "My workers will assemble the chains now."

Harrison smiled. "Tell us when you've completed your tasks, then we'll begin ours."

Rashaa thrust a finger toward the humans again. "This had better work or our deal of protection is over."

"If it doesn't, there won't be anyone to protect," responded Harrison.

The savage rose from his seat along with his cohorts. "I will send someone to let you know when we are ready." With a wave of his hand, he left the group behind, his men following.

Harrison watched them leave, then turned to his team of adventurers. "They're going to fight," he said with a wide smile. "Now it's our turn to lure the dragons into the countryside."

The young warrior and his friends gathered their belongings and prepared to leave the comforts of the woods, knowing that in a very short time they would embark on one of the greatest battles the land had ever seen.

CHAPTER 40

Ɔ

The Scynthians spent the next day and a half forging the metals needed for their task. In the meantime, Gelderand and Allard, along with Swinkle and Tara, perfected what they believed would create the necessary food source to attract the winged beasts.

Harrison paced before his team, awaiting Murdock and Pondle's reconnaissance mission. A short while later, two familiar figures reentered the woods and proceeded to their leader's position.

The two men stopped in front of the group. Murdock stared at Harrison, then shifted his gaze to Nigel, who stood next to him, not happy that this man appeared to hold a position of authority.

Returning his focus to the young warrior, he said, "The immediate countryside is bare. There's no sign of the dragons or those two old men."

"This plan is preposterous!" exclaimed Lord Hammer, jerking his head toward Allard with a glare. "What are we expecting? For the beasts to just materialize from thin air?"

Allard cast his eyes downward, shaking his head. Gelderand, sensing the tension, said, "We have gone over this a thousand times. The dragons will smell the food and come charging for it. However, this will require patience."

Nigel thrust a finger in the mage's direction. "I'm not one for waiting patiently!"

Harrison pushed the older warrior's arm down. Nigel recoiled, then glared at the young warrior. "Your strategy is sound," said Harrison. "Let's proceed as we've discussed." Something beyond Tara and Swinkle caught the young warrior's eye.

"Lance!" shouted the Aegean, finding his canine friend rushing to their position. The dog dashed to his master, stopping on a dime, and barking feverishly.

"What's the matter, boy?" said Harrison, stooping to the canine's level. As much as he tried, he could not get Lance to relax.

The young warrior cupped the dog's little face, massaging his ears. In a soothing voice, he said, "Lance, calm down. What are you trying to tell me?"

The dog's eyes widened into a vacuous stare, the kind that canine's get under extreme excitement. "Elves! Elves! Elves!" he kept repeating in a series of quick barks.

Harrison released his grip on the dog and rose to his feet. Scanning the immediate area, he said, "Elves?"

"What?" said Tara, her eyes wide in surprise. "They've come to help? Where?"

Harrison gazed deeper into the Scynthian compound, finding many of the savages looking in the same direction. The young warrior focused past the beasts, noticing that they stood at attention and appeared to allow a convoy to pass through them.

The young warrior's eyes widened. Pointing to a platoon of smaller beings, he exclaimed, "There they are!"

A familiar group approached the young warrior and his cohorts. "Look who else is with them," said Murdock.

As the group marched closer, Harrison recognized the person at the forefront. "Is that Fallyn?"

The red-haired woman marched toward her friends, with several familiar elven faces in tow. Smiling, she approached Harrison and said, "I hope you're not upset with me, but I took it upon myself to transform into another creature in order to escape the Scynthians' attack." Gazing back at the elven platoon, she continued, "That's when I found them."

Harrison shook his head. "I'm not mad at all, as a matter of fact, we all assumed you'd morphed into another creature to get away." Peering past Fallyn, Harrison outstretched his hand and exclaimed, "Moradoril! Am I glad to see you!"

The elven king accepted the young warrior's gesture of peace with a smile. "Great to see you as well." Moradoril brought his focus to the man standing next to Harrison, raising an eyebrow in the process. "You're playing a risky game, lad."

The Aegean looked over to Nigel. "We still have our differences but have put them aside for the common good."

Moradoril took a step forward, allowing his eyes to wander over the black-clad warrior. "Nigel Hammer," started the elven king. "An odd set of circumstances we find ourselves in, do we not?"

Nigel smirked. "Why do you say that?"

The king did not waver. "Your name is on the opposite side of every human confrontation. It seems most of your land's leaders would rather do away with you than become partners."

"The feeling is mutual," said Lord Hammer in a snide tone. "I have no use for most people in this world."

Moradoril narrowed his eyes. "Then why stand here today?"

Nigel cocked his head, then said, "Even I need a world to live in. One that's not ruled by misguided kings with a killer dragon army."

The elven king made a subtle nod of concurrence, accepting the wicked man's answer, for the time being. Taking his gaze back to Harrison, he added, "You have also made an alliance with a rather brutal race."

Harrison nodded in agreement. "I know, the Scynthians. Do you know of our plan?"

"I have made some assumptions," said the king swiveling his head around the encampment, taking in the multitude of Scynthian warriors.

"They've joined the cause," said Harrison. "We need their help and they need ours."

"Interesting to say the least," said Moradoril, before waving his twenty soldiers forward. Changing the subject, he said, "I am sure someone would like to say hello." The archers stepped aside, revealing a lovely figure.

"Brianna!" exclaimed Harrison. "It's an honor to see you again."

The elven queen stepped forward. "As it is to see you," she said. "However, time is not on our side and the enemy is great."

Harrison nodded. "That may be true, but we have a plan that we're about to set in motion."

Brianna pursed her lips. "Fallyn informed us of your strategy. Ambitious to say the least."

"I know, it's a bit tricky," said Harrison, acknowledging the elven queen's concern. "Not only do we need to defeat dragons, we must also convince two headstrong men to cease their sinister plan."

"Having Fallyn take on the role of your deceased brother is more than risky, Harrison," said Brianna with concern. "We should discuss this further."

"With all due respect, Brianna, we've hashed this plan out and feel that it'll work," said the young warrior. "There aren't many more options."

Brianna's expression did not change. "More than an uphill battle."

"Indeed," said Harrison. "A perilous strategy but one that'll bring the final conflict." The young warrior panned over the elven contingent. Furrowing his brow, he asked, "Is this all the men you have with you?"

Moradoril shook his head no. "Many of my archers are in the foothills and we have brought a weapon of our own."

"What kind of weapon?" asked Harrison, intrigued with this new turn of events.

"Something that can shoot a dragon out of the sky." Moradoril gave a wry smile.

"Has your weapon been proven in battle?" asked the young warrior, trying to temper his excitement.

"Many years ago, well before your current ancestors were born, the mighty dragon Cedryicus terrorized the land," started Moradoril.

"Dracus was her offspring, was he not?" asked Harrison, having recognized the beast's name from their journey to discover the Talisman of Unification.

"You have a good grasp on the land's history," said the elven king. "That he was." Continuing with his story, he said, "Cedryicus destroyed acres of farmland, scorching crops and killing innocent humans. The people of the land sought us to help eliminate the problem.

"Our people constructed a lethal weapon that severely injured the dragon and stopped her from terrorizing the townsfolk again. Your Ancient Kings slayed the dragon in the end."

"And we killed Dracus," said the young warrior, recalling using a magical sword to eliminate the beast. Harrison's brain churned, figuring that the odds of them defeating the dragon race had gone up significantly. Still, their task remained more than daunting.

"We're going to lure the dragons into the countryside," said Harrison. "You arrived just in time."

"And how exactly are you going to do that?" asked Brianna.

Harrison smiled. "I think that should be our first order of discussion." The young warrior waved his men forward. "Let's all find a safe place to talk and we'll fill you in on our strategy."

The small platoon of fighters, along with their new elven counterparts, ventured to an open area where they held a long and contentious dialogue about how to enact their planned battle tactics.

* * *

The newly formed squad of elves and humans debated Harrison's strategy for a few hours, coming to a final agreement. Brianna, still unsure of Fallyn's role being successful, took the woman aside while the others prepared for battle.

"Fallyn, are you sure about your transformational capabilities?" asked the elven queen.

The woman sighed. "With all due respect, Brianna, I can do this."

"I'm not concerned if you can morph into Harrison's brother. I'm worried about how you are going to trick the king into believing you are him."

Fallyn pursed her lips, then changed into Harrison's identical image. Using a male voice, she said, "Does this satisfy your uneasiness?"

Brianna's eyes widened ever so slightly in surprise. Bringing her focus to the doppelganger's face, she said, "Did Troy have green eyes?"

The warrior imposter crinkled his brow. "No, they're blue like Harrison's."

The elven queen pointed at Fallyn. "Yours are green."

At that time, Tara and Kymbra took a greater interest in the other females' activities. Tara, approached the two, confused. "Harrison?" she asked in a guarded tone.

Kymbra folded her arms across her chest and gestured with her head in the warrior's direction. "That's not him."

Tara scrunched her brow. "Fallyn?"

"Yes, it's me," said the woman, still using a male voice. "Do I look like Harrison to you?"

"Identical," said Tara, astonished.

"Aside from your eyes," said Kymbra, staring into Fallyn's green pools.

Tara's eyes widened a bit. "She's right! They're not blue!"

Brianna interlocked her fingers, resting them in front of herself. "This is just the first of your problems."

Fallyn shape changed back to herself, appearing flustered. "I never gave a thought to my eye color."

"The king's going to know," said Kymbra, her tone direct and to the point. "You better fix that problem."

Fallyn gazed to the ground, deep in thought. Nodding, she said in a shallow whisper, "I will, I will."

Kymbra noticed Murdock waving their group over, ready to depart for the countryside. "They're calling for us," said the warrior. "We better go."

Kymbra and Tara turned to leave the small group. Before Fallyn could depart as well, Brianna gripped her forearm. Focusing on her green eyes, the queen said with conviction, "I truly worry for you, Fallyn. Be more than prepared for your encounter."

The red-haired woman gave her a curt nod. "I will be." The two then joined the rest of the platoon for their mission.

Harrison noticed the four women advancing to their ranks. Greeting them with a smile, he said, "We're just about ready to leave the woods. Everything alright with you?"

"Just expressing some last minute concerns," said Tara, hoping to allay the young warrior's fears. "We're ready to leave now."

The Aegean eyed the ladies a second longer before turning away from them in search of the Scynthian leader. Finding the armed warrior a short distance away, he turned to Pondle and asked, "Can you summon Rashaa? The time has come." The thief gave his leader a single nod and went off to fulfill his task.

Murdock, still not enthused with Nigel standing so close, said, "You realize that we have only one shot at this. If we don't succeed, we're dead."

"All of humanity is dead," said Harrison.

Pondle returned with Rashaa and two of his comrades. "Are you ready?" asked the Scynthian.

Harrison nodded. "We are. Assemble your men and have them follow us into the countryside with your weapon. Also, send one of your scouts with us so that he can relay the attack signal to you." Jerking his thumb at Lord Hammer, the Aegean continued, "He'll lead your soldiers into battle." Rashaa looked down at Nigel, then brought his attention back to Harrison and nodded once.

"Your men understand their mission?" asked the young warrior.

Rashaa narrowed his feline-like eyes, their green shimmering in the light. "You don't have to tell a Scynthian twice when to fight. These beasts destroyed our home. They will pay."

Harrison smiled, a glimmer of hope warming his body. "The task ahead of us will be arduous, but we'll succeed."

"I hope you're right," said Rashaa. The Scynthian pointed to one of his sentries. "You go with them and wait for their signal. I'll gather our forces."

The soldier gripped his mace, then stepped toward Harrison's squad while Rashaa departed to ready his warriors. The people gazed upward at the hulking figure, unaccustomed to having one of their hated enemies as part of their close-knit group.

Harrison addressed Nigel. "You good?"

"More than ready to lead this army into battle," said the former governor of Concur. "You do your part and I'll do mine."

"Just await the signal," said Harrison.

Moradoril and his squadron took their cue to move into position. "I have assigned several sentries to accompany your scouts," said the elven king. "The rest will march with us and provide protection."

Harrison nodded in agreement. "I concur with that." With all of their moving parts in place, the young warrior made eye contact with Murdock and Pondle. "Lead us to the countryside."

The two men adjusted their packs, then started heading away from the woodlands. Lance scooted ahead with them, while the Scynthian soldier trekked behind. A short way back, scores of Scynthians grunted, having started the grueling task of moving their creation from the woods to the open plains.

Harrison brought his attention to the robed members of the group, finding them awaiting his next command. "All of you, follow me and Kymbra. We'll determine a safe haven when we reach the countryside. We shouldn't have anything to worry about now that the Scynthians are on our side."

The young warrior turned and took a step in the opposite direction, before stopping and saying, "Except for the dragons." The Aegean smiled, hoping to lighten the mood a bit.

His friends showed no emotion. Instead, they remained stoic as they took up their positions behind the warriors and began their trek out of the forest.

* * *

The bright sunshine stood out as a stark contrast to the shade of the woodlands. Harrison had to shield his eyes from the glare in order to get a better read of the landscape. Low foothills rolled from the woods toward the flat plains. The young warrior gazed at the level ground in the distance and knew where they would fight the land's next great conflict. Tara and Swinkle sidled up to him while battle plans swirled in his head.

"This is going to be very dangerous, isn't it?" asked the young maiden, more than a hint of anxiety in her voice.

"The most difficult task we've ever faced," said Harrison.

"Can we really defeat these monsters?" asked Tara.

The young warrior stopped and gazed into her worrisome eyes. "I won't live in a world ruled by fear and hate. I'd rather die for our cause than be subjected to that kind of treatment every day." Harrison approached his mate, taking hold of her hands.

"I made a promise that I'd protect you and I will. Even the most menacing of creatures have a weakness. I think we've found it and we'll exploit it."

"I am ready to do my part," said Swinkle, confident.

Harrison turned to face the young cleric. "I hope Pious looks on you with favor as you perform your task."

"I have prayed as much as any time in my life," said Swinkle. "I am ready for the consequences should things go wrong."

Harrison placed a hand on his friend's shoulder, giving it a firm squeeze. "You'll do just fine. Let's continue moving."

As the group continued its trek, the young warrior's thoughts shifted to what lay ahead. The serene landscape, with its lush rolling hills and high grasses, appeared more inviting for a group picnic than a battle space. However, the Aegean understood what his friends needed to do.

With the platoon marching from the woodlands, Harrison turned his attention to the robed members of the group. "Gelderand," called the young warrior.

The mage turned upon hearing his name. "Yes, Harrison?"

"How deep into the countryside should we venture?" asked the young warrior. "The Scynthians can only move so fast after we give the signal."

The magician pondered the question, then said, "We need to be clear of the trees in order for the dragons to see and smell their meal. However, we can perform our magic anywhere you deem fit."

The young warrior absorbed the information. "Thanks, Gelderand, I think I know what we must do."

"And Harrison," said the mage, "Remember, creating the food source is not the problem. It will be relying on the Scynthian's execution."

"My fear exactly," said the young warrior, gazing ahead to the lumbering beast who walked amongst their squad, wondering if its race had the fortitude to complete their mission. Harrison then brought his gaze back behind him. The small convoy had ventured less than a quarter mile from the woodlands. Just about far enough, the young warrior thought to himself. His mind made up, he brought his attention to the woman trekking close to him.

"Kymbra, go and tell Murdock and Pondle that we've reached out stopping point." The blonde warrior nodded, then ran off to fulfill her task.

"Everyone!" shouted Harrison, gaining the attention of the people who marched with him. "Stop your procession and prepare for the next phase of our mission." All members of the platoon heeded their leader's command and began their preassigned tasks.

The young warrior gazed about the immediate area, pleased that everyone had taken it upon themselves to start their responsibilities; however he knew it was time for the Scynthians to provide an essential piece to the plan.

Harrison sought Moradoril, finding him with his elven contingent. "It's time to send one of your scouts back to the Scynthian camp."

"That it is," said the king. Moradoril panned his people before his eyes rested on a trusted archer. "Floriad, alert the Scynthians. It is time for them to bring us their forged tool."

"Yes, my king," said the elf, who ran from his position with incredible quickness, heading back into the forest's depths.

Moradoril cast his eyes on Harrison. "Do you think the Scynthians have created something that can withstand a dragon's wrath?"

Harrison swallowed. "We can only hope so."

"How about the people you sent to Concur?"

The young warrior cast his eyes downward. "I have faith that they made it back alive and help is on its way."

Moradoril took a step toward the Aegean, planting a hand on the young man's shoulder. "Son, you have great trust in your friends and your strategies, and you should be commended for that. However, the world does not always work according to plan."

Harrison harked back to his training, how his leaders instilled in him to be ready for any scenario, that the best laid plans can suddenly go awry. "I realize the gambles that I'm making, but inaction will lead to certain death for all peoples. Look at what they've done to the dwarves, to the Scynthians, to you."

"These beasts are horrific, no doubting that," said the elven king. "But many will perish on the battlefield today, it is inevitable."

The young warrior tried to check his anxiety, knowing what Moradoril said was true. Images of his friends flashed through his mind, the burden of knowing that they trust in his leadership, even if it meant to their deaths.

Harrison lifted his eyes, catching a glimpse of Tara assisting Swinkle with some parchments. His heart pounded, the love for her greater than anything he could ever imagine. With conviction in his voice, he said, "Then we better win more often than we fail."

Moradoril squeezed his hand a little tighter, agreeing with the young warrior's words. "Shall I send scouts to scour the countryside for these wicked beasts?"

"No," said Harrison. "Those dragons are airborne and they'll see your sentries coming well before they can ascertain their position. Risking their wellbeing in such wide openness is not a good idea." The Aegean smirked. "We have something else to bait the dragons to our position."

Moradoril furrowed his brow, unaware of the new tactic. "What do you have in mind?"

Harrison placed a hand on the elven king's back, turning him toward his men. "You'll see. Come, we need to ready ourselves for the upcoming battle."

The Aegean led the king back to the rest of the platoon, while Moradoril's brain churned, wondering what new battle tactic his young counterpart had in mind.

CHAPTER 41

Ơ

Seven winged beasts darkened the otherwise clear blue sky, their green scaly hides shimmering in the sunlight. Way below, two much smaller figures walked through the countryside, escorted by two more dragons.

"How much further is our trek, Finius?" asked King Holleris to his counterpart.

"The coastal cities are still several days away, my king," wheezed the warlock, the constant traveling wearing thin on his weary bones.

The king flashed a wicked smile. "The land's dignitaries will bow to me like peasants! Argos' destruction is only the beginning!"

"That they will," said Finius. "However, all the land is now alerted to our presence."

"Good," said the king, a certain cockiness to his voice. "Let them all know what they're up against. They'll soon realize they can't defeat us."

"Don't be so proud of our creations," warned the magician. "People can surprise you, especially when they have nothing to lose."

The king waved a dismissive hand at his dark mage. "You give them too much credit. I've seen these 'leaders' in the past and nothing has changed. They're all so predictable."

"Be that as it may, I still say we proceed with caution." Dancing shadows on the ground caused the warlock to gaze skyward. High above, a few of the winged beasts performed a spiraling dance, as if something had piqued their interest.

King Holleris noticed his counterpart's actions and looked to the heavens as well. Furrowing his brow, he asked, "What are they doing?"

Finius squinted, bringing a hand to shade his eyes. Another much smaller creature darted around the flying beasts, drawing their attention. "It appears something has distracted our children."

The king squinted as well. "What is it? A bird?"

Finius cocked his head. Maintaining his upward stare, he said with concern, "I believe you're right."

* * *

The majestic eagle swooped by another of the two-headed beasts, doing its best to steer clear of its massive jaws. The bird had zipped through the squadron of dragons, gaining their attention, teasing them to play. After the eagle's third pass, three of the creatures decided to pursue.

The bird of prey gauged the unfolding scene, finding that a few of the dragons had altered their course, their curiosity getting the better of them. The eagle screeched, signaling to the dragons that it was time to chase.

The eagle swooped below the monsters, flying dangerously close to one of them. The dragon nearest the soaring bird lurched at the elusive animal, snapping its jaws close to the fleeing creature. Missing its target only infuriated the beast. Incensed, the monster roared and intensified its hunt for the bird.

Recognizing that it had more than gained the dragon's attention and wrath, the eagle straightened its path and started to fly due east. Swiveling its head back, the bird's green eyes focused on the three monsters that had decided to follow it, the creatures closing fast. The eagle zig zagged but maintained its eastward course, trying its best to lead the dragons away from the rest of the pack while also ensuring its escape.

* * *

Harrison surveyed the Scynthian's handiwork. "They forged this metal a lot better than I expected."

Swinkle nodded. "Maybe we did not give their race enough credit. We always expect the worst from them."

"They're still brutal killers, Swinkle," said the young warrior, taking his gaze to his friend. "They won't hesitate to kill us if our plans go south." The young cleric nodded, agreeing with his friend's statement. "Let's proceed with our strategy. Time to find our magicians."

The two men strolled deeper into their encampment, locating Gelderand, Allard, and Tara. "The Scynthians are ready. How about you?"

Gelderand brought his focus to Allard, who nodded once. "Where shall we perform our next trick?" asked Gelderand.

Harrison took his gaze westward, just beyond their campsite. Pointing to that location, he said, "Over there."

The magicians followed his line of sight, then gathered their belongings. "Follow us," said Gelderand.

Tara approached her love as the two men began their short trek. "My uncle asked me to help him with their task."

"You're going to do great," said Harrison before leaning over and kissing her on the forehead. "Come on, let's go."

The young people followed Gelderand and Allard through the camp. By this time, the rest of their team noticed their actions and wandered toward the edge of the encampment, too. Lance bounded to his master, eager to see what would happen next.

Upon reaching a flat stretch of land a short way from the fighters, Gelderand looked up to the heavens, then back to the forest. Feeling good about his choice, he pointed to the ground and said, "This is the spot."

Allard made a quick survey of the land. "I agree."

Gelderand brought his attention to Swinkle. "Do you have the parchment?"

Swinkle stepped forward. "Yes, I do."

"And are you ready to recite your prayer?"

The young cleric nodded. "Just tell me when to start."

Gelderand looked west for a second, peering at nothing in particular. The mage took a deep breath, then exhaled slowly. "Now is the time."

Harrison heard the mage's request. In a booming voice, the young warrior barked, "Everyone, the time has come to enact the next phase of our mission. No one knows what the future entails; however, we must all be brave and remember that we're fighting for our existence, our way of life. If we succeed, all the peoples of the land will sing our praises. If we're defeated, at least we know we tried to do what was right."

Moradoril stepped forward after Harrison's speech. "The elven race is with you, Harrison. May the gods shine down on us today."

The Scynthian sentry also took the opportunity to speak his mind. "The Scynthians pledge to help on this day. We all fight together."

The young warrior gazed at the men and women who stood around him, ready for the fight of their lives. Win or lose, he felt a sense of pride wash over the crowd, something that he could use in the ensuing battle.

Taking his gaze to his dear friend, he said, "Swinkle, maybe a prayer is in order before we get started."

The holy man did not disappoint. First, he took a vial of holy water and sprinkled it on the ground. "Dear Pious, bless the people who stand before you today. In a matter of moments, we will embark on the most difficult task of our lives and we pray that you will be on our side."

Swinkle corked his vial and secured it to his belt once again. Next, he said, "Bless all the good people and creatures of the world, for we are all coming together to battle an unspeakable evil. Many of us here have lost our homes or way of life, but we cannot be deterred. With your help, Pious, there is no way that we can lose. Look down on us with favor and we promise to do what is right."

The young cleric motioned for everyone to step back, which they did, giving the holy man ample room to pray. Swinkle then clasped his hands together and mumbled to himself. Bending down, he placed his hands close to the ground while continuing his mantra. Seconds later, a soft glow sprung from his fingertips.

After the light subsided, a small object appeared on the ground, taking on the look and texture of an oversized loaf of bread.

"This is going to feed a dragon?" said Murdock to Kymbra under his breath, yielding a guffaw from the woman. The female warrior poked the ranger in the ribs for good measure.

Swinkle rose from his position, taking his gaze to Gelderand. "The product may be small, but it is a highly enriched food base. Now we need for you to create a larger portion."

Gelderand summoned Allard to join him, both men stepping to the forefront. The men made eye contact with each other and, with a simple nod, began to recite their simultaneous spells.

Harrison's eyes remained riveted on the beige, bread-like food that rested on the ground. As the magicians continued their chant, the substance began to wiggle. To the young warrior's surprise, as well as to those congregated in the vicinity, the loaf split into two, then three, then many more iterations, ending with an impressive pile of food. The young warrior's eyes widened at the eight foot high heap of dragon bait.

With a broad smile and a sparkle in his eye, Harrison exclaimed, "You did it!"

Swinkle raised a finger in the Aegean's direction. "We're not done yet." Turning to the young maiden, he said, "Tara, can you help me?"

The girl approached Swinkle, who in turn handed him a scroll. The young cleric helped Tara unfurl the parchment, then both youngsters held it for one of the mages to read. Gelderand stepped forward and, spreading his arms wide with his palms toward the food pile, began reading the scroll's contents.

"Behold, I command thee to multiply the food before us, creating an abundant supply of nourishment."

Harrison again watched with wide eyes, waiting for some kind of transformation to take place. He did not have to wait long, for moments later the pile of food began to grow higher while its base widened. The process accelerated, spreading the substance across the ground, forcing everyone around them to scurry away from the ever-growing mass. A minute later, a huge mountain of bread-like food littered the immediate area.

The young warrior panned the newly created mound of nutrients. "I don't believe my eyes!" he exclaimed, barely able to contain his smile.

Gelderand's expression remained stoic. "We still have a lot of work to do and little time to get it done."

Harrison reeled in his excitement. Taking on his leadership role, he shouted, "Everyone, start your assigned tasks now!"

Murdock and Pondle hurried to Harrison's side. "You want us to separate this into two mounds?" exclaimed the ranger, jerking his thumb at the immense pile. "We need more men!"

"We can only work with what we have," said Harrison. "Listen to Gelderand and start splitting up the dragon food."

Gelderand and Allard assessed the huge mound in front of them. Allard pointed to the left, saying, "We need to create two feeding stations in order to trap two dragons."

"Agreed," said Gelderand, concentrating on the best course of action. "And they should be apart from each other. We do not want the dragons fighting over the food."

"Twenty feet between piles should suffice," concluded Allard. Gelderand nodded in concurrence. Allard brought his gaze to the beings surrounding him. "Put twenty feet between the piles! Now!"

Moradoril's soldiers began the arduous task of taking the food substance from the center of the singular mass and carrying equal shares to the left and right.

Harrison, taking the elves' cue, rolled up his sleeves and thrust his hands into the soft doughy substance. As he carried a handful to the right, he caught the members of his team staring at him.

"What are you all looking at?" he exclaimed. "Start separating the piles!"

Pondle gazed at Murdock, who rolled his eyes in frustration. Kymbra acknowledged the gesture, saying, "This might not be glamorous, but it's what we have to do." The female warrior then plunged her hands into the sloppy mess, just as Harrison had.

The two men watched as Tara, Swinkle, and Gelderand followed Harrison and Kymbra's lead. With a huff, Murdock panned to Pondle and said, "Let's get this over with." The men then helped with the mundane task at hand.

The group toiled for thirty minutes and, when they completed their task, two giant mounds of a bread-like food substance stood twenty feet apart from each other.

Harrison, his breathing heavy, placed two sticky hands on his hips. "Am I glad that's over with," he said before feeling a warm tongue licking his fingers. The young warrior instinctively lifted them, finding Lance swallowing the leftovers of Harrison's chore.

"Looks like Lance gives your creation the stamp of approval," said the young warrior in Gelderand's direction.

The mage flashed a quick smile. "I am sure the dragons will, too."

Harrison, the light moment over, went back to his commanding ways. "Time to use the Scynthian's tool." The young warrior gathered his team and proceeded to where the instrument lay on the ground.

The Aegean peered at the object, a large hook attached to a massive chain. Harrison followed the links into the distance until they disappeared into the woods.

Murdock slapped his arm, then pointed to the food mountain. "How are we going to get that thing in there?"

"I know, it's heavy," said the young warrior. "But we must find a way."

Moradoril approached the two, lending his advice. "This protein source is thick," he started. "We will have to carry it to the center and manually embed it into the mound. It will fall into the substance under its own weight."

Harrison glossed over the scene, coming to the same conclusion. "Alright, let's position our bait hook."

The elven king waived his hand, summoning his soldiers to the Scynthian's chain. To his surprise, a large shadow enveloped his body, darkening the area around him. Turning his head upwards, he gazed into the Scynthian scout's green eyes.

"This metal is dense," said the being in a low, guttural voice. "Very heavy."

"Can you help?" asked the elven king.

The Scynthian dropped his mace and proceeded to hunch over the hook where the base met the first link. The creature then panned his finger to all those standing around. "Help lift."

Several elves, along with the Scynthian squatted next to the object. The larger being placed his big, hairy hands under the hook, lifting it an inch above the ground. The elves, noticing an opening for their hands, slid their fingers under the metal object and took hold.

Harrison pointed at Murdock and Pondle, then rushed to the Scynthian's side. The ranger and the thief did likewise. Kymbra followed suit a second later. With everyone in place, the mixed team counted to three, then lifted the hook.

The density of the object surprised the young warrior. Though he assumed beforehand that the Scynthian's creation would be heavy, he still could not fathom its true weight. His muscles strained as he worked with the others to move the object into the awaiting mound.

Shaped like a massive fish hook, it took all the humans, elves, and Scynthians congregated around the food mass to lift the five foot long cast of metal. Harrison felt his legs sinking into the mush, diminishing his ability to gain solid footing. As sweat beaded on his brow, he panned over to the others next to him, finding them in the same predicament.

"We need to get this thing as close to the top as possible," grunted Murdock, struggling to gain adequate footing as well. "That's the only way this hook will sink into this stuff."

After several minutes of sloshing around the pile, the mixed group of humanoids positioned the object near the mound's apex and as close to the center as possible. They then allowed the hook's own weight to take over, gravity plunging the metal piece deep inside the thick substance.

Harrison, along with the others, waited for the object to find its resting point. Moments later, sensing that the hook had finished its descent, the young warrior said, "I think we're good." Everyone around him lingered a moment more, waiting to see if the Scynthian's creation had indeed come to a stop. Several seconds went by without incidence.

The young warrior, satisfied with their work, took care in stepping out of the food mass, his body covered with the bread-like substance. Again, Lance bolted to his side, licking the sweet tasting food.

Allard pointed to the dog. "Keep him away from this pile," said the mage, taking his focus to the undisturbed heap. "As a matter of fact, everyone should stay away from it after I'm finished."

"What are you going to do?" asked Harrison, scraping the food stuff from his body.

"I am going to inject it with a fatal toxin, something capable of taking down a beast the size of a dragon," said the dark magician. "There will be more than enough poison to kill the dog or any of us for that matter."

The Aegean soaked in Allard's information, then bent down to address Lance. "No more eating this stuff," said Harrison, pointing to the mounds. "It will make you sick." The canine cocked his head and appeared to frown.

"I mean it," said the young warrior, pointing a finger directly in the dog's face. "No more eating!" Lance shuffled away from the pile with his head hung a bit lower.

"He's all set," said Harrison in Allard's direction.

The mage then called out to the beings around him. "I am going to inject a lethal toxin into this pile. Do not, I repeat, do not come in contact with it after I am done with my spell. None of us have an antidote to combat the poison."

Everyone took a few steps back from the second mound of food, doing their best to keep away from the soon to be tainted substance. Satisfied that everyone heeded his warning, Allard removed several vials from his pack, mixing them carefully into a bowl. He then took a small tube from his belt, uncorked it, and placed precisely three drops into the mixed substance. With a puff of smoke, the liquid turned black.

Harrison, watching from afar like everyone else, got a whiff of the sweet scent as soon as the last drop hit the bowl. "It smells like sugar," said Harrison in Swinkle and Tara's direction.

"More like vanilla," said the young maiden.

"It is a highly concentrated syrup," added Swinkle. "For that smell to reach us so fast, it must be very intense."

"And it will attract a lot of critters not just dragons," said Harrison.

Allard took his creation and brought it to the massive food mountain devoid of the Scynthian's hook. Removing a knife from his belt, he stirred its contents, then began to splatter the poison onto the mound. Minutes later, he had emptied the bowl of his toxin, allowing the liquid to saturate the substance. Next, he took the knife and container, and placed them into a sack.

"Again, stay away from the pile," said Allard. "I also suggest that we move away from this area immediately."

Harrison took the mage's cue. "Everyone, to their battle positions!" he shouted. All members of the group scurried off to their assigned posts, anticipating combat.

Before heading to his spot, Harrison approached Allard once again. "What are your thoughts?" he said, motioning with his head to the two traps disguised as food.

Allard shook his head. "I have no idea. All I know is that this aroma will attract the beasts. Once they arrive, it's anyone's guess."

The young warrior nodded, then brought his gaze to the countryside. Somewhere past the horizon he knew that Fallyn had started her part of the mission and now their portion was complete. Harrison allowed his gaze to linger a moment more, then he proceeded to his battle station, ready for whatever would happen next.

C H A P T E R 42

Ϙ

Harrison and the groups of men, elves, and Scynthians waited less than an hour for the first signs of trouble. One of the elven sentries, his gaze fixed on the western skyline, pointed toward the horizon.

"Something's coming!" shouted Gaelos, his focus sharp and unwavering.

The young warrior, along with his friends, had pulled back their position to just in front of the forest, away from the large stacks of generated food. The elf's exclamation more than piqued his interest.

Harrison rushed to the archer's side, scanning the horizon as well. Finding nothing, he asked, "What do you see?" By this time, the rest of the humans and elves congregated to Harrison's position.

"In the sky," said Gaelos. "They're heading this way!" The elf squinted, then added, "And I see a smaller flying creature as well."

"An eagle?" asked Harrison, still unable to see anything unusual in the sky.

"It appears to be," said the elf.

"Fallyn," said the young warrior, a sense of pride washing over him, knowing that the woman had fulfilled her mission to perfection.

494

Moradoril and Brianna took up position on either side of their kinsman. Both of their eyes widened. "Dragons on the way!" exclaimed the elven king.

Harrison shook his head in agitation. "I don't see anything!"

"Our eyesight is superior to yours," said Brianna. "Time is of the essence. Our adversary will be on our doorstep very soon."

The young warrior heard the elven queen's words; however, he remained determined to see the beasts with his own eyes. Finally, in the distance he noticed a dark speck against the blue sky, the image growing larger with every passing second.

Harrison swallowed. "There's three of them," he said with gravity. Swiveling to Moradoril, he said with anxiety in his voice, "We only planned for two!"

The elven king's belly tightened. "War is unpredictable. We best be ready for battle."

Tara approached Harrison, trying her best to allay her fears. "Harrison, what do we do about the third one?" she asked, her voice quivering. The young warrior began to speak, but just shook his head instead.

Gaelos turned to his king. "They're coming in fast! What are your orders?"

"Sound the elven alarm!" bellowed Moradoril. The sentry brought a horn to his lips and blew three short, high-pitched bursts, signaling the number of creatures to expect.

Harrison gazed at his friends. "Get ready for battle! Let the dragons feed on the food before we act!" The young warrior's eyes sought the Scynthian scout. Locking his gaze on the savage's, he said, "Wait for my mark!" The beast nodded once in affirmation.

All heads turned to the two piles of manufactured food. Just as Brianna had said, the dragons quickly closed the gap between them and the awaiting trap. Harrison watched in anticipation, his mind whirling, unsure what ramifications the third dragon might add to their battle equation. To his relief, though, a majestic bird of prey swooped past the mounds and glided over the elves and humans before seeking sanctuary in the awaiting forest. At least Fallyn made it back safe, he thought.

Bringing his attention back to the matter at hand, Harrison held his breath as the monsters filled the immediate area, their green, scaly hides darkening the otherwise clear sky. A chill ran down his spine as he clearly distinguished two long necks and large, leathery wings on each dragon. An earth-shaking shriek rattled his bones.

Tara tugged on his arm, shaking. "We should leave!" she cried with round eyes. "We're no match for them!" Lance scurried between the two, trembling with fear.

Harrison had to check his flight instinct, his brain screaming for him to take cover in the woodlands. However, his warrior training kept his feet planted on the ground.

Taking his focus to his mate, he said, "You can hide! I'll find you but I must stand my ground and lead these men into battle!"

The young maiden, frightened almost to tears, understood Harrison's predicament. "No, I'm staying with you."

Never removing his stare, he said, "I will protect you. I'll keep you safe." Bringing his focus to the scared dog, he ordered, "Lance, stay with Tara at all times!" The canine gazed up at the young maiden, ready to fulfill his task.

Harrison returned his gaze to the incoming monsters. The beasts descended from the sky, their dual necks bobbing and weaving. Within seconds the three dragons landed on the ground and took a strong interest in the awaiting food source.

The young warrior clutched his battle axe, his eyes glued to the scene. One of the dragons approached the first mound that contained the hidden bait hook. The emerald-colored beast furled its wings on its back, then leaned forward with both its necks. The young warrior waited in anticipation as they drew ever closer to the food source, hoping that they would succumb to their hunger desires.

The dragon craned its necks in two separate directions, the nostrils on each head flaring, taking in the substance's sweet aroma. To everyone's surprise, both necks sprung high, then dove into the mound with open mouths.

Harrison and Tara stared wide-eyed at the scene unfolding before them. The creature ravaged the food, tearing at the pile and swallowing massive chunks at a time. In the meantime, the two other dragons turned their attention to the second mound.

Similar to the first beast to the scene, both creatures lowered their heads to the mound, taking turns sniffing their awaiting meal. As the two dragons maneuvered closer to their prize, one of the beasts swung both of its necks in its counterpart's direction, shrieking at the top of its lungs. Startled by its kin's actions, the surprised creature hopped back, raising its long necks high and returning an equally earth-rattling screech.

The first dragon was relentless. Determined to claim the food source as its own, the monster lunged at its equal, using one head to snap its jaws while the other straightened its neck high. Without warning, a stream of fire spewed from the dragon's mouth, scorching the earth to the left of the second dragon, forcing it to reel backwards. Infuriated, the staggering beast righted itself, then volleyed a cone of flames to the left of the first dragon, torching the ground. Unwavering in its claim to the awaiting food source, the first creature lunged with both heads at its counterpart, incinerating the area around the monster.

The second creature retreated, flapping its wings, and lifting off the ground in an effort to avoid the ever increasing flames. The first beast, taking advantage of its current situation, turned its attention to the heap of food. In a blink of an eye, both necks lunged at the pile, devouring chunks of the sweet, tainted substance with both mouths.

Harrison's eyes remained riveted on the feeding frenzy. "They're both going for the food!" he exclaimed.

"Will our traps work?" asked Tara, her eyes fixed on the monsters as well.

Before the young warrior had a chance to answer, the dragon feeding nearest them clamped down on something hard, then used its other head to screech so loud that it knocked all humanoids to the ground.

Harrison scrambled to his feet, then gazed with wide eyes at the unfolding scene. The monster, its mouth clamped shut next to the food pile, lifted its neck up slowly, revealing a thick, steel chain hanging out of its mouth. The other neck remained straightened and shrieked at the top of its lungs.

Tara pointed to the struggling creature. "It's caught on the hook!"

The young warrior's eyes sought the Scynthian scout. Finding him a short way behind his position, he shouted, "Send the signal!"

The sentry did not waver. The Scynthian brought the large oxen horn from around his neck to his lips and, turning to face the woodlands, blew as hard as he could. A low, resonating sound boomed from his instrument, reverberating from his position and into the depths of the forest.

Harrison swiveled back to the maddening beast, his mouth falling agape, finding it flapping its wings in a vain attempt to flee its pain. Blood spewed from the monster's injured mouth, the Scynthian's massive hook lodged deep in its throat while the beast's other head continued its Banshee-like screaming.

The young warrior, though his focus remained riveted on the injured dragon, recognized an audible rumble that reverberated along the ground. Harrison turned his shocked eyes downward just in time to see the Scynthian's steel chain become taut. His eyes followed the links skyward, ending at the dragon's mouth and extending back to the forest. A voracious roar erupted from the denseness of the trees, then the dragon's head made a wicked lurch toward the woodlands. The steel hook tore deeper into the beast's mouth, blood gushing from its orifice like a waterfall. The uninjured head wailed, sending shock waves throughout the huddled humanoids.

Harrison watched in amazement, knowing that at this particular moment, the land's greatest battle had commenced. His militaristic mind churning, he bellowed to those surrounding him, "Attack positions!"

The elven archers fanned out, creating a semicircle in front of their human counterparts. Harrison and his friends, along with Moradoril and Brianna, awaited the beast's next move.

The infuriated monster, hook firmly entrenched in its mouth, jerked its injured head back, the beast's long neck hauling the chain in the opposite direction. Harrison gazed toward the woods, finding that the force of the dragon's actions had pulled the links away from the safety of the forest and deeper into the countryside. To his dismay, several Scynthian warriors came flying into the grassy plain, no longer safe in the shadow of the trees, their hands still gripping the cable. The chain thudded to the ground, scattering the fur-covered creatures in all directions.

The dragon, beginning to decipher the problem at hand, stared down the links of the chain with its good head, following it into the forest. The beast raised its uninjured neck back and, taking a deep inhale, unleashed a stream of flames down the length of the chain. The cone of fire entered the woods, igniting everything in its path. Those positioned in the countryside clearly heard the screams and wails of agony. However, the chain remained taut.

Harrison pointed to the links, still intact. "The Scynthians are still hanging on!" Seconds later, an audible grunt, made by hundreds of creatures in unison, filled the battlefield. The chain pulled toward the forest once again, driving the monster's bloody head downward.

The young warrior sensed something different this time. The beast's injured head struck the ground, where it remained dazed. The second head lowered down toward its counterpart, the young warrior swearing he witnessed a look of concern on the dragon's face.

Locating the Scynthian scout again, Harrison exclaimed, "Sound the second alarm!"

The Scynthian blew his horn again, this time in quick bursts, as if to encourage his kinsmen to the battle. Moments after the sentry issued the second signal, the chain pulled violently toward the woods, the Scynthians using all the strength they could muster as a team to continue applying pressure to the injured beast. This time, the dragon's massive body toppled over, falling to the ground with a resounding thud. At the same time, hundreds of Scynthian warriors, screaming at the top of their lungs, rushed from the woods with weapons in hand.

Harrison felt a hand grip his shoulder. "Look," said Murdock, pointing to the monster that had consumed copious amounts of the tainted food. "That one's looking pretty sick!"

The young warrior jerked his head in the opposite direction just in time to see the second dragon lurch its two heads toward the ground. The monster heaved, dumping semi-digested sludge to the earth.

"Both of them are weakened!" exclaimed Harrison. "Time to finish them off!"

Murdock gripped his friend's shoulder tighter. Pointing to the third dragon," he said, "Don't forget about that one!"

The young warrior took his focus to the third monster, noticing something peculiar. "Murdock, something's wrong with it."

The ranger stared at the beast, looking for something out of character. The dragon appeared lucid and sluggish, not aggressive as he would have expected, considering his fellow mates were suffering.

"I'd have to agree," said the ranger. "Either way, we need to take action now!"

Harrison nodded, then searched for Moradoril. Finding him a short distance away, the young warrior dashed to the elven king's side. Noticing Brianna a few steps behind the king in a meditative state, the Aegean asked, "Is she preparing herself for her task?"

"She is nearly there," said Moradoril. "In the meantime, we must keep these monsters at bay."

A voracious roar reverberated throughout the immediate area. The first dragon, the hook tearing a jagged gash from the corner of its mouth and ripping the flesh in a zig zag fashion down toward its neck, had started to flap its wings again in an attempt to flee. With Scynthian fighters charging from the woods, those warriors who remained hidden behind the trees yanked on the massive chain one more time.

The dragon, its wings still flapping, began to lift from the ground, only to fall forward after the Scynthian's latest maneuver. The monster stumbled and dropped to the earth just as the fur-covered beings entered the fray. Clubs and maces flailed at the incapacitated dragon as the Scynthians pounded without mercy on the hook-ravaged head.

Sensing the escalation in danger, the dragon lifted its uninjured head high and expanded its chest. Without hesitation, the beast unleashed a torrent of flames upon the battling

500

Scynthians, igniting scores of them and torching the surrounding earth. Screams and bedlam erupted at the scene as the battle's intensity turned up a notch.

Harrison watched in horror. Before him massive beasts, surprised by such small, insignificant beings, fought for their lives, while all he could do was stand and watch. Gazing at his weapon, a sinking feeling overtook him, knowing that any effort to join the fray would be futile. *Stick to the plan*, he lamented to himself.

Fireballs rocketing toward the dragon's exposed underbelly shook him from his trance. The projectiles hit their mark with ease, bursting into flames and singeing the beast. As Gelderand and Allard readied themselves for another attack, Harrison noticed Brianna step to the forefront. Maneuvering in front of her archers, the elven queen spread her arms wide, unleashing a powerful spell.

The young warrior gazed at the queen, knowing that her actions signaled the final phase of their first mission. "What is she doing?" asked Tara, unsure of the elf's intentions.

"She's holding the dragon in place," said Swinkle. "And she's completely vulnerable at this time."

"Her archers are protecting her," said Harrison, peering at the elves bent on one knee, their bows locked onto the flailing beast. "She'll be fine."

Brianna held her ground while her body lightly shook, the spell taking its toll. The monster tried to flee but could not, the queen's magic keeping it in place. Between the flames, Scynthian warriors regrouped and continued their attacks on the tiring beast.

In a last gasp effort, the floundering dragon raised its good head again but this time pivoted toward Harrison's team and the elves. For a second time, several projectiles struck the monster just before it could spew flames at the inferior creatures. The dragon reeled back, lost its footing, and fell to the ground.

Scynthian warriors, sensing the tide turning in their favor, converged on the dragon. Like thousands of ants attacking a debilitated enemy, the Scynthians pounced from all angles. The savages climbed onto the monster, slashing the creature's thick scales, doing whatever they could to slay the wretched beast.

Meanwhile, with the situation more or less in control with the first dragon, the young warrior took a keen interest in the health of the other one that had eaten the tainted food.

"What should we do about that one?" asked the young warrior in Moradoril's direction. The monster continued to vomit, its health weakening by the second.

"Leave it be," said the elven king. "The poison is doing its work." Taking his gaze to the third beast, he continued, "I'm more worried about that one."

Harrison brought his attention to the fully healthy dragon. To his dismay, the creature, recognizing the peril that had befallen its kin, unfurled its wings and, in one smooth motion, took off for the heavens. The young warrior watched in horror as the dragon flew higher into the sky, then headed due west.

"It's going for help," said the Aegean, knowing full well that seven more dragons would soon be on their way.

"We can't worry about the others!" exclaimed Moradoril. "Our focus must remain with these two for now."

Harrison nodded in agreement before a hellish screech from above caused him and all those around his position to cower. The dragon had called to his unseen brothers and sisters in the distance, surmised the young warrior, then had circled back toward its injured counterparts.

The young warrior realized the monster's intention. Yelling to anyone that remained in earshot, he exclaimed, "Take cover!"

The dragon, its massive wings boosting its acceleration, flew down from the heavens and began its attack run. Finding a multitude of targets, the creature's chest expanded, then both heads began spewing cones of flames in all directions, torching the area around the injured beasts.

Harrison hit the ground hard, fires igniting the vegetation around him. The young warrior raised his head skyward, finding the beast's dark silhouette flying higher, readying itself for another attack run. His heart pounding, he took the lapse in time to locate his friends. Frantically panning the immediate area, he searched in earnest for one person in particular. Quick barks alerted him to her position.

Lance lay next to the young girl, calling for his master. Harrison sprinted across the charred earth, covering the fifty feet between him and Tara in no time. His heart sank upon reaching his mate. The girl remained motionless, face down on the ground with Lance laying by her side.

"Oh, Tara," lamented the young warrior, as he reached down for her frail body. Harrison took care in turning her over, taking the young maiden in his arms. A small gash above her left eye graced her forehead and her lids remained shut.

"Tara," said Harrison, looking for a response. Lifting the girl's mouth to his ear, the young warrior did his best to hone in on any sign of life. At first he did not hear a thing, but moments later he felt Tara's soft breath against his ear.

The young warrior, satisfied that the girl was still alive, lifted his head and searched for the one person that he knew could help her. Several yards away, he saw Swinkle on all fours, shaking the cobwebs from his head.

"Swinkle!" shouted Harrison, trying to garner his friend's attention. "Swinkle!"

The young cleric stared right at Harrison upon hearing his name called. The holy man did not have to ask a single question, realizing that the girl in Harrison's arms needed assistance. Swinkle rose to his feet, sidestepping pockets of flames as he dashed to the couple's position.

Lowering his head to Tara's face, he asked, "Is she alive?" The young cleric brought a delicate hand to the young maiden's forehead, feeling her injury.

"Yes," said Harrison, anxiety in his voice. "Can you help her?"

Swinkle's eyes lingered on Tara's wound a second longer, then he nodded, "Yes."

Positioning his hands close to the young girl's laceration, the holy man mumbled a prayer to himself. A soft white glow encompassed the injury, almost closing the cut completely. When finished, the young cleric backed away and waited for Tara's reaction.

Seconds passed before the girl's eyes opened wide, darting in every direction. Her eyes softened upon seeing Harrison's. "I have you," said the young warrior, squeezing his love closer.

Tara did not say a word and began to cry. "You're going to be alright," reassured Harrison, though he knew that the gravity of the situation was far from over. "But we need to move now."

Swinkle pointed to the sky. "It's coming back!" Lance sprung to his feet and began to bark.

"Can you walk?" asked Harrison, not really waiting for an answer, instead plopping the girl on her feet. Tara nodded, still trying to gather her bearings.

"Move!" said the young warrior, pointing away from the dragons and toward the woods. "Head for the cover of the trees!"

Everyone in the general area heard an ominous whooshing, the massive beast's wings creating panic to all humanoids present. Harrison pushed Tara's back, more than encouraging her to sprint toward the cover of the forest. The young warrior's eyes darted, trying to gauge his surroundings. Lance bolted ahead of the pack, leaving him, Tara, and Swinkle behind. Scynthians continued to pound the first dragon into submission, while the second one wretched again. Elven archers secured their bows and dashed toward the poisoned beast. Brianna held her ground, Moradoril beside her, sword drawn and ready to strike anything that might attack his queen. Try as he might, though, Harrison could not locate the rest of his friends.

Unaccustomed to running from battle, the young warrior knew what he needed to do next. The tree line loomed a mere fifty yards away when he shouted, "Everyone, stop!"

Swinkle halted, as did Tara, the two of them gasping for air. Harrison gestured to Swinkle and, between ragged breaths, said, "Take her into the woods and find a safe place to hide. I'm going back to help the others."

"No!" exclaimed Tara. "I'm coming with you!"

"You're hurt," said the young warrior, leaving no room for debate. Focusing on the young cleric, he ordered, "Take her, now!" Lance darted back to their position, barking feverishly.

Harrison understood the dog's antics. Turning around, he watched as the flying beast torched the landscape, scattering humanoids in every direction. Clutching his battle axe tighter, he pointed to the woods and yelled, "Go!"

Tears streamed down Tara's face as Swinkle gripped her forearm, pulling her away from Harrison. Lance continued his yipping, imploring them to leave.

The young warrior stared at his love, then said, "I'll find you." Setting his emotions aside, he turned away from Tara and Swinkle, then ran toward the ensuing chaos.

"Tara, we must go now!" said Swinkle, knowing every second wasted could cost them their lives. "Harrison will be back."

The young maiden watched through teary eyes as Harrison sprinted toward the flaming battlefield. Knowing that there was nothing more she could do, she turned and ran with Swinkle and Lance toward the relative safety of the awaiting forest.

CHAPTER 43

◻

The battlefield before Harrison was ominous. Clouds filtered across the once sunny sky, while flames and smoke erupted in the immediate countryside. The young warrior sprinted back toward the melee as three dragons, two critically wounded and the third trying to avoid a similar fate, fought their relentless adversaries.

Harrison scampered back to the elves, finding Moradoril standing his ground while Brianna continued with her spell. The elven king caught Harrison's eye, exclaiming, "She can't hold on much longer!"

A wild screech stopped the young warrior before he could respond. The third dragon dropped from the heavens and landed near its counterparts with a resounding thud. The beast took two purposeful steps in the direction of the first dragon, concerned with its injured state. Scynthians and elves had climbed atop of the monster, slashing and clubbing the beast over and over again. Lowering both necks at the same time, the dragon shrieked, then lunged its heads at the closest creatures, snagging some in their mouths, crushing them to death.

Scynthians and elves alike began to flee, knowing that they were no match for the infuriated dragon. The beast raised both its long necks and expanded its chest before spewing more flames toward the retreating humanoids. The dragon's fiery attack doused everyone in the immediate area, garnering screams of anguish from those affected by the flames.

Continuing with its fury, the dragon swung its necks in the opposite direction, finding its equal that had fallen victim to the tainted food. Allard's poison had done its job, completely incapacitating the monster, bringing it one step closer to death. The uninjured dragon lowered its heads to its sick counterpart, sniffing and examining its body.

Harrison and Moradoril watched with great interest as the fallen dragon's chest finally stopped expanding. The healthy dragon, sensing that its kin had died, stumbled backwards, almost falling over.

"Did you see that?" said Harrison with wide eyes. "The one that ate the poison is dead!"

Moradoril grabbed Harrison's shoulder, pointing to the one still alive. "Look what its brother's death did to him!"

The young warrior stared at the healthier dragon, finding something odd with its current state. "Is it me or did that one become sick?"

"Not sick," said Moradoril, "weakened by the other one's death!"

Harrison panned to the king, scrunching his brow. "What does that mean?"

"I think they're all physically connected," said the king. The two jerked their heads in the direction of the dragon that had swallowed the hook. With a final gasp, the beast mimicked its brethren and succumbed to its injuries.

"That one's dead, too!" exclaimed Harrison. The men then panned back to the last living monster.

"He's having a hard time," said Moradoril, the two of them finding the dragon disoriented, flapping its wings while trying to regain its senses.

Harrison's mind churned. "You know, I'm willing to bet the other dragons that aren't here are effected by their deaths, too."

Moradoril flashed the young warrior a grave look of concern. "I'm thinking that we will find out before too long."

While the two men conversed, the last remaining dragon righted itself and began to flap its wings in earnest, lifting from the ground and heading upwards. The massive beast let out a blood-curdling screech toward the western horizon, then flew higher into the sky.

"I don't like the looks of this," said Harrison, keeping his eyes fixed on the beast that ascended to the heavens. Making one last aerial maneuver, the two-headed creature reached its apex, then began its attack run.

Moradoril grabbed Harrison's arm, then yelled, "Run!"

The young warrior looked on in horror as the elven king ran off toward his queen, gathering her and his men, and making haste toward the forest. Harrison panned the vicinity, searching for his friends. To his left he found Murdock, Pondle, and Kymbra trying to navigate through the ensuing chaos. Elves dashed from the scene, while scores of Scynthian warriors scattered in all directions.

Harrison rushed toward Murdock's position. Reaching the ranger, he pointed skyward, saying, "We need to seek shelter! Head for the woods!"

"Are you crazy!" exclaimed Murdock, spreading his arms out wide. "That dragon's going to torch the forest!"

The young warrior's heart sank upon hearing Murdock's statement, knowing that he had sent Tara and Swinkle to that very same location. Kymbra shoved Harrison, breaking his train of thought.

"Keep moving!" yelled the female warrior. "That monster's coming back fast!"

The young warrior gazed upwards again, finding the dragon hurtling toward their position. Harrison swallowed hard as the beast reared back its heads, getting ready to spew flames from both mouths. Without warning, a majestic eagle flew over their position and headed toward the incoming projectile. With a screech of its own, the bird of prey swooped at one of the heads, distracting it just enough to force the monster off course.

Harrison pointed into the sky. "It's Fallyn!"

Kymbra continued pushing the young warrior, encouraging him to move. "We need to go! Fallyn's giving us time to flee!"

"Where's Gelderand and Allard?" asked Harrison, swiveling his head. "We must find them, too!"

Kymbra scanned the area as well. "They're here somewhere!"

"Not a good enough answer!" said Harrison as bodies of all races continued to scramble. Catching Murdock and Pondle's eye, he exclaimed, "Fan out and find the mages, then head for cover!"

The two men nodded once, then scattered in search of the magicians. Harrison grabbed Kymbra by the wrist. "You're with me!" The lithe warrior nodded once in affirmation as well.

The two fighters dodged fleeing Scynthians and roaming flames alike as they searched for the missing magic men. A high pitched screech halted their search, both gazing upward to locate the source of the horrifying sound. The dragon, momentarily pausing its attack run, snapped at the eagle with one of its long necks. The bird eluded the monster's attack, looping around its massive jaws and zipping over the top of its other head.

The eagle's antics further infuriated the two-headed monster, sending it into a frenzy. Though the beast was immense, it made several aerial maneuvers that allowed it to keep pace with the smaller winged animal. The eagle, sensing a change in the dragon's fighting tactics straightened its trajectory before diving toward the earth. The flying beast chased the feathered creature, mimicking its maneuvers to perfection.

Harrison followed the aerial show with grave concern, knowing that Fallyn had her limitations while in animal form. "Kymbra!" shouted the young warrior, pointing to the chase scene. "Fallyn needs our help first!"

The blonde warrior scrunched her brow and shook her head. Flashing the Aegean an incredulous look, she said with a shrug, "What do expect us to do against that thing?"

The young warrior stared at the eagle, losing ground to the dragon with every passing second. The bird of prey slowed its descent before landing on the ground hard, taking a tumble fifty yards away from Harrison's position. In one smooth motion, the eagle transformed into a familiar female figure, the auburn-haired woman swiveling her head in a panic, trying to get a read on her surroundings.

"Fallyn!" called Harrison at the top of his lungs.

The woman heard her name, finding the young warrior frantically waving her over. Fallyn had just started her sprint when she felt the ground behind her shake. Jerking her head back, she found the massive beast right behind her.

"Harrison!" screamed the panic-stricken woman.

The young warrior heard the plea for help, but froze instead. One of the monster's necks lurched forward, snatching the hysterical woman in its jaws, lifting her high into the air. The dragon bit down with a disgusting crunch, taking Fallyn into its mouth and swallowing her whole.

"Fallyn!" cried Harrison, horror stricken at the woman's horrendous death. However, he had no time to mourn Fallyn's loss for the dragon's other neck rose high and stared directly at the young warrior.

Harrison locked eyes with the beast, standing no more than fifty yards away. A moment later he felt his head start to warm, then an odd sensation, as if something other than himself tried to manipulate his thoughts. Recalling his mind control training at the Fighter's Guild, the Aegean recognized the mental attack that the monster had employed, similar to the one the swamp creature had used during their encounter while searching for the Treasure of the Land.

Harrison strained to break the beast's grip, using all the mental power he could muster to visualize cutting an invisible rope that tethered him to the dragon. As each second ticked by, he imagined severing the thread one strand at a time. After a minute of intense concentration, the young warrior felt the imaginary cord snap. The link between the two broken, Harrison reeled backwards to the ground, covered in sweat.

The dragon, though temporarily defeated, did not end its pursuit. Enraged once again, the beast bellowed out its chest, drawing in vast quantities of air, then spewed a cone of flames in the young warrior's direction. Harrison dropped to the ground, allowing the monster's attack to blast overhead, as the vegetation around him sparked and burned, the temperature taking a dramatic turn upwards. Screams and wails of agony erupted all around him, along with fires and fanning flames.

Harrison patted his armor coverings, extinguishing small fires that had ignited his clothing. The monster, satisfied with scorching the vicinity, turned its attention to the woodlands, shrieking yet again.

The young warrior scrambled from the immediate danger, sidestepping burning pockets of brush, his eyes wide in shock. His breathing coming in ragged breaths, he scanned the area for the person who had stood closest to him only moments ago.

"Kymbra!" he shouted, swiveling from side to side, trying not to fall into an irreversible panic. "Kymbra!"

Something ran toward him through the smoke and orangey haze of the landscape. "Help me!" yelled the woman, fire burning her clothing and exposed skin.

Harrison recognized Kymbra and sprinted to her. The woman had felt the brunt of the dragon's fury, the attack scorching her whole being. The young warrior grabbed the injured person and dropped her to the ground, rolling her wherever he could find a patch of earth not set ablaze, extinguishing any remaining fires. Her body no longer burning, Harrison held the woman in his arms and stared at her with concerned eyes.

"Kymbra," said the young warrior, swallowing hard. "Are you alright?"

The dragon's attack had damaged the blonde warrior's body. Her once white pigment now appeared black and charred, with cuts and abrasions littering her exposed skin.

Kymbra opened her mouth to speak. "No, I'm not," she said in a shallow whisper, closing her eyes.

Harrison lightly shook the fighter. "Kymbra, stay with me!" he shouted. His actions worked, the woman lifting her heavy lids.

"I'm going to get you to safety and have Swinkle heal you," said the young warrior. Kymbra nodded, then closed her eyes again.

The Aegean lifted the woman to her feet, throwing one of her arms around his shoulder in order to assist in moving the warrior forward. A hellish screech stopped the two in their tracks.

Harrison gazed skyward, but saw nothing in the ever-thickening smoky haze. Confused, he tried to hone in on the sound again. Just as before, he heard a shriek, however it did not come from the dragon that had just torched the area, rather this sound emanated from the opposite direction and it grew louder.

The young warrior's heart sank when several massive shadows flew overhead. "Reinforcements," said the Aegean in disbelief, realizing that their harrowing predicament had taken a turn for the worse.

"What did you see?" whispered Kymbra, her eyes still closed.

"The remaining dragons from King Holleris' army," said the young warrior before noticing something odd with Kymbra. "The cuts on your arm," he said, shaking his head. "And your face!"

Kymbra rolled her head to meet Harrison's gaze. "What are you talking about?"

"Your body's healing!" Harrison's mind raced in thought, recalling something that Brianna had told him after their adventure in Rovere Moro. "The troll's blood! We're healing the way they do!"

"I am feeling a bit better," said the woman, starting to follow Harrison's rationale. "Little by little."

A low rumbling stopped their conversation, both people feeling the ground reverberate under their feet. "What's that?" asked Kymbra, her nerves beyond frayed.

"I have no idea," said Harrison, "but we need to get to a safe place." The young warrior restarted his trek toward the forest when an explosion ahead of him halted their procession.

The two fighters stared wide-eyed at the scene before them. Dragons, hovering in the air above the tree tops, spewed flames into the vegetation below, igniting everything in their path. Harrison's thoughts immediately shifted to Tara, knowing that he had ordered her and Swinkle into the same forest that the beasts' now attacked. Anxiety coursing through his veins, he plodded forward, determined to help his mate.

The ground continued to quake under his feet and a low rumble began to permeate the area. To his surprise, a thickening fog had started to envelope the battlefield, making things harder to see.

Kymbra pointed skyward at two of the dragons. "They're coming down."

Harrison took his eyes to the scene as well and, sure enough, two of the monsters had lowered to the ground. The young warrior strained to see through the fog and smoke, and as he did so, he sensed something amiss. Then, his eyes widened.

"Those dragons just lowered two people to the ground!" he exclaimed. "It's King Holleris and Finius Boulware!"

Kymbra, her wounds healing, removed her arm from around Harrison's shoulder and gazed into the distance. She, too, saw the massive beasts guarding two smaller figures.

"I think you're right!" she exclaimed. "We need to stop them!"

Harrison pointed away from where the dragons had dropped their cargo. "That way," he said. "Away from the heat's intensity. We'll loop around and hopefully regroup with our friends." Kymbra nodded, accepting the young warrior's plan.

With the fog getting thicker, the two warriors headed on their new path. The Aegean banked on entering the forest, which loomed two hundred yards away, and finding their friends close by. Harrison's thought process changed when the first horse raced ahead of them.

The low rumble that had consumed the landscape before turned into a stampede of armed horsemen. Harrison recognized the burgundy and gold markings, as well as the lances held in the riders' hands.

"The Arcadians are here!" exclaimed the young warrior, welcoming the additional reinforcements. The horsemen galloped by, avoiding burning vegetation, and creating a perimeter along the forest's edge.

"We still need to take cover," said Kymbra, concerned with the added chaos the Arcadians had created, as well as the mysterious thickening fog.

Harrison agreed, doing his best to bypass the reinforcements and navigate to the woodlands. The two ventured through the haze, reaching the outskirts of the forest. Before entering, the young warrior turned back to gauge his surroundings. Squinting, he managed to see one horseman in particular prancing back and forth in front of the rest of the stationary riders, barking out commands.

513

"Bracken Drake is here!" said Harrison with a smile.

Kymbra leered in the same direction, coming to the same conclusion. "I'll take that as a good sign," said the woman. The warrior stretched her aching muscles, then said, "I'll getting better by the second."

Harrison nodded. "That's a very good thing." Pointing to the cover of the trees, he said, "Let's head that way."

The two fighters left the fiery countryside behind and began their trek to regroup with their friends. Harrison's brain churned with a myriad of scenarios, but one thought rose above all others. *I must find Tara and make sure that she's safe.*

CHAPTER 44

 Q

Harrison and Kymbra entered the forest, the dragons' devastating attacks creating an eerie orange glow that spread throughout the area. To make matters worse, the fog that had enveloped the battlefield began to roll into the woods, making it harder to see.

Kymbra, who had sustained serious burn wounds only a few moments ago, stopped the young warrior. "Harrison, look at me!"

The Aegean took a moment to inspect the blonde warrior, his eyes riveted on her wounds. "Your injuries are nearly healed!"

"I feel so much better," said the lithe warrior, hardly containing her smile. "I guess those trolls almost killing me wasn't such a bad thing after all."

"I suppose," said Harrison before taking his gaze all about the area, looking for any points of reference. "This haze is getting too thick to see anything."

"Thoragaard's here," said Kymbra, confident. "He made this fog."

The young warrior cocked his head. "He's here?"

"Look around you," said the woman. "This isn't natural."

"If he's here from Concur, then there's a good chance Brendan, the Forge brothers, and the Unified Army are close behind."

"We already saw the Arcadians," said Kymbra. "It would only make sense."

Harrison nodded, his brain churning in thought. "We need to regroup with the others and form a new strategy." A deafening crash more than startled the two as a monstrous tree fell to the earth, flames erupting all around them.

The young warrior grabbed Kymbra's arm, leading her away from the fallen tree. Pointing toward the forest's depths, he said, "That way!"

The two sprinted from their position, running as far away from the sprouting fires as possible. The young warrior did his best to gauge his situation but the increasing fog and smoky haze made that task almost impossible. Shadows of beings crisscrossing the landscape only added to the confusion.

Several large forms in the distance grabbed Harrison's attention. "Scynthians," he said in Kymbra's direction.

"They're still on our side until those dragons are dead, right?" asked the lithe warrior, a bit of concern in her voice.

"That was the deal," answered Harrison, scanning the vicinity, recognizing the remnants of the former Scynthian encampment.

The warriors took a few steps further into the forest before Harrison stopped in his tracks. The young warrior held up his hand, halting Kymbra's forward progress. Cocking his head, he strained to hone in on something only he seemed hear.

"What is it?" asked Kymbra, her heart pounding.

The sound of a dog barking brought a wide smile to the young warrior's face. "It's Lance!"

"Where is he?" The blonde warrior surveyed the landscape, seeing no sign of the canine.

"Don't use your eyes," said Harrison, "use your ears." The young warrior did just that, doing his best to pinpoint the dog's location.

Honing in on Lance's yelps, he pointed in front of him and said, "That way."

The two fighters traversed the forest, steering clear of flames and burning underbrush, all the while homing in on Lance. The little dog continued his call, leading the two to his position.

Sensing that the animal was very close to their location, Harrison yelled, "Lance!" The canine's barking ceased. The young warrior gazed back at Kymbra, giving her a look of concern. "Lance!" called Harrison again.

A welcome, familiar figure bounded out of the haze. "Lance!" cried Harrison, dropping to one knee to greet his canine friend. The little dog jumped at his master, licking Harrison's face with excitement.

"I'm glad to see you, too, boy," said the young warrior, then his demeanor turned serious. "Where are Tara and Swinkle?"

Lance took two steps away from the couple, yapping, "Follow!"

Harrison turned to Kymbra and said, "Follow him!"

Lance darted off into the thick fog, Harrison and Kymbra following close behind. The little dog weaved through the underbrush, stopping several times to make sure his human masters did not get lost. Several minutes later, the Aegean saw a shadowy figure milling around a large oak tree.

"Here!" yapped the excited animal, darting between the figure, Harrison, and Kymbra.

"Harrison? Is that you?" came a voice through the haze.

"Swinkle?" called the young warrior, straining to see his friend.

"It is I!" said the young cleric, genuinely happy to see his friend again. "Follow us!"

Harrison and Kymbra chased after Swinkle and Lance, circling around the massive trunk to reach the other side. The person sitting against the tree almost took Harrison's breath away.

"Tara!" said the young warrior, his heart full of joy.

The young maiden gazed up from her seat on the ground. "Harrison," she said in a shallow voice, maintaining her seated position, unable to rise.

Concern over the girl's wellbeing overtook Harrison. "Tara, are you alright?"

"The knock on her head has made her more woozy than anticipated," said Swinkle. "I have been administering herbs and giving her plenty of water."

The young warrior bent to Tara's level. Raising her frail body, Harrison held her close. "We're going to take care of you," he said in a loving tone.

Tara smiled weakly. "I know you will." She closed her eyes for a moment, before opening them again. "I knew you'd find me."

"I promised you that I would," said the young warrior. "I'll never leave you alone in this world." Tara smiled hearing those words.

"She needs to rest, Harrison," said Swinkle.

The young warrior nodded, placing the young girl down again. Tara closed her eyes and curled in a ball. Lance scooted to her side and laid next to her.

Harrison stepped away and, in a low voice, asked Swinkle, "Will she be alright?"

The young cleric shrugged. "I believe so but time will tell. This landscape is not the best place for a person in her condition."

"Where's everybody else?" asked Kymbra, noticing that none of their friends were in the vicinity.

Swinkle shook his head. "I don't know."

Harrison grimaced. The battlefield had taken on an unexpected dynamic with the thick fog making visibility nearly zero, which only added to the confusion.

"We need to find our people and make a new plan," said the young warrior. "The sooner we confront King Holleris and his warlock, the faster we can end all of this."

"What do you propose?" asked Kymbra, shaking her head in exasperation. "No one can see a thing with this smoke and fog."

"Our other senses need to come to the forefront," said Harrison. Bending down, he looked into Lance's eyes and said, "Lead us to Murdock and Pondle." The little dog jumped to his feet, yapping once in affirmation, his tail wagging at a feverish rate.

Kymbra cocked her head and raised an eyebrow. "You're counting on the dog finding them in this mess?" she said, crossing her arms across her chest.

"His sense of smell is better than our eyesight right now," said Harrison. "He'll find them."

"What about us?" asked Swinkle with concern. "We are very vulnerable here."

Harrison longed to stay close to the young maiden, wishing to be her personal protector and to take her away from this hideous scene; however, he also understood his leadership role in the war.

The young warrior gazed at his love laying on the ground. With a heavy heart, he said, "Take cover and tend to Tara. I'll find you when this is all over."

"How?" asked the young cleric, spreading his arms wide. "We are in the middle of the woods without any identifying markings!"

Harrison panned the vicinity, finding nothing out of the ordinary that would clue him to their whereabouts. Still deep in thought, he went over to Tara, bending on one knee next to her. Swinkle had healed the gash on her forehead but her internal pain remained. The young warrior brushed a lock of hair from her face, causing her to stir.

Gazing at Swinkle from his position, he reiterated, "I'll find you." The young cleric pursed his lips and nodded, accepting the fact that the circumstances were less than optimal and his friend's conviction was all he could count on at this time.

"Be careful, Harrison," said the young cleric.

"Stay hidden and keep her safe." With an audible sigh, the young warrior rose to his feet before commanding Lance, "Go find Murdock and Pondle!"

The canine barked once, then lowered his snout to the ground, sniffing for a scent. Harrison stared at Swinkle, then nodded once before going after the little dog.

"I believe him," said Kymbra. "We'll be back." The blonde warrior then turned and left the two young people behind.

As they left, Swinkle prayed to Pious, then said aloud, "Good luck, my friend."

* * *

Lance continued pressing his nose to the ground, searching for their elusive friends. Harrison and Kymbra followed close behind Lance, keeping clear of burning embers while trying to navigate through the foggy woods.

The young warrior scanned the general area. Burning trees created ghoulish shadows throughout the forest, their outlines forming black, spindly streaks on an otherwise orangey canvas. Figures darted in all directions, Scynthians running amuck in chaos. Harrison, with no clear direction, noticed several creatures ahead of them, their weapons drawn.

Glancing back at Kymbra, he said, "Three Scynthians up ahead. Follow my lead."

The young warrior, holding his battle axe in an attack position, called to the beasts. "Hey! Where are your leaders?"

The startled warriors glared at the approaching humans, raising their weapons. The trekking people halted upon seeing the Scynthians' actions, as did Lance.

Harrison motioned for Kymbra to stay put, then lowered his battle axe and took purposeful steps toward the Scynthian warriors. Thrusting an open palm at the beasts, he exclaimed, "Relax and listen to me!" Befuddled by the human's order, the creatures dropped their weapons by their side as well.

Having garnered the warriors' attention, Harrison asked again, "Where's your commander? Nigel Hammer?"

After hesitating for a moment, one of the warriors barked, "Lost! All of us are on our own!"

The young warrior shook his head. "What were your last orders?"

"Kill the dragons!" said another of the fighters.

"You can't do that alone," said Harrison. "There must be a plan to regroup if you got separated."

The three Scynthians glanced from side to side. "Can't find anyone! We're supposed to meet away from our original camp."

"Do you know where that is?"

One of the Scynthians pointed to his right, which led deeper into the forest but closer to the raging inferno. "That way!"

Harrison stared in the direction the Scynthian pointed. "Who ordered this command?"

"Human like you," said the first Scynthian.

Harrison waved Kymbra over, the female warrior stepping by his side. Raising his own weapon, he said to the savages, "Lead us all that way. This chaos ends now!"

After exchanging glances, the three Scynthians gestured for the humans to follow. Before trailing their new leaders, Harrison peeked back at Kymbra, recognizing her look of concern at following the three creatures. Lance bolted next to his master, keeping pace with the sprinting humans.

The Scynthians led the trio deeper into the forest, sidestepping glowing embers and ever increasing flames. The thickening fog coupled with hideous shrieks in the distance did nothing to allay their already frayed nerves. As before, shadowy figures of all races darted through the underbrush. After several minutes of harried trekking, the unusual party came to a halt.

One of the Scynthians pointed ahead of them. "There they are!"

Harrison squinted, smoke stinging his eyes. A short distance away he found many more Scynthian warriors congregating in the area, weapons drawn and awaiting orders.

"I don't see Nigel Hammer," said Kymbra, sidling up to Harrison.

"Neither do I," said the young warrior, scouring the area for a familiar face. Taking the lead, he said, "Stay close to me."

Harrison walked past the Scynthians, gesturing with his head for them to follow as well. The Aegean headed in the direction of an orange glow inside the Scynthian's area, the forest in the distance ablaze.

The young warrior panned the camp, finding half-empty carts, excess metal that they had used for the hook and chain links, extinguished camp fires, and various weaponry and armor.

"Looks like they left everything and ran," said Kymbra, panning the scene as well.

Harrison pointed at a large Scynthian ahead of them. "That's Rashaa. We need to speak with him." The two left their Scynthian sentries behind and approached their leader.

Rashaa, fully aware of the situation before him, barked new battle orders to any of his comrades within shouting distance. Harrison maintained a firm grip on his battle axe, always wary of their fragile alliance. The burly creature thrust his gauntlet-covered hand in the opposite direction, hurling commands to whoever was left of his troops.

Swiveling his head right at the young warrior, the Scynthian leader made eye contact with the humans, then took purposeful steps toward them. Pointing at the Aegean, he said with a snarl, "You're still alive!"

"Yes, we are," answered Harrison. Taking the tone of an ally leader, he said, "What's the status of your army?"

Rashaa spread his arms wide. "Engaged in battle!" A massive explosion in the distance forced the three beings to cower. Regaining their composure, the Scynthian exclaimed, "Two dragons dead!"

"Seven more to slaughter," responded Harrison. "What are your orders?"

"Your general says fight to the death," said Rashaa. "We will vanquish those that destroyed Mahalanobis!"

The Scynthian's statement curbed the young warrior's anxiety about this brutal race's commitment to battle. "Where's Lord Hammer now?"

Rashaa gazed about the vicinity, appearing disoriented with the hazy environment. "Hard to say," said the commander. "Don't know the last time I saw him."

Harrison nodded, accepting the fact that the chaos has rippled through warriors of all creeds. "Continue with the battle," said the young warrior. "A new plan will be forthcoming." Rashaa gave the Aegean a curt nod, then went about searching for more of his troops.

The young warrior brought his attention to Lance. "Find our friends, boy!" The little dog yapped once, then stuck his nose to the ground again in earnest.

Harrison and Kymbra followed Lance deeper into the forest, this time looping away from the action. "This is a good sign," said the young warrior.

"How so?" asked Kymbra. "We're getting further and further away from the battle."

"Murdock and Pondle know we need a safe perimeter to regroup," said Harrison. Just as he finished his statement, Lance barked once, then sprinted forward toward thick underbrush.

Harrison watched as the canine dashed into the thickets, reappearing with a bark and his tail wagging. The two warriors rushed to the dog's position.

"What did you find, boy?" asked Harrison with great anticipation.

Before Lance barked again, a voice called out to the two, "Keep that dog quiet!" Murdock spread apart the vegetation, agitated as usual. "Get back here now!"

Harrison and Kymbra waded through the thickets with Lance in tow. Reaching the other side of the undergrowth, the two warriors found several familiar faces staring back at them.

"Glad to see everyone's still alive," said Harrison, as Murdock, Pondle, Gelderand, and Allard peered back at the young warrior.

"Where's Tara?" asked Gelderand with concern.

"I found her with Swinkle," said Harrison, allaying her uncle's fears. "They're hidden away in this forest, hopefully out of sight."

"Is she alright?" pressed the mage, knowing that she had sustained an injury while trying to escape the chaos in the countryside.

"Swinkle's attending to her head wound," said the young warrior. "She needs to rest, which is what she's doing now."

"In this environment?" said Murdock, taking his gaze around the hazy woodlands. "I hope you tucked her away well."

Harrison had hoped the same thing when he left her and Swinkle behind. "She's as safe as she's going to be."

"How about Fallyn?" asked Gelderand. "No one has seen her in a while."

The young warrior hung his head, her gruesome death playing out in his mind again. "One of the dragons killed her. She's gone." All the men averted their eyes, allowing the fact that one of their group had perished to sink in.

"If it wasn't for Fallyn's efforts, we wouldn't be here today," said Harrison. "Those of us injured at the trolls' hands probably would've gotten sick and maybe even had died. She was an important member of our team and is going to be missed."

Changing the subject, he panned the small group and asked, "What do you make of the battle scene?"

"Pure chaos," said Pondle. Pointing into the forest's depths, he added, "We moved away from the action once the dragons arrived. They're going to destroy everything."

"Did anyone see Holleris or Finius Boulware?" asked the young warrior.

"Not after they descended from their dragon escorts," said Murdock. "Those beasts started torching the landscape."

"How about the elves?" pressed Harrison. "They retreated back into the woods as well."

Murdock shrugged. "I'm sure they're around, as well as the Scynthians."

Harrison nodded, then asked, "Nigel?"

"Controlling the Scynthians," said Allard. "However, his patience will run thin very soon if the battle turns sour."

"It already has," retorted the ranger. "I wouldn't count on him at this point, not that I ever did."

"Be that as it may," said Harrison, "we must regroup or take on King Holleris and his army alone."

"What are we going to do against those dragons?" said Murdock, spreading his arms wide. "We'll never get close to them."

Harrison nodded in concurrence. "I know we can't defeat them, but we need to get back in the action."

"I told him that Thoragaard's here," added Kymbra to the conversation. "That means the Unified Army is close by."

"And we saw the Arcadians setting up a perimeter in the countryside," added Harrison.

Murdock furrowed his brow, nodding. "That changes things."

"I had a feeling this foggy haze wasn't natural," said Pondle. "I can lead us toward the battlefield."

Harrison did not have to think hard about their next course of action. "Let's do it. No use waiting around for something to happen, and I have assurances that the Scynthians will fight to the death."

"Nigel Hammer and the Scynthians?" lamented Murdock, placing his hands on his hips, shaking his head. "Too many wildcards for me to feel secure in anything we do."

"Still, we must press forward, force the action," said Harrison. Gesturing to Pondle, he said, "Head us toward the battlefield."

The thief removed his small sword from its sheath, then waved it forward, signaling to the group for them to follow his lead. One by one, the fighters and mages headed out of the underbrush and into the awaiting landscape.

Gripping his battle axe tighter, Harrison stared at the forest's hazy inner depths and awaiting flames. The orangey backdrop littered with ghoulish shadows seemingly beckoned him to join the fray. The Aegean swallowed hard before advancing with his friends, knowing the next phase of their mission would most likely be the hardest battle of their lives.

CHAPTER 45

◻

Tara's head pounded even though Swinkle had prayed over her multiple times. Still asleep, the smell of smoke and burning underbrush filled her senses, fabricating dreams full of fire, rage, and colossal creatures.

Wake up, Tara! The young maiden stirred in her sleep, a soft yet forceful voice calling to her beyond images of scorched landscapes. *Rise, child!*

Tara stood just outside the burning forest in her dream, staring into its depths, searching for Harrison. A two-headed monster crashed through the woods, tearing down trees in its path, heading straight for the young girl. Tara's heart raced. She panned the vicinity, finding no place to hide in the grassy countryside. The monster lumbered out of the woodlands, then stared right at the young maiden. The beast raised its wings, lifting both necks, and expanding its chest.

With nowhere to run and no place to hide, the girl began to wail. "No!" she cried, tears streaming down her face. The dragon reared back both heads and opened its mouths but a figure appeared beside the lass before the monster could rain flames down upon her.

Tara turned her head and stared at the beautiful figure. "Brianna?"

The elven queen waved her hands in front of herself, directing an electric charge at the dragon. The bolts struck the monster, holding it in place, prohibiting the beast from spewing flames.

Keeping the creature at bay, Brianna brought her gaze to the young maiden. Using a soothing voice, the elven queen said, "Tara, you must find your inner strength and rise. Your role in all of this is about to come to fruition."

"What role?" asked the girl, her brow crinkled in confusion.

The dragon, still incapacitated, mustered the inner fortitude to roar. Brianna, sweat breaking on her brow, managed to keep the monster stationary, however it was gaining strength.

"Search for me!" exclaimed the elven queen, her powers weakening. "Before it's too late!" Widening her eyes, she screamed, "Wake up!"

Tara's eyes flew open and her breaths came in short bursts. Swinkle noticed the girl's antics and rushed to her side.

"Tara? Is everything alright?" asked the concerned cleric. "Did you have a nightmare?"

The young maiden, her blonde hair matted to her forehead with sweat, gazed past Swinkle, then reached for the ground in an effort to get up.

"Why don't you settle down before you do anything strenuous," said the young cleric, lightly gripping her forearms, trying to get her to relax.

"We have to find Harrison!" exclaimed Tara, her eyes darting as if her love were just out of view. She jerked her head and stared at Swinkle, all the while panting to catch her breath. "We need to find Brianna, too!"

Swinkle did his best to keep his composure, figuring that the young girl's head wound had become more serious. In a calming tone, he said, "You just had a nightmare. Let's try to relax."

Tara jumped to her feet. "No! I need to join the action! I must find Harrison and Brianna!"

Swinkle rose to a standing position as well. "Hold on, Tara! Harrison ordered me to remain with you."

Tara nodded once. "That he did. Follow me and I promise we'll stay together." The young maiden methodically collected her belongings and, when finished, began her trek deeper into the woods and toward the awaiting flames.

"That's not what he meant!" lamented Swinkle.

Taking a phrase from her love, she said, "It's not open for discussion. Either come with me or stay behind."

Swinkle, sensing that Tara had already made up her mind and course of action, hung his head. Slumping his shoulders and admitting defeat, he said, "Allow me to gather my things."

"Make haste, Swinkle," said Tara with conviction in her eyes. "The time has come."

* * *

Harrison, with Lance running by his side, sprinted in the direction of the ever increasing flames. Just as he witnessed in Arcadia with the Scynthian uprising, King Holleris and his dragon army had decided to torch the area in hopes of flushing out their enemy. However, instead of waiting for his foe to find him, Harrison and the others took the initiative to force the action.

Murdock gestured to the young warrior from up ahead. Motioning toward the right, he said, "Lots of commotion that way."

The young warrior gazed in the direction the ranger had pointed. Smoldering vegetation and Thoragaard's fog only added to the confusion, making breathing and navigation through the woodlands a much more difficult chore for the group. Harrison hoped these same obstacles had a similar effect on the dragons.

Squinting to focus on the landscape before him, the Aegean began to understand what his friend had meant about increased activity. Large, monstrous shadows lumbered within the hazy fog, while bursts of flames and bright flashes illuminated the area.

"Are they all together?" asked Harrison, alluding to the dragon army.

"Hard to say," said the ranger. "We need to get closer."

"If we do, we risk those monsters seeing us," added Pondle, holding his ground, unsure of their next move.

Harrison's mind was set. "Keep moving forward. We need to regroup with everyone else."

Pondle pursed his lips, then waved the small group forward. Branches hung low, forcing the adventurers to duck in order to avoid walking into them. Harrison did not care for the haze, its thickness a hindrance in observing his enemy. The young warrior knew the ramifications of their current predicament. King Holleris and his dragons did nothing to give away their position, rather they seemed to beckon them to their location, which worried Harrison the most.

"Harrison," said Gelderand in a cautious tone. "Tread very carefully."

"What do you think they're doing?" asked the young warrior, keeping his eyes fixed on the flashes.

"Holleris believes he has the upper hand," said the mage. "And he probably does."

"He's overconfident," said Harrison, not willing to admit defeat just yet.

"The king does have seven dragons," added the magician. "I would be overoptimistic as well." Thunderous steps stopped everyone in their tracks.

The young warrior's eyes widened in horror. A hideous shriek permeated the area, then a cone of flames whooshed through the surrounding trees. Everyone ducked for cover as the woods around them ignited. Harrison tried to regain his senses but a second volley of fire torched the underbrush, scattering the young warrior's team again.

Harrison fell to the ground, landing on all fours, trying to compose himself. Lance darted to his position, shaking. The young warrior focused on the small dog, sensing his canine companion's terrified state.

"Lance, go find Tara, stay with her!" he ordered. The animal cocked his head, unsure if he should leave his master in such a perilous time. Another screech more than startled the two.

"Go now, boy!" ordered Harrison again. Lance whimpered, then scooted away from the chaos to start his new mission.

Somewhat relieved that Lance had gone off to protect his love, the young warrior went back to the task at hand. Gathering his bearings, he saw the rest of his friends moving in the underbrush and dashed to their position.

Through heavy breaths the young warrior said to Murdock, "I sent Lance to find Tara."

"Good call," said the ranger, the thickets hindering his analysis of the area. "He'd be a liability in this mess."

"What are we going to do now?" asked Kymbra, watching the group's backside, hoping to thwart any attempt at a surprise attack.

Harrison's brain churned with battle strategies. "We need to find out just what Holleris is up to," said the young warrior. "And steer clear of these beasts."

"Easier said than done," said Pondle, pointing into the forest. "Those dragons are everywhere." A horn blaring in the distance gained their attention.

"What was that?" asked Kymbra, her eyes wide. "The Scynthians?"

"No," said Harrison, a wide smile spreading across his face. "That's Brendan and the Unified Army!"

"Where are they?" asked the blonde warrior, panning the vicinity for the hidden troops.

The young warrior scoured the area as well. "I can't get a read on their position with all the commotion." A second burst helped the group hone in on their whereabouts.

Pondle pointed into the woodlands to his right. "It came from that way! Follow me!"

The thief led the small platoon away from the dragons and deeper into the forest before gesturing toward matted vegetation. "They're over there!"

Harrison rushed through the smoky underbrush, navigating his course as best he could under the circumstances. The emergence of human soldiers stopped him in his tracks. The young warrior, weapon firmly in hand, watched as wave after wave of fighters ran past. Several short horn bursts, along with explosions, added to the chaos.

Two soldiers from the Unified Army headed for the young warrior. Harrison thrust his hand in their direction, forcing them to stop. "Who's the commander?" exclaimed the Aegean.

"Generals Brigade and Forge," shouted one of the men. "They're back that way!" The warrior pointed behind his position.

530

Harrison nodded, then said, "Go!" The two fighters restarted their task, running off in the opposite direction. Meanwhile, the young warrior regrouped with his team.

Finding Pondle ahead of him, he pointed and yelled, "Brendan's that way!" The small platoon raced from their position until they found more familiar soldiers. Another explosion, followed by high-pitched shrieks kept the team focused.

A short distance away, Harrison recognized a warrior barking orders to his men through the haze. "Brendan!" exclaimed the young warrior, taking the lead and running to his leader.

The elder Aegean warrior swiveled upon hearing his name, then focused on the person advancing toward him. Widening his eyes in recognition, the leader said, "Harrison! Thank the gods you're alive!" Gazing past the young warrior to his adventurer friends, he added, "All of you!"

"I guess Thoragaard got you our message," said Harrison.

"He did and he's here with us," said Brendan. "Good thing he arrived when he did or these monsters would have advanced on the coastal cities."

"At least we helped stop their progress," said the young warrior. Harrison noticed Brendan grimace. "What is it?"

The elder Aegean's expression turned dour. "Several of these beasts destroyed Argos," started the warrior. "They burned the city to the ground."

Harrison's heart sank. "What happened to the people?"

Brendan shook his head, taking a moment to reflect on the awful day. "Many people died, Harrison, including Caidan Forge."

The young warrior's shoulders slumped, as if someone dropped a heavy weight on them. "What about Octavius?"

The elder Aegean pointed his sword toward the burning forest. "He's out there, leading whatever's left of the Argosian army. He's become a man possessed."

Harrison recalled the pain of losing his own brother and could relate to the elder Forge's mental state at this time. "He's seeking vengeance."

Brendan nodded. "I hope it just doesn't get him killed." Regaining his focus, the general added, "Remember all the battle strategies we taught you at the Fighter's Guild? Well, throw them out. This battlefront is nothing like we've ever seen."

Harrison understood the gravity of the situation. Ever since he and his friends fled back into the forest to avoid the dragon's fiery attacks, they had become mostly disoriented between the mysterious fog and smoky atmosphere.

"Where exactly are we?" asked the young warrior.

"Closer to the countryside than you think," started the elder Aegean. "Octavius and I led the Unified Army into the woodlands from the plains while Bracken Drake has encircled the woods with his troops."

"We saw them just before we entered the forest as well," said the young warrior. "And, believe it or not, Nigel Hammer is leading the Scynthian army." A large explosion stopped his train of thought.

Gazing about the area, Harrison asked, "The dragons are close by. How's the army holding up?"

Brendan shook his head. "We're losing, Harrison. Numbers are on our side, but these monsters are too massive." More blasts erupted in the immediate area and, afterwards, moans and screams of agony. "They're torching the forest and hitting us with projectiles."

"Have you determined their strategy?" asked the young warrior, hopeful for any kind of clarity.

"It feels like they want an epic battle," said the elder warrior. "To settle the score once and for all."

"We were able to destroy two of the beasts," said Harrison. "After that, everything went to hell."

"Appropriate metaphor," said Brendan, taking his gaze around a landscape that resembled more of a netherworld than a serene forest. "Our best bet is to surround them somehow, get them all together."

"Can we accomplish that?" asked Harrison, his brow furrowed with concern.

"No idea, but it's our only hope." Flames erupted in the forest several hundred yards from their position. "I don't care for these flare-ups either."

Harrison looked in the direction of the new disturbance, realizing something. "King Holleris has seven fire-breathing dragons. Why hasn't he commanded them to burn the whole place down?"

Brendan nodded, acknowledging the young warrior's assessment of the battle scene. "That's what I would have done if I wanted to vanquish my adversaries in one fell swoop. Why he hasn't done this is disturbing."

The young warrior stared at the latest explosion, deep in thought before a chilling scenario entered his mind. Maintaining his gaze on the burning trees, he said with calmness, "He wants to watch us die."

The elder warrior creased his brow. "That makes no sense. Tactically, he's setting himself up for unnecessary conflict."

Allard stepped forward, pointing at Harrison. "He's right," said the mage, "this man is a lunatic with a killer army. I believe he thinks he's invincible."

Brendan, mildly surprised to see a onetime adversary in Harrison's group, absorbed the new information. "Intriguing premise," said the Aegean. "How do we exploit his overconfidence?"

"We need to hurt his creatures," added Gelderand. "Injure one, weaken them all."

"Not an easy task," said Brendan with a shake of his head. "What do you propose we do?"

Gelderand gazed over to Allard. "If we," the magician pointed to his fellow mage, "can hit one of them with our own projectiles, that should distract it enough for a subsequent attack."

"Which would be?" asked the warrior leader, raising his eyebrows high on his forehead.

"That's where your men come in," said Allard. "There's only so much we two can do."

Brendan brought a hand to his chin, thinking. "The elves have a weapon." The Aegean smiled. "Time for them to use it."

* * *

"Tara!" shouted Swinkle, not happy with the young girl's unfettered adventurer spirit. "Slow down!"

"Time is of the essence, Swinkle!" responded the young maiden, wading through the haze and underbrush.

"Rushing to our death will not help Harrison!" exclaimed the young cleric through ragged breaths. The two youngsters had ventured in the direction of the ensuing chaos, much to Swinkle's chagrin.

Tara had no intention of listening to Swinkle's advice; however, rustling in the bushes stopped the girl in her tracks. She raised a palm toward the holy man, signaling for him to stop, then hunched over in an effort to conceal herself.

The young cleric heeded her call, bending down, too. Whispering, he said, "What do you think you're doing?"

Tara stared at the moving bush, sure that something behind it had caused it to sway, then leaned a bit closer to get a better understanding of what might lie on the other side. A little dog burst through the shrubbery, jumping at the girl with joy.

The young maiden toppled over, surprised at the canine's antics. Swinkle rushed to her side, helping Tara regain her senses. "Lance!" cried Tara as she scrambled to her feet. "You scared the living daylights out of me!"

The small dog hopped around, circling the two, all the while yipping with excitement. "Where's Harrison?" asked Swinkle, trying to get the dog to focus. Instead, the animal held his ground and barked once with force.

"What did he say?" asked Tara with round eyes, gazing at the young cleric.

"I don't know," said Swinkle. "Only Harrison can interpret his barks."

Tara kneeled down to the dog's level. Outstretching her hand, she said, "Come here, Lance." The dog obliged. "Take us to Harrison."

Lance held his ground and again let out one forceful bark. Swinkle placed his hands on his hips. "If I had to venture a guess, I would say Harrison told him to watch over us."

Tara huffed. "That's *exactly* what he told him!" Staring into the little dog's eyes, the young maiden said, "We're pressing onward, no matter what Harrison commanded you to do!"

Lance cocked his head and whimpered, coming to the realization that his mission would not be a success. The animal then glared at the underbrush behind them, sensing something out of the ordinary. The dog took two steps forward, growling.

"What's the matter?" asked Swinkle, his anxiety rising.

"I don't know," responded Tara, her worries surfacing as well. "Should we inspect the area?"

Swinkle swallowed hard. "I suppose so. Follow me."

The two stepped past Lance, who followed to walk side by side with his masters. Swinkle did not hear anything, but the relative stillness of the area caused him concern. Through the smoke and haze, he thought he saw something move.

Pointing ahead, he said, "Did you see that?"

Tara shook her head. "See what?" Seconds later they saw several armed figures milling about the vicinity. "Soldiers!"

The young cleric took hold of Tara's forearm, stopping their procession. "They're Scynthians, we better tread carefully."

Tara swallowed hard as well, understanding that the Scynthians were fighting with them but also recalling that Harrison had referred to the race as brutal savages countless times. More Scynthians poured into the general area, raising their concern level. However, the beings who followed the armored creatures piqued her interest.

"Swinkle, are those Scynthians a little shorter than usual?" asked the girl.

The young cleric focused on the new set of characters. "Yes, they are," he said before coming to a realization. "Wait a minute! Those are dwarves!"

Tara squinted, recognizing several members of the stubby race. Making a bold decision, she said, "I think we should come out from behind these bushes and show ourselves to them. They're on our side."

"That's a risky maneuver, Tara," said Swinkle, not sure of the lass's idea.

Several beings approaching from behind altered their plan. Five Scynthian warriors surrounded the humans, while Lance barked at the intruders. The little dog's antics alerted more creatures to their predicament.

A smaller being, with a huge axe in hand, stumbled through the thickets along with ten of his comrades who formed a semi-circle behind their leader. Seeing the frightened humans, he said, "What do we have here?"

Swinkle recognized the latest figure to the party. "Drogut, the dwarf king? Is that you?"

The dwarf acknowledged the young cleric's statement with a single nod. "You're one of the people with Harrison, aren't you?"

"Yes," said the holy man. "My name is Swinkle. This is Tara." Swinkle gestured to the young maiden.

"I remember both of you," said Drogut. Extending his hand to another familiar member of his party, he said, "I think you remember my brother, Rogur." The second dwarf nodded when the king mentioned his name.

"Yes, we do," said Swinkle. Knitting his brow, he asked, "How did you end up here?"

"My people did not expect to enter the fray of this conflict so soon," started Drogut, "however extenuating circumstances have arisen." Lowering his weapon, he added, "We need to find Harrison immediately."

"Why is that?" asked Tara, her brow furrowed with concern.

"Someone needs to speak with him." Drogut turned and gestured toward his brother. Rogur peeled back the underbrush, allowing several larger figures to enter the arena.

Swinkle recognized the newest player. "Naa'il?" said the young cleric with surprise in his voice.

The juvenile Scynthian stepped forward. "You remember me?"

The holy man nodded. "That I do." Swinkle shook his head, confused. "Why are you here and traveling with the dwarves?"

"Our city destroyed," started Naa'il. "Dragons burned Mahalanobis. They must pay for their deeds."

The young cleric brought his eyes to Drogut. "Where do you come into the picture?" he asked, shaking his head.

"I sent a reconnaissance team outside our mountain home to get a better read on the world's situation," said the dwarf king. "They encountered the Scynthians, who in turn told them about the recent destruction of their homeland. After putting aside our differences, we decided to seek a common person, Harrison Cross."

"He's in this forest somewhere," said Tara, hopeful to find her love as well. "No one knows where he is."

"Must find him," said Naa'il. "He must see Alabaar's treasure."

Swinkle crinkled his brow, unfamiliar with the term. "What exactly is this treasure?"

The Scynthian shook his head. "Only for him to see."

"It's all part of this same game," interjected Drogut. "We've all been led to this common point."

"However, we're all still scattered," said Tara, spreading her arms wide. "And those monsters are lurking everywhere." Thunderous booms echoed throughout the forest, driving home the young maiden's point.

Drogut flashed a sly smile. "Their time is coming, lass, as is Finius Boulware's. Let's find Harrison and start their demise."

Tara gazed over to Swinkle, who shrugged, signaling to the young girl that they did not have much of a choice in the matter. The young maiden also felt a little more at ease, having armed soldiers to protect her instead of a weaponless cleric.

The young girl pointed at Lance. "He's the last one to see Harrison and not too long ago."

Drogut smiled. "Then get that pup back on his master's trail!"

Tara bent to one knee, getting to the dog's face. "Lance, find Harrison!"

The little dog glanced between the two humans, unsure of his actions. The young maiden ordered again, "Go! Find Harrison!"

Lance barked once, then placed his snout to the ground, embarking on yet another trip to find his master.

"Follow that dog!" ordered Drogut, as the mixed group of humans, dwarves, and Scynthians began their trek to reunite with Harrison and his team.

CHAPTER 46

ⵔ

Harrison and his friends pressed forward, along with Brendan Brigade and contingents of the Unified Army, trekking deeper into the forest and closer to the dragons' position. The young warrior's heart pounded, as Harrison did his best to keep his anxiety at bay. The forest continued to burn as it had throughout the long day, a blanket of smoke and fog enveloping the constricting area. To make matters worse, the Aegean gazed upwards, noticing that twilight would soon be approaching.

King Holleris' dragons wreaked havoc dangerously close to the young warrior's position, though he could not pinpoint their exact location. Harrison took in the scenery; however, all was not well. Pondle and Murdock trekked ahead of him, as Kymbra, Allard, and Gelderand took cautious steps from behind.

"What's your plan once we find the dragons?" asked Kymbra, breaking the silence.

"I need to get King Holleris to back down," answered the Aegean.

Kymbra shook her head. "He never will. Each step we take brings us closer to death."

"Not if I can help it," said the young warrior. Movement up ahead forced the small contingent to stop.

The blonde warrior stared at Harrison with round eyes. "What's happening?"

"The final battle's close at hand," said Harrison, a myriad of battle scenarios racing through his mind. "The time has come."

Unified soldiers raced past the small platoon, forming a large, elaborate semi-circle defense shield within the forest. Fighters shuffled throughout the woodlands, taking up positions behind trees, waiting for their next move.

Harrison waved Kymbra, Gelderand, and Allard forward as the young warrior sought to team with Murdock and Pondle again.

Reaching the two trackers, Harrison asked, "What do you think?" Everyone gazed in the direction of the dragon army as the forest grew dark around them.

Murdock shook his head. "I'm trying not to."

"Those monsters are about three hundred yards away and I'm sure King Holleris and Finius Boulware are with them somewhere," said Pondle, relaying his assessment.

"Why aren't they doing anything?" asked Kymbra, a hint of worry in her voice.

"They are waiting for us to make the first move," said Gelderand.

"Then we better really think this through," said Murdock. Staring at Harrison, he asked, "Now that Fallyn's gone, what's it going to be?"

The young warrior remained stoic, staring in the direction of his enemies. All his journeys, all his training, everything he lived for came down to this very moment. Harking back to his studies at the Fighter's Guild, he said, "We'll form a circular perimeter and surround them with our armies, leaving them with no escape route. After that's accomplished, I'll talk to King Holleris."

Murdock sidled up to his friend, placing a hand on his shoulder. "Harrison, those monsters can blow a hole through our defenses and we have nothing to stop them."

The young warrior maintained his focus into the woods before turning to the ranger and saying, "I know. It's a chance we have to take. There are really no other options."

Murdock, usually one to protest, understood the ramifications of the Aegean's plan. "They will kill you in an instant."

Harrison stared at Murdock without saying a word. After a brief moment of contemplation, he addressed his team. "Time to gather our forces and surround these beasts. There's no turning back now."

The young warrior gazed at the anxious faces that stared back at him. No one had any alternate strategy to offer. With reluctance, they all nodded and waited for their leader's next move.

"Let's find Brendan," said Harrison. "Time to get this engagement started."

Pondle waved the team forward, gesturing for them to follow his lead. The thief led the platoon through the underbrush, taking mere minutes to locate the Aegean leader. Pondle pointed into the forest's depths where soldiers maneuvered throughout the landscape.

Harrison took purposeful steps in the direction his friend had pointed, finding the field general barking orders and readying his troops. "Brendan," said Harrison, "I think there's a strategy we should employ."

"We already have one," said the Aegean leader. "We're going to wait these monsters out, get them to move, then have the elves attack them."

"I'm not sure I agree," said Harrison with confidence.

"Really? What did you have in mind?" said Brendan, raising an eyebrow.

"I must speak with King Holleris," said the young warrior. "I really believe that I can get him to change his mind."

Brendan shook his head. "Harrison, he'll discard you like a piece of trash. Your intentions are noble, but wrong."

A fire lit inside the young warrior's belly. "With all due respect, I believe *you're* wrong," responded Harrison. "Finding the Treasure of the Land, uncovering the Talisman, the quest to reunite humanity, this all didn't happen by chance. I was led to these things that culminate with whatever happens today. I believe it's my destiny."

The elder Aegean warrior looked away toward the impending confrontation, then refocused on Harrison. "You're a brave warrior, Harrison, and I don't want to lose you over this. King Holleris will never listen to you or anybody else."

"Then we just quit?" responded the young warrior, spreading his arms wide. "The king might unleash his creations at any moment. At least if I engage him it'll buy you some time so that you can determine a strategy to defeat his army. We haven't seen the elves' weapon yet and I have no idea if Naa'il is going to return in time with his gift for us, whatever that means. If we don't confront Holleris, all's lost anyway."

Brendan shook his head. "Since our options are limited, I'll go along with this plan. You need to keep him occupied for as long as you can. I'm going to send scouts to our factions throughout the forest and update them on our strategy."

Harrison nodded in concurrence. "Thank you, Brendan. I can do this."

The elder warrior extended his hand, the young warrior accepting. "Good luck, Harrison. I'm expecting to regroup with you after all this is done."

"As am I," said the young warrior. The two released their handshake and went their separate ways. Harrison took a moment, then went back to his team.

"What's the consensus?" asked Murdock.

"Brendan's forces are going to surround the area," started the young warrior. "Then I'm going to start a dialogue with King Holleris."

The ranger shook his head. "You really think you can change his mind?"

Harrison sported a blank expression. "At least I need to try."

Murdock drew a heavy sigh. "Then I suppose I have no choice than to join you."

Pondle had moved close enough to the two to overhear their conversation. "Don't think I'll let you two go it alone. Count me in."

"Me too," said Kymbra, stepping forward. "We've come this far. We need to see how this ends."

Harrison gazed over to the mages. "Gelderand, Allard," he said, as both men moved closer to the small group. "Position yourselves in the underbrush and get ready to attack."

Gelderand furrowed his brow. "Attack how?"

The young warrior flashed him a nervous smile. "You'll know what to do when the time comes." The magicians exchanged anxious glances, then nodded.

"How do you want to go about engaging Holleris?" asked Pondle. "Are you going to simply walk right into his camp?"

"That's kind of what I had in mind," said Harrison.

Murdock shook his head in disgust. "I hate this plan!"

"You said it yourself, what more can we really do?" said the young warrior. "Brendan's sentries are scouring the forest, relaying the plan to the Arcadians, Unified Army leaders, elves, and hopefully the Scynthian brigade. A great battle is readying. My actions will either prevent a lot of bloodshed or begin the carnage."

Murdock rested a hand on Harrison's shoulder. "How do you want this to go down?"

Harrison gazed into the forest, toward the menacing dragon army. "Follow me into the woods until we reach their position. Once we get there, fan out, seek cover, and wait for something to happen. You all will have to make your own decisions from there."

Murdock and Pondle locked eyes, neither one enamored with the Aegean's plan, but understanding what they must do. "I'll lead the way," said Pondle.

Harrison scanned the vicinity. Soldiers littered the landscape on either side of the men, as well as behind their position. The young warrior could only hope that just as many fighters surrounded the dragons on the other side of the perimeter. His heart pounding, the Aegean gestured for the thief to lead them forward.

As they had done so many times in the past, Murdock and Pondle ventured off before the group with Harrison, Kymbra, Gelderand, and Allard following close behind.

Underbrush branches trembled as if fearful of the dragons while the young warrior, deep in thought, marched toward the biggest meeting of his life. Up ahead, Pondle and Murdock halted their procession as Scynthian warriors flooded the area. Harrison gripped his battle axe tighter out of instinct, remembering his past bloody confrontations with the brutal race.

"Harrison," called a familiar voice. The young warrior's eyes darted in all directions searching for the unseen intruder. To his left, Nigel Hammer appeared out of thin air.

The black-clad warrior showed his hand, flashing a gold ring at the young warrior. "You really need to get yourself one of these things."

"Nigel!" exclaimed the Aegean, while his friends closed in around their one-time adversary. "I figured you would've left the forest by now."

Lord Hammer frowned, slipping the ring into a small pouch attached to his belt. "And miss all the fun? You think too little of me."

"Are you here to help?" asked the young warrior.

"The Scynthians are ready for a battle," said Nigel, waving his hand to the ensuing wilderness. Harrison brought his gaze to the woods, finding scores of anxious fighters, waiting for their next melee.

"What's your plan?" asked Lord Hammer, stepping closer to their inner circle.

"I'm going to speak with King Holleris and end this madness," said Harrison.

Nigel cocked his head. "A foolish strategy, but if anyone could pull this stunt off it would be you."

"Harrison, we don't need this now!" said Murdock, trying to keep his cool under the circumstances.

The former governor of Concur raised a gloved hand toward the ranger in hopes of silencing him. "Listen to me good," said Nigel, his eyes locked on Harrison's. "Say your piece to the king, but be wary of his words. He's a liar and he's in control of this situation. Trust your instincts."

Lord Hammer's words took Harrison by surprise. "You're giving me actual advice?"

Nigel stepped forward again. "I'm not making a ploy here. This is the end game, Harrison. Either you convince the king of your intentions or we all die." Lord Hammer paused, allowing his comment to sink in. "I've been in more battles than I can remember, but this one is the end all. Your heart is good, better than any of ours, but the king's evil is strong."

Harrison nodded, appreciating the warrior's words. "What are you going to do?"

Nigel panned the forest. "Get the Scynthians to attack at the right moment. They might be stupid, but they're relentless." The dark warrior extended his hand to the Aegean.

Harrison took it, the two former foes embarking in a firm handshake. "Thank you for sticking around so long."

Nigel nodded once, then fished the magical ring from his pouch. "This will be the last time you see me," he said with a sly smile before slipping the ring on his finger, disappearing from view. "Allard, we'll meet at the rendezvous point when this is all over."

All eyes swiveled to the dark mage, who gave a sheepish nod, not knowing where Nigel had gone. "Do you still have what we discussed in your possession?" asked the magician. No answer came.

"There are more important things to worry about now," said the young warrior, changing the subject, getting his team to refocus on the matter at hand. Just as the group began to concentrate on their upcoming meeting, the fog that had enveloped the forest began to thicken.

"Thoragaard's at it again," said Kymbra, darting her eyes left to right, taking in the new haze.

"He is doing what he feels gives us the best chance to defeat this dragon army," said Gelderand. "All of our pieces are in place. The time is now."

Harrison took his eyes to the vegetation before him. "Pondle, how far away is the king?" he asked, swallowing.

The thief rechecked his calculations. "No more than a hundred yards."

The young warrior digested the information. "Let's trek together another fifty yards; then I want everyone to fall back in the underbrush."

"What do you want us to do?" asked Murdock.

Harrison pointed to the magicians. "Give them a chance to do their work." Focusing on the ranger, he said, "You're in charge once I step foot into the king's area."

Murdock's eyes widened a bit. Nodding, he said, "It'll only be temporary. You'll be back before you know it."

Harrison gripped Murdock's shoulder. "Let's go."

Pondle led the small platoon closer to the king's position, navigating the underbrush as best they could through the growing thickness. The thief stopped their procession a few minutes later.

"This is the halfway point," said Pondle.

Harrison gazed ahead of the group. "I guess this is it," said the young warrior. "Fan out, take cover, and be ready for battle. Expect the unexpected."

The young warrior turned away from his friends and took a moment to collect his thoughts. Though he understood that the odds of King Holleris changing his evil strategy were slim, a higher call of duty resonated throughout his being. Harking back to his studies, particularly on how to engage an enemy with the clear upper hand, Harrison moved toward the greatest confrontation of his life.

CHAPTER 47

Ｑ

Brendan Brigade's Unified Army remained poised for battle, encircling an area of the forest just north of the dragon army that had taken position in a clearing. His equal, Octavius Forge, joined him as the two peered into the woods.

"What's our next move?" asked the Argosian leader.

Brendan surveyed the landscape. "Our soldiers are in place. We're just waiting for Holleris to do something irrational."

The elder Forge scrunched his brow. "Like what?"

The Aegean shook his head, unsure. "Anything out of the ordinary." A lone figure venturing toward the clearing caught his attention. Pointing at the person, he exclaimed, "It's Harrison!"

Octavius stared into the distance as well. "What's he doing?" he asked.

Brendan gritted his teeth. "He's forcing the action!" The Aegean gestured in his fellow general's direction. "Ready the troops for battle! Things are going to get mighty interesting!" The elder Forge nodded and scampered away to alert the anxious soldiers.

Brendan peered at his onetime pupil. "Take what you learned, Harrison," he said softly aloud, knowing that his prize student's big heart will put him in jeopardy. "Remember your studies."

* * *

Liagol rushed passed the royal guardians and to his leader's side. Nodding at Moradoril and Brianna, he spoke so fast the words tripped over each other, "Harrison is approaching the evil king!"

Moradoril tempered his response, not surprised at the information. "Have the troops ready the weapon and aim it at the dragon closest to King Holleris." The elven king paused, then said, "Make haste."

Liagol nodded in acknowledgement, then dashed away to fulfill his task. Brianna sidled next to her king as the scout left his superiors behind.

"This plan must work, Moradoril," said the queen, more stoic than usual. "There is no alternative plan."

The elven king, deep in thought with eyes fixed on the break in the forest's landscape, replied solemnly, "I know."

* * *

Arcadian horsemen from the south guided their steeds deeper into the Dark Forest, taking up residence in the perimeter between the countryside and where the dragon army had taken root. Advanced scouts returned to their leader Bracken Drake with important news.

"Harrison's small team is moving toward the enemy," said one of the scouts.

Bracken clenched his jaw. "They're initiating their plan," said the general. "Time to execute ours."

"What are your orders, sir?" asked the second soldier.

The Arcadian leader did not hesitate, his thought process clear. "Take ten men, gather all of the steeds, and bring them to the countryside. When you see the first dragon appear from the forest, shoo them to the west."

The first sentry cocked his head. "Sir, why would we want to rid ourselves of our horses?"

Bracken drew a heavy sigh. "The animals might act as a diversion. Dragons love horse meat and, if they chase them, it might provide us a chance to flee." Both soldiers exchanged anxious glances. "Go!" ordered their leader.

The general watched as his men scrambled to fulfill their task, hoping that he and his men would not need to run from a battle that was heavily stacked against them.

* * *

"Your little friend is advancing toward the monsters," said Rashaa, learning about Harrison's maneuver from his guards. "And warriors dressed in red are close by."

"He's not my friend," said Nigel, stroking his beard as he took in the information. "But he's brave."

"When do we attack?" asked Rashaa, more than ready for battle.

Lord Hammer panned the vicinity. Scynthian warriors littered the forest to the south and west of the dragon's clearing. He knew a simple command would suffice.

"Blow your horns as loud as you can at the first sign of battle," said the former governor of Concur. "Not a second before. Do you understand?"

Rashaa nodded. "Understood."

"Because if you do something foolish, like starting this fight prematurely, then we're all dead before we even get started," said Nigel with a sneer.

The Scynthian warrior took two heavy steps in Lord Hammer's direction, stopping in front of him. Glaring down at the smaller human, he bellowed, "We will not let Mahalanobis burn in vain! We will destroy the dragons!"

Nigel turned away and stared into the forest, unfazed. "Good."

* * *

"Why's the fog so thick over here?" asked Tara, with a slight quiver in her voice.

"I don't know," responded Swinkle, peering through the thickets, the mist hindering his sight. "Thoragaard must be close by."

"Closer than you think," came a monotone voice from behind the haze. The illusionist stepped forward, flanked by Adrith and Marissa. Lance scampered to greet their long lost friends, his tail wagging in happiness. The Scynthian and dwarf contingents raised their weapons upon seeing the intruder.

"Thoragaard!" exclaimed Tara, happy to see a familiar face. "No one knew if you made it to Concur or if you were all still alive!"

The mage nodded once in concurrence, but his demeanor quickly changed. "Harrison is going to try and talk to King Holleris. We must be ready for any outcome."

Swinkle stepped forward. "Engage with the king? He knows better than that!"

"Be that as it may," said the illusionist, "he is moving forward with his own plan."

"He doesn't know Naa'il's here!" Tara gazed back to the juvenile Scynthian who listened to the humans' conversation with great interest. "We need to take him to see Harrison!"

"Impossible at this time," said Thoragaard. "What is so important that he must meet with Harrison?"

"Alabaar's gift," said the Scynthian. "Only for Harrison to see."

"Why is that?" pressed Thoragaard, intrigued.

"Direct orders," said Naa'il, shaking his head. "No one else."

The illusionist pursed his lips, knowing that no meeting could take place at this very moment. "The dragons are in a clearing not far from here. Others are in the woods, preparing for battle. Let's get closer to Harrison's position where we can await the outcome of his event."

"Very important to see Harrison," reiterated Naa'il.

Drogut, Rogur, and the rest of the combined warriors fanned around the humans. "My people will provide protection," said Drogut. "As will the Scynthians, right?" Naa'il gazed at his comrades, who nodded in agreement.

"Very well," said Thoragaard. Bringing his focus to the female warriors, he said, "Adrith and Marissa will guide us forward. Have Lance go with them, he can pick up Harrison's scent."

Adrith bent down and waved the little dog forward. "Find Harrison," she said, the dog's eyes widening upon hearing his master's name. With a single yap, the little dog darted to the head of the group.

Drogut approached Tara. "Fear not, lass, we'll protect you."

"I know you will," said Tara, trying to keep her nerves at bay. Swinkle took hold of her hand.

"All will turn out as Pious has planned," said the young cleric, locking eyes with the girl. "You must have faith."

After a moment, Swinkle released her hand and the mixed team of adventurers started their trek toward the ensuing encounter.

* * *

Harrison ventured away from his friends, entering deeper into the ever-thickening fog. The lack of light rendered his sight moot, making the decision to ignite his torch an easy one. Though he knew he had just alerted his enemy to his position, his fighter instincts told him they already knew where he stood. Furthermore, to the young warrior's chagrin, the mist reflected the torch's flame, making things more difficult to see not easier.

The forest grew very quiet, eerily so. The young warrior neither saw nor sensed any birds, animals, or even the sound of chirping crickets and swore he heard the thump of his beating heart. Though the haze hung low to the ground, even a simple tracker like Harrison could tell that the area before him began to thin. The young warrior scanned the vicinity, searching for any sign of his enemy.

The muted sound of heavy breathing caused the hairs on the back of his neck to rise, stopping him in his tracks. Harrison concluded that massive beasts had created the noise. Taking measured steps, he gripped his battle axe tighter, knowing that his adversary's army loomed very near. The young warrior outstretched his torch bearing arm, hoping that its light would allow him a glimpse of one of the beasts but Thoragaard's fog kept them well hidden.

Harrison swallowed, then brought his gaze upwards. There, some twenty feet above his position, he saw the glow of red, piercing eyes. Many sets of red, piercing eyes. The young warrior swallowed hard again, a nervous sweat breaking on his brow.

"Step forward," called a voice from behind the mist. "So that we can get a better look at you."

Harrison knew that he was at the king's mercy and the time had come to face his adversary. The young warrior ventured closer to his enemy, stepping further into the awaiting clearing. Taking in his surroundings, seven large, two-headed dragons formed an intimidating semi-circle, each set of eyes boring a hole in the puny skull of the human who had dared to enter their realm. Before them stood two men: an ancient, disheveled soul and his superior, King Holleris.

The haze thinning a bit, the royal man asked, "Where is your brother?"

Before answering, Harrison recalled how he had wanted to use Fallyn's talents to try and trick this man. The word suicide sprung from the recesses of his mind after reevaluating that strategy now, just like his friends had said.

"He died shortly after killing you," said the young warrior, maintaining his focus on the evil man.

A wide smile graced the king's face. "As you can see, I am not dead!"

"No, you're not," answered Harrison, "and your very existence is putting the rest of the world in jeopardy."

The king began to laugh. "My existence? You have no idea how long I've waited for this day! Your brother would have appreciated it as well if you hadn't tainted him."

Harrison knew he had to keep his emotions in check, to avoid whipping this man into a crazed frenzy. Brushing off the comments about Troy, he asked, "Why do you hate us so? What have we done to you?"

King Holleris' demeanor turned dour as a scowl flashed across his face, a millennium of pent up rage ready to spew. "You have no idea what I've witnessed over the past one thousand years," he bellowed. "After my sovereignty was wrongly taken away from me, I watched as rulers like you tried to pick up the pieces. I looked on while unworthy leaders dismembered The Kingdom, helping themselves instead of those who deserved assistance, and the rise of those barbaric Scynthians. None of this would have happened had I remained in power!"

Harrison did not back down. "How can you stand there and say those things? You've listened to your own lies for so long that you believe them as unwavering truths. You couldn't be more wrong."

The king clenched his jaw and narrowed his eyes, if just for a second. Allowing his rage to abate, he asked, "Is that so? How can a boy like you possibly comprehend the undercurrents of ruling the land?"

"I'm learning," started the Aegean, "and soon all will come to understand what you two," Harrison pointed to the king and his warlock, Finius, "did to set your wicked plan into motion."

King Holleris let out a little laugh. "Met with them, didn't you?"

Harrison knew who the king alluded to. "Yes, and they filled me in on the history of the land. Your fellow kings wanted to help those who had little, to ease their way of life and protect them from Scynthian uprisings. But you wanted absolute authority in order to eliminate the peasants and the less fortunate, to rob the land of its riches and keep them for yourself. Those are the lies you told Troy and the ones you continue to believe today."

One of the dragons lowered its heads and snorted in the young warrior's direction, as if to warn the human to treat its master with respect. The king's eyes lit up.

"What do you think of my creations?" said the king, raising a hand to caress the monster's scaly hide. "A force to be reckoned with, no?"

Harrison swallowed, knowing that the king could unleash the dragon's fury at any time. "I must admit, they're impressive creatures but using them to instill fear and hate sends the wrong message to the people of the land."

"Is that so?" chided the king. "Then what should I tell them?"

Harrison had waited a long time for this moment, racking his brain night after night, wondering what he would say to the king, and now he had his chance. Mustering all the strength and conviction he had, he said, "A true ruler listens to his people, leads them when times are tough, provides safety when enemies attack, and helps with their problems.

"Most people's lives are filled with burdens, trying to provide for their families, raise children, and be part of a strong society. Benevolent leaders understand their daily sacrifices and help them reach their goals. Those in authority should not be the only ones to benefit from the land's riches, to take more than their fair share of taxes, to suppress the weak. You want to instill fear and pain in the people of this land, and that's the wrong thing to do."

The king listened to the young warrior's speech, then smirked. "Such the righteous, honorable warrior, always looking out for his fellow man." King Holleris cocked his head. "A noble crusade but one deeply flawed. You are a mere boy. What are you? Eighteen, nineteen years old? What do you know about raising a family, providing for your children? You have neither! And what about all those peasants who litter our streets, add nothing to the world, and stick their hands out looking for scraps and coins to get them through another pathetic day?"

The king paused, his anger rising. "You think you have all the answers! Well, let me tell you something, I've seen this charade play out for centuries and you know what? People don't change. Oh, they'll play along with your little benevolent strategy at first, but in due time you'll have a world filled with people looking to you for relief every single day. Not with me. Ruling with an iron fist sends the right message." The king looked up to the dragon closest to him. "Having an invincible force hammers home the point."

"You're a jaded man," responded Harrison. "Your exile has only fueled your misguided rage and led to the creation of killer monsters. Imagine what good you could have done if you had put your energy into something more beneficial."

"More beneficial?" The king laughed again. "My dragons will restore order to this world! Everyone will bow to my sovereignty and I will provide the people with leadership they will understand. This is *my* land and I intend to rule as I see fit."

Harrison shook his head. "Then we've reached an impasse. There's no way I would ever abide by your laws." The young warrior drew a heavy sigh. "I'll say this only once. Pull back your army of dragons and join us in making this a land ruled by the people, for the benefit of all. Otherwise, suffer the consequences."

The king smirked. "Consequences?" A wave of fury coursed through the royal man's body, his face reddening with anger. "How dare you threaten me? My dragons will crush the armies that have encircled us. Don't think for a second that I didn't know about them."

Harrison felt the invisible noose tighten around his neck, knowing that he had no means to defend himself from the king's monsters. Time seemed to stand still for the young warrior, imaginary gears churning in the Aegean's mind desperate to formulate a plan. Harrison locked his eyes on the king, watching him gesture in his warlock's direction. Finius stepped to the forefront, then pointed a large wooden staff at the young warrior.

From the forest's depths bright missiles passed over the young warrior and whooshed toward the dragon army. The projectiles impacted an invisible shield, destroyed before they could reach their intended target. Harrison swiveled toward the king who laughed hysterically at his adversary's first failure.

Glaring at Finius, the king pointed at Harrison and shouted, "Do it!"

The ancient mage gripped his staff tighter, then mumbled something inaudible. Harrison took his cue to turn and run, entering the woods just as balls of fire burst from the warlock's weapon. The fiery orbs smashed through the thickets, igniting the forest around the young warrior, dispersing flames and heat yet again. Harrison dropped to the forest's floor, feverishly patting his smoldering clothing in an effort to prevent them from igniting. Within chaotic seconds, a whistling sound from overhead more than startled the young warrior. The Aegean sprung to his feet in time to see a long, silvery bolt hurtle through the air, penetrate the king's defense shield, and strike the dragon closest to the royal man. The beast wailed in pain, the elves' weapon impaling the creature.

To Harrison's delight, each of the monsters shuttered, appearing to feel the brunt of the elves' attack. The young warrior then brought his eyes to the king and his warlock, finding them buckling as well, seemingly feeling the effects of the projectile.

The injured dragon shrieked in agony, then used one of its mouths to latch onto the lodged bolt. Harrison watched with wide eyes as the beast yanked the projectile out of its side. The dragon stumbled, injured, but before it could regain its footing, a second bolt penetrated its scaly hide just below its right wing. The creature wailed once again and then, to the young warrior's surprise, burst into hundreds of smaller, dragonfly-sized monsters, dispersing in all directions. To add to the surreal scene, a Scynthian horn bellowed from deep in the woods.

The Aegean, shocked at the monster's sudden transformation, scrambled to his feet and fled the vicinity. His actions did not go unnoticed.

"Harrison!" called a voice from the woods. The young warrior spun, trying to locate the person. "Over here!"

The Aegean panned right to discover Murdock waving him over. Harrison sprinted to the ranger's position just as a large fireball exploded near his previous location.

"Did you see that?" exclaimed the young warrior in astonishment, regrouping with his friends. Before they could answer, a low hum started rumbling throughout the area, grabbing everyone's attention.

"What's that sound?" asked Harrison, spinning his head in all directions.

Kymbra's eyes widened as she pointed back to the clearing. "Look over there!"

All heads swiveled where Kymbra pointed. Harrison looked on in shock, for an onslaught of miniature dragons headed toward them. The flying menaces swarmed around the small group, spewing quick bursts of flames.

Harrison flailed his battle axe at the smaller foes, only to find the dragons maneuvering away from the young warrior's weapon with ease. To make matters worse, the diminutive beasts' breath attacks had started to ignite his clothing.

Nearby, shrieks and explosions reverberated throughout the forest as King Holleris' army began attacking. The young warrior, transfixed on ridding himself of the annoying beasts, had barely enough time to react to his changing surroundings before a heavy dose of water doused the whole group, extinguishing their burning clothes, and dispersing the harassing dragonflies in the process.

Allard appeared from the underbrush, waving the adventurers toward him, his spell effective for the time being. "That'll keep them at bay for now," said the magician in Harrison's direction. "We have bigger problems to contend with."

"Where's Gelderand?" asked the young warrior, wiping the excess water from his brow.

"Searching for Finius Boulware," said Allard. "I need to help him, too."

"This way!" exclaimed Pondle, waving his friends deeper into the woods and further from the clearing. The thief led his team on an elaborate loop, steering clear of burning underbrush and guiding them around the chaotic scene. However, the dragons began torching the immediate area, including anyone or anything in their path.

Harrison panned the vicinity, taking in the flaming trees, dead soldiers, and frenzied atmosphere, but one thought remained clear in his mind.

"We need to apprehend the king!" he shouted, making sure everyone understood their ultimate goal.

"Let's concentrate on staying alive," responded Murdock, taking cover after a fiery limb crashed to the ground.

Pondle signaled for them to halt. Pointing, he exclaimed, "There's Gelderand!"

All eyes focused on where the thief pointed. The mage had situated himself behind a large tree, waiting to get a better glimpse of the advancing monsters. Harrison and his friends rushed to his position.

Gelderand nodded to his right. "Holleris and Boulware!"

The young warrior stared into the hazy forest, finding the king and Finius close to their dragon protectors. "How do we separate them from the beasts?" asked Harrison.

"We can't," said the mage. "They will never move from their side and why would they? Plus they easily defended themselves against our missiles."

"Then what's our best means of attack?" asked the young warrior, concern in his voice.

The older man did not have to think long. "The elves have a devastating weapon that they just used to perfection. We need to let them exploit it."

Harrison gazed into the smoky woods, searching for the elusive race. "Why haven't they fired their weapon again?" A volley of roars and flames answered his question.

"That's why," said the magician, pointing deeper into the forest. "The king's monsters are disrupting their means of attack."

Before anyone could ask another question, an ever-loudening rumble began to reverberate throughout the woodlands. To the young warrior's surprise, wave upon wave of Scynthian warriors flooded the area, hollering at the top of their lungs, brandishing an assortment of weaponry. The young warrior smiled as the fur-covered beings entered the clearing and began their attack on the dragon army. Another Scynthian horn bellowed in the distance, signaling for more combatants to enter the fray.

"That will buy us some time," said Gelderand, waving for his friends to follow his lead.

The Aegean scurried after the mage before blood-curdling shrieks forced him to cower for safety. A bright orange flash and an intense explosion preceded the unmistakable cries of dying souls.

Gelderand remained vigilant, ignoring what sounded like a massive loss of life, while fleeing deeper into the woods. "Hurry!" he shouted.

The young warrior, along with his other friends, understood the older man's strategy as he took an elongated route in an effort to get a better reading on the king's position. After several minutes of running, the mage stopped on the other side of the clearing, opposite from where they had begun their trek.

Harrison caught up to the older man. Between gasps, he asked, "What's your plan?" Murdock, Pondle, Kymbra, and Allard formed a semi-circle around the magician, awaiting his answer, trying to catch their breath as well.

Gelderand took in the scene before him. Pointing toward the melee, he said through ragged breaths, "The Scynthians have gained the dragon's attention and those monsters are doing whatever they can to protect their masters," started the mage. "Holleris and Finius are still near that one."

Harrison gazed into the clearing, finding the two older men in close proximity to one of the larger beasts, not daring to venture far from its side. "We can't run toward them. That'll be suicide."

"We need to somehow separate them from the dragons," said Murdock.

"Not going to happen," said Gelderand. "No way do they stray from its side."

The ranger spread his arms wide, exasperated. "Then what do you suggest?"

"Hit them from afar," said Allard, as all eyes focused on him. "We use our magic against their magic."

"Enlighten us," said Murdock, using his customary sarcastic tone.

Before Allard could answer, another bolt whistled from the forest, striking one of the dragons in the side, causing it to screech in pain. The beast burst into scores of dragonflies, then swirled and swarmed in the direction of the elves' devastating weapon.

"That can only help us," said Harrison, letting his eyes follow the smaller fire-breathing creatures, then watching the forest light up in the area they had fled. Moments later, brighter flashes comingled with the dragonflies.

"The elves are taking care of that beast," said Murdock, looking at the same scene. Panning in the opposite direction, he said, "Take a look at what's happening over there."

The young warrior watched in stunned silence as the Scynthians attempted to butcher the remaining dragons. Though the creatures maintained the upper hand, swatting away the inferior beasts and torching even more in the process, Harrison marveled at the Scynthians' resolve. However, howls of pain and anguish resonated throughout the battlefield, reminding the young warrior how far they still had to go in order to win the war.

Pondle waved the magicians to the forefront. "Follow me," he said. "I'll lead you closer to the men while staying out of sight." Gelderand and Allard approached the thief with Harrison, Murdock, and Kymbra guarding the rear.

Maneuvering deeper into thickets and underbrush, Pondle concealed the small platoon as best as he could. From their vantage point, the clearing resided a mere twenty yards away, close enough for the mages to work their magic.

"Stop here!" said Gelderand. The group halted their procession, allowing the magicians to gauge their situation.

Allard approached Gelderand, gripping his shoulder and pointing to the opening in the forest. "Forget about the king," he said. "It's Finius we must compromise."

Gelderand nodded in concurrence. "Do you have any tricks that will be effective from this distance?"

Allard's eyes darted in all directions, the bright flashes, fog, and smoke hindering his sight. Between explosions, he found Finius launching fireballs from his staff, spinning in every direction, torching an untold number of Scynthians.

"As you are proposing, a round of fireballs and missiles should do the trick," said Allard. "We don't need to hit him with a direct shot, just explode near him."

"I agree," said Gelderand.

Allard gazed about at the multitude of flashes that occurred during the battle, hindering him from pinpointing the warlock's exact position. "I can't get a good read on Finius with all these bursts of light."

"I can provide a constant light source," said Gelderand. "Will that help?"

The magician nodded. "Let's make it happen," said Allard. "Quickly."

"What about us?" asked Harrison, unsure of his role in the new plan.

"Grab the king after we take Finius out of the equation," replied Allard.

"Got it," said the young warrior, his friends agreeing with a series of nods.

The mages looked back into the clearing, ready to put their plan into action. Allard fished materials out of a sack attached to his belt, then stared at Gelderand. "Ready when you are."

Gelderand stepped forward, wringing his hands while mumbling a spell. Seconds later, he threw open his hands and a bright light enveloped the battlefield, turning darkness into day. All combatants stopped for a brief moment, surprised at the unexpected new light source.

Allard took his cue to release his own spell. Three bright orange fireballs rushed from his fingertips and hurtled toward the unsuspecting mage. Finius spun toward the incoming projectiles, raising both his hands in the process. The fireballs burst around the warlock with majestic explosions.

Harrison's eyes widened and he gave a slight smile, sensing that their first victory had finally come. Utilizing Gelderand's light source to better enhance his vision, the young warrior waited as the detonations dissipated, readying himself to apprehend the king. His elation turned to horror in a matter of seconds. Finius Boulware stared right at the adventurers, unscathed. The ancient warlock had negated Allard's spell and now prepared a counterattack, knowing exactly where his next targets stood.

The sounds of trampling underbrush caught everyone by surprise. Armies of human foot soldiers converged on the area from out of the forest's depths. The dragons, sensing a new battle, roared and started spewing flames in all directions.

Harrison, the whole forest erupting in chaos once again, brought his focus back to Finius and King Holleris. Pointing at the two men, he screamed in a panic, "They're getting away!"

Everyone stared at the large dragon that spread its wings, providing protection for its masters, while encouraging the two men to huddle close to it. Soldiers flooded the area, holding their ground, not wanting to attack the agitated monsters.

The dragon appeared to assess its situation and, feeling that the scores of humans did not pose a significant threat, instead stared directly at Harrison and his friends. The young warrior felt the beast's glare, the monster recognizing that the projectiles intended to harm his masters had come from them. Meanwhile, the remaining four dragons began flapping their wings and lifting from the ground.

"This isn't good!" exclaimed Harrison, keeping his focus on the large dragon's piercing red eyes, eerily reminiscent to those of the minotaurs he had faced in the Sacred Seven Rooms. The creature then took purposeful steps in their direction, forcing the soldiers to break their lines, flattening the underbrush and bending back small trees.

"Run!" exclaimed the young warrior. His friends heeded their leader's command, dispersing into the chaotic night, joining the myriad of human and Scynthian soldiers who fled the area as well.

In an effort to take control of the battlefield, the massive beast lowered both its heads toward the ground and unleashed dual cones of flames into the underbrush. Harrison, along with many scurrying soldiers, felt the brunt of the attack, as a wave of heat and flames washed over them, the landscape igniting. Screams of anguish and horror permeated the area. Harrison, his clothing singed and scorched, dropped to the ground.

The young warrior's body burned, his flesh melting under his armor. The Aegean heard the monster's heavy steps approaching but his singular focus remained patting out the flames that tried to engulf him. Though the forest erupted all around him, the young warrior succeeded in stopping the fire's rapid advancement from overtaking his exposed clothing. Hurt and with pain coursing through every part of his being, the young warrior lay on the ground trying to assess his dire predicament. Two sets of red eyes from above the raging inferno stopped his train of thought.

"Halt, Torch!" commanded King Holleris from the dragon's back.

Harrison strained to focus on the evil man who sported a wicked grin. Next to him sat Finius Boulware, his staff ready to strike.

The king called to the broken warrior. "Your pathetic battle is lost before it even started," taunted Holleris. "All of your armies are either under attack or are retreating for their lives." As if on cue, circling dragons spewed flames in all directions, torching the area from high above, forcing their enemies to flee in a panic.

Harrison understood his dire situation. "Evil may win battles," he started, straining to be heard above the crackling flames, "but it never wins the war."

King Holleris glared at the young warrior. "It does this time!" The evil man lurched forward, commanding its creation, "Destroy him!"

The dragon's two heads rose high and its underbelly inflated. Harrison managed to gaze up at the enormous beast, knowing that his time was all but over. Three red projectiles flew by breaking him from his trance, striking the king and his warlock, knocking them off the creature.

The monster, infuriated at seeing its masters attacked again, glared in the direction where the fireballs originated, searching for a new target. Both heads spewed flames into the awaiting woodlands, igniting more patches of land, before backpedaling to aid its creators.

Harrison felt hands grab his armor, then the sensation of being pulled through the forest's fiery floor, passing tree after burning tree. After what seemed an eternity, he came to an abrupt stop. Woozy, the young warrior lifted his eyes, finding Murdock and Pondle gazing down at him.

"Stay with us, Harrison," said the ranger.

"They're not that far away!" said Kymbra, keeping watch for the small pack, her eyes fixed on the monster in the distance.

"Where are we?" mumbled the young warrior, closing his eyes. Harrison felt a hand lightly slap his face.

"Don't close your eyes!" demanded Murdock, taking a flask of water to the young warrior's lips. "Drink up!"

Harrison swallowed some of the cool liquid, then coughed. "I feel awful," he said, before closing his eyes again.

* * *

Gelderand pointed to his left. "That way," he said in Allard's direction. The dark mage nodded, then scurried off to fulfill his task.

The elder mage brought his focus to the snorting monster that loomed yards ahead, then to the two men who positioned themselves near their creation. With disdain, he watched Finius place his hands on either side of Holleris' head. A soft white glow radiated from them, healing the king's superficial wounds. Gelderand then brought his attention back to the creature and swallowed hard, knowing he had nothing in his arsenal that could destroy the dragon.

Flames rained from above as circling menaces went about making attack runs on the various armies running amok throughout the forest. Gelderand gazed overhead at one of the flying beasts, its breath lighting up the woodlands, flashes revealing its ghoulish slender necks and flapping wings.

The mage tried to refocus his energies to the matter at hand. Gelderand knew he had limited abilities with an attack and run strategy as his only option for survival. The magician peered through the underbrush, hoping to find Allard in position across from him. The darkness, coupled with the changing lighting, made it hard to see a man in a black cloak, let alone determine his figure for certain.

Gelderand squinted, finding movement where he thought Allard should be. Good enough, he thought as he gathered ingredients from a pouch attached to his belt. Keeping an eye on Finius, he began to mumble a spell under his breath, his outstretched hands starting to glow orange. A silver bolt shot through the woods and penetrated the dragon, the injured beast screeching in pain, breaking the mage's concentration and sending shockwaves throughout the forest.

The wounded monster's eyes glowed red with rage. In one smooth motion, one of the necks latched onto the projectile and tore it out of its midsection. The other head hollered in agony, but instead of attending to its wounds, the beast glared into the forest. Its fury beyond the point of reason, the creature bolted from its position and headed in the direction where the missile originated. The dragon blew through the woodlands, knocking over trees while arrows whistled in the air, bouncing off its massive body.

Gelderand, his mouth agape, still had his spell's ingredients in his hands. Gazing in the king's direction, he found that the two men now stood unprotected. Focusing on the task at hand, the mage began to recite his spell again. As he did so, fog thickened in the area, telling him that help was on its way.

* * *

Lance scurried back to Tara after hearing the injured beast's hideous roar. The young maiden shuddered and cowered close to the frightened dog.

"Stay next to me, Lance!" she exclaimed, trying to keep her sanity amongst the chaos. Scynthian and Dwarven warriors formed a semi-circle around the young girl, panning the vicinity, ready to engage in combat.

"Tara," said Swinkle, "we must find Harrison before all is lost."

"Where could he be," lamented the young maiden, her voice trailing off as she scanned the forest with wide eyes.

"Let Lance find him," said the young cleric in a soothing voice. "He is our best chance."

Tara nodded in understanding, then bent to one knee. "Lance, find Harrison!"

The little dog whimpered, apprehensive at continuing with so much violent activity throughout the immediate area. With a huff, the canine pressed his nose to the ground and continued his search for his master in earnest.

"He'll find him, Swinkle," said Tara, rising to stand next to the holy man. "I know he will." With visions of her love playing in her head, the small platoon pressed deeper into the fiery forest.

* * *

"Where's Swinkle when you need him," lamented Murdock, doing his best to keep his friend alive.

"Our best option is to stay put," said Pondle, panning to locate the next inevitable obstacle in their quest to stop the king.

"Well, we certainly can't continue with Harrison in his present condition," added Kymbra. "I'll maintain a defensive position for us."

"Good idea," said Murdock, trying to get the young warrior to drink more water. The sight of a little creature bursting into their makeshift triage both startled and excited the small team.

"Lance!" shouted Pondle with joy. "Where's everybody else?"

The dog bounded between Pondle, Kymbra, and Murdock before dashing to Harrison's side, sniffing his master's body. He then licked the young warrior's face in an effort to wake him.

The dog's slick tongue snapped Harrison out of his funk, awakening him to find his canine companion's face close to his own.

"Lance?" said Harrison, gazing at the dog through half-closed eyes. The little dog began to bark with fervor upon hearing his name.

"Quiet, boy!" said Pondle, afraid that the animal's antics would alert unsavory beings to their location. Instead, Lance's barks grew louder.

Seconds later, Adrith and Marissa appeared from the woods followed by the rest of their contingent. Scynthian warriors, along with their Dwarven counterparts, flooded the area. Amongst the throngs of beings emerged Swinkle and Tara.

The young maiden found Harrison lying on the ground and rushed to his side. "Oh, Harrison," she cried, dropping to his level, her eyes darting over his burn-riddled body. Tears forming, she said, "You're going to be alright. Swinkle's here."

The young cleric bent to one knee before fishing a vial of holy water from his pouch. No examination was needed; just the sight of his friend lying broken on the forest's floor drove home the intensity of his injuries.

Taking the container, Swinkle administered the sacred liquid over Harrison's body while reciting a prayer. Finished with that task, he placed his hands around the young warrior's midsection, then prayed again. A soft white glow radiated from his extremities before subsiding.

Tara stared at Harrison, seeing little change in his wellbeing. "Did your prayers work?" she asked.

"Time will tell," said the young cleric, taking his friend's hand in his. Closer examination showed that some of the burns had begun to heal. Swinkle crinkled his brow. "This is odd."

"What have you found?" asked Tara while the others moved in closer to hear.

"Harrison's body is healing faster than expected," said Swinkle.

"That's good, right?" asked Tara with a shake of her head.

"It is, but my prayers do not cure wounds that fast." The young cleric threw up his hands. "It's as if my actions have kick started a reaction."

"The trolls caused this," said Kymbra who had listened to the conversation with intent. "Those hideous monsters slashed Harrison just like they clawed me up. The elves' remedy used their blood, which gave us regeneration qualities."

"And my prayer has accelerated the process," added Swinkle. The young cleric showed his palms, waving his friends away. "Everyone, step back and let whatever is happening run to completion."

The rest of the group did as Swinkle asked, stepping a few feet away from Harrison, Swinkle, and Tara. The young cleric made a closer inspection of his friend, finding Harrison's exposed skin mending. Smiling, he said, "I think he's going to be alright."

"How long until he's healed?" asked Murdock. "We're in the midst of a battle, you know."

"No idea," said Swinkle. "We need to keep him safe."

Two men stepped to the forefront. "What's the battle scene?" asked Drogut, his brother Rogur by his side. Naa'il approached the dwarves, along with his warriors.

Pondle alternated his glance between the two warrior races. "The king's main dragon took a bolt to its midsection, then went off in a rage after the elves." The thief motioned with his head. "The king and Boulware are somewhere out there with Allard and Gelderand on their trail."

"Thoragaard, too," said Marissa.

"He was with us," added Adrith.

Drogut narrowed his eyes. "These humans, are they magicians?"

"Yes," said Pondle.

The dwarf king nodded to his brother. "Boulware's ours! My people seek retribution for his actions!"

"You can have him," said Murdock, "but we haven't won anything yet. And, those monsters are sure to come to their masters' aid."

"Then we help the warlocks," said Drogut. Taking his stare to Naa'il, he asked, "Can we count on your support?"

"I must stay with Harrison," said the juvenile Scynthian. "Must see Alabaar's gift."

The dwarf king shook his head in disgust. "What's with that stupid gift? We need fighters now!"

Naa'il turned to his warrior comrades. "They go with you!"

Drogut focused on the Scynthians, their weapons ready for battle. "Good enough." The dwarf scanned the human contingent. "What about you people?"

Murdock panned his friends. Pointing at Harrison, he started, "He's not going anywhere." Looking over to Tara and Swinkle, he said, "Neither are they. But the rest of us will fight with you."

"They stay back for protection," said Kymbra, pointing to her female counterparts. "We can't leave them unguarded."

"Works for me," agreed Drogut. "We're losing valuable time."

Pondle stepped forward, Murdock following. "Follow us," he said with a wave, then scampered into the burning landscape. Murdock and Kymbra trailed the thief, along with the dwarves and Scynthians.

Lance darted after the fighters, then stopped and retreated to Harrison's side. "Good boy, Lance," said Tara, stroking the little dog's fur. "You stay back here with us."

Adrith unsheathed her small sword, as did Marissa. "This isn't over yet by a longshot," said Adrith. "We'll keep an eye out for intruders but be prepared for anything."

The two female warriors went about securing the area, leaving Naa'il behind with Tara and Swinkle. "When he wake up?" asked the Scynthian, pointing down to Harrison.

"A little while," said the young cleric.

Tara sat by the young warrior's side, lifting his head onto her lap, stroking his hair. "I'm not leaving him ever again." The young maiden locked eyes with Swinkle. "If we die, we die together."

"Let's hope it does not come to that," said the young cleric, positioning himself near his friends, while Naa'il crouched alongside his human allies.

Swinkle gazed in the direction his friends had fled, then said a prayer to provide a small sanctuary for those left behind. His nerves frayed and his job done for now, he prayed to Pious yet again for help and guidance. When finished, he looked to the heavens and said softly, "The battle is in your hands now."

CHAPTER 48

Ω

Gelderand cast three massive fireballs in King Holleris' direction. The flaming projectiles sped toward the king; however, Finius' fiery counterattack saved the pair once again. The warlock, using his own staff, intercepted the missiles, destroying them on contact. His adversary's position now known, the ancient mage fired back at Gelderand.

Three missiles whooshed through the thickening haze and headed right for the mage. Gelderand had nowhere to flee. Dropping to the ground his only option, the magician hit the earth just as the projectiles slammed into a large tree. The massive trunk ignited on impact, bursting flames in all directions, starting yet another fire in the embattled forest. A huge branch snapped and dropped to the forest's floor, striking Gelderand and pinning him to the ground. Finius, having incapacitated one of his adversaries for the time being, turned his focus on Allard, pointing his staff in the dark mage's direction.

Meanwhile, King Holleris had seen enough. "Blaze! Cinder!" he wailed from the forest's fiery depths. Hideous shrieks filled the area, his monsters heeding his call.

Allard, fixed in the crosshairs of Finius' staff, scampered away in an effort to hide himself from the warlock. The thickening haze made things tougher to see, but a monotone voice calling his name startled him even more.

"Allard, follow my voice," said Thoragaard, hidden from view.

The dark mage squinted, trying to locate the illusionist. "Finius is going to attack again!"

"I know," said Thoragaard, "we must stop him."

The fog grew denser near Allard. Panicking, he cried, "Where are you?"

A hand from behind covered Allard's mouth. "Keep your voice down," whispered Thoragaard into the mage's ear. The illusionist released his grip, presenting himself to the magician.

Allard's eyes darted, not believing who stood before him. Thoragaard, still wearing his dark hooded robe, gestured back toward the king and Finius, but the heavy mist exuding from his body caught the dark mage's attention the most.

Eyes wide, he asked, "How are you doing that?"

Thoragaard waved a dismissive hand. "That does not matter right now. We must aid Gelderand and stop the wicked king." The illusionist glared at Allard. "Are you with me?"

The magician nodded repeatedly, his eyes still round with shock. More shrieks and loud crashes snapped him from his trance. "We can't defeat them!" cried Allard, his anxiety level skyrocketing.

Thoragaard took a purposeful step in the mage's direction, pinning his arms to his side. "Focus, Allard!" The illusionist pointed to the thick branches above the king's position. "Aim your missiles at them! Force those limbs to fall on the two men!"

Allard looked at the boughs, then at Thoragaard. Nodding, he said, "I can do it."

"Good," said the illusionist, releasing his grip. "I'm going to loop around and help Gelderand." Thrusting a finger in the mage's face, he said, "Make it happen on a count of three." Just as Thoragaard had emerged, he disappeared from view enveloped in a thick fog.

The dark mage was alone again, the haze dissipating around him. Gazing upward, Allard started counting to three, aiming at the branches. Heavy footsteps startled the magician, causing him to lose count and disrupting his planned spell.

Allard panicked. Swiveling his head in all directions, the one voice that echoed in his brain kept telling him to flee. "Where's the king?" he said, looking for the elusive target. Fog and flames hindered his vision, and his thoughts started getting the better of him. A heavy crash from behind made him jump, exposing himself to the monsters that lurked in close proximity.

King Holleris noticed the magician first. "There's one of them!" he bellowed. "Blaze! Cinder! Kill him!" The dragon closest to the king swiveled its heads toward Allard, making direct eye contact with the magician.

Fear overtook the dark mage. Not bothering to think about his predicament anymore, Allard fled deeper into the forest. The older man ran away as fast as he could, his breathing coming in ragged gasps. Heavy steps from behind only heightened his anxiety.

The terrified man located a large oak just ahead of him. Sprinting, he hid behind its massive trunk, hoping that the monsters did not see him. The earth shook behind him, as two dragons plodded toward his location. Allard, his nerves shattered, had no way of concentrating on a spell, let alone having anything in his arsenal to defeat the beasts. The mage swung his pouch in front of him and sifted through its contents, yet nothing he found gave him confidence in his survival.

Allard desperately searched the surrounding landscape, hoping to find a cave or opening somewhere that would provide him shelter from the impending doom. He found neither. The next step crashed behind the tree, one of the dragons looming only a few feet behind him. The dark mage closed his eyes and tried his best to concentrate, mumbling the words that might provide an invisible sanctuary. To his surprise, it worked.

The magician gazed through his imperceptible shield, all the while sensing the beasts' presence. One of the creatures lumbered to his right, while the other remained motionless behind the tree. Allard's breathing came in shallow, horrified spasms as he stood completely still. The dragon in front of him lowered its heads, both of them sniffing the ground around them.

Massive heads from behind appeared on either side of the trunk, taking the forest's air into their nostrils, searching for its elusive prey. Allard barely breathed, remaining motionless. The monster before him swung both of its head right at Allard, glaring at the dark mage. It then maneuvered its massive body to face the terrified human, making a low guttural clicking sound.

The second dragon interpreted the clicks, then shrieked at the top of its lungs. Swinging its massive necks, the creature leveled the top of the oak, smashing the trunk, splintering it to pieces.

Allard pressed his eyelids shut as the once impressive tree transformed into a jagged stump. The terrified magician slowly peeled open his eyes and, to his horror, found four sets of red piercing orbs glaring at him from above. *By the gods, they can see me!*

His invisible sanctuary compromised, the defenseless human cowered into a ball, awaiting the inevitable. The two dragons drew in copious amounts of air, their chests expanding, then released a torrent of flames onto the terrified mage. Allard vaporized before the pain could overtake his body.

* * *

A thick haze enveloped Gelderand but the sounds of death and destruction haunted him more. The elder mage tried to maneuver from underneath a very heavy limb. Shooting pain from his left thigh stopped him cold. Sweat beading on his brow and anxiety coursing through his veins, the magician clenched his teeth and pushed the branch again. Excruciating pain halted his second attempt.

Gelderand knew the outcome before looking at his leg. The tree limb that fell from the sky smashed his femur. Though he possessed a myriad of spells, none could help him at this time. Furthermore, deadly monsters lurked just beyond eyesight.

The mage peered at the thickening mist, thankful for its concealment from Finius and Holleris. To his surprise, a man emerged from the darkness.

"There's no time to spare," said Thoragaard, doing away with pleasantries. "The king and his warlock are close."

Gelderand stared at his equal. "My leg is broken," he said with dejection.

The illusionist frowned, examining the magician's dire predicament. Taking his gaze upwards, Thoragaard found more heavy limbs protruding from the grand oak. Moving with purpose, the illusionist looped a rope around one of the massive branches, then secured the loose ends to the fallen limb. Giving the twine a tug and satisfied that it would support his weight, Thoragaard ascended the rope until he reached its apex, then climbed onto the branch. Shimmying toward the trunk, the illusionist stood and planted a hand on the tree for support, then gazed into the distance.

Thoragaard watched as the two dragons lumbered around a torched tree. Bringing his focus downward, he found Finius and Holleris awaiting their creations' return. Satisfied with his assessment, the illusionist opened his hands and appeared to toss several blue and red beacons into the forest, past the men's position. The soft lights wobbled harmlessly into the darkness, blipping every few seconds, catching the attention of the menacing beasts. The dragons focused on the lights and began following them into the forest, away from Thoragaard and Gelderand's position.

Safe for the time being, Thoragaard scaled down the rope and came to his fellow mage's aid. "They will be diverted for only so long," said the illusionist.

"I can't move my leg," said Gelderand, still in harrowing pain.

Thoragaard did not respond; instead he untied one end of his rope and clutched it tightly. Gazing at the branch that had pinned the elder mage, he said, "I'm going to use all my strength to lift this log. You must pull yourself away when it's off your leg." Gelderand swallowed hard, then nodded.

The illusionist gripped the twine, then pulled down with all his might, allowing the tree's limb to act as a winch. The branch that crushed Gelderand's leg lifted ever so slightly, allowing the mage to maneuver away from it. Shooting pains reverberated from the magician's injury, nearly causing him to black out.

Thoragaard, sensing that Gelderand had moved out of the branch's path, lowered the thick log back to the ground. He then made haste in untying and stashing the rope, before rushing to the elder mage's side.

Bending to be closer to Gelderand, he said, "I'm going to throw your arm around my shoulder and carry you to safety." Returning the mage's blank stare, he added, "Rest assured, this is going to hurt."

Thoragaard, knowing that time was of the essence, hoisted Gelderand's arm over his shoulder, propping up the injured mage. The elder magician gasped as shooting pains radiated from his broken leg.

"The rest of the team is this way," said the illusionist, heading toward Tara and Swinkle's position. The duo ventured a mere few steps before their next encounter. A mixed party of dwarves and Scynthians halted their procession upon seeing Thoragaard and Gelderand.

Drogut pointed to the chaos beyond the magicians. "Did you cause that?"

"More or less," said Thoragaard. Gesturing with his head, he continued, "We have more pressing concerns. Gelderand is injured badly and he needs immediate attention."

"Is Boulware over there?" asked the dwarf, disregarding the illusionist's plea. "I want him!"

"He is but we need your help," said Thoragaard. At that moment, several familiar faces burst through the underbrush.

"What happened to him?" asked Murdock, while Pondle and Kymbra rounded out the small team.

"Dragons and fire," said Thoragaard. "Is Swinkle close by?"

"Yes, not too far from here," answered the ranger.

"Take Gelderand to him," said the illusionist, passing the injured mage to Murdock. "We are all still in great danger. I must go now."

Murdock hoisted Gelderand up, just as Thoragaard had done, then watched as the magician disappeared into the underbrush.

"Follow that wizard!" said Drogut, his brethren heeding their leader's command, leaving the humans behind. The

Scynthian warriors, following the dwarves' lead, started to do the same.

Murdock, uncomfortable with his current assignment, called to one of the savages. "Hey! I need your help!" Two of the warriors turned their attention to the ranger.

"You two!" exclaimed Murdock, locking eyes with the Scynthians. "Take Gelderand back to the others, then come back and fight with us."

The larger beings heeded the ranger's request, lifting the elder mage up, his legs dangling above the ground. Murdock heard Gelderand's anguish-filled grunts as the Scynthians rushed him through the forest and back to their original position.

Murdock, his task finished, brought his gaze to Pondle and Kymbra. "Let's follow the rest of them!" The three people gripped their weapons and headed toward the ensuing melee.

* * *

Lance jumped to his feet, stuck his tail straight up, and growled into the darkness. Tara, nerves frayed, knew something loomed in the forest, just out of sight.

"What is it, Lance?" she asked with trepidation, while the remaining team members clutched their weapons a little tighter, staying within their sanctuary.

Three figures burst from the woods, panning to find their counterparts. Lance scampered forward, exiting the safe haven and exposing himself to the bewildered Scynthians.

"It's Gelderand," said Adrith, rushing to his side, along with Marissa. The two women helped guide the mage from the Scynthians and laid him on the ground.

"He's injured," said Swinkle, scampering to the magician.

Tara placed Harrison's head on the ground and came to her uncle's side. "What happened to him?" she lamented.

Swinkle halted his quick examination as soon as he saw Gelderand's damaged leg. "This is not good," he said, before kneeling beside the elder mage.

"Swinkle, you have to do something," cried Tara, her eyes wandering all over her uncle's hurt body.

"I will pray over his injured area," said the young cleric. Swinkle placed his hands on either side of Gelderand's broken leg, then started to pray. A familiar white glow enveloped the mage's limb, healing it a bit.

Swinkle brought his attention to Gelderand himself. "Are you in a lot of pain?"

The older man, sweat breaking on his brow, nodded. "Yes."

"What happened, uncle?" asked Tara, taking his head in her hands.

"Finius' weapon launched fireballs in my direction," started the mage through measured breaths. "Missiles exploded against the tree behind me. A huge branch fell on my leg."

"He needs a splint," said Adrith, inspecting the man's body as well. "Marissa, help me find suitable sticks." Both women went off in search of something that they could use to brace Gelderand's leg.

Naa'il had allowed the humans to tend to their wounded comrade before asking, "Can I help?"

Swinkle smiled, then said, "Thanks for offering, but providing protection is what we need most from you."

The juvenile Scynthian nodded. Pointing to his fellow warriors, he ordered, "Guard our camp!" The fighters returned a nod and went off to set up a defensive perimeter.

Harrison, trying to allow his own injuries to heal, lifted his head to see what had started so much commotion. The young warrior elevated himself off the ground, gritting his teeth to stop from howling in pain. Though his burns had started mending, they still had a long way to go before he would consider himself fully healed.

Pushing the pain to the back of his mind, he joined his friends, asking, "What's wrong with Gelderand?"

"The king's warlock did this," said Tara, maintaining her stare on her uncle.

"Swinkle, what do you need to do to fix him?" asked the young warrior.

"He has a broken leg," said the holy man with a sigh. "I must set his bone, place him in a splint, and let time heal his wound."

Harrison panned the vicinity. His senses heard, saw, and smelled the battle raging throughout the forest. In a hushed tone, he said, "Gelderand needs to be mobile or he'll never get out of these woods."

The young cleric lifted his eyes to his friend, agreeing without saying a word. "I will do my best." At that time, Adrith and Marissa returned to the encampment with several splint candidates.

"Let me have a look at these," said Swinkle, accepting the female warriors' offerings. Finding two sturdy sticks, he said, "These will do."

Swinkle went into his pack and returned with some bandages and twine. "Does anyone else have rope?"

Marissa raised her hand. "I do," she said, then went to her backpack to retrieve the important item.

"Thank you," said Swinkle, accepting the fighter's rope. Taking his focus to Gelderand, he said, "I need to set your leg. This is going to hurt a lot."

"Wait!" said the elder mage. "Is there no other way?"

Swinkle shook his head. "No. The bone is broken and needs to be aligned. If I don't do this now, you may never walk right again." The young cleric paused to allow the severity of his comments to sink in. "I will pray over you as soon as I am done." Gelderand, knowing that he had no other options, nodded with reluctance.

"Alright," said the young cleric, ready to start his procedure. Pointing to Adrith and Marissa, he said, "Lightly hold him down and don't let him squirm." The two women placed their hands on Gelderand's shoulder and chest, applying pressure.

Swinkle gazed over to Tara. "Please step away." The young maiden kissed her uncle on the cheek, then moved aside.

The young cleric took a firm hold of Gelderand's leg, causing the mage to wince. Staring at the magician, he asked, "Are you ready?" The mage gave the boy a quick nod, then closed his eyes.

Swinkle, in one smooth motion, pulled on Gelderand's leg, snapping the bone back into place. The mage let out an audible gasp, then passed out due to the intense pain.

Tara hurried to her uncle's side. "Uncle!" she cried, unable to register a response from the older man. Lightly tapping his face, she said again, "Uncle!" Still, the magician did not move.

Swinkle rushed to Gelderand, placing a hand on his sweaty forehead. "The pain was too much for him," he said, feeling his neck for a pulse. "His heart is still beating and he is breathing. He will awaken in time."

Tara brought a hand to cover her mouth, tears forming in her eyes. Harrison shuffled over and took the frightened girl in his arms. "Swinkle will make him feel better. You'll see."

The young cleric returned to Gelderand's injury. Waving at Adrith and Marissa, he said, "Place those sticks on either side of his leg."

The women did as ordered, allowing Swinkle to secure them to the mage's damaged limb with the rope they had provided. The young cleric made sure the splint was firm but not tight enough to stop blood flow to Gelderand's leg. After his examination, he prayed over the hurt man again before sitting back, his chores complete.

"That should do it for now," said Swinkle, trying to catch his breath. "He will not be out cold for long."

Sensing that the immediate threat had diminished, Naa'il strolled over to Harrison. Focusing on the young warrior, he asked, "You feel better?"

Harrison cocked his head from side to side. "A little, why?"

"Need to talk to you."

CHAPTER 49

◻

Pondle overtook Murdock, leading the ranger and Kymbra in pursuit of the Dwarven and Scynthian contingents. Dragons roared, men screamed, and battles raged all around the adventurers. A violent crash stopped the trio in their tracks.

Murdock placed a firm hand on Pondle's shoulder, garnering his attention. "The king and his wizard are very close," he said. "We need to find them."

"Just follow the dragons," said Kymbra, flames reflecting in her eyes.

"That won't be hard to do," said Pondle. "It's keeping hidden from them that worries me."

The forest around the small team burned as screams and hollers reverberated throughout the woodlands. Scynthians scampered toward their area, while human armies encircled the region, ready to engage in more battles.

Murdock did not have to look far to find his adversaries. "The two monsters are right there," said the ranger, pointing to the dragons that had returned to their masters, protecting them.

"The king and Finius are going to ride those beasts right out of the forest," said Kymbra. "Why else would they stay here?"

"To crush us once and for all," said Murdock. A low but steady hum broke his train of thought. "What's that?"

Pondle looked past Murdock and Kymbra, his eyes widening. "Dragonflies!"

Scores of the miniature creatures made their return, joining the chaos. The diminutive beasts spewed flames at anything that moved, lighting the clothing on human fighters and Scynthians alike.

"We need to find the elves," said Murdock. "They're the only ones who can take down those beasts." Shrieks from above more than startled the trio.

"More dragons are in the sky!" cried Kymbra. "We're trapped!"

The ranger panned the battlefield. The dragons had torched the clearing, keeping the humans and Scynthian armies at bay. Smaller menaces darted *en masse* through the ranks of soldiers. The dwarves and elves were nowhere to be found and above the forest more creatures rained fire from the heavens.

Murdock felt the gravity of the situation and, for the first time, had the feeling that all was lost. A blast from beyond their position sent a chill down his spine. Although fires burned all around him, to his surprise the ranger felt a sudden but temporary coldness. Immediately, the dragonflies dropped to the forest's floor, frozen and paralyzed.

"Hurry, this way!" came a voice calling for the three adventurers. The ranger, still trying to gather his bearings, gazed upon welcome familiar faces.

Floriad and Liagol waved to the trio, encouraging them to follow. Murdock sprinted to the elves first. "Where's your weapon?"

"Destroyed," said Liagol. "And we're running out of options."

Ahead the ranger found a contingent of elven archers and soldiers protecting their leaders. Brianna stepped forward upon seeing the people.

"Where are the rest of your team?" asked the queen with grave concern.

"Is Harrison still alive?" asked Moradoril. "Brendan Brigade? The Forge brothers?"

Murdock alternated his glances between the two. "Harrison, yes," he said, fumbling for words. "I'm not sure about the others."

"The situation is dire," said Brianna, pursing her lips. "Finius must be apprehended."

The ranger nodded. "I agree but how? Our mages are hurt and your weapon is gone," said Murdock, his voice trailing. A hideous roar from above forced everyone to cower.

The sound of flapping wings preceded a cone of flames that torched the ground below. Murdock instinctively dove for cover. Beings wailed in agony, the dragon's attack scorching their skin, forcing everyone to flee. A second burst of fire cascaded from above, another monster entering the fray.

Murdock hid behind a burning tree, his heart pounding, knowing that another fiery volley would end them all. The next attack never came. Instead, the two beasts flew higher into the night, leaving the forest to burn.

"Something got their attention," said Kymbra, startling the ranger.

Murdock grabbed the woman and pulled her close. "Thank the gods you're alive," he said in her ear, hugging Kymbra tight. "Where's Pondle?"

"I don't know," she said sniffling. Another bellow in the distance drew them even closer together.

"If I'm going to die," said Murdock, "I want to be holding you in my arms when it happens." The two maintained their embrace while the forest around them burned uncontrollably.

* * *

"Move him over there!" directed Adrith, pointing to an empty patch of forest that the fires had not consumed. Marissa scurried ahead, securing the area.

The two warriors helped Swinkle and Naa'il lower Gelderand to the ground. Tara and Harrison shuffled to the group, bringing up the rear, while Lance scampered through the underbrush.

"Is he still unconscious?" asked Tara, full of nerves.

"Yes," said Adrith, "and he needs to awaken very soon."

Swinkle bent down to assess Gelderand's condition. Harrison came to his friend's side. "What are your thoughts?"

"I will pray over him again," said the young cleric before placing his hands around the mage's injured leg.

Harrison watched his friend administer the familiar white glow; however, he noticed something else. For the first time in a long time, he worried about Swinkle. Sweat beaded on the young man's forehead and he struggled with his prayers. When finished with his task, he sat back and caught his breath.

"Swinkle, are you alright?" asked Harrison with concern, placing a caring hand on the holy man's back.

"I need some rest. That is all," said the young cleric.

"Rest is a luxury," said Adrith before taking her gaze around the surroundings. Howls of anguish permeated the area, adding to everyone's heightened anxiety.

"If we don't fight," added Marissa, "then we better find a way out of this burning hell."

"Retreat?" said Harrison, furrowing his brow. "We can't! All of our friends are scattered throughout the woods. This battle is far from over!"

"Harrison, look at us!" said Adrith. "You're hurt, Gelderand's out cold, and now Swinkle's exhausted. There's not much fight left in us!"

The young warrior contemplated the woman's statement. His fighter's training told him never to give up on a battle; however, his friends did not share his beliefs. Naa'il approached him while battle tactics raced through his mind.

"Must talk now," said the Scynthian. "Before it's too late."

Harrison's shoulders slumped. "What's so important that you've stayed with us instead of fighting with your comrades?"

"Alabaar's gift," said Naa'il. "You must open it now."

"Naa'il," started Harrison, trying to remain calm, "this is not the time to accept a gift from you or your race. Can it wait ..."

"No!" exclaimed the juvenile. "Now!"

Harrison showed the Scynthian his palms, acquiescing to Naa'il's demand. "Alright," said the young warrior, his eyebrows arched. "Bring me your gift."

Naa'il dropped his backpack and retrieved a heat-damaged wooden box. The Scynthian opened it, then grasped the contents from its resting place.

"For you," he said, opening up his large hand to reveal his prize.

Harrison's eyes widened in shock as he gazed upon the curved piece of metal in Naa'il's hand. "Where did you get that?" asked the young warrior before staring at his friend. "Swinkle! Get over here!"

"Where did you get this?" reiterated Harrison, his energy level rising.

"Alabaar told us to seek humans if our city got attacked," started Naa'il. "All Scynthians know this." The juvenile's voice turned somber. "My city is gone. My friends dead. I went back to get this for you."

Naa'il's words softened the young warrior's heart. Placing a hand on the Scynthian's shoulder, he said, "You did a brave thing, returning to your burning city, and you did the right thing to seek us. Let's not let your efforts go to waste."

Swinkle approached the two, focusing on the object in Naa'il's hand. "Is that what I think it is?"

"I believe so," said Harrison with a grin, feeling a pang of remorse for rebuffing Naa'il so many times in the past.

The young warrior fumbled through his pack searching for a similar artifact. Moments later, he held a familiar piece of metal forged from the same material as the one in Naa'il's hand.

"Let's put these together," said Harrison, taking his relic and bringing it closer to Naa'il's.

When the objects were six inches apart, the smaller piece of curved metal leaped from the Scynthian's hand and fused with the silvery object that Harrison held.

Everyone gathered around Harrison to get a better look at the perfectly circular silver artifact. The young warrior held it closer to his face in order to make a better examination. Aside from the Dwarven runes, seven letters encircled the relic.

"S, H, E, T, H, A, R," muttered Harrison aloud. "Shethar? What does that mean?"

"Are the letters in the right order?" asked Tara, gazing at the object in Harrison's hand.

"Maybe there's another combination," said Swinkle. "However, these letters must mean something."

Naa'il craned his neck to get a better view of the artifact. "Why did Alabaar's gift make a circle?"

Harrison pondered the question for a second. "The circle is now complete," he said, thinking aloud. "The four sections came from each humanoid group—the humans, elves, dwarves, and now Scynthians."

"What does all this mean?" said Adrith, trying her best to solve the puzzle.

A loud crash and several explosions startled the group. All eyes turned to the clearing where an ominous silhouette lumbered about, spewing flames in all directions.

"There isn't much time," exclaimed Marissa. "We need to figure this out now!"

"I know, I know," said Harrison, thinking. The young warrior raised a finger, his eyes widening slightly as a thought came to mind. "Is it possible that the word Shethar is the name of the dragon race?"

Swinkle raised an eyebrow. "A very distinct possibility." The young cleric nodded repeatedly. "The more I think about it, yes, it must be the name!"

"What makes you believe that?" asked Tara, in need of convincing.

"Why would the Ancient Kings go through all this trouble and not give us the name of the evil race?" said Swinkle. "It only makes sense!"

Harrison agreed with his friend's line of reasoning. "Do you have the Genocide Scroll?"

Swinkle went into his backpack and retrieved the parchment. Unfurling it, he said, "Here it is!"

"Can you read it?" asked Harrison, his excitement rising.

Swinkle shook his head, then gazed at Gelderand. "It is magically encrypted and only a magician can read the text."

"Gelderand's unconscious," said the young warrior, exasperated. "How can he read it in his condition?"

The young cleric drew a heavy sigh. "He can't."

* * *

585

Fires raged all around Murdock and Kymbra, the heat intensifying. "I can't take this much longer," said Kymbra, a tear rolling down her cheek, still embracing the ranger.

"We're going to get out of this alive," said Murdock, releasing his hold on the woman. The forest burned everywhere; a smoldering formation of very large trees with massive trunks loomed ahead.

Murdock pointed to the cluster. "See those trees over there?" Kymbra looked where he pointed, then nodded. "We're going to run to them. The flames look less intense."

"Can we make it?"

"Unless you want to fry here, there's no other choice," said Murdock. Sweating profusely, he grabbed Kymbra's hand and said, "Let's go!"

The two fighters scampered through the blazing underbrush, heading for the darker mass of trees ahead of them. The whole woodlands roared like an out of control bonfire, embers flying through the air, pops and cracks from burning vegetation flooding the area. The couple reached the outcrop moments later.

Murdock pushed Kymbra forward between two massive trunks. Though the trees burned, less fires had erupted beyond the grouping. Kymbra passed through the natural opening with Murdock close behind.

Kymbra examined the gigantic trunks. "These oaks are so big they're blocking the fire from spreading."

The ranger pointed to the fiery branches and scorched bark. "They're burning nonetheless. Keep moving!"

The two fled further away from the inferno, stopping a couple of minutes later to catch their breath and assess their situation. "Where do we go from here?" asked Kymbra, her spirits lifting a bit now that the flames had lost some of their intensity.

Murdock remained focused. "We find Pondle."

Kymbra's eyes widened, having momentarily forgotten about the ranger's friend. "Where could he be?"

Murdock shook his head. "Anywhere."

"Those dragons torched the whole area," said Kymbra. "We're lucky to be alive."

"He's alive," snapped Murdock. "We just need to find him."

Kymbra raised her palms. "Alright, let's keep searching but where should we start?"

Murdock thought for a moment. "He'd head straight for the action, where we last saw the king and his wizard."

The lithe warrior gripped her sword. "Then let's go over there, too."

The ranger surveyed the landscape, taking in the devastation. "We looped away from the dragons to escape the fires but we need to head back in the other direction."

Kymbra took a step toward Murdock, kissing him on the lips. "Let's do this. We'll going to find your friend." The ranger nodded but said nothing, then led the two back into the awaiting chaos.

* * *

"Swinkle, if you can't read this scroll, we need to find someone who can," said Harrison. The young cleric shrugged, agreeing.

Harrison panned the area, looking for someone just out of sight. "Where are Allard and Thoragaard?" he lamented.

"They left us a while ago," said Tara. "Who knows where they both are now!"

As the young warrior pondered his predicament, Lance approached his master and whimpered. Harrison paid him no attention, still deep in thought. The little dog nudged the Aegean, whining again.

Harrison gazed at the animal. "Not now, Lance."

The dog yapped once, then gazed to his right. Harrison noticed the canine's subtle antic, taking his line of sight to that of the dog's. It took the young warrior a moment to comprehend what Lance was trying to convey, but his eyes widened when he fully understood.

Harrison stared at Tara, who had taken a moment to check on her uncle, fixing his dressing and patting his forehead with a rag. The young warrior stood up and approached the young maiden while everyone else watched.

"Tara," he said, garnering her attention. The young girl looked up, surprised at seeing so many eyes gazing back at her.

"Yes?" she answered with apprehension in her voice.

Harrison smiled. "You're a mage," he started, confident. "You can read the scripture."

Tara's eyes grew round and her eyebrows arched high on her forehead. "*Me?*" she said in an incredulous voice. "This parchment must be too difficult for someone with my limited experience to read."

"On the contrary," said Swinkle. "Look at our situation. Allowing King Holleris to rule the world because no one could read a magical scroll is not what the Ancient Kings had in mind."

"Swinkle's right," said Harrison. "We've already succeeded in finding all the pieces to this puzzle. This is the end game."

"Can't the elves read it?" asked the young maiden, still unsure of the situation or her abilities.

"I am willing to believe that only a human mage can read this scripture," said Swinkle.

"We don't know where the elves are and we might not find them in time," added the young warrior. Harrison stepped closer to the girl, taking her hands in his. Gazing into her blue eyes, he said, "This is your destiny. Brianna told you so much."

Tara averted her eyes, recalling the elven queen's cryptic prognostications. Maybe this is my time, she thought, my contribution to mankind. Gazing back to Harrison, she said, "I'll do it."

* * *

Murdock and Kymbra sidestepped burning limbs and flaming underbrush while trying to avoid tripping on the scores of crisp carcasses that littered the forest's floor. Though they had trekked for several minutes, they saw no sign of Pondle.

Kymbra pointed up ahead. "It's the king!"

Murdock gazed into the distance. Sure enough, King Holleris and Finius watched over the burning battlefield as their two dragons protected them.

"What's he waiting for?" asked the female warrior, shaking her head. "He has the upper hand."

"I don't know," said the ranger, "this battle's over."

The two scanned the woodlands, finding human fighters, elven soldiers, and Scynthian warriors scattered throughout without any semblance of order.

"No one's in charge anymore," said Murdock, "we're all on our own." Several figures moving through the underbrush caught their eye. The ranger pointed to the beings. "Dwarves!"

Murdock gestured for Kymbra to follow him, the two reaching the band of stocky fighters. The ranger recognized Drogut and Rogur at the head of the pack.

"Hey!" he called, causing the fighters to stop and take up a defensive posture. Upon seeing the humans, the Dwarven soldiers lowered their weapons.

"Finius is close by!" exclaimed Drogut, still consumed by the thought of apprehending the warlock. "We want him!"

"No problem by me," said Murdock, "but how in the world do you think you're going to capture him?"

"That plan needs working out," said the dwarf king. Arrows started whizzing through the air, originating from the right of their position. "That can only help us!"

Murdock gazed upon the monsters that loomed twenty yards ahead. The projectiles no longer hit an invisible shield; rather they pelted the beasts' thick, scaly hides.

"The king and Finius can stand behind those creatures forever," said Kymbra. "We don't possess anything that will hurt those monsters."

A familiar low hum resonated near their position. Murdock turned around, finding more unwanted guests. "Dragonflies!" he exclaimed before scores of miniature monsters entered the region yet again.

The fighters all hunched over, covering their heads as the diminutive beasts spewed short bursts of flames on all those who stood in their path. This time, however, no mages would come to their rescue.

Murdock grabbed Kymbra's forearm. Knowing that they had little chance of defeating the creatures, he shouted, "Run!" The two then fled the scene, hoping to get away from their smaller adversaries before fire consumed them.

* * *

Swinkle handed Tara the parchment. The young maiden felt her heart race as she accepted the scroll. Unfurling it revealed a short amount of illegible text, words that Tara knew only she could unlock. Doubt crept into her mind.

"What if I fail?" she lamented, not wanting to let everyone down.

"You won't," reassured Harrison. "However, I can tell you that all will be lost if you don't at least try." A series of explosions and crashing trees drove home the young warrior's point. "You can do this."

Tara gazed at the magical text again, recalling her teachings with Thoragaard. She then peered over at her uncle, who was still unable to regain consciousness, and considered how she would not want to disappoint him. Summoning her inner strength, she drew a deep breath, then slowly exhaled her nervous energy.

"I'll read the scroll," she said, then went into her pack to retrieve the necessary ingredients for her spell.

Harrison bent closer to the girl. "Take your time but be thorough. We only have one chance at this." Tara nodded, understanding the gravity of the situation.

The young warrior turned his attention to Adrith and Marissa. "Set up a perimeter around us. We don't want anything to interfere with Tara's preparations." The female warriors nodded and fanned out to set up defensive positions. Satisfied with that, Harrison focused on Naa'il.

"I'll need to you protect us as well," said the young warrior.

"I help," said the Scynthian, clutching his mace and heading in the opposite direction.

Harrison concentrated on Tara again. "The perimeter is secure," he said. "Are you ready?"

"Yes," said the young maiden, but before she could start her spell, the low hum of dragonflies droned in the nearby forest.

"Oh, no," said Harrison to himself, knowing that the diminutive beasts would disrupt Tara's concentration.

"They're heading this way!" exclaimed Adrith, pointing to the approaching swarm.

Harrison stared at the incoming creatures bearing straight for them. The young warrior glared at his weapon, knowing that his battle axe would not defeat the miniature enemy. As the dragonflies closed in on the small group, Naa'il rushed to the forefront, waving his weapon at the beasts.

Turning his head in Harrison's direction, he yelled, "Do your magic!" The Scynthian then dashed into the forest, waving his mace and hollering at the top of his lungs. To everyone's surprise, the dragonflies targeted the fleeing Scynthian, leaving them alone.

Harrison watched the smaller dragon-like insects close on the fleeing warrior. Moving as one, the winged creatures swarmed around Naa'il, spewing flames over the poor creature. The Scynthian flailed his mace at the monsters, howling in pain as his fur ignited. Adrith and Marissa broke ranks and raced to help Naa'il.

The young warrior stared at Tara. "Read that scroll! Now!"

Tara sprinkled her ingredients on the parchment, pushing the horrible cries of anguish from her mind. As she did so, the young maiden recited the words that Thoragaard and Gelderand had taught her in the not too distant past. When finished with her spell, she held the scroll out in front of her. The text remained the same.

The young maiden's heart raced, fearing that she had let the group, or the whole world for that matter, down. At that moment a strange aura came over her and she started to feel lightheaded. The text on the parchment began to swirl, the symbols transforming.

Tara could hear Adrith and Marissa shouting, the dragonflies attacking them as they tried to help Naa'il, who wailed in agony. However, the sounds appeared muted, as if she were listening from underwater. Then, the writings became crystal clear.

The girl's eyes widened as the once illegible text transformed into understandable words. Summoning an inner will, she proclaimed using a loud forceful voice, "*Evil has run rampart across the land. Creatures that were created, not born, adhere to the wishes of the wicked, but no more. The time has come to rid the world of these malicious beasts. With the power bestowed on me through the creators of this scroll, I hereby eradicate the Shethar from existence!*"

The invisible aura that Tara had felt while reading the scroll disappeared. To her surprise, Harrison and Swinkle stared at the young maiden, then started panning their heads in all directions. The forest continued to burn and the screams of anguish did not abate. However, changes did happen.

* * *

Murdock and Kymbra had positioned themselves closer to the clearing, watching King Holleris and Finius relish their apparent victory against the overmatched armies. With nothing more to prove, the two men stood next to one of their dragons and climbed on top. The beast roared again, spewing flames at the retreating beings who littered the forest.

King Holleris beamed. "Victory is ours, Finius!" he exclaimed, as the monster began to flap its enormous wings, lifting off the ground. Next to it, another dragon and then a third started to rise upwards.

"We'll ride our creations high above the world, then guide them to the cities in the west where we'll stake our claim to the throne," said the king, dreams of ruling the land he had lost over a millennium ago swirling in his head. "Soon, this will all be ours!"

The dragons rose twenty feet before the unthinkable happened. In an instant, all three creatures vanished, leaving the two evil men falling back to earth with a resounding thud.

"What the ..." said Murdock, his brow creased, unsure of what just happened.

"Where did the dragons go?" asked Kymbra, just as shocked as the ranger.

A wide smile stretched across Murdock's face. "They read the scroll!" The ranger turned to Kymbra, grabbing her arms and pinning them to her side with excitement. "The dragons are gone because Gelderand eradicated them!"

The lithe warrior felt her body relax, the stress and anxiety melting away in an instant. "They're all gone?" Kymbra swiveled her head in all directions, trying to get a read on the landscape.

Murdock pulled the woman close to him, hugging her tightly. "It's all over!"

Kymbra, though just as excited as the ranger, leaned back, her demeanor turning serious. "It's not over until we find all of our friends in one piece."

Murdock nodded. "You're right," he said. "We got more work to do." The two separated, then set out to search for those who had gone missing.

* * *

Drogut, Rogur and several Scynthian warriors had escaped another harrowing experience at the hands of the miniature dragon's vicious breath attack. Sweating profusely and not accustomed to such extreme temperatures, all beings had faded back from the clearing, biding their time.

"Drogut," said his brother, panting and near exhaustion, "this obsession with Finius Boulware might get us all killed."

The Dwarven king glared at his kin. "Better to die trying to kill that warlock than to know he defeated us again!"

Rogur nodded, not wanting to upset his brother further. The younger dwarf turned his attention to the beasts torching the clearing and decimating so many soldiers. The fighter had to look away when the cries of horror and anguish echoed throughout the forest.

A fellow dwarf fighter grabbed Rogur's shoulder and pointed to the opening in the forest. "They're leaving," he said, watching the massive beasts flap their wings and rise above the ground. "All this is for naught!"

Before Rogur could process his feelings, the monsters vanished and the wicked men plummeted to the ground. His eyes round, the younger dwarf shouted, "The dragons disappeared!"

"Well, I'll be ..." said Drogut, his voice trailing as he stared at the sight of the two men rolling on the ground. Raising his axe over his head, he commanded, "Storm the clearing and bring me Boulware!"

The rest of the dwarves and Scynthians roared in unison, then bolted to the unprotected men.

* * *

Moradoril, bent on one knee, did his best to comfort his injured archers, the massive beasts scorching several of his soldiers, rendering them to the verge of death. In an instant, the monster's ominous shadows disappeared.

The elven king rose from his position and gazed into the smoky forest. Brianna, her clothing singed, torn, and damaged, sidled up to Moradoril as he tried to comprehend the unthinkable.

With wide eyes, the elven king said, "I think they did it."

Brianna took hold of Moradoril's arm. Smiling, she said, "*She* did it."

* * *

"Send word to Bracken Drake!" commanded Brendan Brigade. "The dragons are dead!" The Aegean leader could hardly believe his eyes, still searching the immediate area for the beasts as if their disappearance had been a wicked trick.

Octavius Forge scrambled to meet his equal, an incredulous look gracing his face. "Did I just see what I thought I saw?"

Brendan nodded with a smile. "That you did," said the Aegean before gathering his weaponry. "Summon whatever men you have left and storm the battlefield." Octavius nodded, then turned away.

The Aegean grabbed General Forge's forearm before he could depart. "I want the king and his wizard alive." Brendan stared into Octavius' eyes, raised an eyebrow, and cocked his head, driving home his point. The Argosian leader smirked and nodded once, then took off to command his army.

* * *

Bracken Drake directed his remaining men to flank either side of him, creating a phalanx of soldiers. The Arcadian general raised his sword high into the sky, then turned to the sentry next to him. "Sound the horn!"

The fighter heeded his leader's command and blew hard into his instrument. Bracken lowered his weapon in one smooth motion, signaling for his men to start their final march toward the enemy.

* * *

Two Arcadian sentries shooed their horses east as winged monsters arose from the forest, hungry for fresh meat. Three dragons quickly made up ground as the frantic animals galloped away.

"This is going to be a massacre," said one of the sentries, watching the two-headed beasts gain ground on their steeds. In a sudden turn of events, the winged creatures disappeared from the sky.

"Where did they go?" asked another guardian, gazing skyward, swiveling his head in all directions.

"Did they turn invisible?" asked the first man.

"I don't think so," said the other sentry. "They would have attacked by now."

"Then they're defeated!" exclaimed the first Arcadian. His excitement quickly faded as he gazed at the frightened steeds that galloped away. Placing his hands on his hips, he said with a huff, "We have to get our horses back."

* * *

Scynthians ran in all directions, unsure of their next maneuver. "Charge the clearing," yelled Nigel Hammer. "Attack the enemy!"

The former governor of Concur panned the battlefield with a cold, steely gaze. No one appeared to be listening to him. Rashaa, the Scynthian leader, had perished on one of the runs toward the flame-throwing beasts and scores of other warriors died in similar fashion.

Lord Hammer strained to see in the distance, sensing something amiss. Clutching his weapon tighter, he left the decimated Scynthian army behind and trekked toward the clearing. A few moments later, hundreds of human soldiers began to flood the area, encircling the region where King Holleris and Finius Boulware had arranged their dragons.

Footsteps trampled from behind. The dark warrior wheeled around, weapon ready to strike. Several soldiers from the Unified Army approached his position.

"They're gone!" shouted a young fighter, oblivious to the outcast general who stood before him.

Nigel grabbed his arm, halting the boy in his tracks while the soldier's comrades pressed forward.

"What do you mean gone?" questioned Lord Hammer.

"The dragons!" exclaimed the fighter with a wide smile. "They disappeared!"

Nigel released his grip on the young man, allowing him to scamper away to catch up with his squadron. Lord Hammer panned the vicinity, finding more human soldiers heading in his direction and no dragons. The black-clad warrior quickly removed the gold ring from his pouch and slipped it onto his finger. Now invisible, the dark lord headed toward the commotion in a different direction.

* * *

"The dragonflies vanished!" shouted Adrith before she and Marissa started patting out the flames that had overtaken Naa'il's body.

Harrison focused on the immediate landscape. Though chaos still erupted and fires engulfed the region, he could no longer find the menacing beasts that had wreaked so much destruction.

Turning his attention to Tara, he said, "I think you did it! The dragons are gone!"

The young maiden stared at the blank parchment, all semblance of text removed. "The words were right here," she said, shaking her head. "I swore I just read them."

"You did," said Swinkle. "And the world will be a better place because of your efforts." Lance bounded over, wagging his tail and rubbing his body against the young girl.

"If what you say is true," started Tara, "then what do we do now?"

Harrison knew exactly what they had to do next. "I must face the king."

"Harrison," said the young cleric, "you are still injured and we cannot leave Gelderand behind."

The Aegean pondered the situation. "Confronting him is inevitable. Especially with this sudden change in the battle."

Harrison took inventory of his surroundings. Gelderand lay hurt and still unconscious, Adrith and Marissa had extinguished the flames that had engulfed Naa'il, and Tara and Swinkle awaited his next move.

The young warrior whistled for Lance. "Come on, boy, you're coming with me. Everyone else, remain here and wait for my return."

Tara approached Harrison. "Don't do anything foolish," she lamented, knowing how the young warrior's intentions might be good but reckless at the same time.

"This ends now," said Harrison with conviction. "I'll be back but someone needs to lead us to this final battle." The young warrior leaned over and kissed Tara on the lips. "Stay safe and out of sight. I will return."

The young warrior gazed over to Swinkle. "Relay my intentions to the others."

The young cleric nodded. "Be careful, Harrison. The king's back is against the wall and he will do anything to survive."

Harrison nodded once, then gestured for Lance to trek with him. Though he hurt all over, he could sense the troll's regeneration process overtaking his body. Staring into the smoky woods, he started his journey to right the wrongs of the past one thousand years.

CHAPTER 50

Ｑ

Fires burned all around Harrison as he and Lance trudged toward the clearing. Just out of eyesight, soldiers manned their stations and Scynthian warriors raced to their positions, all stopping at the outskirts of the forest's opening. Ahead, the young warrior found two older men on their hands and knees.

Harrison made a slow pan of the vicinity, absorbing the utter destruction. Aside from a forest reminiscent of one found in hell, charred bodies and dismembered corpses littered the area. Broken weaponry lay scattered on the ground, the death toll in the hundreds. His own injuries notwithstanding, the young warrior began to seethe. A phalanx of soldiers appearing from the forest's depths more than startled him.

Bracken Drake positioned his men just behind the Aegean, creating a formidable perimeter. The general commanded his men to await his orders, then approached the young warrior.

"Harrison," he started, "it's good to see you alive, but if you don't make the first move, I'm going to kill those men on my own."

The young warrior met the Arcadian's steely gaze. "This war ends now," said Harrison. "Prepare your men to apprehend our adversaries on my mark."

"As you see fit," said Bracken before adding, "Be careful. The wizard's hurt but may still have some tricks up his sleeve."

Harrison nodded, then turned his focus back to the clearing. Clutching his battle axe tighter, he gazed down to Lance and said,

599

"Let's go, boy." The young warrior shuffled into the open space, revealing himself to King Holleris and Finius Boulware.

Both men rose to their feet when they saw Harrison with Finius grasping his wooden staff and pointing it at the young warrior. An arrow whizzed through the clearing, piercing the ancient wizard's upper chest, forcing him to release his weapon, and dropping him to the ground.

"Apprehend him!" yelled Murdock, lowering his longbow. The ranger stood twenty yards to Harrison's right with Kymbra by his side.

Three elven scouts burst from the underbrush, rushing to the warlock's slumped body. To everyone's surprise, they removed the arrow and began healing the wicked mage.

Liagol waved Harrison over, while Floriad and Gaelos attended to Finius. "Your generals want the warlock alive, to pay for his crimes through the centuries," said Liagol. Seconds later, a band of dwarves and Scynthians rushed from the thickets.

Drogut stepped forward, bellowing, "The wizard's ours!"

Harrison felt the momentum swing. Hissing sounds began to permeate the local woodlands as once raging infernos began to dissipate. From the smoldering embers emerged soldiers from the Unified Army, with Brendan Brigade and Octavius Forge leading them into the clearing.

Across from Harrison, Brianna, Moradoril, and a band of elves, their bodies burned and scarred from the dragons' last volley of flames, appeared for support.

Lance, sensing more movement in the underbrush, barked once, then bolted toward Murdock and Kymbra, entering the forest behind them. A moment later he came back out, yapping with delight. Adrith and Marissa assisted Naa'il, while Swinkle and Tara, each having one of Gelderand's arms draped over their shoulders, helped the mage to the edge of the forestation.

Scynthians, their numbers woefully smaller, blocked off the opposite edge of the region, preventing any possible escape for the evil king. Lord Nigel Hammer, appearing out of thin air, commanded the savage army.

Taking his cold stare to Harrison, he said, "End this now."

"I don't usually agree with him," said a voice near Murdock. "But I do this time." Both Murdock and Kymbra turned, finding Pondle emerging from the forest's depths with Thoragaard by his side. The four hugged, happy to see everyone alive, then turned with conviction to the new battle front.

The young warrior with newfound strength and purpose approached the king, stopping ten feet from his position. Both men stared each other down, neither saying a word.

"Look at you," said King Holleris, breaking the silence. "Just as broken as your brother when he last visited me."

"I'll heal," said Harrison, "but your rule of tyranny is over before it ever got started."

"Is that what you think?" said the king, bating the young warrior. "That you can destroy my creations without retribution? I have more wealth in my possession than you'll ever have in a lifetime."

"A lot that's going to do you in a prison cell," said Harrison, gripping his weapon tighter.

"What are you going to do now? Bring me to a trial, then imprison me for eternity?" asked the wicked man. "I've already spent an eternity to get here. Whoever guards me will gladly accept a handsome reward for setting me free."

"You'll be held under the strictest of military prisons until your sentencing," said Harrison. "No one will rescue you."

"So willing to take that chance," said the king with a smirk. "Finius might be useless now, but another can take his place. A wise man makes contingency plans."

Harrison did not want to believe the king's words, but a pang of doubt crept into the young warrior's mind. His blood simmering, he said, "Anyone found helping you will be hung on the spot. Your time is over."

The king laughed, then held out his hands. "Go ahead, bind my wrists so that a frail old man won't escape a surrounding army. Throw me in the deepest gallows, away from all humanity. Do whatever you must, but remember this. I survived a millennium already and know the secret to do it again.

"Do you think Finius was the only person who created my dragons? I had a hand in that, too! My blood coursed through their veins and, in a matter of time, I will use whatever life I have left to create an even greater species." The king gestured with his outstretched hands. "Please, bind me."

Harrison's heart pumped harder and his blood boiled. Though evil had consumed the king, the young warrior could not shake the thought of this man reconstituting another wretched race of monsters.

King Holleris rattled his hands. "Bind me! Bind me!"

"You will pay for your sins," said Harrison, squeezing his axe handle.

"Bind me!" screamed the king. "Do it!"

Harrison raised his axe, took two steps, and leveled his blade through the king's neck, severing the wicked man's head for the second time in the royal man's lifetime. King Holleris' headless corpse slumped to the ground in a pool of blood, his head rolling a few feet away.

The young warrior, his heart still racing, went over to the severed appendage, kicking it lightly with his boot. The king's eyes remained round and his mouth wide open, unable to finish his last words. Lowering his blade, an uncanny sense of calm overtook Harrison.

Within seconds, a myriad of beings flooded the clearing. Drogut and his kin swarmed Finius, forcing the wicked warlock to the ground, pinning his arms behind his back.

"This wretched monster is ours!" exclaimed the Dwarven king.

"Everyone, wait!" cried Brendan Brigade, navigating through the people who had formed a tight circle around the decapitated king and his sorcerer. "Finius must stand trial for his crimes!"

"That's not going to happen," said Drogut. "He almost killed every dwarf on this planet!"

"Brendan," interjected Octavius. "These two destroyed Argos and killed Caidan. I seek justice for my people as well."

Moradoril and Brianna stepped forward. "The elves have a vested interest in this man, too," said the elven king, images of their destroyed homeland swirling in his head. "A trial is a necessity."

"Finius is still a dangerous man," added Brianna. "My people can contain him best."

Drogut gestured for his men to continue to bind the warlock. "We're taking him!"

"Kill him, too!" said a deep voice. All eyes shifted to Naa'il, who pushed his way into the circle, his fur singed and body badly burned. "His dragons torched Mahalanobis. Scynthians demand him!"

Brandan raised his palms, trying to restore order. "I understand everyone's emotions right now but we need to figure out the best course of action."

Shouts and exclamations followed the Aegean's last statement, each contingent strongly voicing their opinion. Amidst all the commotion, Harrison gazed down at the lifeless corpse, watching the wicked king's blood trickle out of his body. The young warrior's thoughts drifted to his deceased brother and how this man had poisoned Troy's mind from the moment the king's henchmen had snatched him from his cradle.

Finding an inner strength, he exclaimed above the din, "My brother Troy died because of this wicked man." Everyone stopped their arguments and stared at the young warrior. Having gained everyone's attention, he continued, "King Holleris' men could just have easily kidnapped me instead of Troy when they stole him from my parents. These two wicked souls twisted his young mind, getting him to believe his actions were just.

"We've all rendered colossal losses because of these monsters and their devastating creations. However, there won't be a trial, ever. King Holleris is dead."

Brendan approached Harrison, placing a caring hand on his shoulder. "You did what you needed to do to silence King Holleris' evil once and for all, and no one will hold you accountable. However, Finius has caused immeasurable destruction to so many races that he must stand trial."

Harrison brought his focus to his mentor. "Brendan, we're in a state of war, correct?"

The general arched his eyebrows, surprised at the question. "Yes, we are. Why do you ask that question?"

"During wartime isn't it customary for generals to hold trials on the battlefield to ensure quick judgments and sentencings without having to trudge prisoners along with their armies?"

The elder Aegean smirked, understanding Harrison's line of thinking. "Yes, field generals use that practice often."

Harrison extended his arm, fanning it in a wide arc to those who stood around them. "And we have all the leaders of the land with us now. I can't think of a better time to try this man for his crimes."

Brendan nodded, then turned his attention to the land's leadership. "Harrison's reasoning is sound. I agree that we should try this man for his crimes at this moment. Any objections?"

Bracken Drake stepped forward. "The city of Arcadia agrees."

Octavius Forge raised his hand. "As does Argos."

"The elves have no problem with a trial at this time," said Moradoril.

"Agree," said Naa'il.

All eyes turned to Drogut. "Do you even have to ask?" The dwarf king pointed to Rogur. "Get that monster on his feet!" Drogut's brother and his comrades forced the wicked warlock to stand.

Finius, a shell of his former self with his hands bound behind his back, stood before all the races of the land with his head hung low. Several of Drogut's men had to stand next to the evil wizard, propping him up to hear the charges against him.

Brendan maintained his lead role. "Finius Boulware, you have conspired with the deceased King Holleris to put forth a wicked plan to overthrow all the governments of the land. During your millennium of destruction, you are responsible for the deaths of countless lives, a plan to eradicate entire races, and a plot to enslave the free people of this world. How do you respond to these charges?"

The warlock swayed under the weight of his indictment, knowing he had no words that could rectify his situation. Trying to stand tall, he hissed, "I have no remorse for my actions. Nothing I can say will change your minds. King Holleris had a grand vision for this land and you should have given him a chance to bring it to fruition. Instead," Finius glared at Harrison, "you killed him!"

"Utter destruction and chaos are no way to drive home your point of saving this land!" exclaimed Harrison.

"We didn't have a chance," barked Finius.

"Enough!" said Brendan. "Since you have no remorse and no worthy defense for your actions, we will now sentence you."

"Kill him," said Bracken Drake, coldly.

"Death is his sentence!" exclaimed Octavius.

"Let us do it!" bellowed Naa'il as several Scynthian warriors gripped their clubs tighter.

"Everyone, wait," said Harrison before turning his sights on the dwarves. "What did you have in mind since your people wanted him the most?"

Drogut did not say a word, instead he walked right up to the warlock. Glaring up at him, he said, "This monster's actions were the reason the elves' entombed my people, keeping us alive for the sole purpose of feeding ravenous spiders. For a thousand years my kinsmen watched in horror as those creatures consumed them one at a time. Those that survived the horrific ordeal are now mad, never to be well again."

The dwarf king thrust a finger in the evil mage's face. "You, Boulware, will suffer a similar fate!" Everyone cringed at the thought of spiders slowly digesting the wicked warlock.

Harrison brought his gaze to Brendan. "I agree with Drogut that this form of death is suitable for the crimes this man has committed."

The Aegean general nodded, then turned his attention to the group before him. "Does anyone have an objection to this death sentence?" No one protested. "Then it's settled."

Brendan stared at the bound mage. "Finius Boulware, I hereby sentence you to death at the hands of the dwarves, who will administer their manner of execution. You can save any last words until the time the dwarves are ready to implement their plan."

Drogut turned and approached Brendan. The dwarf king extended his hand. "Thank you for honoring the wishes of my people." Brendan accepted, returning a firm shake.

The dwarf king then addressed his men. "Ready yourselves for our trip back home. It's time to leave this hellish forest." Several dwarf fighters pushed Finius forward, forcing him to start walking away from the clearing.

Harrison intervened before the stocky warriors went too far ahead. "Drogut," said the young warrior. "We need someone to represent your people when we start setting policy for the land."

Drogut thought for a moment, then turned to his brother. "Rogur, I appoint you to represent our race."

"Me?" said the younger dwarf. "Don't you need me to help with Finius' sentence?"

"Oh, we'll await your return," said the dwarf king with a smile. "This is going to be a long process for the old warlock." Drogut gestured for two fellow fighters to accompany Rogur. "You'll need someone to talk to on your return trip."

"On the contrary," said Moradoril, entering the conversation. "It would be our honor to escort your kinsmen home."

Drogut nodded once to the elf king. "A noble gesture." The dwarf addressed his brother again. "We'll see you soon enough, brother."

The dwarf king then gestured for his men to begin their trek out of the forest. Moments later, the contingent of dwarves left with their prize, leaving the rest of the armies behind.

Brendan approached Harrison after the dwarves departed. "What's your plan here, Harrison?"

"Order needs to be restored to the land, with all races participating," said the young warrior. "Everyone's here. I suggest we leave this desolate place and return to Concur to convene our meeting. It's been a long war."

Brendan smiled. "That it has. Lady Meredith will be happy to see us, too."

"Yes, she will," said Harrison, smiling back. The young warrior gazed back to the corpse that lay on the ground. "What do we do about the king's body? Give it a burial?"

The elder Aegean narrowed his eyes. Without saying a word, Brendan lit a torch and ignited the wicked man's corpse. While the flames consumed the dead body, he said, "This man does not deserve a burial." The general took his boot and kicked the severed head next to the burning carcass, the appendage catching fire as well.

Harrison stared at the impromptu pyre. With a heavy sigh, he said, "Let's get out of here."

The Aegean leader nodded, then addressed the many faces staring at the two men. "This battle is over!" exclaimed Brendan to the cheers of the soldiers in the clearing. "We'll all leave this burning forest behind and head for the countryside where we'll regroup before traveling to Concur. Upon reaching the walled city we'll convene the first meeting of all the land's races in over a thousand years." Brendan spread his arms wide. "To all my fellow leaders, gather your troops and let's begin the trek out of this forsaken place."

Bracken Drake gathered the Arcadians, while Octavius worked with Brendan to collect the various troops that made up the Unified Army. The elves formed their marching order and headed through the forest, Moradoril and Brianna leading the way.

Naa'il sought Harrison, saying, "I take Scynthians with you."

The young warrior smiled. "Gather your comrades. We'll march into Concur together."

The juvenile Scynthian flashed a rare smile, then went about to gather his scattered troops. As Harrison watched him leave, three dwarves approached him.

"Might we trek with you?" asked Rogur.

"By all means," said Harrison. "It will be my honor to escort you as well."

"Thank you," said the dwarf. "We're ready whenever you are."

"Give me a few minutes to gather my friends, then we'll leave," said the young warrior. The dwarves nodded, then backed away, allowing their human friends to ready themselves.

Harrison panned the vicinity, searching for the people most important to him. Murdock, Pondle, and Kymbra approached the young warrior first.

The ranger slapped his friend's back. "We did it!" exclaimed Murdock with a wide smile. "We actually did it!"

Harrison nodded. "I know, I can hardly believe it, too! How much did we really go through to get to this point?"

"More than I care to remember," responded Murdock, shaking his head.

"Let's go home," said Kymbra, taking hold of the ranger's arm.

"I'd be more than happy to lead us out of here," said Pondle.

"In a few minutes," said Harrison, looking past the thief. Lance bolted toward his master while Adrith and Marissa assisted Gelderand, his arms slung over each woman's shoulder. Behind them, Thoragaard and Swinkle ushered Tara. The young maiden dashed toward Harrison as she entered the clearing.

The young warrior could hardly contain his smile, scooping the girl into his arms. "You did it!" said Harrison, planting a kiss on the young maiden's lips. "The dragons are gone because of you!"

Tara blushed. "I only did what I was taught," said the young maiden. "I'm glad I didn't let everyone down."

"You're too modest," said Harrison. "Your efforts proved to be the most important aspect of this war. Without you, King Holleris would have enslaved the world using his dragons as enforcers."

Tara smiled. "I'm just happy that I succeeded while doing my part."

"The history books will reflect just that," beamed Harrison. "I'm so proud of you!"

The young maiden took hold of her mate's hand. "Thank you but can we finally go home?"

"Of course we can," said Harrison, kissing her on the cheek. The young warrior then addressed his friends.

"It's been an honor fighting with you, adventuring with you, and most of all, succeeding with you," started Harrison. "Our journey had many pitfalls along the way. We lost Marcus and Fallyn, Aidan and Jason, as well as Teleios and Troy. I'd like to dedicate our victory today to them."

Swinkle, Harrison's closest friend, took a step forward. "Everyone, please bow your heads," said the young cleric, all his friends complying. "Pious, we thank you for your guidance, allowing us to rid the land of these wicked beasts, and avoiding evil men ruling with an iron fist. Please take care of the friends we have lost, knowing that we all will see them again another day."

The young cleric brought his gaze to Harrison. "Thank you as well, Harrison, for leading us to victory, for persevering in the darkest of times, and getting us all to believe in the ultimate goal."

Harrison placed a caring hand on Swinkle's shoulder. "It's what I was born to do." The young warrior looked upon all of his friends. "We accomplished this together, each and every one of us." Harrison pulled Tara close to him again. "It's time to go home."

Without an argument from the rest, the group of adventurers gathered their belongings, joined the rest of the armies, and began their trek back to the great city of Concur.

CHAPTER 51

The journey back to Concur took well over a month. Harrison and the land's leadership team had deemed it necessary to take their time, allow soldiers to heal their battle wounds, get everyone back to health, and, most important, to discuss parameters for a lasting peace. Along the way, Harrison and Tara made plans of their own.

"I see Concur!" exclaimed the young maiden, her heart bursting with joy knowing that their long trek from the Dark Forest was all but over.

"I never thought I'd be so happy to see a city again," said Harrison, clutching his love's hand tighter. "Our future begins very soon." The young warrior planted a kiss on top of the girl's head.

"Meredith's going to be happy to see everyone," said Tara, leaning her head on Harrison's chest.

The young warrior smiled. "That she will."

Within the hour, a large convoy of men, elves, dwarves, and Scynthians approached the east gate. Sentries posted on top of the wall blew their horns, alerting the city to the approaching army. Harrison, his friends, and the land's leaders positioned themselves at the head of the procession.

Harrison gazed through the wall's opening, finding soldiers and townsfolk bustling inside. As they drew nearer, several figures exited the city in order to meet the advancing army.

The young warrior focused on a very familiar figure. Meredith with Percival and Catherine flanking her on either side stepped ahead of the platoon of soldiers who had escorted her from the city. A wide smile graced her face upon seeing the young warrior.

The Governor of Concur approached Harrison with tears in her eyes. "Welcome home!" she said, hugging him tightly. The woman then brought her gaze to Tara. "Both of you."

"We're so glad to be back," said Harrison. Shaking his head, he continued, "There's so much to tell." The young warrior released his hug. "Someone else is here with us."

Meredith stepped back, peeking behind Harrison. Thoragaard stepped forward, along with Adrith and Marissa. "Meredith," said the illusionist in his customary monotone voice, "how nice to see you again."

"Thoragaard!" exclaimed Meredith, racing to embrace the mage. "I wasn't sure if you had made it to the Dark Forest alive. Thank the gods you've returned!"

"A harrowing experience to say the least," said the magician. "We all have battled enough. It is time to rest."

Meredith stepped back to address the crowd. "That it is," she started before raising her voice. "It's an honor to accept the land's utmost fighters back to our great city. Our citizens are most grateful for your sacrifices and will do everything in our power to make you all as comfortable as possible. Please, accept our hospitality as you acclimate yourselves back to everyday life."

The troops cheered in unison, everyone happy to hear that they would have good food and a warm bed to rest in after months of travel and battle. Brendan addressed Meredith, along with Harrison and Octavius.

"Thank you for your hospitality, Lady Meredith," said Brendan with a slight bow.

"You're more than welcome after what you all did for the benefit of this land," said the governor. "Please, take a couple of days to relax before we engage in any activities."

"I'll direct our armies and visitors accordingly," said the elder Aegean. "Again, thank you." Brendan then turned to

Harrison. "Fill Meredith in on everything while we handle accommodating the men."

The young warrior nodded. "I shall do just that."

Brendan Brigade took his cue and gathered the land's leadership in order to work out a strategy to get their troops comfortably inside the walled city. Meanwhile, Harrison and his friends surrounded Meredith and her servants.

"It's so wonderful to see everyone," said the governor. "I'll make special arrangements for all of you in the governor's mansion. Your days of fighting are over." Meredith focused on her help. "Percival, Catherine, be sure that our guests have everything they need during their stay."

"Of course, milady," said the thin servant. "Please, everyone, follow us back to the governor's residence." Before he could gather Harrison and his friends, Meredith added one more thing.

"Also prepare the ballroom for an historic meeting," said the governor. "I'm sure there'll be much to talk about."

Percival nodded and bowed. "Consider it done." The house servant waved the people forward. "Please, everyone, follow me."

Harrison and his friends started their walk inside the city with Meredith venturing alongside the young couple. "I truly mean it when I say it's good to see you," said Meredith, taking Harrison by the arm. "I'm sure you've seen horrific things."

"More than you can imagine," said Tara, gripping Harrison's hand tighter.

The young warrior, a little embarrassed at having two beautiful women struggling for his attention, said, "The worst is behind us now and we're looking forward to a long break in the fighting."

"I pray for the same," said the governor. "Did you see Nigel in your travels?"

The question took Harrison by surprise. "As a matter of fact we did," said the young warrior. "He actually took command of the Scynthian army."

"He did?" said Meredith with genuine disbelief. "That's not like him at all."

"We were all just as amazed," said Harrison. "I guess he understood the gravity of the situation."

"Only if it suited himself," huffed Meredith. "Where did he go?"

Harrison lifted his eyebrows. "Come to think of it, he disappeared after our final confrontation with the king and his wicked warlock."

"Disappeared?"

"Into thin air," said Harrison. "He still has the ring that makes him invisible."

Meredith shook her head in disgust. "He'll use it to push along his agenda. What about Allard?" she asked with a scowl, not bothering to hide her disdain for Lord Hammer's dark mage. "Was he with him?"

"Yes, Allard joined Gelderand and Thoragaard against the evil king," said Harrison. "No one's seen him either."

Meredith pursed her lips. "They're probably both conspiring against us as we speak."

"Possibly," said the young warrior with a shrug. "After we settle in, we'd like to have a treaty ceremony with the land's leadership. We couldn't think of a better place than Concur to hold the event."

The governor smiled, knowing that her city's rebuilding effort could use the boost from the land's dignitaries. "I wouldn't have it any other way. I'll have my staff ready the ballroom for the historic summit."

"That would be fantastic." Changing the subject, Harrison said, "I have something personal to ask of you." The young warrior peered down to Tara, both smiling. "Actually, it's a request."

Meredith raised an eyebrow. "A request?"

* * *

Two days after entering the walled city, the land's leaders congregated around a large oak table. Meredith ordered her staff to ready the mansion's ballroom for the occasion, sparing no expense. Fine tapestries and artwork adorned the walls, sculptures rested in the room's corners, and brilliant carpets lay on the floor. Fresh cut flowers and the finest tableware graced the hard surface's top.

Harrison, Brendan Brigade, and Octavius Forge took a seat at the long table while his friends found chairs along a wall directly behind them. The young warrior nodded to his fellow fighters who had already taken their places and waited for the meeting to begin.

To the young warrior's left, Naa'il fidgeted in an undersized chair. Two of his fellow comrades stood behind the juvenile. "Try to relax," said Harrison with a smile, figuring that the Scynthians did not hold such formal events.

"Chair too small," said the warrior, trying to get comfortable. "Scynthians stand at our meetings."

Harrison laughed. "We don't. Just try and make the best of it." Naa'il nodded but did a poor job looking comfortable.

Meredith, in a large ornately decorated chair, sat alongside Thoragaard at the head of the table. "Welcome to Concur," she started. "I hope you've found everything to your liking over the past couple of days."

Moradoril, positioned across from Harrison's team, said, "Your hospitality has been wonderful." Liagol, Floriad, and Gaelos, like Harrison's friends, filled seats behind their king and queen.

"We thank you for everything you have done for us," added Brianna with a smile. Meredith nodded, accepting their compliments.

"Milady," started Bracken Drake, situated near the elves with two of his Arcadian advisors behind him, "your generosity with our troops cannot be overstated. Our men have suffered for a long time but you have made them feel right at home."

"The dwarves want to recognize your hospitality as well," added Rogur, seated beside Naa'il with his two companions behind him.

"Scynthians grateful," stammered Naa'il, unsure of the strange human protocol.

"As always, milady," said Brendan, "we cannot begin to thank you enough for your generosity."

"I'm glad we could tend to everyone's needs," said Meredith with a smile. "My servants will prepare a buffet while we commence with our meeting."

On cue, several servers delivered warm plates filled with tender meats and roasted vegetables to a long table at the end of the room, while others strategically placed loaves of warm bread, flagons of ale, and carafes of wine. The aroma of fine foods began to fill the room.

Meredith addressed her guests once again. "I'm sure our dinner spread will hasten this meeting," she said with a smile. "Brendan has informed me of the plans everyone agreed to while journeying back to Concur." The governor turned her attention to the elder Aegean fighter. "Brendan."

The Aegean leader rose from his seat. "Thank you, Meredith. As you all know and agreed to, we have the formal treaty documentation prepared for signatures." Brendan gestured to Swinkle, who handed him two rolled parchments. The Aegean leader unfurled each scroll, flattening them out on the table.

"I set before you a treaty that, if enforced, will provide peace for all the peoples of the land." Brendan addressed Meredith again. "Milady, the wording in this agreement states that the Scynthians will keep the land west of the Dark Forest and all of the Empire Mountains, save for the Dwarven mines. The Scynthians will also not disrupt any of the dwarves' activities in the region."

Harrison gazed over to Naa'il. "This is what you agreed to," he said in a low voice. "You understand that, right?"

The Scynthian fidgeted in his seat. "Last time you show map."

The young warrior motioned toward the second parchment on the table. "That's it right there."

"Naa'il," said Brendan. "The colors shaded in red are your lands. We will not enter them unless there's a dire emergency, like we just witnessed with King Holleris and his dragon army." The Aegean remained focused. "In return, your people promise to no longer attack innocent men, women, and children."

The juvenile Scynthian rose from his seat and stood next to Brendan, examining the map in the process. Using a clawed finger, he pointed at the southern region of the land.

"My people here, too," he said, in reference to the Great Ridge of King Solaris.

"Understood," said Brendan. Taking his line of sight to Bracken Drake, he continued, "and the Arcadians will escort a platoon of your fighters to the mountain range where you can inform them of this treaty."

"Might be fighting," said Naa'il. "We talked about this."

The Aegean nodded. "Again, understood. Do we have your acceptance to this pact?"

"Yes," said Naa'il, before returning to his seat.

"At this time, I would like all the leaders of the land to sign this Treaty of Peace, which as of today will be known as the Concurian Accord," said Brendan, giving a slight nod to Meredith.

The governor spoke again. "Before this document is signed, we must also hear verbal confirmation from all parties." Meredith turned to Brendan. "Is Aegeus in agreement to this pact?"

Brendan nodded. "Yes, milady."

Meredith turned her attention to Octavius Forge. "Argos?"

The elder Forge sat tall. "Yes."

"Arcadia?"

"Arcadia shall abide by this pact," said Bracken Drake.

Meredith brought her focus to Moradoril. "The elves?"

"It would be an honor to be part of this alliance," responded Moradoril. "Yes."

The governor shifted her gaze to Rogur. "The dwarves?"

The Dwarven representative nodded. "Yes, we agree."

Meredith gazed at Naa'il. "And will the Scynthians agree to the parameters outlined here today?"

The Scynthian hesitated for a moment, then said, "Scynthians agree."

A wide smile flashed across Meredith's face. "Concur also pledges allegiance to this pact." The governor rose from her seat and outstretched her arms. "Then we've reached a consensus. All parties shall abide by this agreement as soon as it is signed."

Swinkle rushed over and placed an ink well and fancy, feathered pen next to the Concurian Accord. Brendan picked up the pen and dabbed it in the black liquid. "Aegeus shall sign first."

After the elder Aegean signed the treaty, each leader took their turn signing as well, ending with Naa'il. As soon as the Scynthian affixed his race's symbol, Meredith summoned her servants to hand everyone their choice of a flagon of ale or chalice filled with fine wine.

"Congratulations to us all," said Meredith, raising her goblet along with everyone else.

"To an everlasting peace," said Harrison as all people in the room saluted one another before taking a swig from their cups.

"Now, everyone, please enjoy a meal for the ages," said Meredith. Servants once again flew around the room, loading plates, filling flagons, and attending to everyone's needs.

Tara sidled up to Harrison. "This is quite a fancy get together."

Harrison took a sip from his chalice. "It's not always like this," he said with a laugh.

"Well, you finally got what you wanted," said Murdock, joined by the rest of his friends. "Everyone's together and they're all happy."

"For now," said Kymbra, sipping from her chalice and draping an arm around Murdock's waist.

"Let's hope we never have to go through another devastating ordeal again," said the young warrior, taking Tara's hand.

"So, does that mean we'll go adventuring again soon?" asked Pondle, visions of treasures dancing in his head.

"I'm up for that," said Adrith, smiling.

"Me too!" chimed Marissa.

Harrison gazed down at Tara, then smiled. "Not right now," he said, then added, "in the future. Let's enjoy some much needed downtime."

"You can say that again," said Gelderand, limping toward the couple. "My adventuring days are over."

"Really?" said Harrison, his brow scrunched. "I figured you'd want to get back in the wilderness after you've healed."

The mage shook his head slowly. "I promised an old man that I'd return to care for him and I intend to do just that."

Harrison nodded, recalling Gelderand's pledge to his mentor, Martinaeous. The couple approaching caught his eye.

"Meredith," said the young warrior. "Once again, you did not disappoint."

"Was there ever any question?" said the governor with a sly smile.

"What you did was remarkable," said Thoragaard, in Harrison's direction. "Your efforts have taken the land to a state of peace."

"Don't give me all the credit," said the young warrior. "This was a total team effort, involving every faction in this land."

"You're too modest," said Meredith. "You brought everyone together, like it or not."

Harrison lowered his head, embarrassed at the compliment. Tara tugged on his arm, smiling. "I guess I can take a little credit," he said with a smile.

Meredith laughed, then shifted her gaze to Tara. "Has Catherine found you yet?"

The young maiden shook her head no. "Is she looking for me?"

"As a matter of fact, yes," said the governor, pointing with her chalice to her handmaiden who traversed the room. "She has something for you."

Tara crinkled her brow as Catherine drew closer. The object in her hands brought an exclamation of joy. "Rufus!"

"He's waited so long for your return," said Catherine, handing the tabby cat to Tara.

"How's he feeling?" asked the girl, snuggling the feline to her chest.

"He's pretty much healed from his wounds," said the handmaiden. "Meredith wanted you to know how much we cared for him while you were away."

Tara turned to the governor. "I can't thank you enough!"

"Rufus got the best care," said Meredith. "I'm sure he's going to make Lance jealous."

"He already has," said Harrison with a laugh as Lance bounded toward Tara, placing his legs on hers in order to sniff the creature in her arms. Rufus peered down at the dog and meowed, eliciting laughs from the people around them.

Harrison maneuvered closer to Meredith. Under his breath, he asked, "Are we all set for tomorrow?"

A wide smile beamed across the governor's face. "Oh, we are more than ready!"

Harrison brought his gaze around the room, a feeling of satisfaction coursing through his body. The land's leadership shared drinks and laughs, Scynthians talked with dwarves, and an intense feeling of accomplishment began to set in.

Taking a sip from his flagon, he turned to Meredith with a smile and said, "Good."

* * *

"I can't believe we're actually doing this," said Tara with a grin, taking Harrison's hands.

"I've never wanted something more in my whole life," said the young warrior before planting a kiss on the young maiden's lips.

Three days had passed since the better part of the kingdom entered through Concur's east gate. Today, the young couple stood in a posh room inside the governor's mansion.

The double doors to the chamber opened a crack. Catherine, flowers in her hair, peeked her head in and said, "It's time!"

"Give me another second," said Harrison. The girl nodded once and closed the door.

Harrison squeezed Tara's hands. "I never thought I'd find someone like you, especially adventuring across the land. I thought I'd be hunting down treasure my whole life; however, Pious had different plans for me."

Tara giggled. "You sound like Swinkle!"

Harrison laughed at the mention of his friend's name. "He's made a tremendous impact on my life, which ultimately led me to you." The young warrior repositioned a flower in Tara's hair. "And today he's going to make things permanent for us."

Harrison placed a strong hand on the young maiden's belly. "All of us."

Tara smiled, then reached up on her tiptoes to kiss Harrison again. "Let's not keep everyone waiting."

Harrison received her kiss, then held out his arm. Tara intertwined hers with his and the two walked to the doorway. The young warrior knocked twice. Catherine opened the portal a crack, her eyes staring at his.

"We're ready," said Harrison through the opening. Catherine nodded and a second later threw open the doors.

Harrison and Tara stepped out onto the terrace, the warm midday sun hitting their faces. Flanked on either side of the runway sat royalty and leaders from throughout the land.

Tara beamed in her white dress adorned with jewelry from Meredith's collection and fresh flowers in her hair. "You know my uncle's not happy that he can't escort me," said the young maiden under her breath.

Harrison located the magician, seated next to the makeshift altar. "No one wanted to see him limp down the runway."

Musicians started playing a wedding march as everyone rose from their seats. Harrison and Tara, arm in arm, began their walk down the red carpet that Meredith's servants had laid for the ceremony. The young couple passed Brendan Brigade and Octavius Forge, along with Bracken Drake and a couple of his lead men. Across from them stood Moradoril and Brianna with Liagol, Floriad, and Gaelos flanking them. Alongside the elves stood Rogur and his comrades, making up the dwarf contingent while Naa'il and two Scynthian warriors rounded out the guest list.

Their friends loomed closer as the young couple advanced toward the platform. Murdock and Pondle smiled, while Kymbra, Adrith, and Marissa, who had shed their battle wear for elegant garments, stood next to the men, beaming as well. Across from them stood Meredith with Thoragaard by her side, the governor unable to contain the smile on her face.

Swinkle waited at the makeshift altar in his customary robe, a holy book in his hand. Lance sat next to him, his tail wagging on the ground, wearing a new red collar for the occasion. Rufus, not happy about a small bell attached to his collar, nevertheless cuddled up against the dog. To the right sat Gelderand, who struggled to stand as the young couple approached.

Harrison went over to the magician and helped him to his feet, then led him over to Tara. The young maiden, a tear in her eye, took her uncle's arm, righting him.

"There is no way I'm letting you get married without me giving you away," whispered Gelderand in Tara's ear.

"I'd have it no other way," said the girl through happy tears.

Swinkle raised a hand, signaling for the music to cease. After the musicians finished their tune, the young cleric opened his book, then said, "Who gives this woman away in marriage?"

"I, Gelderand, do give this beautiful girl to her prospective husband," said the elder mage.

"Let it be known," started Swinkle, "that Gelderand releases his niece, Tara Underwood of Tigris, to be wedded to Harrison Cross of Aegeus. Are there any objections?"

Gelderand gazed upon Tara and, when no one protested, turned to the young warrior. The elder mage placed Tara's hand in Harrison's. "I give to thee, my niece, Tara, to be your wife."

Harrison accepted the young maiden's hand into his own. "It's an honor to join your family," said Harrison.

"I could not be a prouder uncle than I am today," said Gelderand with a smile. "Take good care of her."

"I intend to do just that," said Harrison. Gelderand gave him a nod, then with Thoragaard's assistance, took his seat near the platform.

The young couple then turned to face Swinkle, finding a broad smile on the young cleric's face. "Today, Harrison and Tara express their love for each other in front of Pious, their friends, and the land's dignitaries." Percival, doubling as Swinkle's assistant, handed the young cleric a vial of holy water.

Swinkle placed a small wand in the tube, then flicked it toward the couple, sprinkling them with the sacred liquid. "Pious, make this couple pure in your eyes, giving them strength to love one another through triumphs and hardships, happiness and doubt, good times and bad." The young cleric placed the wand back in the tube and handed it to Percival before reading from his sacred book.

"Bless this couple with an abundance of children, to show that their love goes beyond one another." Swinkle turned a page, then continued, "and bless them with good health, to be strong for each other, and the blessed family they shall create."

Swinkle gestured for Percival to bring him a small silver platter. Percival held it out to Swinkle, who recited a prayer over two gold rings. Handing the smaller of the two to the young warrior, he said, "Harrison, please express your commitment to Tara."

Harrison took the girl's small hand and began slipping the gold ring onto her finger. "Tara, I love you with all of my heart and soul. I cannot think of anyone else in this world that I would want to be my wife. Please accept this ring as my commitment to you, for the rest of my life." The young warrior gazed lovingly into Tara's eyes with blissful contentment.

Swinkle then retrieved the larger ring and handed it to the young maiden. "Tara, please express your commitment to Harrison."

Tara took Harrison's rugged hand and began to place the gold ring on his finger. "Harrison, there's no one in this world I'd rather call my husband. I love you, will honor you, and be your loving wife for the rest of my days. You are my true soulmate and I can't wait to see what our life's next adventure brings."

Swinkle waited for Tara to finish her vow, then said, "Pious has brought you two together in love. Let no person break you apart." The young cleric closed his book, then spread his arms wide. "With the power vested in me, I now pronounce you husband and wife." The young cleric sprinkled holy water over the couple a final time, then whispered to the two, "Turn and face your friends."

As the couple pivoted, the young cleric proclaimed to thunderous applause, "Everyone, I present to you Harrison and Tara Cross!" All guests cheered as Meredith's servants released doves from the terrace. Lance yapped with joy and scurried to his master's side, Rufus following.

Harrison squeezed Tara's hand tightly. Gazing into her eyes, he said, "This is the happiest day of my life."

The young maiden beamed. "The same goes for me."

The newlywed couple then engaged in a kiss as their friends cheered. After separating, Catherine handed Tara a bouquet of white flowers, which she gladly accepted. The young maiden then intertwined her arm with Harrison's.

Harrison looked down to Lance. "Lead the way, boy!"

The little dog barked once, then turned to start the procession down the red carpet, Rufus scurrying alongside. The young warrior took in the excitement and joy that their friends showered upon them and knew, at that very moment, everything was finally right with the world.

Epilogue

Harrison returned home to be with Tara after a long day helping train warriors at Aegeus' Fighter's Guild. The young couple's home sat on the outskirts of Aegeus, away from the bustle of the town and closer to the woods, which suited them well.

The young warrior opened the front door and was immediately greeted with the sounds of barks and yaps. Lance bolted to his master while Kora, the little dog's mate, rushed to Harrison's side. The Aegean greeted the dogs, as he always did, but his main focus went to the toddler on the other side of the room.

"Daddy!" cried Teaken, running to her father. Tara had named the couple's three year old daughter after her favorite character from a children's story that her mother used to read to her when she was of a similar age.

"She's been waiting for you all day," said Tara from the kitchen, stirring ingredients for dinner in a mixing bowl.

"Come here, baby," said Harrison, dropping to one knee and corralling his daughter into his arms. The young warrior picked the toddler up and raised her above his head, eliciting squeals of joy from the little girl.

"How are both of my ladies today?" asked Harrison, stepping into the kitchen area and planting a kiss on Tara's lips.

"We had a full day, didn't we Teaken?" said the young woman, accepting her husband's kiss.

"Puppies are messy!" said the child.

"Yes, they are," said Tara with a frown. "Those little guys are zipping everywhere."

"What do you mean?" asked Harrison, but before Tara could respond three little pups teleported around the people. Teaken named the two females Zoe and Piper, while Harrison called the larger male Lance Jr., affectionately known in the household as Junior.

The young warrior teetered on one foot, trying not to step on the little canines that appeared out of thin air. Laughing, he said, "I think they're getting the hang of teleportation!" Kora scurried over to her puppies, herding them together while Lance gave the little ones some space.

Tara, returning to her meal preparation duties, asked, "Did anything come of those reports from Arcadia?"

Harrison did a poor job trying to hold back his grimace. "The Scynthians in the southern part of the land are having a hard time abiding by the Concurian Accord," said the young warrior. "I'm afraid more fighting's going to break out."

Tara placed her bowl on the countertop, her interest piqued. "You're not going to Arcadia to help, are you?"

Harrison shook his head. "Not if I can help it." Taking his young daughter to her mother, he said, "I'm not leaving you again."

Tara smirked, accepting Teaken from her husband. "You better not." Changing the subject, she added, "Your daughter's learning a little bit of her mother's magic."

Harrison gazed at the little girl. Tickling her belly, he said, "Is this true?"

The toddler squealed with delight. "Yes," she said, then focused on her mother's mixing bowl. The wooden spoon began stirring on its own.

The young warrior's jaw dropped, beyond surprised. Tara cocked her head and lifted a single eyebrow, signaling that their little one might harbor many more undiscovered talents.

"Why don't you let me finish preparing dinner," said Tara, handing Teaken back to Harrison, "and you two can check on the boys."

Teaken jumped into her father's arms, breaking her spell in the process, the spoon spinning out of the bowl and plopping to the ground. The three pups quickly scampered to the newfound food source, licking the yummy ingredients from the spoon and floor. Tara huffed, letting the dogs play with the dirty utensil while she searched for a clean one.

Harrison carried his daughter through their sitting area to the back bedroom. Putting Teaken down, the little girl ran to find a favorite toy as the young warrior approached two cradles. Rufus, laying on his soft, ornate matting, meowed, then scooted out of the room, avoiding the commotion before it began.

"How are my little warriors doing?" asked the Aegean, gazing at his twin baby boys.

Harrison had insisted that they name one of their sons after his deceased brother Troy, ensuring that he receive the proper surname he had so deserved. The couple named their second son Griffin, after Harrison's father.

The three puppies burst into the room, jumping on Teaken's bed, wreaking their usual havoc.

The Aegean bent over the cradles allowing each child to hold one of their father's fingers. "Someday, you'll help save this world, just like me."

The two boys cooed as they gazed up at their father. Harrison smiled, recalling how the elder's prophecy stated that brothers would someday reunite the land.

Biography

Mike has been writing The Overlords Fantasy Book Series for over twenty years. Currently, he lives in Tiverton, RI with his wife Lea, and their Australian Cattle Dog, Zoe. Mike speaks at local elementary and middle schools, colleges, libraries, and writer's groups where his sincere hope is to inspire everyone he meets to be creative and follow their dreams. He's also the Vice President of the Association of Rhode Island Authors (ARIA).

When not working on the Overlords series, Mike is very active in fitness and sports. He continues to play baseball where he's a knuckleball pitcher for the Rhode Island Brewers, which won the 2008 and 2014 National Championships in Phoenix, AZ. He also runs 4 to 5 miles on a regular basis, does interval weight and cardio training, and takes Vinyasa yoga classes twice a week. Did we mention that he's an engineer working on Homeland Defense projects, too?

The first three books in The Overlords Fantasy Book Series, *LEGEND OF THE TREASURE*, *THE TALISMAN OF UNIFICATION*, and *JOURNEY TO SALVATION* can be purchased from the website listed below or other online and local retailers.

Stay up to date with all of Mike's events, new releases, and fan extras when you sign up for his newsletter at www.The-Overlords.com.

FOR MORE ON MIKE SQUATRITO

www.The-Overlords.com
www.facebook.com/TheOverlordsBookSeries
Twitter: @Overlords
Instagram: @mikesquatrito

Made in the USA
Monee, IL
09 June 2023

35140053R00371